SelectEditions

SELECTED AND EDITED

SelectEditions

BY READER'S DIGEST

THE READER'S DIGEST ASSOCIATION, INC.
MONTREAL • PLEASANTVILLE, NEW YORK

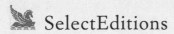 SelectEditions

Vice President, Books & Home Entertainment: Deirdre Gilbert

INTERNATIONAL EDITIONS
Executive Editor: Gary Q. Arpin
Senior Editor: Bonnie Grande

253-270-0501

CONTENTS

THE RESCUE
Nicholas Sparks
PUBLISHED BY WARNER BOOKS

6

CODE TO ZERO
Ken Follett
PUBLISHED BY DUTTON

142

MY MOTHER'S DAUGHTER
Judith Henry Wall
PUBLISHED BY SIMON & SCHUSTER

284

EVEN STEVEN
John Gilstrap
PUBLISHED BY POCKET BOOKS

434

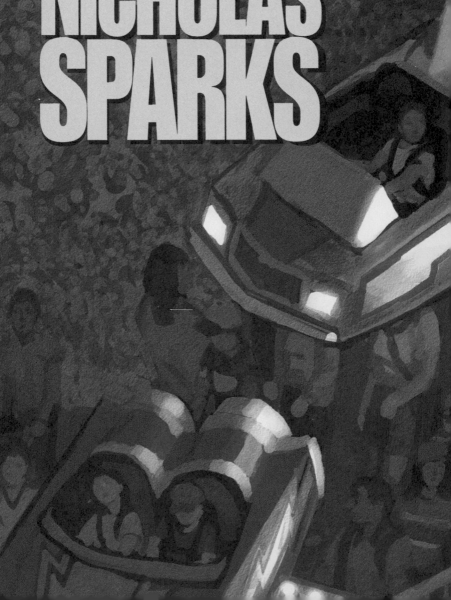

The Rescue

*S*ometimes the biggest risks
are those we take with our hearts. . . .

One

IT WOULD later be called one of the most violent storms in North Carolina history. Because it occurred in 1999, some of the most superstitious citizens considered it an omen, the first step toward the end of time. Others simply shook their heads and said that they knew something like that would happen sooner or later. In all, nine documented tornadoes would touch down that evening in the eastern part of the state, destroying nearly thirty homes in the process. Telephone lines lay strewn across roads, thousands of trees were felled, flash floods swept over banks of three major rivers, and lives changed forever with one fell swoop of Mother Nature.

It had begun in an instant. One minute it was cloudy and dark, but not unusually so; in the next, lightning, gale-force winds, and blinding rain exploded from the early summer sky. People who could took cover inside, but people on the highway, like Denise Holton, had no place to go. Rain fell so hard in places that traffic slowed to five miles an hour. Rain poured across Denise's windshield, obscuring nearly everything. Pulling the shoulder strap of the seat belt over her head, she leaned over the steering wheel. Her headlights seemed absolutely useless.

Then, just as suddenly as it had started, the storm weakened, and it was possible to see again. She'd reached the front edge of the system. Cars began to speed up, racing to stay ahead of the front.

Denise sped up as well, staying with them. She glanced at the gas gauge and felt a knot form in her stomach. She didn't have enough gas to make it home. Another ten minutes passed before she heaved a sigh of relief. Gas, less than a mile away, according to the sign. She exited and stopped at the first open pump.

The storm was still on its way. At forty miles an hour, it would reach this area within the next fifteen minutes. As quickly as she could, Denise filled the tank and then helped Kyle out of his car seat. She insisted he hold her hand as they went inside to pay. The station was crowded. Denise grabbed a can of Diet Coke, then found strawberry-flavored milk for Kyle. It was getting late, and Kyle loved milk before bedtime. Hopefully, if she could stay ahead of the storm, he'd sleep most of the way back.

By the time she went to pay, she was fifth in line. Everyone was on edge. Hurry up, their expressions said, we need to get out of here. In the aisles behind her she heard a mother arguing with her young son. Denise glanced over her shoulder. The boy appeared to be about the same age as Kyle, four and a half or so.

The child whined, "But I want the cupcakes!"

"I said no. You've had enough junk today."

"But *you're* getting something."

They got into line behind Denise, their argument continuing.

"Aw, c'mon, Mom! I'm hungry."

"Then you should have eaten your hot dog."

Denise finally reached the register, paid with cash, then turned toward the door. She smiled at the mother behind her, as if to say, Kids are tough sometimes, aren't they?

In response the woman rolled her eyes. "You're lucky," she said. She nodded toward her son. "This one here never shuts up."

Denise nodded with tight lips, then took Kyle's hand and left the store. Walking toward the car, Denise suddenly felt the urge to cry.

"No," she whispered to herself. "You're the lucky one."

DENISE hit the highway again, staying ahead of the storm. For the next twenty minutes rain fell steadily, but not ominously, while she made her way back to Edenton, North Carolina. The Diet Coke, she hoped, would keep her alert and focused on the drive instead of on Kyle. But Kyle was always there.

Kyle, she felt sure, was a gift from God. He had been born four years to the day after her mother had died of a brain aneurysm. Other than him, she was alone in the world. Her father had died when she was four, and she had no siblings. Kyle immediately became the sole recipient of the love she had to offer. She showered him with attention, but it somehow hadn't been enough. Now she led a life she hadn't anticipated, a life where Kyle's daily progression was carefully logged in a notebook. Kyle, of course, didn't complain about the things they did every day. Kyle, unlike other children, never complained about anything. She glanced in the rearview mirror.

"What are you thinking about, sweetie?"

Kyle hadn't said anything since he'd been in the car. He turned at the sound of her voice. She waited for his response. Nothing.

DENISE Holton lived in a house that had once been owned by her grandparents. After their deaths it had become her mother's; then eventually it had passed on to her. It wasn't much—a small ramshackle building set on three acres, built in the 1920s. The two bedrooms and the living room weren't too bad, but the kitchen was in dire need of modern appliances. Both the front and back porches were sagging, and without the portable fan she sometimes felt as if she would bake to death. But she could live there rent free. It had been her home for the past three months.

Staying in Atlanta, the place she'd grown up, would have been impossible. Once Kyle was born, she'd used the money her mother had left her to stay at home with him. When he was a little older, she had planned to go back to teaching. Now, years later, she was still at home with Kyle, and teaching was a distant memory. Instead she worked the evening shift at a diner called Eights, a busy hangout on the outskirts of Edenton. The owner, Ray Toler, was a sixty-something black man who'd run the place for thirty years. He and his wife had raised six kids, all of whom went to college. Copies of their diplomas hung along the back wall, and everyone who ate there knew about them. Ray made sure of that.

Ray understood how hard it was for single mothers. "There's a small room in the back," he'd said when he hired her. "You can bring your son with you, as long as he doesn't get in the way." There were two cots, a night-light—a place where Kyle would be safe.

She worked four nights a week, from seven to midnight, earning barely enough to get by. Though coming in a little later meant less in tips, she couldn't in good conscience leave Kyle in the back room for an extra hour all by himself while he was still awake. By arriving later, she could put him down in the cot and he'd sleep.

On those evenings she didn't work at the diner, Denise usually sat in the rocking chair on the porch. She enjoyed reading outside. In Atlanta she used to read novels for pleasure. Now she never checked novels out when she went to the local library. Instead she used their computers, which had free access to the Internet. She searched through clinical studies sponsored by major universities, printing the documents whenever she found something relevant. The files she kept had grown to nearly three inches wide.

She had an assortment of psychological textbooks as well, and she would sit outside for hours, studying them. When she'd finally finished for the night, she would go inside to check on Kyle, then head back outside.

A gravel walkway led to a path through the trees, eventually to a broken fence that lined her property. She and Kyle would wander that way during the day; she walked it alone at night. Past the fence, the forest pressed in around her, the darkness almost stifling, but by then she could hear the water; the Chowan River was close. A quick turn to the right, and all of a sudden it was as if the world had unfolded before her. The river, wide and slow moving, powerful, eternal, as black as time. She would cross her arms and gaze at it, taking it in, letting the calm it inspired wash over her. She would stay a few minutes, seldom longer, since Kyle was still in the house.

Then she'd sigh and turn, knowing it was time to go.

IN THE car, still ahead of the storm, Denise remembered sitting with the doctor in his office at Duke University earlier that day while he read the results from the report on Kyle.

The child is male, four years eight months old at the time of testing. . . . Kyle is a handsome child. No recorded head trauma. Pregnancy described by mother as normal. . . .

The doctor continued for a few minutes, outlining specific results from various tests, until finally reaching the conclusion.

IQ normal range. Child severely delayed in both receptive and expressive language . . . probably central auditory processing disorder (CAPD). Cause undetermined. Overall language ability estimated to be that of a twenty-four-month-old.

When the doctor was finished, he looked at Denise sympathetically. "In other words," he said, "Kyle has problems with language. For some reason—we're not sure why—he isn't able to speak at a level appropriate for his age, even though his IQ is normal. Nor is he able to understand language equal to other four-year-olds."

"I know."

The assurance of her response caught him off guard. "There's a note here that says you've had him evaluated elsewhere."

Denise nodded. "I have. I didn't give you the report."

His eyebrows rose slightly. "Why?"

She hesitated and finally said, "May I be frank?"

He studied her, then leaned back in his chair. "Please."

"Kyle has been misdiagnosed again and again over the past two years—everything from deafness to autism to ADD. In time none of those things turned out to be accurate. Do you know how hard it is for a parent to hear those things about her child, to believe them, to learn everything about them, then be told they were in error?"

The doctor didn't answer.

Denise met his eyes. "I know Kyle has problems with language, and believe me, I've read all about auditory processing problems. I wanted his language skills tested by an independent source so that I could know specifically where he needed help."

"So none of this is news to you."

Denise shook her head. "No, it's not."

"Do you have him in a program now?"

"I work with him at home."

He paused. "Does he see a speech or behavioral specialist?"

"No. He went to therapy for over a year, but it didn't seem to help, so I pulled him out last October. Now it's just me."

"I see." It was obvious that he didn't agree with her decision.

Her eyes narrowed. "You have to understand—even though this evaluation shows Kyle at the level of a two-year-old, that's an improvement from where he once was. Before he worked with me, he'd never shown any improvement at all."

In truth, it was easier to defend Kyle to a doctor than to herself. Even though he'd improved, the language ability of a two-year-old wasn't much to cheer about. Kyle would be five in October.

Still, she refused to give up on him. She would never give up. She drilled him on the mechanics of speech for four hours a day, six days a week. Some days he could comprehend new things easily; other days he seemed further behind than ever.

Yesterday they'd spent the afternoon on the banks of the Chowan River. He enjoyed watching the boats, and it provided a change from his normal routine. Usually when they worked on his speech he was strapped in a chair in the living room. The chair helped him focus.

Denise carefully logged his progress in a notebook and finished jotting down the latest information. Without looking up, she asked, "Do you see any boats, sweetie?"

Kyle didn't answer. Instead he lifted a tiny toy jet in the air, pretending to make it fly.

"Kyle, honey, do you see any boats?"

He made engine sounds. He wasn't paying attention to her.

She looked out over the water. No boats in sight. She reached over and touched his hand. "Kyle? Say, 'I don't see any boats.' "

"Airplane." (*Owpwane.*)

"I know it's an airplane. Say, 'I don't see any boats.' "

He raised the toy a little higher, one eye still focused on it. After a moment he spoke again. "Jet airplane." (*Jet owpwane.*)

She sighed. "Yes, a *jet* airplane." She looked at his face, so perfect, so beautiful, so normal-looking. She used her finger to turn his face toward hers. "Even though we're outside, we still have to work, okay? You have to say what I tell you to, or we go back to the living room, to your chair. You don't want to do that, do you?"

Kyle didn't like his chair. Once strapped in, he couldn't get away, and no child enjoyed something like that. Still, Kyle moved the toy airplane back and forth with measured concentration.

Denise tried again. "Say, 'I don't see any boats.' "

Nothing.

She pulled a piece of candy from her pocket. Kyle reached for it, but she kept it out of his grasp. "Say, 'I don't see any boats.' "

Finally he whispered, "I don't see any boats." *(Duh see a-ee boat.)*

Denise leaned in and kissed him, then gave him the candy. "That's right, honey. Good talking! You're such a good talker!"

Kyle ate the candy, then focused on the toy again.

Denise jotted his words in her notebook and went on with the lesson. She glanced upward, thinking of something he hadn't said that day. "Kyle, say, 'The sky is blue.' "

After a beat: "Owpwane."

TWENTY minutes from home. Outside, dark clouds spanned the sky above; rain fell steadily. In the back seat Kyle was dreaming, his eyelids twitching. Denise wondered what his dreams were like. Were they devoid of words, a film running through his head of rocket ships and jets blazing across the sky? Or did he dream using the few words he knew? She liked to imagine that in his dreams he lived in a world where everyone understood him, where children wouldn't shy away because he didn't speak.

She thought about Brett Cosgrove, Kyle's father. He was the type of man who'd always caught her eye: tall and thin, with dark eyes and ebony hair. She was twenty-three at the time, single, in her second year of teaching. She'd seen him at a party, and she asked her friend Susan who he was. She was told that Brett worked for a New York investment-banking firm. She glanced his way, he glanced back, and their eyes kept meeting for the next forty minutes before he finally came over and said hello. They left the party together a little after eleven, had drinks in the hotel bar, flirted with an eye toward what might happen next, and ended up in bed. It was the first and last time she saw him. He went back to New York, and she went back to her life. At the time it didn't seem to mean much; a month later it meant a whole lot. She went to the doctor, who confirmed what she already knew. She was pregnant.

She called Brett, reached his answering machine, and left a message to call; three days later he finally did. He listened, then sighed with what sounded like exasperation. He offered to pay for an abortion. As a Catholic, she said it wasn't going to happen. Angered, he asked if she was sure the baby was his. She closed her eyes, calming herself, not rising to the bait. Yes, it was his. What did she want him to do? he asked her. She said she didn't want anything; she just needed to know if he wanted to be involved in the child's life. She listened to the sound of his breaths on the other end. No, he finally said. He was engaged to someone else.

She'd never spoken to him again.

Would Kyle have had these problems if his father were around? In her heart she wasn't sure. Had it been something she'd done while pregnant? Was all of this somehow her fault? Through sheer force of will she pushed the questions from her mind. But sometimes late at night they would come creeping back. Like kudzu spreading through the forests, they were impossible to keep at bay forever, and she would feel sorrow in her heart.

Yet she would also feel joy. For despite all his difficulties, Kyle was a wonderful child. He didn't hurt other children; he never took their toys, and he shared his own even when he didn't want to. Every day there were times when she wanted to come to his defense, to make others understand that though he looked normal, something was wired wrong in his brain. Most of the time, however, she didn't. If they didn't give him a chance, then it was their loss.

He was the sweetest child she'd ever known, and when he smiled, he was so beautiful. She would smile back, and he'd keep smiling, and for a split second she'd think that everything was okay. She'd tell him she loved him, and the smile would grow wider, but because he couldn't talk well, she sometimes felt as if she were the only one who noticed how wonderful he actually was. And he couldn't even tell her he loved her.

Her thoughts followed this familiar track as she guided her old Datsun onto now recognizable roads. She was ten minutes away. Round the next curve, cross the bridge toward Edenton, then left onto Charity Road. Another mile after that and she'd be home. She was driving through a nameless swamp, one of dozens in the low country fed by the waters of the Albemarle Sound. Few people lived here. There were no other cars on the highway. Rounding the curve at nearly sixty miles an hour, she saw a doe standing in the road, facing the oncoming headlights, frozen by uncertainty.

Denise slammed on the brakes. She heard the screeching of tires, felt them lose their grip on the rain-slicked surface. Still, the doe did not move. She was going to hit it. Denise screamed as she turned the wheel hard. The car began to slide diagonally across the road, missing the deer by a foot. Too late to matter, the deer finally broke from its trance and darted away safely, without looking back.

The trees were less than thirty feet off the highway. Frantically Denise turned the wheel again, but the car rocketed forward as if she'd done nothing. She blasted into a cypress tree, heard the twisting of metal and shattering of glass as the front of the car exploded toward her. Because the seat belt was across her lap and not over her shoulder, her head shot forward, slamming into the steering wheel. A sharp, searing pain in her forehead.

Then there was nothing.

"Hey, lady, are you all right?"

With the sound of the stranger's voice, the world came back slowly. Denise couldn't feel any pain, but on her tongue was the salty-bitter taste of blood. She struggled to force her eyes open.

"Don't move. I'm gonna call an ambulance."

The words barely registered. Everything was blurry. She turned her head toward the shaded figure in the corner of her eye. A man, dark hair, yellow raincoat . . . turning away . . .

She felt rain blowing in the car. A hissing sound was coming from the darkness as steam escaped from the radiator. Her vision was returning slowly. Shards of glass were in her lap . . . blood on the steering wheel in front of her. Nothing made sense. She forced herself to concentrate. Steering wheel . . . the car . . . dark outside.

"Oh God!" With a rush it all came back. The deer . . . swerving out of control. She turned in her seat, focusing on the back seat. Kyle wasn't in the car. His safety seat was open, as was the back door on his side of the car.

Through the window she shouted for the figure who'd awakened her. He turned, making his way toward her. A moan escaped her lips. Later she'd remember that she wasn't frightened right away. She felt certain that the person—whoever he was—had helped Kyle out of the car. Now he was at the window, saying, "Listen, don't try to talk. You're pretty banged up. My name is Taylor McAden, and I'm with the fire department. I'm gonna radio for help."

She rolled her head, focusing on him with blurry eyes. "You have my son, don't you?"

She knew what the answer would be, what it should be, but strangely, it didn't come. Instead he shook his head. "No. I just got here. Your son?"

It was then that the first jolt of fear shot through her.

"My son was in the back!" Denise unbuckled the seat belt quickly, ignoring the pain in her wrist and elbow. The man took an involuntary step backward as she forced the door open, using her shoulder because the door had crumpled slightly from the impact. She almost lost her balance as she stood.

"I don't think you should be moving—"

Holding on to the car for support, she ignored the man as she moved around the car, toward the opposite side, where Kyle's door stood open. No, no, no, no . . .

"Kyle!" In disbelief she bent inside to look for him. Blood rushed to her head, bringing with it a piercing pain that she ignored.

"Lady—"

She grabbed his arm. "You haven't seen him? A little boy . . . brown hair? He was in the car with me!"

"No, I—"

"You've got to help me find him! He's only four!"

She whirled around, the rapid movement making her lose her balance. She grabbed hold of the car again. "Kyle!" Pure terror now.

Finally understanding, the man scanned the area. "I don't see him."

"Kyle!" She screamed it as loud as she could, praying inside as she did it. Despite being nearly drowned out by the storm, which was in full fury now, the sound prompted Taylor into further action.

They took off in opposite directions, both shouting Kyle's name. The rain, however, was deafening. After a couple of minutes Taylor ran back to his truck and called the fire station. The two voices—Denise's and Taylor's—were the only human sounds in the swamp. The rain made it impossible for them to hear each other, let alone a child. Eventually two other firemen arrived, flashlights in hand.

"You've got to help me find my baby!" Denise sobbed.

More help was requested; more people arrived. Six people searching now. It was Taylor who found Kyle's blanket, fifty yards from where Denise had crashed, snagged on the underbrush.

"Is this his?" he asked.

Denise started to cry as soon as it was handed to her.

But after another thirty minutes of searching, Kyle was still nowhere to be seen.

IT MADE no sense to her. One minute he was sleeping soundly in the back seat, and the next he was gone. Just like that.

As she sat in the back of the ambulance with the doors open, and the flashing blue lights from the trooper's car illuminated the highway in regular, circular sweeps, her mind raced with such thoughts. Half a dozen other vehicles were parked haphazardly, headlights on, as a group of men in yellow raincoats discussed what to do, their words lost in the roar of the storm.

Once the ambulance had arrived, they'd forced her to stop searching for Kyle. Still dizzy, she was shivering badly, and her vision was blurred. The ambulance attendant suspected a concussion and wanted to bring her in immediately. She steadfastly refused to leave until Kyle was found. He could wait another ten minutes, he said; then he had no choice. The gash in her head was still bleeding, despite the bandage. She would lose consciousness, he warned, if they waited any longer than that. I'm not leaving, she repeated.

More people had arrived. A state trooper, another three volunteers from the fire department, a trucker who had stopped as well. The man who'd found her—Taylor?—was filling them in on what he knew, which wasn't much, other than the location of the blanket. Taylor and the state trooper, a heavyset man losing his hair, started toward the ambulance.

She held Kyle's mud-stained blanket in her lap, nervously rolling it into a ball. She continued to shiver. It was so cold out here. . . . And Kyle was out there without even a jacket. Oh, Kyle. She lifted his blanket to her cheek and closed her eyes. Where are you, honey? Why did you leave the car? Why didn't you stay with Mom?

Taylor and the trooper stepped into the ambulance. Taylor gently put his hand on Denise's shoulder. She opened her eyes. "I know this is hard," he said, "but we have to ask you a few questions."

She bit her lip before nodding slightly, then took a deep breath.

The trooper squatted before her. "I'm Sergeant Carl Huddle with the state troopers office," he said. "I know you're worried, and we are, too. Most of us out here are parents, with little ones of our own. We all want to find him as badly as you do, but we need some general information—enough to know who we're looking for."

Denise sat up a little, trying her best to stay composed. The bandage wrapped around her head had a large red spot just over her right eye. Her cheek was swollen and bruised.

They went over the basics for the report: name, address, phone number, employment, her previous residence, when she'd moved to Edenton, the reason she was driving, the accident itself. Sergeant Huddle noted it all on a flip pad. He looked at her almost expectantly. "Are you kin to J. B. Anderson?"

John Brian Anderson had been her grandfather, and she nodded.

Sergeant Huddle, like everyone in Edenton, had known the Andersons. "Could you give me a general description of Kyle?"

Denise turned away, trying to order her thoughts. Who can describe their kids exactly, in terms of numbers and figures? "Three and a half feet tall, forty pounds or so. Brown hair, green eyes."

"Do you remember what he was wearing?"

"A red shirt with a big Mickey Mouse on the front. Mickey's

hand has a thumbs-up sign. And jeans—stretch waist, no belt. White shoes. I don't know the brand. Something from Wal-Mart."

"How about a jacket?"

"No. It was warm today, at least when we started to drive."

Sergeant Huddle raised his voice over the sound of the pounding rain. "Do you still have family in the area? Parents? Siblings?"

"No. No siblings. My parents are deceased."

"How about your husband?"

Denise shook her head. "I've never been married."

"Has Kyle ever wandered off before?"

Denise rubbed her temple, trying to keep the dizziness at bay. "A couple of times. At the mall once, and once near my house. But he's afraid of lightning. I think that might be the reason he left the car Whenever there's lightning, he crawls into bed with me."

"How about the swamp? Would he be afraid to go there in the dark? Or do you think he'd stay close to the car?"

A pit of fear yawned in her stomach. "Kyle isn't afraid of being outside, even at night. He loves to wander in the woods by our house. I don't know that he knows enough to be afraid."

Huddle paused for a moment, glancing at his watch. It was now 10:22 p.m. More than an hour had passed since the accident. A few hours in this rain without proper clothing could lead to hypothermia. Neither he nor Taylor mentioned to Denise the danger of the swamp itself. It wasn't a place for anyone in a storm like this, let alone a child. A person could literally vanish forever.

Sergeant Huddle closed his flip pad. "We'll continue this later, if that's okay, Miss Holton. We'll need more for the report. Getting started with the search is the most important thing right now."

Denise nodded.

"Anything else we should know? A nickname he'll answer to?"

"No. Just Kyle. But . . ." Then it hit her—the obvious. Oh, no. Why hadn't she mentioned it earlier?

"Miss Holton?"

Everything seemed to wash over her at once: shock, fright, anger, denial. He can't answer them! She lowered her face into her hands.

"Miss Holton?" she heard again.

She wiped her tears away, unable to meet their eyes. "Kyle won't answer if you simply call his name. You'll have to find him; you'll have to actually *see* him. He won't answer." How many times had she said these words before? How many times had it simply been an explanation? How many times had it really meant nothing when compared with something like this?

They stared at her quizzically, not understanding. Drawing a ragged breath, Denise went on. "Kyle doesn't talk very well, just a few words. He can't understand language for some reason." She turned from one man to the other, making sure they understood. "Simply shouting for him won't do any good. He won't understand what you're saying. He can't answer. You'll have to find him."

Why him? Of all the children, why did this have to happen to Kyle? Denise started to sob.

With that, Taylor put his hand on her shoulder. "We'll find him, Miss Holton," he said. "We'll find him."

Two

FIVE minutes later, as Taylor and the others were mapping out the search pattern, four more men arrived to help. It was all that Edenton could spare. Lightning had sparked three major fires, and downed power lines were still a hazard. Calls were flooding in to police and fire departments; every one was logged by priority, and unless a life was in immediate jeopardy, the caller was informed that nothing could be done right away.

A lost child took priority over nearly everything.

The first step was to park the cars and trucks as close to the edge of the swamp as possible, headlights set on high beams, about fifteen yards apart. Flashlights and walkie-talkies were handed out. Eleven men would be involved. They would fan out in three directions—south, east, and west—from where Taylor found the blanket. East and west paralleled the highway; south was the last direction Kyle had appeared to be headed. It was decided that one man would stay behind, on the off chance that Kyle would see the headlights and return on his own. He would send a flare up every hour on the hour so that the men would know where they were.

After Sergeant Huddle had given them a brief description of Kyle, Taylor spoke. He had hunted in the swamp before, and now he laid out what they were up against. Here, on the outer fringes of the swamp, the ground was damp but not usually underwater. It wasn't until half a mile farther in that water formed shallow lakes. Mud was a real danger, though; it closed in around the foot and leg, sometimes holding it like a vise, making it difficult for an adult to escape, let alone a child. Tonight the water was already half an inch deep near the highway. Mud pockets combined with rising water would make for a deadly combination. On the plus side, none of the men imagined that Kyle could have gotten far. Trees and vines made the going rough, possibly limiting the distance he might have traveled. "But," Taylor went on, "according to the mother, the boy won't answer if we call him. Look for any physical sign of him—you don't want to walk right by him."

"He can't talk?" asked one of the men, clearly baffled.

"That's what his mother said."

"Is he retarded?" another asked.

Taylor stiffened at the question. "What does that matter? He's a little boy lost in the swamp who can't talk. That's all we know right now." He turned on his flashlight. "Let's do it."

DENISE was lying in the back of the ambulance on the way to the hospital in Elizabeth City, a town thirty miles to the northeast, which had the nearest emergency room. She stared at the ceiling, still shivering and dazed. Her breathing was rapid but shallow, her skin pale and sickly. She'd begged to stay but was told she would only hinder things. She'd said she didn't care and had stubbornly stepped out of the ambulance, back into the storm, knowing that Kyle needed her. She'd asked for a raincoat and flashlight. After a couple of steps the world had begun to spin. She'd pitched forward and fallen to the ground, opening her head wound again. Two minutes later she was in the ambulance and on her way.

"Have faith, Miss Holton," the attendant soothed. He'd just taken her blood pressure and believed she was suffering from shock. "I mean, I know these guys. Kids have been lost around here before, and they always find 'em."

Denise continued to stare upward.

"Is there anyone you want me to call from the hospital?"

"No," she whispered. "There's no one."

TAYLOR and two other men headed south, deeper into the swamp, while the rest of the search team headed east and west. Visibility, even with the flashlight, was only a few yards at most. Within minutes Taylor couldn't see or hear anyone. He had searched for lost people before, and he suddenly knew there weren't enough men out here. The swamp at night, the storm, a child who wouldn't answer when called. . . . Fifty people wouldn't be enough. The most effective way to search for someone lost in the woods was to stay within sight of the person to the right and left, everyone moving in unison. With ten men that was impossible. Minutes after they'd split up, they were reduced to simply wandering in the direction of their choosing, pointing the flashlights here, there, anywhere.

Reminding himself not to lose faith, Taylor pressed forward, around trees, over the ever softening earth. Though he didn't have any children himself, he was godfather to the children of his best friend, Mitch Johnson, and Taylor searched as though looking for one of them. Mitch was also a volunteer fireman, and Taylor wished fervently that he was out here searching as well. His main hunting partner for the past twenty years, Mitch knew the swamp almost as well as he did. But Mitch was out of town for a few days.

With every few steps the swamp was becoming denser, darker. Rotted trees lay across the ground. Vines and branches tore at Taylor as he moved, and the water had risen past his ankles. He pointed his flashlight at every clump of trees, at every stump, behind every bush, looking for any sign of Kyle. Several minutes passed, then ten. Then twenty. Then thirty.

Taylor checked his watch: 10:56. Kyle had been gone for an hour and a half, maybe more. How long before he got too cold? Or . . . Taylor shook his head, not wanting to think beyond that.

Lightning and thunder were regular occurrences now, the rain hard and stinging. Despite his mother's insistence that Kyle wouldn't answer him, Taylor kept calling his name.

Taylor knew the swamp as well as, if not better than, anyone he knew. It was here that he'd shot his first deer at the age of twelve; every autumn he ventured forth to hunt ducks as well. He had an instinctive ability to track nearly anything. The people of Edenton often joked that he had a nose like a wolf. When asked to explain his secret skill, he simply replied that he tried to think like a deer. People laughed. Think like a deer? What did that mean?

He closed his eyes. Think. Where would a four-year-old go? A kid afraid of storms but not afraid of the woods?

His eyes snapped open at the burst of the signal flare in the evening sky, indicating the turn of the hour. Eleven o'clock.

After another thirty minutes the water was halfway up his shin. He checked in on his walkie-talkie—everyone else said the same thing. Not a sign of the boy anywhere.

Think. Would he have made it this far? Would someone his size be able to wade through water this deep? No, he decided. Kyle wouldn't have gone this far, not in a T-shirt and jeans.

The wind gusted, and trees swayed above him. Rain stung his cheeks as lightning flashed in the eastern sky. The worst of the storm was finally passing them by.

Kyle was small and afraid of lightning. Taylor stared up at the sky, concentrating, and felt the shape of something there, something in the recesses of his mind slowly beginning to emerge. Gusting wind, stinging rain, afraid of lightning . . .

Taylor grabbed his walkie-talkie and directed everyone back to the highway as quickly as possible. He would meet them there.

"It has to be," he said to no one in particular.

LIKE many of the volunteer firemen's wives who called in to the station, concerned about their husbands on this dangerous night, Judy McAden, Taylor's mother, couldn't resist calling, too. All evening long she'd felt instinctively that something bad had happened. At first she tried to dismiss it, but the nagging suspicion persisted. Finally she made the call, almost expecting the worst; instead she'd learned about the little boy—"J. B. Anderson's great-grandkid"—lost in the swamp. Taylor, she was told, was involved in the search. The mother was on the way to the hospital in Elizabeth City.

Judy was relieved that Taylor was okay but suddenly worried about the child. Like everyone else in Edenton, she'd known the Andersons. More than that, Judy had known Denise's mother when they were both young girls, before Denise's mother had moved to Atlanta and married Charles Holton. That had been forty years ago. Now the memories of their youth came rushing back. She also remembered how sad she'd been when she'd learned of her death. She had no idea that her friend's daughter had moved back to Edenton. And now her son was lost. What a homecoming.

Judy didn't debate long. She had always been the take-charge type, and at sixty-three she hadn't slowed down at all. Years earlier, after her husband died, Judy had taken a job at the library and had raised Taylor by herself. Not only did she meet the financial obligations of her family, but she did what it usually took two parents to do. Though those days were behind her, she was busier than ever now. Her attention had shifted to helping the town of Edenton itself, and she participated in every aspect of the community's life and still managed to work at the library thirty hours a week.

She understood a mother's fear when children were concerned. Taylor had been in precarious situations his entire life—indeed, he seemed to attract them. Judy knew the little boy must be absolutely terrified, and the mother . . . well, she was probably a basket case. She pulled on her raincoat. The prospect of driving in the storm didn't frighten her. A mother and son were in trouble. Even if Denise Holton didn't want to see her—or couldn't because of injuries—Judy knew she wouldn't be able to sleep if she didn't let her know that people in the town cared about what was going on.

AT MIDNIGHT the flare again ignited in the evening sky. Taylor was nearing the highway, and he heard people calling to one another. As he cleared the last of the trees, he saw that more than a dozen extra vehicles had arrived, their headlights blazing. Not only had the other searchers returned, but they were now surrounded by people who'd heard about the search and come out to help. People Denise had probably never met. Good people.

The mood, however, was gloomy. Those who'd been searching were soaking wet, covered with mud and scrapes, and exhausted. As Taylor approached them, they quieted. So did the new arrivals.

Sergeant Huddle turned to Taylor. "So did you find something?"

Taylor shook his head. "No. But I think I have an idea of which way he headed."

"How do you know?"

"It's just a guess, Carl, but I think he was moving to the southeast. That's where we found the blanket, for one thing, and if he kept heading that way, the wind would be at his back. I don't think a little boy would try to fight the wind. The rain would hurt too much. I think he'd want to keep the lightning at his back, too. His mother said he was afraid of lightning."

Sergeant Huddle looked at him skeptically. "That's not much."

"No. But I think it's our best hope."

"You don't think we should continue searching like before?"

"We'd still be spread too thin—it wouldn't do any good. You've seen what it's like out there. Look, we've got, what? More than twenty people now? We could fan out wide and cover everything in that direction."

Huddle squinted at him doubtfully. "But what if you're wrong? Just because he's afraid of lightning doesn't mean he'd know enough to move away from it. He's only four years old. Besides, we've got enough people now to head in different directions."

"Trust me, Carl."

"It's not that easy. A little boy's life is at stake."

"I know."

With that, Huddle sighed and turned away. Ultimately it was his call, and in the end he'd be the one who had to answer for it. "All right," he said. "We'll do it your way. I just hope to God you're right."

TWELVE THIRTY now.

Arriving at the hospital, Judy McAden approached the front desk. No stranger to hospital protocol, she asked to see Denise Holton, her niece. The clerk didn't question her—the waiting room was still filled with people—and hurriedly checked the records. Denise Holton, she explained, had been moved to room 217, upstairs, but visiting hours were over. If she could come back tomorrow morning . . .

Judy stepped away from the desk and made sure that the clerk's attention was on the next person in line. Then she exited through a set of double swinging doors. In a matter of minutes she was sailing past a vacated nurses station, heading for room 217.

She opened the door slightly. A small lamp glowed dimly in the corner of the room as she quietly made her way inside. As she was closing the door, Denise turned her head and peered at her. Denise had been staring at the clock on the wall, watching the minutes pass with frightening regularity. Kyle had been missing for almost four hours now. Four hours!

Even in the semidarkness, when Judy saw Denise lying in the bed, she froze. Despite the bandage around her head, Judy recognized Denise as the young woman who used the computers at the library. The one with the cute little boy who liked the books about airplanes. Oh, no, the cute little boy . . .

Denise, however, didn't make the connection as she squinted at the lady standing before her. Her thoughts were still hazy. "Do I know you?" she finally croaked out.

Judy spoke softly. "I've seen you in the library. I work there."

Denise's eyes were half open. The library? The room began to spin again. "What are you doing here?"

"I heard about your son getting lost. My son is one of the ones out there looking for him right now."

Denise's eyes flickered with a mixture of hope and fear. "Have you heard anything?"

Judy shook her head. "No, nothing. I'm sorry."

Denise pressed her lips together, staying silent. She seemed to be evaluating the answer before finally turning away.

"I'd like to be alone," Denise said.

Still uncertain of what to do, Judy said the only thing she herself would have wanted to hear. "They'll find him, Denise."

At first Judy didn't think that Denise had heard her; then she saw Denise's jaw quiver, followed by a welling of tears in her eyes. Denise made no sound at all. She seemed to be holding back her emotions. Judy acted on motherly impulse and gave her hand a squeeze.

"But what if they don't?" Denise faced Judy with red, swollen eyes. "I don't even know if they're still looking for him."

Up close, Judy flashed upon the resemblance between Denise and her mother. That thought was quickly replaced as Denise's words sank in. Judy furrowed her brow. "Do you mean to say that no one's kept you informed of what's happening out there?"

"I haven't heard a thing since I was put in the ambulance."

At once Judy picked up the phone. Not telling the mother? Completely unacceptable. Not only that, but cruel.

Dialing quickly, she reached the fire station in Edenton. "This is Judy McAden, and I'm with Denise Holton at the hospital, the one whose boy's in the swamp. No one's told her what's happening out there. . . . I see. Well, can you radio someone at the scene? . . . No. I'd rather not call back. She needs to know now. . . . All right."

Looking at Denise: "I'm holding now. He's radioing over there. We'll know in just a couple of minutes. How're you holding up?"

Denise smiled for the first time in hours. "Thank you," she said.

A minute passed, then another, before Judy spoke again. "Yes, I'm still here." Judy was silent as she listened to the report, and despite everything, Denise found herself growing hopeful. As the silence continued, Judy's mouth formed a straight line. She finally spoke into the handset. "Oh, I see. Thanks, Joe. Call here if you find out anything. And we'll check back in a little while."

Denise felt a lump rise in her throat. Kyle was still out there.

Judy hung up the phone. "They haven't found him yet, but a bunch of people from town showed up to help. The weather's cleared up some, and they think Kyle was moving to the southeast."

Denise barely heard her.

IT WAS COMING UP ON 1:30 a.m. The temperature—originally in the sixties—was nearing forty degrees now, and they'd been moving as a group for over an hour. Twenty-four men in total, with only enough distance between them to allow them to see the neighboring flashlights, they stretched nearly a quarter of a mile wide. A cold northern wind was pushing the temperature down quickly, and the searchers began to realize that if they hoped to find the little boy alive, they needed to find him in the next couple of hours.

They'd reached an area of the swamp that was a little less dense, where they were able to search more quickly. Taylor could see flashlights in each direction. Nothing was being overlooked.

Taylor had hunted in this part of the swamp before. Because the ground was elevated slightly, it was usually dry, and deer flocked to the area. A half mile or so ahead the elevation dropped again to below the water tables, and they would come to an area of the swamp known to hunters as Duck Shot. During the season men could be found in the dozens of duck blinds that lined the area. It was also the farthest point that Kyle could have traveled.

If, of course, they were going in the right direction.

IT WAS now 2:26 a.m. Kyle had been missing for almost five and a half hours. Judy wet a washcloth and gently wiped Denise's face. Denise hadn't spoken much. She looked shell-shocked: pale and exhausted, her eyes red and glassy. Judy had called again at the top of the hour and been told that there still wasn't any news. This time Denise had seemed to expect it and had barely reacted.

"Can I get you a cup of water?" Judy asked.

Denise didn't answer.

"Would you like me to leave so that you can rest?"

Denise turned to Judy and still saw a stranger, but a nice stranger, someone who cared. "I don't think I'll be able to sleep," she said. "What was your name again?" she asked weakly.

"I'm Judy McAden."

"And you work in the library?"

She nodded. "I've seen you and your son there."

"Is that why . . . ?" Denise asked, trailing off.

"No. Actually, I came because your mother and I were friends a long time ago. I didn't want you to think you were in this all alone."

Denise squinted, trying to focus on Judy as if for the first time. "My mother?"

"She lived down the road from me. We grew up together."

The telephone rang. It startled them both, the sound ominous.

A FEW minutes earlier Taylor and the others had reached Duck Shot. Here the marshy water began to deepen, a mile and a half from the accident. Kyle could have gone no farther, but still they'd found nothing. One by one the group began to converge, and when the walkie-talkies clicked to life, there were more than a few disappointed voices.

Taylor, however, didn't call in. He again tried to put himself in Kyle's shoes. He wouldn't have wanted to fight the wind, and heading this way would have kept the lightning behind him. He had to have moved in this direction.

Lightning flashed again, startling Taylor. As the night sky was illuminated, he saw it in the distance: rectangular and wooden, overgrown with foliage. One of the dozens of duck blinds. Duck blinds. They looked almost like a kid's playhouse.

Despite himself, Taylor felt the adrenaline begin to race through his system. He did his best to remain calm as he rushed to the first duck blind he'd seen. It hadn't been used since last fall and was overgrown with climbing vines and brush. He pushed his way through the vines and poked his head inside. Sweeping his flashlight around the interior, he almost expected to see a young boy hiding from the storm.

But all he saw was aging plywood.

Another bolt of lightning lit the sky, and Taylor caught a glimpse of another duck blind not fifty yards away. He took off, running. He reached the second blind, searched quickly, and found nothing. He cursed, filled with an even greater sense of urgency. He took off again, heading for the next blind. He knew from experience that it wouldn't be more than a hundred yards away. And he was right.

This time, when he reached the blind, he steeled himself to

expect nothing. Shining his light inside, he almost stopped breathing.

A little boy, sitting in the corner, muddy and scratched, filthy but otherwise seemingly okay. Taylor blinked, thinking it was a mirage, but when he opened his eyes again, the little boy was still there, Mickey Mouse shirt and all.

Kyle looked up at the big man in the long yellow coat with an expression of surprise on his face, as though he'd been caught doing something that would get him in trouble.

"Hewwo," Kyle said exuberantly, and Taylor laughed aloud. Grins immediately spread across both their faces. Taylor dropped to one knee, and the little boy scrambled to his feet and then into his arms. He was wet and shivering, and when Taylor felt those small arms wrap around his neck, tears welled in his eyes.

"Well, hello, little man. I take it you must be Kyle."

"HE'S okay. I repeat, he's okay. He's with me right now."

With those words spoken into the walkie-talkie, a whoop of excitement arose from the searchers, and the word was passed along to the station, where Joe called in to the hospital. It was 2:31 a.m.

Judy handed the phone to Denise, who was barely breathing as she picked up the receiver. All at once she brought her hand to her mouth. Her smile, so heartfelt and emotional, was contagious, and Judy had to fight the urge to jump up and down.

The questions Denise asked were typical. "He's really okay? . . . Where did you find him? When will I see him? . . . Thank you, thank you all so much. I can't believe it!"

When she hung up the phone, Denise sat up, despite the pain, and spontaneously hugged Judy while filling her in. "They're bringing him to the hospital to make sure he's okay. He should be here in an hour or so. I just can't believe it."

BACK in the swamp, Taylor had removed his raincoat and wrapped it around Kyle to keep him warm. Then, carrying him from the blind, he met up with the others, and they waited in Duck Shot just long enough to ensure that all the men were accounted for. Once they were assembled, they started back as a group.

The five hours of searching had taken their toll on Taylor, and carrying Kyle was a struggle. The boy weighed at least forty pounds, and the extra weight not only made his arms ache, it also made him sink even deeper in the mud. By the time he reached the road, where an ambulance was waiting, he was spent.

At first Kyle didn't want to let Taylor go, but Taylor was finally able to coax him down to let the attendant examine him.

The long night was finally over.

THE ambulance reached the hospital a little after 3:30 a.m. By that time the emergency room had calmed down. The doctors were waiting for Kyle. So were Denise and Judy.

Judy had surprised the nurse on duty by walking up to the station in the middle of the night to request a wheelchair for Denise Holton. "What are you doing here? Don't you know what time it is?" A little cajoling was necessary, but the nurse granted the request.

Kyle was wheeled in on a gurney. Both the doctors and the nurses stepped back so that Kyle could see his mother.

In the ambulance he'd been stripped down, then wrapped in warm blankets to get his body temperature back up. His face was pink, and in every respect he looked far better than his mother did.

Denise struggled to her feet and bent close so that Kyle could see her. Kyle sat up immediately and climbed into her embrace. They held each other tightly.

"Hello, Mommy," he finally said. (*Hewwo, Money.*)

"Hi, sweetie," she said. "Are you okay?"

Kyle didn't answer, but this time Denise couldn't have cared less.

THE following day dawned cloudy with sporadic rain. The newspapers were filled with coverage of what had happened the night before, the headlines focusing largely on a tornado near Maysville that had left four people dead and another seven injured.

Denise and Kyle were still in the hospital and had been allowed to sleep in the same room. Though Kyle could have been discharged the following afternoon, the doctors wanted to keep Denise in for an extra day of observation. Even though the dizziness had subsided for the most part, bright lights still hurt her eyes, and she had trouble keeping food down.

Denise and Kyle spent the morning watching cartoons. Both were on her bed, watching *Scooby-Doo,* Kyle's favorite.

"He's running," Kyle said, pointing at the screen, watching Scooby's legs turning in circles. *(Eez runny.)*

"Yes. He's running from the ghost. Can you say that?"

"Running from the ghost," he said. *(Runny fraw ah goz.)*

Her arm was around him, and she patted him on the shoulder. "Did you run last night?"

Kyle nodded, his eyes still on the screen. "Yes, eez runny."

She looked at him tenderly. "Were you scared last night?"

"Yes, he's scared." *(Yes, eez scairt.)*

Though his tone changed slightly, Denise didn't know whether he was talking about himself now or about Scooby-Doo. Kyle didn't understand the differences among pronouns (I, you, me, he, she, and so on), nor did he use verb tenses properly. The concept of time (yesterday, tomorrow, last night) was also beyond him. One day maybe he'd be able to tell her about the experience.

With a slow push the door squeaked open. "Knock, knock."

Denise turned toward the door as Judy McAden peeked inside. "I hope I'm not coming at a bad time. They said you were up."

Denise sat up. "No, of course not. We're just watching TV. C'mon in." Using the remote, she turned down the volume slightly.

"Well, I just wanted to come by to meet your son. He's quite the topic of conversation around town now."

Denise angled her head, glancing proudly at her son. "Well, here he is, the little terror. Kyle, say hello to Miss Judy."

"Hello, Miss Judy," he whispered. *(Hewwo, Miss Jeewey.)* His eyes were still glued to the screen.

Judy pulled up a chair and sat beside the bed. She patted him on the leg. "Hello, Kyle. I heard you had a big adventure last night. You had your mother really worried."

After a moment of silence Denise prodded her son. "Kyle, say, 'Yes, I did.' "

Kyle didn't respond.

"Kyle doesn't talk too well yet," Denise offered quietly. "He's delayed in speech."

Judy leaned in a little farther. "Oh, okay. What're you watching?"

Again he didn't answer, and Denise tapped him on the shoulder. "Kyle, what's on TV?"

"Scooby-Doo." (Scoody-Doo.)

Judy brightened. "Oh, Taylor used to watch that when he was little." Then, speaking a little slower, "Is it funny?"

Kyle nodded exuberantly. "Yes, it's funny." *(Yes, eez fuh-ee.)*

Denise's eyes widened just a little when he answered, then softened again. Thank God for small favors.

Judy turned to Denise. "So how are the two of you holding up?"

"Kyle here is healthy as can be. From the looks of him you'd think that nothing happened. Me, well, I hope I'll be getting out tomorrow. I'm sorry I didn't get a chance to thank you last night."

Judy raised her hands to stop her. "Oh, don't worry about that. I'm just glad everything worked out. Has Carl—Sergeant Huddle—stopped by yet?"

"No, not yet. He'll be coming by?"

Judy nodded. "Taylor told me this morning that Carl still had to wrap up a few things."

"Taylor? That's your son, right?"

"My one and only."

Denise struggled with the memory from the night before. "He was the one who found me, right?"

"Yes. He was trying to find some downed power lines when he came across your car."

"I should thank him, too."

"He wasn't the only one out there, you know. By the end, more than twenty people from all over town went out to help."

Denise shook her head, amazed. "But they didn't even know me."

"Edenton's a small town, but it has a big heart."

"Have you lived here your whole life?"

Judy nodded, putting her hand over her heart like Scarlett O'Hara, and slowly drawled out the words. "Darlin', I could tell you stories that would make your eyebrows curl."

Denise laughed. "Maybe we'll have a chance to visit sometime and you could fill me in."

"We'll do that. And I'll tell you what your mom was like as a little girl, too."

AFTER lunch Carl Huddle met with Denise and finished up the remaining paperwork. Lighthearted and far more alert than the evening before, Denise answered everything in detail. Kyle was sitting on the floor, playing with an airplane. When they were finished, Sergeant Huddle folded everything into a manila file, stifling a yawn with the back of his hand. "Excuse me," he said, trying to shake the drowsiness that had come over him.

"Tired?" she asked sympathetically.

"A little. I had an eventful evening."

"Thank you for what you did last night," Denise said. "You can't imagine how much it means to me."

"You're welcome. That's my job, though. Besides, I have a little girl of my own, and if it had been her, I would have wanted everyone within a fifty-mile radius to drop what they were doing to help find her." Sergeant Huddle rose to leave.

Denise sat up higher in the bed. "Before you go, can I ask you a couple of questions about last night?"

"Sure. Ask away."

"How were you able to find him? I mean, it was so dark, and with the storm . . ."

"Well, I'd like to say it was all skill and training, but it wasn't. We got lucky. Damn lucky. For a while there we had no idea which way he'd gone, but Taylor figured that Kyle would follow the wind and keep the lightning behind him. Sure enough, he was right."

He nodded toward Kyle, who was still playing with his airplane. "You've got one tough boy there, Miss Holton. Most kids would have been terrified, but your little boy wasn't. It's pretty amazing."

Denise's brow furrowed as she thought about what he'd just told her. "Wait—was that Taylor McAden?"

"Yeah. The guy who found you." He scratched his jaw. "He found Kyle in a duck blind, and Kyle wouldn't let go of him until we got him to the ambulance. Clamped on to him like a crab claw."

"Taylor McAden found Kyle?"

Carl nodded. "Taylor seemed to have a bead on him all night—don't ask me how."

After saying good-bye, Sergeant Huddle slipped out the door. Denise looked upward, toward the ceiling, without really seeing it.

Taylor McAden? Judy McAden? She couldn't believe the coincidence, but then again, everything that happened last night had fluke written all over it. The storm, the deer, the seat belt over her lap but not her shoulder, Kyle wandering away. Everything, including the McAdens. One here for support, the other one finding her car. One who knew her mother long ago and one who ended up locating Kyle. Coincidence? Fate? Something else?

Later that afternoon, with the help of a nurse and the local telephone directory, Denise wrote thank-you notes to Carl and Judy, as well as a general note (addressed in care of the fire department) to everyone involved in the search.

Last she wrote out her note to Taylor McAden, and as she did so, she couldn't help but wonder about him.

Three

THREE days later, under a cloudy sky, Taylor McAden walked beneath the archway entrance to Cypress Park Cemetery, the oldest cemetery in Edenton. He was dressed in jeans and a work shirt. He'd come directly from a project he'd been working on, quietly slipping away during the lunch break. He cut across the lawn, weaving around ancient memorials, stopping only when he reached the shade of a giant willow tree. Here, on the west side of the cemetery, was a nondescript granite block, inscribed simply on the upper face.

Grass had grown tall around the sides, but it was otherwise well tended. Directly in front of it, in a small tube set into the ground, was a bouquet of dried carnations. His mother had left eleven of them, one for every year of their marriage. She left them every May, on their wedding anniversary, as she had for the past twenty-seven years. She'd never told Taylor about leaving them, and Taylor had never mentioned that he knew. Unlike his mother, Taylor didn't visit the grave on his parents' anniversary. He visited in June, on the day his father died. That was the day he'd never forget.

Taylor bent and started to pull the longer blades of grass along the sides. His memory of Mason Thomas McAden had ended abruptly on that dreadful day. No matter how hard he tried, he couldn't picture what his father would look like if he were still alive. In Taylor's mind his father would always be thirty-six, the same age Taylor was now. A photo of his father was on the mantel in his living room. He had seen it every day for the past twenty-seven years.

The photo had been taken a week before the accident, on a warm June morning, right outside their home. In the picture his father was stepping off the back porch, fishing pole in hand, on his way to the Chowan River. Taylor was still in the house collecting his lures. His mother was hiding behind the truck, and when she called his father's name, Mason turned and she snapped the picture.

Because the film was sent away to be developed, it hadn't been destroyed with the other photos. Judy didn't pick it up until after the funeral and had cried while looking at it, then slipped it into her purse. To others it wasn't anything special—his father walking in midstride, hair uncombed—but to Taylor it had captured the very essence of his father, that irrepressible spirit that defined the man he was. A month after his father died, Taylor had sneaked it out of her purse and fallen asleep while holding it. His mother had come in and found the photo pressed into his small hands. She'd taken the negative in to have a copy made, and Taylor glued four Popsicle sticks to a piece of glass and mounted the photo. In all these years he'd never considered changing the frame.

Thirty-six. His father seemed so young in the picture, his lean face showing only the faintest outlines of wrinkles. Why, then, did his father seem so much older than Taylor felt right now? Was it because he'd lived more deeply? Or was this impression simply the product of a young boy's feelings for his father, including their last moment together? Taylor didn't know, but then he never would. The answers had been buried with his father a long time ago.

He could barely remember the weeks immediately after his father died: the funeral, staying with his grandparents, suffocating nightmares when he tried to sleep. It was summer—school was out—and Taylor spent most of his time outside, trying to blot out what had happened. Then they found a new place to live, and Taylor knew what his mother was trying to tell him. It's just the two of us now. We've got to go on.

After that fateful summer Taylor had drifted through school, progressing steadily from one grade to the next; he played football, basketball, and baseball. He was remarkably resilient, some would say; yet in many ways he was considered a loner. Mitch was, and always had been, his only real friend, and in the summers they'd go hunting and fishing, just the two of them. Though Mitch was married now, they still did it whenever they could.

Taylor bypassed college in favor of work, learning the carpentry business and taking classes to earn his contractor's license. He supported himself by working in the gypsum mine near Little Washington, a job that left him coughing almost every night, but by twenty-four he'd saved enough to start his own business. No project was too small, and he often underbid to build up his business. Over the past eight years he'd nurtured it to the point where he made a decent living. His house was small and his truck was six years old, but it was enough for him to lead the simple life he desired, a life that included volunteering for the fire department. His mother had tried to talk him out of it. It was the only instance in which he'd deliberately gone against her wishes.

Of course, she wanted to be a grandmother, and she'd let that slip out every now and then. Taylor usually made light of the comment and tried to change the subject. He hadn't come close to marriage, though in the past he'd dated two women fairly seriously. The first time was in his early twenties, when he'd started seeing Valerie. She was coming off a disastrous relationship when they'd met, and Taylor was the one she'd turned to. She was two years older, smart, and they had gotten along well for a time. But Valerie wanted something more serious; Taylor had told her honestly that he might never be ready. In time they simply drifted apart. The last he'd heard, she was married to a lawyer and living in Charlotte.

Then there was Lori. She had moved to Edenton to work for the bank. She had a childlike innocence that aroused Taylor's protective interests, but eventually she too wanted more than he was willing to commit to. They broke up soon afterward. Now she was married to the mayor's son and had three children.

By the time he was thirty, he'd dated most of the single women in Edenton; by the time he was thirty-six, there weren't that many left. Mitch's wife, Melissa, had tried to set him up on various dates, but those had fizzled as well. But then again, he hadn't really been looking, had he? Both Valerie and Lori claimed that there was something inside of him they were unable to reach. And though he knew they meant well, their attempts to talk to him about this distance of his didn't—or couldn't—change anything.

When he was finished, he stood, his knees aching from the position he'd been kneeling in. Before he left, he said a short prayer in memory of his father, and afterward he bent over to touch the headstone. "I'm sorry, Dad," he whispered. "I'm so, so sorry."

ONCE Denise and Kyle were reunited in the hospital and she saw that he was okay, everything was right in the world. But a week later reality had settled in. Denise was seated at the Formica table in her small kitchen, poring through the papers in front of her, doing her best to make sense of them.

The hospital stay was covered by insurance, but not the deductible. Her car was totaled, and she'd had only liability insurance. Her boss, Ray, bless his heart, told her to take her time coming back. Eight days had gone by without her earning a penny. The regular bills—phone, electricity, water, gas—were due. And to top it off was the bill for seventy-five dollars for the towing service.

She could cover the regular bills with what was left in the checking account and still have enough for food if she was careful. Lots of cereal this month, that was for sure. She could use her credit card for the hospital deductible—five hundred dollars. Luckily, Rhonda, another waitress at Eights, had agreed to help Denise get to and from work. That left the towing service, and fortunately, they'd offered to clear the bill in exchange for the remains of her car.

The net result? An additional credit-card bill every month, and she'd have to start riding her bicycle for errands around town. A bicycle. Lord have mercy. Well, at least she'd get in shape. "Look at those legs," she imagined people saying. "Why, they're just like steel. However did you get them?"

"I ride my bike."

She couldn't help but giggle. She was twenty-nine years old and she'd be telling people about her bike. Lord have mercy.

EARLY the next morning Kyle padded through the bedroom and crawled into bed with Denise. He whispered, "Wake up, Money, wake up," and when she rolled over with a groan, he climbed over her and used his little fingers to try to lift her eyelids. He thought this was hilarious. "Open your eyes, Money," he kept saying, and despite the ungodly hour, she couldn't help but laugh as well.

To make the morning even better, Judy McAden called a little after nine to see if they were still on for their visit. Judy would be coming over the following afternoon. Hurray! A little later, after breakfast, Denise got the bikes ready. After she'd helped Kyle put on his helmet, they started toward town under a cloudless sky, Kyle riding out in front. To Kyle, riding his bike was an adventure, and he rode with reckless abandon. Even though traffic was light, Denise found herself shouting instructions every few seconds.

"Stay close to Mommy. . . . Stop!"

"Pull over, honey, a car's coming. . . . Stop!"

"Watch out for the hole. . . . Stop!"

"Stop" was the only command he really understood, and whenever she said it, he'd hit the brakes, put his feet on the ground, then turn around with a big grin, as if to say, This is so much fun. Why're you so upset?

Denise was a nervous wreck by the time they reached town. Riding a bicycle wasn't going to cut it, and she decided to ask Ray for two extra shifts a week. Pay off the hospital deductible, save every penny, and maybe she'd be able to afford another car in a couple of months. A couple of months? She'd probably go nuts by then.

Edenton's small downtown was a historic gem. Homes dated back to the early 1800s. Giant oaks lined the streets, providing pleasant cover from the heat of the sun.

Though Edenton had a supermarket, it was on the other side of town, and Denise decided to drop into Merchants instead, an old-fashioned store that sold everything from food to bait to automotive supplies. Adding to the atmosphere were four rocking chairs and a bench out front, where a regular group of locals dropped by for coffee in the mornings.

In the store, Denise filled a plastic basket with the few things she needed, and the owner packed everything into two brown paper bags. She would have preferred plastic, like at the supermarket, so she could have slipped the loops over her handlebars—but bags? How was she going to get all this home? Pondering the problem, she noticed Kyle staring through the glass entrance door, toward the street. "What is it, honey?"

She didn't understand his answer; it sounded like *fowman*. She bent down so she could watch his lips as he said it again. "Fowman." This time he pointed through the door, and Denise looked in that direction. All at once she knew what he'd meant. Not fowman, though it was close. *Fireman.*

Taylor McAden was outside the store. Kyle ran up to him as Taylor stepped inside. He almost bowled Kyle over.

"Whoa, sorry—didn't see you," he said. Then, sudden recognition crossing his face, he broke into a wide smile, squatting so he could be at eye level. "Oh, hey, little man. How are you?"

"Hello, Taylor," Kyle said happily. *(Hewwo, Tayer.)* Kyle wrapped his arms around him as he had that night in the duck blind. Taylor hugged him back, looking content and surprised at the same time.

Denise watched in stunned silence. After a long moment Kyle finally loosened his grip, allowing Taylor to pull back. Kyle's eyes were dancing, as if he'd recognized a long-lost friend. "Fowman," Kyle said again excitedly. "He's found you." *(Eez foun you.)*

Taylor cocked his head to one side. "What's that?"

Denise finally snapped to attention and moved toward them. Even after spending a year with his speech therapist, Kyle had hugged the lady only when Denise prodded him, and she wasn't exactly sure how she felt about Kyle's new attachment. At the same time, the comfortable way that Taylor had reacted to Kyle—and vice versa—made it seem anything but threatening.

"He's trying to say that you found him," she said. Taylor glanced up and saw Denise for the first time since the accident. Despite the fact he'd seen her before, she looked more attractive than he'd remembered. Granted, she was a mess that night, and the way she might look under normal circumstances hadn't crossed his mind.

"Yes. He's found you," Kyle said again, nodding for emphasis.

"That's right, I did," Taylor said with a friendly hand still on Kyle's shoulder, "but you, little man, were the brave one."

Denise watched as he spoke to Kyle. Taylor was wearing jeans and well-worn work boots covered with dried mud. His white shirt was short-sleeved, revealing tight muscles in his sun-darkened arms. When he stood, he seemed taller than she'd remembered.

"Sorry about almost knocking him over back there," he said. "I didn't see him." He stopped, as if not knowing what else to say.

"It wasn't your fault. He kind of snuck up on you." She smiled. "I'm Denise Holton, by the way. I know we met before, but a lot of that night's fairly foggy." She held out her hand, and Taylor took it. She could feel the calluses on his palm.

"Taylor McAden," he said. "I got your note. Thanks."

"Fowman," Kyle said again. He wrung his hands almost compulsively, something he did when he was excited. "Big fowman."

Taylor reached out, grabbing Kyle by his helmet in a friendly, almost brotherly way. "You think so, huh?"

Kyle nodded. "Big."

Denise laughed. "I think it's a case of hero worship."

"Well, the feeling's mutual, little man. It was more you than me."

Kyle's eyes were wide. "Big."

Taylor said, "Kyle looks good. After all that happened, I was sort of wondering how he was doing."

"He seems okay. The doctor gave him a clean bill of health."

"How 'bout you? You were pretty banged up."

"I guess I'm doing okay, too," she said. "A little sore here and there, but otherwise fine."

The bruises on her cheek were still slightly visible. The gash on her forehead had been closed neatly with stitches, and though she would always have a scar, it was near the hairline.

"Good. I'm glad. I was worried about you, too."

There was something in the quiet way he spoke that made Denise take a closer look at him. Though he wasn't the most handsome man she'd ever seen, there was something about him that caught her attention—a gentleness, perhaps, an unthreatening perceptiveness in his steady gaze. Glancing at his left hand, she noticed he wasn't wearing a ring. She quickly turned away.

As she looked away, Taylor couldn't help but watch her. The lovely, almost mysterious face accented by high cheekbones and exotic hazel eyes, long, dark wavy hair pulled into a messy ponytail that reached past her shoulder blades, a shapely figure accented by the shorts and blouse she was wearing.

Before she caught him staring at her, Taylor spoke again. "So I take it you're in town for a few errands?" Small talk, nothing talk, Taylor knew, but for some reason he was reluctant to let her leave.

Denise ran her hand through her disheveled ponytail. "Yeah. We needed to grab a few things. How about you?"

"I'm just here to pick up some soda for the guys."

"At the fire department?"

"No—I only volunteer there. The guys who work for me. I'm a contractor. I remodel homes, things like that."

"He's hungry," Kyle said to his mother. (*Eez hungwy.*)

"Well, we'll be home soon, sweetheart. Okay?" Denise looked at Taylor again. "It was good seeing you," she said.

"You, too," he said. He gave Kyle's helmet a shake as before. "And you, too, little man."

Kyle waved. "Bye-bye, Tayer," he said exuberantly.

"Bye." Taylor gave him a wink before heading toward the soda. Denise turned to the store owner, motioning toward the bags.

"Would you mind if we left this here for a few minutes?" she asked. "We have to get some bags that loop over the handlebars."

Despite the fact he was already halfway across the store, Taylor strained to hear what was going on.

Denise continued, "We're on our bikes, and I don't think I can get this all home. It won't take long—we'll be right back."

He heard the owner answer, "Sure, no problem."

Denise was shepherding Kyle out of the store. Taylor made up his mind on the spot. "Hey, Denise, wait up."

She turned and stopped as Taylor approached. "I couldn't help but overhear what you said, and, well . . ." He paused, that steady blue gaze holding her motionless. "Can I give you a hand getting your groceries home?" He motioned to the truck parked outside.

"Oh no, that's all right."

"Are you sure? It's right on the way. Take me two minutes, tops."

Though she knew he was trying to be kind, a product of a small-town upbringing, she wasn't sure she should accept. Had she been on her own so long that she didn't know how to accept other people's kindness anymore? Or was it that he'd done so much for her already? Go ahead. It's not like he's asking you to marry him. . . .

She swallowed, thinking of the bag hunt, then loading up the groceries to transport home. "If you're sure it's not out of your way."

Taylor felt as if he'd achieved some sort of minor victory. "No, not at all. Just let me pay for this soda and I'll help carry your things to the truck." He went and paid, then picked up her grocery bags.

"How do you know where I live?" she asked.

He looked over his shoulder. "It's a small town. I know where everyone lives."

LATER that evening Melissa, Mitch, and Taylor were in the backyard, steaks and hot dogs sizzling over charcoal. The yellow sun hovered low in the sky just above the dogwoods, motionless in the still evening air.

Mitch stood, tongs in hand. Taller and thinner than Taylor, he was six two and weighed about a hundred and sixty pounds. Most of his hair was gone—he'd started losing it early—and he wore wire-rimmed glasses. He worked at his father's hardware store and was regarded around town as a mechanical genius. He'd majored in business at college and met a psychology major from Rocky Mount named Melissa Kindle before moving back to Edenton. They'd been married twelve years and had four boys. Taylor had been best man at the wedding.

Mitch, like Taylor, was a volunteer with the Edenton Fire Department. At Taylor's urging, the two of them had gone through training together and had joined at the same time. Though Mitch considered it more a duty than a calling, he was someone Taylor always wanted along when a call came in.

Taylor nursed a beer, his third of the evening. He had a nice buzz going. After catching them up on what had been happening recently—including the search in the swamp—he mentioned that he'd seen Denise at the store and that he'd dropped her groceries off. "They seem to be doing fine," he observed, slapping at a mosquito.

Though it was said in all innocence, Melissa eyed him carefully, then leaned forward in her chair. "So you like her, huh?" she said.

Mitch cut into the conversation. "What did he say? He liked her?"

"I didn't say that," Taylor said quickly.

"You didn't have to," Melissa said. "I could see it in your face, and besides, you wouldn't have dropped her groceries off if you didn't." She turned to her husband. "Yeah, he likes her."

"You're putting words in my mouth."

Melissa smiled wryly. "So is she pretty?"

"What kind of question is that?"

Melissa turned to her husband again. "He thinks she's pretty, too."

Mitch nodded, convinced. "So you gonna ask her out?"

Taylor turned from one to the other, wondering how the conversation had spun in this direction. "I hadn't planned on it."

Melissa leaned back in her chair. "You're not getting any younger, you know. You're already past your prime."

Taylor shook his head. "Thanks a lot."

Melissa giggled. "You know we're just teasing." Her eyebrows danced up and down. Melissa was thirty-four but looked and acted ten years younger. Blond and petite, she was quick with a kind word, loyal to her friends, and never seemed to hold a grudge about anything. Her kids could be fighting, the dog might have messed on the rug, the car wouldn't start—it didn't matter. On more than one occasion Taylor had told Mitch that he was a lucky man. Mitch's answer was always the same: "I know."

"Why are you so interested, anyway?" Taylor asked.

"Because we love you," Melissa answered sweetly.

And don't understand why I'm still alone, Taylor thought. "All right," he finally said. "I'll think about it."

"Fair enough," Melissa said, not bothering to hide her enthusiasm.

THE next day Denise spent the morning working with Kyle. Now that summer had arrived, he seemed to work best if they were able to finish before noon. After that it was too warm in the house to concentrate. Right after breakfast she'd called Ray, and he consented to giving her the extra shifts. Starting tomorrow night, she'd work every evening except Sunday.

She'd found herself thinking about Taylor McAden ever since she'd run into him the day before. Just as he'd promised, the groceries had been placed on the front porch, in the shade provided by the overhang. While Taylor had carried the grocery bags to his truck, he'd also offered to put their bikes in the back and give them a ride, but to that Denise had said no. It had less to do with Taylor than Kyle—he was already getting on his bike, and she knew he was looking forward to another ride. Besides, the last thing she wanted was for him to expect a truck ride back every time they came to town.

Still, part of her had wanted to accept Taylor's offer. The way he'd looked at her made it plain that he found her attractive, yet it didn't make her uncomfortable the way the scrutiny of other men sometimes did.

Of the many things she'd learned from her mother, there was one that always came to mind when evaluating others. "You're going to come across people in your life who say all the right words. But in the end, it's always their actions you should judge them by."

Maybe, she thought, that was the reason she'd responded to Taylor. He'd already proven that he could do heroic things, but it wasn't simply his dramatic rescue of Kyle that inspired her interest in him—if that's what it was. No. It was the way he'd offered to help without expecting something in return, the way he seemed to care about how Kyle and she were doing, the way he'd treated Kyle. Especially that.

Even though she didn't want to admit it, over the last few years she'd come to judge people by the way they treated her son. She remembered compiling lists in her mind of the friends who tried with Kyle and the ones who hadn't. Even though Taylor didn't understand everything Kyle had said, Taylor kept talking to him as if he did. He looked Kyle in the eye when he spoke. He'd made sure to say good-bye. Little things, but they were incredibly important to her. Taylor had treated Kyle like a normal little boy.

Ironically, Denise was still thinking about Taylor as Judy pulled up and parked in the shade of a looming magnolia tree. After the traditional preliminaries Denise and Judy seated themselves on the front porch so they could keep an eye on Kyle. He was playing with his trucks near the fence, rolling them along make-believe roads. Before Judy arrived, Denise had coated him with sunscreen and bug spray, and the lotions acted like glue when he played in the dirt. His face looked as if it hadn't been washed in a week.

On the small wooden table sat two glasses of chilled sweet tea that Denise had made that morning. Judy took a drink from her glass, her eyes never leaving Kyle.

"Your mother used to love getting dirty, too," Judy said.

"My mother?"

Judy glanced at her, amused. "Your mother was quite a tomboy."

"Are we talking about the same lady? My mother wouldn't even collect the morning paper without putting makeup on."

"Oh, that happened right around the time she discovered boys. She turned into the quintessential southern lady practically overnight. But don't let that fool you. Before that your mother was a regular Huckleberry Finn. She caught frogs, she cussed like a shrimper who'd lost his net, she even got in a few fights with boys. She was one tough young lady."

Denise stayed silent, waiting for her to go on.

"I remember she'd go the whole summer without wearing shoes, except when she had to go to church. Her feet would be so dirty by September that her mother couldn't get the stains out unless she used a Brillo pad and Ajax. When school started up again, your mother would limp for the first couple of days. I never figured out whether it was because of the Brillo pad or simply the fact that she wasn't used to wearing shoes."

Denise laughed in disbelief.

Judy continued, "Do you know the Boyle place down the road? That white house with the green shutters?"

Denise nodded. She passed by it on the way into town.

"Well, that was where I lived when I was little. Your mom and I were the only girls who lived out this way, so we ended up doing everything together. She was probably the best friend I ever had."

"Why didn't she keep in touch? I mean . . ."

"You mean why, if we were such good friends, didn't she tell you about it? I guess it mainly had to do with her moving away. We kept in touch for a few years, but back then your mother was in love, and when women fall in love, it's all they can think about. That was why she left Edenton in the first place. A boy—Michael Cunningham. Did she ever tell you about him?"

Denise shook her head, fascinated.

"I'm not surprised. Michael was kind of a bad boy, but a lot of girls found him attractive. Same old story. Well, your mother followed him to Atlanta right after she graduated."

"But she told me she moved to Atlanta to go to college."

"Oh, that may have been in the back of her mind, but the real reason was Michael. He was also the reason she didn't come back. Her mom and dad—your grandparents—saw Michael for what he was and said that if she didn't come home right away, she wasn't welcome here anymore. They were as stubborn as can be, and your mom was just the same—each waiting for the other one to give in. But they never did, even after Michael went by the wayside.

"Your father came along after I lost contact with her. I do remember your grandparents heading off to the wedding—and being a little hurt that your mother hadn't sent me an invitation. But your father came from a very respectable family in Atlanta, and I think your mom was a little embarrassed about where she'd come from. Not that your father minded, obviously, since he married her. But I remember that your grandparents didn't say much after they returned from the wedding. I think they knew they didn't fit into their daughter's world anymore, even after your father passed away."

"That's terrible."

"It's sad, but like I said, it went both ways. Please don't think poorly of your mother. I certainly don't. She was always so full of life, so passionate—she was exciting to be around. And she had the heart of an angel. She was as sweet a person as I ever knew." Judy turned to face her. "I see a lot of her in you."

Denise tried to digest this new information about her mother as Judy took another sip of her tea. Then, as if knowing she'd said too much, Judy asked, "So why did you move to Edenton?"

Denise watched Kyle playing with his trucks. "There's a couple of reasons. I guess mainly it has to do with Kyle. I told you he has trouble speaking, right?"

Judy nodded.

"Well, right now they say he has an auditory processing problem. Basically, it means that for some reason—no one knows why— understanding language and learning to speak is hard for him. I guess the best analogy is that it's like dyslexia, only instead of processing visual signals, it has to do with processing sounds." Denise ran her hand through her hair. "Are you sure you want to hear all of this? It's kind of a long story."

Judy reached over and patted Denise on the knee. "Only if you feel like telling me."

Strangely, it felt good to tell Judy about it. Denise explained Kyle's problem and the numerous diagnoses doctors had given her.

"It must have been so hard on you," Judy said. "Where was the father during all of this?"

Denise shrugged, a guilty expression on her face. "The father wasn't around. Suffice it to say, I hadn't expected to get pregnant."

Judy seemed neither surprised nor shocked by the revelation.

Denise cleared her throat. "After Kyle was born, I took a leave of absence from the school where I was teaching. My mom had died, and I wanted to spend the first year or so with the baby. But after all this started happening, I couldn't go back to work. I was shuttling him all day long to doctors and evaluation centers and therapists, until I finally came up with a therapy program that we could do at home. None of that left me with enough time for a full-time job. Working with Kyle is full-time. I'd inherited this house, but I couldn't sell it, and eventually the money just ran out. So I had to move here out of necessity so that I could keep working with Kyle."

She glanced at Judy, a rueful expression on her face. "It seems like all I do is work with Kyle and work at the diner."

Judy patted her on the knee. "Well, pardon the expression, but you're a helluva mother. Not many people would make those kinds of sacrifices."

Denise watched Kyle playing. "I just want him to get better."

"He sounds like he already has."

"But he still has trouble speaking."

"So did Einstein and Teller, but they turned out to be the greatest physicists in history."

"How would you know about their speech problems?" Though Denise knew (she'd read nearly everything on the subject), she was surprised—and impressed—that Judy knew it as well.

"Oh, you'd be amazed at the amount of trivia I've picked up over the years. I'm like a vacuum cleaner with that stuff."

From there the conversation drifted easily to Judy's job and other things. A half hour later Kyle tired of playing with his trucks and wandered up to his mother. "Can I have some macaroni and cheese?" (*Ca-ah haf son concor cheese?*)

"Sure, sweetie."

Denise and Judy stood and went into the kitchen. Kyle went to the table and sat while Denise filled a saucepan with hot water and set it on a burner. "Would you like to stay for lunch?" she asked.

Judy checked her watch. "I'd love to, but I can't. I have a meeting downtown about the festival this weekend."

"Festival?"

"Yeah. It's an annual event and sort of gets everyone in the mood for summer. You should go. Kyle would love it. They have food and crafts, contests—a carnival is in town. There's something for everyone." Judy picked up her purse from the counter. They walked toward the front door and stepped out on the porch again.

Denise ran her hand through her hair, adjusting a few loose strands that had fallen in her face. "Thanks for coming by. It was nice to have an adult conversation for a change."

"Thanks for inviting me," Judy said, leaning in to give her an impulsive hug. "Let's do this again sometime."

"I'd like that."

Judy made her way down the steps. "You know, Taylor's gonna be at the festival on Saturday, with the fire department," she called out conversationally. "Their softball team plays at three. In case you come by, that's where I'll be."

Denise waved as Judy slipped behind the wheel, the faint outlines of a smile playing softly on her lips.

Four

"HEY there! I wasn't sure you two were going to make it," Judy called out happily.

It was Saturday afternoon, a little after three, when Denise and Kyle made their way up the bleachers toward Judy.

The softball game hadn't been hard to find—it was the only area of the park with bleachers. As they'd parked their bikes, Denise had easily spotted Judy sitting in the stands. Seeing them as well, Judy had waved as Denise held on to Kyle, doing her best to keep her balance as she made her way toward the upper seats.

"Hey, Judy. It took us a while to get through the crowds."

The streets downtown had been closed to traffic and were teeming with people. Banners stretched across the main road, booths lining both sidewalks. In the square the carnival was in full swing.

Judy scooted over to make room, and Kyle wedged himself

between them. As he did so, he leaned into Judy almost flirtatiously and laughed as if he thought the whole thing were funny. Then he pulled out one of the toy airplanes he'd brought.

"Oh, people come from all over for the festival," Judy said in explanation. "It pretty much draws from the whole county."

"It sure looks that way."

Judy nudged Kyle in the ribs. "Hi, Kyle. How are you?"

He held his toy up for her to see. "Owpwane," he said.

Though Denise knew it was his way of trying to communicate on a level he understood, she prodded him to answer correctly. She tapped his shoulder. "Kyle, say, 'I'm fine, thanks.' "

"I'm fine, thanks." *(I'n fie, kenks.)* He bobbed his head in rhythm with the syllables, then turned his attention back to his toy.

Denise slipped her arm around him and nodded toward the action on the field. "So who are we rooting for, Judy?"

"Either team, really. Taylor's in the field now at third base for the red team—that's the Chowan Volunteers, the fire department. The blue team's the Chowan Enforcers—the police, the sheriffs, and local troopers. They play for charity every year. The losing team has to pony up five hundred dollars for the library."

"And whose idea was that?" Denise inquired knowingly.

"Mine, of course."

"What's the score?"

"Four to two—the fire department is leading."

For the next hour Denise and Judy watched the game, chatting about Edenton and cheering for both teams. Kyle, however, had grown bored with the game and had taken to playing under the bleachers. It made Denise nervous to lose sight of him, and she stood up to look for him on more than a few occasions.

Whenever she did, Taylor found his eyes darting that way. He'd seen her arrive with Kyle, holding his hand and scanning the bleachers, oblivious of the fact that men were turning their heads as she passed them, her white shirt tucked into black shorts, long legs stretching down to sandals, dark windblown hair flowing past her shoulders. He found himself envious of the fact that his mother— not he—would be sitting with her.

Once, his stare had lasted a little too long, and she waved. He waved back with an embarrassed grin and turned away.

IN THE seventh inning, with the score 14–12, the Volunteers were trailing when Taylor was waiting for his turn at bat. Kyle was standing near the fence when he saw Taylor taking his practice swings.

"Hewwo, Tayer," he said happily.

Taylor turned at the sound of his voice and approached the fence. "Hey there, Kyle. Good to see you. How you doing?"

"He's fowman," Kyle said, pointing.

"I sure am. Are you having fun watching the game?"

Kyle held up his airplane for Taylor to see. "Owpwane."

"You're right. That's a nice airplane."

"You can hold it." *(You kin hode it.)*

Kyle handed it to him through the fence. Taylor examined it as Kyle watched him, a look of pride on his little face. Taylor heard his name being called to the plate.

"Thanks for showing me your airplane. Do you want it back?"

"You can hold it," Kyle said again.

Taylor debated for a moment before deciding. "Okay. This'll be my good-luck charm. I'll bring it right back." He made sure that Kyle could see him put it in his pocket. "Is that all right?"

Kyle didn't answer, but he seemed to be fine with it.

Both Denise and Judy had seen what just transpired.

"I think Kyle likes Taylor," Denise said.

"I think," Judy answered, "the feeling's mutual."

On the second pitch Taylor smashed the ball into right field—he batted left-handed—and took off at a full clip while two others in scoring position made their way around the bags. The ball reached the infield just as Taylor arrived safely at third. The game was tied, and Taylor scored when the next person batted. On his way to the dugout he handed Kyle the airplane, a big grin on his face.

"I told you it would make me lucky, little man. That's a good airplane."

"Yes—the airplane is good." *(Yes—ee owpwane ess goo.)*

It would have been the perfect way to end the game, but it wasn't meant to be. In the bottom of the seventh the Enforcers scored the winning run when Carl Huddle knocked one out of the park.

After the game was over, Denise and Judy made their way down from the bleachers, ready to head over to the park, where food and beer were waiting. Judy pointed out where they'd be sitting.

"I'm already late," Judy explained. "I was supposed to be helping set up. Can I meet you over there?"

"Go ahead," Denise said. "I have to get Kyle first."

Kyle was still standing near the fence, watching Taylor gather his gear. Denise tapped him on the shoulder. "Kyle, c'mon, let's go."

"No," he answered with a shake of his head.

"The game's over."

Kyle looked up at her, a concerned expression on his face. "No, he's not." *(No, eez not.)*

"Kyle, would you rather go play?"

"He's not," he said again, frowning now, his tone dropping.

Denise knew exactly what that meant—it was one of the ways he showed frustration at his inability to communicate. It was also the first step toward a genuine screamfest. Of course, all children threw tantrums now and then, but for Kyle tantrums mostly arose because he couldn't get his point across. He'd get mad at Denise for not understanding, Denise would get angry because he couldn't say what he meant, and the whole thing would spiral downward from there. Once things had calmed down, she'd feel terrible, believing herself to be the most mean-spirited mother on the planet.

More than anything, she didn't want to have that happen here. She steadied herself, vowing not to raise her voice. Okay, take your time. He's trying his best.

"He's not," Denise said, repeating after Kyle.

"Yes."

She held his arm gently. "Kyle, he's not what?"

"No . . ." The word came out with a whine, and Kyle made a low growling sound in his throat. He tried to pull away. Definitely on the verge of a screamfest.

She tried again, with things she knew he understood.

"Are you tired?"

"No."

"Are you hungry?"

"No."

"Kyle—"

"No!" he said, cutting her off. He was angry now.

"He's not what?" she asked with as much patience as possible.

Kyle groped for the words. "He's not . . . Kye."

Denise was completely lost now. "You're not Kyle?"

"Yes."

Huh? Denise thought about it, trying to figure it out. "What's your name? Is it Kyle?"

Kyle shook his head. "He's not Kye. He's linno man."

"Little man?"

Kyle nodded triumphantly and smiled, his anger suddenly receding. "Eez linno man," he said. All Denise could do was stare at him.

Little man. Oh Lord, how long was *this* going to last?

At that moment Taylor approached them, his gear bag over his shoulder. "Hey, Denise, how are you?"

"I'm not exactly sure," Denise answered. She recounted her exchange with Kyle as the three of them began walking across the park together.

Taylor patted Kyle on the back. "Little man, huh?"

"Yes. Eez linno man," Kyle said proudly in response.

"Don't encourage him," Denise said with a shake of the head.

Taylor seemed to find the whole thing extremely humorous, and Kyle was gazing at him as though he were one of the seven wonders of the world. "But he is a little man," Taylor said. "Aren't you?"

Kyle nodded, pleased to have someone on his side. Then he spotted a children's play area. "He wants to run," Kyle said, looking expectantly at his mother. "Over there." *(Ee wanta wun. O'er dare.)*

"Say, 'I want to run.' "

"I want to run," he said softly. *(I wanta wun.)*

"Okay—go ahead," she said.

Kyle dashed toward the play area.

"That's one cute kid," Taylor offered with a grin.

"Thanks. He's a good boy."

"That little man thing isn't really a problem, is it?"

"It shouldn't be. He went through a phase where he pretended to be Godzilla a couple of months ago. He wouldn't answer to anything else. He slipped away at the store once, and I was walking through the aisles calling for Godzilla. You wouldn't believe the looks I got—like what kind of mother names her kid Godzilla?"

Taylor laughed. "That's great."

"Yeah, well." She rolled her eyes, communicating a mixture of contentment and exasperation. Glancing at him, her eyes caught his and lingered just an instant too long before each of them turned away. They walked on in silence. From the corner of his eye, however, Taylor watched her. She was radiant in the warm June sunlight. Her eyes, he noticed, were the color of jade, exotic and mysterious. She was shorter than he was, maybe five six, and she moved with the easy grace of people who were confident of their place in the world. More than that, he sensed her intelligence in the patient way she dealt with her son and, most of all, how much she loved him. To Taylor those were the things that really mattered.

"So why did you get involved with the fire department?" Denise finally said, interrupting his thoughts.

The question brought his father's image to mind. Taylor forced it away. "It's something I've wanted to do since I was a kid."

Though she heard a slight change in his tone, his expression seemed neutral as he studied the crowds in the distance.

"Do they just call you up when there's an emergency?"

He shrugged, suddenly relieved for some reason. "Pretty much."

"Is that how you found my car that night?"

Taylor shook his head. "There were downed power lines, and I was out setting flares so that people could stop in time. I came across your car and pulled over to see what was wrong."

"And there I was," she said.

He met her gaze, his eyes the color of the sky. "And there you were."

They reached the tables, which were piled high with food for the small army of people milling about. Over by the grills where burgers and franks were being cooked were four large coolers filled with ice and beer. Taylor tossed his gear bag to one side and grabbed a beer. He held up a can of Coors Light. "Would you like one?"

"Sure, if you have enough."

"There's plenty." He handed the can to her. The beer was refreshing on such a hot day.

Judy walked over to meet them. She gave Taylor a quick squeeze. "Sorry your team lost," she said playfully. "But you owe me five hundred bucks."

"Thanks for the moral support."

Judy laughed.

Denise scanned the area for Kyle. Like radar, she was able to zero in on him. He was playing on the slide, and his face was red. "Would it be okay if I got Kyle a soda or something to drink?"

"Absolutely," Judy answered. "Coke, Sprite, root beer?"

"Sprite."

Just then Taylor saw Melissa and Mitch coming over to say hello. Melissa was wearing the same triumphant expression that she'd had the night he'd been over for dinner.

"Here, let me bring it to him," Taylor offered hurriedly.

"Are you sure?" Denise asked.

"I'm positive," he answered, and headed for Kyle, narrowly avoiding Melissa and Mitch.

Over the next half hour or so Judy introduced Denise to a few dozen people. The casual setting—kids running from here to there, people laughing and joking—made it easy for her to relax.

Supper for the kids came next, and they came rushing to the tables from all over. Kyle, of course, didn't come to the table with the rest of the children, but strangely, she didn't see Taylor, either. She looked toward the play area, and it was then that she saw the two of them, facing each other. When she realized what they were doing, her breath caught in her throat. She almost didn't believe it. She watched as Taylor gently lobbed a baseball in Kyle's direction. Kyle stood with both arms straight out, his forearms close together. As if by magic, the ball dropped directly into his little hands.

All she could do was stare in wonder.

Taylor McAden was playing catch with her son.

KYLE'S LATEST THROW WAS OFF the mark—as many of them had been—and Taylor scrambled as the ball went past him, coming to a stop in the short grass. As he stepped over to retrieve it, he saw Denise approaching. "We were just playing catch," he said casually.

"Have you been doing this the whole time?" she asked, unable to hide her amazement. Kyle had never wanted to play catch before. She'd tried numerous times. Her surprise, though, wasn't limited simply to Kyle; it had to do with Taylor. It was the first time that someone else had ever taken the time to teach Kyle something new. He was playing with Kyle. Nobody played with Kyle.

Taylor nodded. "Pretty much. He seems to like it."

Kyle saw her and waved. "Hewwo, Money," he called out.

"Are you having fun?" she asked.

"He throws it," he said excitedly. (*Ee frows it.*)

Denise couldn't help but smile. "I see that. It was a good throw." She turned to Taylor. "How did you get him to do it?"

"What? Play catch? Actually, it was his idea. He sort of sailed one at me, so I tossed it back and gave him some pointers on how to catch it. He caught on pretty fast."

"Frow it," Kyle called. His arms were straight out again.

Taylor looked at her to see if it was all right.

"Go ahead," Denise said. "I've got to see this again."

Taylor took his position. "You ready?" he asked Kyle.

Kyle, concentrating hard, didn't respond. Denise crossed her arms in nervous anticipation.

"Here it comes," Taylor said, lobbing the ball. It hit Kyle on the wrist and bounced toward his chest like a pinball before finally falling to the ground. Kyle immediately picked it up, aimed, then threw the ball back. This time the ball was on target, and Taylor was able to catch it without moving. "Good one," he said.

The ball went back and forth a few more times before Denise finally spoke. "You ready for a break?" she asked.

"Only if he is," Taylor responded.

"Once he finds something he likes, he doesn't like to stop."

"So I've noticed."

Denise called out to Kyle, "Okay, sweetie, last one."

Kyle knew what that meant, and he eyed the ball carefully before throwing it. It went off to the right, and once again Taylor scrambled to catch it. Kyle started toward his mother.

When he reached her, she hugged him. "Good job playing catch."

"Yes," Kyle said happily.

"Would you like to play on the slide?" she asked.

Kyle nodded, and he immediately headed toward the play area.

Once they were alone, Denise faced Taylor. She could see beads of perspiration dripping down his cheek. His dark hair peeked out from under his hat, curling slightly, and his shirt was tacked to his chest. Her son had kept him busy. "That was really nice of you, but you didn't have to stay out here the whole time."

"I know I didn't. I wanted to. He's a lot of fun."

She smiled gratefully. "The food's ready."

"I think I'll have a burger. I take it you already ate."

Denise checked her watch. "Actually, I haven't, but we can't stay. I've got to work tonight—I waitress at Eights—and I've still got to feed Kyle."

"He can eat here. There's plenty of food."

"Kyle doesn't eat meat. Or chips. He's kind of a picky eater."

Taylor nodded. "Can I give you a lift home?" he asked.

"We rode our bikes here."

Taylor nodded. "I know."

She didn't need the ride, and he knew it; he'd asked despite the fact that friends and food were waiting. It was obvious that he wanted her to say yes.

It would have been easy to say no. Her mind was telling her that her life was complex enough, that she barely knew him. The thoughts registered in quick succession, making perfect sense, but she surprised herself by saying, "I'd like that."

Her answer seemed to surprise him as well. He nodded without a word. It was then that Denise recognized the same shyness in him that she'd seen at Merchants, and she suddenly acknowledged the very thing she'd been denying to herself all along.

She hadn't come to the festival to visit with Judy, nor had she come to meet new people. She'd come to see Taylor McAden.

"MONSTER TRUCK!" KYLE exclaimed. *(Monstew twuck!)*

A Dodge four-by-four, it was black with oversize wheels. It had two spotlights mounted on a roll bar, a heavy-duty tow cable hooked to the front bumper, a gun rack mounted above the seats in the cab, and a silver toolbox in the bed. Unlike others she'd seen, however, this one was no showpiece. The paint job had dulled, with deep scratches throughout, and there was a dent in the front side panel, right near the driver's door. The entire lower half of the truck was crusted with a thick layer of mud.

"Do you like it?" Taylor asked.

"Yes," Kyle said, nodding enthusiastically.

Taylor loaded the bikes into the bed of the truck, then held the door open for them. Because the truck was high, he had to help Kyle scramble inside.

Taylor started the engine, and they headed toward the outskirts of town with Kyle propped up between them. As if knowing Denise wanted to be alone with her thoughts, Taylor didn't say anything, and she was grateful. She watched pine trees whistle by, still amazed she was in the truck with him. She wondered if he'd ever been married. Neither he nor Judy had mentioned it, but people were often reluctant to talk about past mistakes. Lord knew she didn't bring up Kyle's father unless she had to. Still, there was something about him that made her suspect he'd never made the commitment.

Taylor reached the gravel driveway and turned in, bringing the truck to a stop. Pushing the clutch in, he let the car idle.

"Hey, little man," he said. "You wanna drive my truck?"

It took a moment before Kyle turned.

"C'mon," Taylor said, motioning. "You can drive it."

Taylor pulled him into his lap. He placed Kyle's hands on the upper part of the steering wheel while keeping his own hands close enough to grab it if necessary. "You ready?"

Kyle didn't answer, but Taylor slowly let the clutch out, and the truck began to inch forward. "All right, little man, let's go."

Kyle, a little unsure, held the wheel steady as the truck began to roll up the drive. His eyes widened as he realized he really had control, and all at once he turned the wheel hard to the left. The truck responded and moved onto the grass, bouncing slightly and heading toward the fence before Kyle turned the wheel the other way. They were moving no more than five miles an hour, but Kyle broke into a wide grin, with a "look what I'm doing" expression on his face. He laughed in delight.

"He's driving!" Kyle exclaimed. *(Eez dryfeen!)*

Taylor winked at Denise. "My dad used to let me do this when I was little. I just figured Kyle might like it, too."

With Taylor's verbal—and manual—guidance, Kyle pulled the truck into the shade of the magnolia tree before finally stopping. After opening the driver's door, Taylor lifted Kyle down.

"Let me go get your bikes," Taylor said, jumping out of the cab.

Denise sat, feeling slightly unraveled. Twice in a single afternoon Taylor had done something kind for Kyle, something considered normal in the lives of other children. As Kyle's mother, she could love and protect him, but she couldn't make other people accept him. It was obvious, though, that Taylor already did, and she felt her throat close up a little. After four and a half years Kyle had finally made a friend. She opened her door and jumped down.

Taylor lowered the bikes to the ground, then hopped out of the truck bed in one easy, fluid movement.

"Thanks for driving us home," Denise said.

"I was glad to do it," he replied quietly.

She knew then that she wanted to know more about Taylor McAden. "I've still got a little time before I've got to start getting ready for work," she said, following her instincts. "Would you like to come in for a glass of tea?"

Taylor pushed his hat higher on his head. "That sounds good."

Kyle followed them as they rolled the bikes around to the back porch, then walked inside. Trying to hide her sudden nervousness, Denise pulled out the jar of tea from the refrigerator, then added a few ice cubes to glasses she retrieved from the cupboard. She passed Taylor a glass, leaving her own on the counter, conscious of how small the kitchen was. She turned to Kyle. "You ready for a tub? You're all sweaty."

"Yes," he said.

"Can you give me a minute to get his tub ready?" she asked, glancing at Taylor.

"Sure. Take your time."

Denise led Kyle from the kitchen, and a few moments later Taylor heard the water start up. He took in the kitchen with a contractor's eye. Though it was obvious that Denise had done her best to make it presentable, the kitchen still showed signs of neglect. The floor was warped slightly and the linoleum yellow with age. Three of the cupboard doors were hanging crooked, and the sink had a slow drip that had left rust marks on the porcelain.

By the back door he saw a table with a series of textbooks stacked on top. Curious, he walked over and scanned the titles. Every one of them had to do with child development. On the shelf below was a pile of thick blue binders labeled with Kyle's name.

Denise shut the water off and returned to the kitchen, conscious of how long it had been since she'd been alone with a man. Taylor was perusing the titles when she picked up her glass and made her way toward him.

"Interesting reading," he said, glancing up. "Kyle?"

She nodded, and he motioned to the binders. "What are those?"

"Those are his journals. Whenever I work with Kyle, I record what he's able to say, how he says it, what he's having trouble with, things like that. That way I can follow his progress."

"It sounds like a lot of work."

"It is." She paused. "Would you like to sit?"

They sat at the table, and she explained what—as far as she could tell—Kyle's problem was, just as she'd done with Judy.

"Why is language so hard for him?" he asked.

"That's the magic question. Nobody really knows."

"You know, he doesn't talk all that bad," Taylor said. "When we were throwing the ball back and forth? He was telling me to throw the ball, and whenever he caught it, he would say, 'Good job.' "

Four words, essentially. *Throw it. Good job.* Denise could have said, That's not much, is it? and she would have been right. But Taylor was being kind, and she didn't really want to get into a discussion about the limitations of Kyle's language abilities. "I think that has a lot to do with you, not just Kyle. You're very patient with him, which most people aren't. You remind me of some of the teachers I used to work with."

"You were a teacher?"

"I taught for three years, right up until Kyle was born."

"Did you like it?"

"I loved it. I worked with second graders, and that's just such a great age. Kids like their teachers and are still eager to learn."

Taylor took a sip, watching her closely over the rim of his glass. Sitting in her kitchen, observing her expressions—it all made her seem softer, less guarded. He also sensed that talking about herself wasn't something she was used to.

"Are you going to go back to it?"

"Someday. But what about you? You said you're a contractor?"

Taylor nodded. "Twelve years now."

"And you build homes?"

"I have in the past, but generally I focus on remodeling. To me it's a little more challenging than building something new. You have to work with what's already there, and nothing is ever as easy as you suspected it would be. Plus, most people have a budget, and it's fun to try to figure out how to get them the most for their money."

"Do you think you could do anything with this place?"

"I could make it look brand-new if you wanted. It depends on how much you wanted to spend."

"Well," she said gamely, "I just happen to have ten bucks burning a hole in my pocket."

Taylor assumed a serious expression. "Mmm. We might have to eliminate the Corian countertops and the Sub-Zero refrigerator."

They both laughed.

"So how do you like working at Eights?" he asked.

"It's all right. It's what I need right now. And Ray's wonderful. He lets Kyle sleep in the back while I work."

"Has he told you about his kids?"

Denise raised her eyebrows slightly. "Your mother asked that exact same question."

"It's a small town. In time everyone's going to ask the same questions. Most people don't really care. They're just passing the time. There's not much else to do around here."

"So what do you like to do? In your spare time, I mean."

"If I can get away, I go hunting."

"That wouldn't be popular with some of my friends in Atlanta."

"What can I say? I'm just a good ol' boy from the South."

Again she was struck by how different he was compared with the men she used to date. Not only in what he did and how he looked, but because he seemed content in the world he'd created for himself. He wasn't yearning for fame or zillions of dollars.

Kyle called out from the bathroom, and Denise answered, "I'll be there in a second, sweetie."

Taylor finished his glass. "I should be going."

"Are you going back to the barbecue?"

Taylor nodded. "They're probably wondering where I am."

She gave him a mischievous smile. "Do you think they're whispering about us?"

"Probably."

"I'm going to have to get used to this, I guess."

"Don't worry. I'll make sure they know it didn't mean anything."

Before she could stop the words, they were already out. "It meant something to me."

Taylor seemed to study her, considering what she'd said, as an embarrassed blush surged through her cheeks. "Are you working tomorrow evening?" he finally asked.

"No," she said a little breathlessly.

Taylor took a deep breath. God, she was pretty. "Can I take you and Kyle to the carnival tomorrow? I'm sure he would love the rides."

"I'd like that," she said quietly.

LATER that night, unable to sleep, Taylor mused that what had started as simply an ordinary day had turned into something he hadn't anticipated. The whole situation with Denise had sort of snowballed.

Sure, she was attractive and intelligent, but he'd met attractive and intelligent women before. There was something about her, something about their relationship already, that had caused his normally tight control to slip just a notch. It was almost like comfort, for lack of a better word. Which didn't make any sense, he told himself, flipping his pillow over and mashing it into shape. He barely knew her. Besides, he didn't want to get involved. He'd been down that road before.

Taylor shook off his blanket in sudden irritation. Why on earth had he asked to drive her home? Why had he asked her out tomorrow? And more important, why did the answers to those questions leave him feeling so uneasy?

Five

SUNDAY was mercifully cooler than the day before, and the evening breeze had picked up. Denise stepped out onto the porch just as Taylor pulled up the driveway.

She hoped she didn't look as nervous as she felt. It was her first date in what seemed like forever. Okay, Kyle would be with them, and it wasn't technically a *real* date, but even so, it felt like one.

"Hey there," he said. "I hope I'm not late."

"No, not at all," she said. "You're right on time."

"Hewwo, Tayer," Kyle called out.

Taylor held the truck door open for him and helped him up. "Hey, Kyle. Are you looking forward to the carnival?"

"Ess a monstew twuck," he said happily. Immediately after scrambling onto the seat, he climbed behind the wheel again, trying unsuccessfully to turn it from side to side, making engine sounds.

"He's been talking about your truck all day," Denise explained.

Taylor nodded toward the cab. "Should I let him drive again?"

"I don't think he's going to give you the chance to say no."

As Taylor opened the door for her to climb up, she caught the trace of his cologne. Nothing fancy, probably something from the local drugstore, but she was touched that he'd put it on. Kyle crawled into his lap once Taylor was situated.

Denise shrugged, an "I told you so" expression on her face.

Taylor turned the key. "All right, little man, let's go."

They did a big figure S, bumping haphazardly over the lawn before finally reaching the road. At that point Kyle scooted off his lap, satisfied, and Taylor turned the wheel, heading into town.

It was the last night of the festival, the crowds were light, and they found a parking spot close to the main road. The carnival was still going strong, however—mainly kids and their parents hoping to enjoy the last couple of hours of entertainment. By tomorrow everything would be on its way to the next town.

"So, Kyle, what do you want to do?" Denise asked.

He pointed to the mechanical swing—a ride in which dozens of metal swings on chains rotated in circles. Each child had his or her own seat, and kids were screaming in terror and delight. Kyle watched it, transfixed. "It's a swing," he said. (*Ess a sweeng.*)

"Do you want to ride the swing?" Denise asked him.

"Swing," he said with a nod.

"Say, 'I want to ride the swing.' "

"I want to ride the swing," he whispered. (*Wonta wide ee sweeng.*)

"Okay." Denise spotted the ticket booth and reached into her purse.

Taylor stopped her. "My treat. I asked, remember?"

"But Kyle—"

"I asked him to come, too."

After Taylor bought the tickets, they waited in line. The ride stopped and emptied. Denise led Kyle to his seat. She lifted him up, then lowered the safety bar.

"Ess a sweeng," Kyle said again.

She put his hands on the bar. "Now hold on and don't let go."

Kyle's only response was to laugh in delight.

"Hold on," she said again, more seriously this time.

She walked back to where Taylor was standing and took her place, praying that Kyle would listen to her. The ride started and slowly began to pick up speed. By the second rotation the swings were beginning to fan out. As Kyle swung by, he was laughing. As he came back around, Denise noticed that his hands were still right where they should be. She breathed a sigh of relief.

"You seem surprised," Taylor said.

"I am. It's the first time he's ever been on a ride like this."

"Haven't you ever taken him to a carnival?"

"I didn't think he was ready for one before."

"Because he has trouble talking?"

"Partially. There's a lot about Kyle that even I don't understand." Suddenly she wanted Taylor to understand Kyle, to understand what the last four years had been like—to understand her.

"I mean," she began softly, "for children, language is much more than conversation. It's how they learn about the world. It's how they learn that stoves are hot without having to touch them, that crossing the street is dangerous without having to be hit by a car. If Kyle can't understand the concept of danger, how can I teach him those things? When he wandered away into the swamp that night, he didn't seem frightened when you found him. Because I hadn't shown him what might happen, he didn't know enough to be afraid. Of course, if you consider every possible danger and the fact that I have to literally show him what it means, instead of being able to *tell* him—I can't tell you how many close calls there have been. Climbing too high and wanting to jump, riding too close to the road, walking up to growling dogs . . . it seems like every day there's something new."

She closed her eyes for a moment, as if reliving each experience. "Most of the time I worry about the obvious things. Whether he'll ever be able to talk normally, whether he'll go to a regular school, whether he'll ever make friends, whether I'll have to work with him forever. Those are the things that keep me awake at night."

She paused then, the words coming slower, every syllable edged with pain. "I don't want you to think that I regret having Kyle. I love him with all my heart. But"—she stared at the swings—"it's not exactly what I imagined raising children would be like."

"I didn't realize," Taylor said gently.

As if suspecting that she'd confided too much, she offered a rueful smile. "I probably made it sound pretty hopeless, didn't I?"

"Not really," he lied. In the waning sunlight she was strangely radiant. She reached over and touched his arm. Her hand was soft and warm.

"You're not very good at that," she said. "You should stick to telling the truth. I know I made it sound terrible, but I didn't tell you about the good things."

Taylor raised his eyebrows slightly. "There are good things, too?" he asked, prompting an embarrassed laugh from Denise.

"Next time I pour my heart out, remind me to stop, okay?"

Though she tried to pass off the comment, her voice betrayed her anxiety. Taylor suspected that he was the first person she'd ever really confided to in this way and that it wasn't the time for jokes.

The ride finally came to a stop. Kyle, his legs pumping back and forth, called out from his seat, "Sweeeng!"

"Do you want to ride the swing again?" Denise shouted.

"Yes," he answered, nodding.

Taylor handed the man more tickets, then returned to Denise's side. As the ride started up again, he rested his elbows on the railings. "So tell me about the good things," he said quietly.

The ride circled twice, and she waved to Kyle each time before saying anything. "Do you really want to know?" she finally asked.

"Yes, I do."

She cleared her throat. "Okay, the good things. Kyle's getting better, slowly but surely. Last year his vocabulary was only fifteen to twenty words. This year it's in the hundreds, and at times he puts three and four words together in a single sentence. And now he tells me when he's hungry, when he's tired, what he wants to eat. He's only been doing that for the last few months."

She took a deep breath. "You have to understand, Kyle works so hard every day. While other kids can play outside, he has to sit in his chair staring at picture books. It takes him hours to learn things that other kids might learn in minutes." She stopped, an almost defiant look in her eyes. "But you know, Kyle just keeps on trying, day after day. He doesn't complain; he just does it. If you only knew how hard he has to work to understand things, how much he tries to make people happy, how much he wants people to like him, only to be ignored . . ." She struggled to maintain her composure.

"You have no idea how far he's come, Taylor. You've only known him for a short while. But if you knew where he started and how many obstacles he's overcome so far, you'd be so proud of him." Despite her efforts, tears began to flood her eyes. "Kyle has more heart, more spirit, than any other child I've ever known. He is the most wonderful little boy any mother could wish to have. Despite everything, Kyle is the greatest thing that's ever happened to me."

All those years of having these words pent up inside, all those years of wanting to say the words to someone—it was such a relief to finally let it all go.

Taylor tried to swallow the lump in his throat. Watching her talk about her son—the absolute fear and absolute love—made the next move almost instinctive. He took her hand gently in his. The feeling was strange, a forgotten pleasure. She didn't try to pull away.

With her free hand she wiped at a tear that had drifted down her cheek. She sniffled. She looked spent, still defiant, and beautiful.

"That was the most beautiful thing I've ever heard," he said.

THEY spent another hour at the carnival, riding the Ferris wheel—the three of them crammed into a wobbly seat—and the Octopus, a spinning, dipping, gut-twisting ride that Kyle wanted to ride over and over again.

Once they got home, Denise helped Kyle change into his pajamas. While she led him through his prayers, his eyes were already closing. Taylor was waiting for her in the kitchen, his long legs stretched out under the table. "That was fast."

"It's been a big day for him. Would you like a drink?"

"I'll take a beer if you have one."

"My selection isn't quite that big."

"What do you have?"

"Iced tea."

"And?"

She shrugged. "Water?"

He couldn't help but smile. "Tea's fine."

She poured two glasses and handed one to him, wishing she had something stronger to take the edge off the way she was feeling. "It's a little warm in here. Would you like to sit on the porch?"

"Sure."

They made their way outside and sat in the rockers. The evening was alive with sound—frogs and insects, the rustling of leaves. The moon had risen and now hovered above the tree line.

"Now, this is nice," Taylor said. "I feel like I'm on an episode of *The Waltons*."

Denise laughed. "Don't you like to sit on the porch?"

"Sure, but I never seem to have time for it anymore."

"A good ol' boy from the South like yourself?" she said, repeating the words he'd used before. "I would have thought you would sit outside on your porch playing a banjo, a dog lying at your feet."

"With my kinfolk, a jar of moonshine, and spittoon o'er yonder?"

She grinned. "Of course."

He shook his head. "If I didn't know you were from the South, I'd think you were insulting me."

"But because I'm from Atlanta . . ."

"I'll let it slide this time." He felt the corners of his mouth curling into a smile. "So what do you miss the most about the big city?"

"Not a lot. I suppose if I were younger and Kyle wasn't around, this place would drive me crazy. But I don't need big malls or fancy places to eat or museums anymore. How about you? Didn't you ever get the urge to just pack up and move away?"

"Not really. I'm happy here, and besides, my mom is here. She's a widow, you know, and I'd feel bad leaving her alone."

Denise nodded. "I don't know that I would have moved if my mom were still alive, but I don't think so."

Two raccoons scurried out of the woods, across the lawn. Denise stood, trying to get a better view. Taylor joined her at the porch railing. With her hair moving slightly in the breeze, he was struck again by how pretty she was.

"So what was your life like? Growing up in Atlanta, I mean?"

"Probably a little bit like yours." She met his eyes. "We were both only children, raised by widowed mothers who grew up in Edenton."

Taylor felt something flinch inside.

Denise went on. "You know how it is. You feel different because other people have two parents, even if they're divorced. I remember hearing my friends talking about how their fathers wouldn't let them stay out late. It used to make me so angry, because they didn't even realize what they had. Do you know what I mean?"

Taylor nodded, realizing how much they had in common. "Do you mind if I ask you a question?" he asked almost tentatively.

"It depends on the question," she answered, trying not to tense up.

Taylor glanced away. "Where's Kyle's father?" he asked.

Denise had known it was coming. "He's not around. I didn't really even know him. Kyle wasn't supposed to happen."

"Does he know about Kyle?"

"I called him when I was pregnant. He told me straight up he didn't want anything to do with him."

Taylor frowned. "How can he not care about his own child?"

Denise shrugged. "I don't know."

"Do you ever wish he was around?"

"Oh, heavens, no," she said quickly. "I would have liked Kyle to have a father, but it wouldn't have been someone like him. Besides, for Kyle to have a father—the right kind and not just someone who calls himself that—he'd also have to be my husband."

Taylor nodded in understanding.

"But now, Mr. McAden, it's your turn," Denise said, turning to face him. "I've told you everything about me. So tell me about you."

"I already told you I'm a contractor. And you know that I volunteer with the fire department. There's really not much more than that. What did you want to know?"

"Well, tell me about your father," she said softly.

The words startled him, and Taylor felt himself stiffen slightly. It wasn't the question he'd expected.

"My father passed away when I was nine," he began. "But he was more than my father. He was my best friend, too. I know that sounds strange. I mean, I was just a little kid and he was grown, but he was. We were inseparable. When five o'clock would roll around, I'd camp out on the front steps and wait for his truck to come up the driveway. He worked in the lumbermill. As he opened his door, I'd run for him and put my arms around him. Even in winter I could smell the sweat and sawdust on his clothes. He called me 'little man.' "

Denise nodded in recognition.

"My mom always waited while he asked me what I did that day or how school went. And I'd just talk so fast, trying to say as much as I could before he went inside. But even though he was tired and probably wanting to see my mom, he never rushed me."

Taylor swallowed hard. "Anyway, we used to go fishing every weekend. We'd go out in the boat and sit together for hours. Sometimes he'd tell me stories—it seemed like he had thousands of them—and he'd answer whatever questions I asked as best he could. My father never graduated from high school, but even so he was pretty good at explaining things. And if I asked him something he didn't know, he'd say that, too. I never saw him get angry. When I'd act up, all he had to do was say, 'That's enough now, son.' And I'd stop because I knew I was disappointing him. I know that probably sounds strange, but I guess I just didn't want to let him down."

"He sounds like a wonderful man," Denise said.

"He was." The finality of his voice made it clear that the subject was closed to further discussion, although Denise suspected there was far more left to be said. They sat without speaking for a long time, listening to the music of the crickets.

"How old were you when your father died?" he asked finally.

"Four."

"Do you remember him like I remember mine?"

"Not really. I remember images—him reading me stories or the feeling of his whiskers when he kissed me good night. I was always happy when he was around. Even now not a day goes by when I don't wish I could turn back the clock and change what happened."

Taylor turned to her with a startled expression. In just a few words she'd explained the very thing he'd tried to explain to Valerie and Lori. Even though they'd listened with compassion, they'd never really understood. They couldn't. Neither of them had ever awakened with the terrible realization they'd forgotten the sound of their father's voice. Neither had cherished a single photograph as the only means of remembrance. For the second time that evening he reached for her hand.

They held hands in silence, fingers loosely intertwined. Lazy clouds, silver in the moon, lay scattered in the sky. Denise watched shadows play over Taylor's features. A sea breeze had blown through earlier, leaving a stillness in its wake. An owl called from the darkness. The evening was coming to an end, she could feel that.

He finished his glass, then set it on the railing.

"I should probably go. I have an early day tomorrow." But he stood there another minute without saying anything more. For some reason he kept remembering how she'd looked when she'd poured out her fears about her son: her defiant expression, the intense emotion as the words had flooded out. It moved him to see that her fears only made her love grow stronger for her son. It was natural to find beauty in that. But there was more to it, wasn't there? Something deeper, a commonality he'd never found in anyone else.

Even now not a day goes by when I don't wish I could turn back the clock and change what happened. How had she known?

With great reluctance Taylor turned away from the railing and turned from the feelings inside him. The floor of the porch creaked as he moved to the steps, Denise beside him, her hand still in his.

She looked up at him, and he almost kissed her then. In the soft light of the porch her eyes seemed to glow with hidden intensity. Even so, he couldn't tell if she really wanted that from him, and he held back. The evening had already been more memorable than any he'd spent in a long time; he didn't want to spoil that. Instead he took a small step backward, as if to give her more space.

"I had a wonderful time tonight," he said.

"So did I," she said.

He finally let go of her hand, felt longing as it slipped away from him. He made his way down the steps, toward his truck.

Standing on the porch, she waved one last time as Taylor headed down the drive, his headlights shining in the distance.

After he left, Denise walked to her bedroom and sat on the bed. She opened the drawer of her bedstand. It was empty except for a small bottle of perfume, a birthday gift from her mother before she died. Since then she hadn't used it, but kept it as a reminder. Now it reminded her of how long it had been since she'd worn any perfume. She was a mother above everything else. Yet she was also a woman, and after years of keeping it buried, she felt its presence. Sitting in the bedroom, gazing at the perfume, she was overcome with a sense of restlessness, a longing to be desired, to be loved.

She turned out the light and went to the window. Outside, the sky was full of stars, stretching to eternity, and she stared at them, smiling, thinking about Taylor McAden.

TAYLOR was in his kitchen two evenings later, doing paperwork, when he got the call. An accident on the bridge, between a gasoline tanker and an auto. Grabbing his keys, he was out the door less than a minute later; within five minutes he was one of the first on the scene. Cars were backed up in either direction on the bridge.

The cab of the tanker had rolled up onto the back of a Honda, completely crushing the rear. In the midst of the accident the tanker driver had locked the wheel as he'd slammed on the brakes, and the truck had whipsawed across both lanes of the road, completely blocking both directions. The car, pinned beneath the front of the cab, hung precariously off the bridge like a diving board. Its roof had been torn open. The only thing that kept it from falling into the river some eighty feet below was the weight of the tanker's cab. Its engine was smoking badly, fluid leaking steadily onto the Honda beneath.

Mitch came rushing forward to fill Taylor in. "The truck driver's all right, but there's still someone in the car."

"What about the tanks on that truck?"

"Three quarters full."

"If that cab explodes, will the tanks go with it?"

"The driver says that it shouldn't if the lining wasn't damaged. I didn't see a leak, but I can't be sure."

Two fire trucks arrived—the pumper and the hook and ladder—and seven men jumped out, already in their fire-retardant suits. Mitch and Taylor scrambled for the suits that had been brought for them. Carl Huddle arrived; so did two police officers. After a quick consultation they turned their attention to the cars on the bridge. Drivers were ordered to vacate the area by half a mile.

Rescuing the trapped passenger was foremost in people's minds. But how to reach him? Putting any extra weight on the car itself might cause it to tip.

When a blast of water from the hose was aimed toward the cab, their fears were justified. The water gushed violently toward the cab's engine, then cascaded inside the shattered back windshield of the Honda at the rate of five hundred gallons per minute, partially filling the car's interior. It then flowed with gravity toward the engine, out of the passenger area. The nose of the car dipped slightly, then rose again. The firemen manning the hose shut it down.

"Let's use the ladder on the truck," Taylor urged. "We'll extend it out over the car and use the cable to haul the person out."

"It might not support the two of you," Joe said. As the chief, he was the only full-time employee of the fire department. It was his job to drive one of the trucks, and he was always the calming influence in a crisis like this.

From where the hook and ladder could be parked, the ladder would have to extend over the car an additional twenty feet and nearly horizontally out over the river. Edenton's hook and ladder was old, and the ladder wasn't designed to be used in a situation like this.

"What other choice do we have? I'll be out and back before you know it," Taylor said.

Joe had almost expected him to volunteer. Twelve years ago, during Taylor's second year with the crew, Joe had asked him why he was always the first to volunteer for the riskiest assignments. Taylor offered a simple explanation: "My dad died when I was nine, and I know what it's like for a kid to grow up alone. I don't want that to happen to anyone else." There had been dozens of occasions where Taylor's offer had been declined. But this time . . .

"All right, Taylor," Joe said with finality.

By the time the hook and ladder was in position, seven minutes had elapsed. Small flames were now visible beneath the truck engine, scorching the rear of the Honda. Time was running out.

When the ladder truck was in place, Taylor climbed up, a rope clipped to his own harness, and secured the other end of the rope to the ladder a few rungs from the end. A much longer cable was also run from the rear of the hook and ladder up to the ladder itself. Attached to the hook at the far end of the cable was a safety harness. Once the safety harness was secured around the passenger, the cable would slowly be rewound, lifting the passenger out.

As the ladder began to extend, Taylor lay on his belly. When there were still ten or twelve feet to go to the car, Taylor felt the ladder creaking beneath him, like an old barn in a windstorm.

Six feet. Taylor could feel the heat from the flames.

Four feet. He was over the car now, getting close to the front windshield. Then the ladder came to a rattling halt. Taylor knew that it was extended as far as it would go.

Grabbing the harness for the passenger, he began inching forward, toward the edge of the ladder, taking advantage of the last three rungs. He needed them now to position himself over the windshield and lower himself to reach the passenger. As he crawled forward, the night sky opened before him. Eighty feet below, the water was the color of coal. He could feel his heart thudding in his chest. Beneath him the ladder bounced and shuddered with every movement.

Without warning, the car beneath him dipped slightly and straightened. He heard a low, muffled moan. "Don't move!" Taylor shouted. The moan grew louder, and the Honda started to rock in earnest. "Don't move!" Taylor shouted again, his voice full of desperation.

He moved quickly. He secured his rope on the final rung. Pulling his legs forward, he squeezed through the rungs, doing his best to move as fluidly as possible while still staying in the harness. The ladder rocked like a teeter-totter, groaning and creaking. Holding on to the rope with one hand, he reached down toward the passenger with the other. Pushing through the shattered windshield to the dashboard, he saw that he was too high. He caught sight of the person he was trying to save: a male in his twenties or thirties, seemingly incoherent and thrashing his arms and legs. The man was unbuckled, lying half on the seat, half on the floor.

Taylor reached above him to the ladder and grabbed the safety harness, then pulled it toward him. The cable grew tight. But he still couldn't reach the man. He needed another couple of feet.

"Can you hear me?" Taylor called into the car.

The passenger shifted, causing the car to rock violently.

The flames beneath the truck suddenly flared and intensified. Taylor shifted his grip on the rope to the lowest spot he could, then stretched for the passenger again. Closer this time, but the passenger was still out of reach. Sweat began to drip down Taylor's face. Suddenly, as if in a nightmare, he heard a loud whooshing sound, and flames exploded from the engine of the truck, leaping toward Taylor. He covered his face instinctively as the flames receded.

No time to debate. Taylor pulled the cable toward him. He worked his boot into the hook that held the safety harness. Then, supporting his weight with his foot, he unhooked his own harness and slid his hands down the cable until he was almost crouching. Now low enough to reach the passenger, he let go of the cable with one hand and grabbed the safety harness. He had to work it around the passenger's chest, beneath his arms. The ladder was bouncing hard now. Flames began to sear the roof of the Honda. Adrenaline surged through his limbs. "Wake up!" he shouted. "You've got to help me here." Taylor worked one end of the harness toward the man's arm, then slipped it underneath.

One down. "Help me! Wake up!" Taylor screamed.

The man opened his eyes and began to struggle out from between the steering wheel and the seat. The car was rocking heavily now. Weakly he freed his other arm, and Taylor worked the safety harness around him, cinching it tight.

"We're gonna pull you out now. We're almost out of time." The man simply rolled his head. "Bring him up!" he screamed. "Passenger is secure!"

Taylor worked his hands up the cable until he was in a standing position. The firefighters slowly began to unwind the cable. The ladder began to groan and shudder, but instead of the passenger coming up, the ladder seemed to be lowering. Taylor could feel it on the verge of buckling. "Stop!" he shouted. "The ladder's gonna go!"

He had to get off the ladder. After making sure that the man wouldn't get snagged, he reached for the ladder rungs above him. Then he carefully removed his foot from the hook, letting his legs dangle free, and started to go hand over hand across the ladder. Suddenly the flames ripped into a frenzy. He'd seen engine fires numerous times—and this one was seconds away from blowing. He looked toward the bridge. As if in slow motion, he saw the firemen motioning frantically at him to hurry. But he knew there was no way he could make it back to the truck in time and still get the passenger out.

"Pull him out!" Taylor shouted. "He's got to come up now!"

Dangling high above the water, Taylor let go completely. In an instant he was swallowed by the evening air.

"THAT was the dumbest thing I've ever seen you do," Mitch said matter-of-factly. It was fifteen minutes later, and they were sitting on the banks of the Chowan River. "I mean, that one takes the cake."

"We got him out, didn't we?" Taylor said. He was drenched and had lost one boot while kicking for safety. His muscles seemed rubbery; his hands were shaking uncontrollably.

"You didn't have to let go. You could have made it back."

Even as he said it, Mitch wasn't quite sure it was true. Without Taylor's weight the ladder had enough tensile strength to allow the passenger to be lifted through the windshield. Once he was free, the ladder swung out, away from the accident, rotating back toward the bridge. Just as the ladder reached the bridge, the engine of the truck blew. The car was tossed free and followed Taylor into the water. Taylor had made his way beneath the bridge, foreseeing just such an occurrence. As it was, the car had come down close—too close—and he'd narrowly avoided being crushed by the wreckage.

"What if the engine had blown twenty seconds earlier?" Mitch went on. "What if you'd hit something submerged in the water?" .

Then I'd be dead, Taylor thought. He shook his head. "I didn't know what else to do," he finally said.

Mitch studied him with concern. He'd seen this look before, the shell-shocked appearance of someone who knew he was fortunate to be alive. He noticed Taylor's shaking hands and reached over, patting him on the back. "I'm just glad you're all right."

Taylor nodded, too tired to speak.

ONCE the situation on the bridge was fully under control, Taylor got in his car and headed home. Though Joe had been as angry as Taylor had ever seen him, Taylor did his best to convince him that he hadn't acted recklessly. "Look," he said, "I didn't want to jump. But if I hadn't, neither of us would have made it."

He'd left the lights on in his haste to leave, and the house was almost welcoming when he entered. The paperwork from his business was still spread on the table; the calculator had been left on. The ice in his water glass had melted. In the living room he could hear the television playing in the background. The ball game he'd been listening to had given way to the local news.

He took a quick hot shower, then walked through the house, turning everything off before slipping into bed. He turned out the lights almost reluctantly. Despite his exhaustion, he knew that sleep wouldn't come. Instead the images of the past several hours began to replay in his mind. Almost like a movie, some moved in fast-forward, others in reverse, but in each case they were different from what had actually happened. In one sequence after another he watched helplessly as everything went wrong.

His eyes snapped open. His hands were trembling again, his throat dry, and he was breathing rapidly. He checked the clock. It was nearly eleven thirty. Knowing he wouldn't sleep, he turned on the lamp and dressed quickly. He knew he needed to talk. Not to Mitch, not to Melissa. Not even to his mother.

He needed to talk to Denise.

THE PARKING LOT AT EIGHTS was mostly empty when he arrived. The diner would be closing in ten minutes.

He pushed open the door and heard a bell jingle, signaling his entrance. The air smelled of bacon despite the lateness of the hour.

Beyond the counter, he saw Ray cleaning up. Ray turned at the sound of the door. He waved, a greasy dishtowel in his hand. "Hey, Taylor. Long time no see. You comin' in to eat?"

"Oh, hey, Ray. Not really."

Ray shook his head, chuckling to himself. "Somehow I didn't think so," he said almost mischievously. "Denise'll be out in a minute. She's putting some stuff in the walk-in."

Denise pushed through the swinging door from the kitchen.

"Taylor?" she said, clearly surprised. "What are you doing here?"

"I wanted to see you," he said, not knowing what else to say.

She wore a white, work-stained apron over her marigold yellow dress, and white sneakers. Her hair was pulled back into a ponytail, and her face was shiny from perspiration. She was beautiful.

As she neared, she saw something in his eyes. "Are you okay?" she asked. "You look like you've seen a ghost."

"I don't know," he muttered, almost to himself.

She stared up at him, concerned, then looked over her shoulder. "Hey, Ray? Can I take a quick break here for a second?"

"Take your time, sweetheart. I'm about done here, anyway."

She faced Taylor. "Something happened tonight. What was it?"

"There was an accident on the bridge."

Denise nodded. "I know. Hardly anyone came in here, because the bridge was closed. Were you there?"

Taylor nodded.

"I heard it was terrible. Was it?"

Taylor nodded again.

She reached out, gently taking hold of his arm. "Hold on, okay? I've got a few things to do, and then I'll be ready to go. Wait for me, okay? We can talk at my house."

TAYLOR carried Kyle into the house and put him in bed. Denise pulled the sheet over him, and they both crept out of his room. In the living room, Denise turned a lamp on as Taylor sat on the couch. Denise sat in a chair. Neither one of them had said anything on the way home for fear of waking Kyle, but once they were seated, Denise went straight to the point. "What happened on the bridge tonight?"

Taylor told her everything: about the rescue, what Mitch and Joe had said, the images he'd been tormented by afterward.

When he was finished, she leaned forward. "You saved him?"

"We all did," Taylor said, automatically making the distinction.

"But how many of you went out on the ladder? How many of you had to let go because the ladder wouldn't hold?" Taylor didn't answer, and Denise rose to sit next to him on the couch. "You're a hero," she said. "Just like you were when Kyle was lost."

"No, I'm not," he said.

"Yes, you are." She reached for his hand. For the next twenty minutes Denise did her best to keep Taylor's thoughts away from the accident. They talked about inconsequential things. As a child, when she'd had nightmares, her mother used to do the same thing.

Taylor gradually began to relax, his answers coming more slowly. His eyes closed and opened, closed again. His breath settled into a deeper rhythm as the demands of the day began to take their toll.

He finally nodded off. She retrieved an extra blanket from her bedroom and draped it over him. Half asleep, he mumbled something about having to go. Denise whispered that he was fine where he was. "Go to sleep," she murmured, turning off the lamp.

She went to her room and slipped out of her work clothes, into her pajamas. She untied her ponytail, brushed her teeth, and scrubbed her face. Then, after crawling into bed, she closed her eyes.

The fact that Taylor McAden was sleeping in the other room was the last thing she remembered before she, too, nodded off.

"HEWWO, Tayer."

Taylor opened his eyes, squinting against the early morning sunlight streaming in the living-room window. He saw Kyle standing over him, his face very close. It took a second for Taylor to register where he was. He ran both hands through his hair. Checking his watch, he saw that it was a little after six in the morning.

"Good morning, Kyle."

"He's on the couch." *(Eez on-ah coush.)*

Taylor straightened up, feeling stiffness in his joints. "I sure was."

"Good morning," he heard behind him. Over his shoulder he saw Denise coming out of her room, wearing pink pajamas and socks.

"Good morning," he said, standing and turning around. "I must have dozed off last night. Sorry about that."

"It's okay," she said. "You were tired." Denise went over to Kyle and kissed him on the top of the head. "Good morning, sweetie."

"Morning," he said. *(Mawneen.)*

"Are you hungry?"

"No."

Denise returned her attention to Taylor. "How about you?"

"I don't want you to have to cook up something special."

"I was going to offer you some Cheerios," she said, eliciting a smile from Taylor. "Did you sleep okay?"

"Like a rock," he said. "Thanks for last night."

She shrugged. "What are friends for?"

Embarrassed, he began folding the blanket, glad for something to do. He felt out of place here, at her house, so early in the morning.

"Sure you don't want to stay for breakfast? I've got half a box."

Taylor debated. "And milk?" he finally asked.

"No. We use water in our cereal here," she said seriously.

He looked at her as if wondering whether or not to believe her. Denise laughed. "Of course we have milk, you goob."

"Goob?"

"It's a term of endearment. It means that I like you."

The words were strangely uplifting. "In that case I'd be glad to stay."

After they finished breakfast, Denise walked him to the door. Taylor still had to make it home to change before heading off to meet his crew. They stepped out onto the porch.

"Listen," Taylor said, "about last night, thanks for everything."

"You already thanked me earlier, remember?"

"I know," Taylor said earnestly. "But I wanted to do it again."

Denise took a small step forward. She could see the surprise in his eyes when she kissed him softly on the lips.

It wasn't more than a peck, really, but all he could do was stare at her afterward, thinking how wonderful it was.

"I'm glad I was the one you came to," she said.

DURING the next week and a half Taylor spent more and more time at Denise's house, dropping by after she'd finished working with Kyle. One afternoon he taught Kyle to hit the ball with a small bat and tee that Taylor had used when he was young. By the time Kyle was ready to stop, Taylor's shirt was soaked. Denise kissed him for the second time after handing him a glass of water.

On Sunday, the week after the carnival, they spent the day at the beach. They shared a picnic lunch, then waded in the surf as terns fluttered overhead. They built sandcastles that Kyle, roaring like Godzilla, delighted in stomping.

On the way home they picked up some fresh corn at a farmer's road stand. While Kyle ate macaroni and cheese, Taylor had his first dinner at Denise's house. The sun and wind at the beach had worn Kyle out, and he fell asleep. Taylor and Denise talked in the kitchen until almost midnight. She showed him one of the journals.

"Whenever Kyle has a bad day—and he does quite often—I'll open this up and remind myself of all the challenges he's made it through so far. One day, once he's better, I want him to read it so that he knows how much I love him."

"He already knows that."

"I know. But someday I want to hear him say that he loves me."

"Doesn't he do that now? When you tuck him in at night?"

"No," she answered. "Kyle's never said that to me."

"Haven't you tried to teach him that?"

"No. I want to be surprised when he finally does it on his own."

At midnight, on the doorstep, they kissed again, this time with Taylor's arm around her.

A few days later Taylor let Denise borrow his truck to head into town to run errands. By the time she got back, he'd rehung the sagging cabinet doors in her kitchen. "I hope you don't mind," he said.

"Not at all," she cried, clapping her hands together. "Can you do anything about the leaky sink?" Thirty minutes later that was fixed as well.

In their moments alone Taylor found himself mesmerized by her simple beauty and grace. But there were also times when he could see written in her features the sacrifices she'd made for her son. It was an almost weary expression, like that of a warrior after a long battle, and it inspired an admiration in him that he found difficult to put into words. She seemed to be a stark contrast to those people who were always on the go, searching for personal fulfillment. So many people these days, it seemed, believed that these things could come only from work, not from parenting, and many believed that having children had nothing to do with raising them.

On Wednesday of the following week Taylor invited both Denise and Kyle to his home. Similar to Denise's in many ways, it was an older house that sat on a large parcel of land. Kyle loved the toolshed out back, and after pointing out the "tractor" (actually a lawn mower), Taylor took him for a ride around the yard.

Watching them together, Denise realized that Taylor was already more than a friend. But he did hold things back about himself. He remained strangely silent about his father. Nor had he said anything about the women he'd known in the past.

LATER in the week Taylor surprised her by bringing over an old-fashioned ice-cream maker. He cranked the handle, sweat running off his face, as the cream thickened slowly.

"Would you like to take over?"

"No, that's okay. It's more fun watching you do it."

Taylor nodded, then played the martyr as he pretended to struggle with the handle. She giggled. Taylor wiped his forehead with the back of his hand. "Do you want to go out for dinner Sunday?"

"Sure. But you know Kyle won't eat anything at most places."

Taylor swallowed, his arm never stopping. His eyes met hers. "I meant, could I take just you? My mom said she'd be happy to come over and watch Kyle."

Denise hesitated. "I don't know how he'd do with her."

"How about if I pick you up after he's already asleep? You can tuck him in bed, and we won't leave until you're sure it's okay."

She relented. "You've really thought this through, haven't you?"

"I didn't want you to have the opportunity to say no."

She grinned. "In that case I'd love to go."

ON SUNDAY, Denise kept Kyle busy outside all day, and after giving him a bath and putting on his pajamas, she read him three books. When she closed his door, Kyle was already sound asleep.

Taylor had said they were going to Fontana, a restaurant in the heart of downtown. She had decided on a simple black cocktail dress that had been in the back of her closet for years, still draped in a plastic sheath from a dry cleaner in Atlanta. She couldn't remember the last time she'd worn it. She was pleased to see that it still fit well. After drying and styling her hair, she put on a little makeup, then pulled out the perfume from her bedstand drawer. A little on her neck and hair, then a dab on her wrists. It was then that she heard Judy knocking. Taylor arrived two minutes later.

Fontana was owned by a middle-aged couple originally from Berne, Switzerland, who had moved to Edenton from New Orleans. They'd brought a touch of elegance to the town. Taylor and Denise were seated at a small table in a corner. The dinner was wonderful in every detail—the food delicious and the setting undeniably intimate. Over dessert Taylor reached for her hand across the table.

As the evening wore on, Taylor told Denise about his past with the fire department and some of the more dangerous blazes he'd helped to battle; he also talked about Mitch and Melissa, the two friends who'd been with him through it all. Denise shared stories of college and the years she'd spent teaching and how utterly unprepared she'd felt the first time she stepped into a classroom. To both of them this night seemed to mark the beginning of their life as a couple. It was also the first time they'd ever had a conversation in which Kyle's name never came up.

After dinner, as they stepped out onto the silent, deserted street, Denise noted how different the old town seemed at night. Meandering along brick sidewalks that had cracked over time, they held hands, neither of them feeling the urge to speak.

Denise was struck by how much her world had changed recently, and all of it, she realized, could be traced to the man beside her. Yet despite all he'd done for her, he never pressured her for anything in return. He was content to get to know her first, to listen to her problems, to hang crooked cabinet doors and make homemade ice cream. In every way, he had presented himself as a gentleman. But because he'd never pushed her, she found herself wanting him with an intensity that surprised her. She wondered what it would feel like when he finally took her in his arms. Thinking about it made something tighten inside, and she squeezed his hand.

As they neared the truck, they passed a storefront whose glass door had been propped open. Stenciled on it was TRINA'S BAR. Aside from Fontana, it was the only place open downtown. When she peeked in, Denise saw couples talking quietly over small circular tables. In a corner was a jukebox. A country song was winding down. There was a short silence until the next song rotated through: "Unchained Melody." Denise stopped in her tracks. "I love this song," she said.

"Would you like to go inside? We could dance if you'd like."

"No. I'd feel funny with all those people watching," she said.

The street was deserted. A single light, set high on a pole, flickered slightly, illuminating the corner. The music drifted from the bar. They stepped away from the open door, and without a word Taylor slipped one arm around her back, pulling her closer. With an endearing smile he raised her hand to his mouth and kissed it, then lowered it into position. Suddenly realizing what was happening, Denise took an awkward step before beginning to follow his lead.

For a moment both were slightly embarrassed, but after a couple of turns Denise closed her eyes and leaned into him. She could hear his breathing as they rotated in slow circles, swaying gently with the music. Suddenly it didn't matter whether anyone was watching. Except for the feel of his warm body against hers, nothing mattered at all, and they danced and danced, holding each other close beneath a flickering streetlight in the tiny town of Edenton.

KYLE, JUDY SAID, HADN'T EVEN stirred while they'd been away. "Did you two have a good time?" she asked.

"Yes, we did," Denise answered. "Thanks for watching Kyle."

"My pleasure," she said sincerely, eyeing Denise's flushed cheeks.

Denise went back to check on Kyle as Taylor walked Judy to her car. He didn't say much, and Judy hoped that it meant he was as taken with Denise as she seemed to be with him.

When Denise emerged from Kyle's room, Taylor was back in the living room, squatting by a small cooler he'd removed from the back of the truck. He didn't hear her close her son's door. Silently Denise watched as he removed two crystal flutes and set them on the table in front of the couch. He reached in again, this time pulling out a bottle of Champagne. The bottle went onto the table, next to the flutes. Satisfied, he glanced toward the hallway. At the sight of Denise standing there, he froze, an embarrassed expression on his face. "I thought this would be a nice surprise," he said.

She looked toward the table and back at Taylor again, realizing she'd been holding her breath. "It is," she murmured. "I haven't had Champagne in years."

Taylor opened the bottle and poured two glasses. He handed one to her wordlessly.

"Wait, okay?" she said, and ran to the kitchen. She emerged with two small candles and a book of matches. She set them on the table, then lit them. As soon as she turned out the lamp, the room was transformed, shadows dancing against the wall.

"To you," he said as they tapped their glasses together. She took a sip. The bubbles made her nose twitch, but it tasted wonderful.

He motioned to the couch, and they sat close to each other. Outside, the moon had risen, and its light spilled through the clouds. Taylor took another sip of Champagne, watching Denise.

"What are you thinking?" she asked.

"I was thinking about what would have happened had you never been in that accident."

"I would have had my car," she declared.

Taylor laughed before growing serious again. "But do you think I'd be here now if it hadn't happened?"

Denise considered it. "I don't know," she said at last. "I'd like to think so, though. My mom believed that people were destined for one another. I guess part of me still believes it."

"My mom used to say that, too. I think that's one of the reasons why she never remarried. She knew there could never be anyone to replace my father."

"But your mom's only human. We all need companionship."

As soon as she'd said it, she realized she was talking about herself as much as she was about Judy. Taylor, however, didn't seem to notice. Instead he smiled. "You don't know her as well as I do."

"Maybe, but remember, my mother went through the same things your mom did. She mourned my father always, but I know she still felt the desire to be loved by someone."

"Did she date?"

Denise nodded, taking a sip of her Champagne. "After a couple of years. But none of them ever worked out."

"Did that make you angry? Her dating, I mean?"

"No, not at all. I wanted my mom to be happy."

"What about you? Did you think you'd be married by now?"

"Of course," she said wryly. "I had it all worked out. Graduate at twenty-two, married by twenty-five, my first child at thirty. A great plan."

"You sound disappointed."

"I was," she admitted, "for a long time. I mean, my mom always had this idea of what my life would be like, and she never missed the opportunity to remind me. She meant well. I know she did. She wanted me to learn from her mistakes, and I was willing to do that. But when she died . . . I don't know. I guess for a while there I forgot everything she'd taught me." She stopped, a pensive look on her face.

"Because you got pregnant?" he asked gently.

Denise shook her head. "No, not because I got pregnant, though that was part of it. It was more that after she died, I felt like she wouldn't be looking over my shoulder all the time. And I took advantage of that. It wasn't until later that I realized the things my mom said were for my own benefit."

"We all make mistakes, Denise—"

She held up a hand, cutting him off. "I'm not saying it because I feel sorry for myself. Like I said, I'm not disappointed anymore. I know my mom would be proud of the decisions I've made over the last five years." She hesitated. "I think she'd also like you."

"Because I'm nice to Kyle?"

"No. My mom would like you because you've made me happier in the last two weeks than I have been in the last five years."

In the glowing candlelight, sitting close, she looked at him squarely, her eyes lit with compassion, and it was at that moment that Taylor McAden fell in love with Denise Holton. All the years of loneliness had led to this place, this here and now. He reached out and took her hand as a well of tenderness rose within him.

Denise knew intuitively the meaning of Taylor's touch, the words he'd left unspoken. She knew because she'd fallen in love with him at exactly the same time.

MOONLIGHT spilled through the bedroom. Taylor lay on the bed, Denise resting her head on his chest. She lifted her head, marveling at the naked beauty of his form, seeing at once the man she loved and the blueprint of the young boy she never knew. With guilty pleasure she recalled the sight of their bodies intertwined in passion. When Taylor saw her staring, he reached over and traced her cheek with his fingers, a melancholy smile playing on his lips, his eyes unreadable in the soft gray light.

In silence they lay together as the digital numbers on the clock radio blinked forward steadily. Later Taylor rose and walked to the kitchen to get two glasses of water. When he came back, he saw Denise's figure intertwined with the sheet. He took a drink of water, then set both glasses on the bedstand. Kissing her between her breasts, he whispered, "You're perfect."

She put one arm around his neck, then ran her hand down his back. "I'm not, but thank you. For everything." He sat on the bed then, his back against the headrest. Denise moved up, and he draped one arm around her, pulling her close to him.

It was in that position that the two of them finally fell asleep.

Seven

WHEN she awoke, Denise was alone. The covers on Taylor's side had been pulled up. It was a little before seven. Puzzled, she got out of bed, put on a short silk bathrobe, and checked the house quickly before glancing out the window. Taylor's truck was gone.

Kyle, who'd heard her get up, staggered out of his bedroom, plopping down on the living-room couch. "Hewwo, Money," he mumbled.

Just as she answered, she heard Taylor's truck coming up the drive. A minute later he was opening the front door, a grocery bag in his arms. "Oh, hey," he said when he saw them, "I didn't think you two would be up yet."

"Hewwo, Tayer," Kyle cried, suddenly alert.

Denise pulled her robe a little tighter. "Where did you go?"

"I ran to the store." Taylor closed the door behind him and walked across the living room. "Sorry about leaving this morning, but my stomach was growling. So I decided that I would make you two a real breakfast. Eggs, bacon, pancakes, the works."

Denise smiled. "You don't like my Cheerios?"

"I love your Cheerios. But today is special."

"Why is today so special?"

He glanced toward Kyle and simply raised his eyebrows at Denise. "Well, today is special for the obvious reason," he said conversationally. "But even more, after I make your gourmet breakfast, I'd like to take you and Kyle to the beach today."

"But I have to work with Kyle, then head into the diner tonight."

As he walked past her toward the kitchen, he stopped, leaning toward her ear as if sharing a secret. "I know. I'm supposed to work today, too. But I'm willing to play hooky once if you are."

Smiling, Denise pulled the eggs from the bag. "Scrambled?"

"With you looking so good, how could I not feel scrambled?"

She rolled her eyes. "You really are a goob."

TWO HOURS LATER THEY WERE sitting on a blanket at the beach near Nags Head, Taylor applying sunscreen to Denise's back. Kyle was using a plastic shovel nearby, scooping sand from one spot and moving it to another. Neither Taylor nor Denise had any idea what he was thinking as he did it, but he seemed to be enjoying it.

Later, as the sun began its midafternoon march across the sky, they packed up their things, ready to head home. Taylor carried the blanket and picnic basket they'd brought with them. Kyle was walking ahead of them, carrying his pail and shovel through the dunes. All along the footpath a sea of orange and yellow blossoms bloomed. Denise bent and plucked one, bringing it to her nose.

"Around here we call it the Jobellflower," Taylor said. She handed it to him, and Taylor wagged a finger at her in mock reproach. "You know it's against the law to pick flowers on the dunes. They help protect us from the hurricanes."

"Are you going to turn me in?"

Taylor shook his head. "No. But I'm going to make you listen to the legend of how they got their name."

Denise took a step closer to him. "So tell me about the flower."

"The Jobellflower was named for Joe Bell, who lived on this island a long time ago. Supposedly Joe had been in love with a woman, but she ended up marrying someone else. Heartbroken, he moved to the Outer Banks to live the life of a recluse. On his first morning in his new home he saw a woman walking along the beach in front of his house, looking terribly sad and alone. Every day he would see her. Eventually he went out to meet her, but when she saw him, she ran away. The next morning she was walking along the beach again. This time she didn't run, and Joe was immediately struck by how beautiful she was. They talked all day, then the next, and soon they were in love. Surprisingly, at the same time, a small batch of flowers began to grow right behind his house, flowers never seen before in this area. As his love grew, the flowers continued to spread, and by the end of the summer they'd become a beautiful ocean of color. It was there that Joe knelt and asked her to marry him. When she agreed, Joe picked a dozen blossoms and handed them to her, but strangely, she recoiled, refusing to take them. Later, on their wedding day, she explained her reason. 'This flower is the living symbol of our love,' she said. 'If the flowers die, then our love will die as well.' This terrified Joe, so he began to plant or seed Jobellflowers all along the stretch of beach where they'd first met, then throughout the Outer Banks. And every year, as the flowers were spread, they fell deeper and deeper in love."

When he was finished, Taylor bent and picked a few more of the blossoms, then handed the bunch to Denise.

She said, "I like that story, but didn't you just break the law, too?"

"Of course. But this way we'll each have something to keep the other in line."

"Like trust?"

"That, too," he said as he leaned in and kissed her on the cheek.

TAYLOR drove her to work that night, and he offered to watch Kyle at Denise's house. At midnight he loaded Kyle into the car, then went to pick up Denise. Kyle woke only briefly when she got in, then curled up onto her lap as he usually did. Fifteen minutes later everyone was in bed—Kyle in his room, Denise and Taylor in hers.

Just before dawn Taylor slipped out of Denise's room. Not wanting Kyle to see them sleeping together, he dozed on and off on the couch until Denise and Kyle came out of their bedrooms.

Denise scanned the room. Pieces of popcorn were scattered on the floor and the couch. On top of the television were two movies, *The Rescuers* and *The Lion King,* the cases open, videos on top.

Denise said, "I didn't notice the mess you two made last night when I came in. It looks like you had yourselves a good time."

Taylor sat up from the couch and wiped his eyes. "We had fun. But did you see what else we did?"

"You mean aside from spraying popcorn all over my furniture?"

"C'mon, Kyle. Let's show your mom what we did last night."

To Denise's surprise Kyle seemed to understand what Taylor had said and obediently followed him to the back door. Taylor led them to the rear steps, motioning to the garden on either side of the door.

All along the back of the house were freshly planted Jobellflowers.

"You did this?" she asked.

"Kyle did, too," he said, a touch of pride in his voice.

"SO WHAT'S happening with Denise?" Mitch asked.

They were at Mitch's house on Monday, repairing the roof. During the past week Denise and Taylor had seen each other virtually every day. On the Fourth of July, Taylor had taken Denise and Kyle out on his rebuilt ancient motorboat; later they had set off their own fireworks.

The sun was blisteringly hot, and both Mitch and Taylor had their shirts off as they pried off the torn shingles one by one. Taylor wiped the sweat from his face with his bandanna. "Not much."

"That's it?" Mitch snorted. "Not much?"

"What do you want me to say?"

"The works. Just start rambling, and I'll stop you if I need something explained."

Taylor glanced from side to side. "Can you keep a secret?"

"Of course."

Taylor leaned a little closer. "So can I." He winked, and Mitch burst out laughing.

Mitch shook his head. "You know, the way I figure it—you're going to tell me sooner or later, so it may as well be sooner. Besides, Melissa won't let you out of here until you do. Trust me, that gal can throw a frying pan with deadly accuracy."

"Well, you can tell Melissa that we're doing fine."

"Does she make you happy?"

It took a moment for Taylor to answer. "Yeah," he said finally, "she really does. I've never met anyone like her before. She's pretty, she's intelligent, she's charming, she makes me laugh. And you should see the way she is with her son. She's so patient, so dedicated, so loving. It's really something."

"Can I give you some advice?"

"Could I stop you?"

"No. I'm like Ann Landers when it comes to things like this."

Taylor adjusted his position on the roof, making his way toward another shingle. "Then go ahead."

Mitch tensed slightly, anticipating Taylor's reaction. "Don't screw it up this time."

Taylor stopped in midmotion. "What's that supposed to mean?"

"Remember Valerie? Remember Lori? You go out with 'em, you pour on the charm, you spend all your time with them, you get them to fall in love with you, and then wham—you end it."

Reluctantly Taylor considered what Mitch had said. "They were different from Denise. I was different. I've changed since then."

"It's not me you have to convince, Taylor."

Taylor shook his head. "You're a pain in the ass, you know that?"

"Yeah, I know. Melissa tells me that, too, so don't take it personally. It's just the way I am."

THROUGHOUT the summer the relationship between Taylor and Denise remained constant. They spent most afternoons together— to escape the heat, Taylor's crew started early in the morning and would finish by two o'clock—and Taylor continued to shuttle Denise to and from her job at the diner. Occasionally they ate dinner at Judy's house; sometimes Judy came by to baby-sit Kyle again.

Denise looked forward to everything they did. On a warm night toward the end of July he took her up to Elizabeth City and they went dancing. He moved her around the floor with surprising grace, waltzing and two-stepping to a local country band. Later, in bed, Taylor pulled her close as a thunderstorm raged outside the window. "This," he confided, "is as good as it gets."

Kyle, too, blossomed under his attention. He began to talk more frequently, though much of it didn't make sense. By late summer he'd learned to hit the ball off the tee consistently, and his ability to throw the ball had improved dramatically.

But as idyllic as everything seemed, there were moments in which Denise sensed an undercurrent of restlessness in Taylor she couldn't pin down. He would sometimes get an unreadable, almost distant look after they made love. He would hold her and caress her as usual, but she could sense something dark and unknowable in him. It scared her sometimes, although when daylight came, she often berated herself for letting her imagination run away with her.

Toward the end of August, Taylor left town to help fight a major fire in the Croatan forest for three days. Denise found it difficult to sleep while he was gone. Worrying about him, she called Judy, and they spent an hour talking on the phone. Denise followed the coverage of the fire in the newspaper and on television, searching in vain for any glimpse of Taylor. When he finally returned to Edenton, he drove straight to her house. With Ray's permission she took the evening off, but Taylor was exhausted and fell asleep on the couch. She covered him with a blanket, but in the middle of the night he crept into her room. He had the shakes for hours. Taylor refused to talk about what had happened, and Denise held him in her arms, concerned, until he was finally able to nod off again. His demons gave him no relief. Twisting and turning, he called out in his sleep. The next morning he apologized, but he offered no explanation. Somehow, she knew, it wasn't simply memories of the fire that were eating him up.

Her mother had once told her that men who kept secrets bottled up inside spelled trouble for the women who loved them. Instinctively, she knew that was true, yet sometimes she found herself dreaming of walking down the aisle with him. She could deny it, she could ignore it, she could tell herself that neither of them was ready yet. If he asked her tomorrow, she liked to think she would have the wisdom to say exactly that. But, she admitted to herself, she wouldn't say those words. She would say, "Yes . . . yes . . . yes."

In her daydreams she could only hope that Taylor felt the same.

"You seem nervous," Taylor commented, studying Denise as she put on her makeup. "It's only Mitch and Melissa."

Holding up two different earrings, one to each ear, she debated between the gold hoop and the simple stud. "I only met them one time, three months ago, and we didn't talk that long. What if I make a bad impression?"

"Don't worry." Taylor gave her arm a squeeze. "You won't."

"Well, it wouldn't be so nerve-racking if you'd taken me to meet them sooner, you know. You've waited an awful long time to start bringing me to meet your friends."

"Hey, you're the one who works six nights a week, and I'm sorry if I want you all to myself on your night off." He slipped both arms around her. "Have I told you how wonderful you look?"

"You're changing the subject."

"I know. But look at you. You're beautiful."

"Good enough for a barbecue with your friends?"

"You look fantastic," he said sincerely, "but even if you didn't, they'd still love you."

THIRTY minutes later Taylor, Denise, and Kyle were walking toward the door when Mitch appeared from around back. "Hey, y'all," he said. "Glad you could make it. The gang's out back."

They followed him through a gate to the deck. Melissa was sitting at the table, watching her four boys jump in and out of the swimming pool. "Hey there," she called out, getting to her feet.

Taylor drew Melissa into a bear hug and gave her a quick kiss on the cheek. "You two have met, right?" he said.

"At the festival," Melissa said. "How are you doing, Denise?"

"Good, thanks," she said, still feeling a little nervous.

Mitch motioned to the cooler. "You two want a beer?"

"That sounds great," Taylor said. "Would you like one, Denise?"

"Please."

As Taylor went to fetch the beers, Melissa made herself comfortable at the table again, followed by Mitch and Denise. Kyle, wearing a bathing suit, stood shyly by his mother's side.

Melissa leaned toward him. "Hi, Kyle. How are you?"

When he didn't answer, Denise said, "Say, 'I'm fine, thanks.' "

"I'm fine, thanks." *(I'n fine, kenks.)*

Melissa smiled. "Well, good. Would you like to go get in the pool with the other boys? They've been waiting for you to show up."

Kyle looked from Melissa to his mother.

"Do you want to swim?" Denise asked, rephrasing the question.

Kyle nodded excitedly. "Yes."

"Okay, go ahead. Be careful."

Denise took his towel as Kyle ambled toward the water. He reached the pool and stepped down, the water up to his knees. He bent over and splashed, breaking into a wide grin, and finally waded in.

"How old is he now?" Melissa asked.

"He'll be five in October."

"Oh, so will Jud. That's him over there by the diving board."

Denise saw him, the same size as Kyle. Melissa's four boys were jumping, splashing, screaming—in short, having a great time.

Denise felt herself relaxing a little. "How old are the boys?"

"Ten, eight, six, and four."

"My wife had a plan," Mitch said, cutting into the conversation. "Every other year, on our anniversary, she'd let me sleep with her."

Melissa rolled her eyes. "Don't listen to him. His conversation skills aren't meant for civilized people."

Taylor returned with their beers. "What are y'all talking about?"

"Our sex life," Mitch said, and Melissa punched him in the arm. Mitch asked Denise, "I'm not making a bad impression, am I?"

Denise smiled, deciding that she liked these two. "No."

"Why don't you two guys leave us alone so we can do some girl talk?" Melissa said. "Go clean the grill or something."

"I just got here," Taylor complained.

"Go on," Melissa said as if shooing a fly from her plate.

Mitch turned toward Taylor. "I don't think we're wanted."

"I think you're right, Mitch."

Melissa whispered conspiratorially, "These two should have been rocket scientists. Nothing gets by them."

Mitch said, "I think she just insulted us, Taylor."

"I think you're right."

"C'mon, Taylor," Mitch said, pretending to be offended. He and Taylor rose from the table, leaving Denise and Melissa alone.

Denise was laughing. "How long have you two been married?"

"Twelve years."

"How did you meet?"

"At a party in college. The first time I ever saw him, Mitch was balancing a bottle of beer on his forehead while trying to cross the room. If he could do it without spilling it, he'd win fifty bucks. He ended up soaked from head to toe, but it was obvious he didn't take himself too seriously. I guess that's what I was looking for. We started dating, and a couple of years later we got married."

She looked toward her husband, obvious affection in her eyes. "He's a good guy. I think I'll keep him."

"SO HOW was it down in the Croatan?"

When Joe had asked for volunteers to fight the forest fire, only Taylor had raised his hand. What he didn't know was that Joe had called Mitch in confidence afterward, telling him that Taylor had nearly been killed when the fire suddenly closed in around him. Had it not been for a slight shift in the wind, he would have been dead. His latest brush with death hadn't surprised Mitch.

Taylor took a drink of his beer. "Pretty hairy, but luckily no one got hurt. You should have come along. We could have used you."

Mitch began to work the scraper back and forth on the grate. "No. That's for you young guys."

"I'm older than you are, Mitch."

"Sure, but I have children. If there's a problem here in Edenton, that's one thing, but I'm not going to search them out. I used to think that I'd do this forever, but I'm not so sure anymore."

"Does Melissa still want you to give it up?"

Mitch nodded. "She just doesn't want anything to happen to me."

"We need you," Taylor said seriously.

Mitch laughed. "You sound like an army recruiter when you say that. There are people who can replace me at a moment's notice."

"You sound like your mind's already made up."

Mitch took a second before nodding. "Well, actually, it is. I mean, I'll finish out the year, but that'll be it for me."

Taylor handed a rag to Mitch to wipe the scraper. "You're really going to give it up?"

"Yep."

"No regrets?"

"None." Mitch paused. "You know, you might want to consider giving it up, too."

"I'm not gonna quit. I'm not afraid of what might happen."

"You should be," Mitch said. "If you care about Denise and

Kyle, you gotta start putting them first, like I put my family first. What we do is dangerous, no matter how careful we are. We've been lucky more than a few times." He was silent as he set the scraper aside. Then his eyes met Taylor's. "You know what it's like to grow up without a father. Would you want to do that to Kyle?"

Taylor stiffened. "Jeez, Mitch—"

Mitch raised his hands to stop Taylor from continuing. "Before you start in on me, it's something I had to say. A dead hero is still dead, Taylor. Over the years you've been testing fate more and more often, like you're chasing something. It scares me sometimes."

"You don't have to worry about me."

Mitch put his hand on Taylor's shoulder. "I always worry about you. You're like my brother. I think that entitles me to speak my mind once in a while. I know you're not going to quit, but you should try to be a little more cautious in the future. See this?"

Mitch pointed to his balding head. "I used to have a full head of hair. And I'd still have it if you weren't such a damn daredevil. Every time you do something crazy, I can feel my little hairs committing suicide by jumping right out of my head. So you owe me."

Taylor laughed. "Gee, and I thought it was hereditary."

"Oh no. It's you, buddy."

"I'm touched."

"You should be. It's not like I'd go bald for just anybody."

"All right." Taylor sighed. "I'll try to be more cautious."

"Good. Because in a while I won't be there to bail you out."

"WHAT do you think they're talking about?" Denise asked, watching Taylor from the table. She saw the change in his demeanor, the sudden stiffness, as if someone had turned on a switch.

Melissa had seen it as well. "Mitch and Taylor? Probably the fire department. Mitch is giving it up at the end of the year. He probably told Taylor to do the same thing."

"But doesn't Taylor enjoy being a fireman?"

"I don't know if he enjoys it. He does it because he has to."

"Why?"

Melissa looked at Denise. "Well . . . because of his father."

"His father?" Denise repeated.

"Didn't he tell you?" Melissa asked carefully.

"No." Denise shook her head. "He just told me that his father had died when he was a child."

"Taylor's father died in a fire."

A cold hand seemed to settle on Denise's spine.

Melissa leaned forward. "Taylor doesn't talk about it to anyone, ever. He's never even talked about it with Mitch."

Denise considered this. "That makes me feel better." She paused, furrowing her brow. "I think."

"He's a charmer, isn't he? Cute, too."

Denise leaned back in her seat. "Yes, he is."

"How is he with Kyle?"

"Kyle adores him. Lately he likes Taylor more than me."

"Taylor's always been good with kids. My kids'll call him up to see if he can come over to play. I was beginning to wonder if he'd ever meet somebody. You're the first person in years he's actually brought over."

"So there've been others?"

Melissa smiled wryly. "He hasn't talked about them, either?"

"Nope."

"Well, girl, it's a good thing you came over," she said conspiratorially, and Denise laughed. "So what did you want to know?"

"What were they like?"

"Not like you. You're a lot prettier than they were. And you've got a son."

"Whatever happened to them?"

"That I can't tell you. Taylor doesn't talk about it. All I know is that one day they seemed to be doing fine, and the next thing you knew, it was over. I never did understand why."

"That's a comforting thought."

"I'm not saying it's going to happen with you. He likes you a lot more than he liked them. I can see it in the way he looks at you. Have you two talked about getting married?"

"No. He hasn't brought it up at all."

"Mmm," Melissa said. "I'll try to find out what he's thinking."

"You don't have to do that," Denise protested, flushing.

"Don't worry. I'll be subtle. He won't know what I'm getting at."

"SO, TAYLOR, are you gonna marry this wonderful girl or what?" Denise almost dropped her fork onto her plate. Taylor was in the middle of taking a drink, and he inhaled a bit of it, causing him to cough. He brought his napkin to his face, his eyes watering. "Excuse me?" The kids had already eaten, and now the four adults were eating their meal of steaks, green salad, cheddar-cheese potatoes, and garlic bread. They'd been laughing and joking when Melissa dropped her bombshell. Denise felt the blood rush to her cheeks.

"I mean, she's a babe, Taylor," Melissa went on matter-of-factly. "Smart, too. Girls like her don't come along every day."

Taylor stiffened. "I haven't really thought about it," he said.

Melissa patted his arm. "Taylor, I was kidding. I just wanted to see your expression. Your eyes got as big as saucers."

"That's because I was choking," Taylor answered.

She leaned toward him. "I'm sorry. But I just couldn't resist. You're easy to pick on. Just like Bozo over here."

"Are you talking about me, darling?" Mitch broke in.

"Who else calls you Bozo?"

"My three other wives, of course—no one really."

"Mmm," she said, "that's good. Otherwise I might get jealous." Melissa leaned over and gave her husband a quick kiss on the cheek.

"Are they always like this?" Denise whispered to Taylor, praying he wouldn't think she'd put Melissa up to the question.

"Ever since I've known them," Taylor said.

"Hey, no talking behind our backs," Melissa said. Turning toward Denise, she moved the conversation back to safer ground. "So tell me about Atlanta. I've never been there."

Though Melissa, Denise, and Mitch chatted for the next hour, Taylor, Denise noticed, didn't say much at all.

After dinner Mitch and Taylor played tag with the boys in the yard out front. "I'm gonna get you!" Mitch shouted as he chased Jud, who was screaming, alternating between delight and fear.

"You're almost on base! Run!" Taylor yelled.

Jud reached base, joining the others. Mitch, his hands on his hips, looked around the yard at the five kids, his chest heaving. They were all within a few feet of each other.

"You can't get me, Daddy!" Cameron taunted.

"Try to get me, Daddy!" his brother Will added.

Mitch bent over and put his hands on his knees. Cameron and Will, sensing weakness, darted in opposite directions. "Okay, now you asked for it!" Mitch said. He began trudging toward Will, heading past Taylor and Kyle, who remained safely on base.

"Run, Daddy, run!" Will teased.

Mitch chased one son after the other. Kyle, who had taken a while to pick up on the game, finally understood it well enough to run with the other kids. Soon his screams were joining theirs.

"Hey, Taylor, I need a little break here," Mitch said, gasping.

Taylor darted out of reach. "Then you gotta catch me, pal."

Taylor ran toward the middle of the yard, slowed down, and allowed Mitch to tag him.

"C'mon!" Cameron shouted to Taylor. "You can't catch me."

Taylor rubbed his hands together. "All right, here I come!"

Taylor took a giant step toward the kids, and with jubilant screams they scattered in different directions. But Kyle's voice was unmistakable. "C'mon, Daddy!" (*C'maw, Da-ee!*)

Daddy.

Taylor, frozen for a moment, simply stared in Kyle's direction.

Mitch teased, "Is there something you haven't told me, Taylor?"

But Taylor barely heard what Mitch had said. *Daddy.* Though he knew it was simply Kyle mimicking the other children, it nonetheless brought Melissa's statement to mind again. *So are you going to marry this girl or what?*

"Earth to Taylor, come in, big *daddy,*" Mitch said, grinning.

Taylor glanced toward him. "Shut up, Mitch. I'm not his daddy."

Though Mitch whispered the next words to himself, Taylor heard them clearly. "Not yet, anyway."

"DID you guys have fun?" Melissa asked as the children came pounding through the front door, calling it quits for the night.

"We had a blast. Dad's getting awful slow, though," Cameron offered.

"I am not," Mitch said defensively. "I let you get to base."

"Right, Dad."

"I put some juice in the living room. Don't spill, okay?" Melissa said as the kids trudged past her. Mitch headed toward the back-yard in search of a beer. Taylor brought up the rear, Kyle right in front of him. Kyle followed the other kids to the living room.

"How did he do?" Denise asked.

"Fine," Taylor said simply. "He had fun."

Denise looked at Taylor carefully. "Are you okay?"

Taylor glanced away. "Yeah, I'm okay," he said, and followed Mitch outside.

"Hey, why so glum?" Mitch asked, filling a plastic garbage bag with the remains from the table.

Taylor shrugged. "Just preoccupied, that's all."

"About what?"

"Just work. Since I've been spending so much time with Denise, I've let my business slide a little. I've got to get back into it."

"Haven't you been heading in every day?"

"Yeah, but I don't always stay all day. You know how it is. You do that long enough, and little problems start cropping up. I've learned that when things go wrong, they go wrong in a hurry."

Mitch felt a strange sense of déjà vu. The last time Taylor had used that expression, he'd been dating Lori.

THIRTY minutes later Taylor and Denise were driving home, Kyle between them, a scene that had been repeated dozens of times. Yet now, for the first time, there was an air of tension.

Okay, Denise thought, so Taylor had almost choked when Melissa had asked if marriage was in the plans. That would have surprised anyone, wouldn't it? Three months isn't a long time. But if he wasn't as serious about their future together as he seemed to be, then why the full-court press these last few months?

All I know is that one day they seemed to be doing fine, and the next thing you knew, it was over. I never did understand why.

Was the same thing going to happen to her? Denise felt a knot form in her stomach, and she glanced at Taylor uncertainly.

From the corner of his eye Taylor caught her glance and turned to face her. "Did you have a good time tonight?"

"Yeah, I did," Denise answered quietly. "I like your friends."

"So how did you and Melissa get along?"

"We got along fine."

"One thing you've learned is that she'll say the first thing that pops into her head. You just have to ignore her sometimes."

His comment did nothing for her nerves. Denise wondered why the things Taylor hadn't said suddenly seemed more important than the things he had. She willed herself to keep her voice steady.

"Taylor, why didn't you tell me about your father?"

Taylor's eyes widened just a little. "My father?"

"Melissa told me that he died in a fire."

She saw his hands tighten on the wheel.

"How did that come up?" he asked, his tone changing slightly.

"I don't know. It just did."

Taylor didn't respond; his eyes were locked on the road ahead.

"Did you become a fireman because of your father?"

Taylor expelled a sharp breath. "I'd rather not talk about it."

"Maybe I can help—"

"You can't." He cut her off. "Besides, it doesn't concern you."

"It doesn't concern me?" she asked in disbelief. "What are you talking about? I care about you, Taylor, and it hurts me to think that you don't trust me enough to tell me what's wrong."

"Nothing's wrong. I just don't like to talk about my father."

Once again silence descended in the truck. This time it lasted the rest of the way home.

After Taylor carried Kyle into his bedroom, he waited in the living room until Denise had changed him into his pajamas. When she came out, she noticed that Taylor was standing near the door.

"You're not going to stay?" she asked, surprised.

He shook his head. "I've got to get to work early tomorrow."

Though he said it without a trace of bitterness or anger, his words didn't dispel her unease. He began to jingle his keys.

Denise walked across the room to be closer to him. "All right. See you tomorrow?"

Taylor cleared his throat. "I'll try, but I've got a pretty full schedule tomorrow. I don't know if I'll be able to swing by."

Denise studied him carefully, wondering. Their eyes met only briefly before Taylor glanced away. "Will you be able to take me in to work tomorrow night?"

"Yeah, sure," he finally said. "I'll take you in."

He left after kissing her only briefly, then walked to his truck.

EARLY the next morning, while Denise was drinking a cup of coffee, the phone rang. She recognized Taylor's voice instantly.

"Oh, hey, I'm glad you're up," he said.

"I'm always up this early," she said, feeling a sense of relief wash over her at the sound of his voice. "I missed you last night."

"I missed you, too," Taylor said. "I didn't sleep too well."

"Neither did I. I kept waking up because I had all the covers for once." She chuckled. "Hey, how about an early supper?"

"No, I can't, but I'll be by to bring you in to work."

"Oh, all right. I'll see you this evening."

GOOD to his word, Taylor was waiting in the kitchen as she collected the last of her things. He hadn't come by with much time to spare. "Where is the little guy?"

"Out back. Let me go get him."

Denise called for him, and Kyle came running into the house. "Hewwo, Tayer," he said, a big grin on his face.

Taylor caught him and lifted him to eye level. "Hey, little man. How was your day? Did you miss me?"

"Yes," Kyle answered. "I missed you."

It was the first time he'd answered a new question properly, without being told how to do it, shocking both of them into silence.

For just a second Denise's worries from the night before were forgotten. But if she expected Kyle's simple statement would alleviate her concerns about Taylor, she was mistaken.

Not that it went bad right away. Though Taylor—still citing work as the reason—had stopped coming by in the afternoons, he continued to drive Denise to and from the diner. They'd also made love the night Kyle had answered Taylor's question.

Yet things were changing. Denise had been around long enough to know that the initial feelings associated with love were like an ocean wave in their intensity, but the wave wouldn't last forever. It couldn't—nor was it meant to be—but if two people were right for each other, a truer kind of love could last forever in its wake. With Taylor, however, it seemed as if he was trying to fight the current, using work as an excuse to avoid the new realities of their situation. So she kept as busy as she could, doing her best not to dwell on what might be happening between them. She threw herself into her work with Kyle with renewed energy. Now that he was speaking more, she began working on more complex phrases and ideas. She worked her shifts; she paid her bills. In short, she lived her life much the same as she had before she'd met Taylor McAden. Nonetheless, she spent most afternoons hoping to see him coming up the drive. Usually, however, he didn't. Despite herself, she heard Melissa's words once more. *All I know is that one day they seemed to be doing fine, and the next thing you knew, it was over.*

Eight

"IT'S just for a few days," Taylor said, shrugging.

They were sitting on the couch while Kyle watched a cartoon on television. It was Tuesday, and he'd come by early to take her in to work. Her pleasure at this had evaporated almost immediately when he'd informed her that he was leaving for a few days.

"When did you decide this?" Denise asked.

"Just this morning. South Carolina opens the hunting season two weeks earlier than we do. A couple of the guys are going down, and I figured I'd head down with them. I feel like I need a break."

Are you talking about me or work? "You're leaving tomorrow?"

Taylor shifted slightly. "Actually, it's more like the middle of the night. We'll be leaving around three."

"You probably shouldn't pick me up tonight," Denise offered. "You need a little sleep."

"Don't worry about that. I'll be there."

Denise shook her head. "No. Rhonda'll bring me home."

Taylor slipped his arm around Denise, surprising her. He pulled her close. "I'll miss you."

"You will?" she said, hating the plaintive note in her voice.

"Of course. Especially around midnight. I'll probably wander out to my truck through force of habit."

Denise smiled, thinking he'd kiss her. Instead he turned away, motioning toward Kyle. "And I'll miss you, too, little man."

"Yes," Kyle said, eyes glued to the television.

"Hey, Kyle," Denise said, "Taylor's leaving for a few days."

"Yes," Kyle said again, obviously not listening.

Taylor crawled down from the couch, creeping on all fours toward Kyle. "Are you ignoring me, Kyle?" he growled.

Kyle squealed as he tried to get away. Taylor grabbed him easily, and they began to wrestle on the floor. "He's wrestling!" Kyle shrieked, his arms and legs flailing. *(Ees wesswing!)*

For the next few minutes there was pandemonium on the living-room floor. When Kyle finally tired, Taylor let him pull away.

"Hey, when I get back, I'm going to take you to a baseball game. If that's okay with your mom, of course."

"Bessbaw game," Kyle repeated wonderingly.

"It's fine with me," Denise said.

Taylor winked. "Did you hear that? Your mom said we can go."

A couple minutes later they were on their way to the diner. Taylor walked Denise and Kyle to the front door. "Call me?" she said.

"I'll try," Taylor promised.

They stood gazing at each other for a moment before Taylor kissed her and hugged Kyle good-bye. Denise hoped that the trip would help clear his mind of whatever had been bothering him.

Perhaps it did, but Denise had no way of knowing. For the next four days she didn't hear from him at all.

SHE HATED WAITING FOR THE phone to ring. It made her feel helpless, a sensation she detested. So he hadn't called. So what?

Denise forged on. On Friday she took Kyle to the park; on Saturday they went for a long walk in the woods. On Sunday she took Kyle to church, then spent the early afternoon running errands.

With enough money now to begin looking for a used car, she picked up two newspapers for their classified ads. Next stop was the grocery store. Kyle was staring at a crocodile on a cereal box when Denise heard her name being called. Turning, she saw Judy.

"I thought that was you," Judy said cheerfully. "How are you?"

"Hi, Judy. I'm fine."

"Hey, Kyle," Judy said.

"Hewwo, Miss Jewey," he whispered.

Judy moved her cart a little off to the side. "So what have you been doing lately? You and Taylor haven't come by for dinner."

Denise shrugged, feeling a pang of unease. "Just the usual. Kyle's been keeping me pretty busy these days."

"How's he coming along?"

"He's had a good summer, that's for sure. Haven't you, Kyle?"

"Yes," he said quietly.

Judy turned her attention to Denise again. "I didn't expect to see you here. Taylor told me he was going to spend the day with you."

Denise ran her hand through her hair. "He did?"

Judy eyed her. "Yesterday. He came by after he got home."

"So . . . he's back?"

The next words came out carefully. "Didn't he call you?"

"No." Denise turned away, trying not to show her discomfiture.

"Well, maybe you were already at work," Judy offered softly, but even as she spoke the words, both of them knew it wasn't true.

Two hours after she got home, Denise spotted Taylor coming up the drive. Kyle was playing out front and immediately started for the truck. Taylor opened the door; Kyle jumped up into his arms.

Denise stepped out onto the porch wondering if he'd come because Judy had called him. Wondering if he would have come otherwise, why he hadn't called while he was gone, and why, despite all that, her heart still leaped at the sight of him.

After Taylor put Kyle down, the two of them began making their way to the porch. "Hey, Denise," Taylor said warily.

"Hi, Taylor."

When she made no move off the porch toward him, Taylor hesitated before coming up the steps. When he tried to kiss her, she pulled back slightly. "Are you mad at me?" he asked.

"I don't know, Taylor. Should I be?"

"Tayer!" Kyle said. "Tayer's here!"

"Could you go inside for a minute, sweetie?" She opened the screen door and then led Kyle inside. After making sure he was occupied with his toys, she returned to the porch.

"So what's up?" Taylor asked.

"Why didn't you call while you were gone?"

Taylor shrugged. "I don't know. I guess I just didn't have the time. We were out all day, and I was pretty worn out by the time I got back to the motel. Is that why you're mad?"

Denise didn't answer. "Why did you tell your mother you were going to spend the day here if you didn't plan on doing so?"

"I did come by—what do you think I'm doing now?"

Denise exhaled sharply. "Taylor, what's going on with you?"

"What do you mean? I got back into town yesterday, I was beat, and I had a bunch of things to take care of this morning. Why are you making such a big deal out of this?"

"I'm not making a big deal out of this."

"Yes, you are. If you don't want me around, just tell me."

"It's not that. I just don't know why you're acting this way."

"And how am I acting?"

"Like you're not sure what you want anymore. With us, I mean."

"Where is all this coming from? Did you talk to Melissa again?"

"No," she said, frustrated and a little angry. "It's just that you've changed, and sometimes I don't know what to think anymore."

"Just because I didn't call?" He took a step closer to her, his expression softening. "There wasn't any time, that's all."

Kyle pushed open the screen door. "C'mon, guys," he said. "Let's go inside." *(C'mon, guys. Wess go issite.)*

For a moment, however, they simply stood without moving.

"C'mon," Kyle prodded, reaching for Denise's shirt.

Denise looked down, forcing a smile, before glancing up again, her emotions warring within her. His explanations seemed reasonable. So why didn't she believe him?

Taylor did his best to break the ice. For dinner he did the cooking, or rather part of it. He'd brought venison, along with some potato salad and baked beans from the supermarket.

After Kyle was asleep, Denise and Taylor sat together on the couch in the living room. She felt better than she had for the past couple of weeks. "So when are you taking Kyle to his baseball game?"

"I was thinking about Saturday. There's a game in Norfolk."

"Oh, that's his birthday," she said, disappointed. "I was planning to throw a little party for him."

"What time's the party?"

"Probably around noon or so. I still have to work that night."

"The game starts at seven. How about if I take Kyle with me while you're at work? I'd have him home in time to pick you up."

"All right. But don't keep him too long if he gets tired."

Taylor raised his hand. "Scouts' honor. I'll pick him up at five, and by the end of the night he'll be eating hot dogs and peanuts and singing 'Take Me Out to the Ball Game.' "

She nudged him in the ribs. "Yeah, sure."

"Well, it won't be for lack of trying."

Denise rested her head against his shoulder. "You're a good guy, Taylor. You've made me feel special these last couple of months."

"So have you."

She could feel his chest rising and falling with every breath. "Do you ever think about the future, Taylor? About us, I mean?"

Taylor didn't respond, and Denise went on.

"These last couple of weeks it feels like you're pulling away. You've been working such long hours that we haven't had much time to spend together, and then when you didn't call . . . ."

She trailed off, knowing she'd already said these things before. She felt his body stiffen as his answer came out in a hoarse whisper. "I care about you and about Kyle. Isn't that enough for now?"

She lifted her head from his shoulder and met his eyes. "Yeah," she lied. "That's enough for now."

Later that night, after making love and falling asleep together, Denise woke and saw Taylor standing by the window, looking toward the trees but obviously thinking of something else. He finally crawled back into bed.

"Are you okay?" she whispered. "What's wrong?"

"Nothing. I just couldn't sleep."

"Is it something I did?"

He drew a long breath. "No. There's nothing wrong with you at all." With that, he cuddled against her, pulling her close.

The following morning Denise woke alone.

This time Taylor wasn't sleeping on the couch. This time he didn't surprise her with breakfast. He'd slipped out unnoticed.

She reviewed their evening, trying to get a better read on it. For every positive thing, there seemed to be something negative as well. She shook her head, doing her best to put it all out of her mind, at least until she saw him again. He'd be by later to take her in to work, and she felt sure that she would know more as soon as she saw him.

A little after five she changed into her work clothes, made Kyle a grilled-cheese sandwich, watched the news.

Time continued to pass. Six thirty and there was no sign of him. He's coming, she told herself. Isn't he? She dialed his number, but there was no answer. She went to the living-room window. Looking out, she waited, her lips pressed together. And waited.

Fifteen minutes to get there, or she'd be late.

At five until seven she called Ray, apologizing and telling him she'd be a little late.

"We've got to go, Kyle," she said. "We're going to ride our bikes."

"No," he said.

"I'm not asking, Kyle, I'm telling you."

Hearing the tone of her voice, Kyle knew not to press her.

Cursing, she went to the back porch. Rolling her bike off the porch, she noticed it wasn't gliding smoothly. A flat tire. "Oh, c'mon, not tonight," she said in disbelief.

She let the bike fall onto a couple of cardboard boxes, then went into the kitchen again just as Kyle was coming out the door.

"We're not taking our bikes," she said. "Come inside."

She went to the phone and tried Taylor again. Not in. She slammed the phone down. Who else to call? Rhonda was already at the diner. Judy? She dialed her number and let it ring a dozen times before hanging up. Who else did she know? Only one other person. She found the number. "Melissa? Hi, it's Denise."

"Oh, hey, how are you?"

"Actually, I'm not too good right now. I'm really calling for a favor. Is it possible for you to drive me in to work tonight? I know it's last minute and I'm sorry, but a tire on my bike is flat—"

"Don't worry," Melissa interrupted. "I'll be there in ten minutes."

Denise hung up, then noticed Kyle watching her. "Mommy's not mad at you, sweetheart. I'm sorry for yelling."

She was, however, still angry at Taylor. How could he?

"So what happened?" Melissa asked when she arrived. "You said your tire was flat?"

"Yeah. But I didn't expect that I'd have to ride my bike in the first place. Taylor didn't show up." Denise buckled Kyle up and got in.

"And he said he would?"

"We didn't talk about it specifically," she admitted, "but he's been driving me all summer, so I just assumed he'd keep doing it."

"Did he call?" Melissa turned onto the main road.

"No."

Melissa's eyes darted in Denise's direction. "I take it things have changed between you two."

"You knew this was going to happen, didn't you?"

"I've known Taylor a long time," Melissa answered carefully.

"So what's going on with him?"

Melissa sighed. "Taylor always seems to turn gun-shy whenever he starts getting serious with someone. It's not you, trust me. When we were at dinner, I wasn't kidding when I said he really cares about you, more than I've seen him care about anyone. Mitch says the same thing. But sometimes I think that Taylor doesn't feel that he deserves to be happy, so he sabotages every opportunity."

Denise balled her fists in frustration. "The question is why?"

Melissa didn't respond right away. "If you ask me, it's because of something that happened a long time ago."

"His father?"

Melissa nodded. "He blames himself for his father's death."

Denise felt her stomach dip. "What happened back then?"

They came to a stop in front of the diner. "You should probably talk to him about that."

"I've tried."

Melissa shook her head. "I know, Denise. We all have."

DENISE worked her shift, barely concentrating, but because it was slow, it didn't really matter. Rhonda left early, leaving Ray as the only option to bring her and Kyle home. Though she was thankful Ray was willing to drive her, he usually spent an hour cleaning up after closing, so it meant a later night than usual. Just before it was time to lock up, the front door opened. Taylor stepped inside.

"Melissa called," he said, "and said you might need a ride home."

"Where were you earlier?"

"I was working. I didn't know you needed a ride today."

"You've been driving me for the last three months," she said.

"But I was gone last week. You didn't ask me to drive you in last night, so I just figured Rhonda would bring you in. I didn't realize that I was supposed to be your personal chauffeur."

Her eyes narrowed. "That's not fair, Taylor, and you know it."

Taylor crossed his arms. "Hey, I didn't come here to get yelled at. I'm here in case you need a ride home. Do you want one or not?"

Denise pursed her lips together. "No."

If Taylor was surprised, he didn't show it. "All right, then," he said. "I'm sorry about earlier, if that means anything."

Denise didn't say anything.

When Taylor realized she wasn't going to speak, he pulled the door open again. "Do you need a ride tomorrow?" he asked.

Again she thought about it. "Will you be there?"

He winced. "Yes," he answered softly. "I will."

"Then, okay," she said.

He nodded, then made his way out the door.

Denise saw Ray scrubbing the counter as if his life depended on it. "Ray?"

"Yes, honey?"

"Can I take tomorrow evening off?"

He glanced up from the counter, looking at her as he probably would have looked at his own child. "I think you'd better."

TAYLOR was surprised when Denise opened the door dressed in jeans. It had been raining most of the day, but Taylor was clean and dry—it was obvious he'd changed before coming over. "Aren't you supposed to be dressed for work?" he asked.

"I'm not working tonight," she said evenly.

Taylor followed her inside, curious. "Where's Kyle?"

Denise sat. "Melissa said she'd watch him for a while." She patted the couch. "Sit down."

Taylor did as she suggested. "So what's up?"

"We've got to talk," she said, "about what's going on with you."

"Is there something I don't know about?" He grinned nervously.

"This isn't the time for jokes, Taylor. I took tonight off in the hopes that you'd help me understand what the problem is."

"About what happened yesterday? I said I was sorry. I mean it."

"It's not that. I'm talking about you and me."

"Didn't we just talk about this the other night?"

Denise sighed. "Yeah, or rather, I talked. You didn't say much. But then, you never talk about the things that are bothering you."

"That's not true."

"Then why are you treating me differently than you used to?"

"I'm not—"

Denise stopped him by raising her hands. "You didn't call while you were away, you snuck out of here yesterday morning, then didn't show up later. Don't you see the pattern?"

He stared at the wall, stubbornly avoiding her question.

Remembering what Melissa said, Denise decided to go to the heart of the matter. "What happened to your father?"

She saw him tense. "Why does that matter?" he asked.

"Because I think that it might have something to do with the way you've been acting lately."

"He died, okay? I've already told you that."

"And?"

"And what?" he burst out. "What do you want me to say?"

She took his hand in hers. "Melissa said that you blame yourself."

Taylor pulled his hand away. "She doesn't know what she's talking about."

Denise kept her voice calm. "There was a fire, right?"

"Damn!" he spat out. "Can't you just drop it?"

His outburst surprised her, and her eyes widened. "No," she persisted, her heart racing. "Not if it's something that concerns us."

He stood up. "It doesn't concern us! I'm getting sick and tired of you grilling me! We're not married, Denise. Where the hell do you get off trying to pry?"

The words stung. "I'm not prying," she said defensively.

"Sure you are. You're trying to get into my head so you can try to fix what's wrong. But nothing's wrong. I am who I am. If you can't handle it, maybe you shouldn't try." He took a step backward. "Look, you don't need a ride, and I don't want to be here right now. Think about what I said, okay?" With that, Taylor made his way out the door, leaving Denise on the couch, stunned.

Think about what I said?

"I would," she whispered, "if you'd made any sense at all."

FLOWERS arrived the next day. The note was simple: "I'm sorry for the way I acted. I just need a couple days to think things through."

Part of her wanted to throw the flowers away; another part wanted to keep them. Part of her wanted to end the relationship right now; another part wanted to plead for another chance. Outside, rain was sheeting against the windows, strong winds bending the trees.

She called Rhonda, then turned her attention to the classifieds. This weekend she'd buy a car. Then she wouldn't feel so trapped.

On Saturday, Kyle celebrated his birthday. Melissa, Mitch, and their four boys, and Judy were the only ones in attendance. When asked about Taylor, Denise explained that he was coming by around five to take Kyle to a baseball game. Kyle had been looking forward to it all week. Denise didn't worry. Despite everything, Taylor hadn't changed at all when it concerned her son. He would come, she knew. There was no way on earth that he wouldn't.

The hours ticked by, more slowly than usual.

But at twenty past five Denise was playing catch with Kyle in the yard, a pit in her stomach and on the verge of crying.

Kyle looked adorable, dressed in jeans and a baseball hat. With his new mitt—courtesy of Melissa—he caught Denise's latest toss.

"Taylor's coming," he said. *(Tayer's cummeen.)*

Denise swallowed hard. She'd called three times; he wasn't home. Nor, it seemed, was he on his way. "I don't think so, honey."

"Taylor's coming," he repeated.

That one brought tears to her eyes. Denise squatted to be at eye level. "Taylor is busy. I don't think he's going to take you to the game. You can come with Mommy to work, okay?"

Kyle looked up at her, the words slowly sinking in. "Tayer's gone," he finally said.

Denise reached out for him. "Yes, he is," she said sadly.

Kyle dropped the ball and walked past her, toward the house, looking as dejected as she'd ever seen him.

TAYLOR came by the following morning, a wrapped gift for Kyle under his arm. Before Denise could get to the door, Kyle was outside, reaching for the package, the fact that Taylor hadn't shown up yesterday already forgotten.

She stepped outside. Kyle was already ripping the paper off the gift in an excited frenzy. Denise watched as his eyes grew wider.

"Legos!" he cried joyfully, holding up the box for Denise to see. *(Weggoes.)*

"It sure is," she said. Without looking at Taylor, she brushed a loose strand of hair from her eyes. "Kyle, say, 'Thank you.' "

"Kenk you," he said, staring at the box.

"Here," Taylor said, squatting, "let me open that for you." He cut the tape on the box and removed the cover. Kyle reached in and pulled out a set of wheels for a model car.

Denise cleared her throat. "Kyle? Why don't you take that inside. Mommy's got to talk to Taylor."

She held open the screen door, and Kyle went in. Setting the box on the coffee table, he was immediately engrossed in the pieces.

Taylor stood, not making a move toward her.

"I'm sorry," he said sincerely. "There's really no excuse. I just forgot about the game. Was he upset?"

"You could say that."

Taylor's expression was pained. "Maybe I could make it up to him. There's another game next weekend."

"I don't think so," she said quietly. She motioned to the chairs on the porch. Taylor hesitated before moving to take a seat. Denise sat as well but didn't face him. Instead she watched a pair of squirrels hopping across the yard.

"You have every right to be angry with me," Taylor said.

Denise finally turned to face him. "I was. Last night if you had come into the diner, I would have thrown a frying pan at you."

The corners of Taylor's mouth upturned slightly, then straightened again. He knew she wasn't finished.

"But I'm over that. Now I'm less angry than I am resigned."

Taylor looked at her curiously as Denise exhaled slowly. When she spoke again, her voice was low and soft. "For the last four years I had my life with Kyle. It's not always easy, but it's predictable, which helps me keep some semblance of control. Kyle needs me to do that, and I need to do it for him. But then you showed up. When we first met, I didn't want to get involved with anyone. But you were so good with Kyle, and I got swept up in that. And little by little I found myself falling in love with you."

Taylor put both hands in his lap as he stared at the floor.

Denise leaned back in her rocker, gazing at him through lowered lashes. "Do you remember the night we met? When you rescued my son? After that you delivered my groceries and then taught Kyle how to play catch. It was like you were the handsome prince of my girlhood fantasies, and the more I got to know you, the more I came to believe it. And part of me still does. You're everything I've ever wanted in a man. But as much as I care for you, I don't think you're ready for me or my son."

Taylor stared at her with pain-darkened eyes.

"I'm not blind to what's been happening with us. You're pulling away from me—from both of us—no matter how much you try to deny it. What I don't understand is why you're doing it. I know you're holding something back, and if you can't or don't want to talk about it, there's not much I can do. But whatever it is, it's driving you away." She stopped, her eyes welling with tears. "Yesterday you hurt me. But worse than that, you hurt Kyle. He waited for you, Taylor. He jumped up every time a car went by, thinking it was you. But it wasn't. Finally even he knew that everything had changed. He didn't say a single thing the rest of the night. Not one word."

Denise looked toward the horizon, a single tear drifting down her cheek. "I can put up with a lot of things. But I'm a grown-up, and I'm old enough to choose whether I want to keep letting that happen. In my heart I know you didn't mean to hurt Kyle. But I can't take the chance of that happening again."

"I'm sorry," he said thickly.

"I am, too."

He reached for her hand. "I don't want to lose you." His voice was almost a whisper.

She took his hand and squeezed it, then let it go. She fought the tears again. "But you don't want to keep me, either, do you?"

To that he had no response.

"So you went ahead and ended it, huh?" Mitch said.

They were in a dingy bar later that evening. "It wasn't me, Mitch," Taylor said defensively. "She's the one who called it off."

"Just came out of the blue, right? You had nothing to do with it."

"It's over, Mitch. What do you want me to say?"

Mitch shook his head. "You know, Taylor, you sit here thinking you've got it all figured out, but you don't understand anything."

"Thanks for your support, Mitch."

Mitch glared at him. "Don't give me that crap. You don't need my support. What you need is someone to tell you to get your ass back over there and fix whatever it was you did wrong."

"You don't understand—"

"Like hell I don't!" Mitch said, slamming his beer glass onto the table. "Who do you think you are? You think you're the only one with a lousy past? I have news for you. Everyone has things they wish they could undo. But most people don't go around doing their best to screw up their present lives because of it."

"I didn't screw up," Taylor said angrily. "Didn't you hear what I said? *She's* the one who ended it. Not me. Not this time."

"Taylor, you can go to your grave thinking that, but both you and I know it ain't the whole truth. So get back over there and try to salvage it. She's the best thing that ever happened to you."

"I didn't ask you to come here so you can give me some of your advice, Mitch."

"Well, do me a favor and listen to it, okay? Your father would have wanted you to."

Taylor squinted at Mitch. "Don't bring him into this."

"Why, Taylor? Don't forget, I knew your father, too. I knew what a great guy he was. He was a guy who loved his family, loved his son. He would have been disappointed by what you're doing now. I guarantee it."

The blood drained from Taylor's face. "Screw you, Mitch."

"No, Taylor. You've already done that to yourself."

"I don't need this crap," Taylor snapped, rising from the table. He started for the door. "You don't even know who I am."

Mitch stood and grabbed Taylor roughly by his shirt.

"I don't know you? Hell, I do! You're a damn coward, is what you are! You're afraid of living, because you think it means giving up this cross you've been carrying your whole life. But you've gone too far. This time you aren't just hurting one person. It isn't just Denise—you're hurting a little boy. Doesn't that mean anything to you? What would your father say to that? 'I'm proud of you, son'? Not a chance. Your father would be sickened, just like I am now."

Taylor, his face white, grabbed Mitch and lifted him, driving him backward into the jukebox. Taylor raised his fist.

"What are you gonna do? Hit me?" Mitch taunted. "Go ahead."

"Knock it off!" the bartender shouted. "Take it outside. Now!"

Taylor pulled his arm back, ready to strike, his hand shaking.

"I'll always forgive you, Taylor," Mitch said almost calmly. "But you gotta forgive yourself, too."

Taylor released Mitch and turned away, a few faces staring at him. Stifling the curses in his throat, he strode out the door.

Nine

JUST before midnight Taylor returned home to a message flickering on his answering machine. Since leaving Mitch, he'd been driving to clear his mind. Guessing that Mitch had left him a message, and regretting his outburst at his friend, Taylor pressed the PLAY button.

To his surprise it was Joe from the fire department, his voice straining to stay calm. "There's a warehouse fire on the outskirts of town. Arvil Henderson's place. A big one. Lives are in danger. If you get the message in time, we'll need your help."

The message had been left twenty-four minutes ago.

Taylor raced to the truck, cursing himself for having turned off his cell phone when he left the bar. Henderson's was a large regional wholesaler of house paint. Trucks were loaded day and night; at least a dozen people were always working inside the warehouse. It would take him about ten minutes to get there.

Gravel shot from his tires as he turned around in the driveway, barely slowing as he turned onto the road. He took every shortcut he knew. In time he could see the sky glowing orange in the distance. The air was already thick with greasy black smoke, fueled by the petroleum in the paint. The warehouse was blazing violently when Taylor made a final turn, coming to a halt.

Pandemonium everywhere. Three pumper trucks were already on the scene, blowing water toward one side of the building. The other side was still undamaged but looking as if it wouldn't stay that way for long. Five people were on the ground being attended to. Two others were being helped out of the warehouse.

As he scanned the scene, Taylor noticed Mitch's car, although it was impossible to make him out in the chaos of bodies and vehicles. Joe was barking orders, trying to gain control of the situation.

Taylor leaped from his truck and scrambled to get his gear. Two minutes later, fully outfitted, he ran toward Joe. As he moved, the evening was suddenly shattered by a series of paint cans exploding, one right after the other. People nearest the building hit the ground as burning portions of the building shot toward them.

Taylor dove and covered his head. More explosions erupted, rocketing debris as firemen scattered backward, away from the heat. From the inferno emerged two men, limbs on fire; hoses were trained on them, and they fell to the ground, writhing.

Taylor pushed up from the ground and ran toward the two men. An external wall suddenly collapsed outward, barely missing them. Taylor's eyes were tearing and burning as he reached them. Both were unconscious. He grabbed them by the wrists and dragged them to safety. Another fireman arrived and took charge of them.

Taylor saw Joe waving wildly and knew something was terribly wrong. Only one part of the building was left standing now, the south end, which housed the offices. Judging by the smoke pouring out, that section was getting ready to blow as well.

Taylor rushed toward Joe. Drawing near, he heard the soul-numbing words. "They're still inside! Two men! Over there!"

He blinked, a memory rising from the ashes. *A boy, nine years old, in the attic, calling from the window . . .*

It stopped him cold. Taylor looked toward the flaming ruins of the warehouse. As if in a dream, he rushed past the men holding the hoses, ignoring their calls to stop. Straight ahead was a doorway that had been torn open by the firemen, and black smoke poured out. Taylor rushed through the door, his gloved hand over his face. His eyes burned as he inhaled acrid air. Everything blazed with unearthly fury. He heard the splintering sound of a beam crashing and leaped aside instinctively as part of the ceiling collapsed beside him.

Taylor could see someone lying on the ground. From the shape of his gear he could see it was a fireman. Taylor staggered toward him, narrowly avoiding another falling beam. Trapped in the last standing corner of the warehouse now, the wall of flames was closing in around them. Almost out of breath, he grabbed the man's wrist and hauled him up over his shoulder. Moving on instinct alone, he made it to a shattered window and in one motion threw the man through.

Taylor took two harsh breaths and coughed violently. Then, taking another breath, he turned and made his way inside one more time. Everything was a roaring hell of acid-tongued flames and suffocating smoke. One more man was inside.

A boy, nine years old, in the attic, calling from the window that he was afraid to jump.

The wall of the office collapsed, toppling in on itself like a stack of cards. The roof above him sagged. Taylor dropped to his knees, his eyes beginning to spasm. He was crawling now, the heat like a sizzling anvil. Ahead of him was an unending wall of rippling heat. It was then that he came across the body. With smoke completely surrounding him, he couldn't tell who it was. The man lay on his stomach, arms out to either side. His helmet was still fastened on his head. Two feet of rubble covered his legs from the thighs down.

Taylor gripped both arms and pulled. The body didn't budge. With the last vestiges of his strength he began to move the charred debris off the man. Taylor's lungs were about to explode. He moved to the head of the body and tugged. This time the body moved. Taylor pulled again, but out of air completely, his body reacted instinctively. He suddenly went dizzy, coughing violently. He let go of the man and rose, staggering in pure panic now, toward the window. After a few yards he stopped and turned back toward the body. The world suddenly exploded into fire. Flames engulfed him, setting his suit on fire as he lunged for the window. He threw himself blindly through the opening. The last thing he felt was his body hitting the earth with a thud, a scream of despair dying on his lips.

ONLY one person died that early Monday morning.

Six men were injured, Taylor among them, and all were taken to the hospital. Three were discharged that night. Two were transferred by helicopter to the burn unit at Duke University in Durham.

Taylor lay alone in the darkness of his hospital room, his thoughts filled with the man he had left behind who had died. One eye was heavily bandaged, and he was staring up at the ceiling with the other when his mother arrived. She sat with him in his hospital room for an hour, then left him alone with his thoughts.

He never said a word.

Denise showed up Tuesday morning when visiting hours began. As soon as she arrived, Judy looked up from her chair, her eyes red and exhausted. When Judy called, Denise had come immediately, Kyle in tow. Judy took Kyle's hand and silently led him downstairs.

Denise entered Taylor's room, seating herself where Judy had been. He turned his head the other way.

"I'm sorry about Mitch," she said gently.

THE funeral was to be held three days later, on Friday. Taylor was released from the hospital on Thursday and went straight to Melissa's. Her family had come in from Rocky Mount, and with Mitch's parents and siblings the house was filled with people.

As soon as Taylor saw Melissa, he started toward her. She broke off her conversation with her sister and brother-in-law and made her way to him. He wrapped his arms around her, putting his head on her shoulder as he cried into her hair. "I'm so sorry," he said. "I'm so, so sorry."

Melissa began to cry as well.

"I tried, Melissa. I didn't know it was him. . . . I couldn't . . . " he finally choked out, before breaking down completely.

They stood holding each other for a long time. An hour later he left without talking to anyone else.

The funeral service was overflowing with people. Every fireman from the surrounding counties, as well as every law-enforcement official, made an appearance. The crowd was among the largest ever for a service in Edenton; nearly everyone in town came to pay their respects. Melissa and her four children sat weeping in the front row.

When it came time for eulogies, Joe went first and spoke of Mitch's dedication, his bravery, and the respect he would always hold in his heart. Mitch's older sister shared remembrances from their childhood. When she finished, Taylor stepped forward.

"Mitch was like a brother to me," he began. "We grew up together. Once, when we were twelve, Mitch and I were fishing. I stood up too quickly in the dinghy. I slipped and hit my head, then fell into the water. Mitch dove in and pulled me to the surface. He saved my life that day, but when I finally came to, he only laughed and said, 'You made me lose the fish, you clumsy oaf.' "

A low murmur of chuckles rose, then faded away.

"Mitch was the kind of man who added something to everything he touched and everyone he came in contact with. He saw life as a big game, where the only way to win was to be good to other people. Mitch"—he closed his eyes, pushing back the tears—"Mitch was everything I've ever wanted to be."

Taylor stepped from the microphone, then made his way back into the crowd. The minister finished the service, and people filed by the coffin, where a picture of Mitch had been placed. In it he was smiling broadly, standing over the grill in his backyard.

The house was even more crowded after the funeral, with everyone who'd been at the service. Judy and Melissa's mother tended to feeding the masses. After hugging Melissa and sharing a few words of grief and sympathy with her, Denise wandered into the backyard to watch Kyle and the other children who'd also attended the funeral. Mainly nephews and nieces, they were young and, like Kyle, unable to fully understand everything that was going on. Dressed in formal clothes, they were running around as if it were nothing more than a family reunion.

Later, as the crowd was finally thinning, Taylor was standing in Mitch's den alone when Denise approached him. "Your words at the service were beautiful," she said.

Taylor simply nodded.

Denise ran her hand through her hair. "I'm really sorry. I just wanted you to know that if you need to talk, you know where I am."

"I don't need anyone," he whispered. With that, he walked away.

What neither of them knew was that Judy had witnessed the whole thing.

TAYLOR BOLTED UPRIGHT IN BED, his heart pounding, his mouth dry. For a moment he was inside the burning warehouse again. Flames were everywhere, and though he tried to scream, no sounds escaped from his throat. Then, just as suddenly, he realized he was imagining it. He looked around the room as reality pressed in around him, making him ache in a different way. Mitch Johnson was dead.

It was Wednesday. Since the funeral he hadn't left his house, hadn't answered the phone. He had to get back to the job. It was already past nine. He should have been there an hour ago. Instead of getting up, however, he simply lay back down.

He had hardly eaten anything in days. He couldn't sleep, nor did he want to. Each hunger pang would remind him of his guilt. Because of him, his friend had died. Just like his father.

Last night, while sitting on the porch, he had tried to bring Mitch to life again, but Mitch's face was already frozen in time. Soon his image would be gone forever. Just like his father's.

EARLY Saturday morning, awakened by nightmares once more, Taylor forced himself out of bed. He'd made a decision. Ten minutes later he was parked in front of Melissa's house.

"I drove by and saw the lawn was getting a little high," he said without meeting her eyes. "How're you holding up?" he ventured.

"Okay," she said, her eyes rimmed with red. "How about you?"

Taylor shrugged, swallowing the lump in his throat.

He spent the next eight hours outside, making her yard look as if a professional landscaper had come by. Then he donned his tool belt and reattached a few broken planks in the fence, caulked three windows, mended a screen. He didn't go inside to visit with Melissa until he was ready to leave, and even then he stayed only briefly.

"There are a few more things to do," he said on his way out the door. "I'll be by tomorrow to take care of them."

The next day he worked until nightfall, possessed.

As he'd done with Denise, he began swinging by Melissa's home nearly every day. He felt a sense of responsibility regarding the boys. They needed a father figure. He knew he couldn't take Mitch's place, but he could be there for them, doing the things that Mitch had done. The lawn. Ball games and fishing trips. Whatever.

He knew what it was like to grow up without a father. For Mitch's sake he wouldn't let that happen to the boys. Melissa didn't seem to mind that he'd begun to come over.

He began to eat again, to make it in to work, and the nightmares stopped. He knew what he had to do.

But the following weekend when Taylor arrived to take care of the lawn, he inhaled sharply. A realty sign: FOR SALE.

Melissa emerged from the house. Pushing open his truck door, he started toward her. He could hear the boys in the yard out back.

Melissa gave him a hug. "How are you, Taylor?" she asked.

Taylor took a step back, avoiding her gaze. "All right, I guess," he answered. "What's with the sign? You're selling the house?"

"Hopefully."

"Why?"

Melissa's whole body seemed to sag. "I just can't live here anymore," she answered. "Too many memories."

"You're not moving away, are you?" he asked in disbelief.

After a long moment Melissa nodded.

"Where're you going?"

"Rocky Mount."

"But why?" he asked, his voice straining. "You've lived here for years; you've got friends here. Is it the house?" He didn't wait for a reply. "If the house is too much, there might be something I could do. I could build you a new one for cost, anywhere you want."

"It's not the house. My family's in Rocky Mount. I need them right now. So do the boys. All their cousins are there."

"You're moving right away?"

Melissa nodded. "Next week," she said. "My parents have a rental house they said I could use until I sell this place. And if I do have to take a job, they can watch my boys for me."

"I could do that," Taylor said. "I could give you a job doing all the billing and ordering. You could do it here from the house."

She smiled sadly at him. "Why? Do you want to rescue me, too?"

The words made him flinch.

"That's what you're trying to do, isn't it? Taking care of the yard, spending time with the boys, the offer for a house and a job. I appreciate it, but it's not what I need right now."

"I wasn't trying to rescue you," he protested. "I just didn't want you to have to handle everything alone."

She slowly shook her head. "Oh, Taylor," she said in almost a motherly tone. "It's what you've been doing your whole life. You sense that someone needs help, and if you can, you give her exactly what she needs. And now you're turning your sights on us."

"I'm not turning my sights on you," he denied.

Melissa reached for his hand. "Yes, you are," she said calmly. "It's what you did with Denise when you found out how hard her life was. You feel the need to make things better. You always have. You may not believe it, but everything in your life proves that over and over. Even your jobs. As a contractor, you fix things that are broken. As a fireman, you save people. It's who you are."

Taylor had no response, his mind reeling from her words.

"That's not a bad thing. But it's not what I need. It's not what you need, either. Once you think I'm saved, you'd move on, looking for the next person to rescue. And I'd probably be thankful for everything you did, except I'd know the truth about why you did it."

She stopped there, waiting for Taylor to say something.

"What is that?" he rasped out finally.

"That you were trying to rescue yourself, because of what happened to your father. And no matter how hard I try, I'll never be able to do that for you. That's a conflict you're going to have to resolve on your own."

The words hit him with almost physical force. Random memories flashed through his mind: Mitch's angry face at the bar, Denise's eyes filled with tears, the flames at the warehouse, his father turning in the sunlight as his mother snapped his picture.

Melissa watched a host of emotions play across Taylor's face before pulling him close, hugging him tightly. "You've been like a brother to me, and I love the fact that you would be here for my boys. And if you love me, too, you'll understand that I didn't say any of these things to hurt you. I know you want to save me, but I don't need it. What I need is for you to find a way to save yourself, just like you tried to save Mitch."

"How?" he finally croaked out.

"You know," she whispered. "You already know."

He left Melissa's home in a daze. It was all he could do to stay focused on the road. He had never searched for hidden meanings or motivations, either in himself or others. His father's death had been horrible. Talking about it, understanding it, wouldn't bring his father back. But now Melissa's words were making him question the meaning of everything he had once thought so clear and simple. Had his father's death really influenced everything in his life? Were Melissa and Denise right in their assessment of him? No, he decided. Neither one of them knew what happened the night his father died. No one, besides his mother, knew the truth.

Taylor, driving automatically, now realized where he was. He stopped the truck and began the short trek to his final destination.

Judy was waiting for him at his father's grave.

"What are you doing here, Mom?" he asked.

Judy didn't turn at the sound of his voice. Instead, kneeling down, she tended the weeds around the stone. "Melissa called me and told me you'd come." From her voice he could tell she'd been crying. "She said I should be here."

Taylor sat beside her. "What's wrong, Mom?"

"I'm sorry." She wiped her cheek. "I wasn't a good mother."

"You were a great mother," he said firmly.

"When you hit bad patches in your life, you don't turn to me, you don't turn to friends. You come here. No matter what the problem, you always decide that you're better off alone. That hurts me. I think how sad it must be for you to live your life without people—people who could offer you support or simply lend an ear when you need it. And it's all because of me." She sat on the ground.

"No—"

She didn't let him finish. "When your father died, I was so caught up in my own sadness that I ignored how hard it was for you. I didn't teach you how wonderful it is to love someone and have them love you back. Your father and I had a wonderful relationship. He made me happy. He was the best person I ever knew."

Taylor slipped his arm around her. "I know you loved Dad."

"That wasn't my point. My point is that I don't regret it."

He looked at her, uncomprehending.

Judy's eyes were suddenly fierce. "Even if I knew what would happen to your father, I would have married him. I wouldn't have traded those eleven years for anything. Yes, it would have been wonderful to grow old together, but that doesn't mean I regret the time we spent together. Loving someone and having them love you back is the most precious thing in the world. But you don't seem to realize that, even when love is right there in front of you.

"I know," Judy went on, "that you feel responsible for your father's death. I've tried to help you understand that you shouldn't, that it was a horrible accident. You were just a child. But no matter how many ways I tried to say it, you still believed you were at fault. Because of that, you've shut yourself off from the world. Maybe you don't think you deserve to be happy. I don't know what it is."

Judy sighed. "This summer, when I saw you with Kyle, I thought about how much you looked like your father. He was good with kids, just like you. The way you used to look at him always made me smile. Kyle looked at you the same way. I'll bet you miss him."

Taylor nodded reluctantly. "He's a great kid."

Judy met his eyes. "Do you miss Denise, too?"

Taylor shifted uncomfortably. "That's over now, Mom."

She hesitated. "Are you sure?"

Taylor nodded.

"That's a shame," she whispered. "She was perfect for you."

A light autumn shower began to fall, forcing them back to the parking lot. Judy got in the car. Closing the door, she smiled sadly at her son, then pulled away, leaving him standing in the rain.

He'd lost everything. He knew that as he left the cemetery and began the short trip home. *She was perfect for you.*

Despite Mitch's death, he hadn't been able to stop thinking about Denise. Her image had flashed through his mind over and over, but he'd forced it away with stubborn resolve. Now, though, it was impossible. With startling clarity he saw her expression as he'd fixed her cupboard doors, heard her laughter echo across the porch. She was here with him, and yet she wasn't. Nor would she ever be again. The realization made him feel emptier than he'd ever felt before.

As he drove along, the explanations he'd made to himself suddenly rang hollow. Yes, he'd been pulling away. Despite the denials, Denise had been right about that. Why, he wondered, had he let himself? Was it for the reasons his mother had said?

Taylor shook his head, unsure of every decision he'd ever made. If his father hadn't died, would he have acted the same way over the years? Thinking back to Valerie or Lori—would he have married them? Maybe, he thought, but probably not. He couldn't honestly say that he'd ever really loved either of them.

But Denise? His throat tightened as he remembered the first night they'd made love. He knew now that he'd been in love with her. So why hadn't he told her so? And more important, why had he ignored his own feelings in order to pull away?

You always decide that you're better off alone. . . .

Was that it? Did he really want to face the future alone? An empty house, a world where he avoided love at all costs?

In the truck, rain splashed against the windshield as if driving that thought home. For the first time in his life he knew he had been lying to himself. Snatches of other conversations replayed themselves in his mind. Mitch warning him: *Don't screw it up this time.* Melissa teasing: *So are you gonna marry this wonderful girl or what?* Denise saying *We all need companionship.* His response? *I don't need anyone.* It was a lie. His entire life had been a lie, and his lies had become reality. Mitch was gone. Melissa was gone. Denise was gone. Kyle was gone.

Everyone is gone. I'm alone.

The realization made Taylor pull off the road, his vision blurring. Wondering how on earth he'd let it happen, he clung to the steering wheel as the rain poured down around him.

DENISE pulled into the drive in her new used car, tired from her shift. The rain had kept business slow all night—just enough to keep her constantly moving, but not enough to make decent tips.

But on the bright side, she'd been able to leave a little early. She turned up the drive. A few more minutes, a nice cup of cocoa, and she'd be under the covers. The thought was almost intoxicating.

The rain had stopped, and the night was foggy. As she neared the house, she nearly slammed on the brakes at the sight of Taylor's truck parked out front. Then she saw Taylor sitting on the steps, waiting for her. A dozen possibilities raced through her head.

Taylor approached the car as she got out. He looked terrible. His eyes were red-rimmed, his face pale. "I see you got a car," he said.

The sound of his voice triggered a flood of emotions in her: love and joy, pain and anger, loneliness and desperation. She couldn't go through all this again. "What are you doing here, Taylor?"

Taylor took a deep breath. "I came to tell you how sorry I was," he began. "I never meant to hurt you."

She glanced over her shoulder at the car, spying Kyle's sleeping figure in the back. "It's too late for that," she said.

He forced a thin-lipped smile, then took a hesitant step toward his truck. Had it been any other day, any other person, he would have kept moving, telling himself he'd tried. Instead he stopped. "Melissa's moving to Rocky Mount," he said, his back to her.

"I know. She told me. Is that why you're here?"

Taylor shook his head and turned to face her. "No. I'm here because I wanted to talk about Mitch. I was hoping that you'd listen, because I don't know who else to turn to."

His vulnerability touched and surprised her, but she couldn't forget what he had done to Kyle—or to her, she reminded herself. "Taylor, it's really late. Maybe tomorrow?" she suggested softly.

Taylor nodded, as if he had expected her to say as much. "I also wanted to tell you about my father," he said slowly.

From his strained expression she knew how hard it had been for him to say the words.

It's not the right time, Taylor. It's late, and Kyle's already asleep. I'm tired and don't think I'm ready for this just yet. That's what she imagined herself saying. The words that came out, however, were different.

"All right," she said.

HE STARED AT THE COFFEE table from his position on the couch. With the room lit by only a single lamp, dark shadows hid his face.

"I was nine years old," he began, "and for two weeks the temperature had hovered near a hundred. It had been one of the driest springs on record. Our house was old—it didn't have air-conditioning or much insulation—and just lying in bed would make me sweat. It was impossible to sleep.

"Back then there was this set of plastic soldiers that I saw in the Sears catalogue. It came with tanks, jeeps, tents. When I finally got it for my birthday, I don't think I'd ever been more excited about a gift. But my bedroom was small—it used to be a sewing room. There wasn't enough space to set it up, so I put the whole collection in the attic. When I couldn't sleep that night, that's where I went."

He shook his head as if he still didn't believe it. "It was late, past midnight, when I snuck past my parents' door to the attic steps. I could play with those soldiers for hours and not even realize it. I just kept setting them up and fighting these imaginary battles. I'd miss dinner or forget my chores. I couldn't help it. Even on that night, hot as it was, I couldn't think of anything else but those damn soldiers. I guess that's why I didn't smell the smoke."

Denise felt the muscles in her neck tighten as he continued.

"I didn't realize anything was happening at all until I heard my parents come scrambling out of their bedroom, yelling for me. But I was too afraid to answer. They'd told me a hundred times that once I was in bed, I was supposed to stay there. I had a baseball game that weekend, and I knew they'd ground me for sure, so instead of coming out when they called, I decided to wait until they were downstairs. Then I was going to sneak into the bathroom and pretend that I'd been in there the whole time. I turned out the light and hid. I heard my father open the attic door, shouting for me, but I kept quiet until he finally left. Eventually the sounds of them tearing through the house died down, and I went for the door. When I opened it, I was stunned by a blast of heat and smoke. The walls and ceiling were on fire. I probably could have made it out, but I just stared at the fire, thinking how strange it was. I wasn't even afraid."

Taylor tensed, hunching over the table. "Before I knew it, everything seemed to catch on fire at once, and the way out was blocked. I began to scream for my father, but he was already gone. I scrambled to the window. When I opened it, I saw my parents on the front lawn. My mom looked up. She brought her hand to her mouth, and then she started screaming. My dad stopped what he was doing, and he saw me, too. That was when I started to cry."

On the couch, a tear spilled out of the corner of his eye, though he didn't seem to realize it. "My dad . . . my big strong dad came running across the lawn to the spot right beneath the window. By then most of the house was on fire. I remember him reaching up his arms, yelling, 'Jump, Taylor! I'll catch you! I'll catch you, I promise!' But instead of jumping, I just started to cry all the harder. 'Jump, Taylor! I'll catch you!' He kept shouting it over and over, until I finally shouted out that I was afraid. The more my dad called for me to jump, the more paralyzed I became. I can still see my father's face when he realized I wasn't going to jump. His eyes never left mine. It was like time stopped right then. It was just the two of us. I couldn't hear my mom anymore. I couldn't feel the heat. I couldn't smell the smoke. Then my father nodded ever so slightly, and we both knew what he was going to do. He finally turned and started running for the front door. He moved so fast that my mom didn't have time to stop him. By then the house was completely in flames. The fire was closing in around me."

With great effort Taylor went on. "It must have been less than a minute before he got to me, but it seemed like forever. Even with my head out the window I could barely breathe. Smoke was everywhere. The fire was deafening. People think they're quiet, but they're not. It sounds like devils screaming in agony when things are consumed by flames. Despite that, I could hear my father's voice, calling that he was coming."

Here Taylor's voice broke, and he turned away to hide the tears that began to spill down his face. "I remember seeing him rushing toward me. He was on fire. His skin, his arms, his face, his hair— just this human fireball rushing at me. He pushed me toward the window, saying, 'Go, son.' He forced me out, holding on to my wrist until I was dangling above the ground. He finally let go. I landed hard enough to crack a bone in my ankle; I heard the snap as I fell onto my back, looking upward. I watched my father pull his flaming arm back inside."

Taylor stopped. Denise sat frozen in her chair, tears in her eyes. When he spoke again, his voice was barely audible. "He never came back out. I remember my mom pulling me away from the house, and by then I was screaming, 'Daddy, no! Get out, Daddy!' "

Taylor seemed to crumple into himself. "Please, God, I'll jump this time. Please let him come out."

Denise moved instinctively to his side, wrapping her arms around him as he rocked back and forth, her own tears falling unheeded as she pressed her face into him. After a while she heard nothing but the creak of the sofa as he rocked himself into a rhythmic trance. He kept whispering over and over, "I didn't mean to kill him. . . ."

Taylor finally fell silent, spent and exhausted. Denise had heard terrible things in her life, but nothing like this. Releasing him, she rested her hand on his leg, and he took hold of it.

"Are you okay?" she asked.

"No," he answered earnestly, "but then maybe I never was."

She squeezed his hand. "Probably not," she agreed. He smiled wanly. They sat in silence a moment before she spoke again.

"Why tonight, Taylor?"

"I've been thinking about Mitch ever since he died, and with Melissa moving away . . . I felt like it was starting to eat me alive."

It always was, she said to herself. "Why me, then? Why not someone else?"

He glanced up at her. His blue eyes registered nothing but regret. "Because I care about you more than I ever cared about anyone."

Her breath caught in her throat. When she didn't speak, Taylor reluctantly withdrew his hand. "You have every right not to believe me," he admitted. "I probably wouldn't, given the way I acted. I've been lying to myself for so long I'm not sure I'd know the truth if I saw it. All I know is I screwed up the best thing I've ever had."

"Yeah, you did," she agreed.

"I guess a second chance is out of the question, huh?"

Denise was silent. Her anger toward Taylor had dissipated. The pain was still there, though. "You used that one a month ago," she said calmly. "You're probably somewhere in the twenties by now."

He heard an unexpected glimmer of encouragement in her tone and looked up at her, his hope barely disguised. "That bad?"

"Worse," she said. "If I were queen, I'd have had you beheaded."

"No hope, huh?"

Was there? Denise hesitated. She could feel her resolve crumbling as his eyes held her gaze. "I didn't exactly say that. But we can't just pick up where we left off."

It took a moment for the words to sink in, and when he realized that the possibility was still there, Taylor felt a wave of relief. "I'm sorry, Denise," he repeated. "I'm sorry for what I did to Kyle, too."

She simply nodded and took his hand.

For the next few hours Taylor talked steadily as Denise listened. He filled her in on the last few weeks: what Melissa and his mother had said; the argument he'd had with Mitch the night he'd died. He spoke about how Mitch's death had resurrected the memories of his father's death and his lingering guilt about both deaths.

It was nearly four in the morning when he left. Denise watched him drive away. She still didn't know where their relationship would go, but she knew it wasn't simply up to her to give him another chance. As it had been from the beginning, it was still up to Taylor.

THE following afternoon he called to ask if it would be all right for him to stop by. "I'd like to apologize to Kyle, too," he said. "And besides, I have something to show him."

Still exhausted from the night before, she wanted time to mull things over. But in the end she reluctantly consented, more for Kyle's sake than her own. Outside, the day was blustery; cool autumn weather had arrived in full force.

An hour later Taylor arrived. Denise could hear Kyle's excited screams from the front yard. She went to the front door, still feeling a little uneasy. Opening it, she saw Kyle jumping into Taylor's arms, his face beaming. Taylor hugged him for a long time, putting him down as Denise walked up.

"Hey there," he said quietly.

She crossed her arms. "Hi, Taylor."

"Tayer's here!" Kyle said jubilantly, latching on to Taylor's leg.

Denise smiled thinly. "He sure is, sweetie."

Taylor motioned over his shoulder. "I grabbed a few things from the store on my way over here. If it's okay to stay awhile."

"Tayer's here," Kyle said again.

"I don't think I have much of a choice," she answered honestly.

Taylor carried a grocery bag inside containing the makings for beef stew. They spoke for a couple of minutes, but he seemed to sense her ambivalence about his presence and went outside with Kyle.

Denise started preparing the meal. As she stood over the sink watching Taylor and Kyle play, she was struck once more with a paralyzing sense of uncertainty about Taylor. Could she trust him?

She watched Kyle climb onto Taylor, covering him with dirt. She could hear Kyle laughing; she could hear Taylor laughing as well. Denise shook her head. He hurt us once; he could hurt us again. With the stew cooking over low heat, she walked out and sat on the porch steps. Taylor and Kyle were still immersed in their playing.

Despite her thick sweater, the nip in the air made her cross her arms. A flock of geese in triangular formation flew overhead, heading south for the winter. A cold front blowing in from the Midwest had descended through the low country of North Carolina.

After a while Taylor glanced toward the house and saw her. He prompted Kyle to turn in her direction. Kyle waved happily, and both of them stood and started toward her.

"You two look like you were having fun," she said.

Taylor grinned. "I think I'll give up contracting and just build dirt cities. It's a lot more fun, and the people are easier to deal with."

She leaned toward Kyle. "Did you have fun, sweetie?"

"Yes," he said, nodding enthusiastically. Kyle moved closer, his arms outstretched. He wrapped them around her neck.

"What's wrong, honey?" Denise asked. With his eyes closed, Kyle squeezed tightly, and she put her arms around him.

"Thank you, Mommy." (*Kenk you, Money.*)

For what? "Honey, what's wrong?" she asked again.

"Kenk you," Kyle said again. "Kenk you, Money."

"Honey . . ." Denise tried again, a little more desperately this time. She shot a "See what you've done now" look at Taylor, when all of a sudden Kyle spoke again. "I wuff you, Money."

It took a moment to understand what he was trying to say. *I love you, Mommy.*

Denise closed her eyes in shock. As if knowing she still didn't believe it, Kyle said it a second time. "I wuff you, Money."

Oh, my God. . . . Unexpected tears began to spill from her eyes.

For five long years she'd waited to hear the words other parents take for granted, a simple declaration of love. "I love you, too, sweetie. I love you so much."

I'll never forget this, she thought, memorizing the feel of Kyle's body, his little-boy smell, his halting, miraculous words. Never.

Watching them together, Taylor stood mesmerized.

She finally released him, and he turned to Taylor, a grin on his face. Denise turned to gaze at Taylor, her expression full of wonder. "Did you teach him to say that?"

Taylor shook his head. "Not me. We were just playing."

Kyle turned back to his mother, the same joyous expression on his face. "Kenk you, Money," he said simply. "Tayer's home."

As soon as he said it, Denise wiped the tears from her cheeks, her hand shaking slightly. Her shock was evident.

Taylor reached for a twig on the ground, twirled it absently in his fingers. He looked up at her, meeting her gaze with steady determination. "I hope he's right," Taylor said. "Because I love you, too."

It was the first time he'd ever said the words to anyone. Though he'd imagined they would be hard to say, they weren't. He'd never been so sure about anything.

Denise could almost feel Taylor's emotion as he reached for her hand. In a daze she took it, allowing him to pull her to her feet, drawing her close. She felt his lips against hers. The tenderness of the kiss seemed to last forever, until he buried his face in her neck.

"I love you, Denise," he whispered. "I'll do anything for another chance. If you give it to me, I promise I'll never leave you again."

Denise closed her eyes, letting him hold her before finally, reluctantly pulling back. She turned away, and Taylor didn't know what to think, listening as she took a breath. Still, she didn't speak.

Above them, cumulus clouds, rolling white and gray, were drifting steadily with the wind. In an hour rain would come, but by then they would be in the kitchen, listening as raindrops pelted the tin roof.

Denise sighed and faced Taylor again. He loved her. It was as simple as that. And she loved him. She moved into his arms, knowing that the coming storm had nothing to do with them.

Epilogue

EARLIER that morning Taylor had taken Kyle fishing. Denise opted to stay behind; she had a few things to do around the house before Judy came over for lunch. Kyle was in kindergarten now, and though he'd come a long way in the past year, he was still having a little trouble adjusting to school. But the recent move to their new house hadn't bothered him at all. He loved his new room and delighted in the fact that it overlooked the water. She had to admit, she loved it, too. From the porch she could see Taylor and Kyle perched on the seawall, fishing poles in hand. How natural they looked together. Like father and son, which of course they were.

After the wedding Taylor had legally adopted Kyle, and when they returned from the honeymoon, Taylor surprised Denise with a set of blueprints he'd had drawn up. The plans were for a graceful low-country home, with wide porches, a modern kitchen, and hardwood floors. They purchased a lot on the water and began building within a month; they'd moved in as the school year started.

Denise had stopped working at Eights as well. She and Taylor went in for dinner now and then, simply to visit with Ray.

Though Taylor still suffered from the occasional nightmare, he'd surprised her with his devotion over the past year. He came home for lunch every day. He coached Kyle's T-ball team last spring, and they spent every weekend as a family.

She went to the kitchen and stirred the chicken stew. Though

Kyle still avoided eating meat for the most part, a few months earlier she'd made him try chicken. He'd finally taken a bite; over the next few weeks he'd gradually started eating a little more. Now, on days like these, they ate as a family, everyone sharing the same food. Just as a family should.

A family. She liked the sound of that.

Glancing out the window, she saw Taylor and Kyle walking up the lawn, toward the shed where they kept their fishing poles. A moment later they were mounting the steps to the porch.

"Hey, Mom," Kyle chirped.

"Did you catch anything?" she asked.

"No. No fish."

Like everything else in her life, Kyle's speech had improved dramatically, and he was closing the gap between himself and his peers. More important, she'd stopped worrying about it so much.

Taylor kissed Denise as Kyle made his way inside. "So where is the little fella?" Taylor asked.

She nodded toward the corner of the porch. "Still asleep."

"Shouldn't he be awake by now?"

"In a few minutes. He'll be getting hungry soon."

Together they approached the basket in the corner, and Taylor bent over, peering closely. He reached out and gently ran his hand over his son's hair. At seven weeks there was barely anything at all. "He seems so peaceful," he whispered.

Denise put her hand on Taylor's shoulder, hoping that one day the baby would look just like his father. "He's beautiful," she said.

Taylor looked at the woman he loved, then turned back to his son. He leaned in close, kissing his son on his forehead.

"Did you hear that, Mitch? Your mom thinks you're beautiful."

NICHOLAS SPARKS

The author of *The Rescue* knows first-hand the kind of speaking difficulties he attributes to Kyle Holton. One of his own three sons experienced the same problems.

Nicholas Sparks and his wife, Cathy, did a great deal of research into their son's difficulty, which Sparks says is best described as "dyslexia of sound." The couple found two books particularly useful: *Late-Talking Children* by Thomas Sowell and *Let Me Hear Your Voice* by Catherine Maurice.

"Those books explained that we weren't alone in having a child like ours," says Sparks. And the teaching techniques that Denise Holton employs in *The Rescue* are ones the couple used to help their boy.

The Sparks family lives in New Bern, North Carolina.

To read more about Nicholas Sparks and *The Rescue,* visit the Select Editions website:

ReadersOnly.com
Password: *happy*

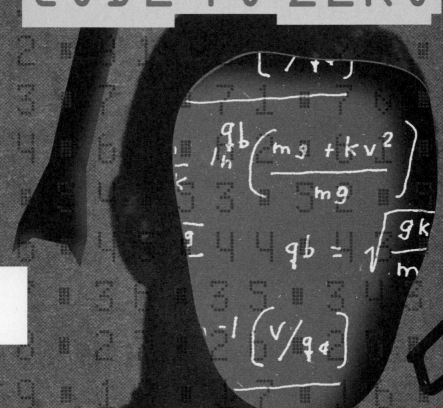

KEN FOLLETT

Meet Luke X.

Luke is a man without a memory, thrust into a treacherous game of hide-and-seek. And someone has hidden the rule book.

Historical note: The launch of the first American space satellite, *Explorer I,* was originally scheduled for Wednesday, January 29, 1958. Late that evening it was postponed to the following day. The reason given was the weather. Observers at Cape Canaveral were puzzled: It was a perfect sunny Florida day. Next night, there was another postponement, and the same reason was given.

The launch was finally attempted on Friday, January 31.

PART 1

The Jupiter C *missile stands on the launchpad at Cape Canaveral. For secrecy it is draped in vast canvas shrouds that hide everything but its tail, which is that of the army's familiar* Redstone *rocket. But the rest of it, under the concealing cloak, is unique. . . .*

5:00 A.M. He woke up scared.

Worse than that: He was terrified. It was like a nightmare, except that waking brought no sense of relief. He felt that something dreadful had happened, but he did not know what it was.

He opened his eyes. A faint light illuminated his surroundings, and he made out vague shapes. Somewhere nearby, water ran. He tried to make himself calm and attempted to think straight. He was lying on a hard floor. He was cold, and he had some kind of hangover, with a headache and a feeling of nausea.

He sat upright, shaking with fear. There was an unpleasant smell of disinfectant. He recognized the outline of a row of washbasins.

He was in a public toilet.

He felt disgusted. He had been sleeping on the floor of a men's room. What the hell had happened to him? He concentrated. He was fully dressed, wearing some kind of topcoat and heavy boots, though he had a feeling that these were not his clothes. His panic was subsiding, but in its place came a deeper fear.

He needed light. He got to his feet and peered into the gloom. Holding his arms out in front of him in case of invisible obstacles, he made his way to a wall. Then he walked crabwise, his hands exploring. He found a cold, glassy surface he guessed was a mirror, then a towel roller. At last his fingertips touched a switch, and he turned it on.

Bright light flooded white-tiled walls. In a corner was what looked like a bundle of old clothes. He asked himself how he got here. What had happened last night? He could not remember. *He could not remember anything at all.*

What was his name? He did not know.

He turned toward the mirror. He saw a filthy hobo dressed in rags, with matted hair, a dirty face, and a crazy stare. Then he was hit by a terrible revelation. He started back with a cry of shock, and the man in the mirror did the same. The hobo was himself.

In a voice that shook with terror he shouted, "Who am I?"

The bundle of old clothes moved. It rolled over, a face appeared, and a voice mumbled, "You're a bum, Luke. Pipe down."

His name was Luke. He was pathetically grateful for the knowledge. A name was not much, but it gave him a focus. He stared at his companion. The man wore a ripped tweed coat with string for a belt. He rubbed his eyes and muttered, "My head hurts."

Luke said, "Who are you?"

"I'm Pete, you retard, can't you see?"

Luke swallowed. "I've lost my memory!"

"I ain't surprised. You drank most of a bottle of bourbon yesterday. It's a miracle you didn't lose your entire mind."

Bourbon would explain the hangover, Luke thought. "But why would I drink a whole bottle?"

Pete laughed mockingly. "That's about the dumbest question I ever heard. To get drunk, of course."

Luke was appalled. He was a drunken bum who slept in public toilets. He bent over a washbasin, ran the cold water, and drank from the tap. It made him feel better. He wiped his mouth, then forced himself to look in the mirror again. The reflection showed a man in his late thirties, with dark hair and blue eyes. He had no beard or mustache, just a heavy growth of dark stubble.

He turned back to his companion. "Luke what?" he said. "What's my last name?"

"How the hell am I supposed to know?" Pete got to his feet. "I need some breakfast."

Luke realized he was hungry. He searched his pockets for money. All were empty. "I think I'm broke," he said.

"No kidding," Pete said sarcastically. "Come on." He stumbled through a doorway, and Luke followed.

When he emerged into the light, he suffered another shock. He was in a huge temple, empty and eerily silent. Mahogany benches stood in rows on the marble floor, like church pews waiting for a ghostly congregation. Around the vast room, atop rows of pillars, surreal stone warriors with helmets and shields stood guard over the holy space.

The insane thought crossed Luke's mind that he had been the sacrificial victim in a weird rite that had left him with no memory. "What is this place?" he asked.

"Union Station, Washington, D.C.," said Pete.

Luke felt foolish. He was in a grand train station, early in the morning before it filled up with passengers. He had scared himself, like a child imagining monsters in a darkened bedroom.

Pete headed for a triumphal arch marked EXIT, and Luke hurried after him.

An aggressive voice called, "Hey! Hey, you!"

Pete said, "Oh-oh." He quickened his step.

A stout man in a railroad uniform bore down on them, full of righteous indignation. "You bums been sleeping here, ain't you?" he said. "You know that ain't allowed."

Luke suppressed a retort and walked faster.

"This ain't a flophouse," the man went on. "Now scat!" He shoved Luke's shoulder.

Luke turned suddenly. "Don't touch me," he said.

The man took a big step backward, looking scared.

Pete took Luke's arm. "Let's go."

They passed through the arch. It was dark outside, the streets quiet. The air was bitterly cold, and Luke drew his ragged clothes closer about him. It was winter, maybe January or February.

He wondered what year it was.

"Where are we headed?" he asked Pete.

"I know a gospel shop on H Street where we can get free breakfast, so long as you don't mind singing a hymn or two."

"I'm starving. I'll sing a whole oratorio." Luke's mind seethed with anxious questions. How long had he been a drunk? Did he have any family? Where had he met Pete?

They came to a small church standing defiantly between a cinema and a liquor store. They entered by a side door and went down to the basement. At one end of a long, low room Luke saw a piano and a small pulpit; at the other, a kitchen range. In between were trestle tables with benches.

Three bums sat there, one at each table, staring patiently into space. At the kitchen end a dumpy woman stirred a big pot. Beside her a gray-bearded man wearing a clerical collar looked up from a coffee urn and smiled. "Come in, come in," he said cheerfully.

"Morning, Pastor Lonegan," Pete said.

The pastor said, "Have you been here before? I've forgotten your name."

"I'm Pete. He's Luke."

"Two disciples!" His bonhomie seemed genuine. "You're a little early for breakfast, but here's fresh coffee." He poured it into thick mugs. "Milk and sugar?"

Luke did not know whether he liked milk and sugar in his coffee. "Yes, thank you," he said, guessing.

The coffee tasted sickeningly creamy and sweet. He guessed he normally took it black, but it assuaged his hunger.

Luke and Pete sat at a table. Until now Luke had noticed only Pete's dirty face and ragged clothes. Now he saw that Pete had none of the marks of a long-term drunk: no broken veins, no dry skin flaking off the face. Perhaps he was too young—only about twenty-five, Luke guessed. He had a dark mustache and a dark red birthmark that ran from his right ear to his jawline. Luke sensed suppressed anger in him. He guessed that Pete resented the world, maybe for making him ugly, maybe for some other reason.

"What are you staring at?" Pete said.

Luke shrugged and did not reply. On the table was a newspaper folded open at the crossword, and a stub of pencil. Luke picked up the pencil and started to fill in the answers.

More bums drifted in. Luke got all the crossword clues but one—"small place in Denmark," six letters.

Pastor Lonegan looked over his shoulder and said quietly, "Oh, what a noble mind is here o'erthrown."

Luke immediately got the clue. "Hamlet," he wrote in. Then he thought, How did I know that?

He unfolded the paper and looked at the front page. It was dated Wednesday, January 29, 1958. His eye was caught by the headline: U.S. MOON STAYS EARTHBOUND.

Cape Canaveral, Tuesday: The U.S. Navy today abandoned a second attempt to launch its space rocket, *Vanguard*, after technical problems.

The decision comes two months after the first *Vanguard* launch ended in humiliating disaster when the rocket exploded two seconds after ignition.

American hopes of launching a space satellite to rival the Soviet *Sputnik* now rest with the Army's rival *Jupiter* missile.

The piano sounded. Mrs. Lonegan was playing a familiar hymn, "What a Friend We Have in Jesus." Luke joined in the singing, pleased he could remember the song. Bourbon had a strange effect, he thought. He could do the crossword and sing a hymn from memory, but he did not know his mother's name.

After the hymn they said grace. Then the men lined up, and Mrs. Lonegan served them hot oatmeal. Luke ate three bowls. Afterward, feeling better, he approached the pastor. "Sir, have you seen me here before? I've lost my memory."

Lonegan looked hard at him. "I don't believe I have. How old are you?"

"I don't know," Luke said, feeling foolish.

"Late thirties, I'd say. You haven't been living rough very long. It takes its toll on a man. Quit drinking now and you could lead a normal life again."

Luke wondered how many times the pastor had said that. "I'm going to try," he promised.

"If you need help, just ask." Then he turned away.

Luke spoke to Pete. "How long have you known me?"

"I don't know. You been around a while."

"I have to find out where I'm from."

Pete hesitated. "What we need is a beer," he said. "Help us think straight." He turned for the door.

"I don't want a beer," Luke said decisively. He had more important things to do than keep Pete company. "In fact, I think I'd like to be alone for a while."

"What are you, Greta Garbo?"

"I'm serious."

"You need me to look out for you. You can't make it on your own. Hell, you can't even remember how old you are."

Pete had a desperate look in his eyes, but Luke was unmoved. "I appreciate your concern, but I need to find out who I am."

After a moment Pete shrugged. "You got a right. See you around, maybe."

"Maybe."

Pete went out.

Luke thanked Pastor Lonegan, then went up the stairs and out into the street. Pete was on the next block, speaking to a man in an olive gabardine raincoat—begging the price of a beer, Luke guessed. He turned and walked in the opposite direction.

It was still dark. Luke's feet were cold. He realized he wasn't wearing socks. As he hurried on, a light flurry of snow fell. After a few minutes he eased his pace. He had no reason to rush.

6:00 A.M. Elspeth woke up worrying about Luke. She lay in bed for a few moments, her heart heavy with concern for the man she loved. Then she switched on the bedside lamp and sat upright.

Her motel room was decorated with a space-program theme. The floor lamp was in the shape of a rocket, and the pictures on the walls showed planets and crescent moons in a wildly unrealistic night sky.

The Starlite was one of a cluster of new motels that had sprouted in the area of Cocoa Beach, Florida, eight miles south of Cape Canaveral. The decorator had obviously thought the space theme appropriate, but it made Elspeth feel as if she were borrowing the bedroom of a ten-year-old boy.

She picked up the bedside phone and dialed Anthony Carroll's office in Washington, D.C. At the other end the phone rang unanswered. She tried his home number, with the same result. Had something gone wrong? She felt sick with fear. She would call his office again in half an hour.

As she showered, she thought about Luke and Anthony when she had first known them. They were at Harvard, and she was at Radcliffe, before the war. Best friends, Luke and Anthony had made an odd couple. Both were tall and athletic, but there the resemblance ended. The Radcliffe girls had called them Beauty and the Beast. Luke was Beauty, with his wavy black hair and elegant clothes. Anthony was not handsome, with his big nose and long chin, and he always looked as if he were wearing someone else's suit, but girls were attracted to his energy and enthusiasm.

Elspeth showered quickly. In her bathrobe, she sat at the dressing table to do her makeup. She had been wearing a bathrobe the first time she ever spoke to Luke. It was during a panty raid by a group of Harvard boys. By chance Luke had come to her room.

Once alone with her, he had seemed embarrassed. Elspeth had smiled, pointed to the closet, and said, "Top drawer." He had taken a pair of pretty white panties with a lace edging. The next day he asked her for a date.

She tried to concentrate on her makeup. The job was more difficult than usual this morning because she had slept badly. Foundation smoothed her cheeks, and salmon-pink lipstick brightened her mouth. She had a math degree from Radcliffe, but still she was expected to look like a mannequin at work. She brushed her hair. It was reddish brown and cut in the fashionable style: chin length and turned under at the back. She dressed quickly in a sleeveless green-and-tan-striped shirtwaist dress.

She picked up the phone and dialed Anthony's office again. There was no reply.

1941

Elspeth Twomey fell in love with Luke the first time he kissed her, at five minutes to midnight in the shadows of the Radcliffe dormitory quad.

That had been six months ago, and the feeling had grown stronger since. Now she was seeing Luke almost every day. They met for lunch or studied together. He was a math major, like her. Weekends they spent almost all their time together.

It was not uncommon for Radcliffe girls to get engaged in their final year to a Harvard boy or a young professor. But Luke had never spoken about marriage.

She looked at him now, sitting in a booth at the back of Flanagan's bar, arguing with Bern Rothsten, a graduate student. Bern was a Communist, like many Harvard students and professors.

"Your father's a banker," Bern said to Luke with disdain. "You'll be a banker, too. Of course you think capitalism is great."

Elspeth saw a flush rise at Luke's throat. His father had recently been featured in a *Time* magazine article as one of ten men who had become millionaires since the Depression.

Luke said, "Banking is an honorable job. Bankers help people."

"Like they did in 1929."

"They make mistakes. Soldiers make mistakes—they shoot the wrong people—but I don't accuse you of being a murderer."

It was Bern's turn to look wounded. He had fought in the Spanish civil war—he was older than the rest of them.

Luke added, "Anyway, I don't aim to be a banker."

Bern's dowdy girlfriend, Peg, asked, "What, then?"

"A scientist. I want to explore beyond our planet."

Bern laughed scornfully. "Space rockets! A schoolboy fantasy."

Elspeth leaped to Luke's defense. "Knock it off, Bern. You don't know what you're talking about."

"I think it's going to happen," Luke said. "And I believe science will do more than communism for ordinary people in our lifetime."

Elspeth winced. She felt Luke was naïve about politics. "The benefits of science are restricted to the privileged elite," she said.

"That's just not true," Luke said.

A tall figure cast a shadow over the table. "Are you kids old enough to drink alcoholic liquor?" It was Anthony Carroll. With him was someone so striking that Elspeth uttered an involuntary murmur of surprise. She was a small girl, fashionably dressed in a short red jacket, with curls of dark hair escaping from under a little red hat. "Meet Billie Josephson," said Anthony.

Bern Rothsten said to her, "Are you Jewish?"

She was startled to be asked so directly. "Yes."

"So you can marry Anthony, but you can't join his country club."

Anthony protested, "I don't belong to a country club."

"You will, Anthony, you will," said Bern.

Luke stood up to shake hands and knocked over a glass. It was unusual for him to be clumsy, and Elspeth realized with annoyance that he was instantly taken with Miss Josephson. "I'm surprised," he said, giving her his most charming smile. "When Anthony said his date was called Billie, I imagined someone six feet tall and built like a wrestler."

Billie laughed and slid into the booth beside Luke. "My name is Bilhah," she said. "It's biblical. She was the handmaiden of Jacob and the mother of Dan. But I was brought up in Dallas, where they called me Billie-Jo."

Anthony sat next to Elspeth and said quietly, "Isn't she pretty?"

Billie was not exactly pretty, Elspeth thought. She had a narrow face, with a sharp nose and large, intense, dark brown eyes. It was the whole package that was so stunning: the angle of the hat, the Southern accent, and most of all her animation. While she talked to Luke, telling him some tall Texas story, she smiled, frowned, rolled her eyes, and pantomimed all kinds of emotion.

"How did you meet her?" Elspeth asked.

"I noticed her in the Fogg Museum. She was wearing a green coat with brass buttons and a beret. I thought she looked like a toy soldier fresh out of the box."

Billie was not any kind of toy, Elspeth thought. She was more dangerous than that. Billie laughed at something Luke had said and swiped his arm in mock admonishment. The gesture was flirtatious, Elspeth thought. Irritated, she interrupted them and said to Billie, "Are you planning to beat the curfew tonight?"

Radcliffe girls were supposed to be in their dormitories by ten o'clock. To stay out later, they had to put their name in a book with details of where they planned to go and what time they would be back. Billie said, "I'm supposed to be spending the night with a visiting aunt who has taken a suite at the Ritz. What's your story?"

"No story, just a ground-floor window that will be left open."

Billie said, "In fact, I'm staying with friends of Anthony's."

"Some people my mother knows who have a large apartment," Anthony said to Elspeth. "Don't give me that old-fashioned look. They're terribly respectable."

"I should hope so." Elspeth turned to Luke. "Honey, what time's the movie?"

He looked at his wristwatch. "We've got to go," he said.

Luke had borrowed a Ford roadster for the weekend. They drove into Boston to see Alfred Hitchcock's *Suspicion*. In the darkness of the theater Luke put his arm around Elspeth, and she laid her head on his shoulder. She felt it was a pity they had chosen a film about a disastrous marriage.

Around midnight they returned to Cambridge and pulled off Memorial Drive to park facing the Charles River, next to the boathouse. The car had no heater, and Elspeth turned up the fur collar of her coat and leaned against Luke for warmth.

They talked about the movie. Elspeth thought that in real life the Joan Fontaine character, a repressed girl brought up by stuffy parents, would never be attracted to the kind of ne'er-do-well Cary Grant had played. Luke said, "But that's why she fell for him— because he was dangerous."

Elspeth looked at the reflection of the moon on the restless surface of the water. Billie Josephson was dangerous, she thought.

Luke changed the subject. "This afternoon Professor Davies told me I could do my master's degree right here at Harvard."

"What made him say that?"

"I mentioned that I was hoping to go to Columbia. He said, 'What for? Stay here.' I explained that my family's in New York."

Luke was the eldest of four children. His mother was French. Elspeth knew that Luke was fond of his two teenage brothers and doted on his eleven-year-old sister.

"Have you thought about doing a master's?" he asked. "You're a better mathematician than most of the Harvard men."

"I've always wanted to work at the State Department."

"That would mean living in Washington."

Elspeth was sure Luke was just thinking aloud, but he seemed dismayed that they might move to different cities.

"Have you ever been in love?" he said suddenly.

"As a matter of fact, I have." She watched his face in the moonlight and was gratified to see the shadow of displeasure flicker across his expression. "When I was seventeen, there was a steelworks dispute in Chicago. I went to help as a volunteer. I worked for a young organizer called Jack Largo, and I fell in love with him."

"And he with you?"

"Goodness, no. He was twenty-five. He thought of me as a kid." She hesitated. "He kissed me once, though. We were packing leaflets, and I said something that made him laugh. Then he kissed me. I nearly died of joy. But he just went on packing leaflets as though nothing had changed."

"Are you still in touch with him?"

She shook her head. "He was killed." She fought back sudden tears. "Two off-duty policemen hired by the steelworks got him in an alley and beat him to death with iron bars."

"No!" Luke stared at her.

"Everyone in town knew who had done it, but nobody was arrested. The mills must keep rolling."

"You make it sound as if industry were no better than organized crime."

"I don't see a big difference," she said, "but I don't get involved anymore. What about you? Have you ever been in love?"

"I don't think I know what love is." It was a typical boy's answer. But then he kissed her and she relaxed. After a while he drew away from her and sighed heavily. "I wonder how married people ever get bored. They never have to stop."

"Their children stop them, I guess," she said with a laugh.

"Do you want to have children someday?"

She felt her breath come faster. "Of course I do."

"I'd like four. How would you feel about four?"

She smiled happily. "If they were yours, I'd love it," she said.

He kissed her again.

Soon it became too cold to stay where they were, and reluctantly they drove back toward the Radcliffe dorms. As they were passing through Harvard Square, a figure waved to them from the side of the road. "Is that Anthony?" Luke said incredulously.

It was, Elspeth saw. Billie was with him.

Luke pulled over, and Anthony came to the window. "I'm glad I spotted you," he said. "I need a favor. My friends have gone away for the weekend—they must have got the dates mixed up. Billie has nowhere to go."

Billie had lied about where she was spending the night, Elspeth recalled. Now she could not return to her dorm.

"I took her to the house." He meant Cambridge House, where he and Luke lived. "I thought she could sleep in our room and Luke and I could spend the night in the library."

Elspeth said, "You're crazy."

Luke put in, "It's been done before. So what went wrong?"

"We were seen."

"Oh, no!" Elspeth said. For a girl to be found in a man's room was a serious offense. Both of them could be expelled.

Luke said, "Who saw you?"

"Geoff Pidgeon and a whole bunch of men. It was half dark, and they were all drunk. I'll talk to them in the morning."

Luke nodded. "What are you going to do now?"

"Billie has a cousin who lives in Newport, Rhode Island. Would you drive her there?"

"What?" said Elspeth. "But it's fifty miles away!"

"What do you say, Luke?" Anthony asked.

"Of course," Luke said.

"Hey, thanks."

Elspeth opened the door and got out. "Be my guest," she said sulkily. Luke was right to rescue a friend in trouble, but she hated the thought of him spending two hours in this little car with sexy Billie Josephson.

Luke sensed her displeasure and said, "Elspeth, get back in. I'll drive you home first."

"No need," she said. "Anthony can walk me to the dorm."

Billie kissed Elspeth's cheek. "I don't know how to thank you," she said. She got into the car and closed the door.

Luke waved and drove off.

Anthony and Elspeth stood and watched the car recede into the darkness.

■ ■ I

6:30 A.M. Daylight crept stealthily over the cold city. Men and women came out of houses, narrowing their eyes against the biting wind, and hurried toward the warmth and bright lights of offices.

Luke had no destination: One street was as good as another. He began to study the people he passed. He kept hoping that one of them would stop and say, "Luke, what happened to you? Come home with me. Let me help you." He began to feel he was not going to be lucky. Simply walking around fantasizing about a lucky break was no kind of strategy. He needed a plan.

He wondered if he might be a missing person. There was a list, he felt sure, of such people. Who kept the list? It had to be the police.

He seemed to remember passing a precinct house a few minutes earlier. He turned abruptly to go back. As he did so, he bumped into a young man in an olive-colored gabardine raincoat. He had a feeling he might have seen the man before. Their eyes met, but the man looked away and walked on. Swallowing his disappointment, Luke tried to retrace his steps. It was difficult, because he had turned corners and crossed streets more or less at random. However, he had to come across a police station sooner or later.

As he walked, he tried to deduce information about himself. He watched a tall man in a gray homburg hat light a cigarette and take a long, satisfying drag, but he had no desire for tobacco. He guessed he did not smoke. Looking at cars, he found he knew the names of most of the models he saw. That was the kind of information he had not forgotten. These trifling victories over his amnesia gave him an inordinate sense of triumph.

Soon he had completely lost his way. He was on a street of cheap shops. He stopped suddenly and looked back. Thirty yards behind him he saw the man in the olive raincoat, watching the TV in a store window. Luke frowned, thinking, Is he shadowing me?

It was easy enough to check. Luke walked to the end of the block, crossed the street, and walked back along the other side. When he reached the far end, he stood at the curb and looked both ways. The raincoat was thirty yards behind him. Luke crossed again. To allay suspicion, he studied doors as if looking for a street number. The raincoat followed.

Luke was mystified, but his heart leaped with hope. A man who was following him must know something about him. For a real test Luke needed to travel in a vehicle, forcing his shadow to do the same. That would cost money.

He began to look at his surroundings with different eyes. He saw newsstands to be robbed, handbags that could be snatched, pockets ready to be picked. He stepped inside a coffee shop.

His eyes raked the tables, looking for change left as tips, but it was not going to be that easy. He approached the counter. A radio was playing the news. "Rocket experts claim America has one last chance of catching up with the Russians in the race to control outer space."

What would a bum say? "Any stale doughnuts?" he asked.

"Get out of here," the counterman said roughly.

Luke saw what he needed. Beside the till, within easy reach, was a can with a slit in the top and a label saying REMEMBER THOSE WHO CANNOT SEE. Now Luke just had to distract the counterman. "Gimme a dime?" he said.

The man said, "Okay, that's it. You get the bum's rush." But he had to duck under the counter to get out, and for a second he could not see Luke. In that moment Luke took the collection can and slipped it inside his coat.

The counterman grabbed Luke by the collar and propelled him rapidly across the café. At the door the man gave him a painful kick. Forgetting his act, Luke spun around, ready to fight. The man suddenly looked scared and backed inside.

In an alleyway, Luke busted the can open. The money, mostly pennies, amounted to two or three dollars. He put it in his coat pocket and returned to the street. He thanked heaven for charity and made a silent promise to give three bucks to the blind if he ever got straight. All right, he thought, thirty bucks.

The man in the olive raincoat was standing by a newsstand.

A bus pulled up a few yards away. Luke had no idea where it went, but he boarded. The driver gave him a hard look. "The fare is seventeen cents, unless you got a token," he said. Luke paid with some of the change he had stolen. As he walked toward the back of the bus, he looked anxiously out the window. The man in the raincoat was walking away. Luke frowned. If the man were a shadow, he should have been trying to hail a taxicab.

At the third stop Luke got off the bus. He looked up and down the street. There was no sign of the man in the olive raincoat. As he hesitated, he noticed that one of the passengers who had got off the bus with him had paused in a shop doorway and was fumbling in his pockets. As Luke watched, the man lit a cigarette and took a long, satisfying drag. He was a tall man, wearing a gray homburg hat. Luke realized he had seen him before.

7:00 A.M. Anthony Carroll drove along Constitution Avenue in a yellow Cadillac Eldorado. He pulled into the parking lot of Q Building in Alphabet Row, a strip of barrackslike structures hastily erected during the war on parkland near the Lincoln Memorial. He had spent much of the war here, working for the Office of Strategic Services, precursor of the CIA.

A multimillion-dollar CIA headquarters was under construction across the Potomac River in Langley, Virginia. When it was completed, Alphabet Row would be demolished. Anthony had fought hard against the Langley development, and not merely because Q Building held fond memories. Right now the CIA had offices in thirty-one buildings, and it was very difficult for foreign agents to figure out the size and power of the Agency. When Langley opened, anyone would be able to estimate its resources simply by driving past.

Anthony had lost that argument. The pen pushers and accountants in charge were determined to manage the CIA more tightly. Secret work was no longer for daredevils and buccaneers, the way it had been in the war.

Anthony Carroll was still a hugely powerful figure within the Agency. He was head of technical services, a euphemistic name for burglary, phone tapping, and other illegal activities. The division's nickname was Dirty Tricks. However, he had enemies: pen pushers who disliked the whole notion of the government doing secret operations. They were ready to destroy him as soon as he made a slip. And today his neck was stuck out farther than ever before.

As he strode into the building, he deliberately put aside his worries and focused on the problem of the day: Dr. Claude Lucas, known as Luke, the most dangerous man in America, the one who threatened everything Anthony had lived for.

He had been at the office most of the night and had gone home only to shave and change his shirt. Now the guard in the lobby said, "Mr. Maxell's in your office, sir."

Anthony frowned. Pete Maxell was supposed to be with Luke. Had something gone wrong? He ran up the stairs.

Pete was sitting in the chair opposite Anthony's desk, still dressed in ragged clothes, a smear of dirt partly covering the red birthmark on his face. As Anthony walked in, he jumped up, looking scared.

"What happened?" Anthony said.

"Luke decided he wanted to be alone. But it's okay. Simons has him under surveillance, and Betts is there for backup."

"What about his memory?"

"Completely gone."

Anthony took off his coat and sat behind his desk. Luke was causing problems, but Anthony had expected as much, and he was ready.

He looked at the man opposite. Pete was a good agent—competent, careful, and fanatically loyal to Anthony. He was also inexperienced, however.

Anthony said, "Tell me exactly what happened."

Pete sat down again. "He woke up crazy, yelling, 'Who am I?' and stuff like that. Then he asked who I was, and I said, 'I'm Pete.' It just came out, I was so concerned to stop him yelling. I took him to the gospel shop, the way we planned, but he kept asking shrewd questions."

Anthony nodded. "We shouldn't be surprised. In the war he was the best agent we had. He's lost his memory but not his instincts."

"I kept trying to steer him away from inquiring into his past, but I think he figured out what I was doing."

"Where is he now?" Anthony asked.

"I don't know. Simons will call in as soon as he gets a chance."

"When he does, get back there and join up with him. Whatever happens, Luke mustn't get away from us."

The white phone on Anthony's desk rang, his direct line. He stared at it for a moment. Not many people had the number. He picked it up.

"It's me," said Elspeth's voice. "What's happened?"

"Relax," he said. "Everything is under control."

7:30 A.M. It was now full light, and although the street was busy, Luke easily kept track of the gray homburg hat. But after he crossed Pennsylvania Avenue, the hat disappeared from view. Once again he wondered if he might be imagining things. A minute later he spotted the olive raincoat coming out of a bakery.

"Toi, encore," he said under his breath. "You again." He wondered briefly why he had spoken in French.

Two people were following him in a smoothly executed relay operation. They had to be professionals. He tried to figure out what that meant. They could be KGB or CIA, although it seemed unlikely that a deadbeat such as he could be involved in espionage.

He decided he would split the team. He stepped into a smoke shop and bought a pack of Pall Malls. When he went outside, Raincoat had disappeared and Homburg had taken over again. He walked to the end of the block and turned the corner.

A Coca-Cola truck was parked at the curb, and the driver was unloading crates. Luke walked to the far side of the truck, dropped to the ground, and rolled under it. Looking along the sidewalk at ground level, he picked out Homburg's blue suit pants and tan oxfords.

The man quickened his pace, presumably concerned that Luke had disappeared. He walked around the truck, then returned to the sidewalk and broke into a run.

Luke was pleased. He did not know how he had learned this game, but he seemed to be good at it. He crawled to the front of the truck and scrambled to his feet. He looked around. Homburg was still hurrying away.

Luke crossed the sidewalk and turned the corner. He stood in the doorway of an electrical store, opened the pack of cigarettes, and took one out.

Raincoat appeared. He spotted Luke, gave a nervous start, and continued walking, edging to the outside of the sidewalk.

Luke stepped into his path and said, "Got a light, buddy?"

Raincoat hesitated. "Sure," he said, trying to act casual. He reached into the pocket of his raincoat, took out a book of matches, and struck one.

Luke said, "You know who I am, don't you?"

The man stared at Luke, dumbstruck, until the match burned down. Then he dropped it and said, "I don't know what you're talking about, pal."

"You're following me," Luke said. "You must know who I am."

"I'm not following anyone."

The man tried to walk past Luke. Luke moved sideways, blocking his path. "Excuse me, please," Raincoat said.

Frustrated, Luke grabbed him by the lapels of the raincoat and slammed him against the shopwindow, rattling the glass.

"Get your damn hands off me," the man said in a level voice.

"Who am I?" Luke screamed at him. "Tell me. Who am I?"

"How should I know?"

Luke took the man by the throat. "You're going to tell me."

Behind Luke the frightened voice of a passerby said, "Hey, what's going on here?"

Luke let his hands fall to his side. Raincoat backed away. "You crazy bastard," he said. "You're out of your mind."

"You're lying!" Luke yelled. He reached out to grab the man again.

Raincoat turned and ran away. Luke could have chased him, but he hesitated. What was the point?

After a moment Luke walked away, heading in the direction opposite to that taken by his two shadows. "Great job," he said to himself. "You achieved precisely nothing."

And he was alone again.

8:00 A.M. Dr. Billie Josephson was running late. She had got her mother up, made her put on her hearing aid, and sat her in the kitchen with coffee. She woke her seven-year-old, Larry, and told him he had to shower, then returned to the kitchen.

Her mother, a small, plump woman of seventy known as Becky-Ma, had the radio on loud. Perry Como was singing "Catch a Falling Star." Billie put bread in the toaster for her mother and poured cornflakes into a bowl for Larry. Then she made a peanut-butter-and-jelly sandwich for his lunch. She put the lunch box in his schoolbag and added his baseball glove, a present from his father.

On the radio a reporter was interviewing sightseers on the beach near Cape Canaveral who were hoping to see a rocket launch.

Larry came into the kitchen. She got him started on his corn-flakes and began to scramble eggs. It was eight fifteen, and she was almost caught up. She loved her son and her mother, but a secret part of her resented the drudgery of taking care of them.

The radio reporter was interviewing an army spokesman. "What if the rocket goes off course and crash-lands right here on the beach?"

"There's no danger of that, sir," came the reply. "Every rocket has a self-destruct mechanism triggered by a radio signal. If it veers off course, it will be blown up in midair."

Larry said, "I have to make a space rocket today. Can I take the yogurt container to school?"

"No, you can't. It's half full," she told him.

"But Miss Page will be mad if I don't. She told us last week."

Billie sighed. "Larry, if you had told *me* last week, I would have saved a whole bunch of containers. What kind do you need?"

"Rocket shape."

Billie went around the house and got a cardboard detergent container, a liquid soap bottle, and an ice-cream tub. Most of the packages showed families using the products—generally a pretty housewife, two kids, and a pipe-smoking father in the background. She had never lived in a family like that. Her father, a poor tailor in Dallas, had died when she was a baby, and her mother had brought up five children in poverty. Billie herself had been divorced since Larry was two.

She put all the containers in a shopping bag for Larry to carry to school.

"Oh, boy. I bet I have more than anyone," he said. "Thanks, Mom."

A car horn tooted outside, and Billie quickly checked her appearance in the glass of a cupboard door. Her curly black hair had been hastily combed, she had no makeup on, and she was wearing an oversize pink sweater, but the effect was kind of sexy.

The back door opened, and Roy Brodsky came in. Roy was Larry's best friend. He was followed by his father, Harold, a good-looking man with soft brown eyes. Harold Brodsky was a widower, who taught chemistry at George Washington University. He looked at her adoringly and said, "Sweetheart, you look gorgeous." She grinned and kissed his cheek.

Like Larry, Roy had a shopping bag full of cartons. Billie said to Harold, "Did you have to empty half the containers in your kitchen?"

"Yes. I have little bowls of soap flakes everywhere, and six toilet rolls without the cardboard cylinder in the middle."

"Darn, I never thought of toilet rolls!"

He laughed. "Would you like to have dinner at my place tonight?"

She was surprised. "You're going to cook?"

"Not exactly. I thought I'd ask Mrs. Riley to make a casserole. Roy's going to a cousin's birthday party tonight, and he'll sleep over. We'll have a chance to talk without interruption."

"Okay," Billie said thoughtfully. They could talk without interruption at a restaurant, of course. Harold had another reason for inviting her to his house when his child would be away. "That'll be great," she said.

"I'll pick you up around eight. Come on, boys." He shepherded the children out the back door.

Billie cleared the table. Rushing now, she stripped the beds and bundled the sheets into a laundry bag. She said, "Hand this bag to the laundryman when he calls. Okay, Ma?"

Her mother said, "I don't have any of my heart pills left."

"Ma!" Billie was at the end of her rope. "Ma, I have a busy day at work today, and I don't have time to go to the pharmacist."

"I can't help it. I ran out." She started to cry.

Billie relented immediately. "I'm sorry, Ma," she said. Five years ago, when the three of them had set up house together, Ma had helped care for Larry. But nowadays she was barely able to look after him for a couple of hours when he came home from school.

The phone rang. She picked it up. It was Bern Rothsten, her

ex-husband. Billie got on well with him, despite the divorce. "Hey, Bern, you're up early."

"Yeah. Have you heard from Luke?"

"Luke Lucas? Lately? No. Is something wrong?"

"I don't know—maybe."

Bern and Luke shared the intimacy of rivals. When they were young, they had argued endlessly. Their discussions often seemed acrimonious, yet they had remained close all through the war. "What's happened?" Billie said.

"He called me on Monday. I was surprised. I don't hear from him often."

"Nor do I," Billie said. "Last time I saw him was a couple of years ago."

"He was coming to Washington and wanted to see me. Something had happened."

"Did he tell you what?"

"Not really. He just said, 'It's like the stuff we used to do in the war.' "

Billie frowned anxiously. Luke and Bern had been in OSS during the war, working behind enemy lines, helping the French Resistance. "What do you think he meant?"

"I don't know. He said he'd call me when he reached Washington. He checked into the Carlton on Monday night. Now it's Wednesday, and he hasn't phoned. Could you let me know if you hear from him?"

"Sure, of course."

Billie hung up, then sat at the kitchen table, her chores forgotten, thinking about Luke.

1941 ▮▮▮

Route 138 meandered south through Massachusetts toward Rhode Island. The old Ford had no heater. Billie was wrapped up in coat, scarf, and gloves, but her feet were numb. She did not really mind. It was no hardship to spend a couple of hours alone with Luke Lucas, even if he was someone else's boyfriend.

They talked about the war in Europe. That morning in Radcliffe

Yard, rival student groups had handed out leaflets, the Interventionists passionately advocating that America should enter the war, the America Firsters opposing it with equal fervor.

"I have cousins in Paris," Luke said. "I'd like us to go over there and rescue them. But that's kind of a personal reason."

"I have a personal reason, too. I'm Jewish," Billie said. "But rather than send Americans to die in Europe, I'd open our doors to refugees. Save lives instead of killing people."

"That's what Anthony believes."

Billie was still fuming about the night's fiasco. "Anthony should have made sure I could stay at his friends' apartment," she said.

She was hoping for sympathy from Luke, but he disappointed her. "I guess you both were a little too casual about the whole thing."

Billie was stung. "I think Anthony had a duty to protect my reputation."

"Yes, but so did you."

She was surprised he was so critical. "I'll never do that again, with any man."

"Could I ask you a personal question?" Luke met her eyes for a moment. "Are you in love with Anthony?"

"I'm fond of him, I enjoy his company, but I don't love him." She thought about Luke's girlfriend, the most striking beauty on campus. "What about you? Are you in love with Elspeth?"

"Well, to be honest, it's as close to love as I've come, but I don't know if it's the real thing."

"Didn't you put Elspeth in a vulnerable situation tonight, too, keeping her out in your car until the early hours?"

"You're right," he said. "We all took risks."

She shuddered. "I don't know what I'd do if I got thrown out."

"Study somewhere else, I guess."

She shook her head. "I'm on a scholarship. My father's dead; my mother's a penniless widow. I couldn't study anywhere without a scholarship. Why do you look surprised?"

"I have to say you don't dress like a scholarship girl."

She was pleased he had noticed her clothes. "It's the Leavenworth Award," she explained.

"Wow." The Leavenworth was a famously generous grant. "You must be a genius."

"I don't know about that," she said. "I'm not smart enough to make sure I have a place to stay the night."

"On the other hand, being thrown out of college is not the worst thing in the world. Some of the cleverest people drop out."

"It would be the end of the world for me."

"You're planning to be a doctor?"

"Psychologist. I want to understand how the mind works. It's so mysterious and complicated. Things like logic, the way we think. Imagining something that isn't there in front of us—animals can't do that. The ability to remember. Fish have no memory. Did you know that?"

He nodded. "And why is it that just about everyone can recognize a musical octave?" he said. "Two notes, the frequency of one being double that of the other—how come your brain knows that?"

"You find it interesting, too!" She was pleased. "Tell me about why you want to explore outer space."

"I think it's the most exciting adventure mankind has ever had."

"And I want to map the mind." She smiled. "We have something in common—we both have big ideas."

He laughed, then braked the car. "Hey, we're coming to a fork in the road."

She switched on a flashlight and looked at the map on her knee. "You'll have to pull over. I can't find it."

He stopped the car and leaned across to look at the map. "Maybe we're here," he said. He reached out to point, and his touch was warm on her cold hand.

Instead of looking at the map, Billie found herself staring at his face. His hair fell forward over his left eye. Without thinking, she lifted her hand and stroked his cheek with the outside edge of her little finger. He stared back at her, and she saw bewilderment and desire in his eyes.

He moved away suddenly and put the car in gear. "We take"—he cleared his throat—"we take the left fork."

Billie wondered what the hell she was doing. Luke had spent the evening with the most beautiful girl on campus. Billie had been out with his roommate.

"Why did you do that?" Luke said angrily.

"I don't know," she said. "I didn't intend to; it just happened."

He took a bend too fast. "I don't want to feel like this about you," he said.

She was suddenly breathless. "Like what?"

"Never mind."

Billie recognized the road. "Next left," she said. "If you don't slow down, you'll miss it." Half of her wanted to get out of the car and leave behind this unbearable tension. The other half wanted to drive with Luke forever.

"We're here," she said.

They stopped outside a neat one-story frame house with gingerbread eaves. The Ford's headlights picked out a cat sitting motionless on a windowsill, looking at them with a calm, disdainful gaze.

"Come in," Billie said. "My cousin will make some coffee."

"No, thanks," he said. "I'll just wait here until you're safely inside." She held out her hand to shake.

"Are we friends?" Luke asked, taking her hand.

She lifted his hand to her face, kissed it, and pressed it against her cheek, closing her eyes. After a moment she heard him groan softly. She opened her eyes and found him staring at her. His hand moved behind her head, he pulled her to him, and they kissed. A gentle kiss. She held the lapel of his rough tweed coat and pulled him closer. If he grabbed her now, she knew she would not resist. She pulled away. "I could fall in love with you in about twenty minutes," she said. "But I don't think we can be friends."

She stared at him a moment longer, seeing in his eyes the same churning conflict she felt in her heart. Then she looked away, took a deep breath, and got out of the car.

As she crossed the yard, she heard the car move, and turned to wave. As it swung by, she saw Luke's face and the glint of something shiny on his cheeks.

Then he disappeared into the darkness.

8:30 A.M. Secret agents in America had never been as powerful as they were in January 1958.

The director of the CIA, Allen Dulles, was the brother of John Foster Dulles, Eisenhower's Secretary of State. The CIA's Plans Directorate, also known as CS for Clandestine Services, carried out coups against left-leaning governments in Iran and Guatemala, and the White House was delighted at how cheap and bloodless these coups were by comparison with the war in Korea.

Within the Plans Directorate was technical services, the division that Anthony Carroll headed. The fact that the CIA was prohibited by law from operating within the United States was no more than a minor inconvenience to technical services. Theoretically it was a training division, but "training" also served as an all-purpose cover for covert actions inside the U.S.A. Just about anything Anthony wanted to do—from bugging phones to testing truth drugs on prison inmates—could be labeled a training exercise. The surveillance of Luke was no exception.

Six agents were gathered in Anthony's office. Pete Maxell passed around a mug shot of Luke while Anthony briefed them. "Our target is a middle-ranking State Department employee with a high-security clearance. He's having some kind of nervous breakdown. He flew in from Paris on Monday, spent Monday night in the Carlton Hotel, and went on a drinking binge on Tuesday. He stayed out all last night and went to a homeless shelter this morning. The security risk is obvious."

Anthony's office door opened, and Carl Hobart came in. A plump, bald man, he was Anthony's immediate boss. Anthony groaned inwardly and continued with his briefing. "But before we tip our hand, we want to see what the subject does, where he goes, who he contacts. It could be that he's giving information to the other side. If he's involved in some kind of treason, we need all the information we can get *before* we pick him up."

Hobart interrupted. "What's this?"

Anthony said, "A little training exercise. We're conducting surveillance on a suspect diplomat."

"Give it to the FBI," Hobart said. "It's their job, not ours."

Anthony gave Hobart a 'cool look. "A case like this can unlock a horde of information if we handle it right," he said. "But the Feds are only interested in getting publicity for putting Reds in the electric chair. When was the last time they gave us anything?"

"The last time was never," Hobart said. "But I've got another assignment for you today. I need you and your people to brief me on Cuba for a top-level meeting later this morning."

Anthony was worried. He had no time for distractions today, and he needed all his best people to keep an eye on Luke. "I'll see what I can do," he said.

"My conference room, with all your most experienced agents, at ten o'clock—and no excuses." He turned away.

Anthony made a decision. "No," he said.

Hobart's bald head reddened. "You'll hear more about this," he said. "A lot more." He went out and slammed the door.

"Back to work," Anthony said. "Simons and Betts are with the subject now. They're due to be relieved by Rifenberg and Horwitz. We'll run four shifts, six hours each. That's all for now."

The agents, except for Pete, trooped out. He had shaved and put on his regular business suit, with a narrow Madison Avenue tie. He said to Anthony, "Aren't you taking a risk with Hobart?"

"I can't let him close down an important surveillance operation."

"But you lied to him. He could easily find out that Luke isn't a diplomat from Paris."

Anthony shrugged. "Then I'll tell him another story."

Pete looked dubious but nodded assent and moved to the door.

Anthony stayed at his desk, watching the phone, trying to be patient. It rang after five minutes, and he picked it up. "Carroll here."

"You've been upsetting Carl Hobart again."

"Good morning, George," Anthony said. George Cooperman was deputy chief of operations and a wartime comrade of Anthony's. He was Hobart's immediate superior. "Hobart should stay out of my way."

"Get over here, you arrogant young bastard," George said amiably.

"Coming." Anthony hung up. He opened his desk drawer and took out an envelope. Then he put on his coat and walked to Cooperman's office, which was in P Building.

Cooperman was a tall, gaunt man of fifty. He was reading the Moscow newspaper *Pravda*. He threw it down and growled, "What's your excuse this time?"

Anthony tossed the envelope onto the desk. Cooperman looked inside. "Blueprints," he said. "Of a rocket. So what?"

"I took them from the surveillance subject. He's a spy."

"And you chose not to tell Hobart that."

"I want to follow this guy around until he reveals his whole network. Hobart would hand the case over to the FBI. They'd throw him in jail, and his network would fade to black."

"You're right, but I need you at this Cuba meeting. You can let your team carry on the surveillance, and if anything happens, they can get you out of the conference room."

"Thanks, George." Anthony got up to leave.

Cooperman said, "And make damn sure you run this surveillance right. If you screw up on top of insulting your boss, I may not be able to protect you."

BACK in his office in Q Building, Anthony found Pete with the team that had been shadowing Luke: Simons, carrying a gray homburg; Betts, wearing an olive raincoat. The team that should have relieved them was also there.

"What the hell is this?" Anthony said. "Who's with Luke?"

"Nobody," Pete answered. "We, uh"—he swallowed—"we've lost him."

PART 2

The Jupiter *missile that will carry the* Explorer I *satellite into space is 68 feet 7 inches high, taller than a town house. It weighs 64,000 pounds on the launchpad, but most of that is fuel. The satellite itself is only 2 feet 10 inches long and weighs just 18 pounds.*

10:00 A.M. The Georgetown Mind Hospital was a red brick Victorian mansion with a modern extension at the back. Billie Josephson parked her red Thunderbird and hurried into the building.

She hated to arrive this late. It seemed disrespectful of her work and her colleagues. She was late because of her mother. Billie had gone to get the heart pills and returned home to find Becky-Ma lying on her bed, fully dressed, gasping for breath. The doctor had come, but he had nothing new to say. Becky-Ma had a weak heart. If she felt breathless, she should lie down. She must remember to take her pills. Stress was bad for her. Billie had wanted to say, "What about me? Isn't stress bad for me, too?" Instead, she resolved anew to walk on eggshells around her mother.

She stopped by the admissions office and glanced at the overnight register. A new patient had been brought in late yesterday, after she had left: Joseph Bellow, a schizophrenic. Surprisingly, the patient had been discharged during the night. That was odd.

She passed through the dayroom on the way to her office. The subjects of Billie's research sat around, some watching TV or playing games. A few gazed vacantly into space. She waved to Tom, a young man with aphasia. "How are you, Tommy?" she called. He grinned and waved back. He could read body language well, so it had taken Billie months to figure out that he did not understand a single word.

Through the glass wall of an interview room she saw Ronald, a brilliant architect who had suffered head injuries in a car crash. He could look at a group of objects on a tray and say whether there were three or four of them, but if there were twelve and he had to count them, he had trouble. This suggested to Billie that the ability to see at a glance how many items are in a small group is a separate skill from the ability to count.

In this way, she was slowly mapping the depths of the mind, locating memory here, language there, mathematics somewhere else. At her present rate of progress it would take about two hundred years. With a team of psychologists she could progress much faster. She might see the map completed in her lifetime. That was her ambition.

She went up the stairs to the next floor, thinking about the mystery patient, Joseph Bellow. Why had he been discharged in the middle of the night?

She reached her office and looked out the window onto a construction yard. A new wing was being added to the hospital—and a new post was to be created to go with it: director of research. Billie had applied for the job, but so had one of her colleagues, Dr. Leonard Ross. Len was older, but Billie had wider experience and had published more. She wanted the job badly.

On the building site she noticed, among the workmen, a small group of men in business clothes. Looking more closely, she saw that Len Ross was with them.

She asked her secretary, "Who are those guys being shown around by Len Ross?"

"They're from the Sowerby Foundation."

The foundation was financing the new post. They would have a big say in who got the job. And Len was making nice to them. "Did we know they were coming?"

"Len said he had sent you a note. He came by this morning, but you weren't here."

There had never been a note, Billie felt sure. Len had deliberately failed to warn her.

"Damn," Billie said. She rushed out to join the party.

She did not think about Joseph Bellow again for several hours.

11:00 A.M. As Luke negotiated the grid of streets leading to Union Station, he found himself checking every minute or two to see whether he was being followed.

He had lost his shadows more than an hour ago, but they might now be searching for him. Who were they, and what were they doing? He had to find out.

But first he had to clean himself up. His plan was to steal a suitcase from a train passenger. It would not be easy. If he were arrested, the police would never believe he was anything but a deadbeat. He would end up in jail. It was not prison itself that scared him, so much as the prospect of weeks or months of ignorance and confusion, not knowing who he was and helpless to make any progress in finding out.

Thinking ahead, he figured that after the theft he would have to disappear fast. He needed a car. Close to the station, the street was lined with parked cars. He slowed his pace as a car pulled into a slot ahead of him. It was a two-tone Ford, blue and white, new but not ostentatious. It would do fine.

A man in a dark topcoat got out of the Ford, took a briefcase from the trunk, locked the car, and headed for the station.

To save time later, Luke decided he would unlock the car now. He waited until there was no one around; then he walked to the driver's door. Pressing his hands flat against the glass of the window, he pushed down. Nothing happened. He stood on tiptoe to add the weight of his body to the pressure on the window mechanism. At last the pane of glass slid slowly down. When the window was fully open, he reached in and unlocked the door. He opened it, wound up the window, and closed the door again. Now he was ready for a fast getaway.

He returned to Union Station. The best time to steal a suitcase would be immediately after the arrival of a large, crowded train, when the concourse was thronged with hurrying people. He studied the information board. An express from New York was due in a few minutes. Perfect. He hurried to the gate and waited.

As the first passengers emerged, Luke watched them intently. He was looking for a man his own size and build. He dismissed an elderly traveler who was the right height but too thin. At least a hundred more passengers had passed before Luke saw his mark. He was Luke's height, build, and age. His topcoat was unbuttoned to show a tweed sport coat and flannel pants—which meant he probably had a business suit in the leather bag he carried.

Luke slipped into the crowd and shoved through until he was directly behind the man. Then he kicked upward, bending the target's leg at the knee. The man cried out and fell forward, letting go of both his briefcase and suitcase, and crashed into a woman in a fur coat. She, too, stumbled, giving a little scream, and fell to the ground. While other passengers gathered around trying to help, Luke calmly picked up the man's suitcase and walked away.

At the exit, he glanced back. A tall man was scanning the concourse keenly, as if looking for something. His head swiveled suddenly toward Luke. Luke stepped quickly through the door.

Outside, he headed down Massachusetts Avenue to the Ford Fiesta. He looked back toward the station. The tall man was running across the traffic circle in front of the station, heading Luke's way.

Luke slung the bag onto the back seat. He got in and slammed the door. He reached under the dash and found the wires on either side of the ignition lock. He pulled them out and touched them together. Nothing happened. He felt sweat on his forehead, despite the cold. There was another wire to the right of the ignition. He pulled it out and touched it to the wire on the left.

The engine started. He put the transmission into drive, released the parking brake, and pulled out. Then he drove off.

A smile crossed his face. Unless he was very unlucky, he had a complete set of fresh clothes in the bag. Now he needed somewhere to shower and change.

12:00 NOON The countdown stood at X minus six hundred and thirty minutes, and Cape Canaveral was buzzing. For most of the *Explorer* team tonight's launch would be the fulfillment of a lifetime's hopes. Elspeth felt the same way.

They were based in hangar D and hangar R, which were side by side. Elspeth was in hangar R. She had a desk in the office of her boss, Willy Fredrickson, the launch conductor. Her job was to prepare and distribute the launch timetable.

Trouble was, the timetable changed constantly. Nobody in America had sent a rocket into space before. New problems arose all the time, and the engineers were forever improvising ways to jury-rig a component or bypass a system. Here duct tape was called missile tape. So Elspeth produced regular updates of the timetable and distributed them. The job required her to go everywhere and know almost everything. Her title was secretary, and she was paid a secretary's wages, but no one could have done the job without a science degree.

Her noon update was ready, and she set out to distribute it. She was rushed off her feet today, but that suited her. It stopped her worrying about Luke. She went first to the press department. The missile men had learned from bitter experience that a routine postponement could be made to look like a failure when the newspapers reported it, so they had a deal with the news organizations. They gave advance notification of launches only on condition that nothing would be published until there was "fire in the tail," which meant the rocket engine had been ignited.

It was an all-male office, and several men stared at her as she walked across the pressroom. Elspeth knew she was attractive, with her pale Viking looks and tall, statuesque figure, but there was something formidable about her, too, that made men who were inclined to whistle or call her honey think again.

In the missile-firing laboratory she found five shirtsleeved scientists standing at a bench, staring worriedly at a flat piece of metal that looked as if it had been in a fire. The group leader, Dr. Keller, said, "Good afternoon, Elspeth." He spoke in heavily accented English. Like most of the scientists, he was a German who had been captured at the end of the war and brought to America to work on the missile program.

She handed him a copy of her update, and he took it. Elspeth nodded at the object on the table and said, "What's that?"

"A jet vane," he explained. "With normal alcohol fuel the vanes last long enough to do their job. Today, by contrast, we are using a new fuel, which has a longer burning time and higher exhaust velocity. We have not had time to run sufficiently many tests."

"Is this going to delay the launch?" she asked.

"That's what we're trying to decide. I think our answer is going to be 'Let's take the chance.'" The others nodded gloomily.

"I'll keep my fingers crossed," Elspeth said.

She went outside into the scorching Florida sun, crossed a dusty apron, and entered hangar D.

In the telemetry room she saw Hans Mueller, known as Hank. He pointed a finger at her and said, "One hundred thirty-five."

It was a game they played. She had to say what was unusual

about the number. "Take the first digit, add the square of the second digit plus the cube of the third, and you get the number you first thought of." She gave him the equation: $1^1 + 3^2 + 5^3 = 135$.

"Correct! You win the big prize." He fished in his pocket and brought out a dime.

She took it. "I'll give you a chance to win it back," she said. "One hundred thirty-six."

"Ah." He frowned. "Wait. Sum the cubes of its digits: $1^3 + 3^3 + 6^3 = 244$. Now repeat the process and you get the number you first thought of: $2^3 + 4^3 + 4^3 = 136$."

She gave him back his dime and a copy of her update.

Her boss, Willy Fredrickson, was in the communications room with two technicians. The Teletype machine was not working, and Willy was frustrated. But he gave her a grateful look as he took the update and said, "Elspeth, you are twenty-two-carat gold."

A moment later a young army officer carrying a chart, and Stimmens, one of the scientists, approached Willy. The officer said, "We got a problem." He handed Willy the chart and went on. "The jet stream has moved south, and it's blowing at one hundred and forty-six knots."

Elspeth's heart sank. The jet stream was a wind in the stratosphere between thirty thousand and forty thousand feet. It did not normally extend over Cape Canaveral, but it could move. And if it was too fierce, it might throw the missile off course.

Willy turned to Stimmens. "We've allowed for this, haven't we?"

Stimmens said, "We figure the missile can withstand winds up to one hundred and twenty knots, no higher."

Willy turned back to the officer. "What's the forecast for tonight?"

"Up to one hundred and seventy-seven knots."

Willy ran a hand over his head. Elspeth knew what he was thinking. The launch might have to be postponed. "Send up a weather balloon, please," he ordered. "We'll review the forecast again at five o'clock."

Elspeth made a note to add the meeting to her timetable; then she left, feeling despondent. They could solve engineering problems, but there was nothing they could do about the weather.

Outside, she got into a jeep and drove to launch complex 26. She pulled up beside the blockhouse and looked across to launchpad 26B. The gantry was a derrick from an oil rig, adapted for this purpose and coated with orange rust-resistant paint to protect it from corrosion by the humid, salty Florida air. The long, white pencil of the *Jupiter C* rocket seemed caught in the tangle of orange girders, like a dragonfly in a spiderweb. The men called it "she," despite its phallic shape, and Elspeth, too, thought of the rocket as female. A bridal veil of canvas had concealed the upper stages from prying eyes since it arrived here, but that had now been removed, and *Jupiter C* stood revealed, sunshine gleaming off its spotless paintwork.

The scientists knew that the eyes of the world were on them. Four months ago the Soviet Union had stunned the United States by sending up the world's first space satellite, the *Sputnik*. A month later they had sent up a second satellite, *Sputnik 2,* with a dog on board. Americans were devastated. A dog today, a man tomorrow.

President Eisenhower promised an American satellite before the end of the year. On the first Friday in December the U.S. Navy launched the *Vanguard* rocket. It rose a few feet into the air, burst into flames, toppled sideways, and smashed to pieces on the concrete. IT'S A FLOPNIK! said one headline.

The *Jupiter C* was America's last hope. There was no third rocket. If this failed today, the United States was out of the race. The American space program would be in total disarray, and the U.S.S.R. would control outer space for the foreseeable future.

All that, Elspeth thought, resting on this one rocket.

Vehicles were banned from the launchpad area, so she left her car and walked across the open space. At the back of the derrick was a long steel cabin containing offices and machinery. Elspeth entered by a metal door.

The gantry supervisor, Harry Lane, sat on a folding chair studying a blueprint. "Hi, Harry," she said brightly.

He grunted. He did not like to see women around the launchpad, and no sense of courtesy constrained him from letting her know it.

She dropped an update on a metal table and left. Driving back to the hangar, she realized she had a perfect excuse for calling Anthony. She would tell him about the jet stream, then ask about Luke.

In her office, she dialed Anthony's direct line and got him right away. "The launch is likely to be postponed until tomorrow. There are strong winds in the stratosphere. There's a weather-review meeting at five. How's Luke?"

"Well, we have a problem there. We've lost him."

Elspeth's heart missed a beat. "What?"

"He slipped away from my men."

"God help us," she said. "Now we're in trouble."

1941

It was dawn when Luke got back to Cambridge House. He slipped in through the back door, climbed the service stairs to his room, and fell into bed in his underwear. The next thing he knew, Anthony was shaking him, saying, "Get up."

He opened his eyes. "What's the time?" he mumbled.

"It's one o'clock, and Elspeth is waiting for you downstairs."

The mention of her name jogged his memory. He did not love her anymore. He had fallen in love with Billie. It would make a train wreck of all their lives: his own, Elspeth's, Billie's, and Anthony's.

Luke got up and pulled on a pair of flannels, a sweater, and tennis shoes and staggered downstairs.

Elspeth was waiting in the lobby, the only part of the building where girls were allowed. It was a spacious hall, with a fireplace and comfortable chairs. She was as eye-catching as ever, in a wool dress the color of bluebells and a big hat. She laughed when she saw him. "You look like a small boy who can't wake up."

He kissed her cheek and slumped into a chair. "It took hours to get to Newport," he said.

"You've obviously forgotten you're supposed to take me to lunch," Elspeth said brightly.

He looked at her. He did not love her, and felt he was the worst kind of heel.

He had to say something. "Can we skip lunch? I haven't even shaved."

A troubled shadow crossed her face, and he realized that she knew perfectly well something was wrong, but her reply was carefree. "Of course," she said.

"I'm sorry you got dressed up for nothing," he said.

"It wasn't for nothing—I saw you. And your fellow housemen seemed to like my outfit." She stood up. "Anyway, Professor and Mrs. Durkham are having a party. I'll go there."

Luke stood and helped her into her coat. "We could meet later."

"That'll be fine," she said gaily. "Pick me up at six."

He returned woefully to his room. "Has anyone said anything about last night?" Luke asked Anthony.

"Not a thing."

"Billie's quite a gal," Luke said.

"Isn't she great?" Anthony said. Luke observed with dismay the look of pride on his roommate's face. To steal someone else's girlfriend was despicable in any circumstances, but the fact that Anthony was obviously crazy about Billie made everything even worse.

Luke groaned, and Anthony said, "What's the matter?"

Luke decided to tell him half the truth. "I'm not in love with Elspeth anymore. I think I have to end it."

Anthony looked shocked. "That's too bad. You two are quite an item."

"I feel like a jerk."

Anthony raised his eyebrows. "Have you proposed?"

"No. But we've talked about how many children we'd have."

"You're still not engaged."

"I guess you're right, but all the same I feel like a heel."

There was a tap at the door, and a man Luke had never seen before came in. He was carrying two envelopes, and Luke had a feeling he knew what they were.

"The dean of students has asked me to hand you these notes in person." He gave them each an envelope and left.

Anthony ripped his open. "Damn it." Luke opened his and read the short note inside, asking him to come to the dean's study at three o'clock that afternoon.

Such letters always meant disciplinary trouble. Someone had reported to Dean Ryder that there had been a girl in the house last night. Anthony would probably be expelled.

Then there was a knock at the door, and in came Geoff Pidgeon, the amiable, chubby occupant of the room opposite. "Didn't I just see the dean's clerk? Look, Anthony, I haven't said a word to anyone about seeing you with that girl."

"But who did? The only sneak is Jenkins, and he's away for the weekend."

"No, he's not," Pidgeon said. "He changed his plans."

"Then it's him," Anthony said. "I'm going to strangle that s.o.b. with my own hands."

"I wonder if Elspeth and Billie have had letters," Luke said.

Pidgeon said, "If Jenkins knows their names, we can be sure he reported them. That's what he's like."

"Elspeth is safe. She wasn't here," Luke said, "but Billie could be expelled. Then she'd lose her scholarship."

"I can't worry about Billie now," Anthony said.

Luke was shocked. Anthony had gotten Billie into trouble, and by Luke's code he should be more worried about her than about himself. But Luke saw a pretext to talk to Billie, and he could not resist it. Suppressing a guilty feeling, he said, "Why don't I go to the girls' dorm and see whether Billie's back from Newport yet."

"Would you?" Anthony said. "Thanks."

Luke shaved and changed his clothes. It was two o'clock when he reached the Radcliffe dormitory. A uniformed maid let him into the lobby. He asked for Billie. The maid sat at a desk, picked up a speaking tube of the kind used on ships, blew into the mouthpiece, and said, "Visitor for Miss Josephson."

Billie came down wearing a dove-gray cashmere sweater and a plaid skirt. She looked lovely but distraught, and Luke longed to take her in his arms and comfort her. She and Elspeth had been summoned to the office of Peter Ryder.

She showed him into the smoking room, where girls were

allowed to receive male visitors. "What am I going to do?" she said. Her face was drawn with distress, but Luke found her even more ravishing than yesterday.

"Anthony could say it was someone else in the room."

"They wouldn't believe it." With a bitter smile she added, "I'll have to go back to Dallas and be a secretary to an oilman in cowboy boots."

Two girls burst into the lounge, their faces flushed. "Have you heard the news?" said one.

Luke was not interested in news. He shook his head, and Billie said desultorily, "What's happened?"

"We're at war!"

Luke frowned. "What?"

"It's true," said the second girl. "The Japanese have bombed Hawaii. Everyone's talking about it on the street. People are stopping their cars."

Billie looked at Luke. "I'm frightened," she said.

He took her hand. He wanted to say he would take care of her, no matter what. Two more girls rushed in, talking excitedly. Someone brought a radio downstairs and plugged it in. There was an expectant silence while they waited for it to warm up. Then they heard an announcer's voice. "The battleship *Arizona* is reported destroyed, and the *Oklahoma* sunk in Pearl Harbor. American casualties are estimated to be at least two thousand dead and a thousand more injured."

Luke felt a surge of rage. "Two thousand people killed!"

Billie said, "It means war, doesn't it?"

"You bet it does," Luke said angrily. He was still holding Billie's hand.

"I don't want you to be in a war," she said with tears in her eyes.

His heart felt ready to burst. "I'm so happy you feel that way." He smiled ruefully. "The world is falling apart, and I'm happy." He looked at his watch. "I suppose we have to see the dean, even though we're at war." Then he was struck by a thought, and he fell silent.

"What?" Billie said. "What is it?"

"Maybe there *is* a way for you and Anthony to stay at Harvard."

ELSPETH WAS NERVOUS WHEN the four of them met outside the dean's study, but she told herself that she did not need to be afraid. She had broken the curfew last night, but she had not been caught. Anthony and Billie were the ones who were in trouble.

Dean Ryder summoned them inside. He was a fussy, old man in a neat black jacket and waistcoat with gray pants. His bow tie was a perfect butterfly, and his oiled hair looked like black paint on a boiled egg. With him was a gray-haired spinster called Iris Rayford, who was responsible for the moral welfare of Radcliffe girls.

They sat in a circle of chairs, as if for a tutorial. The dean lit a cigarette. "Now, boys, what happened in your room last night?"

"Where's Jenkins?" Anthony said curtly. "He's the sneak, isn't he? A man has a right to be confronted by his accuser."

"This isn't a court, Mr. Carroll," the dean said. "Miss Rayford and I have been asked to establish the facts. Disciplinary proceedings, if necessary, will follow in due course."

"Enough of this," Luke said with an impatient gesture. "I brought a woman into the house last night, sir."

Elspeth gasped. What was he talking about?

The dean frowned. "My information is that it was Mr. Carroll who invited the woman in."

"I'm afraid you've been misinformed."

Mystified, Anthony said, "Luke, I don't know what you're doing, but—"

"Let me tell the story," Luke said. "I met the girl at the Dew Drop Inn. She's a waitress there. Her name is Angela Carlotti."

The dean said, "I was told that the person seen in Cambridge House was Miss Bilhah Josephson here."

"No, sir," Luke said. "Miss Josephson is a friend of ours, but she spent last night at the home of a relative in Newport."

Miss Rayford spoke to Billie. "Will the relative confirm that?"

Billie shot a bewildered look at Luke, then said, "Yes."

The dean said to Luke, "Can you produce this . . . waitress?"

"Yes, sir, I can, but I don't intend to bring her into this."

"In that case, you make it difficult for me to accept your story."

"I don't think Miss Carlotti's evidence will be necessary."

"I beg to differ, Mr. Lucas."

Then Luke dropped his bombshell. "I'm leaving the college tonight, sir. I'm going to join the army."

Elspeth cried, "No!"

The dean stared at Luke with his mouth open. He muttered something about making his report and leaving others to decide. Miss Rayford wrote down the address of Billie's cousin, but it was all camouflage. They had been outwitted, and they knew it. At last the students were dismissed.

As soon as the door closed, Billie burst into tears. "Don't go to war, Luke," she said.

Anthony said, "You saved my life." He embraced Luke. "I'll never forget this."

Luke turned to Elspeth. She raised her hand and slapped his face, once, very hard.

"You bastard," she said. Then she turned and walked away.

■ ■ I

1:00 p.m. Luke was looking for a quiet residential street. Driving away from Union Station, he headed west. He crossed a river and found himself in a charming suburb of narrow streets lined with trees. He passed a building with a sign that read GEORGETOWN MIND HOSPITAL, and he guessed the neighborhood was called Georgetown. He parked the stolen Ford on a dead-end street, facing the way he had come, in case he had to make a fast getaway.

He needed a screwdriver and a hammer. There was probably a repair kit in the trunk—but the trunk was locked. It took him about thirty seconds to pick the lock. As he had hoped, there were a few tools in a box next to the jack. He chose the largest screwdriver. There was no hammer, but there was a heavy wrench that would serve. He put them in the pocket of his raincoat.

He took the stolen bag from the car and walked around the corner. He knew he was conspicuous, a ragged bum walking in a nice neighborhood. If somebody called the cops, he'd be in trouble in minutes. On the other hand, if all went well, he might be washed and shaved and dressed like a respectable citizen in half an hour's time.

He crossed a front yard and knocked at the door of the first house on the street.

ROSEMARY Sims saw a nice blue-and-white car drive slowly past her house. She wondered whose it was. She had good eyesight still, and she could watch most of the street from her comfy chair by the second-floor window. So she saw the stranger when he came walking around the corner. "Strange" was the word. He wore no hat, his raincoat was torn, and his shoes were tied up with string.

He went to Mrs. Britsky's door and knocked. Mrs. Britsky—a widow, living alone—looked out the window and waved him away.

He went next door and knocked at Mrs. Loew's. She was a tall black-haired woman. She spoke a few words with the caller, then slammed the door.

He went to the next house. Young Jeannie Evans came to the door with Baby Rita in her arms. She fished in the pocket of her apron and gave him something, probably a few coins. So he was a beggar.

Old Mr. Clark came to the door in his bathrobe and slippers. The stranger got nothing out of him.

The owner of the next house, Mr. Bonetti, was at work, and his pregnant wife had left five minutes ago, heading for the store. The stranger studied the door and glanced up and down the street.

Mrs. Sims turned away from the window and lifted the handset of the phone. Slowly she dialed the number of the local police station.

Luke had been unlucky, having to knock on five doors to find an empty house. Now he had to act fast. He inserted the screwdriver between the door and the jamb at the level of the lock. Then he struck the handle with the wrench, trying to force the blade into the socket of the lock. The first blow failed. He wiggled the screwdriver and used the wrench again. Still the blade would not slip into the socket. He felt perspiration break out on his forehead. He told himself to stay calm. He had done this before. When? He had no idea. It did not matter. The technique worked, he was sure of that.

He hammered again, as hard as he could. The screwdriver sank in an inch. He pulled sideways on the handle. To his profound relief the door opened inward.

He stepped quickly inside and closed the door behind him.

WHEN Rosemary Sims finished dialing the number, she looked out the window again, but the stranger had vanished.

That was quick.

The police answered. Feeling confused, she hung up the phone without speaking.

IT WAS the home of a young couple. They had a new couch and a big TV set in the living room, but they were still using orange crates for storage in the kitchen. An unopened letter on the hall radiator was addressed to Mr. G. Bonetti.

Luke went upstairs. Of three bedrooms, only one was furnished. He threw the suitcase on the bed. Inside it he found a carefully folded blue pinstripe suit, a white shirt, and a conservative striped tie. There were dark socks, clean underwear, and a pair of black wing tips that looked only about half a size too big.

He stripped off his filthy clothes and kicked them into a corner. It gave him an odd feeling to be naked in the home of strangers. He thought of skipping a shower, but he smelled bad.

He crossed the tiny landing to the bathroom. It felt great to stand under the hot water and soap himself all over. When he got out, he dried himself with a pink bath towel and put on undershorts, pants, socks, and shoes from the stolen suitcase.

In a toiletry bag Luke found a safety razor and a shaving brush. He lathered his face and shaved quickly. In the same bag was a hundred dollars in twenties, neatly folded—emergency money. He pocketed the cash, resolving to pay the man back one day.

He put on the shirt, tie, and jacket. They fitted well: He had been careful to choose a victim his own size and build. There was a mirror on the back of the bedroom door. He had not looked at his reflection since early this morning, in the men's room at Union Station, when he had been so shocked to see a filthy hobo staring back at him. He stepped to the mirror, bracing himself.

He saw a tall, fit-looking man in his middle thirties, with black hair and blue eyes. A weary sense of relief swept over him. Take a guy like that, he thought. What would you say he does for a living? His hands were soft and did not look like those of a manual worker. He had a smooth face, one that had not spent much time out in bad weather. His hair was well cut. The guy in the mirror looked comfortable in the clothes of a corporate executive.

There was no hat or coat in the bag. Luke knew he would be conspicuous without either on a cold January day. He opened the closet. Mr. Bonetti had a sport coat, and a black suit he probably wore to church. There was no topcoat, but there was a light raincoat. Luke took it off the hanger and put it on. There was no hat in the closet, just a tweed cap that was too small. Luke would have to buy a hat, but the cap would serve for an hour or so—

He heard a noise downstairs. He froze, listening.

A young woman's voice said, "What happened to my front door?"

Another voice replied, "Looks like someone tried to break in. Maybe you should call the cops."

Luke cursed under his breath.

"I don't know. . . . Looks like the thieves didn't get in."

"How do you know? Better check if anything's been stolen."

Luke realized he had to get out of there fast. He opened the bedroom window. There was no convenient tree or drainpipe down which he could climb.

"I'm going to look upstairs. We'd feel pretty silly if we call the cops and there's no one here."

Luke heard footsteps on the stairs. He crossed the landing to the bathroom and stood behind the door.

The footsteps mounted the staircase, crossed the landing, and entered the bedroom. A voice said, "Whose bag is that?"

Luke slipped silently out of the bathroom and tiptoed down the stairs.

"What kind of burglar brings luggage?"

"I'm calling the cops right now. This is spooky."

Luke opened the front door and stepped outside.

He smiled. He had done it.

MRS. SIMS FROWNED, MYSTIFIED. The man leaving the Bonetti house had on Mr. Bonetti's black raincoat and his tweed cap, but he was larger than Mr. Bonetti.

She watched him walk down the street and turn the corner. A minute later the blue-and-white car she had noticed earlier came around the corner, going too fast. She realized then that the man who had left the house was the beggar she had been watching. He must have broken in and stolen Mr. Bonetti's clothes!

As the car passed her window, she read the license plate and memorized the number.

2:00 P.M. In a menswear store Luke bought a gray felt hat and a navy wool topcoat. He wore them out of the store and felt, at last, that he could look the world in the eye.

Now he was ready to attack his problems. First he had to learn something about memory—what caused amnesia and how long it might last. Where did one go for information? A library. He got a street map of Washington at a newsstand. Prominently displayed was the Central Public Library, at the intersection of New York and Massachusetts avenues. Luke drove there.

It was a grand classical building, raised above ground level like a Greek temple, with a pillared entrance. Luke hesitated at the top of the steps, then walked in. A gray-haired librarian behind the counter said, "Can I help you, sir?"

"I want to look at books on memory," Luke said.

"That'll be the psychology section." She led him up a grand staircase to the next floor and pointed to a corner.

Luke looked along the shelf. There were plenty of books on psychoanalysis, child development, and perception, none of which were any use. He picked out a fat tome called *The Human Brain* and browsed through it, but it seemed highly technical. There were some equations and a certain amount of statistical material, which he found easy enough to understand.

Then his eye was caught by *An Introduction to the Psychology of Memory* by Bilhah Josephson. He pulled it out and turned to the chapter on disorders of the memory. He read:

The common condition in which the patient "loses his memory" is known as "global amnesia." Such a patient does not know his identity and will not recognize his own parents or children. However, he may be able to drive a car, speak foreign languages, and name the prime minister of Canada. The condition would be more appropriately called "autobiographical amnesia."

Luke was elated. This was exactly what had happened to him. He could still check whether he was being tailed and start a stolen car without the key. He was not the only person to whom this had happened.

Dr. Josephson outlined her theory that the brain contained several different memory banks:

The autobiographical memory records events we have experienced personally. The long-term semantic memory holds general knowledge such as the capital of Romania and how to solve quadratic equations. The short-term memory is where we keep a phone number for the few seconds in between looking it up in the phone book and dialing it.

She gave examples of patients who had lost one form of data but retained others, as Luke had. He felt profound relief, and gratitude to the author of the book.

Then he was struck by an inspiration. He was in his thirties, so he must have followed some occupation for a decade. His professional knowledge should still be in his head, lodged in his long-term semantic memory. He ought to be able to use it to figure out his line of work. Thinking back over the last few minutes, he noticed that he had easily understood the equations in *The Human Brain*. Maybe he was in a profession that involved numbers—perhaps a math teacher.

He found the math section, and a book called *Number Theory* caught his attention. He browsed through it. It was clearly presented but some years out of date. Suddenly he looked up. He had discovered something. He understood number theory, and the book was not written for the layman. It was an academic work. He had to be some kind of scientist.

He located the chemistry shelf and picked out *Polymer Engineering*. He found it comprehensible but not easy. Next he moved to physics and tried *A Symposium on the Behavior of Cold and Very Cold Gases*. It was fascinating, like reading a good novel.

He was narrowing it down. His job involved math and physics. But what branch of physics? Cold gases were interesting, but he did not feel that he knew as much as the author of the book. He scanned the shelves and stopped at geophysics, remembering the newspaper story headlined U.S. MOON STAYS EARTHBOUND. He picked out *Principles of Rocket Design*. It was an elementary text, but nevertheless there was an error on the first page he looked at. Reading on, he found two more. "Yes!" he said aloud, startling a nearby schoolboy who was studying a biology text. If he could recognize mistakes in a textbook, he had to be a rocketry expert.

He hurried to the information desk and asked the librarian, "Is there any kind of list of scientists?"

"Sure," she said. "The *Dictionary of American Scientists.*"

He found the book easily. He sat and went through the index, searching for anyone named Luke. He found a biologist called Luke Parfitt, an archaeologist called Lucas Dimittry, and a pharmacologist called Luc Fontainebleu, but no physicist.

He thought of another approach. The name Luke might not be his own, but his face was. The *Dictionary of American Scientists* carried photos of only the most prominent men, such as Dr. Wernher von Braun. Somewhere there were people who knew him—friends and colleagues who would recognize him. Where did one find scientists? At a university.

He looked up Washington in the encyclopedia. The entry included a list of universities in the city. He picked Georgetown because he had been in the area earlier and knew how to get back. On his street map he saw that the university had a large campus. It would probably have a big physics department with dozens of professors. Surely one of them would know him.

Full of hope, he left the library and got back into his car.

2:30 P.M. The Cuba meeting took a coffee break, and Anthony ran back to Q Building for an update, praying his team would have come up with something—any clue to Luke's whereabouts.

Pete met him on the stairs. "Here's a weird report from the police in Georgetown," he said. "A housewife came back from the store to find that her home had been broken into and her shower used. The intruder left behind a pile of filthy old clothes."

"At last a break," Anthony said. "Give me the address."

"You think this is our guy?"

"I'm sure of it. He's fed up with looking like a bum, so he's broken into an empty house, showered, shaved, and put on some decent clothes. Come on, let's go. Grab some photos of Luke."

ANTHONY left the building with Pete following, and they jumped into his old yellow Cadillac. "This may need delicate handling," he said to Pete as he headed for Georgetown. "We don't have a hundred men to chase up leads, so my plan is to get the Washington Police Department working for us."

Anthony drove quickly to the address in the police report. It was a small one-family home on a quiet street. A police cruiser was parked outside.

Before going into the house, Anthony studied the opposite side of the street, scrutinizing the houses. After a moment he spotted what he was looking for: a face in an upstairs window. It was an elderly woman, who returned his stare with unabashed curiosity. She was just what he needed, a neighborhood busybody.

They went to the house that had been broken into. The door was opened by an attractive young woman who was expecting a baby. She took Anthony and Pete into her living room, where two men were sitting on the couch, drinking coffee and smoking. One was a uniformed patrolman, the other a detective. An open suitcase was on the coffee table in front of them.

Anthony showed his identification to the cops, but he did not want Mrs. Bonetti—and all her neighbors—to know that the CIA was interested in the case, so he said, "We're colleagues of these police officers."

The detective was Lewis Hite. "You know something about this?" he said guardedly.

"We may have some information that will help, but first I need to know what you've got."

"We've got a suitcase belongs to a guy named Rowley Anstruther, Jr., from New York. He breaks into Mrs. Bonetti's house, takes a shower, and goes away, leaving his suitcase behind. Go figure!"

Anthony looked through the contents of the leather bag. There were clean shirts and underwear, but no shoes, pants, or jackets. "Looks like Mr. Anstruther arrived in Washington from New York today," he said.

Mrs. Bonetti said, "How do you know that?"

"The bag contains clean underwear but no laundry," he explained, "so he probably hasn't yet spent a night away." He paused. "I believe some old clothes were also left behind."

The patrolman said, "I got 'em." He lifted a cardboard box from beside the couch.

Anthony recognized the rags Luke had been wearing. "I don't believe Mr. Anstruther came to this house," he said. "I think the bag was stolen from him this morning, probably at Union Station." He looked at the patrolman. "Would you call the precinct nearest the railroad station and ask if such a theft has been reported?" Anthony went on. "We have a picture of the man we believe stole the suitcase and broke into this house." He nodded to Pete, who handed Hite a photograph. He studied it.

"He's six foot one, one hundred and eighty pounds, athletic build, and may pretend to have lost his memory."

The patrolman came back. "Dead right about the theft. Union Station, eleven thirty this morning."

"So what's the story?" Hite was intrigued. "This guy wanted Anstruther's clothes and came here to change?"

"Something like that."

"You think he's still in town?"

"Yes," Anthony said. He was not as sure as he pretended.

"I presume he's in a car."

"Let's find out." Anthony turned to Mrs. Bonetti. "What's the name of the white-haired lady who lives across the street, a couple of doors down?"

"Rosemary Sims."

"She spends a lot of time looking out her window?"

"We call her Nosy Rosie."

"Excellent." He turned to the detective. "Let's have a word with her."

They crossed the street and knocked on Mrs. Sims's door. She opened it instantly. "I saw him!" she said. "He went in there looking like a bum and came out dressed to the nines."

Hite said, "Did he have a car, Mrs. Sims?"

"Yes. A nice little blue-and-white model."

"Did you happen to notice the license plate?" Hite asked.

"Yes," she said triumphantly. "I wrote it down."

Anthony smiled.

3:00 P.M. Luke drove through the iron gates of Georgetown University and parked in front of the main entrance, a triple-arched portico marked HEALY HALL. Inside, a receptionist told him the way to the physics department. Following her directions, he found a large laboratory where a professor and a group of students were working with the components of a microwave spectrograph. The professor wore a clerical collar, and Luke realized this must be a Catholic university. He approached the group with an expectant look.

The older man asked, "Can I help you?"

"I hope so," Luke said. "Is there a department of geophysics here?"

"Goodness, no," he said. "At this university even physics is considered a minor subject." The others laughed.

"What about astronomy?"

"Why yes, of course. Our observatory is famous."

His spirits lifted. "Where is it?"

The man gave him directions.

On the flat roof of a small two-story house was a large revolving observatory, its dome having a sliding roof section. Luke approached it with mounting anticipation.

Inside, the rooms were arranged around a massive central pillar that supported the enormous weight of the dome. Luke opened a door and found an attractive woman about his own age sitting behind a typewriter. "Good morning," he said. "Is the professor in?"

"You mean Father Heyden?"

"Uh, yes."

"And you are?"

"Um . . . Luke. Professor Luke."

"To which university are you attached, Professor Luke?"

"Um . . . New York. Look, I didn't come here to be cross-examined. Just tell Father Heyden that Professor Luke, the rocketry physicist, has dropped by and would like a word with him."

"I'm afraid that won't be possible," she said firmly. "Father is at a lecture on rocket fuels in the Aircraft Building at the Smithsonian Institution."

Luke felt a surge of hope. "Where's the Smithsonian Institution?"

The secretary raised her eyebrows. "It's downtown, right in the Mall, around Tenth Street."

"What time is the lecture?"

"It started at three."

Luke checked his watch. It was three thirty. "Thank you," he said, and he ran down the stairs and out of the building.

3:30 P.M. Billie was furious with Len Ross for trying to ingratiate himself with the people from the Sowerby Foundation. She was still annoyed that afternoon when the hospital's chief executive asked her to come to his office.

Charles Silverton waved Billie to a chair and said, "Did you speak to the people from Sowerby this morning?"

"Yes. Len was showing them around, and I joined the party."

"Do you think you could have said anything to offend them?"

"I don't think so. We just talked about the new wing."

"You know, I really wanted you to get the job of director of research. Len Ross is a competent scientist, but you're exceptional."

"The foundation is backing Len for the job?"

He hesitated. "I'm afraid they're insisting on it as a condition of their grant."

"The hell they are!" Billie was stunned.

"Do you know anyone connected with the foundation?"

"One of my oldest friends, Anthony Carroll, is a trustee. He's my son's godfather."

"Does he have a grudge against you?"

For a moment Billie slipped back in time. She had been angry with Anthony after the catastrophe that led to Luke's leaving Harvard, and they had never dated again. But she forgave him because of how he behaved toward Elspeth, who had gone into a decline, letting her academic work slip. She was in danger of failing to graduate until Anthony rescued her. They studied together, and she caught up enough to pass. Anthony won back Billie's respect, and they had been friends ever since.

She told Charles, "I got kind of mad at him back in 1941, but we made up long ago."

"Maybe someone on the board admires Len's work."

Billie considered. "Len's approach is different from mine. He's a Freudian. He looks for psychoanalytical explanations."

"So there might be a keen Freudian on the board who is against you. Why don't you ask your friend?"

"That's exactly what I'm going to do," she said.

3:45 P.M. Luke checked his watch as he drove along K Street. The institute was in a park called the Mall. He would be there in about ten minutes, just as the talk was ending. As he turned right on Ninth Street, he heard a police siren blip once, and his heart skipped a beat.

He looked in his rearview mirror. A cruiser was on his tail, lights flashing. There were two cops in the front seat. One pointed toward the curb and mouthed, "Pull over."

Could he have committed some minor traffic violation? If they asked for his driver's license, he had no kind of identification, and he was driving a stolen car.

Ahead of him on the one-way street was a truck. Without further thought Luke stamped on the gas pedal and pulled around the truck. The cops switched on their siren.

Luke cut in front of the truck, going fast. Acting on instinct now, he yanked the parking brake and spun the wheel hard to the right. The Ford went into a long skid. The truck swerved left to avoid it. Luke's car came to rest facing the wrong way. He stepped on the gas, heading against the traffic on the one-way street.

Cars veered wildly left and right to avoid a head-on collision. Luke swung right to miss a city bus, then clipped a station wagon. He made it to the next crossing and swung right onto a broad avenue. He raced two blocks, running red lights, then looked in his mirror. There was no sign of the police car.

He turned again, heading south now. It was four o'clock, and he was farther from the Smithsonian than he had been five minutes ago. He stepped on the gas.

His luck changed. All the lights were green. He hit seventy crossing Constitution Avenue, and he was in the park.

He saw the big dark-red building, like a castle in a fairy tale. He stopped the car and checked his watch. It was five past four. The audience would be leaving. He cursed and jumped out.

He ran across the grass. The secretary had told him the lecture was in the Aircraft Building. He went inside what looked like a hangar. All kinds of old aircraft were suspended from the ceiling: biplanes, a wartime jet, even a hot-air balloon. He spoke to a guard. "I'm here for the lecture on rocket fuels."

"You're too late," the man said. "The lecture's over."

"Where was it held? I might still catch the speaker."

"Far end of the hall," the man said.

Most of the audience had left the lecture theater, and attendants were already stacking the metal chairs. But a small knot of eight or nine men remained in a corner, deep in discussion, surrounding a white-haired man who might have been the lecturer.

Luke walked up to the group. The white-haired man glanced at him, then looked back to the others. He carried on without a pause. "Nitromethane is almost impossible to handle. You can't ignore safety factors."

"You can build safety into your procedures," said a young man.

The argument was a familiar one to Luke. A variety of rocket fuels had been tested, many more powerful than the standard combination of alcohol and liquid oxygen, but they had drawbacks.

A man with a southern accent said, "What about unsymmetrical dimethylhydrazine? I hear they're testing that at the jet propulsion laboratory in Pasadena."

Luke suddenly said, "It works, but it's deadly poison."

They all turned to him. The white-haired man frowned, looking slightly annoyed, resenting the interruption from a stranger.

Then the young man said, "My God, what are you doing in Washington, Luke?"

Luke felt so happy he could have wept.

PART 3

The satellite is bullet-shaped rather than spherical. In theory a sphere should be more stable, but in practice the satellite must have protruding antennas for radio communication, and the antennas spoil the round shape.

4:15 P.M. Luke found he could not speak.

The other scientists resumed their conversation, oblivious to his distress, except for the young man, who looked concerned and said, "Hey, are you okay?"

Luke nodded. After a moment he managed to say, "Could we talk?"

"Sure." He led Luke into a small room with a couple of chairs, a desk, and a phone. They sat down. "What's going on?" said the man.

"I've lost my memory."

"My God!"

"Autobiographical amnesia. I still remember my science—that's how I found my way to you guys—but I don't know anything about myself."

The young man said, "Do you know who I am?"

Luke shook his head. "Tell me what you know about me."

"You're Dr. Claude Lucas, but everyone calls you Luke. I'm Will McDermot."

Luke closed his eyes, overwhelmed by relief and gratitude. "Thank you, Will. Do you know where I live?"

"Huntsville, Alabama. You work for the Army Ballistic Missile Agency, based at Redstone Arsenal in Huntsville. Your boss is Wernher von Braun."

"I can't tell you how good it is to know this stuff."

"I was surprised to see you, because your team is about to launch a rocket that will put an American satellite in space for the first time. They're all down in Cape Canaveral, and word is it could be tonight."

"I read about it in the paper this morning, but did I really work on that rocket?"

"Yeah. The *Explorer*. It's the most important launch in the history of the American space program."

Only hours ago Luke had imagined himself a drunken bum. Now it turned out he was a scientist at the peak of his career. "I ought to be there!" he said.

"Exactly. So do you have any idea why you're not?"

Luke shook his head. "I woke up this morning in the men's room at Union Station."

Will gave a man-to-man grin. "Sounds like you went to a great party last night."

"Is that the kind of thing I do? Get so drunk I pass out?"

"I don't know you well enough to answer that. I'd be surprised, though. You know us scientists. Our idea of a party is to sit around drinking coffee and talking about our work."

That sounded right to Luke. "I'm going to call Cape Canaveral."

"Great idea." Will picked up the phone on the desk and handed it to Luke.

Luke got the number from information and dialed. "This is Dr.

Lucas," he said. He felt inordinately pleased to be able to give his name: He would not have thought it could be so satisfying. "I'd like to speak to someone on the *Explorer* launch team."

A moment later a voice said, "Army security. Colonel Hide speaking."

"This is Dr. Lucas—"

"Luke! At last! Where the hell are you? We've been going crazy. We got army security looking for you, the FBI—even the CIA!"

"I'm in Washington. Listen, a strange thing has happened. I lost my memory. I've been wandering around town trying to figure out who I am. Finally I found some physicists who know me."

"But that's extraordinary. How did it happen?"

"I was hoping you could tell me that, Colonel."

"You always call me Bill."

"Bill."

"Okay, well, I'll tell you what I know. You took off Monday, saying you had to go to Washington. You flew from Patrick."

"Patrick?"

"Patrick Air Force Base, near Cape Canaveral. Marigold made the reservations."

"Who's Marigold?"

"Your secretary in Huntsville. She made an appointment for you to see General Sherwood at the Pentagon yesterday, but you didn't keep the appointment."

"Did I give a reason for wanting to see the general?"

"Apparently not. His area of responsibility is army security, but he's also a friend of your family's."

"Is the launch going ahead tonight?"

"No. We've got weather problems. It's been postponed until tomorrow at ten thirty p.m."

"Do I have friends here in Washington?"

"Sure. One of them's been calling me every hour. Bern Rothsten." Hide read out a phone number.

Luke scribbled it on a scratch pad. "I'll call him right away."

"First you should talk to your wife."

Luke froze. Wife, he thought. I have a wife. He wondered what she was like.

"You still there?" Hide said.

Luke started to breathe again. "Uh, Bill . . ."

"Yes?"

"What's her name?"

"Elspeth," he said. "Your wife's name is Elspeth. I'll transfer you to her phone. Hold the line."

Luke had a nervous sensation in his stomach. This was dumb, he thought. She was his wife.

"Elspeth speaking. Luke, is that you?" She had a warm, low voice.

He said, "Yes, this is Luke."

"I've been so worried. What on earth happened?"

"I really don't know. I woke up this morning in the men's room at Union Station, and I spent the day trying to find out who I am."

"Everyone's been looking for you. Where are you now?"

"At the Smithsonian, in the Aircraft Building. A fellow scientist has been helping me, and I have a number for Bern Rothsten."

Elspeth said, "You don't remember why you took off for Washington in such a hurry?"

"No. Didn't I tell you?"

"You said it was better for me not to know. But I was frantic. I called an old friend of ours in Washington, Anthony Carroll. He's in the CIA. He called you at the Carlton on Monday night and arranged to meet you for breakfast on Tuesday morning, but you didn't show up. I'm going to call him now and tell him everything's all right."

"Obviously something happened to me between Monday evening and Tuesday morning."

"You ought to see a doctor, get yourself checked out."

"I feel fine, but there's a lot I want to know. Do we have children?"

"No. We've been trying for a baby ever since we got married, which is four years ago, but we haven't succeeded."

"Do we know why?"

"No. But we've been talking about adopting."

"Are my parents alive?"

"Your mom is. She's in New York. Your pa died five years ago."

Luke felt a sudden wave of grief, though he'd lost his memories of his father.

Elspeth went on. "You have two brothers and a sister, all younger. Your baby sister, Emily, is your favorite. She's ten years younger than you, and she lives in Baltimore."

"I could go on asking you questions all day. But what I really want is to find out how this happened to me. Would you fly up here tonight?"

There was a moment of silence. "Why?"

"To figure out this mystery with me. I could use some help—and companionship."

"Luke, I can't leave Cape Canaveral now. We're about to launch the *Explorer!* I can't leave the team at a moment like this."

"I guess not." He understood but felt let down. "Who's Bern Rothsten?"

"He was at Harvard with you and Anthony Carroll."

"He's been trying to reach me. Maybe he knows what this is all about."

"Call me later, won't you? I'll be at the Starlite Motel tonight."

"Okay."

"Take care of yourself, Luke, please," she said earnestly.

"I will, I promise." He hung up.

He felt emotionally drained. Part of him wanted to go to his hotel and lie down, but he picked up the phone again and called Bern Rothsten. "This is Luke Lucas," he said.

"Luke, thank God! What the hell happened to you?"

"I don't really know except that I've lost my memory."

"You lost your memory? Do you know how this happened?"

"No. I was hoping you might have a clue. Why have you been trying to reach me?"

"I was worried. You called me on Monday from Huntsville."

"Huntsville? I thought I flew from Florida."

"You did, but you stopped off in Huntsville because you had an errand to run. You said you were on your way here and would call me from the Carlton, but you never did. Listen, there's someone you have to call. Billie Josephson is an expert on memory."

The name rang a bell. "I think I came across her book in the library."

"She's also my ex-wife and an old friend of yours." Bern gave Luke the number.

"I'm going to call her right away. Bern . . ."

"Yeah."

"I lose my memory, and it turns out that an old friend of mine is a world expert on memory. Isn't that a hell of a coincidence?"

4:45 P.M. Billie had an hour-long interview with a patient, but she was distracted during it, thinking about the Sowerby Foundation and Anthony Carroll. When it was over, she called Anthony and said, "I was passed over for the post of director of research here at the hospital. Len Ross got the job. Did you know that?"

"Yeah, I guess I did."

"I don't understand it. I thought I might lose to a highly qualified outsider—Sol Weinberg, from Princeton, or someone of that order. But everyone knows I'm better than Len."

"Do they?"

"Anthony, come on. You know it yourself. So why didn't I get the job? The foundation is insisting on Len."

"I guess they have the right."

"Anthony, it's very unusual for a trust to interfere in this kind of decision. They normally leave it to the experts. You must know why they took this step."

"Well, I don't. There hasn't been a meeting about it."

"Charles was very definite."

"Most likely the director and one or two board members had a chat over a drink at the Cosmos Club. One of them has called Charles and given him the word."

"Charles was shocked. He can't understand why they would do such a thing."

"Maybe the director doesn't approve of women earning high salaries when there are men like Ross trying to support a family."

"For Christ's sake, I have a child and an elderly mother to take care of!"

"I didn't say it was logical. Listen, Billie, I have to go."

She hung up and stared at the phone. The conversation rang false to her. It was perfectly plausible that Anthony might not know about machinations among the other board members of the foundation. So why didn't she believe him?

Anthony was lying.

WHEN Anthony hung up the phone, it rang again immediately. He picked it up and heard Elspeth say, "I've been on hold for a quarter of an hour!"

"I was talking to Billie. She—"

"Never mind. I just spoke with Luke. He was at the Smithsonian in the Aircraft Building with a bunch of physicists."

"I'm on my way." Anthony dropped the phone and ran out the door. Pete saw him and ran after him. They went down to the parking lot and jumped into Anthony's Cadillac.

It took them four minutes to drive to Independence Avenue and Tenth Street. Inside the Aircraft Building, Anthony said, "I'll go right, you go left." He walked through the exhibits, scrutinizing the faces of the men as they stared up at the aircraft suspended from the ceiling. At the far end of the building he met up with Pete, who made an empty-hands gesture.

The men's room and offices were checked and yielded nothing.

Anthony said, "This is a catastrophe."

Outside, on Independence Avenue, Anthony saw two cops checking out a car parked on the other side of the road. Anthony went closer and saw that the car was a blue-and-white Ford Fiesta with the same license plate Nosy Rosie had given him.

He showed the patrolmen his CIA identification. "Did you just spot this car illegally parked?" he said to them.

"No. We saw a man driving it on Ninth Street," one cop said. "But he got away from us. Few minutes later we see the car parked here."

Anthony took a business card out of his billfold. "This fugitive may have stolen another car in this neighborhood and made his get-away. If you get a report of a car stolen nearby, would you please call me at this number?"

The cop read the card and said, "I'll do that, Mr. Carroll."

As Anthony and Pete returned to the yellow Cadillac, Pete said, "What do you think he'll do now?"

"I don't know."

Anthony was silent, thinking while they drove to Q Building. Reaching his office, he said, "I want you to go with two men to the Carlton. Take a room, then stake out the lobby. I'll join you later."

Anthony shut the door of the office. This really was a catastrophe. Now that Luke knew his identity, there was no telling what else he might find out. If he could find him, he could still patch things up. But he would have to take drastic measures.

With a heavy heart he went to the photograph of President Eisenhower that hung on the wall. He pulled on one side of the frame, and the picture swung out to reveal a safe. He dialed the combination, opened the door, and took out his gun.

It was a Walther P38 automatic. This was the handgun used by the German army in the Second World War. Anthony had been issued it before he went to North Africa. He also had a silencer that had been specially designed by OSS to fit the gun.

He took the silencer from the safe, fitted it over the barrel of the pistol, and screwed it tight. He put on a long camel-hair winter coat, single-breasted, with deep inside pockets. He placed the gun, handle down, in the right-hand pocket.

He buttoned his coat and went out.

6:00 P.M. Luke took a taxicab to the Georgetown Mind Hospital and gave his name at the reception desk, saying he had an appointment with Dr. Josephson.

She had been charming on the phone: concerned and intrigued to know that he had lost his memory, eager to see him as soon as she could. Now she came running down the stairs, a short woman in a white lab coat, with big brown eyes and a flushed expression of excitement. Luke could not help smiling at the sight of her.

"It's so great to see you!" she said, and threw her arms around him in a hug.

He felt an impulse to respond to her exuberance, but afraid that he might do something to cause offense, he froze, his hands in the air like the victim of a holdup.

She laughed at him. "You don't remember what I'm like," she said. "Relax. I'm almost harmless."

He let his arms fall around her shoulders. Her small body was soft under the lab coat.

"Come on, I'll show you my office." She led him up the stairs.

Billie had a small room with a plain desk and a steel file cabinet, but she had made it pretty with flowers and a splashy abstract painting in bright colors. She gave Luke coffee and opened a package of cookies, then asked him about his amnesia.

She made notes as he answered her questions. Luke had had no food for twelve hours, and he ate all the cookies. She smiled and said, "Want some more?" He shook his head.

"Well, I have a pretty clear picture," she said. "You have global amnesia, but otherwise you seem mentally healthy. I can't assess your physical state, but you look all right, just shook."

"Is there a cure for this type of amnesia?"

"No, there's not. The process is generally irreversible."

That was a blow to Luke.

"Don't be downhearted," Billie said kindly. "Sufferers are able to relearn what has been forgotten, so they can usually pick up the threads of their lives and live normally."

Even while he was hearing horrible news, he found himself watching her with fascination, concentrating on her eyes, which seemed to glow with sympathy. He said, "What might have caused the amnesia?"

"Brain damage is the first possibility to consider. However, there's no sign of injury."

"So what else?"

"It can be brought on by prolonged stress, a sudden shock, or drugs. It's also a side effect of some treatments for schizophrenia, involving electric shock and drugs."

"Any way to tell which affected me?"

"Not conclusively. You need to find out what happened to you between Monday night and this morning."

"At least I know what I'm looking for: shock, drugs, or schizophrenia treatment."

"You're not schizophrenic," she said. "You have a good hold on reality. What's your next step?"

Luke stood up. "I'm going to see Bern Rothsten. He may have some ideas."

"I'll see you out."

As they walked down the stairs, Luke asked, "How long have you been divorced from Bern?"

"Five years. Long enough to become friends again."

"This is a strange question, but I have to ask. Did you and I ever date?"

"Oh, boy," said Billie. "Did we ever."

1943

On the day Italy surrendered, Billie bumped into Luke in the lobby of Q Building. At first she did not know him. She saw a thin man of about thirty, and her eyes passed over him without recognition. Then he spoke. "Billie? Don't you remember me?"

She knew the voice, of course, and it made her heart beat faster. But when she looked again at the emaciated man from whom the words issued, she gave a small scream of horror. His head looked like a skull. His shirt collar was too large, and his jacket looked as if it were draped over a wire hanger. His eyes were the eyes of an old man. "Luke," she said, "you look terrible!"

"Gee, thanks," he said with a tired smile.

"I'm sorry," she said hastily.

"Don't worry. I've lost some weight, I know. There's not a lot of food where I've been."

She wanted to hug him, but she held back, not sure he would like it.

He said, "What are you doing here?"

"A training course—maps, radio, firearms, unarmed combat."

He grinned. "You're not dressed for jujitsu."

Billie still loved to dress stylishly, despite the war. She could not afford to buy the latest fashions on her army wages, but her father had taught all his children to sew. "I'll take that as a compliment," she said. "Where have you been?"

"Do you have a minute to talk?"

"Of course."

"Let's go outside."

It was a warm September afternoon. They walked alongside the reflecting pool. "How come you're in OSS?" Luke asked.

"Anthony Carroll fixed it," she said. The Office of Strategic Services was considered a glamorous assignment, and jobs here were much coveted. "He's Bill Donovan's personal assistant now." General "Wild Bill" Donovan was head of OSS. "He's brought in all his old friends from Harvard. Elspeth is in London, Peg is in Cairo, and I gather you and Bern have been behind enemy lines somewhere."

"France," Luke said.

"What was that like?"

"The first man I killed was a Frenchman," he said abruptly. "He was a cop, a gendarme. Claude—same name as me. He blundered into a farmhouse where my group was meeting. There was no doubt what we were doing—we had maps on the table, rifles stacked in the corner, and Bern was showing the Frenchies how to wire a time bomb." Luke gave an odd kind of laugh, with no humor in it. "Damn fool tried to arrest us."

"What did you do?" Billie whispered.

"Took him outside and shot him in the back of the head."

"Oh, my God."

"He didn't die right away. It took about a minute."

She took his hand and squeezed it. He held on, and they walked around the long, narrow pool hand in hand. He told her another story, about a woman Resistance fighter who had been captured and tortured, and Billie cried. The afternoon cooled, and still the grim details spilled out of him: cars blown up, German officers assassinated, Jewish families led away to unknown destinations.

They had been walking for two hours when he stumbled, and she caught him and prevented his falling. "I'm so tired," he said.

She hailed a taxi and took him to his hotel.

He was staying at the Carlton. She recalled that his family was wealthy. He had a corner suite with a grand piano in the living room and—something she had never seen before—a telephone extension in the bathroom.

She called room service and ordered chicken soup and scrambled eggs, hot rolls, and milk. He sat on the couch and began to tell another story, but before he could finish it, the food came.

Billie signed the check and tipped the waiter. When she turned around, Luke was asleep.

She woke him just long enough to get him into the bedroom and onto the bed. "Don't leave," he mumbled; then his eyes closed again.

She took off his boots and loosened his tie, then sat on the edge of the bed watching him for a while, remembering that long drive to Newport almost two years ago.

Then she slipped off her jacket and skirt and lay down on the bed. She got her arms around Luke's bony shoulders, put his head on her bosom, and held him. "Everything's all right now," she said. "When you wake up, I'll still be here."

AT DAWN he got up to go to the bathroom. He got back into bed a couple of minutes later, wearing only his underwear. He put his arms around her and hugged her. "Something I forgot to tell you, something very important," he said.

"What?"

"In France I thought about you all the time. Every day."

"Did you?" she whispered. "Did you really?" But he did not answer. He had gone back to sleep. She lay in his embrace, thinking about him in France, risking his life and remembering her, and she was so happy she felt her heart would burst.

At eight o'clock in the morning she called in and said she was sick. It was the first day she had taken off for illness in more than a year in the military. She had a bath, got dressed, and ordered coffee and cornflakes from room service.

She was reading the Washington *Post* when Luke came stumbling out of the bedroom in his underwear, his jaw blue with stubble. She smiled at him, happy that he was awake.

"How long did I sleep?"

She checked her wristwatch. "About eighteen hours."

"I haven't slept like that for a year." He rubbed his eyes. "You stayed all night?"

"You asked me to."

He went to the phone "Room service? Let me have a T-bone steak, rare, with three eggs, sunny-side. Plus orange juice, toast, and coffee."

Billie frowned. She had never spent the night with a man, so she did not know what to expect in the morning, but this disappointed her. It was so unromantic. She was reminded of her brothers waking up—they, too, emerged stubbly, grouchy, and ravenous.

He sat beside her on the couch. "I talked a lot yesterday."

"About five hours straight."

He took her hands. "I'm so glad we met again."

Her heart jumped. "Me, too."

"I'd like to kiss you."

She felt a sudden leaping sensation inside, but she held back. The war had brought about a new moral laxity in Washington, but she was not part of it. She clasped her hands in her lap and said, "I sure don't aim to kiss you until you're dressed."

He gave her a skeptical look. "Are you afraid of compromising yourself? We already spent the night together."

"I stayed here because you begged me to!"

"I appreciate it."

"Then don't imply I've already compromised myself so that anything else I might do makes no difference."

He gave a big sigh. "Well, I didn't intend to imply that. You're making a hell of a fuss about a casual remark." He went into the bedroom.

Billie heard the shower running. She felt exhausted. She had spent hours in the grip of a profound romantic passion, then in a few minutes it had turned sour. How could such things happen?

Whatever the reason, he had made her feel cheap. In a minute or two he would come out of the bathroom, ready to sit down and have breakfast with her as if they were a married couple. But they were not, and she was feeling more and more uncomfortable.

Well, she thought, if I don't like it, why am I still here?

She put on her hat and left the suite, closing the door quietly behind her.

SHE saw him almost every day for the next four weeks.

At first he was in Q Building for daily debriefing sessions. He would seek her out at lunchtime, and they would eat together in the cafeteria or take sandwiches to the park. His manner reverted to his characteristic relaxed courtesy, making her feel respected and cared for. The sting of his behavior in the Carlton eased. At the end of the week he asked her for a date, and they saw the movie *Jane Eyre*. On Sunday they went canoeing on the Potomac.

Over time Luke put on a little weight, and the haunted look went from his eyes. A little of his boyishness came back.

They talked endlessly and had a major fight about twice a week. Each followed the pattern of their first row, in his hotel suite. He would say something high-handed or make a decision about their evening's plans without consulting her. She would protest hotly, and he would accuse her of overreacting. She would get more and more angry, and in the heat of the argument she would make some wild assertion she knew to be false. Then he would say there was no point in talking to her, because she was willing to say anything to win an argument. But unlike the first fight, when she left, he would walk out. Within minutes she would be distraught. She would seek him out and beg him to forget it and be friends. At first he would be stony-faced; then she would say something that made him laugh, and he would melt.

But in all that time she did not go to his hotel, and when she kissed him, it was a chaste brush of the lips, always in a public place. The sunny September turned into a chilly October, and Luke was posted.

He got the news on a Friday afternoon. He was waiting for Billie in the lobby of Q Building when she left for the day. She could see by his face that something bad had happened. "What's wrong?" she said immediately.

"I'm going back to France. I leave in two days."

Tears came to her eyes. She swallowed hard. "Two days."

"I've got to pack."

"I'll help you."

They went to his hotel.

As soon as they were inside the door, she pulled him to her and tilted her face to be kissed. This time there was nothing chaste about it. Then she slipped off her coat and said, "Touch my breasts."

He looked startled.

"Please," she begged.

His hands closed over her small breasts. She shut her eyes and concentrated on the sensation. They broke apart, and she stared at him, memorizing his face. She wanted never to forget the blue of his eyes, the lock of dark hair that fell over his forehead. "I want a photo of you," she said.

"I might have a family photo. Let me look." He went into the bedroom.

She followed him.

His battered brown leather bag lay on a stand. He took out a silver picture frame that opened up like a book. Inside were two photographs, one on each side. He slipped a picture out and handed it to her. It showed a younger Luke in a polo shirt. With him were an older couple, plus twin boys of around fifteen, and a little girl.

"I can't take this. It's your picture of your family," she said.

"I want you to have it. That's me. I'm part of my family."

"Did you take it to France with you?"

"Yes."

"There are two photos in that frame. Show me the other one."

He seemed reluctant but opened it. The second picture had been cut out of the Radcliffe yearbook. It was a photo of Billie.

She burst into tears. He had cut her picture out of the yearbook and carried it, alongside the photo of his family, all that time his life was in such danger.

"Why are you crying?" he said.

"Because you love me," she replied.

"It's true," he said. "I was frightened to tell you. I've loved you since Pearl Harbor weekend."

"We could have had each other for two years!" The tears streamed down her cheeks. "Now we've only got two days—two lousy days!"

"Then stop crying and kiss me again," he said.

They made love all weekend, frantic with desire and sorrow, knowing they might never meet again.

After Luke left on Monday morning, Billie cried for two days.

Eight weeks later she discovered she was pregnant.

■ ■ ▮

6:30 P.M. "Yes, we dated," Billie said as they went down the stairs.

They came to the door of the building. "Were we in love?" Luke asked.

"Oh, sure," she said, and although her tone was light, there was a catch in her voice. "I thought you were the only man in the world."

How could he have let a woman like this slip away from him? It seemed a tragedy worse than losing his memory. "But you learned better and married Bern."

"Yes."

"What went wrong with him?"

"Conflicting values, and for Bern politics came above all else."

"Do you have anyone now?"

"Sure. His name's Harold Brodsky."

Luke felt foolish. She was a beautiful divorcée in her thirties. Of course she had someone. "I guess he shares your values."

"Yes. The most important thing in his life is his child—he's a widower—and after that comes his academic work."

"Which is?"

"Iodine chemistry. I feel the same about my work." She smiled.

"I may not be starry-eyed about men, but I guess I'm still idealistic about unraveling the mysteries of the human mind."

"I wish you could unravel the mystery of my mind."

"It's strange," she said. "Maybe you suffered a cranial injury that left no visible trace. You're not an alcoholic or a drug addict. I can tell by looking at you."

"Which leaves . . . ?"

She shook her head. "You certainly aren't schizophrenic. You couldn't have been given the combination drug-and-electrotherapy treatment that could have caused—" She stopped suddenly, looking alluringly startled, mouth open, eyes wide.

"What?" Luke said.

"I just remembered Joseph Bellow. He was admitted late yesterday, after I'd gone home. Then he was discharged in the night, which was real strange."

"What was wrong with him?"

"He was a schizophrenic." She paled. "Let's check his file."

She turned and ran back up the stairs to a room marked RECORDS OFFICE. Luke followed. There was no one inside. Billie turned on the light.

She opened a drawer and pulled out a folder. She read aloud, "White male, six foot one, one hundred and eighty pounds."

"You think it was me," Luke said.

She nodded. "The patient was given a treatment that could cause global amnesia."

"My God." If she was right, this had been done to him deliberately. That made sense and explained why he had been followed around—presumably to make sure the treatment had worked. "Who did this?"

"My colleague, Dr. Leonard Ross. A patient is normally kept under observation for days before treatment is given, and I can't imagine any justification for discharging him immediately afterward. This is very irregular."

"Sounds like Ross is in trouble."

Billie sighed. "If I complain, people will accuse me of sour grapes. They'll say I'm bitter because he got the job I wanted."

"When did that happen?"

"Today."

Luke was startled. "A hospital superior must have promised Ross the promotion in return for doing this irregular treatment."

"No." Billie shook her head. "The trust that's funding the post, the Sowerby Foundation, insisted on Ross for the job."

"But who at the foundation would want me to lose my memory?"

"I can guess who," Billie said. "Anthony Carroll. He's on the board."

The name rang a bell. Anthony was the CIA man Elspeth had mentioned. "That still leaves the question why."

"Well, at least now we have someone to ask," Billie said, and she picked up the phone and dialed.

"Let me speak to Anthony Carroll," Billie said. "This is Dr. Josephson. . . . Okay, have him call me at home one hour from now."

"I thought this Anthony was a friend," Luke said.

"Yeah." Billie nodded, a worried frown on her face. "So did I."

7:30 P.M. Bern lived in a neighborhood of large homes and foreign embassies. His apartment had an Iberian theme, with ornate furniture in dark wood. Luke recalled Billie saying that Bern had fought in the Spanish civil war. It was easy to imagine him as a fighter. His dark hair was receding now, but there was a hard set to his face and a knowing look in his gray eyes.

Bern shook Luke's hand warmly and gave him strong coffee in a small cup. "What the hell is going on, old buddy?" Bern asked.

Luke sat down and related what he and Billie had discovered at the hospital. Then he said, "Here's what I think happened to me. I don't know if you're going to buy it, but I'm hoping you can shed some light on the mystery."

"I'll do what I can."

"I came to Washington on Monday to see an army general for some mysterious purpose that I wouldn't tell anyone about. My wife was worried about me and called Anthony, who made a breakfast date with me for Tuesday morning. At breakfast Anthony put something in my coffee to make me fall asleep, then drove me to George-town Mind Hospital. He waited until Billie left for the day, then checked me in under a false name and got hold of Dr. Len Ross. Using his position as a board member of the Sowerby Foundation, he persuaded Ross to give me a treatment that would destroy my memory."

Luke waited for Bern to say the whole thing was ludicrous, but he did not. He simply said, "But for God's sake, why?"

"For the moment let's concentrate on how rather than why. He checked me out of the hospital, dressed me in rags, and dumped me in Union Station with a sidekick to keep an eye on me and make sure the amnesia treatment had worked."

"But he must have known you'd figure out who you were sooner or later."

"Yes, but by then the trail would have gone cold. Billie probably would have forgotten about the mystery patient, and Ross would have destroyed his records."

Bern nodded thoughtfully. "A risky plan, but one with a good chance of success."

"I'm surprised you're not more skeptical."

Bern shrugged. "We've all been in secret work. These things happen."

Luke felt sure Bern was keeping something back. "Bern, if there's something else you know, *please* tell me."

"There is something, but I don't want to get anyone into trouble."

Luke's heart leaped in hope. "Tell me, please. I'm desperate."

Bern took a deep breath. "Toward the end of the war Billie and Anthony worked on a special project for OSS—the Truth Drug Committee. After the war Billie went back to college and did her doctoral thesis on the effects of various legal drugs on people's mental states. When she finally became a professor, she continued to work on the same area, concentrating on how drugs and other factors affect memory."

"But not for the CIA."

"That's what I thought, but I was wrong. In 1950 the Agency started a project about mind control code-named Bluebird. They financed a whole series of legitimate research projects in universities, channeling the money through trusts to conceal their true source. And they financed Billie's work."

"How did she feel about that?"

"We fought about it. I said the CIA was planning to brainwash people. She said that all scientific knowledge could be used for good or evil, and she didn't care who paid the bill."

"Is that why you divorced?"

"Sort of. In 1952, I wrote a screenplay about a secret government agency that brainwashed unsuspecting citizens. Jack Warner bought it, and the movie came out in 1953. It was a huge hit. My career was made—I was deluged with offers from the studios."

"And Billie?"

"I took her to the première. She went into meltdown. She said I'd used confidential information I got from her. She was sure the CIA would withdraw her funding. It was the end of our marriage."

"That's what Billie meant when she said you had a conflict of values."

"She's right. She should have married you."

Luke's heart missed a beat. He was curious to know why Bern said that, but he postponed the question. "I assume the CIA didn't cut off her funding."

"No." Bern looked bitterly angry. "They destroyed my career instead. I was subjected to a loyalty investigation. Of course, I had been a Communist right up until the end of the war, so I made an easy target. I was blacklisted in Hollywood."

"What did you do?"

"I had a couple of bad years; then I thought of a series of children's books." He pointed to a bookcase. The bright jackets made a splash of color. "I wrote the first story under a pseudonym. The book was a big best seller, and I've written two a year ever since."

"Now I understand why you didn't react with total incredulity to my story," Luke said.

"Yes," Bern said. "I believe Anthony did this, but I don't have the least idea why."

8:00 P.M. Billie sat at her dressing table, freshening her makeup. She could hear television gunfire downstairs: Larry and Becky-Ma were watching *Wagon Train*.

She did not feel like a date with Harold tonight. She was angry about not getting the job she wanted, bewildered by what Anthony had done, and confused to find that the old chemistry between herself and Luke was as powerful and dangerous as ever.

The phone rang in the hallway.

She jumped up and crossed the room to the extension by the bed, but Larry had already picked up. She heard Anthony say, "This is the CIA. Washington is about to be invaded by an army of cabbages."

Larry giggled. "Uncle Anthony, it's you!"

"If you are approached by a cabbage, do not—repeat, do not—attempt to reason with it."

"You're making this up." Larry laughed.

Billie said, "Anthony, I'm on the extension."

Anthony said, "Get your jammies on, Larry, okay?"

"Okay," said Larry, and hung up.

Anthony's voice changed. "Billie, you wanted me to call."

"Anthony, what the hell are you up to?" Billie asked. "I could tell you were lying last time we spoke, but I didn't know what the truth was then. Now I do. I know what you did to Luke at my hospital last night. I want an explanation."

"I can't talk about this on the phone. If we could meet in the next few days—"

"I want your story right now."

"I'll explain everything if you'll meet me tomorrow."

She almost agreed; then she remembered what he had done. "You went behind my back in my own hospital. Tell me the truth right now or I'll go to the FBI the minute I hang up."

It was dangerous to threaten men—it often made them obstinate. But she knew how the CIA hated and feared interference from the FBI, especially when the Agency was working on the borderline of legality, which was most of the time.

He sighed. "You may find this hard to believe."

"Try me."

"Well, here goes. Luke is a spy, Billie."

"Don't be absurd."

"He's an agent for Moscow. He's been passing secrets to the Soviets for years. How do you think they managed to put their *Sputnik* into orbit while our satellite was still on the laboratory bench? They had the benefit of all our research as well as their own."

"Anthony, we've both known Luke for twenty years. He'd never betray his country."

"People do. Remember, when he was with the French Resistance, he was working with the Communists. Of course, they were on our side then, but obviously he continued after the war."

Billie sat down, feeling stunned. "Do you have evidence?"

"I have *proof*—top secret blueprints he gave a KGB officer."

"But even if all this is true, why did you wipe out his memory?"

"To save his life. The CIA was going to kill him."

"Why not just put him on trial as a spy?"

"And have the whole world know that our security is so lousy the Soviets have been getting all our rocket secrets for years?"

"So what happened?"

"I persuaded them to try this. Nobody knows except the director of the CIA and the President. And it would have worked if only Luke had believed that he lost his memory after a night of drinking. Even he would never have known what secrets he gave away. Is he with you now?"

"No." Billie felt the hairs prickle on the back of her neck.

"I need to talk to him before he does himself any more damage."

Acting on instinct, Billie lied. "I don't know where he is."

"You wouldn't hide anything from me, would you?"

"Sure I would. You've already said your organization wanted to kill Luke. It would be dumb of me to tell you where he is, if I knew. But I don't."

"Billie, listen to me. I'm his only hope. Tell him to call me, if you want to save his life."

"I'll think about it," Billie said, but Anthony had already hung up.

8:30 P.M. Luke put down the phone with a shaky hand. Bern said, "What did Billie say? You look like a ghost."

"Anthony says I'm a Soviet agent," Luke told him. "The CIA was going to kill me, but Anthony persuaded them that it would be just as effective to wipe out my memory. Could it be true?"

"No."

"You can't be sure of that."

"Yes, I can, because I *was* a Soviet agent. You ended my career."

Luke stared at him.

"It was in the war," Bern said. "The French Resistance was divided into Gaullists and Communists. Roosevelt and Churchill wanted to make sure the Communists couldn't win an election, so the Gaullists were getting all the guns and ammunition."

"How did I feel about that?"

"You just wanted to beat the Nazis and go home, but I wanted to even things up."

"How?"

"I tipped off the Communists about a parachute drop we were expecting, so they could ambush us and steal our ordnance." He shook his head ruefully. "They screwed up royally. They attacked us at the drop point as soon as the stuff hit the ground, so you knew we had been betrayed. And I was the obvious suspect."

"What did I do?"

"You offered me a deal. I had to stop working for Moscow right then, and you would keep quiet about what I had done. We both kept our promises, but our friendship was never the same."

"If I'd been a Communist, I would have covered up for you."

"Absolutely."

"So Anthony is mistaken."

"Or lying," Bern said, "and if he's lying, what was his *real* reason for making you lose your memory?"

"It has to be connected with my sudden departure from Cape Canaveral. I must have learned something so important that I had to rush to the Pentagon to talk to them about it. I guess I told Anthony and he decided he had to wipe out my memory to make sure the secret never got out."

"I wonder what the hell it was."

"I guess my first step to finding out is to go to my hotel room and look through my stuff. Maybe I'll find a clue."

"If Anthony wiped out your memory, he must have gone through your possessions, too."

"But there may be something he didn't recognize as relevant."

"And then?"

"The only other place to look would be Cape Canaveral. I'll fly back tomorrow."

"Spend the night here," Bern said. "My instincts tell me you're in danger. I don't like the idea of you spending the night alone. Go to the Carlton, pick up your stuff, and come back. I'll take you to the airport in the morning."

Luke said, "You've been a heck of a good friend to me over this."

Bern shrugged. "We go back a long way."

"But you just told me after that incident in France our friendship was never the same."

"That's true." Bern gave Luke a candid look. "Your attitude was that a man who betrayed you once would betray you twice."

Luke said thoughtfully, "I was wrong, though, wasn't I?"

"Yes," Bern said. "You were."

9:30 P.M. Anthony's yellow Cadillac was parked outside the Carlton Hotel. Pete hurried out of the building and came to the car. "Ackie Horwitz called in. Luke is at Bern Rothsten's place."

"At last," Anthony said.

"When he leaves, Ackie will follow him on the motorcycle. Do you think he'll come here?"

"He may. I'll wait here." There were two more agents in the hotel lobby who'd alert Anthony if Luke went in by another entrance.

A little later a taxicab pulled into the hotel's driveway, and Luke got out. He was wearing a navy topcoat and a gray hat. Across the street Ackie Horwitz pulled up on his motorcycle. Anthony got out of his car and strolled toward the hotel entrance.

Luke paid the taxi driver. He glanced at Anthony but did not recognize him.

LUKE KNEW HE HAD BEEN followed from Bern's apartment by a man on a motorcycle. Now he was strung taut, all his senses on alert.

The lobby of the Carlton looked like a grand drawing room, full of reproduction French furniture. Two women in fur coats chatted with a group of men in tuxedos near the entrance to the bar. Bell-hops in livery went about their business with quiet efficiency. It was a luxurious place, designed to soothe the nerves of jangled travelers. It did nothing for Luke's.

Scanning the room, he quickly identified two men who had the air of agents: one sitting on a sofa, the other near the elevator. They were dressed in business suits. They definitely were not out for an evening in expensive restaurants and bars. He thought of walking right out again, but where would that leave him? He approached the reception desk, gave his name, and asked for the key to his room. As he turned away, a stranger spoke to him. "Hey, Luke!"

It was the man who had walked into the hotel behind him.

Luke said, "I'm afraid I don't know who you are."

"Anthony Carroll. I'm so glad I've caught up with you at last."

Luke tensed. Anthony did not look like the kind of man who would betray an old friend. Luke said, "How could you do this to me? I'm not a spy."

"It's not that simple."

"Neither Bern nor Billie believes your story about my working for Moscow."

"They don't know everything."

"What do you know that they don't?"

"I'll tell you, but we can't talk here. Shall we go to my office? It's five minutes away."

"Let's go to my suite," Luke said.

Anthony hesitated, then said, "Sure."

They crossed the lobby. Luke checked the number on his room key: 530. "Fifth floor," he said to the elevator operator.

They did not speak as they went up. Luke looked at Anthony's clothes: the old camel-hair coat, the rumpled suit, the nondescript tie. Suddenly Luke saw that the soft material of the coat sagged slightly on the right side. There was a heavy object in the pocket.

He felt cold with fear. He had not thought that Anthony would have a gun. Trying to keep his face immobile, Luke thought furiously. Could Anthony shoot him right here in the hotel?

As the elevator stopped at the fifth floor, Anthony unbuttoned his coat. For a fast draw, Luke thought.

They stepped out. Luke did not know which way to go, but Anthony confidently turned right. He must have been to Luke's room already.

Luke tried to make himself calm. Anthony had the gun, but Luke had guessed Anthony's intentions. It was about even.

They reached the door, and Luke took out his key. If he went inside, he was dead. He unlocked the door and pushed it open. "Come in," he said. He stood aside to let his guest enter first.

Anthony hesitated, then walked past Luke through the doorway.

Luke hooked his foot around Anthony's right ankle, put both hands flat on Anthony's shoulder blades, and pushed hard. Anthony went flying. He crashed into a small table, knocking over a vase. In desperation he grabbed at a brass floor lamp, but the lamp fell with him.

Luke pulled the door shut and ran for his life. He hurtled along the corridor, burst through the fire exit, and ran down the stairs. On the next landing he crashed into a maid carrying a stack of towels. "I'm sorry," he called as the maid screamed and towels flew everywhere.

ANTHONY knew that it was a mistake to enter the room first, but Luke left him no choice. After a stunned moment he picked himself up. He opened the door. Looking out, he saw Luke disappearing into the stairwell.

Anthony followed, running as fast as he could. On the next floor down he was momentarily delayed by a maid who was kneeling on the floor, picking up scattered towels. He slowed his pace to maneuver around her. As he did so, he heard the elevator arrive.

A couple in evening clothes emerged. Anthony barged past them into the elevator and said, "Ground floor, and be quick about it."

The man slammed the doors and threw the lever. The elevator descended slowly.

LUKE EMERGED INTO THE lobby. His heart sank. The two agents he had spotted earlier were now standing in front of the main entrance, blocking his way out. A moment later the elevator door opened and Anthony stepped out. Luke turned and ran back along a corridor into the depths of the hotel. Behind him he heard the pounding footsteps. There had to be a back entrance.

He pushed through a curtain and found himself in a little courtyard decorated like a Mediterranean outdoor café. Barging between the tables, he made it to an exit door, emerging into a kind of butler's pantry. Half a dozen uniformed waiters were heating food in chafing dishes and arranging plates on trays. In the middle of the room was a staircase leading down. Luke pushed through the waiters and took the stairs.

In the basement was the main kitchen, where dozens of chefs cooked for hundreds of people. They were too busy to pay attention to Luke as he dodged between the refrigerators and the ranges.

At the back of the kitchen he found a staircase going up. He guessed it led to the delivery entrance. He raced up the stairs. At the top he burst through a door into the cold night air.

He was in a dark yard surrounded by a high wire fence with a gate. He heard the door behind him bang open and guessed that Anthony had come out.

He ran for the gate. It was closed and secured with a big steel padlock. Heart pounding, Luke scrambled up the fence. As he reached the top, he heard the sigh of a silenced pistol, but he felt nothing. He flung himself over the top. The pistol coughed again. He fell to the ground. He heard a third muffled shot. He sprang to his feet and ran, heading east. At the corner, he looked back. Anthony was nowhere in sight.

He had escaped.

10:30 P.M. Harold Brodsky made a good martini, and his housekeeper's tuna bake was as tasty as promised. For dessert there was cherry pie and ice cream. Billie felt guilty. Harold was trying so hard to please her, but her mind was on Luke and Anthony, their shared past and their puzzling new entanglement.

After dinner Harold suggested they move to the living room. He produced a bottle of expensive French brandy and poured generous measures into two snifters. Was he trying to stiffen his own courage, Billie wondered, or lower her resistance?

Harold was normally an entertaining talker, witty and clever, and she generally laughed a lot when she was with him, but tonight he seemed preoccupied. He took a sip of brandy. "I've been thinking about our future," he said.

Billie's heart sank. He was going to propose. Yesterday she would have accepted; today she could hardly think about it.

He took her hand. "I love you, Billie," he said. "We get on well, and we both have a child. I want us to be together forever." He looked at her, then said, "How do you feel?"

Billie sighed. "I'm fond of you, Harold. Yesterday I would have said yes. But today I met someone from my past, and I remembered what it was like to be in love at the age of twenty-one. I don't feel that way about you."

He was not totally discouraged. "Who does at our age?"

"Maybe you're right," she said.

The doorbell rang, and Billie's heart leaped.

"Who the heck is that?" Harold said. He got up and went out to the hall.

Billie heard Luke's voice at the door. "I need to talk to Billie."

Harold said, "I'm not sure she wants to be disturbed right now."

"It's important."

"How did you know she was here?"

"Her mother told me. I'm sorry, I don't have time to screw around."

Billie heard a cry of protest from Harold, and she guessed Luke had forced his way into the house. She went into the hallway. Luke looked very shaken. "What's happened now?" she said.

"Anthony shot at me."

Billie was shocked. "Anthony? My God, what got into him?"

"I'm going to the Pentagon, but I may not be believed. Will you come and back me up?"

"Sure," she said. She took her coat off the hall stand.

Harold said, "Billie, we were in the middle of a very important conversation."

Luke said, "I really need you."

Billie hesitated. Harold had obviously been planning this moment for some time, but Luke's life was in danger. "I'm sorry," she said to Harold. "I have to go." She lifted her face to be kissed, but he turned away.

"Get out of my house—both of you," Harold said furiously.

11:00 P.M. Anthony found some stationery in the hotel room Pete had rented. He took out an envelope. From his pocket he took three slugs and three cartridge cases, the rounds he had fired at Luke. He put them into the envelope and sealed it, then stuffed it into his pocket to dispose of it.

The assistant manager on duty came into the room. He was a small, bald man. "Sit down, please, Mr. Suchard." Anthony showed the man his CIA identification.

"What can I do for you, Mr. Carroll?" Suchard asked.

"First, I want to apologize for the little fracas we had earlier."

Suchard nodded primly. "Fortunately, few guests noticed anything. Only the kitchen staff and a few waiters."

"It is a pity to disrupt your fine hotel, even over a matter of national security. Of course, I can't give you the details."

"Of course."

"But I hope I can rely on your discretion." Anthony took out a roll of bills. "We have a small fund for compensation in these instances." He slowly counted five twenties and handed them over.

"Thank you, sir," said Suchard. "I'm sure we can handle things."

"If anyone questions you, it might be best to say you saw nothing."

"Of course." Suchard stood up. "If there's anything else . . ."

"I'll be in touch," Anthony said, and Suchard left.

Pete came in. "The head of security at Cape Canaveral is Colonel Bill Hide." He handed Anthony the number.

Anthony dialed it and got through. "This is Anthony Carroll, CIA, technical services division," he said.

Hide spoke with a slow, unmilitary drawl. "Well, what can I do for you, Mr. Carroll?"

"I'm calling about Dr. Lucas. He has been behaving strangely, which is worrying, given his access to classified information."

"It sure is. I talked to him a few hours ago, and he told me he'd lost his memory."

"There's more to it than that. He stole a car and broke into a house."

Hide was buying the story. "My God, he's in worse shape than I thought."

Anthony pressed on. "We think he's not rational, but you know him better than we do. What would you say?"

"Hell, I think he's lost his marbles. In fact, I'd better call the Pentagon and warn them."

"As you wish. Thank you, Colonel. You've set my mind at rest."

"You're welcome."

Anthony hung up and reviewed the situation. There was no evidence left at the hotel. He had prejudiced the Pentagon against any report Luke might make. That just left Billie's hospital.

He stood up. "I'll be back in an hour," he said to Pete. "Take Malone and Curtis and bribe a room-service waiter to let you into Luke's suite. I have a feeling he'll come back."

12:00 MIDNIGHT Billie drove her red Thunderbird into the parking lot of the Georgetown Mind Hospital. Colonel Lopez from the Pentagon pulled alongside her in a Ford Fairlane.

"Lopez doesn't believe a word I say," Luke said angrily.

"You can't blame him," Billie reasoned. "The assistant manager of the Carlton says no one was chased through the kitchens, and there are no cartridge cases at the loading dock."

"Anthony cleaned up the evidence."

"I know that, but Colonel Lopez doesn't."

They got out of their car and walked into the building with the colonel, a patient Hispanic man with an intelligent face. Billie nodded to the receptionist and led the two men up the stairs and along the corridor to the records office.

"I'm going to show you the file of a man named Joseph Bellow," she told the colonel. "You'll see that he was admitted on Tuesday, treated, then discharged at four a.m. on Wednesday. It's very unusual for a schizophrenic patient to be given treatment without observation first, and it's unheard of for a patient to be released from a mental hospital at four o'clock in the morning."

Billie opened the drawer, pulled out the Bellow file, and opened it. It was empty. "Oh, my God," she said.

Luke stared at the folder in disbelief. "I saw the papers myself less than six hours ago!"

Lopez stood up with a weary air. "Well, I guess that's it."

Luke had the nightmare feeling that he was living in a surreal world in which people could shoot at him and mess with his mind and he could never prove it had happened.

"Wait," Billie said. "The register will show his admission. It's kept at the reception desk."

They went down to the lobby. Billie said, "Let me see the register, please, Charlie."

"Right away, Dr. Josephson." The young black man behind the counter searched around for a moment. "Dang, where did that thing go?" he said. "It was here a couple of hours ago."

Billie's face was like thunder. "Tell me something. Has Dr. Ross been here tonight?"

"Yes, ma'am. He left a few minutes ago."

"Next time you see him, ask him where the register went."

Luke turned to Lopez. "Before we saw you tonight, Colonel, had someone else talked to you about me?"

Lopez hesitated. "Yes," he admitted. "We got a call from a Colonel Hide down in Cape Canaveral. He said the CIA had reported that you were behaving irrationally."

Luke nodded grimly. "Anthony again."

Billie said to Lopez, "I don't blame you for not believing us when we have no evidence."

"I didn't say I don't believe you," Lopez said.

Luke was startled and looked at the colonel with new hope.

Lopez said, "I could believe you imagined that a CIA man chased you around the Carlton. I might even accept that you and Dr. Josephson conspired to pretend there used to be a file and it disappeared. But I don't believe that Charlie here is in on the conspiracy. There must be a daily register, and it's gone."

"So you believe me?" Luke said.

"Something is going on, and it must have to do with that rocket we're about to launch. I'm going to order a full security alert at Cape Canaveral."

"But what about Anthony?"

"I have a friend at the CIA. I'll tell him your story and say I don't know whether it's true or not but I'm concerned."

"That's not going to get us far," Luke protested. "We need to know why they wiped out my memory."

"I agree," Lopez said, "but I can't do any more. The rest is up to you."

"So I'm on my own," Luke said.

"No, you're not," said Billie. "You're not on your own."

PART 4

The new fuel is based on a nerve gas and is very dangerous. It is delivered to Cape Canaveral on a special train equipped with nitrogen to blanket it if any escapes. A drop on the skin will be absorbed into the bloodstream instantly and will be fatal. The technicians say, "If you smell fish, run like hell."

1:00 A.M. Billie drove fast, handling the Thunderbird's three-speed manual gear change with confidence. Luke watched in admiration. They sped through the quiet streets of Georgetown, crossed the creek to downtown Washington, and headed for the Carlton.

They parked around the corner from the Carlton. "I'll go first," Billie said. "If there's anyone suspicious in the lobby, I'll come right out again. When you see me take my coat off, you'll know it's clear."

Luke watched her go in through the glass doors of the lobby. A porter approached her, and he guessed she was saying, "I'm Mrs. Lucas. My husband will be along in a moment." Then she took off her coat.

Luke entered the hotel. For the porter's benefit he said, "I want to make a call before we go upstairs, honey." Next to the reception desk was a phone booth with a seat. Luke went inside. Billie followed him and closed the door. He put a dime in the slot and called the hotel. He angled the handset so that Billie could hear.

"Sheraton-Carlton. Good morning."

"Room five thirty, please."

"Sir, it's past one o'clock. Is this an emergency?"

"Dr. Lucas asked me to call no matter how late."

"Very good."

There was a pause, then a ringing tone. After four rings the phone was picked up. A voice said, "Hello?" It was not Anthony, but it might be Pete.

Luke put on a tipsy voice. "Hey, Ronnie, this is Tim. We're waitin' for ya!"

"You got the wrong room, buddy." The man hung up.

"Someone's there," Billie said.

"Maybe more than one."

"I know how to get them out. I did it in Lisbon during the war."

They left the phone booth. Luke noticed Billie discreetly pick up a book of matches from an ashtray by the elevator. On the fifth floor they found room 530 and went past it. Billie opened a door to reveal a linen closet. "Perfect," she said. "Is there a fire alarm nearby?"

Luke saw one down the hall. "There." He pointed.

"Good." In the closet, sheets and blankets stood in neat stacks on wooden shelves. Billie unfolded a blanket and dropped it on the floor. She did the same with several more until she had a pile. She took a breakfast order from a doorknob and lit it with a match. As it flared up, she put the flame to the blankets. "This is why you should never smoke in bed," she said.

She piled on additional bed linen. Soon smoke began to fill the corridor. "Time to sound the alarm," she said. "We don't want any-one to get hurt."

Luke broke the fire-alarm glass and pressed the large red button inside. A moment later a loud ringing shattered the silence.

They retreated along the corridor until they could only just see the door of Luke's suite through the smoke. The corridor filled with people coughing and fumbling through the smoke toward the stairwell.

The door to room 530 opened slowly. Luke saw a tall man step into the corridor. Pete. He hesitated, then joined the rush for the stairs. Two more men came out and followed him.

"All clear," Luke said. He and Billie entered the suite, and Luke closed the door to keep the smoke out.

"Oh, my God," said Billie. "It's the same room." She stared around, wide-eyed. "I can't believe it." Her voice was hushed, and he could hardly hear her. "This is the very suite."

He stood still, watching. She was in the grip of a strong emotion. "What happened here?" he asked her at last.

She shook her head wonderingly. "It's hard to imagine that you don't remember." She walked around. "There was a grand piano in that corner," she said. She looked into the bathroom. "And a phone in here. I had never seen a phone in a bathroom."

Luke waited. "You stayed here in the war," she said at last. Then in a rush she added, "We made love here."

He looked into the bedroom. "On that bed, I guess."

"Not just on the bed." She giggled, then became solemn again. "How young we were."

"I wish I could remember," he said, and his voice sounded thick with desire.

To his surprise she blushed.

He turned aside and picked up the phone. He dialed the opera-tor. "This is Mr. Davies. I sounded the alarm," Luke said rapidly. "The fire is in a linen closet near room five forty." He hung up with-out waiting for a reply.

Billie was looking around, her emotional moment over. "Your clothes are here," she said.

Lying on the bed were a gray tweed sport coat and a pair of charcoal pants. On the floor was a pair of wing-tip shoes. Luke opened the drawer of the bedside table and found a billfold, a checkbook, and a slim appointments diary with a list of phone numbers in the back. He looked quickly through its pages and found the current week, but there were no obvious clues.

A well-worn black leather suitcase rested open on a stand. He rummaged through it, finding clean shirts and underwear, a notebook half full of mathematical calculations, and a paperback book.

Billie looked into the bathroom. "Shaving gear, toiletry bag, toothbrush."

Luke opened all the cupboards and drawers in the bedroom, and Billie did the same in the living room. He found a black wool topcoat and a black homburg hat.

"Your phone messages are here on the desk," Billie said. "From Bern, from a Colonel Hide, and from someone called Marigold."

"She's my secretary in Huntsville. Colonel Hide said she made my flight reservations."

"I wonder if you told her the purpose of the trip."

"It's possible." He looked at the phone numbers in the back of the diary. "Bingo," he said. "Marigold, home." He sat at the desk and dialed the number.

The phone was answered by a sleepy woman with a slow Alabama accent.

He said, "I'm sorry to call so late. Is this Marigold?"

"Dr. Lucas! Thank God. What in heaven happened to you? No one knew where you were at, and now I hear tell you lost your memory. Is that so?"

"Yes. But I'm hoping you might help me figure things out."

"If I can."

"I'd like to know why I suddenly decided to go to Washington on Monday. Did I tell you?"

"No, you sure didn't, and I was curious. You just said you needed to fly to Washington and that you wanted to stop over in Huntsville for a couple of hours."

"I wonder why."

"Then you said something kind of strange. You asked me not to tell anyone that you were coming here."

"Ah. So it was a secret visit?"

"Yes. And I've kept it secret. I've been questioned by army security and the FBI, and I didn't tell either one of them. Did I do right?"

"Gosh, Marigold, I don't know. But I appreciate your loyalty." The alarm stopped ringing. Luke realized he had run out of time. "I have to go now," he told Marigold. "Thanks for your help."

"Well, you bet. Now you just take care, hear?" She hung up.

"I've packed your stuff," Billie said.

"Thanks," he said. He took his own black coat and hat from the closet and put them on. "Now let's get out of here before the spooks come back."

THEY drove to an all-night diner and ordered coffee. "I wonder when the first flight to Huntsville leaves in the morning," Luke said.

"We need an airline guide," Billie said. "I bet Bern has one. It's the kind of thing writers like. They're always looking stuff up."

"He's probably asleep."

"Then I'll wake him."

Billie went to the pay phone beside the rest rooms. Luke sipped his coffee, watching her. As she talked into the phone, she smiled and tilted her head, being charming to someone she had woken up. She looked bewitching, and he ached with desire for her.

She returned to the table and said, "He's going to join us and bring the book."

Luke checked his watch. It was two a.m. "I'll probably go straight to the airport from here. I hope there's an early flight."

Billie frowned. "Is there a deadline?"

"What made me drop everything and rush to Washington? It has to be something to do with the rocket—a threat to the launch."

"Sabotage?"

"Yes. And if I'm right, I have to prove it before ten thirty tonight."

"Do you want me to fly to Huntsville with you? I can leave Larry with Bern."

Luke shook his head. "I don't think so. Thanks."

"You always were an independent son of a gun."

"It's not that," he said. He wanted her to understand. "I'd love you to come with me. That's the trouble—I'd like it too much. Did I always like you so much, or is this new?"

"This is not new. We fight like hell, but we adore one another."

"You said we were lovers once. Was it good?"

She looked at him with tears in her eyes. "The best."

"Then how come I'm not married to you?"

She began to cry, soft sobs that shook her small frame. "Because"—she wiped her face and took a deep breath—"because you got so mad at me you didn't speak to me for five years."

1945

Anthony's parents had a farm near Charlottesville, Virginia. It was a big white timber-framed house, with rambling wings that contained a dozen bedrooms.

Luke arrived there on the Friday after Japan surrendered. Anthony's mother showed him to a small, spotlessly clean bedroom with a polished hardwood floor and a high old-fashioned bed.

He changed out of his uniform—he now held the rank of major—and put on a black cashmere sport coat. As he was tying his tie, Anthony looked in. "Cocktails in the drawing room whenever you're ready," he said.

"I'll be right there," Luke said. "Which room is Billie in?"

A frown flickered across Anthony's face. "The girls are in the other wing, I'm afraid," he said. "The admiral is old-fashioned about that sort of thing." His father had spent his life in the navy.

"No problem," Luke said with a shrug. He had spent the last three years moving around occupied Europe at night; he would be able to find Billie's room in the dark.

When he went downstairs, he found all his old friends waiting. As well as Anthony and Billie, there were Elspeth, Bern, and Bern's girlfriend, Peg. Luke had spent much of the war with Bern and Anthony and every leave with Billie, but he had not seen Elspeth or Peg since 1941. The admiral handed him a martini, and he took a satisfying gulp. This was a time to celebrate if ever there was one.

Luke studied them over dinner, comparing them with the golden youths who had been so worried four years ago about being expelled from Harvard. Elspeth was painfully thin after three years on rations in wartime London. Bern, at twenty-seven, looked ten years older. This had been his second war, and he had been wounded three times. Anthony had come through best: He had spent most of the war in Washington. Billie, too, seemed little changed. After two years of undercover work in Lisbon, she was still a bundle of radiant energy—gay at one moment and fierce at the next.

"We should drink a toast," Luke said, lifting his wineglass. "To those who survived—and those who did not."

They drank; then Bern said, "I have another. To the men who broke the back of the Nazi war machine—the Red Army."

They all drank again, but the admiral looked displeased.

Coffee was served in the drawing room. Luke handed the cups around. As he offered cream and sugar to Billie, she said in a low voice, "East wing, last door on the left."

At ten thirty the admiral insisted the men move to the billiard room. He poured himself a big tumbler of bourbon and took Luke to the far end of the room to show him his guns in a locked display rack.

"I know and respect your family, Luke," the admiral said as they examined an Enfield rifle. "Your father is a very great man."

"Thank you," Luke said. His father had spent the war helping to run the Office of Price Administration.

"You'll have to think of your family when you choose a wife, my boy. Whoever becomes Mrs. Lucas will have a place waiting for her in the upper reaches of American society. You must pick a girl who can carry that off."

"I'll bear that in mind, Admiral," Luke said, putting the rifle back. He was beginning to see where this was going.

The admiral put a hand on his arm. "Whatever you do, don't get stuck with that little Jewess. She's not worthy of you."

Luke gritted his teeth. "If you'll excuse me, this is something I'd rather discuss with my own father."

"But your father doesn't know about her, does he?"

Luke flushed. The admiral had scored a point. Luke and Billie had not met one another's parents. There had hardly been time. Their love affair had been conducted in snatched moments during a war. He said, "Forgive me if I warn you that these remarks are personally offensive to me."

"I understand that, son, but I may know more about the lady in question than you do."

"The hell you do," Luke said.

The admiral put his arm around Luke's shoulders. "Look, I'm a man. I understand. So long as you don't take matters too seriously, there's no harm in screwing a little tart, we've all—"

He never finished the sentence. Luke turned toward him, put both hands on his chest, and shoved him away. The admiral staggered back, arms flailing, and his glass of bourbon went flying through the air. He tried to regain his balance, failed, and sat down hard on the rug.

Anthony grabbed Luke's arm. "Luke, for God's sake, what do you think you're doing?"

Bern stepped between them and the fallen admiral. "Calm down, both of you," he said.

"The hell with calm," Luke said. "What kind of man invites you to his house, then insults your girlfriend?"

"She is a tart," the admiral said. "I should know, damn it. I paid for her abortion."

Luke was stunned. "Abortion?"

"Hell, yes." The admiral struggled to his feet. "Anthony got her pregnant and paid a thousand dollars for her to get rid of the little bastard."

"You're lying."

"Ask Anthony."

Luke looked at Anthony.

Anthony shook his head. "I told my father it was my baby so that he'd give me the money, but it was your child, Luke."

Luke was enraged. He thought he knew Billie, yet she had kept this a secret from him. He had fathered a child. He stormed out of

the room, ran up the stairs and along the east wing. He found
Billie's room and went in without knocking.

She was lying naked on the bed, reading. For a moment the sight
of her took his breath away. She looked up at him with a happy
smile; then her face darkened at his expression.

"The admiral says he paid for you to have an abortion. Is it
true?" Luke shouted. "Answer me!"

Her face paled. She began to cry, and buried her face in her
hands. "I'm sorry," she sobbed. "I wanted to have your baby with
all my heart, but you were in France, and I didn't know if you were
ever coming back. I had to decide all on my own. It was the worst
time of my life."

"You should have told me the next time I came home on leave."

She sighed. "Yes, I know. But Anthony thought I shouldn't tell
anyone, and it's not difficult to persuade a girl to keep something
like that a secret."

"After you've deceived me over something so important, how can
I ever trust you again?"

She looked anguished. "You're going to say it's over, aren't you?"

"Yes."

She began to cry afresh. "You idiot. You don't know anything, do
you, despite the war."

"The war taught me that nothing counts as much as loyalty."

"You still haven't learned that when humans are under pressure,
we're all willing to lie."

"Even to people we love?"

"We lie *more* to our loved ones, because we care what they think."

He despised such easy excuses. "That's not my philosophy of
life."

"Lucky you," she said bitterly. "You come from a happy home.
You've never known bereavement or rejection. You had a hard war,
but you weren't crippled or tortured. Nothing bad has ever happened to you. Sure, you don't tell lies."

"If that's how you think of me, you must be glad our relationship
is over." Disgusted, he turned to leave.

"No, I'm not glad." Tears ran down her face. "I love you. I'm sorry I deceived you, but I'm not going to prostrate myself with guilt because I did a bad thing in a moment of crisis."

Somewhere in the back of his mind a small voice told him he was throwing away the most precious thing he had ever had. But he was too angry, too humiliated, and too painfully wounded to listen. He went to the door.

"Don't leave," she pleaded.

"Go to hell," he said, and he went out.

2:30 A.M. "I can't believe I gave you up," Luke said. "Didn't I understand what you'd been through?"

"It wasn't all your fault," Billie said wearily. "I thought it was, at the time, but now I can see my own role in the whole mess."

"And so you married Bern."

She laughed again. "You can be so egocentric," she said amiably. "I didn't marry Bern because you left me. I married him because he's one of the best men in the world. It took me years to get over you, but when I did, I fell in love with Bern."

"And you and I became friends again?"

"Slowly. I wrote to you when Larry was born, and you came to see me. Then Anthony had a huge thirtieth birthday party and you showed up. You were back at Harvard, getting your doctorate, and the rest of us were in Washington—Anthony and Elspeth working for the CIA, me doing research at George Washington University, and Bern writing scripts for National Public Radio."

"When did I marry Elspeth?"

"Nineteen fifty-four—the year I divorced Bern."

"Do you know why I married her?"

She hesitated. "I'm the wrong person to answer that question."

A white Lincoln Continental pulled up outside, and Bern jumped out and came into the diner.

"I'm sorry we woke you," said Luke.

"Forget it," Bern said. "Here." He tossed a thick booklet onto the table. The cover said *Official Airline Guide—Published Monthly*. Luke picked it up.

Billie said, "Look for Capital Airlines. They fly to the south."

Luke found it. "There's a plane that leaves at six fifty-five, but it stops at every small town in Dixie and gets to Huntsville at two twenty-three this afternoon."

Bern read over his shoulder. "The next plane doesn't leave until nine o'clock, but it has fewer stops, so it gets you to Huntsville a few minutes before noon."

"I'd get the later plane, but I don't relish hanging around Washington any longer than I have to," Luke said. "Maybe I could leave here by car and pick up a plane somewhere down the line. The early flight's first stop is Newport News. It lands there at two minutes past eight. Could I get there in time?"

"It's two hundred miles," Billie said. "Say four hours. You can make it with an hour to spare."

Bern said, "More if you take my car. It has a top speed of a hundred and fifteen."

"You'd lend me your car?"

"We've saved each other's lives. A car is nothing. But you have a second problem."

"What's that?"

"I was followed here."

3:00 A.M. Anthony sat at the wheel of his Cadillac, a block from the diner. It appeared to be a cop hangout: Two patrol cars were parked outside, along with Billie's red Thunderbird and Bern's Continental.

Ackie Horwitz had been stationed outside Bern Rothsten's apartment. When Bern left in the middle of the night, Ackie had followed. Now Ackie came out of the diner carrying a container of coffee and a candy bar. He came to Anthony's window. "Lucas is in there," he said. "He has on a black coat and a black hat now. Rothsten is with him, and the girl."

"I'll wait here until Luke comes out; then I'll follow him."

"Gotcha." Ackie went to his motorcycle and left.

The door of the diner opened. Billie came out first. Next came a man in a black coat and black hat: Luke. They went to the red

Thunderbird. A man in a trench coat got into the Lincoln. The T-bird moved away, followed by the Lincoln. Anthony waited a few seconds, then pulled out.

Billie headed west, and the Lincoln followed. They came to Fourteenth Street and stopped for a red light. When the light turned green, Billie's Thunderbird suddenly shot forward, while the Lincoln remained stationary. Cursing, Anthony swung around the Lincoln and raced after the T-bird.

Billie zigzagged through the neighborhood at the back of the White House, shooting red lights and driving the wrong way on one-way streets. Anthony did the same, but the Cadillac could not match the T-bird for maneuverability, and she drew away.

Then luck intervened. Screeching around a corner, Billie ran into a flood. Water was gushing out of a curbside drain, and the entire width of the road was two or three inches under. She lost control. The Thunderbird swung around in a wide arc and came to a halt slewed across the street. Anthony pulled across its front, blocking it in. Billie could not get away.

Anthony ran to the passenger side. "Get out of the car!" he yelled, drawing his gun. The door opened, and the figure in the black coat and hat got out.

Anthony saw immediately that it was not Luke, but Bern. Rage boiled up inside him. "You idiot!" he screamed at Bern. "You don't know what you've done!"

Bern was infuriatingly calm. "Then tell me, Anthony," he said. "What have I done?"

Anthony turned away and stuffed the gun back into his coat.

4:30 A.M. Bern said to Billie, "You're in love with Luke, aren't you?"

They were sitting in her car outside his building. She did not want to go in; she was impatient to get home to Larry and Becky-Ma.

"In love?" she said evasively. "Am I?"

"It's okay," he said. "I realized long ago that you should have married Luke. You loved me, too, but in a different way."

That was true. Her love for Bern was a gentle, calm feeling. With Luke she felt a sexual craving that left her weak and helpless with desire.

"Luke's married," she said. "And he's the faithful type."

Bern laughed. "I guess you're right." He kissed her cheek and got out of the car. "If you hear from him tomorrow, call me."

"Okay."

Bern walked into the building, and Billie drove off.

She crossed the Memorial Bridge, skirted the National Cemetery, and zigzagged through the suburban streets to her home. She reversed into the driveway, a habit she had developed because she was usually in a hurry when leaving. She entered the house, hung her coat on the hall stand, and went straight upstairs to check on Larry.

When she saw the empty bed, she screamed.

"Larry!" she yelled at the top of her voice. "Where are you?" She went into every room. She looked in the garage and the yard. Going back inside, she went into every room again, opening closets and checking under beds, looking into every space large enough to hold a seven-year-old.

Becky-Ma came out of her bedroom. "What's happening?" she said shakily.

"Where's Larry?" Billie shouted.

"In his bed, I thought," she said.

Fighting down panic, Billie went into Larry's bedroom and studied it. There were no signs of struggle. The teddy-bear pajamas Larry had worn last night were neatly folded. His school clothes were gone. It looked as if he had gone with someone he trusted.

Anthony.

At first she felt relief. Anthony would not harm Larry. But then she thought again. Wouldn't he? She had to get Larry back fast.

She ran downstairs to call Anthony. Before she got to the phone, it rang. She snatched it up. "Yes?"

"This is Anthony."

"How could you be so cruel?" she screamed

"I have to know where Luke is," he said coolly. "It's important."

"He's gone—" She stopped herself. "Where's Larry?"

"He's with me. He's fine. Don't worry. Just tell me what I need to know, and everything will be all right."

"When I see my son, I'll tell you where Luke is."

"Don't you trust me?"

"Is that a joke?"

He sighed. "Okay. Meet me at the Jefferson Memorial at seven o'clock."

She checked her watch. It was after six. "I'll be there."

She hung up.

"What is it?" Becky-Ma said. "What's going on?"

Billie tried to give an impression of calm. "Larry's with Anthony. I'm going to pick him up now."

She went upstairs. In her bedroom she stood on a chair and took a small suitcase from on top of the wardrobe. She placed the case on the bed and opened it. Inside was a .45 Colt Automatic.

They had all been issued Colts in the war. She had kept hers as a souvenir, but some instinct made her clean and oil it regularly. There was a box of bullets in the case. She loaded the gun and chambered a round.

Then she ran out of the house and jumped into her car.

6:30 A.M. It was still dark when Luke arrived at Newport News and pulled Bern's Lincoln into the parking lot next to the closed airport terminal.

He had been up more than twenty-four hours, and he felt desperately weary, but his mind was racing. He was in love with Billie. Now that he was two hundred miles away from her, he could admit that to himself. But what about Elspeth? Why had he married her? He had asked Billie, and she had refused to answer. He checked his watch. He had more than an hour until takeoff. He got out of the car and went to the phone booth.

Elspeth picked up fast, as if she was already awake. Suddenly he felt awkward. "Uh, good morning, Elspeth."

"I'm so glad you called," she said. "I've been worried. Are you okay?"

"Yes, I'm fine now. Basically, Anthony caused me to lose my memory by giving me a combination of electric shock and drugs."

"Good God. Why would he do a thing like that?"

"He says I'm a Soviet spy."

"That's absurd. Where are you calling from?"

He hesitated. His enemies might easily have tapped Elspeth's phone. "I don't really want to say in case someone is listening."

"All right, I understand. What are you going to do next?"

"I need to find out what Anthony wanted me to forget."

"How will you do that?"

"I'd rather not say over the phone."

"Well, I'm sorry you can't tell me."

"Matter of fact, I called to ask you some things. Why can't we have children?"

"We've been trying since we got married. Last year you went to a fertility specialist, but he couldn't find anything wrong. A few weeks ago I saw a woman doctor in Atlanta. She ran some tests. We're waiting for the results."

"Would you tell me how we came to get married?"

"Well, I didn't see you for years. Then we met again in 1954, in Washington," she began. "I was still with the CIA. You were working at the jet propulsion laboratory in Pasadena, but you flew in for Peg's wedding. We were seated together at the rehearsal dinner. We talked and talked—it was as if thirteen years had never happened. Afterward we went back to my apartment and I seduced you. I used the oldest trick in the book."

1954 ▐▐ ▌

Elspeth's place was small and uncluttered, with a few pieces of angular modern furniture. Luke made martinis, and Elspeth started to cook spaghetti in the tiny kitchen. Luke told her about his job.

"I'm so happy for you," she said with generous enthusiasm. "Even back at Harvard you always wanted to explore outer space."

"In those days most people thought it was a foolish dream of science-fiction writers," he said, smiling.

"I guess we still can't be sure it will happen."

"I think we can," he said. "The big problems were all solved by German scientists in the war. They built rockets that could be fired in Holland and land on London."

"I was there," she said. "We called them buzz bombs." She shuddered briefly, remembering herself walking through the dark streets as bombs fell around her. "So our missiles are based on the German buzz bombs?"

"Yes. Their V2 rocket, to be exact." Luke was not supposed to talk about his work, but Elspeth probably had a higher security rating than he did, and she showed more interest in rocketry than any other girl he had ever met.

She asked him to watch the stove while she freshened up. He took off his jacket and tie, then stirred the sauce with a wooden spoon.

He heard her call out, "Luke, could you come here?"

He stepped into the bathroom. Elspeth's dress hung on the back of the door, and she stood in a strapless peach-colored brassiere and matching half-slip. Her hand was to her face. "I got soap in my eye, damn it," she said. "Would you try to wash it out?"

"Bend down. Get your face close to the washbasin," Luke said, encouraging her with his left hand between her shoulder blades. The pale skin of her back was soft and warm to his touch. He cupped water in his right hand and raised it to her eye.

"That helps," she said.

He rinsed her eye until she said the stinging had stopped. Then he stood her upright and patted her face with a dry towel. Her lips parted in a smile. It was the easiest thing in the world to kiss her. She kissed him back, hesitantly at first; then she put her hands behind his neck and pulled his face to hers and kissed him hard.

After a while he picked her up, stepped into the bedroom, and laid her on the bed. When they made love, it was slow and intense. "I've wanted this for so long," she whispered into his ear, and then she cried out with pleasure and lay back, exhausted.

Elspeth fell into a deep sleep, but Luke lay awake, thinking about his life. He had always wanted a family, yet here he was, thirty-four and single. Since the war his career had been his priority, but that was not the real reason he was unmarried. The truth was that only two women had ever touched his heart—Billie and Elspeth. Billie had deceived him, but Elspeth was here beside him.

At daybreak he got up and made coffee. He brought it into the bedroom on a tray and found Elspeth sitting up in bed, looking sleepily delectable. She smiled happily at him.

"I have something to ask you," he said. He sat on the edge of the bed and took her hand. "Will you marry me?"

■ ■ ▮

7:00 A.M.   Anthony drove up to the Jefferson Memorial with Larry sitting in the front seat between him and Pete. It was still dark, and the area was deserted.

The monument was a double circle of pillars with a domed roof. It stood on a high platform approached by steps at the rear. "The statue is nineteen feet high," he told Larry. "You can't see it from here, but it's inside those pillars."

"We should have come in the daytime," Larry said.

Anthony had taken Larry out before, and they always had a good time. But today Larry knew something was wrong. It was too early, and he wanted his mother.

Anthony opened the door. "Stay here, Larry, while I talk to Pete," he said. The two men got out. Their breath misted in the cold air.

Anthony said to Pete, "I'll wait here. You take the kid and show him the monument. Stay on this side so that she'll see him when she arrives."

Anthony opened the car door. "Come on, Larry. Uncle Pete's going to show you the statue."

Larry got out. With careful politeness he said, "After we've seen it, I think I'd like to go home."

Pete took the child's hand, and they walked around the monument toward the steps at the back. A minute later they appeared in front of the pillars, lit by the car's headlights.

A few moments later the Thunderbird arrived. It parked twenty yards from Anthony's Cadillac, and a small, slight figure jumped out, leaving the engine running.

"Hello, Billie," said Anthony.

She looked from him to the monument and saw Pete and Larry up on the raised platform. She stood frozen, staring.

Anthony walked toward her. "Don't try anything dramatic. It would upset Larry."

"Don't talk to me about upsetting him, you bastard." Her voice cracked with strain. She was near to tears.

"I had to do this."

"Nobody has to do something like this."

It was a waste of time arguing with her, he decided. "Where's Luke?"

After a pause she said, "Luke caught a plane to Huntsville."

Anthony breathed a deep sigh. He had what he needed. "Why Huntsville?" he asked. "Why not Florida?"

"I don't know."

Anthony tried to read her face, but it was too dark. "You're holding something back."

"I don't care what you think. I'm going to take my son and leave."

"No, you're not. We're keeping him for a while."

Billie's voice was a cry of anguish. "Why? I've told you where Luke went!"

"There may be other ways you can help us."

"It's not fair!"

"You'll live." He turned away.

That was his mistake.

With her right shoulder Billie hit him in the small of the back. She weighed only one hundred and twenty pounds, but she had surprise and rage on her side. He stumbled and fell forward, coming down on his hands and knees. He grunted with surprise and pain.

Billie took the Colt from her coat pocket. As Anthony tried to get up, she dropped to one knee and shoved the barrel of the gun into his mouth. She felt a tooth break.

"I'm going to take the gun out of your mouth," she said. "You're going to call to your colleague and tell him what I say." She took the gun out of Anthony's mouth. "Now," she said. "Call him."

Anthony hesitated, and she touched the barrel of the pistol to his left eye.

"Pete!" he shouted.

Anthony and Billie were outside the range of the headlights.

"What's happening?" Pete called. "I can't see you."

Billie shouted, "Larry, this is Mom. Get in the T-bird!"

Pete grabbed Larry's arm.

"The man won't let me!" Larry screamed.

"Uncle Anthony's going to tell the man to let you go." She pressed the gun barrel harder into Anthony's eye.

"All right." Anthony shouted, "Let the kid go!"

"Okay." Pete released Larry's arm.

Larry ran toward Billie. "Not this way," she said, struggling to keep her voice calm. "Get in the car, quickly."

Larry ran to the Thunderbird and jumped in.

Billie hit Anthony on both sides of his face with the gun as hard as she could. He lay groaning. She said, "Remember that if you're ever tempted to kidnap a child again."

She backed toward her car, keeping the gun on him. Then she stuffed it inside her jacket and got in the car. "Are you okay?" she asked Larry.

He started to cry. She shoved the gearshift into first and tore away.

8:00 A.M. Bern poured milk over Larry's cornflakes while Billie beat up an egg for French toast. They were giving their child comfort food, but Billie felt the adults needed comfort, too.

"I'm going to kill that s.o.b. Anthony," Bern muttered. "I swear I'll kill him."

Billie was worried. "I'm afraid Anthony may try to kill Luke first," she said. "I didn't think it was possible a few hours ago, but now I know better."

Bern dipped a slice of white bread into the egg mixture. "Luke won't kill easy."

"But he thinks he's escaped. He doesn't know I've told Anthony where he is. I have to find a way to warn him."

"Leave a message at the Huntsville airport?"

"It's not reliable enough. I think I have to go there myself."

Billie picked up the airline guide. Flight 271 left Washington at nine, landing at Huntsville four minutes before noon. Luke's flight did not land until two twenty-three. She could be waiting for him at the airport. "I can do it," she said, but she hesitated, looking at Larry.

"He'll be okay. I'll take care of him."

Bern was a trained agent and could protect his kid from just about anything. Billie made a decision.

"Mommy has to go now," she said to Larry. "You have a fun day with Daddy, and maybe he'll take you swimming."

"Okay."

As she went out, she heard Bern say, "I bet you couldn't eat a slice of that French toast."

"I could too!" Larry replied.

PART 5

Explorer's elliptical orbit will take it as far as 1800 miles into space and swing it back within 187 miles of the earth's surface. Orbiting speed of the satellite is 18,000 miles per hour.

10:45 A.M. Luke's plane refueled at Winston-Salem, and the passengers got off for a few minutes. Luke called Huntsville from the terminal and got his secretary, Marigold, on the phone.

"Dr. Lucas," she said. "Are you okay?"

"I'm fine, but I only have a minute or two, so I'll make this quick. Is the launch still scheduled for tonight?"

"Yes. Ten thirty."

"I'm on my way to Huntsville. My plane lands at two twenty-three. I'm trying to figure out what I did there on Monday. Do you have any idea where I went?"

"Well now, let me see. I met you at the airport in an army car and brought you here to the base. You went into the computation lab, then drove yourself down to the south end."

"What's there, at the south end?"

"The Engineering Building. You sometimes work there."

"And then?"

"You asked me to drive you to your home. I waited in the car while you stepped inside for a minute or two. Then I took you to the airport."

Desperately Luke cast about for another line of questioning. "Was I carrying anything?"

"Just your little suitcase. Oh, and a file."

"A file?" he said. He swallowed.

A stewardess interrupted. "Time to board the aircraft, please, Dr. Lucas."

"Was it any special kind of file?"

"A standard army file folder—thin cardboard, buff-colored."

"And did I still have this file when you took me to the airport?"

The stewardess returned. "Dr. Lucas, please board the plane."

"I'm coming, I'm coming." He repeated his question to Marigold.

"I'm trying to remember. You know, I don't believe you had it at the airport. I'm picturing you walking away from me, and I see you have your bag in one hand, and in the other . . . nothing."

"Are you sure?"

"Yes. You must have left it either at the base or at home."

Luke's mind was racing. The file was the reason for his trip to Huntsville. He felt sure. It contained the secret he had found out, the one that Anthony was so desperate for him to forget. He had stashed it somewhere for safekeeping. Now, if he could find it, he could discover the secret.

"I think that file could be very important. Could you look around and see if it's there?"

"My Lord, Dr. Lucas, this is the army! Don't you know there must be a million of them buff-colored file folders here?"

"Just check around. As soon as I land at Huntsville, I'll go to the house and search there. Then if I don't find it, I'll come to the base."

Luke hung up and ran for the plane.

11:00 A.M. The MATS flight to Huntsville was full of generals. MATS was the military airline. Anthony wore sunglasses to conceal the two black eyes Billie had given him. His lip had stopped bleeding, and the broken tooth showed only when he talked.

Should he simply take the first opportunity to kill Luke? It was temptingly simple. But he worried that he did not know exactly what Luke was up to. He had to make a decision. However, by the time he boarded the plane, he had been awake for forty-eight hours straight, and he fell asleep. He dreamed he was twenty-one again, there were new leaves on the tall trees in Harvard Yard, and a life full of glorious possibilities stretched before him like an open road. Next thing he knew, Pete was shaking him as a corporal opened the aircraft door, and he woke up inhaling a warm Alabama breeze.

Huntsville had a civilian airport, but MATS flights came down on the airstrip within Redstone Arsenal.

"I'm going to make some inquiries at the base," he said to Pete. "I want you to go to the airport and keep watch. If Luke arrives, try to reach me here."

At the edge of the airstrip a young man in the uniform of a lieutenant waited with a card that read MR. CARROLL, STATE DEPARTMENT. Anthony shook his hand.

"Colonel Hickam's compliments, sir," the lieutenant said, and pointed to an olive-drab Ford.

"That'll be fine," Anthony said. He had called the base before catching his plane, brazenly pretending he was under orders from CIA director Allen Dulles.

"Colonel Hickam would be glad if you would drop by headquarters at your convenience." The lieutenant handed Anthony a map. "The headquarters building is marked on the map. And we have a message asking you to call Mr. Carl Hobart in Washington."

"Thank you, Lieutenant. Where's Dr. Claude Lucas's office?"

"That'll be the computation laboratory."

"Does Dr. Lucas have a secretary?"

"Yes. Mrs. Marigold Clark."

"Lieutenant, this is my colleague Pete Maxell. If he needs to reach me here at the base, what's the best way?"

The lieutenant looked at Pete. "Sir, you could leave a message at Colonel Hickam's office and I would try to get it to Mr. Carroll."

"Good enough," Anthony said, and he got into the Ford. He checked the map and started out. It was a typical army base. Arrow-straight roads ran through rough woodland, broken by neat rectangles of lawn, close-cropped like a conscript's haircut. The buildings were all flat-roofed structures of tan brick. He easily found the computation lab.

He went into the building. In an outer office were three small desks. Two were vacant. The third was occupied by a Negro woman of about fifty. "Good afternoon," he said.

She looked up. "Hello. How can I help you?"

"I'm from Colonel Hickam's office," he said. "I'm looking for Marigold Clark."

"That's me."

"I guess you know that Dr. Lucas is on his way here."

"He called me this morning. His plane lands at two twenty-three."

That was useful. "So he'll be here around three."

"Not necessarily. He said he's going home first."

That was perfect. Anthony could hardly believe his luck. Luke was going straight to his house. Anthony could go there and wait, then shoot Luke as soon as he walked in the door. With Elspeth in Florida, the corpse might not be found for days.

"Thank you," he said to Marigold. He left the room before she could ask his name.

He returned to the car and drove to the headquarters building. He found Colonel Hickam's office. The colonel was out, but a sergeant showed him to an empty room with a phone. He called Q Building but did not speak to his boss, Carl Hobart. Instead, he asked for Carl's superior, George Cooperman.

"Did you shoot at someone last night?" said Cooperman, his smoker's voice sounding even more gravelly than usual.

"There's no proof. I picked up all the slugs."

"Did you hit anybody?"

"Unfortunately not."

"You're supposed to come back immediately."

"Then it's a good thing I didn't talk to you."

"Listen, Anthony, I always cut you as much slack as I can, because you get results. But I can't do any more for you on this one. You're on your own from here, buddy."

"That's how I like it."

"Good luck."

Anthony sat staring at the phone. He could disobey orders for only so long. He needed to wrap this up fast.

He called Cape Canaveral and got Elspeth on the phone. "Have you talked to Luke?" he asked her.

"He called me at six thirty this morning." She sounded shaky. "He wouldn't say what he intended to do, but he knows you were responsible for his amnesia."

"He's on his way to Huntsville. I'm at Redstone Arsenal now. I'm going to your house to wait for him there. Will I be able to get in?"

"There's a key under the bougainvillea pot in the backyard. Take care of Luke, won't you?"

"I'll do my best."

As he stood up to go, the phone rang. He wondered whether to answer. It might be Hobart. But Hobart did not know he was in Colonel Hickam's office. He picked up.

It was Pete. "Dr. Josephson's here," he said. "She just got off a plane. She's sitting in the terminal, like she's waiting."

"Damn her. She's come to warn him that we're here. You have to get her out of there."

"How?"

"I don't care. Just get rid of her!"

12:00 NOON   Huntsville airport was small but busy. As soon as she arrived, Billie checked on Luke's flight and learned it was running almost an hour late. She had three hours to kill.

She got a candy bar and a Dr Pepper from a machine. She put down the attaché case that contained her Colt and stood leaning against a wall, thinking. How was she going to handle this?

As she was racking her brains, a girl in a Capital Airlines uniform approached her. "Are you Dr. Josephson?"

"Yes."

"I have a phone message for you." She handed over an envelope.

Billie frowned. Who knew she was here? "Thanks," she muttered. Tearing the envelope open, she read, "Please call Dr. Lucas at Huntsville JE 6-4231."

She was bewildered. Could Luke be here already? There was only one way to find out. She found a pay phone and dialed the number. A man's voice answered: "Components test lab."

"Dr. Claude Lucas, please."

"Just one moment." After a pause the man came back. "Dr. Lucas stepped out for a minute. Who is this, please?"

"Dr. Bilhah Josephson. I have a message to call him."

"Oh, Dr. Josephson. I'm so glad we found you. Dr. Lucas is very concerned to contact you."

"What's he doing here? I thought he was still in the air."

"Army security pulled him off the plane at Norfolk, Virginia, and laid on a special flight. He's been here more than an hour. Can you get yourself down to us?"

"Where are you?"

"The lab is about an hour out of town on the Chattanooga Road."

Billie took a notebook out of her bag. "Give me directions." Then, remembering her southern manners, she added, "If you would, please."

3:00P.M. The landscape gradually became wilder and the roads narrower. Billie wondered why the components testing laboratory was an hour away from the base. Perhaps it was for safety reasons.

The disparity between what she expected and what she saw from behind the wheel of her rented Ford grew until she finally threw up her hands in despair. She was furious with herself and with the fool who had given her directions.

After a couple more miles she came upon a dilapidated feed store with a pay phone outside. She pulled over. She still had Luke's message with the phone number. She put a dime in the slot and dialed. The phone was answered immediately.

"May I speak to Dr. Claude Lucas?" she said.

"You got the wrong number, honey."

"Isn't this Huntsville JE 6-4231?"

"Yep. You've reached a pay phone in Huntsville airport."

"A pay phone?"

"Yes, ma'am."

Billie began to realize she had been hoodwinked. Luke had not been taken off his plane in Norfolk and put on an army flight. That whole story was a lie designed to get her out of the way. With despair in her heart she wondered if he was still alive.

If he was, maybe she could still warn him. She racked her brains. Luke had a secretary at the base, she remembered. A name like a flower. . . .

Marigold.

She called Redstone Arsenal and asked to speak to Dr. Lucas's secretary. A woman with a slow Alabama voice came on the line.

"Is this Marigold?"

"Yes."

"I'm Dr. Josephson, a friend of Dr. Lucas's. We've spoken before, I think. My name is Billie."

"Oh, sure, I remember. How are you?"

"Worried. I need to get a message to Luke urgently. Is he with you?"

"No, ma'am. He went to his house."

"If you see him or if he calls you, would you give him a message from me? Tell him Anthony is in town. He'll understand."

"I'll do that, Doctor."

"Thank you." Billie hung up.

4:00 P.M. Anthony heard a car. He looked out the front window of Luke's house and saw a Huntsville taxicab pull up at the curb. He thumbed the safety catch on his gun.

The phone rang. Anthony stared at it in horror. He was paralyzed by indecision. He looked out the window again and saw Luke getting out of the cab. The call could be trivial, or it could be vital information.

He snatched the phone up. "Yes?"

"This is Elspeth." Her voice was low. "He's looking for a file he stashed in Huntsville on Monday."

Anthony understood in a flash. Luke had xeroxed the blueprints he had brought to Washington. He had made a clandestine stop in Huntsville to hide the copies.

"Who else knows about this?"

"His secretary, Marigold, told me."

Luke was paying the driver. Anthony was running out of time.

"The file's not here," he said. "I've searched the house from top to bottom."

"Then it must be at the base."

"I'll have to follow him while he looks for it."

Luke was approaching the front door.

"I'm out of time," Anthony said, and slammed down the phone.

He heard the key scrape in the lock as he ran through the hall and into the kitchen. He went out the back door and closed it softly. The key was still in the outside of the lock. He turned it silently, bent down, and slipped it under the flowerpot.

4:30 P.M. On top of the TV in the living room was a bamboo picture frame containing a photograph of a strikingly beautiful redhead in an ivory silk wedding dress. Beside her, wearing a gray cutaway, was Luke. He studied Elspeth in the picture. She could have been a movie star.

When he had first seen the outside of the house and the wisteria climbing the pillars of the shady veranda, it had gladdened his heart. But the inside was all hard edges and shiny surfaces and bright paint. Everything was too neat. He knew suddenly that he liked to live in a house where books spilled off the shelves, and the dog was asleep right across the hallway, and a tricycle stood upside down in the driveway.

No kids lived in this house. There were no pets, either. It was like an advertisement in a women's magazine.

He began to search. A buff-colored file folder should be easy enough to find. He sat at the desk in the study and looked through the drawers. He found nothing.

Upstairs, he opened the closet and saw, with pleasure, the rack of navy blue and gray suits and tweed sport coats. He had been wearing this stolen suit for more than twenty-four hours, and he was tempted to take five minutes to shower and change into some of his own clothes. But he resisted. There was no time to spare.

He searched the house thoroughly. Everywhere he looked, he learned something about himself and his wife. They liked Glenn Miller and Frank Sinatra, they read Hemingway and Scott Fitzgerald, they drank Dewar's Scotch and ate All-Bran.

At last he gave up. In a kitchen drawer he found keys to the black Chrysler 300C in the garage. He would drive to the base and search there.

Before leaving, he picked up the mail in the hall and shuffled the envelopes. Desperate for a clue, he ripped them open. One was from a doctor in Atlanta.

Dear Mrs. Lucas,

Following your routine checkup, the results of your blood tests have come back from the lab, and everything is normal. However, you are underweight, you suffer insomnia, and when I saw you, you had obviously been crying. These are symptoms of depression. Depression may be caused by changes in body chemistry, by unresolved mental problems such as marital difficulties, or by childhood trauma such as the early death of a parent. In your case, I have no doubt that the condition is related to the tubal ligation you underwent in 1954.

Luke stopped reading. Tubal ligation was a method of sterilization for women who did not want to have children. When he had asked Elspeth why they could not have children, she had said she didn't know. That was a lie. She knew perfectly well why they could not have children—she had been sterilized. He looked at the next paragraph.

This procedure may cause depression at any age, but in your case, having it six weeks before your wedding . . .

Luke's mouth fell open. Elspeth's deception had begun *before* they got married. Their marriage had been a lie. He had wanted children, yet children were the very thing she had deliberately denied him. And she had lied about it for four years.

He must be a poor judge of people, he thought. He had remained close to Anthony, who had tried to kill him, yet had broken with Bern, who had been a faithful friend. He had quarreled with Billie and married Elspeth, yet Billie had dropped everything to help him, and Elspeth had deceived him.

A large moth bumped into the closed window and startled Luke out of his reverie. He looked at his watch and was shocked to see that it was past seven. Time was pressing. The rocket was scheduled to launch in three hours. If he hoped to unravel the mystery of his life, he needed to start with the mysterious file. It was not here, so it had to be at Redstone Arsenal. Maybe that would be the beginning of understanding.

7:30 P.M. There were no lights on in Luke's house when Billie stopped by. But what did that mean? There were three possibilities. One: The house was empty. Two: Anthony was sitting in the dark, waiting to shoot Luke. Three: Luke was lying in a pool of blood, dead. The uncertainty made her crazy with fear.

She had screwed up royally, maybe fatally. A few hours ago she had been well placed to warn Luke and save him; then she had allowed herself to be diverted by a simple ruse. It had taken her hours to get back to Huntsville and find Luke's house. She had no idea whether her warning message had reached him. She was furious with herself for being so incompetent, and terrified that Luke might have died because of her failure.

What should she do next? One person who might have some answers was Marigold.

She found a pay phone and called information. She asked for a number for Marigold Clark. She was afraid Marigold might not have a phone, but after a moment the voice on the line gave her a Huntsville number.

A man answered. "Marigold's at choir practice," he told Billie.

"I need to talk to her real bad," she said. "Do you think it would be all right if I interrupted the choir for a minute?"

"Guess so. They're at the Calvary Gospel Church on Mill Street."

Billie went back to her car. She found Mill Street on the Hertz map and drove there. The church was a fine brick building in a poor neighborhood. There were only about thirty men and women with the choir, but they sounded like a hundred. They clapped and swayed as they sang, and a large woman with her back to Billie conducted vigorously.

They finished on a high chord, and the conductor looked around and saw her. "Take a short break," she said to the choir.

"I'm sorry to interrupt," Billie said. "I need to talk to Marigold Clark."

"I'm Marigold Clark," the woman said warily.

"We spoke on the phone earlier. I'm Billie Josephson."

"Oh, hi, Dr. Josephson."

Billie said, "Have you heard from Luke?"

"Not since this morning. I expected him to show up at the base, but he didn't. Do you think he's all right?"

"I don't know. I went to his house, but there was no one there. I'm afraid he might have been killed."

Marigold shook her head in bewilderment. "I've worked for the army twenty years, and I never heard of anything like this."

"He's in great danger." Billie looked at Marigold. "Do you believe me?"

Marigold said, "Yes, ma'am, I do."

"Then you have to help me," Billie told her.

9:30 P.M. Anthony was at Redstone Arsenal, sitting in his army Ford, watching the door of the computation laboratory. Luke was inside, searching for his file folder. Anthony knew he would not find it, because he had already searched the lab.

Time was on Anthony's side. Every minute that passed made

Luke less dangerous. The rocket would be launched in one hour.
Could Luke ruin everything in an hour?

The door to the lab opened. Luke emerged and approached the
black Chrysler parked at the curb. He got in and drove off.
Anthony switched on his headlights and followed.

After about a mile Luke slowed in front of a long one-story building and pulled into its parking lot.

LUKE had felt sure he would find the folder in the computation
lab, where his office was, but he found nothing. There was one
more possibility. Marigold had said that he also went to the Engineering Building on Monday. It was his last hope.

Engineering had an atmosphere quite different from that of the
computation lab. Computation was spotlessly clean for the sake of
the massive computers. Engineering was scruffy by comparison,
smelling of oil and rubber.

Luke hurried along a corridor. At the end he came upon a large,
open room with half a dozen steel tables. On the far side an open
door led into a laboratory. Along the wall was a row of lockers, each
with a nameplate. One was his. Maybe he had stashed the file here.

The locker was padlocked. He took out his key ring and found a
likely key. It worked, and he opened the door. Inside was a hard hat
on a high shelf. Below that, hanging from a hook, were blue overalls and on the floor a pair of black rubber boots.

There, beside the boots, was a buff-colored army file folder. This
had to be what he was looking for.

The folder contained a large brown envelope, already ripped
open. Inside were some papers. When he took them out, he could
see immediately they were blueprints for parts of a rocket. His heart
hammering in his chest, he moved quickly to one of the steel tables
and spread the papers out under a lamp. After a few moments'
rapid study, he knew without doubt that the drawings showed the
Jupiter C rocket's self-destruct mechanism.

He was horrified.

Every rocket had a self-destruct mechanism so that if it should
veer off course and threaten human life, it could be blown up in

midair. In the main stage of the *Jupiter* rocket a Primacord igniter rope ran the length of the missile. A firing cap was attached to its top end, and two wires stuck out of the cap. If a voltage was applied across the wires, the cap would ignite the Primacord, causing the fuel to burn and be dispersed, destroying the rocket.

The explosion was triggered by a coded radio signal. The blueprints showed twin plugs—one for the transmitter on the ground and the other for the receiver in the satellite. One turned the radio signal into a complex code; the other received the signal and applied the voltage across the twin wires.

A separate diagram, not a blueprint but a hastily drawn sketch, showed exactly how the plugs were wired, so that anyone having the diagram could duplicate the signal. It was brilliant, Luke realized. The saboteurs had no need of explosives or timing devices, nor did they need access to the rocket. The radio signal could be broadcast from a transmitter miles away.

The envelope was addressed to Theo Packman at the Vanguard Motel. Presumably Packman was, even now, somewhere in Cocoa Beach with a radio transmitter, ready to blow up the rocket seconds after it took off.

Luke could prevent that. It was ten fifteen. He had time to call Cape Canaveral and have the launch postponed. He snatched up the phone.

A voice said, "Put it down, Luke." Luke turned slowly. Anthony stood in the doorway holding a gun, pointing it at him.

Luke stared at the man whom he had so misjudged. "How long have you been working for Moscow?" he asked. "Since the war?"

"Longer. Since Harvard."

"Why?"

Anthony's lips twisted into a strange smile. "For a better world."

Once upon a time, Luke knew, a lot of sensible people had believed in the Soviet system. But he also knew their faith had been undermined by the realities of life under Stalin. "You still believe that?" he said incredulously.

"Sort of. It's still the best hope, despite all that has happened." Anthony raised the gun with a steady hand, aiming at Luke's heart.

Luke dropped behind the steel table.

The silenced gun coughed, and there was a metallic clang as the bullet hit the steel.

Luke rolled under the table and lifted himself into a stoop so that his back was against the underside of the table. Grabbing the two legs at one end, he heaved, standing upright at the same time. The table came up off the floor and teetered forward. As it toppled, Luke blindly ran with it, hoping to collide with Anthony. The table crashed to the floor, but Anthony was not beneath it.

Luke tripped and fell, banging his head on a steel leg. Dazed, he rolled sideways and came up into a sitting position. He looked up to see Anthony facing him, braced with his feet apart, aiming his gun two-handed. Luke was now, literally, a sitting target.

Then a voice rang out, "Anthony, stop!" It was Billie.

Anthony froze. Luke slowly turned his head. Billie stood by the door, an automatic pistol in her hand, leveled at Anthony. Behind her was a middle-aged Negro woman, looking shocked and scared.

"Drop the gun!" Billie yelled.

Slowly Anthony lowered his arms, but he did not drop the gun.

"Drop it or I'll shoot!"

Anthony smiled. "No, you won't," he said. Still pointing the gun at the floor, he began to walk backward, making for the open door that led into the laboratory. "You don't believe that a rocket is worth more than a human life, even if it's a traitor's life."

"Don't test me," Billie cried.

Anthony turned and darted through the doorway.

Luke leaped to his feet. The clock on the wall said ten twenty-nine. He had a minute left to warn Cape Canaveral. He picked up the phone and dialed.

"This is Luke," he said. "Give me the launch conductor. Quick!"

There was a pause. In the background he could hear the count-down in the blockhouse: "Twenty, nineteen, eighteen . . ."

A new voice came on the line, tense and impatient. "This is Willy. What the hell is it, Luke?"

"Someone has the self-destruct code. They're going to blow up the rocket. You have to abort the launch."

The background voice said, "Eleven, ten . . ."

"How do you know?" Willy asked.

"I've found diagrams of the wiring of the coded plugs, and an envelope addressed to someone called Theo Packman."

"That's not proof. I can't cancel the launch on that."

Luke sighed, feeling suddenly fatalistic. "I've told you what I know. The decision is yours."

"Five, four . . ."

"Hell." Willy raised his voice. "Stop the countdown!"

Luke slumped in his chair. He had done it. He glanced up at the anxious faces of Billie and Marigold. "They've aborted the launch," he said.

A new voice came on the line. "Luke? This is Colonel Hide. What the hell is going on?"

"Do you know who Theo Packman is?"

"Yeah. He's a freelance journalist on the missile beat."

"I found an envelope addressed to him containing blueprints of the *Explorer*'s self-destruct system. That's why I persuaded Willy to abort the launch."

"Thank God you did."

"Listen, you have to find this Packman character right now. The envelope was addressed to the Vanguard Motel."

"Got it."

"And Packman was working with someone in the CIA, a double agent called Anthony Carroll. I'm sure of it."

"Okay, I'm on it. I'll call the CIA."

Luke hung up the phone and sat back. He had done all he could. He looked at Billie, who said, "What next?"

"I guess I'll go to Cape Canaveral. The launch will be rescheduled for the same time tomorrow. I'd like to be there."

"Me, too."

Luke smiled. "You deserve it. You saved the rocket." He stood up and embraced her.

"Your life, you idiot. To heck with the rocket, I saved your life." She kissed him.

Marigold coughed. "You've missed the last plane from Huntsville airport," she said. "Next one is a MATS flight that leaves the base at five thirty a.m. Or there's a train. It stops in Chattanooga around one a.m. You could get there in a couple of hours by car."

Billie said, "I like the train idea."

When they were on the highway, Billie said to Luke, "There's a question we haven't talked about."

"I know," he said. "Who sent the blueprints to Theo Packman?"

"It must be someone inside Cape Canaveral, someone on the scientific team."

"Exactly."

"Do you have any idea who?"

Luke winced. "Yes." With a heart full of grief he said, "I think it was Elspeth."

11:00 P.M. Elspeth could not believe it. The triumph of her life had been within her grasp—and now, just a few seconds before ignition, the launch had been postponed.

She was on the flat roof of an administration building, with a small crowd of secretaries and clerks, watching the floodlit launchpad through binoculars. Their fears had grown as the minutes ticked by and the rocket remained on the ground, and now a collective groan went up as technicians in overalls swarmed out of their bunkers and began the complex procedure of standing down all systems.

Elspeth left the others without a word and walked back to hangar R. When she reached her office, the phone was ringing. She snatched it up. "Yes?"

"What's happening?" The voice was Anthony's.

"They've aborted the launch. I don't know why."

"Luke found the papers. He must have called."

"Couldn't you stop him?"

"I had him in my sights—literally—but Billie walked in, armed."

"Is Luke all right?"

"Yes, but Theo's name is on those papers. They'll be on their way to arrest him. You have to find him first."

"Let me think," Elspeth said. "He's on the beach. I know his car. It's a Hudson Hornet."

"Then get going!"

She slammed down the phone and rushed out of the building. She ran across the parking lot and jumped into her white Corvette.

There was no regular road to the beach. From the highway several unpaved tracks led between the dunes to the shore. She planned to take the first, then continue south on the beach. That way she could not miss Theo's car. She had to go slowly for fear of missing the turnoff in the dark. Then she saw a car emerging. It was followed by another and another. Elspeth flashed her left-turn indicator. A constant stream of cars was coming from the beach. The spectators had figured out that the launch was canceled, and they were all going home.

A car behind her honked impatiently. She saw she was not going to be able to get to the beach this way. Could she wait on the highway in the hope of spotting his car? It was too chancy. Her best option was to go to his motel and wait there.

She sped on. There was no sign of police or army security at the Vanguard Motel. She was in time, but Theo's car was not there. She parked near the motel office.

She did not have to wait long. The yellow-and-brown Hudson Hornet pulled in a couple of minutes later. Theo eased into a slot at the far end of the lot and got out, a small man with thinning hair, dressed in chinos and a beach shirt.

Elspeth got out of her car. She opened her mouth to call to him. At that moment two police cruisers arrived. Behind them followed two unmarked cars. They parked across the entry, making it impossible for cars to leave.

At first Theo did not see them. He headed toward the motel office. Elspeth knew in a flash what she had to do. She took a deep breath, then started walking toward him.

As he came close, he recognized her and said loudly, "What the hell happened to the launch?"

Elspeth said in a low voice, "Give me your car keys."

"What for?"

"Look behind you."

He glanced over his shoulder and saw the police cars.

"Stay calm. Give me the keys."

He dropped them into her open hand.

"Keep walking," she said. "The trunk of my car is not locked. Get inside."

"Into the trunk?"

"Yes!" Elspeth went on past him.

She recognized Colonel Hide and another face from Cape Canaveral. With them were four local cops and two tall well-dressed men who might have been FBI agents. None of them were looking her way.

She reached Theo's car and opened the trunk. Inside was the suitcase containing the radio transmitter—powerful and heavy. She dragged it over the lip of the trunk. It hit the ground with a thud. She closed the trunk lid quickly.

She looked around. At the other end of the lot she saw the trunk of her own car closing. Theo was inside. Gritting her teeth, she grasped the handle of the suitcase and lifted. It felt like a box of lead. She walked a few yards, then dropped it. She picked it up with her other hand. She managed another ten yards before she dropped the case again.

Behind her Colonel Hide and his men were crossing the lot toward the motel office. She prayed Hide would not look at her face. The darkness made it less likely he would recognize her.

Giving up carrying the transmitter, she began to drag it across the concrete, hoping the noise would not attract the attention of the cops.

At last she reached her car. As she opened the trunk, one of the uniformed police approached her with a cheerful smile and said, "Help you with that, ma'am?"

Theo's face stared at her from inside the trunk, white and scared.

"I got it," she said. With both hands she heaved up the suitcase and slid it in. There was a quiet grunt of pain from Theo as a corner dug into him. Elspeth slammed the trunk lid.

"Checking out?" the cop said.

"Yeah."

He bent, looked into the car, front and back seats, then straightened up again. "Drive safely."

Elspeth got into her car and started the engine.

The cop went to one of the cruisers and moved it out of the way.

She drove through the gap and pulled onto the highway, then floored the gas pedal.

1:30 A.M. The train pulled slowly out of Chattanooga. In the cramped roomette Luke took off his jacket and hung it up, then perched on the edge of the lower bunk and unlaced his shoes. Billie sat cross-legged on the bunk, watching him. Luke undid his tie, and Billie said, "If this is a striptease, it doesn't have much oomph."

Luke grinned ruefully. They had been forced to share the roomette; only one was available. He was longing to take Billie in his arms, yet he hesitated.

"What?" she said. "What are you thinking?"

"That this is too quick."

"Seventeen years is nothing?"

"To me it's been a couple of days. That's all I can remember. And I'm still married to Elspeth."

Billie nodded solemnly. "But she's been lying to you for years."

"I don't like the feeling that I'm seizing an excuse." She said nothing in reply, so he added, "You don't agree, do you?"

"No. I want to make love to you tonight, but I know you. You've never been one to live for the moment, even when we were kids."

"Is that so bad?"

She smiled. "No. I'm glad you're like that. It makes you rock-solid reliable. If you weren't this way, I guess I wouldn't have . . ." Her voice trailed off.

"What were you going to say?"

She looked him in the eye. "I wouldn't have loved you this much, this long."

She was embarrassed, and covered up by saying, "Why don't you climb up on top and give me room to take off my shoes."

Obediently he climbed the little ladder and lay down on the top bunk. He turned on his side, elbow on the pillow, head resting on his hand. "Losing your memory is like a new start in life," he said. "Every decision you ever made can be revisited."

She kicked off her shoes and stood up. "I'd hate that," she said. With a swift movement she slipped off her black ski pants. Catching his eye, she grinned. "It's okay. You can watch." She reached under her sweater at the back and unfastened her brassiere. Then she drew her left arm out of her sleeve and pulled her bra out of her right sleeve with a conjurer's flourish.

"Bravo," he said.

She gave him a thoughtful look. "So we're going to sleep now?"

"I guess."

"Okay." She stood on the edge of the lower bunk and raised herself to his level, tilting her face to be kissed. He touched her lips with his own. Then she pulled away.

He lay thinking about her lying a few inches below, with her bare legs and her round breasts inside the soft angora sweater. In a few moments he was asleep.

He had an intensely erotic dream and woke up slowly, reluctant to return to the world of rockets and treachery. His shirt was open, and his pants were undone. Billie lay beside him, kissing him. "Are you awake? I don't want to waste this on a guy who's asleep."

He ran his hand along her side. She still had on the sweater, but her panties had gone. "I'm awake," he said thickly.

He reached inside her sweater to touch her breasts. She whispered, "They missed you."

He felt as if he were still half in the dream as the train rocked and Billie kissed him and America flew by the window mile after mile. He wound his arms around her back and held her tightly to convince himself that she was real, not a fantasy. Just as he was thinking that he wanted this to go on forever, his body took control. Waves of pleasure broke over him.

As soon as it was over, she said, "Hold me tight." She buried her face in his neck.

They fell asleep in each other's arms.

PART 6

The countdown reaches zero.

In the blockhouse the launch conductor says, "Firing command!" A crewman pulls a metal ring and twists it. This is the action that fires the rocket. Prevalves open to let the fuel start flowing. The liquid oxygen vent is closed, and the halo of white smoke around the missile suddenly vanishes.

The launch conductor says, "Fuel tanks pressurized."

For the next eleven seconds nothing happens.

8:30 A.M. Anthony flew to Patrick Air Force Base, a few miles south of Cape Canaveral. In his imagination he saw a detachment of FBI agents, with their neat suits and shiny shoes, waiting to arrest him, but there was only Elspeth.

She looked drained. She led him outside to where her Corvette was parked in the hot sun.

As soon as they were inside the car, he said, "How's Theo?"

"Pretty shook, but he'll be okay."

"Where's he hiding?"

"In my motel room. He'll stay there until dark. What about you? Will the CIA give your description to the police?"

"I don't think so. The Agency likes to solve its own problems. They'll think I've gone rogue, and their only concern will be to take me out of circulation before I embarrass them. Once they start listening to Luke and realizing they've been harboring a double agent, that may make them even more eager to hush things up."

"So the three of us are still in play. That gives us a good chance to still pull this thing off."

In twenty-four hours it would be all over, Anthony thought. They would have struck a historic blow for the cause to which they had devoted their lives.

Elspeth glanced across at him. "What will you do after tonight?"

"Go to Moscow. I have everything I need—passports, cash, disguises." Anthony was a major in the KGB. Elspeth had been an agent longer—had in fact recruited Anthony—and was a colonel. "They'll give me some kind of senior advisory role," he went on. "After all, I'll know more about the CIA than anyone else in the Soviet bloc."

"You're not nervous?"

"Sure I am. I'll be lonely at first—no friends, no family, and I don't speak Russian. But maybe I'll get married and raise a brood of little comrades." His flip answers disguised his anxiety. "I decided a long time ago to sacrifice my personal life to something more important."

"I made the same decision, but I'd still be frightened by the thought of moving to Moscow."

"It's not going to happen to you."

"No. They want me to stay in place at all costs."

For the last four years Russian scientists had known everything about the U.S. space program. They saw every important report, all the test results, each blueprint—thanks to Elspeth. She was the reason the Soviets had beaten the Americans into space. She was easily the most important spy of the cold war.

Her work had been done at enormous personal sacrifice, Anthony knew. She had married Luke in order to spy on the space program, but her love for him was genuine, and it had broken her heart to betray him. However, her triumph was the Soviet victory in the space race, which would be sealed tonight. Tonight would make everything worthwhile.

Among the palm trees on the roadside ahead, Anthony saw a huge model of a space rocket above a sign that read STARLITE MOTEL. Elspeth slowed the car and pulled in, parking as far as possible from the road. The rooms were in a two-story building around a large pool, where a few early birds were already sunbathing. Anthony wanted to be seen by as few people as possible, so he pulled his hat low and walked quickly as they went from the car to her upstairs room.

Theo was standing at the window looking out over the ocean. Elspeth introduced the two men. Theo said to Anthony, "How did Luke find me out? Did he explain that to you?"

"He was using the Xerox machine in hangar R. There's a security logbook beside the machine. You have to note the date and the number of copies you made and sign the log. Luke noticed that twelve copies had been signed for by 'WvB,' meaning Wernher von Braun."

Elspeth said, "I always used von Braun's name because no one would question the boss."

Anthony went on. "But Luke knew that von Braun was in Washington that day. He went to the mailroom and found the copies in an envelope addressed to you. He decided he couldn't trust anyone down here, so he flew to Washington. Fortunately, Elspeth called me and I was able to intercept Luke before he told anyone."

Elspeth said, "But now we're right back where we were. Luke has rediscovered what we made him forget."

Anthony asked her, "What do you think the army will do?"

"My guess is they'll change the code."

Anthony said, "If they change the code, we can't make the rocket self-destruct."

"I have to find out what their plan is and figure out a way around it." Elspeth picked up her handbag and slung her jacket over her shoulders. "Buy a car. Drive to the beach as soon as it's dark. Park as near as you can to the Cape Canaveral fence. I'll meet you there." She went out.

After a moment Theo said, "You have to give her credit. She's got a cool nerve."

4:00 P.M. The countdown stood at X minus three hundred and ninety minutes. Elspeth moved about the base restlessly, updating her timetable, alert for any change in procedure. So far she had gained no clue as to how the scientists planned to guard against sabotage, and she was beginning to feel desperate.

Everyone knew Theo Packman was a spy and that Colonel Hide had raided the Vanguard Motel with four cops and two FBI men. The space community quickly linked the news with the last-second cancellation of the launch. The explanation given—that a late weather report had indicated a worsening of the jet stream—was not believed by anyone inside Cape Canaveral's perimeter fence. As midday cooled into afternoon, Elspeth's tension mounted. If she did not learn the plan soon, it would be too late.

Luke had not shown up yet. She was longing to see him and dreading it at the same time. She was working to destroy his dream; her deceit had poisoned their marriage. All the same, she yearned to see his face.

The scientists in the blockhouse were taking a break, eating sandwiches and drinking coffee. She sat next to Willy Fredrickson, her boss, who had his headphones around his neck while he ate a grilled-cheese sandwich. "I guess you know everyone's talking about an attempt to sabotage the rocket," she said conversationally.

Willy looked disapproving, which she took as a sign that he knew exactly what she was talking about. Before he could reply, a technician at the back of the room said, "Willy," and touched his own headphones.

Willy listened to his headset for a minute. "Okay," he said into his mouthpiece. Then he looked up and said, "Stop the countdown. There'll be a ten-minute delay."

Elspeth lifted her notebook and pencil expectantly. "Shall I say why?"

"We have to replace a feed-through capacitor that seems to be chattering."

Capacitors were essential to the tracking system, and chattering—small electrical discharges—could be a sign that the device was going to fail. But Elspeth was not convinced.

She scribbled a note, then got up and left. Outside the blockhouse, the afternoon shadows were lengthening. The white shaft of *Explorer I* stood like a signpost to the heavens. She walked briskly across the sandy lawn to the concrete launchpad and entered the steel cabin in its base that housed the offices and machinery. The gantry supervisor, Harry Lane, was speaking into a phone. When he hung up, she said, "Ten minutes' delay?"

"Could be more."

Writing on her pad, she said, "Reason?"

"Replacing a malfunctioning component," he said.

Just then a technician in oily overalls walked in. "Here's the old one, Harry," he said. In his dirty hand he held a plug.

Elspeth knew it was the receiver for the self-destruct signal.

She walked quickly out the door before Harry could see the triumphant expression on her face. Heart thumping, she hurried to her jeep.

She sat in the driver's seat, working it out. To prevent sabotage, they were replacing the plug. The new one would be wired differently, to work on a different code. A matching broadcast plug must have been fitted to the transmitter. The new plugs had probably been flown here from Huntsville earlier in the day. They always came in sets of four, the duplicate pair being a spare in case of malfunction. It was the duplicate pair that Elspeth had examined last Sunday, when she had sketched the wiring. Now, she thought worriedly, she had to find this duplicate set and do the same all over again.

She drove back to the hangars. She entered hangar D and went to the telemetry room. This was where she had found the duplicate plugs the last time.

When he saw her, Hank Mueller brightened and said, "Eight thousand."

"It's the cube of twenty," Elspeth said.

"Not good enough."

"Okay, it's the sum of four consecutive cubes: 11, 12, 13, 14."

"Very good." He gave her a dime and looked expectant.

Instead, she blurted out, "Do you have the duplicate set of new plugs from Huntsville?"

"No," he replied. "They put them in a safe."

"What safe?"

"They didn't tell me."

"Never mind." She pretended to make a note in her book and went out. She hurried to hangar R. There was only one safe that she knew of. In Colonel Hide's office.

She went to her desk, took an army envelope, and typed on it, "Dr. W. Fredrickson—Eyes Only." Then she slid two blank sheets of paper into the envelope and sealed it.

She went to Hide's office. He was alone, sitting behind his desk. He looked up and smiled. "Elspeth," he said in his slow drawl. "What can I do for you?"

"Would you keep this in the safe for Willy?" She handed him the envelope.

"Sure," he said. He spun around in his chair and opened a cupboard behind him. Looking over his shoulder, Elspeth saw a steel door with a dial. She moved closer. The dial was graduated from 0 to 99, but only multiples of 10 were marked with a figure, the other numbers being indicated by a notch. The first number where Hide stopped the dial was easy: 10. Then he dialed a number just below 30, either 29 or 28. Finally he moved the dial to between 10 and 15. The combination was something like 10-29-13. It must be his birthday, either the twenty-eighth or twenty-ninth of October, in 1911 to 1914. That gave a total of eight possibilities.

Hide opened the door. Inside were two plugs.

Elspeth smiled as he tossed the envelope into the safe and closed the door. "Thank you, Colonel."

Now she had to wait for him to leave his office. She returned to her office just as her phone rang. It was Anthony. "We're leaving here in a few minutes," he said. "Do you have what we need?"

"Not yet, but I will. What kind of car did you buy?"

"A light green Mercury Monterey, fifty-four model."

"I'll recognize it. Just make sure Theo's ready for tonight."

"Okay."

Colonel Hide passed her door. "I gotta go," she said, and hung up.

She went out. Hide stood in the next doorway, talking to the girls in the typing pool. Elspeth loitered for a minute, wishing he would move on. But when he did, he returned to his office and stayed there for two hours.

Elspeth almost went crazy. Her timetable was forgotten. Willy Fredrickson, her boss, would be furious, but what did that matter?

She looked at her wristwatch every few minutes. At eight twenty-five Hide at last walked past. She sprang up and went to her door. She saw him heading down the stairs.

Another man was walking along the corridor toward her. He said, "Elspeth?" Her heart stopped, and she met his eye. It was Luke.

8:30 P.M. He had been dreading this moment.

He had dropped Billie off at the Starlite. She planned to freshen up, then get a cab to the base in time to see the launch. Luke had gone straight to the blockhouse and learned that takeoff was now scheduled for ten forty-five p.m. Willy Fredrickson had explained the precautions the team had taken to prevent the sabotage of the rocket. The new plugs were locked in a safe, Willy told him.

Luke would feel less worried when he had seen Elspeth. He could not bear to accuse her, but when he looked into her eyes and asked her to tell him the truth, he would know.

He came up the stairs in hangar R with a heavy heart. As he reached the top, he saw a tall redhead emerge from an office along the corridor, looking anxious. She was more beautiful than her wedding photograph.

He spoke to her, and then she noticed him. "Luke!" She came quickly toward him. Her smile of welcome showed genuine pleasure, but he saw fear in her eyes. She threw her arms around him and kissed his lips.

He cut short the kiss and detached himself from her embrace. She frowned and looked hard at him, trying to read his expression. Suddenly anger suffused her face. She pushed him away. "You screwed Billie Josephson, you bastard!"

Her betrayal was worse than his, but anything he said was going to sound like an excuse. So he said nothing.

Her mood switched again, just as quickly. "I have to go. We'll talk later."

"I don't think so," he said firmly. "When I was at the house, I opened a letter addressed to you." He took it out of his jacket pocket and gave it to her. "It's from a doctor in Atlanta."

She pulled the letter out of the envelope and began to read it. "Oh, my God," she whispered.

"You had your tubes tied six weeks before our wedding," he said.

Tears came to her eyes. "I didn't want to do it," she said.

He led her into her office, closing the door. She sat down at her desk, fumbling in her purse for a handkerchief. He pulled a chair over, close to her.

"I almost didn't have the operation," she said. "It broke my heart."

He looked carefully at her, trying to be detached. "I guess they forced you to." He paused. Her eyes widened. "The KGB," he went on, and she stared at him. "They ordered you to marry me so that you could spy on the space program, and they made you get sterilized so that you would not have children to divide your loyalties." He saw a terrible grief in her eyes and knew he was right. "Don't lie," he said. "I won't believe you."

"All right," she said.

She had admitted it. He sat back. It was all over.

"I kept changing my mind," she said, and tears rolled down her face as she spoke. "In the morning I'd be determined to do it. Then at lunchtime I'd call you on the phone and you'd say something about a house with a big yard for children to run around in, and I'd make up my mind to defy them, but I couldn't in the end." She sniffed and wiped her face. "What are you going to do now? Call the FBI?"

"Should I?"

"If you do, I'll end up in the electric chair like the Rosenbergs. But there's an alternative."

"What?"

"Let me go. I'll go to Europe. From there I can get a flight to Moscow."

"Is that what you want to do? Live out your days there?"

"Yes." She gave a wry grin. "I'm a colonel, you know. I'd never be a colonel in the U.S."

"You'd have to go now—immediately," he said.

"Okay."

"I'll escort you to the gate, and you'll have to give me your pass so you can't get back in." He looked at her, trying to imprint her face on his memory. "I guess this is good-bye."

She picked up her purse. "Can I go to the ladies' room first?"
"Of course," he said.

9:30 P.M. Elspeth passed the ladies' room and entered Colonel Hide's office. It was empty.

She closed the door behind her and stood leaning against it, trembling with relief. The office swam in her sight as her eyes filled with tears. The triumph of her life was within her grasp, but she had just ended her marriage to the best man she had ever known, and she was committed to leave the country of her birth and spend the rest of her days in a land she had never seen.

She closed her eyes and made herself breathe slowly. Then she turned the key in the office door, went to the cupboard behind Hide's desk, and knelt in front of the safe.

Carefully she repeated the actions Hide had performed when she watched him opening the safe. First she spun the dial four times counterclockwise, stopping at 10. Next she turned it three times in the other direction, stopping at 29. Then she turned it twice counterclockwise, stopping at 14. She tried to turn the handle. It would not move. She heard footsteps outside and a woman's voice, but the footsteps receded.

She knew the first number was 10. She dialed it again. The second number could have been 29 or 28. She dialed 28 this time, then 14 again. The handle still would not turn.

She had tried only two possibilities out of the eight. Her fingers were slippery with sweat, and she wiped them on the hem of her dress. Next she tried 10, 29, 13, then 10, 28, 13. She was halfway through the list.

She heard a siren give a warning blast—two shorts and a long. This meant that all personnel should clear the area. The launch was an hour away.

The combination 10, 29, 12 did not work, but 10, 28, 12 did. Jubilant, she turned the handle and pulled open the door. The two plugs were still there. There was no time now to dismantle them and sketch the wiring. She would have to take them to the beach. Theo could use the actual plug in his own transmitter.

Someone tried the door, and Elspeth stopped breathing.

A man's voice called, "Bill, you in there?" It sounded like Harry Lane. The doorknob rattled. Then she heard departing footsteps. She grabbed the plugs and stuffed them into her purse. Then she closed the safe, spun the dial, and shut the cupboard.

She went to the office door and opened it, then went down the hall and reentered her office. Luke was sitting where she had left him, looking grim. "I'm ready," she said.

He stood up. "After you leave here, you'll go straight to the motel," he said. "In the morning you'll drive to Miami and get on a plane out of the United States."

"Yes." She handed him her security pass.

He nodded, satisfied. Together they went down the steps and out into the warm night. Luke walked her to her car. "I'll follow you to the gate in the jeep," he said as she got into the Corvette.

The lights of Luke's jeep came on and followed her as she drove off. Passing the launchpad, she saw the gantry inching back on its tracks, leaving the huge white rocket standing alone in the floodlights. She checked her watch. It was a minute before ten. She had forty-six minutes left.

She drove out of the base without stopping. The headlights of Luke's jeep diminished and finally disappeared as she rounded a bend. "Good-bye, my love," she said, and began to cry.

The lights of other cars swept by in blurred streaks. She almost overshot the beach road. When she saw it, she jammed on her brakes and slewed across the highway in the path of the oncoming traffic. A taxicab braked hard and swerved, honking and narrowly missing the tail of her Corvette. She bumped onto the uneven sand of the beach and drove on.

AFTER Elspeth left, Luke stayed at the gate in his jeep, waiting for Billie. She arrived at ten fifteen in a taxicab. He signed her in; then they headed for the blockhouse. "Elspeth has gone," Luke said.

"I think I saw her," Billie replied. "Is she in a white Corvette?"

"Yes, that's her."

"My cab nearly hit her car. I saw her face in the headlights. She was turning off the road in front of us."

Luke frowned. "She told me she'd go straight back to the Starlite."

Billie shook her head. "No, she was heading for the beach."

"Damn," said Luke, and he turned the jeep around.

ELSPETH drove slowly along the beach, staring at the groups of people who had gathered for the launch. She was looking for a Mercury Monterey. Anthony had told her it was green, but there was not enough light to see colors.

She started at the end of the beach, nearest to the base, but Anthony and Theo were not there. She guessed they had chosen a more isolated spot. Working her way slowly south, she saw a tall man leaning against a car and looking through binoculars. She stopped and jumped out. "Anthony!" she said.

He lowered the binoculars, and she saw that it was not him. "I'm sorry," she said.

She checked her watch. It was ten thirty. She was almost out of time.

Elspeth drove close to a car that looked right, but it seemed to be empty. She accelerated again—then it honked. She slowed down and looked back. A man had gotten out and was waving at her. It was Anthony. "Thank God!" she said. She reversed back to him and leaped out of the car. "I've got the duplicate plugs."

Theo got out of the other car and opened its trunk. "Give them to me," he said. "Quickly!"

10:48 P.M. The jeep tore along the beach at top speed. Luke scanned the cars, ignoring the cries of protest as his tires showered people with sand. Billie was standing beside him, holding the top of the windshield. She saw a white Corvette parked next to a darker sedan.

"There!" she screamed.

"I see them," Luke shouted back.

At the rear of the sedan three people were clustered around the open trunk. Billie recognized Elspeth and Anthony. The other man must be Theo Packman. But they were not looking into the trunk. Their heads were raised, and they were staring across the sand dunes toward Cape Canaveral.

Billie read the situation instantly. The transmitter was in the trunk. They were in the process of setting it to broadcast the detonation signal. She turned toward Cape Canaveral. There was nothing to see, but she heard a deep, rumbling roar like the sound of a blast furnace in a steel mill. The rocket was taking off.

"We're out of time!" she yelled.

"Hold tight!" Luke said.

She gripped the windshield as he swung the jeep around in a wide arc.

OVER the roar of the rocket, Elspeth heard the scream of a car engine. She looked up and saw a jeep heading for them at top speed. "Hurry!" she screamed.

Theo connected the last wire. On his transmitter were two switches—one marked ARM and the other DESTROY.

Theo threw the ARM switch.

On the beach a thousand faces tipped backward, watching the rocket rise straight and true, and a huge cheer went up as Luke drove straight for the back of the Mercury.

The jeep had slowed as he turned, but he was still traveling at about twenty miles per hour. Billie jumped out, hit the ground running, then fell and rolled.

At the last second Elspeth threw herself out of the way. Then there was a deafening bang and the crash of breaking glass. The Mercury's rear end crumpled, and its trunk lid came down with a bang. Luke thought either Theo or Anthony had been crushed between the cars, but he could not be sure. He was thrown forward violently. The steering wheel caught his chest. He felt the sharp pain of cracked ribs and sensed blood flowing down his face.

He pulled himself upright and looked at Billie. She seemed to have fared better than he. She was sitting on the ground rubbing her forearms, but she did not appear to be bleeding.

He looked across the hood of the jeep. Theo lay on the ground, not moving. Anthony was on his hands and knees, looking shaken but unhurt. Elspeth had escaped injury and was scrambling to her feet. She dashed to the Mercury and tried to open the trunk.

Luke leaped out of the jeep and ran at her. As the trunk lifted, he shoved her aside.

Anthony yelled, "Hold it!"

Luke looked at him. He was standing over Billie with a pistol to the back of her head.

Luke looked up. The red fire tail of *Explorer* was a bright shooting star in the night sky. As long as that was visible, the missile could still be destroyed. The first stage, which contained the explosive detonator, would burn out when the rocket was sixty miles high. It would separate and fall away, eventually to splash down in the Atlantic Ocean.

Separation would take place two minutes and twenty-five seconds after ignition. Luke figured the rocket had been ignited roughly two minutes ago. There had to be about twenty-five seconds left—plenty of time to throw a switch.

Luke looked at Billie. She was on one knee, like a sprinter at the starting line, frozen in position with the long silencer of Anthony's gun pressing into her curly black hair. He asked himself if he was ready to sacrifice Billie's life for the rocket. The answer was no.

Elspeth again bent over the trunk of the car.

Then Billie threw herself backward, hitting Anthony's legs with her shoulders.

Luke lunged at Elspeth and pushed her away from the car.

The silenced gun coughed as Anthony and Billie fell in a heap.

Luke stared in dread. Had Anthony hit Billie? She rolled away from him, apparently unhurt. Then Anthony lifted the gun, aiming at Luke.

Luke looked death in the face, and a peculiar calm possessed him. He had done all he could.

There was a long moment of hesitation. Then Anthony coughed, and blood came out of his mouth. Pulling the trigger as he fell, he had shot himself, Luke realized. Now his limp hand dropped the gun and he slumped back on the sand, his eyes staring up at the sky but seeing nothing.

Elspeth sprang up and bent over the transmitter a third time.

Luke looked up. The fire tail was a glowworm in space. As he watched, it winked out.

Elspeth threw the switch, but she was too late. The first stage had separated. Luke sighed. It was all over. He had saved the rocket.

Billie put her hand on Anthony's chest, then checked his pulse. "He's dead," she said.

At the same moment Luke looked at Elspeth. "You lied again," Luke said.

"We weren't wrong!" she yelled hysterically. "We were not wrong!"

Behind her, families of spectators and tourists were beginning to pack their belongings. No one had been close enough to notice the fighting; all eyes had been turned to the sky.

Elspeth got into her car, slammed the door, and started the engine. Instead of turning toward the road, she headed for the ocean. Luke and Billie watched in horror as she drove straight into the water.

The Corvette stopped, waves lapping at its fenders, and Elspeth got out. In the car's headlights Luke and Billie saw her begin to swim out to sea. Luke moved to go after her, but Billie grabbed his arm and held him.

"She'll kill herself," he said in agony.

"You can't catch her now," Billie said. "You'll kill yourself."

Luke still wanted to try, but then Elspeth passed out of the headlights' beam, swimming strongly, and he realized he would never find her in the dark. He bowed his head in defeat.

Billie put her arms around him. After a moment he hugged her back. Standing on the beach, their arms around each other, they both looked up.

The sky was full of stars.

EPILOGUE

1969

Luke was on the NASA team that put Apollo 11 on the moon.

By then he was living in a big, comfortable old house in Houston with Billie, who was head of cognitive psychology at Baylor. They had three children: Catherine, Louis, and Jane. (His stepson, Larry, also lived with them, but that July he was visiting his father, Bern.)

Luke happened to be off duty on the evening of July 20. Consequently, at a few minutes before nine o'clock, central time, he was watching TV with his family, as was half the world. He sat on the big couch with Billie beside him, and Jane, the youngest, on his lap. The other kids were on the carpet with Sidney, their yellow Labrador.

When Neil Armstrong stepped on the moon, a tear rolled down Luke's cheek.

Billie took his hand and squeezed it.

Catherine, the nine-year-old, looked at him with solemn brown eyes. Then she whispered, "Mommy, why is Daddy crying?"

"It's a long story, honey," Billie said. "I'll tell it to you one day."

Explorer I was expected to remain in space for two to three years. In fact, it orbited the earth for twelve years. On March 31, 1970, it finally reentered the atmosphere over the Pacific Ocean near Easter Island and burned up at 5:47 a.m., having circled the earth 58,376 times and traveled a total of 1.66 billion miles.

KEN FOLLETT

He was not yet thirty years old when his novel *Eye of the Needle* hit the best-seller lists in 1978. Ken Follett has been a name to reckon with ever since and a favorite of Select Editions readers. (Ten of his books have been Reader's Digest selections.) *Code to Zero* is Follett doing what he does best: combining heart-stopping fiction with historical fact.

Follett's leisure pastimes these days range from stirring up the London political waters—his wife, Barbara, is a member of the British Parliament—to making musical waves. He can currently be heard performing vocals and bass guitar on a CD aptly titled *Stranger than Fiction.*

To learn more about Ken Follett and
Code to Zero, visit the Select Editions website:

📖 ReadersOnly.com
Password: *happy*

My Mother's Daughter

a novel by

JUDITH
HENRY WALL

Ever since we were children, my brother Buddy and I couldn't help but wonder what had happened to our family. We seemed to have disappointed our mother in some deep, profound way. Why did our mama sigh? How had her heart been broken? All our lives, the only thing we ever wanted was to make our mother happy.

Cissy

MY BROTHER, Buddy, *never stopped wondering about our birth parents. He was certain that finding out who they were would give us essential knowledge about ourselves and somehow change our lives for the better. We would be happier, more confident. We would have a heritage and lineage. We would be more comfortable with ourselves. Who were those other parents, and why had they given us away? Would we ever meet them? Did they think about us?*

For many years I wondered along with my brother, who was older than me by a year and a half. The romance and mystery of birth parents gave Buddy and me endless hours of shared longing and speculation, mostly spent on a dusty old mattress we'd dragged in front of the round attic window.

When our cousin, Iris, was with us, we would focus instead on the comings and goings of the neighbors who lived on our tree-lined street. But when it was just Buddy and me, we focused on mythical, what-if worlds—on the places where birth parents might dwell.

Sometimes we imagined them together, but mostly we dealt with our birth parents separately, reasoning that a couple who had given away their children would not still be together. Buddy conjured up scenarios with our father an undercover CIA agent in Russia or falsely accused of a crime and locked away in prison. Usually, however, we thought of him as dead. It was tidier that way. He might have been killed in Korea. Or swept out to sea during a hurricane. I preferred a scenario in which he was killed in a fiery car crash as he raced to be with our mother the night I was born.

Mostly, though, we daydreamed about the woman who had given us birth and tried to find excuses for her. Death worked well here, too. Maybe she had wanted to keep us but died giving me birth. I imagined a woman who looked like Audrey Hepburn, kissing us good-bye and promising to watch over us from heaven.

Or maybe she was still alive but suffered from amnesia. Someday she might remember that she was the mother of two children and hire a private detective to find us. She might even be a grand duchess, with Buddy heir to a defunct Russian throne.

Of course, up there in the little attic alcove, I felt disloyal succumbing to birth mother daydreams. Our adoptive mother worked very hard at motherhood. She was always saying how lucky she was to have us for her very own children.

Our daddy probably would have understood our need for birth parent daydreams, but Mama would have been hurt. She had earned the right to be first and foremost in our affection. And in my heart I knew our birth mother was probably just some poor ignorant girl who hadn't the means or courage to raise her own children.

As the years went by, I came to realize that the happiness we yearned for would not come from finding an angelic birth mother but in pleasing the complex woman who was raising us. We seemed to have disappointed her in some profound way. Why did Mama sigh? Had her heart broken when she realized she'd never have children of her own? Or maybe the fear that our aunt, Justine, would swoop into town and reclaim Iris stole away her laughter.

Buddy and I had always known that Iris was the beloved one. Iris was the daughter of our mother's sister and therefore related by blood—not a daughter, but the closet thing our mother would ever have to a blood child. We accepted Iris's special status as rightful. After all, Buddy and I loved her, too. From earliest memory, Iris had been the center of our lives. She spread joy in her wake. She made our mother happy in a way Buddy and I never could. And more than anything, we wanted our mother to be happy.

One

JULY 1945—Justine was coming home!

Martha Claire paused in her weeding and sat back on her haunches to relish the thought. At this very minute her sister was on a ship crossing the Atlantic Ocean.

And surely before the year was out, Grayson also would come back to her. Her life could begin anew.

She rubbed at the small of her back before returning to her task. Whether Justine noticed it or not, when she came down the front walk for the first time in two and a half years, she was going to be greeted by a perfectly manicured yard. And inside, the house was well on its way to being spotless. Daddy was putting down new linoleum in the kitchen. Mother had recovered the seats of the dining-room chairs. Justine's bedroom was freshly painted.

Yesterday Martha Claire had gone across the river to pick wild blackberries so Granny Grace could put up Justine's favorite preserves. Granny Grace already had rows of spiced peaches and pickled okra on the pantry shelf, waiting for her granddaughter's homecoming. Martha Claire would help her grandmother and mother prepare all of Justine's favorite food. Nothing boiled, Justine had written. She was sick of boiled food. And please have a watermelon chilled. She hadn't tasted watermelon for two summers.

Martha Claire decided to cut back the petunias, which had gotten leggy. The lantanas and periwinkles were in full bloom, though. Across the yard the magnolia tree was laden with huge waxy blossoms, and the freshly painted picket fence around Mother's rose garden shimmered whitely in the sunshine. It was a beautiful yard—one of the finest in Columbus, Texas, as was the house, which had been built by Martha Claire's great-great-grandfather. Had Justine missed it? Martha Claire wondered as she surveyed their childhood home—the place she herself loved best on earth.

What letters her sister had found time to write described the wonder of being in London, of doing her small part for the war effort. If she wrote about the war itself, it was only to complain about the hours spent in bomb shelters. Only at the end would she dash off a few words about missing her family back home.

Grayson's letters, on the other hand, had been mostly about missing her, words Martha Claire read over and over again.

Now that the war was over, however, her husband's letters were more about human tragedy than longing. His unit was involved in the repatriation of prisoners liberated from the concentration camp at Dachau. He was overwhelmed with the horror he found there and did not know when he was coming home. Martha Claire tried not to be resentful. She had seen pictures of those poor souls in the newsreels—living skeletons with empty eyes. But her husband had been gone for three endless years, and his father wasn't well. It was time for Grayson to take over the family store, time for him to make a home with his wife and put the war behind him.

Martha Claire wondered what Justine planned to do now that the war was over. Their parents hoped their younger daughter would settle in Columbus or at least someplace not too far away. That's what Martha Claire wanted, too, her sister close by—if not in Columbus, then no farther away than Houston, where Justine had worked in a photography studio before enlisting in the Women's Army Corps. Martha Claire had missed her sister as much as she had missed her husband, in some ways more. She was always thinking of things she wanted to tell Justine.

Her body longed for her husband, but she had a hard time imagining conversations with him. Grayson was only a year older than she was, but she felt as though she had been frozen in time while he had grown older. And sadder.

Martha Claire had been Grayson's wife for three years and one month, but she still lived with her parents, still had no home of her own, still didn't feel like a wife. The only time she had shared a bed with her husband had been on their honeymoon and the few weekends they had together before he shipped out.

But surely by next summer she would have her own house and

garden, she told herself as she returned to her weeding. And a baby on the way. Oh, yes, definitely a baby on the way.

THE porter shook Justine's arm. "Wake up, miss. Next stop's Columbus."

Justine struggled to an upright position, her muscles stiff, her stomach churning, her head throbbing. Grandpa Mayfield would say she wasn't worth shooting. He had died while she was away, she reminded herself. He would not be at the station with the others. Granny Grace was the only grandparent she had left.

She sagged back against the seat. She had envisioned a different sort of homecoming, with her smiling and smart in her uniform as she stepped down from the train—not sick and scared, with her future in jeopardy.

On the ship she had tried to convince herself she was suffering from seasickness. And the crossing had been a rough one. Of course, the seas had also been rough two and a half years ago, when Justine made the crossing from New York to Dover as a member of the Women's Army Corps with orders for London, where she would serve as a file clerk in a military police command. She hadn't been sick then, just scared to death of German submarines.

The cramped quarters she had recently shared with three other Wacs were far below deck—in the deepest bowels of the ship, where claustrophobia was at its worst. Justine wondered if any holdout submarines with swastikas on their sides were still swimming around out there, if she could even muster the strength to make it topside to a lifeboat should the ship founder. By the third day, however, she wouldn't have minded going down with the ship. Nothing she ate or drank stayed down. She would retch so hard, it felt as though she were turning inside out. When the nausea receded, she would crawl inside a cocoon of semiconsciousness. The third or fourth day out her darling Billy was inside the cocoon.

She knew he was a hallucination, brought on by serious dehydration, by fear of what awaited her at the end of the voyage, but she needed the comfort of his presence. Billy Baker from Brisbane. An RAF tail gunner. She had called him her Billy Boy. Just a wartime romance. She wasn't about to fall in love with anyone, much less a boy with the life expectancy of a gnat. Except as the tide of war began to change, she had begun to think that Billy just might make it through, that he just might be alive to celebrate the armistice with her and to wonder what they would mean to each other in a world where there was no war.

In the cave of her bunk bed she would close her eyes and drift with Billy, back to their favorite pub, the Toad in the Hole. At the corner table grizzly old Hugh played the harmonica: "As Time Goes By," "Chattanooga Choo Choo," "Baby Face," "Danny Boy." Billy knew the words to all of Hugh's songs, which he sang in a haunting tenor voice, and his laugh was infectious, his grin adorable, his dart game legendary. Maybe a bomb would fall on them tonight, but for now they were absolutely alive.

When the air-raid sirens began to wail, they would race toward the Baker Street tube. That last night he grabbed her arm and there in the middle of the pavement drew her into his arms. She could feel his heart pounding, the shock waves from exploding bombs traveling up her legs. The air was filled with fire sirens, women calling frantically to children. Billy held her so tightly, she could barely breathe. And they kissed. God, how they kissed.

Later, in the belly of a troopship that was transporting Justine to the rest of her life, Billy was with her again—at least a vision of him. And she was grateful. Sometimes she was aware of the other women yelling at her to shut up while she sang pub songs with him and told him that she loved him and that she was sorry she'd never said the words before. She should have that night in the street when he'd kissed her. She should have said them then, because she had felt them. All the way to her toes she had felt them.

The last morning of the voyage Justine put on her uniform and walked up the narrow steps to the deck. Under the benign eyes of the Statue of Liberty she filled her lungs with fresh air for the first time in seven days. But as they docked, she was heaving again, leaning over the rail. As she retched, she prayed that it would dislodge the tiny spark of life that had taken up residence inside her and send it floating away to its doom.

In Grand Central Terminal, she sent a telegram to her parents, then sat on her duffel bag and thought of her hometown. She conjured up images of the meandering river that wrapped itself around the north half of the town and of the domed courthouse surrounded by a handsome iron fence. But the fence was gone. Her mother had written that the town donated it to the war effort. Most of Columbus's iron fences had been donated, including the one around the family home on Milam Street.

She thought of her room at the top of the stairs, imagined herself in her bed with smooth white sheets, her mother's cool hand on her forehead. She wanted to go home. But she could not stay. Columbus was her past, not her future. Better to have been killed by a bomb in London than to endure stagnation in a backwater Texas town, no matter how much she loved the people there.

When her train was announced, she climbed on board. The train had been full of returning servicemen, with some passengers forced to sit on luggage stacked in the vestibules. The elderly porter had taken one look at Justine and managed to secure a seat for her.

Now her journey was almost over. She was only minutes from home after being away for a lifetime.

She stumbled into the ladies' lounge to splash water on her face. The reflection in the mirror was ghastly. Her hair was matted, her skin ashen. Her uniform hung on her body like a sack.

She made her way back to her seat and watched out the window as the train rolled into town. She could see the roof of the opera house. The train station was just ahead. She was *home*.

She could see her family standing on the platform—Mother, Daddy, Martha Claire, and Granny Grace—dressed in their Sunday best, their faces anxious and excited as they looked for her in the passing windows. She drew back, not wanting them to see her just yet. Her heart swelled painfully. She did love them. She would always love them, always come back to them.

She put on her hat, collected her things, and went down the steps. Martha Claire arrived first. Her sister. The other half of herself. Her even lovelier face was registering shock. "Justine, what happened to you?"

Justine could tell how wasted she was by the feel of her sister's arms around her body and by her daddy's arms engulfing her.

Then her mother took Justine's face between her hands. "Oh, Justine, what have you done to yourself?" Polly asked. Her arms came around her daughter. Justine leaned into her mother's embrace. She had traveled miles for this moment. "We'll work it out, my darling," her mother whispered. "Somehow we'll work it out."

POLLY Mayfield sat on the side of her daughter's bed and took Justine's hand. "Feeling better?"

Justine nodded.

She did look better, Polly thought, now that she'd had a bath and slept most of the day. But dark circles rimmed her eyes, and her cheeks were as white as her nightgown. Doc Hadley had checked her over and said not to worry. She needed rest.

"Then we'd better discuss what to do," Polly said, looking down at Justine's ringless fingers. "I don't suppose you're married?"

Justine rolled her head back and forth on the pillow. No.

"And no man is going to make an honest woman of you?"

Once again Justine rolled her head.

"And your young man is dead."

Justine propped herself up on an elbow. "What young man?"

"The one who flew with the Royal Air Force."

"How do you know about him?" Justine asked.

"You mentioned him in a letter about six months back. You apologized for not writing and said you'd been sad because a friend in the RAF had been shot down and was killed. You never mentioned him again. Did you love him, Justine?"

Justine fell back on her pillow. "I don't know. Maybe. It hurt when he was killed. A lot."

"And then you found someone else?"

"Not someone to love," Justine said quietly. Then turning her face to the wall, she said, "I'm sorry, Mother. Don't hate me."

Polly stroked Justine's shoulders and back, telling her that she could never hate her own daughter, that she would always love her no matter what.

How could this have happened? Polly wondered. She had always assumed that neither one of her daughters would ever disgrace the family in this manner. Martha Claire was the sort of romantic girl who saved herself for marriage. Justine was simply not interested in boys, except as pals. Polly would like to know what happened. Had her daughter's grief over the death of the young airman left her vulnerable? Or had Justine, who had always taken every dare, simply thrown caution to the wind? Polly doubted if she would ever know.

Enough of pondering, though, she decided, adjusting the pillow behind Justine's head. The unthinkable had happened to her daughter, and she had to figure out some way to deal with it. "Does this man know he is going to be a father?" she asked.

Justine's chapped lips formed the word no.

"Don't you want to give him a chance to do the right thing?"

Justine closed her eyes. "No," she whispered.

"He's married, then?"

Justine sighed but didn't answer.

Polly cleared her throat and said the words she had been composing in her mind. "I have decided that you are married, Justine—to a British soldier you met during the victory celebration when everyone was dancing in the streets and kissing everyone in sight. It was a whirlwind courtship, and you had a simple wedding in a country church with only the minister's wife in attendance. Just weeks later the poor boy was killed trying to defuse one of those undetonated German bombs still scattered about London. Your husband was an only child, and his parents were killed in the blitz, so you have no remaining ties to England. You'll have to decide on a last name—for you and the baby."

Justine struggled to sit up, an astounded look on her face. "Mother, no one is going to believe a story like that. I would have written to you if I'd gotten married. You would have told the neighbors and put an announcement in the newspaper."

"It all happened so fast, and then he was dead," Polly went on, honing her story. "You had to deal with your grief before you told anyone, and by then you realized you were in a family way. Doc Hadley said he'll put whatever name you want on the birth certificate. You have to think of what's best for the child, Justine. It's better to have a father's name, even if it's a made-up one."

"What about what is best for me?" Justine demanded.

"And what might that be?"

"Not to have a baby at all." Justine's chin was lifted in defiance.

"It's a little late for that," Polly said, smoothing back her daughter's hair—fair hair that couldn't decide if it was supposed to be red or blond, just like Martha Claire's, just as her own had once been.

"I could get rid of it," Justine said. "Doc Hadley won't do it, but there's that colored woman in Freedmantown."

"Yes. Aunt Sally Washington. She must be close to ninety now, but I've heard she still does abortions—mostly for colored girls, but I expect she does a white girl now and then. I imagine that's where poor Sadie Marie Cordell went. You'd probably live through it, but do you really want to take that risk? And do you want to wonder for the rest of your life about the baby you never had?"

"I want a different kind of life," Justine insisted. "I'm not like Martha Claire. You know that. I want to be a photographer and make my own way in the world."

"You should have thought of that back in London," Polly said, not unkindly. She'd had dreams once herself. She was going to study music and become a concert organist and not just play hymns on Walnut Avenue Methodist's decaying Hammond. But she didn't have the money and life got in the way, and the life she'd ended up with was a good one. She would not change it if she could.

Before the war Justine had refused to follow her sister to college and had taken a job in Houston as an assistant in a photography studio. People couldn't believe that Polly and Walter Mayfield had allowed their young daughter to live alone in a big city. But Polly knew there was no point in telling Justine she couldn't go. She would have gone anyway.

As it turned out, Justine hated the job. All she did was take pictures of babies and develop film. She probably would have come home and found a nice boy to marry if it weren't for the war. As soon as Justine heard about the Women's Army Corps, she knew she wanted to sign up and begged her sister to join with her. After

Pearl Harbor, though, after war became reality, Martha Claire decided to marry Grayson the minute he graduated from Texas A.&M., before he began his military service.

Once Martha Claire was married, Justine traveled to Fort Des Moines, Iowa, where she received her military training. She came home the following summer to say good-bye. At the station, when they put a smartly uniformed Justine on the train for her journey to England and the war, Martha Claire had broken down and thrown herself into Justine's arms. "Promise me you'll come back to Columbus," she begged. Justine hugged her sister and promised. But she hadn't promised she would come home to stay.

In London, Justine had taken pictures of the war-torn city and the people who lived there. One of her photographs had ended up in *Collier's* magazine—almost a full page with Justine's name underneath. It was a picture of two little girls having a tea party with their dolls in the middle of a bomb crater. The local newspaper ran a story about Justine taking pictures in London. "She'll never come back to Columbus now," Martha Claire had predicted mournfully.

Poor Martha Claire, Polly thought. If only she'd been able to get pregnant before Grayson left, she would have managed the separation better. That had certainly been her plan. Until the war came along, Martha Claire had been convinced that if she wanted something badly enough, she could make it happen. After all, she had been elected homecoming queen, been named outstanding student at Mary Hardin Baylor College, and gotten the boy she wanted to fall in love with her. But she had waited out the war childless, and now her unmarried sister was carrying a misbegotten child. How in the world was Martha Claire going to react to that?

Polly felt a swelling in her breast at the thought of a grandchild in her arms. She had already decided there would be no late-night crossing over the tracks into Freedmantown. She would raise the child herself if she had to. "You don't have to decide anything now," Polly told her daughter, "but keep in mind that you have responsibilities—to the life inside you and to your family, your sister especially. Martha Claire plans to stay in Columbus. Manufacturing a husband would give her a way to hold her head up."

"It's not *her* problem," Justine said defiantly.

"You know better than that, Justine Mayfield. Dirty linen is a family matter, especially in a little town like Columbus."

"Do Martha Claire and Daddy know what's going on?"

"I think they've guessed. I'm going to talk to them now."

"Oh, Mother, do you have to?" Justine's eyes filled with tears.

"Yes, dear, I do. They have a right to know." Polly kissed her daughter's forehead. "I love you, my darling girl."

Justine put her arms around her mother's neck. "I love you, too, Mother, but I can't be what you want me to be."

Polly turned out the lamp. From the doorway she said, "Don't underestimate the value of a home and a family who will always love you no matter what. It's your most precious possession."

"I have to be someone," Justine said into the darkness.

"Everyone is someone," Polly said, and closed the door.

THE glow of the streetlight silhouetted the branches of the magnolia tree outside the bedroom window. Justine remembered the day Grandpa Hess had planted that tree. She and Martha Claire had watched—two little girls in pigtails, sitting cross-legged in the grass. Their mother's father had died not long after that, and Justine, Martha Claire, and their parents had moved from their smaller house on Walnut Street to live with Granny Grace in the big house on Milam Street where their mother had grown up.

And now that tree shaded Justine's bedroom window, a legacy from her long-dead grandfather. She would leave a legacy, too, with her photographs. If there were ever a retrospective of her work, it would include only a few of the pictures she had taken thus far. Only a handful were the kind that evoked a genuine emotional response. The little girls playing in the bomb crater was one such picture. Justine turned on the lamp and looked over at the bookcase. Her old Kodak box camera was there beside a rusty pair of roller skates. She had delivered groceries to earn money for film, and she had gotten better with each roll. For the rest of her life that was what she wanted—to get better and better while she photographed life, like Dorothea Lange and Margaret Bourke-White.

She rolled onto her side, pulled her knees up to her pregnant belly. "Go away," she groaned. "I don't want you." If she could have turned back the clock, she never would have gotten on that train to Dover, never would have fallen into the abyss.

THE next morning Justine woke to the sound of her sister whispering from the doorway, "Justine, are you awake?"

Without opening her eyes, Justine nodded. She felt the bed sag as Martha Claire sat beside her and asked, "Is it true?"

Justine opened her eyes and regarded her sister's distraught face. "So it seems," she said, propping herself up with a second pillow.

"Did some man force himself on you?" Martha Claire asked, her eyes wide. Green eyes—a more startling green than Justine's.

"No, nothing like that."

"Then if you loved him, why didn't you get married?"

"I never said I loved him."

"I'm your sister, Justine. I know that you wouldn't have done something like that with a man if you didn't love him."

"Things were different there. The war changed everything. We had too much to drink, and it just happened. I wish it hadn't. I'm sorry. Very very sorry. And that's all I'm going to say about it."

"But we've got to decide what we're going to tell people."

"I don't want you telling anyone anything," Justine said. "Maybe I'll just go off someplace to have it and put it up for adoption."

"You can't give away a baby," Martha Claire said. "We would spend the rest of our lives wondering about it and feeling sorry."

"And if I don't give it away, I'll spend the rest of my life wishing I had. Actually, I came home with something else in mind. I was going to sneak across the tracks and let that old colored woman do whatever it is she does. But Mother knew the instant I got off that train. Can you believe that? Doc Hadley had to poke around, but Mother takes one look at me and knows."

"You can't do *that,* either, Justine," Martha Claire said, a hand on her breast, her eyes wide. "Remember Sadie Marie?"

"Of course I remember Sadie Marie! But at least things got settled for her, didn't they?" Justine felt tears welling and turned her back to her sister. She hated crying. Hated feeling sorry for herself. Maybe she deserved to die like stupid ole Sadie Marie.

Martha Claire began rubbing her sister's back and shoulders, and Justine felt herself relaxing. They used to give each other backrubs all the time. And shared all their secrets. But no longer. Life would never be like that again.

"If you stay here," Martha Claire was saying, "I'll help you with the baby. But we have to tell people that you got married and your husband died, just like Mother says. He got blown up by a bomb."

"Go away, Martha Claire," Justine groaned.

WITHOUT consulting her parents or sister, Martha Claire placed a brief obituary in the next issue of the weekly Colorado County *Citizen:* "Sergeant Major Philip Benston Dover. Born July 12, 1921, in Liverpool, England. Killed in the service of his country June 4, 1945, in London, England. Survived by his wife, Justine Mayfield Dover, of Columbus." Justine burst into tears when she saw it.

Walter, Polly, and Granny Grace were overjoyed.

"I'm sorry, Justine, but I had to do something. Maybe you don't care about this family's reputation. Maybe you think it won't affect us when you get big out to here with no claim to a husband."

Justine blew her nose and handed the newspaper back to her sister. "It's okay. You did what you had to do. But why *Dover?*"

"It sounded English," Martha Claire explained.

Neighbors and friends began showing up at the front door to pay their respects to the grieving family. Reverend Huxley stopped by to ask about a memorial service. A reporter from the Houston *Post,* with a photographer in tow, arrived. He wanted an interview with Mrs. Dover and a photograph of the young widow holding her dead husband's picture but had to settle for a photograph of the Mayfield family's handsome Victorian home with a funeral wreath on the front door. It was printed the following day next to a picture of Justine from a Columbus High School yearbook.

Through it all Justine stayed in bed. She never should have come back home. She knew that now. She felt as though she were sinking into a quicksand bog from which there was no escape.

Two

I NEVER *thought of my aunt Justine as a widow lady, even though that was what she was. Other ladies wore dresses downtown, but Justine—in spite of her widow-lady status—wore slacks, like Katharine Hepburn. In fact, she reminded me of Katharine Hepburn, with her long legs and plain-speaking ways.*

I remember wishing I could have been a little like Justine, but the truth was, I didn't have the courage to alienate my mother. I had a need to please her that came from deep inside me. I was, above all, Martha Claire Stewart's adopted daughter. And perhaps, even though I loved Justine, I also shared my mother's disdain for a woman who would leave her daughter for someone else to raise. Justine was able to travel the world and become a famous photographer because my mother was raising her daughter, Iris.

Since earliest memory, a picture of my aunt and my mother hung among the gallery of framed family pictures that marched up the stair-case wall. The picture had been taken when the Mayfield sisters were teenagers. Tall, athletic Justine was wearing a plaid skirt, white blouse, and saddle oxfords. My mother was dainty in a ruffled frock and white pumps. After the falling-out between them, Mama burned that picture in the backyard, but in my mind's eye I can see it still. The Mayfield sisters portrayed there were so pretty, their arms linked forever in sisterly affection. When that picture was taken, they thought they'd have each other for a lifetime.

"I THINK you'd make a terrific army wife," Justine told her sister as she hammered the lid back on the paint can.

"Why do you say that?" Martha Claire demanded.

"Think of all the 'finishing' you got at Mary Hardin Baylor College for Women. You know as much about etiquette as Emily Post."

"Don't make fun," Martha Claire said as she worked the paintbrush back and forth on the newspaper that protected the floor.

Justine carefully lowered her pregnant body onto the wooden crate that held the photo enlarger she'd ordered from Sears, Roebuck. She'd always felt like a cow next to her dainty sister. Now she felt like an elephant—and still with a month to go. "I'm not making fun of you, Martha Claire," she said with great earnestness. "Officers' wives have to know all about etiquette so their husbands can get promoted. With you managing the home front, Grayson would be a general someday, and a general's wife is like royalty."

Martha Claire shook her head. "If Grayson stayed in the army, we'd spend our lives as vagabonds. We'd always be living among strangers, and our children would be born God knows where. I want to live here, and before the war Grayson did, too."

Even wearing old clothes, with her hair tied up in a bandanna, Martha Claire was lovely. Justine had never known anyone who was so comfortable in her own body, her own face, her own smile. Justine would find herself staring at Martha Claire, waiting for the next smile. Everyone did that. No wonder Grayson had fallen in love with her in high school. Lots of other boys had, too. But Martha Claire had zeroed in on Grayson the first week of her sophomore year, when he marched up onto the stage and sang "When the Moon Comes Over the Mountain" at a back-to-school amateur hour, and she never wavered in her aim.

Justine reached over and stroked her sister's hand. "I just want you and Grayson to be happy, and I worry that if you make him stay here to do something he doesn't want to do, neither one of you will be. He's not the same man that he was before the war. He's been through hell. He deserves a chance at happiness."

"Other men have come back home and settled in. What makes Grayson so different?"

"Other men didn't have a military education," Justine pointed out. "You know how he took to all the regimental stuff up at College Station. He was the number one cadet. And now he's a captain with medals on his chest. He has a chance for a distinguished military career, and you want him to be a shopkeeper!"

"What's so bad about being a shopkeeper? Daddy has tended his pharmacy for twenty-five years. Grayson's family has always had that dry-goods store. He knows what it was like to grow up in Columbus. He'll want the same for our children. Just think of all those canoe rides on the river, the Saturday matinees, the Friday night football games. Think of living among people you've always known. Why would I want to live anyplace else?"

Martha Claire got up and walked around the room, inspecting the walls she'd just painted, signifying the end of the conversation.

Poor Grayson, Justine thought. He would have to hang up his uniform, as his father had done when he came home from World War I. And she herself was facing the same sort of prison, here in this very room. Not that it wasn't a nice room, over their father's pharmacy, with two windows in the front that looked out on the square and a storeroom with no windows where she would set up her darkroom. Justine stared down at her belly. She didn't hate the baby anymore. It hadn't asked to be conceived. But she did hate what was happening to her life.

She would open a photography studio to support herself and her child. They would live in what once had been servants quarters over a carriage-house-turned-garage behind the family home. Everyone had pitched in to make it livable.

She stared at her backward name already painted on one of the front windows: JUSTINE MAYFIELD-DOVER, PHOTOGRAPHER. She'd borrowed the hyphen from Margaret Bourke-White. *Dover.* Strange that Martha Claire had chosen that name, Justine thought.

Poor Grayson. She felt for him from the bottom of her heart. His sentence was for life. Hers would not be, she vowed.

MARTHA Claire stood with her parents and grandmother at the nursery window, peering through the glass at Justine's newborn baby—an absolutely beautiful baby girl, asleep in a bassinet. Martha Claire was transfixed. She longed to hold this child, to kiss her sweet face and inhale her baby scent. Soon she would have her own baby, but in the meantime she would have her sister's child to fill her heart. Iris was her name. Beautiful little Iris.

Martha Claire wished Grayson were here to see Iris in the first hours of her life. He had called from New York yesterday. He was accompanying his command to Fort Bragg, North Carolina, and would muster out there. In just a matter of days he would be home. She felt uneasy about seeing him again. Afraid, even. Grayson had become a stranger to her. His letters talked about the poor souls liberated from Nazi death camps, broken, diseased people who had no possessions, no family, no spirit; people who had lost everything. His heart was heavy for the suffering of others when she wanted it to be light and filled with hope and love and thoughts of her and the wonderful future that awaited them.

Being with Grayson once had seemed the most natural thing in the world. She had been a virgin when they married, but just barely. They had had their secret place in a riverside grove, where they took off their clothes and did everything short of going all the way. She enjoyed their mutual beauty as much as their kissing.

Justine had wanted Martha Claire to join the Women's Army Corps with her. For a heartbeat Martha Claire had been tempted. They could go off together before she settled down with Grayson. But what if he died over there? If that happened, she wanted him to die as her husband. She wanted his child to love and raise.

She abandoned her plans for a big wedding at some point in the unknown future and decided to marry Grayson in her mother's rose garden the same week she graduated from Mary Hardin Baylor and the day after he had graduated from Texas A.&M. and received his commission as a second lieutenant in the United States Army. Grayson had been reluctant about the hurry-up wedding. Maybe they should wait until the war was over, he told her.

"But I need to be your wife," Martha Claire explained. "I couldn't bear to send you off to war otherwise."

They worked around the clock to get the house and garden ready for the wedding. Martha Claire had fretted about the weather, but her wedding day arrived fair and blue. Her wedding dress had been worn by her grandmother and her mother before her. Grayson was married in his cadet uniform. In front of family and friends, with her sister at her side, Martha Claire had proudly said the words that bound her to Grayson for a lifetime.

The newlyweds spent their wedding night in a tourist court outside Sugar Land on the way to a honeymoon on Galveston Island. "Make me pregnant," she whispered as Grayson entered her body for the first time. "Give me a baby, please."

For one week they walked along Galveston's great empty beaches, gorged themselves on fresh seafood, made love morning and night. Afterward they would talk about the future with tears and assurances. He would come back to her. They would be happy. Their love was forever. But Grayson became distant at times, and she knew he was thinking not about their mutual future but his own more immediate one. He tried to hide his excitement, but she could hear it in his voice. He wanted to go, as did Justine. They both would rather go to war than stay in Columbus with her. This knowledge ate at her and altered the nature of her love for them.

After she and Grayson returned to Columbus, they spent one night together in her parents' house. The next day Grayson rode the train to Fort Sill, Oklahoma, where he would attend the twelve-week battery-officer training course. Three times Martha Claire made the seven-hour train ride into southwestern Oklahoma, getting off in downtown Lawton and walking to a hotel, where Grayson would meet her. He would have to be back at the base the next morning, leaving Martha Claire to her long ride home.

She and Grayson had not conceived a child on their honeymoon or during her three visits to Lawton. Their last night together, in the Lawton hotel, she had prayed with fervor. Kneeling beside the bed, she asked Grayson to join her, which he did willingly. He wanted a baby, too. He was thrilled about what lay ahead and scared to the depths of his being. A baby would make facing death easier. As he thrust his way into her body, she floated in a high celestial space. If God loved her at all, He would give her a baby.

Two weeks later Grayson was on his way to war and Martha Claire was staring down at a telltale show of blood on the crotch of her underpants. She wept bitter tears, and a deep-seated fear became embedded in her soul. What if there would be no baby ever? Who would she be if not a mother? Because she was a positive person, though, Martha Claire was able to keep fear at bay. After all, she and Grayson had been married only a short time. He would come home, and she'd have a baby within the year.

For three and a half years she had waited for his return. Waiting became a way of life. And fear became her constant companion, fear that the dreaded military sedan would pull up in front of the house, with a solemn-faced officer coming to the door.

Grayson had been wounded when a mortar shell hit his jeep and killed his driver. He had been in southern France then. There had been some worry that he would lose an eye, but he hadn't written about that until the danger had passed.

When Grayson's father had a heart attack, she began helping out at the store. It was only temporary, of course. When Grayson returned, she would become a full-time homemaker and mother.

She had saved all of his letters with the heavy black blocks where the censors had made their deletions. Now his letters weren't censored. The war had ended. Yet she almost resented them when they arrived. Other men had already returned. How could she complain, though, when what he was doing was so noble and good? But what if he had volunteered for extended duty to put off his return? Was he punishing her for denying him a military career? He had been gracious in defeat, however, writing that Martha Claire was right—there had been an implied promise on his part that they would make their home in Columbus. He had a responsibility to her and his parents. And he could continue his military service on a part-time basis in the Texas National Guard. It wasn't as though he was hanging up his uniform forever.

When he'd called last night, she hadn't recognized his voice. "It's me," he said. He was calling from the pier in New York City. The ship had just docked. He explained about Fort Bragg.

"I love you, Martha Claire," he said. "You are my life."

His voice broke. He meant what he said. But there had also been resignation in his voice. He wanted her *and* something else, and he was having to settle for just her. She had won, and she had lost.

But they would heal themselves with a family. She wanted three, four, maybe five children. She would bring Grayson here to the hospital to see this precious newborn child. Martha Claire pressed her fingertips against the glass. Iris should be *her* baby. Justine didn't want to be a mother. Maybe she would go off and have her career and leave Iris for her sister and brother-in-law to raise.

THE minute Martha Claire saw Grayson step down from the train, she realized her sister had been right. She was getting back a different man. He had seen horrors she couldn't imagine. She had wanted to believe that once he was home the years would roll back and they would be newlyweds again. However, now that he was actually in her arms, she realized there was a part of him she would never know, when once she had known him completely. But oh, how sweet it was to have his arms around her again.

"All that kept me alive was thinking about you," he said, burying his face in her hair.

"My darling," she whispered. "We'll never be apart again."

Reluctantly she relinquished him to his parents. His father had suffered two heart attacks and gone from robust to fragile while his son was at war. Martha Claire had tried to warn Grayson in her letters, but there was shock on his face as he embraced his father.

Later, at the hospital, they viewed Justine's baby through the nursery window. "She's lovely," was all Grayson said.

"I wish she were our baby," Martha Claire told him.

They walked silently down to Justine's room, where Grayson politely kissed his sister-in-law's cheek and listened to her rant a bit about being held captive in a hospital for ten days when poor women had babies at home. Then she stopped abruptly. "Your husband is exhausted, Martha Claire. You need to take him home."

Martha Claire had rented a two-bedroom house next door to her in-laws. She had painted every room, refinished furniture, and made curtains. Now, during the short ride to their own home, her stomach tied itself in knots. She hadn't been this nervous on their wedding night. Grayson carried her across the threshold.

Martha Claire lit candles and opened a bottle of champagne. "To my husband," she said, lifting her glass. He picked up his glass, then put it down again and buried his face in his hands. Martha Claire held him while he cried, unsure of the source of his tears. She helped him out of his uniform and drew a bath for him. He was asleep by the time she crawled into bed beside him.

"WHERE are we going?" Grayson asked.

"It's a surprise," Martha Claire said. She was so nervous, she felt ill. She was taking a risk, something that went against her nature.

Grayson had been home almost two weeks—two very polite weeks. Mealtime was a strain. Sitting in the living room after dinner, they were like two old people, Martha Claire with her sewing basket, Grayson with the newspaper or a book. He was quiet and withdrawn. Deep lines radiated from the corners of his eyes. She wanted him to talk about the war and why he had changed so, but he said he couldn't. "Will you ever?" she asked.

"I don't know," he'd answered.

They made love at dawn that first morning. He cried again and said it wasn't right that he had lived when others had not. Good men. Better than he. Martha Claire stroked his back, kissed his tears. The first time was just something to get over with, she told herself. Next time would be different. And it was. That evening they came together again, quietly, carefully, without tears. And every night since. Martha Claire was left longing for their honeymoon, when their bodies had fused like streams of molten lava.

It was a beautiful evening, with a warm breeze. The river was at its romantic best, all silvery in the moonlight. When she turned down the rutted lane, Grayson sighed. At the end of the lane, in a riverside stand of willow, was their special place, where they had once come to take off their clothes, experience flesh against flesh. Martha Claire wanted to revisit those times of high passion and endless kisses. She stopped the car. "Please," she said.

He put his arms around her. "Ah, sweet Martha Claire. We didn't leave the magic down by the river."

"Then where is it?" She was crying. Great hiccuping sobs escaped from deep inside of her. Where had the passion gone?

"We have to start over," he said, caressing her hair, her back, her wet cheeks. "There's no way to go back to that other time."

"What will happen to us?" she asked.

"We will make our home together, raise a family, run the store. If we make enough money, I'd like to take you to Europe."

"Do you still want to stay in the army?" she asked, her voice small. "If it's what you really want . . ."

He buried his face against her neck. "It's all right. I won't make you leave Columbus. I only want to make you happy."

And his mouth found hers. The kiss was salty. Deep. Full of need. Oh, yes, she thought. Please. And they did revisit that other time. At last she could kiss his body with abandon and make him cry out in passion.

As he drove them home, hope flowed in her veins. She felt it as never before. Their first child had been conceived.

POLLY and Granny Grace kept assuring Justine that the baby was just colicky. She would get over it. And as Justine endured endless nights and miserable days, she felt genuinely sorry for the poor little creature. She didn't doubt that Iris truly was suffering from tummy aches or birth trauma or whatever it was that gave babies colic. Justine was too exhausted to cope, though, too exhausted to care. If asked to choose between a million dollars and an uninterrupted night's sleep, she would take sleep.

Her mother and grandmother showed her about rocking, jiggling, and pacing, activities that Justine performed by the hour. But Iris cried on. The only thing that quieted her was sticking a nipple in her mouth. The baby would nurse greedily for a short time, fall asleep with her mother's nipple in her mouth—and start crying the minute Justine put her down. So Justine sat by the hour, in the uncomfortable spindleback rocker, with her marginally asleep infant. She was a prisoner. A recluse.

Then, during the baby's seventh week of life, Iris smiled at her. Justine was suspicious. Probably it was just gas. Iris did it again. The smile was lopsided, silly, and absolutely precious.

"Does this mean that you are actually a human being?" Justine asked in wonder.

Iris smiled one more time, then promptly closed her eyes and fell asleep.

Justine stared down at her daughter's angelic face, at the tiny hand clutching her finger, and felt something stirring inside her. "Oh, my God," Justine whispered as understanding dawned. This wasn't supposed to happen, but it had. She was in love.

Falling in love with her baby did not end the colic or cure Justine's exhaustion, but it made her eager to get on with her life. She put an announcement in the newspaper offering an opening-month special on baby pictures and began practicing on her daughter. Polly and Grace made sure she had customers that first month—nine in all. The following month Justine photographed her first wedding. Martha Claire organized her life around caring for her husband and her sister's baby. She still wasn't pregnant.

THEY had just crawled into bed when the phone rang. Grayson hurried down the hall to answer it, with Martha Claire following. No one called after ten o'clock unless there was a problem. Standing behind her husband, she could hear his mother's hysterical voice. Frank couldn't breathe; Lily was shrieking.

Martha Claire called Doc Hadley while Grayson pulled on trousers and raced out the door in his bare feet. By the time Martha Claire had thrown on her robe and joined him next door at her in-laws' house, Lily was cradling her husband's body in her arms. Grayson was kneeling beside his mother, sobbing, his face in his hands. They were in the dining room, with an unfinished game of cribbage on the table. Both Lily and Frank were wearing bathrobes.

Martha Claire put one hand over her mouth and the other against the wall for support. Frank was dead. Sometimes she had a hard time convincing herself that she liked her mother-in-law, but she had been genuinely fond of Frank. She went to stand behind Grayson, to put her hands on his trembling shoulders and kiss the top of his head. "My poor darling," she said. "I'm so sorry."

Doc Hadley arrived and called the undertaker. Lily wailed as she watched her husband's body being carried out the front door. She clung to her son and asked, "What will I do without him?"

But after Frank's funeral it was Grayson who retreated inside himself. In the weeks that followed, he left early for the store and stayed late. Lily often came to dinner, and he would reminisce with her about his father, but when it was just him and Martha Claire, however, their conversations were perfunctory. He repaired his father's small outboard and fished away Sunday afternoons. He needed time to come to terms, he told his wife.

Martha Claire spent as much time as she could with her mother-in-law, who was coming to terms in spite of herself. She didn't like wearing black, and she wasn't about to give up bridge and canasta. Not that she didn't get weepy from time to time, and she was lonely when she woke in the night and Frank wasn't there. But after a time sadness became a bore, and she decided to remember her husband fondly but also to work on her bridge game.

Martha Claire was determined to get Grayson out of his funk. Sometimes he didn't want to make love, and that was upsetting. How could she get pregnant if he didn't reach for her in bed?

Two months after his father's death she splurged on a rib roast. She put on a nice dress and set the table with the good china and candles in silver holders. When Grayson arrived, she greeted him with a kiss. "I don't care what we talk about, but we have to talk about something," she said. "I can't stand the silence."

He held her close for a long time. "I'm so sorry," he said.

"No need to be sorry. You had to get through your grief, but now I need my husband back."

They ate dinner first, making careful conversation. Grayson told her the roast was perfect. She was a fine cook. Over coffee, he began to talk in earnest. It was strange, he explained, to suddenly become his father, to become the Mr. Stewart who owned Stewart's Dry Goods, to see the rest of his life laid out in front of him, a replication of his father's and his father's before him. It wasn't such a bad life, he supposed, but Grayson wasn't as comfortable with people as his father was. And he didn't have his father's patience. He got irritated when people couldn't make up their minds after trying on ten pairs of shoes. He had thought he would be better prepared for his father's death. He had known it was coming. But still, Grayson was having a hard time getting used to the idea that he would never see his father again or hear his voice. Just today, down

at the store, he had tried to make sense of an invoice from the notions supplier. He wasn't sure what buttonhole twist was.

Grayson paused. "I guess that was just a long way of saying I miss
my dad and am having a hard time filling his shoes."

She took him upstairs without even doing the dishes.

WITH no baby of her own, Martha Claire relished every minute
she spent with Iris. She never tired of caressing her niece's downy
head, fondling tiny fingers and toes. She frequently kept the baby at
her house while Justine worked, making portraits of children, high
school beauty queens and football players.

With her first two hundred dollars Justine bought a 1936 De Soto
and cast her net wider. She photographed prize bulls, weddings,
church choirs. In the red glow of her darkroom, as she watched the
faces of smiling children and demure brides materialize in the developing tray, she vowed this was just an interim stage in her life.
She could not do this forever.

When she had time, she focused her camera on other subjects—
on the sweating bodies of quarry workers and cotton pickers, the
children of Freedmantown swimming naked in the river. She displayed these photographs on the walls of her studio. Everyone who
came through her door stopped to admire them, but it was the photographs of brides and babies that paid her bills.

Two days before Iris's first birthday Justine was photographing
her first out-of-town wedding, in Texas City, a refinery town on the
Gulf coast. The broad front steps of the church offered a fine view
of the harbor and the huge Monsanto refinery. Justine stood in the
back of the church, waiting to take a triumphant picture of the newlyweds coming down the aisle. The bride was saying "I do" when
Justine heard an explosion, and instantly the entire building began
to shake, the stained-glass windows to implode. Justine was thrown
to the floor and rolled under a pew to protect herself from flying
glass. People were screaming, calling out in pain. A bomb, Justine
thought. Not another war! She grabbed her camera and ran out the
door with one thought. *Iris.* She had to get home to her child.

But the sight that greeted her was not of war. Not a blitzkrieg. No invading airplanes flew overhead. But plumes of orange smoke were rising over the harbor, with burning pieces of debris arcing across the heavens like Fourth of July skyrockets. People were running toward the harbor. A ship had blown up.

Justine ran to her car for a different camera, different film, and prepared to join the river of people racing toward the pier for a view of the burning ship. Suddenly she remembered the small airfield she had passed on the way into town. An aerial photo would be more dramatic. She drove fast, hoping to get to the airfield before the roads were clogged with emergency vehicles.

A pilot who looked too old to drive a car, much less fly an airplane, took her up in an open-cockpit biplane. He flew so close to the burning ship that Justine choked on the smoke. They had just finished a flyby of the shore that allowed her to photograph the crowds of people watching the spectacle when she realized the chemical plant was on fire. She yelled at the pilot and was pointing in that direction when the Monsanto refinery exploded.

An instant later the concussion reached the airplane. Justine held on for dear life as the plane rocked about wildly. As soon as the pilot got it under control, she raised the viewfinder to her eye and photographed the huge fireball rising over the refinery. The people on the pier had been incinerated. They hadn't had a chance. Hundreds of them. As her mind tried to deal with the horror, her hands automatically inserted another roll of film into her camera. She kept on snapping the shutter, frame after frame of profound tragedy worse than anything she had witnessed in London.

Finally, her film exhausted, the pilot flew Justine to the Houston airport. By then she knew her pictures were too important for a state newspaper. She arranged to have the film on the first flight to New York and called the *New York Times*'s newsroom to say that film documenting the Texas City disaster was on its way. It was only then that she thought to call home. Her mother answered the phone and began weeping hysterically. "My God, Justine, when we didn't hear from you, we thought you were dead."

If she had run down to the pier to take her pictures, she would be, Justine realized.

The following day her photographs of the Texas City explosion, which killed more than five hundred people and injured more than three thousand, were on the front page of *The New York Times.* The ship had been a French freighter. The company that owned the freighter insisted it had been carrying fertilizer, not explosives. Already a controversy was brewing. Could fertilizer explode?

A Mr. Silverstein at the *Times* wanted Justine to stay on the scene. He wanted pictures of the mass funeral at the high school football stadium. "You're doing a great job," he told her.

She willed herself to stay dry-eyed throughout the service. After the film was on its way, she would cry.

Her pictures had gone out over the wire, which meant they were in newspapers all over the world. She hadn't felt this alive since London. Her postwar life had finally begun.

Three

MY AUNT Justine used to tell how people back east always thought she came from Alabama or Georgia. "You sound southern," they would insist. Justine would explain that east Texas was right next to Louisiana, and our drawl—and our ways—were more southern than western. Not that we had antebellum plantations with white-columned verandas where we lounged about sipping mint juleps. But most of Columbus's original settlers had come from Louisiana and Arkansas, and they had grown cotton and owned slaves. White folks lived on one side of the railroad tracks and black folks on the other side in Freedmantown. That division still exists today. Our schools are no longer segregated, but our cemeteries certainly are.

Our town was established in the 1830s on the banks of the Colorado River by families from the Stephen F. Austin Colony. Our Colorado River should not be confused with the mighty river that carved the Grand Canyon. Our river loops its way lazily across the coastal plain to the Matagorda Peninsula on the Gulf coast.

The decision to build a town on that particular bend in the river probably had something to do with the majestic live-oak trees that offered huge canopies of shade, a welcome relief from the relentless summer sun. Magnolia trees were brought to town after the turn of the century and now grace many of the older streets.

The Columbus of my childhood hasn't changed greatly from the days when my parents were young. An antiques store occupies the building where my grandfather once operated his pharmacy. A dress shop is in the building that once housed Stewart's Dry Goods. Other businesses are gone, too—the Orphic Theater, Smitty's Sandwich Shop, the depot—but many of the old buildings that housed them are still standing, occupied by tearooms, gift shops, even an art gallery. The courthouse, Stafford's Opera House, and the Stafford Mansion next door look pretty much the same.

Sometimes at twilight I turn my back on the ugly new bank building north of Courthouse Square, so only the old buildings on the west and south sides of the square are in my line of vision, and I can almost see us three kids on our bicycles, a nickel in our pockets for a cherry phosphate at the Sandwich Shop.

After our phosphates we would turn our bikes down Milam Street, toward the big old Victorian house where our mothers, Grandma Polly, and Granny Grace had all grown up. In spite of its cracking paint and sagging front porch, living in such a house had given our family a certain prestige. Our family was "old Columbus," our parents descended from original settlers. Since my brother, Buddy, and I were both adopted, we didn't actually have old Columbus blood flowing in our veins, but I felt proud that we lived in such a wonderful house, with its gingerbread trim, high peaked roof, round gable window, and—best of all—the broad front porch where we spent at least a part of every summer evening. The house would someday belong to Iris, but at that point in our lives it belonged to Buddy and me just as much as it did to her.

"THERE is no place on earth I would rather live than this house," Martha Claire announced as she and Grayson stood back to admire the refurbished parlor. For weeks now they had been refinishing the floors, papering the walls, reupholstering the side chairs. They had just finished rehanging the pictures and replacing her mother's upright piano.

"Well, that's one room down and ten to go," Grayson said with less enthusiasm than his wife. He wished his mother-in-law had sold the house when her husband died rather than invite him and Martha Claire to move in with her and Granny Grace. What at first seemed a way to save money was in reality a fiscal albatross. He hadn't realized the extent of the decay and termite damage to hundred-year-old lumber, hadn't understood the problems that came with antiquated wiring and corroded pipes.

Martha Claire wanted the house to look the way it had when her great-great-grandfather built it. But Grayson had inherited a dry-goods store that was barely able to pay their bills and those of his widowed mother. He and Martha Claire would have a difficult time if it wasn't for the government check he received every three months for his service in the Texas National Guard and the generous check Justine sent every month to cover Iris's keep.

For the past few years Martha Claire and Grayson had been taking care of Iris. Justine was now in Korea covering the end of the war. Her pictures of the first-released American POWs crossing the bridge over the Imjin River had been on front pages all over the country.

Martha Claire had decided that there was a man in Justine's life—based on what, Grayson was unsure. As a result, his wife worried constantly that her sister would fall in love, settle down, and take Iris from them. He feared that, too. Iris was the light of their lives. Already Grayson was anticipating her delight over the finished parlor. He glanced at his watch. Granny Grace and Polly had taken her with them to make Sunday afternoon calls on shut-ins. "All it needs now is an Oriental rug for the floor," Martha Claire was saying. "Then the room will be complete."

"Don't hold your breath on that one," he said as they walked down the hall toward the kitchen.

They sat at the big round table drinking lemonade and munching on sugar cookies. Martha Claire was full of plans for modernizing the kitchen. Grayson only half listened, occasionally reminding her they couldn't afford this or that. But dreaming about the house was good for her, he supposed. It distracted her from the other problem. Grayson always knew when his wife's period came. She would become quiet and wouldn't let him share her sadness. Then, a few days later, she would become hopeful again.

She was asking him if they could put down new linoleum themselves or needed to hire someone, when there was a knock at the front door. Grayson wondered who could be calling on this quiet Sunday afternoon. He hoped it wasn't Reverend Huxley inquiring about Grayson's spotty attendance at church.

When he opened the door, it was Doc Hadley standing on the front porch, holding a baby in his arms—a very small baby wrapped in a faded green shawl. "Hello, Grayson," the doctor said. "I've got someone here I want you and Martha Claire to meet."

Grayson heard Martha Claire call, "Who is it?" But he couldn't seem to answer.

"It's Doc Hadley, Martha Claire," the physician called back. "You got a minute?"

Grayson stepped to one side and allowed the physician into the entry hall. He could hear Martha Claire's footsteps coming from the kitchen. When she arrived at her husband's side, Doc Hadley pulled the corner of the shawl from the infant's face. "It's a girl," he said. "She was born this morning."

Martha Claire took a hesitant step closer. "Whose baby is it?"

"Yours, if you want her," the doctor said.

Grayson stared down at the tiny newborn face. *Their baby if they wanted her?* As the words sunk in, he had to grab the newel post to steady himself.

"But where did she come from?" Martha Claire asked.

"Can't tell you," Doc Hadley said in his usual brusque way. "All I can tell you is that she's a love child—there wasn't a rape or anything like that—and her parents are not from hereabouts. That's all you're ever going to know about this little girl's history. If you take her, it's with a clean slate."

"Grayson and I will have to talk it over," Martha Claire said.

"I don't have time for talking over. This baby needs someone now. If you're not interested, I'm driving her over to the Baptist Children's Home in San Antonio."

"But something as important as taking in a child needs to be discussed," she insisted.

"I don't see it that way, Martha Claire," Doc Hadley said, his voice stern. "You either want a baby or you don't."

Then the doctor fell silent. The two men watched Martha Claire, trying to take a reading from her frowning face, and waited.

His wife was lovely still, Grayson thought, even in a faded house-dress. Her skin was as satiny smooth as a girl's, the line of her jaw as young and lovely as before. But she had changed in other ways. She seldom laughed out loud, was seldom spontaneous. Only when she was playing with Iris could Grayson glimpse the vivacious girl with whom he had fallen so completely in love. But in spite of Martha Claire's diminished spirit, he still loved his wife, still wanted to spend his life with her at his side. And if that life was to be forever lived in this small town, he knew it would be more fulfilling if they took in this small nameless child with her secret history.

Tears were making their way down Martha Claire's cheeks. She looked at Grayson. All he could offer was the smallest of nods. It was Martha Claire's decision. He couldn't ask her to become the mother of a child she could not fully accept as her own.

Martha Claire took a step closer to the doctor. She reached out and touched the baby's cheek, and a whimper escaped from her lips. Suddenly she was gathering the baby into her arms. Grayson's knees gave way, and he sank to the bottom step. *At last, a baby for Martha Claire.* This wasn't the way he would have chosen for her prayers to be answered, but it would do. Yes, it would do.

They would get a call about the legal stuff from the secretary in the county judge's office, Doc Hadley said before leaving them.

Then they were alone with a baby, *their* baby, suddenly parents after years of longing. "Oh, Grayson, isn't she beautiful?" Martha Claire said, her voice filled with such reverence.

Grayson was aware that in the years to follow he would look back on this day as one of the most joyous of his life. He already loved his nameless daughter because she was theirs. Later he would come to love her for herself. But on this first day of his daughter's life he loved her because she had done something he had not been able to do. She had made Martha Claire happy.

They were laughing and crying at the same time now. With their baby between them, they shared salty kisses and stared with adoration at her newborn face. "What do we do now?" he asked.

His question sent Martha Claire into action. She sent Grayson to borrow enough milk from the neighbors to last until the grocery store opened in the morning. Then she dispatched him to the attic for Iris's crib, baby clothes, baby bottles, and a sterilizer.

Granny Grace, Polly, and Iris had already heard the news by the time they came rushing up the front walk. Right behind them was Lily Stewart. Grayson was proud of his mother, who seemed pleased about the baby and showed no disdain when he told her they would never know where the child came from.

Four-year-old Iris never left the baby's side. "Is she going to be my sister?" she asked.

"No, honey, she is your cousin," Granny Grace said.

"I'd rather have her be my sister," Iris insisted.

"She will be just like your sister," Granny Grace explained.

Grayson set up the crib in the corner of their bedroom, and Iris insisted on making a pallet on the floor beside it so she could sleep next to the baby. Already she was calling her new cousin Sissy.

In bed Grayson curled his body against Martha Claire's. He wanted to celebrate their good fortune by making love, but with Iris in the room that was out of the question.

"As soon as Iris is asleep, you can carry her to bed," Martha Claire whispered. While they waited for Iris to fall asleep, they surreptitiously kissed and caressed.

Their lovemaking that night was so infinitely sweet, it made Grayson weep. He loved and was loved in return. He was a husband and father. Life was good. He was just drifting off to sleep when the baby whimpered. "Let me," Grayson told Martha Claire.

He carried the baby downstairs and warmed her bottle, then sat in the rocking chair. "Thank you, sweet child," he told her with tears in his eyes. He kissed his baby's forehead. "I will be the very best father I can possibly be," he promised his daughter.

The following Sunday the baby was christened Cecelia Claire Stewart, but Iris's name for her cousin stuck, only they would spell it with a C, Martha Claire decided. Their baby would be Cissy.

No ONE understood what Martha Claire had gone through in the minutes after Doc Hadley offered her a baby, and she could never explain it, not even to her mother or husband.

She immediately realized that taking the baby would ease the anguish of Justine's visits, when she took Iris to stay with her in the garage apartment for days or weeks on end. Last fall, after Justine announced she was taking Iris to Dallas for an entire week, Martha Claire found herself wishing that something would happen to make Justine cancel the trip. Maybe she'd come down with pneumonia or influenza. Sometimes Martha Claire had thoughts even more troubling than wishing her sister came down with the flu.

Although truce talks were under way in Korea, the fighting continued, and Martha Claire had found herself guiltily imagining a phone call informing the family that Justine had been killed there— a phone call that would make Iris irrevocably hers.

That morning, as she had looked down at the newborn child in Doc Hadley's arms, Martha Claire thought, If I take this baby, maybe I can be a better person; maybe I can stop wishing my sister would die. When she took the baby in her arms, she vowed to pray every night that her sister lived a long and healthy life.

In the months that followed, Martha Claire realized that her husband assumed the baby had put an end to her monthly lapses into depression. And maybe Cissy did help some, but mostly Martha Claire did a better job of concealing them. Because of this child she was supposed to be a whole woman now. She knew, however, that nothing on this earth would ever cure the emptiness inside her except a baby conceived in her own body.

SIX months after Cissy joined their family, Doc Hadley returned with a two-year-old boy in his arms. "This little boy is Cissy's older brother," he announced. By this time Cissy was a sweet, easy baby who delighted in patty-cake and peekaboo.

Holding Cissy on her hip, Martha Claire watched Grayson approach the little boy carefully, his hand outstretched, his expression gentle. The boy was a pretty child, with dark eyes and hair like Cissy's. Without taking his eyes from the boy's face, Grayson asked Doc Hadley, "What's his name?"

"They call him Buddy. He needs a home, too."

"Hello there, Buddy," Grayson said, taking the boy's small hand and shaking it formally. Then he took the child from the doctor's arms. "My, what a nice big boy you are," he said. "Do you like cookies? I'll bet this nice lady here might have a cookie for you."

In the kitchen, Martha Claire gave the doctor a piece of pie and the boy a cookie, which he nibbled while sitting on Grayson's lap.

"Who's been taking care of him?" Martha Claire demanded.

The doctor shook his head. "No questions. This one comes with a clean slate, too. I just thought it would be nice for a brother and sister to be raised together."

Martha Claire was leaning against the sink, her arms folded across her chest. "Why didn't you tell us Cissy had a brother?"

" 'Cause if there'd been two kids, you wouldn't have taken either one of 'em," the doctor said.

Martha Claire sighed. He was right, of course. And she wasn't sure she was going to take a second one now. She was only thirty-one. What if she took this little boy and got pregnant? She already had her hands full with Cissy and Iris, and Granny Grace had had a stroke and needed help doing the simplest tasks. Her mother and Grayson's mother were both helping out down at the store now, leaving her to look after her grandmother and the children and manage all the cooking and cleaning. And she was beginning to think their money problems were never going away. Grayson worked hard at the store, but he wasn't a born businessman like his father. She didn't see how they could afford to take in another child. But there was such longing in Grayson's eyes. A boy to play catch with and take fishing—every man wanted that, she supposed.

She took the child from Grayson's lap. The boy was looking at her with big dark eyes. Then he offered her a bite of his cookie. Martha Claire took a small nibble and told him, "Thank you."

What kind of woman would she be if she said no? Did she really have a choice? "Oh, I suppose," she said. "But no more, you hear? Don't bring me another brother or sister in six months."

"You can count on that," Doc Hadley said. "Mighty fine pie, Martha Claire."

FROM earliest memory Buddy and I loved to hear the story about how Doc Hadley brought us to Mama and Daddy, and how happy our arrival in their lives had made them.

On our birthdays Mama always said that our birth mother would be thinking of us on our special day. Even now, on my birthday, I still wonder if there is a woman out there someplace thinking of the day she gave birth to a baby girl and gave her away, but it is only a passing thought. Mostly I think about Mama and all those celebrations around our dining-room table. Back then kids didn't have major birthday parties with clowns and balloons, but we could invite a friend or two to dinner, and the honoree would sit in Daddy's chair at the head of the table. I remember how special it was sitting in my daddy's chair and how silly it seemed to have him sitting in mine. And I remember Mama standing beside me, smiling, as I blew out the candles, telling me how proud she was to have such a fine big girl as her daughter.

Mama was an intense mother, often grabbing us children midsentence to smother us with kisses and hugs. And she was always grooming us—combing, straightening, retying, sending us back upstairs to rewash faces and scrub fingernails. She never forgot to hand out vitamin pills in the morning. My daddy sometimes accused her of mothering him along with us kids. And she did, reminding him to drink his juice and feeling his forehead if he looked feverish. That was who she was—a mother.

And my cousin Iris was a fiercely devoted niece to her mothering aunt. Iris taught Buddy and me from an early age that our job in life was to please our mother. That's what good children did. We were to rub her neck when she was tired and brush her hair in the evening when the family gathered to watch television. We were to make our beds every morning and never, ever leave clothes on the floor. Pleasing Mama was something I took very seriously. I thought that if I could be a good enough girl and show my mother how much I loved her, it wouldn't matter to her so much that she really wasn't Iris's mother and that Buddy and I were adopted.

We didn't need to worry about pleasing Justine, who periodically swooped into our life with hugs and gifts and enchanting photographs of faraway places. She was now living in New York City, but her visits to Columbus were magical times for us kids. Everyone in town knew Justine, and when we walked downtown, people stopped her on the sidewalk to say how much they enjoyed her photographs. If Justine had not been famous, she surely would have faced censure for not raising her own daughter. But famous people were allowed to play by different rules; after all, how could Justine take all those pictures if she never went anyplace? Folks were proud to know Justine, proud that she still called Columbus home, proud when a picture of their town made its way into one of her magazine spreads. Our bridge had been in Life, our county fair in The Saturday Evening Post.

Every day was an adventure when Justine was with us.

Justine turned somersaults and cartwheels on the lawn and played hide-and-seek with us. She would sit cross-legged on the old mattress in the attic and tell ghost stories by candlelight.

She took us on the train to Houston, where she would buy us new shoes at Krupp and Tuffly's and take us to lunch at the wondrous Forum Cafeteria. She took us to the beach at Galveston and to the Brenham creamery to eat the richest ice cream in Texas.

When she had the chance, Mama went along on our excursions, but not often. First Granny Grace was sick and shouldn't be left alone. And in the last years Justine came to us, it was Grandma Polly who needed looking after. And there was always the housework. We kids helped with the chores, but still there was a lot for Mama to do, and she wasn't one of those people who could leave things until later. Never once do I remember leaving the dishes undone so we could rush off to a ball game or the drive-in movie.

As much as I adored the time we spent with Justine, I sometimes stayed home with Mama while Justine took Buddy and Iris on the adventure of the day. And it wasn't just that I felt sorry for my mother and all the work she had to do; I cherished the times with just her and me. I didn't want her ever to doubt that I loved her.

When Granny Grace began what my mother referred to as slipping away, I helped her to the bathroom and up and down the stairs and constantly tried to bring a smile to her inattentive face. I loved my great-grandmother very much, but looking back, I'm sure a great deal of my motivation for looking after Granny Grace was that it brought words of praise from my mother.

One morning I couldn't make Granny Grace wake up. I don't think I ever had thought through the term slipping away to its inevitable conclusion, for her death came as a terrible shock to me. Afterward I had a difficult time reentering the world of childish pursuits. I couldn't bring myself to jump rope or play jacks when my Granny Grace was dead in the cemetery. Mama took me to see Doc Hadley, who took my face in his hands and told me I was a little girl and it wasn't good for a little girl to ride her bicycle out to the cemetery every day. He said that from then on I could go to the cemetery only once a week, on Sunday afternoon, and if he heard I was going more often, he would have to give me an anti-cemetery shot right in the butt, with a fat needle. Then, like always, he let me listen to my heart with his stethoscope and gave me a roll of gauze so I could play doctor with my dolls. Even back then I knew I wanted to be a doctor when I grew up, just like Doc Hadley.

WHEN Justine wasn't around, Martha Claire sometimes would go on and on about what a negligent mother her sister was and how phone calls and visits didn't take the place of someone who was with the child every day and took care of her when she was sick, and who crawled into bed with her when she had bad dreams.

The irony of it was, of course, that because Justine wasn't a full-time mother, Martha Claire had the privilege of filling in for her. She absolutely doted on Iris, and Iris loved her aunt and wasn't shy about showing it. She hovered around Martha Claire, fixing her cups of tea, helping with Buddy and Cissy. But the pure and simple truth was that Martha Claire was jealous of the love Iris also had for her mother. Iris was always overjoyed when Justine called on the telephone, and would count the days until her mother's next visit. Martha Claire refused to understand that she and Justine weren't competing for Iris's love. The child loved them both but in different ways. Martha Claire was for every day, Justine for fun and trips. Iris didn't think in terms of whom she loved more. She simply loved.

"No, SWEETHEART, think now—nine times seven?"

Buddy looked down at his lap and shrugged. "I don't remember," he said, his voice an agonized whisper.

Martha Claire reached over to caress his soft cheek. Such a beautiful child. At eight years old Buddy had a wonderful head of thick, curly black hair, huge dark eyes, and perpetually rosy cheeks that stood out against fair skin. Buddy was more beautiful than his sister, but he had none of Cissy's quick intelligence. But Buddy could learn, and he would learn. Martha Claire would see to that. Grayson said she pushed the boy too hard, but she couldn't bear the thought that their son might be held back a grade, that people might think she hadn't helped him enough with his homework. Grayson helped some, too, and Iris when she was finished with her own homework. Even Cissy, who was a precocious second grader, would help her brother with his reading. Together they would get him through the third grade and all the grades to follow.

"I'm sorry, Mama," Buddy said.

"Why, sweetie?"

"That I can't remember things."

She opened her arms, and he came to sit on her lap. Soon he would be too big for this, she realized, and she held him tighter, kissing his neck and hair. "Life isn't fair, my darling boy. Some children just have to work harder in school than others."

"I love you, Mama," he said.

"And I love you, Buddy."

"I'M SORRY, Mrs. Richardson, but I can't give your money back on a dress pattern that you've already opened and used."

"But I didn't use it," she protested. "It was too complicated."

"But the pieces are all wadded up," Grayson pointed out. "No one else would buy the pattern now."

"They can be ironed flat," she insisted. "I'm certainly not going to keep a pattern I can't use."

Grayson took a breath to compose himself. He wanted to tell this annoying woman that she could take her piddling purchase and go elsewhere. But he couldn't do that. He couldn't afford to lose even one customer, piddling or otherwise. In the end, he gave Mrs. Richardson her money back on the pattern.

He was no good at dealing with the Mrs. Richardsons of the world. Maybe if his mother or mother-in-law had been there, they might have fared better. But Polly wasn't well, and Lily mostly worked mornings, leaving her afternoons free for bridge.

Grayson's New Year's resolution for 1960 had been to be more innovative at the store. His mother kept telling him that doing things the same old way wasn't working. But here it was August, and he hadn't so much as rearranged the store fixtures. He had laughed when his mother suggested that he eliminate fabric and notions, which never made much money anyway, and add a small sporting goods department. Now he was considering her idea. He could partition off the back and carry shotgun shells, decoys, fishing lures and line, bats and balls.

But would it be worth the effort? He would still be a shopkeeper, and a mediocre one at best. He was never going to be able to fix up the house for Martha Claire or pay for Buddy's and Cissy's college education. Maybe a few changes would make a difference, though. He would discuss it with Martha Claire when he got back from guard camp, he decided. Tomorrow he would be traveling with his unit to North Fort Hood for two weeks of maneuvers, and he looked forward to the time away from the store.

After two weeks he was generally ready to come home, though, ready to see the children, ready to make love to his wife. The center of his universe was still Martha Claire, even though he wasn't sure why. Youthful ardor was pretty much a memory, and at times he still wondered what life would have been like if he'd never come back to Columbus after the war. Whenever he thought of his wife, though, it was with tenderness.

"HEY, Martha Claire, are you high on something?" Justine asked as she stretched out on the blanket.

"What do you mean?" Martha Claire asked.

"You seem so up. I haven't seen you run around and play with the kids in ages. You were actually *frolicking* out there in the surf. And you've laughed more in the past two days than you have in years. You even look younger. What's going on?"

"It's just nice to have you home for two whole weeks. And Grayson's sports corner at the store is beginning to turn a profit. Buddy passed fifth grade. And it's a beautiful day to be with my sister and our children on Galveston Island."

Justine raised herself on her elbow and regarded her sister. "If I didn't know you so well, I'd swear you were having an affair."

Martha Claire gasped. "How dare you say such a thing!"

"Sorry," Justine said. "I know you wouldn't do that. It's just that women I've known get all silly like you are when they're in love." She lay back down. Yes, something was definitely going on with Martha Claire. She hadn't protested that she was too busy for a day at Jamaica Beach, and she'd even dug around in her bureau for a bathing suit to put on, much to the children's amazement.

"Can you keep a secret?" Martha Claire asked.

Justine regarded her. With knees hugged to her chest, Martha Claire was staring dreamily out to sea. The wind was teasing her hair, which shone golden in the sunlight. Her profile was as pure as a Raphael Madonna. Justine reached for her camera and snapped the shutter before Martha Claire was aware what she was doing.

"Of course I can keep a secret," Justine said. "Did I ever tell anyone that it was you who stole that jug of homemade brew off old Mr. Logan's back porch?"

Martha Claire groaned. "That was the sickest I've ever been in my life. Mother thought we had food poisoning."

Justine sat up. "So what's the secret?"

"I'm almost five weeks late with my period."

"You think that you're *pregnant?*"

"Yeah. Wouldn't that be something, after all these years? I have an appointment with Doc Hadley tomorrow."

Justine regarded her sister's slim figure. Her breasts were as small as ever, and obviously she wasn't suffering from morning sickness. She'd been up at dawn, deviling eggs for the picnic. "Remember how sick I was when I was pregnant with Iris?" she asked.

Martha Claire's face clouded. "Not everyone gets sick. And you didn't want to be pregnant. I do."

"Well then, I hope you're right, if that's what you really want."

"I know it's difficult for you to understand, but I've never stopped hoping," Martha Claire said. "Motherhood is no big deal for you, but it's the most important thing in the world for me."

Not trusting herself to respond, Justine rose and started walking toward the surf, then broke into a run. She raced into the water and began swimming. She swam past the breaking waves until she could look back and her sister was only a speck on the distant beach. But Martha Claire's words followed her. *Motherhood is no big deal for you.* The words had stabbed like a knife.

MARTHA Claire regarded Doc Hadley's cluttered office, with medical journals stacked on the table, desk, and floor. Pictures of babies he had delivered over the years covered one wall in a random, thumbtacked montage. Every time Martha Claire saw that wall, she wished that a picture of *her* baby would be up there someday. Maybe now her wish would finally come true.

Doc Hadley had seemed impressed when Martha Claire told him she was thirty-four days late with her period. He had conducted her pelvic examination with his usual briskness, then told her to get dressed; he would talk with her in his office.

Martha Claire could hear voices coming from an adjacent examining room and a child crying. She hoped the doctor wouldn't take too long. What if he had forgotten about her?

But then she heard his footsteps on the wooden floor and the door to his office opened. "Sorry to keep you waiting, Martha Claire," he said, lowering himself into his desk chair. She held her breath while the doctor took off his glasses and cleaned them with his pocket handkerchief. When he put them back on, he looked across the desk at her. "You're entering menopause, Martha Claire."

"*Menopause?* But I'm only thirty-nine years old."

"That's young, but not abnormal. I'll put you on hormones to prevent hot flashes," he said, reaching for his prescription pad.

"Are you saying that I'm not pregnant?"

"Yes. I'm sorry to disappoint you again, but at least you won't have to worry about it anymore. Looks like you're never going to have a baby, Martha Claire. But you've got Iris and Buddy and Cissy. Surely getting pregnant is not as important as it once was."

"Couldn't you be mistaken? Maybe I should see a specialist."

He shrugged. "You can see all the doctors you want, but it isn't going to make you pregnant. Now go on home and count your blessings. You've got a fine husband and three lively young'uns to raise." He handed her a prescription and said something about what a good little ballplayer Buddy was turning out to be.

Martha Claire knew she was supposed to leave now, but she felt as though her body had turned to lead. *Menopause.* No baby, ever.

She didn't realize she was crying until Doc Hadley was thrusting a handful of tissue at her. She sobbed on and on, painful sobs that came from deep inside of her, from a broken heart and a womb that would be forever empty. Finally Doc Hadley called out to his nurse, who brought him a hypodermic needle to inject in Martha Claire's hip. Even as the nurse was leading her to a cot in the back room, Martha Claire could feel blessed oblivion flowing through her veins.

It was night when she awakened, and she was in her own bed with Grayson at her side. He immediately took her in his arms and told her it didn't matter, that she was more precious to him than anything in the world, that he loved their life just the way it was.

"Do Mother and Justine know what happened?"

"Yes, but not the children. When Doc Hadley called, I closed the store and went to bring you home. Tell me, my darling, what can I do or say to make you feel better?"

Martha Claire considered his request. And she thought of Doc Hadley's words—that at least the monthly torment was over. "Just keep loving me," she said. Then she kissed him. She found that she needed the reassurance of passion to reaffirm her womanhood. And this night his love filled her more completely than it had in a long time. She wondered, Could it be a new beginning, with loving just for loving's sake? She clung to him for a long time afterward, relishing the scent and feel of him, this husband for a lifetime.

Four

"ARE you sure everything is all right?" Martha Claire asked.

"My goodness, Martha Claire, you've only been gone since this morning," Polly said. "The children are home from school. Cissy is across the street playing with the Williams girls. Iris put a roast in the oven and is out in the yard playing catch with Buddy. Now stop worrying and enjoy yourself. Get off this phone and go make yourself pretty for your husband. Grayson's been looking forward to this reunion for ever so long, and the man deserves a weekend away with his wife."

Martha Claire hung up the phone and sat on the bed, staring at her reflection in the dresser mirror. Yes, she worried too much, and they had only driven up to College Station, for heaven's sake. But her mother wasn't well. Doc Hadley said her heart was worn out and it was a miracle she had lasted this long. Polly could no longer go up and down stairs, so they had moved the television and morning-room furniture into the dining room and moved Polly's bedroom furniture downstairs to the morning room.

If it weren't for Iris, Martha Claire wouldn't even have considered leaving town. At sixteen Iris was as responsible as any adult and would take good care of her grandmother and fourteen- and twelve-year-old cousins. Martha Claire smiled. Yes, she would relax and have a great time.

Hanging on the closet door was Grayson's dress uniform, silver oak leaves on the shoulders. He was now a lieutenant colonel in the

National Guard, and a battalion commander. Tonight they were attending the twentieth reunion of his class at Texas A.&M. Tomorrow there was a football game against Texas Tech, with the men being honored during halftime.

Grayson was singing the Aggie War Hymn in the shower, which brought a smile to Martha Claire's face. She wanted to look pretty tonight and was glad she'd let Iris talk her into buying a black velvet sheath that showed she still had a decent figure.

When she finished getting ready, Martha Claire did a little pirouette for Grayson's benefit. There was admiration in his eyes as he came to attention and offered her a snappy salute. Martha Claire hadn't seen him in dress blues for years. He looked so handsome, it took her breath away.

She remembered many of the men and their wives from the military balls she'd attended during Grayson's undergraduate years. At dinner they sat with Bobby and Ruth Mitchell, who now lived in Fairbanks, Alaska. Bobby and Grayson had roomed together their senior year and served in the same artillery battalion in France. This was the first time they had seen each other since the war. Martha Claire and Ruth chatted about their children, but mostly they sat quietly while the men reminisced about the war years.

After dinner she and Ruth headed for the ladies' room. When they returned, Bobby was commenting about how good Grayson looked, with not even a scar from his wound. "He would have lost an eye for sure if we hadn't been able to get him on a medevac flight to England," Bobby told his wife.

A flight to England? Martha Claire replayed the words in her head. Grayson had never been to England. She waited for her husband to correct Bobby's statement. But Bobby was still talking, explaining to his wife how Grayson had been wounded during the battle for Le Luc. The Germans had massed a strong defense of the town. Their battalion had been moved in as reinforcements. They were low on fuel, so they walked fifty minutes and rode ten. Grayson was just getting back into the jeep for his ten-minute ride when the jeep took a hit. The driver was killed. Grayson had taken some shrapnel in his right eye and was given emergency treatment at a field hospital, then evacuated to a hospital north of London, where he could be seen by an eye surgeon.

Martha Claire tugged on Grayson's sleeve, but he didn't meet her gaze, didn't say that Bobby was mistaken.

Suddenly the band was playing, and Grayson was pulling her out onto the dance floor. The music was from their era—"Sunrise Serenade," "Falling in Love with Love"—music they had danced to when they were young and filled with sweet longing. Their bodies fit together as perfectly as they had back then. Martha Claire closed her eyes and let the music take her. She mentally pushed puzzlement aside. She would think about Grayson and England another time.

Martha Claire waited until the weekend was over, when she and Grayson were on their way home, to ask him why he'd never told her about going to England during the war.

"I'm sure I wrote to you about it."

"The letter probably got lost along the way," Martha Claire acknowledged.

The next day, while the children were at school, her mother was resting, and Grayson was at work, she went up to the attic and looked in the footlocker where his wartime letters were stored. She found the letter telling her about having to wear a patch over his eye after having a piece of shrapnel removed, but nothing was said about treatment in England, which seemed odd. England was where Justine had been stationed. Wouldn't he have called his sister-in-law? Wouldn't she have gone to see him? Surely a wounded brother-in-law would have warranted a short train ride.

The following morning, without analyzing the reason why, Martha Claire climbed the stairs to Justine's apartment. The walls were covered with photographs she had taken, mostly of family, but also ones of Columbus—the bridges, the courthouse, Stewart's Dry Goods. Having no idea what she was looking for, Martha Claire looked in every drawer, opened every cupboard, shook every book for what might be hidden between its pages. Finally she went through a shoe box that held pictures Justine had taken in London during the war—photos of people digging through bombed-out buildings, medics carrying the injured on stretchers.

One picture in particular captured her attention—of a soldier and little boy kneeling beside a dead dog, with bombed-out row houses in the background. Justine had written on the back: "Charlwood Street, 150 houses destroyed by parachute mines." The focus was on the grief-stricken face of the boy. If Martha Claire's perusal had been a more casual one, she might have passed right over it, taking it for a candid picture of two unknown people—an American soldier comforting a grieving child in war-torn London.

But this American soldier had a bandaged right eye, and she recognized the familiar line of his cheek and jaw. It was a picture of her husband, and her sister had taken it.

THAT night, after Grayson had turned out the light and he and Martha Claire had gone to bed, she told him that she had found a picture of him that Justine had taken in London. He had been comforting a boy whose dog had been killed.

Grayson didn't speak for long, silent minutes; then his voice said into the darkness, "I met her for a drink at a pub."

"That picture wasn't taken in a pub."

"No, it was taken the next day, after an air raid."

"Why did neither of you mention something as remarkable as seeing a relative from back home in London during the war? What reason could you possibly have for not mentioning it?"

"It all happened so suddenly," he said. "Just hours after I was injured, I was on my way to London. Probably I decided to wait until I knew the outcome of the surgery before I wrote. My driver's chest was blown open. I tried to help him, but blood was gushing out of my eye. I thought I was dying, too. It wasn't something I could put in a letter home to my wife."

"So you told Justine?"

"Yes. She was there; you weren't."

Their arms were so close she could feel the warmth from his flesh. She shifted her weight, eliminating the risk of an accidental touch. "Did something happen between you and my sister?"

"Not in the way you mean. Air-raid sirens were going off. Justine helped me figure out how many shillings to leave for our tab. We were putting on our coats; then suddenly the building was caving in. We crawled down to the cellar and ended up trapped. Buildings were burning around us, people screaming. She made me promise I would kill her rather than let her burn to death. It wasn't something either one of us wanted to talk about afterward."

"And nothing else happened? Do you swear on the lives of the children that you didn't have a last fling before the flames got you?"

"No, we didn't, but would it have been so terrible to want that sort of human comfort in the face of death? Hearing Justine's soft south Texas voice made me think of you. Before the bombing started, I remember thinking how I wanted to sit in that pub all night and listen to her sound just like my wife."

Martha Claire allowed him to take her in his arms, to assure her of his love. But the seeds of suspicion had been planted. She believed him, and she didn't. But she would probably never know if her doubt was justified, so she decided to ignore it.

For a time it worked. Life went on. She took care of her children and nursed her mother.

Then one summer evening, while she was sitting at the table paying bills and half-watching an episode of *I Love Lucy,* the cloud of doubt began to lift, leaving sickening realization in its stead.

Polly was lying on the sofa propped up with pillows. Buddy and Cissy were stretched out on the floor in front of the television. Grayson was in his easy chair, with Iris sitting on the floor in front of him, using his legs as a backrest. Martha Claire paused a minute in her check writing to admire her niece's profile. Iris's hair was pulled back into a ponytail, her knees drawn up to her chest. She was slimmer than Justine had been at that age, but Iris had Justine's long legs and her dimpled chin, her widely spaced eyes and full mouth.

Now, however, Martha Claire noticed something about Iris she'd never realized before, something that made her put her hand to her heart and catch her breath. *Iris had Grayson's nose.*

She realized her mother was watching her. Martha Claire met her gaze, and Polly shook her head slowly back and forth, her message clear. Whatever it is that you are thinking, let it go.

Martha Claire pushed back her chair and walked out to the porch, where she stared into the night. Should she have seen it before? Other ways in which her husband and her sister's child were alike began to crowd into her mind. Their perfect teeth. Their laugh. Their beautiful singing voices. But what she was thinking could not be so. Grayson's injury had happened in late summer in 1944. Iris was born in March 1946, which meant she hadn't been conceived until after the war had ended, not until the summer of 1945. Had Grayson gone back after the armistice?

Later, after she had helped her mother into bed, Martha Claire sat on the edge of the bed and said, "Talk to me, Mother."

Polly placed her hands across her chest before she took a breath and said, "You have created a beautiful family and allowed me to be a part of it. I've felt so blessed to spend my last years with you and Grayson and the children in the house where I have lived most of my life. In all those years there has never been anything but love in this house. Don't change that now, Martha Claire."

"I am such a fool that I didn't see it before."

Polly said, "You haven't *seen* anything."

"Come on, Mother. I saw the look on your face. You've wondered, too, haven't you? Wondered if Grayson were Iris's father?"

"If such a thought had ever crossed my mind," Polly said, her voice firm, "I would have put it right out of my head."

Martha Claire stared down at her mother, who had once been plump and pretty and was now little more than wrinkled skin over bones—a woman nearing the end of her days. After a lifetime of caring for those she loved, she wanted a tidy ending for her life. "So you want me to sweep it under the rug?"

"Yes, that is what I want you to do, what I beg you to do."

"I'm not sure I can," Martha Claire said.

Polly squeezed her daughter's hand. "Yes, you can, Martha Claire Mayfield Stewart. For your family, you can do that."

ONCE the floodgate had been opened, however, Martha Claire could not look at Iris and Grayson without seeing some new way in which they were alike. Their earlobes. Their bearing. They both drank tea without sugar. And there was something else that occurred to her. Before the war Justine and Grayson had been great friends, always kidding and horsing around. In the years since the war her husband and sister had had very little to do with one another, she realized. She couldn't remember a single time that just the two of them had gone anyplace together, not even for a walk around the block. They saw each other only in the presence of other family members.

Finally one night, after the lights were out, when the silence in their darkened bedroom grew too heavy to bear, Martha Claire stared up at the ceiling shadows and asked, "Did you go back to England after the war and have an affair with my sister?"

"No," he said.

"Just *no?*" she challenged. "Not, 'My God, Martha Claire, how on earth can you say such a thing?' You swore on the lives of the children that nothing happened between you and Justine during the war. Now I want you to swear on their lives that after the war you did not have an affair with her."

"You have to stop this, Martha Claire," he said.

"Then you won't swear."

"No, I won't swear."

"Then I don't want to sleep in the same bed with you."

Silently he rose from the bed and crossed the hall to Granny Grace's old room.

The next day Martha Claire avoided him. That night he went straight to the spare room. And the night after that.

More and more Polly stayed in her bed, the sickness in her heart taking on an added dimension. The children realized, of course, that all was not well with Martha Claire and Grayson, and tried to be better children. Buddy kept promising he would work harder in school. Cissy kept her bedroom as immaculate as a nun's cell. Iris baked more pies and cakes than they could eat.

For weeks Martha Claire kept her silence, until she could stand it no longer. After the house was dark and quiet, she crept across the hall to the room where her husband now slept and knelt beside the bed. Grayson didn't move, but she could tell he was awake, and she began telling him the ways in which he and Iris were alike. And how, when he came back from the war, he and Justine acted like strangers. "Maybe the reason you never wrote me about going to England was because you knew you would be going back there to be unfaithful to me with my own sister."

"I'm not sure why I didn't write you about it," Grayson said. "Maybe I felt guilty because I had told Justine things I had never been able to tell you. I told her that I didn't want to come back to Columbus, that I didn't want the same things out of life that you did, that I had tried to tell you we shouldn't get married."

"And you went back after the war to finish the conversation?"

He said nothing for the longest time. A freight train's lonely whistle pierced the humid darkness as Martha Claire waited, whatever love was left in her heart for this man ebbing slowly away. *He hadn't wanted to marry her when she thought he loved her more than anything.* "Well?" she demanded, her voice harsh. "You went back after the war to discuss *the Martha Claire problem.*"

"Something like that," he said.

Martha Claire fell back on her haunches. Grayson rolled to a sitting position, his feet on the floor, his forehead in his hands. "I wasn't sure what to do," he said. "I didn't want to come back here, but I didn't want to hurt you. It was tearing me apart. Justine and I had a lot to drink. It just happened. I never planned for it, and I've regretted it ever since. God, how I've regretted it."

Martha Claire put a hand on the bedpost and pulled herself up.

"I don't know if Iris is my child," he went on, the wetness on his face shining in the moonlight. "Justine told me she'd slept around after her boyfriend was killed. When you wrote that she was pregnant, it was easy to convince myself it had nothing to do with me. I never asked her who the baby's father was. Justine never said. After a while I stopped thinking about it."

Martha Claire slapped him hard across his face, the sound reverberating in the silent house. "I hate you with all my heart and soul. I want you to leave this house and never come back."

"I would rather die," he told her, falling to his knees in front of her. "If you will let me stay here with our children, I will do so on whatever terms you set. Please, Martha Claire, for their sake. They shouldn't suffer for something I did. This will be our secret forever. Iris need never know, or Cissy and Buddy."

MARTHA Claire wondered how she could face the rest of her life with the knowledge she now possessed. *Her husband and her sister.* She had no doubt Iris was their child. The child she and Grayson had loved as their own was in fact *his* daughter—his and Justine's. It was too much to endure. The knowledge poisoned her insides and made food taste foul. It stole away her sleep. She was tormented with indecision. She did not want to subject herself and her children to a divorce, yet she could not live under the same roof with Grayson. She wished he would die. Then she could be a respectable widow and get on with her life.

And then, in the middle of all this anguish, on an overcast November day, with the children at school and Grayson at the store, she took her mother a lunch tray and found her gasping for breath. Even as she dialed Doc Hadley's number, she knew it was too late. She raced back down the hall and knelt beside Polly's bed. "Don't go, Mother. I need you. I love you so."

Her mother's last words were, "Grayson loves you."

MARTHA Claire put thoughts of her crumbling marriage on hold and went about the business of planning a funeral.

Justine was traveling throughout the South, photographing demonstrations against school segregation, and did not arrive until the day before the funeral. The children waited up for her and greeted her with hugs and tears.

"Mama and Daddy don't talk to each other anymore," Cissy told her. "Daddy sleeps in Granny Grace's old bedroom."

Justine looked at Iris. "Do you know why?"

Iris shook her head.

While the children fixed her a snack, Justine went upstairs and opened the door to the room where her sister now slept alone.

"I don't want to talk to you," Martha Claire said from the bed.

Justine turned on the dresser lamp. Martha Claire was leaning against the headboard, her arms folded across her chest. "I need for you to tell me about Mother," Justine said.

"I don't think she suffered much."

"The last time I talked to her, she kept telling me how much she loved me. I'm so sorry I didn't drop everything and come then."

"Oh, but you have your *career*," Martha Claire said, "and that's always been more important to you than family."

Justine regarded her sister's face and was shocked by the hatred she saw there. "Tell me what's going on. What's happened?"

"We will talk about it after the funeral."

Icy fingers of dread tickled Justine's neck as she backed out of her sister's room, closing the door behind her. She hesitated outside the room where Grayson now slept. She and Grayson hadn't had a private conversation in seventeen years. She needed to talk to him now. She was aware of Martha Claire's listening ears, though, and went back down to the children. Somehow Martha Claire had figured out her deepest secret.

AFTER the funeral Martha Claire asked Justine to come to her room. She sat on the window seat. Justine sat on the vanity stool. The door was closed. The children had gone home for the evening with Grayson's mother. Justine didn't know where Grayson was. He had been like a shadow all day, saying nothing.

"You are no longer welcome in my home," Martha Claire announced. "I will always love your daughter, but I hope I never have to see you again." Martha Claire held up her hand when Justine started to speak. "And don't tell me I can't know how it was during the war. Grayson has already done that. He told me about the bombs and about the two of you almost dying. Well, I wish you *had* died. Everyone has had close calls in their life. A close call didn't give you the right to have an affair with my husband. How could you? You might as well have plunged a knife in my back."

"You are right to blame me," Justine said. "Grayson was in a fog. I could have stopped it, but I didn't. And I told him if he had an ounce of sense, he'd tell his father to sell the store and give you an ultimatum." She began to pace, fighting down the need to lash back at Martha Claire, but the words came out anyway. "You were always so damned self-righteous. You never did anything wrong. I wanted to be just like my sister. I played by the rules and never made love to a man I loved very much. And then his plane was shot down. He was dead. Just like that. I didn't have the memory of lying naked in his arms. I wish he were Iris's father, but he's not. You know what Grayson and I talked about? We talked about you, about how much we loved you, about how we could convince you to take a risk, to at least give military life a try. We didn't plan for anything to happen. We got drunk and maudlin, and it just did. It wasn't a love affair. It was just two lonely, confused people who needed to touch another human being. I closed my eyes and turned him into an Aussie named Billy. And he turned me into you. I know it was wrong, but it wasn't wrong enough for you to throw away a good man and ruin your wonderful family."

But Justine could tell by the hard, ugly look on her sister's face that she wasn't listening. Suddenly Martha Claire began to shriek. "How dare you come back here year after year! It makes my flesh crawl to think of it. What kind of a monster are you?"

"But I gave you my daughter," Justine protested. "Do you think I wanted to? When you didn't have a baby of your own, I knew that was my penance. I had to let you raise Iris. But now that's changed. I'm taking her with me. I wish I could take Buddy and Cissy, too. This house isn't a fit place for children."

Martha Claire went white. "You will not take her," she said through clenched teeth. "Iris is *mine!*" Then she marched out of the room and down the stairs. She picked up the telephone and called Iris home from Lily's house.

Justine watched from the upstairs railing as Martha Claire paced back and forth across the entry hall. When Justine heard footsteps on the front porch, she hurried down the stairs. The door flew open, and there she was—Iris, the child they would both die for.

Martha Claire presented an ultimatum. "You are the child closest to my heart. I have loved you and cared for you since you were born. But now my sister wants to take you away from me. If you go with her, you will never be welcome in this house again."

Justine felt as though her heart were being twisted from its moorings as she watched her daughter look from her to her aunt. She would have to choose. She could no longer have them both. For an instant Justine wavered. Maybe she should back off. She knew, however, that every time Martha Claire looked at Iris, she would think of who she was. Her love for Iris would be tainted.

Iris had no answer, of course. Not then. She ran upstairs to her room and slammed the door.

IN THE night, Grayson went to Iris's room. She was still dressed, lying on top of the spread. He sat on the side of her bed and held her hand. "You must leave," he told her.

"But what about you and Martha Claire?" Iris said, sobbing. "What about Cissy and Buddy? Why did everything change?"

"It's my fault and no one else's. You must never blame Martha Claire or your mother. You have a right to be happy, and I don't think anyone who stays on in this house will ever be happy again."

He had brought a suitcase and helped her gather the things from her room that were most precious. Then the two of them crept down the stairs and across the yard. He carried the suitcase up the stairs to the landing. He heard the door open. He knew Justine was watching as he hugged Iris's slim body against his chest.

Dearest Iris. He could not imagine life without her.

When Martha Claire emerged from her room the next morning and realized that Iris and Justine were gone, she crawled into bed with Cissy and wept. Buddy came to sit on the floor beside the bed and hold his mother's hand and tell her not to cry.

Never had Martha Claire felt so alone. Her mother was dead. Her sister and husband had betrayed her. Iris, the child she loved more than anything, was gone. All she had left were these two frightened children who counted on her to mother them. And she would do that. But first she had to deal with other things.

She decided Buddy and Cissy were too upset to go to school. Later she realized she should have sent them anyway, as they watched with fearful eyes as she carried all of Justine's memorabilia down from the garage apartment and burned it in the backyard.

She also burned the portrait of the Mayfield sisters that had hung on the stairwell wall for almost twenty-five years.

Then she prepared lunch and left the children to clean up the kitchen. "I'll be all right," she said, "but I have to be alone for a time."

She stayed in her room for three weeks.

IN THE *days after Justine took Iris away, we learned that the Russians had installed missile bases in Cuba.*

While the outside world hovered on the brink of war and other Columbus families were planning evacuation routes in case a nuclear missile armed with a warhead hit the refineries that surrounded Houston, what was left of our family was dealing with its own more immediate crisis. We had no evacuation plans. How could we leave if our mother wouldn't come out of her room? Three times a day I would put her meal tray in front of her door, then knock and tell her it was there. Not a hint of life would come from behind that door except the occasional sound of the shower running or the toilet flushing.

Daddy, Buddy, and I watched on television spy-plane photographs of missile silos in Cuba and President Kennedy giving an ultimatum to the Russians. All the while I kept thinking of Mama up in her room. Did she know that any minute we all could die?

After I was in bed, Buddy would sit on the floor beside the bed and we would speculate about what happened to adopted children if their parents got a divorce. Whom would we belong to then? Often Buddy fell asleep on the floor, and I would slip a pillow under his head and cover him with a blanket. The Russians eventually backed down, but our mother was still upstairs.

Then one afternoon we arrived home from school to the heavenly aroma of baking bread. To this day the smell of baking bread makes me think of the time my mother came out of her room.

At dinner that first evening and ever after not one word was said about Mama's three-week retreat from the family. In fact, words about anything at all were painfully scarce. I remember staring at my plate, desperately trying to think of something to say. Iris could have gotten us talking, but I was not Iris.

The week after Mama came downstairs, Buddy and I got our first letter from Iris. She was going to an all-girl high school where the students wore navy blazers and pleated skirts. Her French teacher was taking the entire class to Paris in the spring. But she was terribly lonely for Columbus. Her mother had promised she could visit next summer if that was all right with Martha Claire.

"Do you think Mama will let her come?" Buddy asked.

"I hope so," I answered, but I wasn't sure. I knew that in Mama's mind Iris had betrayed her by leaving with Justine.

As those first days of the post-Iris era turned into weeks and then months, Buddy and I began to relax a bit. Our parents never kissed, never smiled at one another, but Daddy returned to what I had come to think of as my mother's bedroom. They couldn't still hate each other if they were sleeping in the same bed.

As the school year drew to a close, we waited anxiously while Mama decided if Iris could come visit us. In the end, she decided that no, Iris could not come. Buddy and I could correspond with her, but she wasn't to call on the telephone. I don't think I had ever before talked back to my mother, but that night I told her she was mean. Before she had time to reply, I rushed to my room and slammed the door. I cried so hard, I got sick and threw up on the floor. Daddy found me trying to clean it up and held me while I cried some more. When I had calmed down, he told me to go tell Mama I was sorry.

"But it's the truth," I insisted. "She is mean."

"Go," he said, pointing to the door.

I did as he asked, but had my fingers crossed behind my back. Mama said there were things I didn't understand. I wish now that I had known the reason why Mama wouldn't let Iris come. I think even at age twelve I would have seen the difficulty of my mother's situation and found some understanding for her decision. Buddy and I did not know, however, and we came close to hating our mother for denying us a visit from someone we loved so much.

Iris wrote how disappointed she was about Martha Claire's decision and proposed a plan "to keep us close." I was to call her collect on the first Sunday night of the following month—after Mama and Daddy were asleep—and she would explain.

And so, on the appointed night, with a pounding heart, I crept down the stairs after midnight and carried the phone into the hall closet, where I burrowed behind the coats. Iris answered on the first ring. "Hi, sweetie," she said, and immediately I began to cry. In a soothing voice Iris started telling me what once had been my favorite bedtime story—about the day that Doc Hadley gave me to Mama and Daddy and how Iris decided that I was her sissy and she would take care of me and love me forever and ever. "I love you, Iris," I was finally able to say. "I love you, too, my little Cissy," she said. We talked for more than an hour—a magical hour. Her plan, she explained, was for me to call on the first Sunday night of every month, collect. She had her own phone. Justine said that we could talk all night if we wanted to.

After that I kept an ongoing file in my head of all the things I would tell Iris the next time we talked. She wasn't always home on the first Sunday night of the month. Sometimes she and Justine would be traveling, and I would have to wait until the following month. But that was okay because I knew there would be a next time. My cousin, who had been like a sister to me, had been reduced to a voice in a dark closet, but that voice served as an amulet to soften the pain brought by warring parents and an unsure future.

With the monthly checks no longer arriving from Justine, money was tighter than ever, and the year after Iris left us, Daddy took a job as area sales representative for a company that made children's shoes. He was gone from early Monday morning until late Friday evening, and Mama took over at the store. She didn't talk about fixing the house up anymore. The best she could do was keep the old place painted and patch the leaks.

Every afternoon after school I worked at the store—Buddy, too, sometimes. But usually he had practice—baseball, basketball, football. Academically Buddy struggled, but he was a wonderful athlete. In the fall Daddy always made it home on Friday nights in time for Buddy's football games. Buddy played defensive end, and already people were saying he might be good enough to get a college scholarship. Those evenings spent sitting between my parents were nice. As we cheered together for our Buddy, it felt almost like before, when Mama and Daddy still loved each other.

Daddy took over at the store on Saturday morning. After he closed up, he would work through the list of chores Mama always had waiting for him, spending the rest of the day washing windows, cleaning out the rain gutters, painting whatever. He always did her bidding, even if her request was an irrational one—like crawling up onto the roof to check the television antenna when the TV was working just fine. She never said thank you, but was quick to point out something she considered less than satisfactory. Buddy thought Daddy should stand up to her, tell her he had the right to relax on the weekend, but he never said a word.

Every Sunday evening I baked cookies for Daddy to take on the road. On Monday morning I would wake up early to fix him breakfast and walk him out to the car. I knew that with his college degree from Texas A.&M. he could have found a job in town, but he drove away every Monday morning and spent four evenings a week alone in run-down tourist courts because that was what my mother wanted. I could not understand how our beautiful family had come to this.

I didn't want to love one parent more than the other, but my feelings for my daddy became more and more tender. Even if he had once done some terrible, hurtful thing to Mama, he had a good heart and had by now surely earned the right to be forgiven.

Five

HE HAD always wanted to travel, Grayson would remind himself as he drove up and down the state highways and county roads of his sales territory, which stretched across southern and eastern Texas. And he did try to find satisfaction in what had become his lot in life, as he went from one small town to the next. After he had made his calls on local merchants, giving his spiel about the perfect fit for growing feet, he would explore the surrounding countryside. But after a time everything took on a sameness.

The day Kennedy was shot, he was in Navasota. He called

Martha Claire, who was beside herself to the point of hysteria. But she didn't want to be consoled. She needed to get back to the television. Not even in a foxhole in France had he felt this lonely.

He hated all the jokes about traveling salesmen but did consider taking up with a woman in Tucker. Pretty, plump Loretta ran a homey little café with checkered curtains, and her pies rivaled Martha Claire's. He looked forward to Loretta's welcoming smile, but he couldn't bring himself to deceive Martha Claire a second time. His hope was that if he did Martha Claire's bidding without question, she would someday find it in her heart to forgive him. But Grayson hated for his children to watch silently from the sidelines while their mother constantly carped at him. What sort of memories would they have of this awful time?

"REMEMBER those times up in the attic when we used to daydream about finding our birth mother?" Buddy asked.

"Of course I remember," Cissy said.

They were waxing the station wagon, which Buddy had permission to use tonight—for a date, Cissy suspected. Buddy refused to admit he was going on a date, even though he had polished his shoes, gotten a haircut, and talked Cissy into helping him make the ten-year-old vehicle more presentable. Buddy didn't go on many dates. Cissy knew it was because he didn't treat girls very well. Buddy didn't want to be like their father. He didn't want any girl to treat him the way Mama treated Daddy. Buddy loved Daddy, she knew, but he didn't respect him.

"I'd like us to do that," he said, dabbing wax on a faded fender.

"Do what? You're not talking about searching for her?"

"Why not?" he asked.

Cissy sat on the open tailgate. "Buddy, we don't have a single clue to go on. We don't even know where we were born."

"You must have been born close by, since you were only a couple of hours old when Doc Hadley brought you to Mom and Dad." He sat down beside her and said, "We could put a personal ad in the newspaper: 'Seeking information about a white woman who gave birth to a baby girl October 17, 1950.' "

"What if Mama found out? It would break her heart."

"But we have a right to know."

"Not really. The law protects the identity of women who put their babies up for adoption."

"I asked Doc Hadley about her," Buddy admitted.

"What did he say?" Cissy asked.

Buddy shrugged. "That part of his job was knowing when to keep his mouth shut. He said doctors take an oath about that. I asked him to at least tell me why she gave us away, if she was sick or in prison or something like that. He just shook his head."

"Let it drop, Buddy. All you're going to do is hurt Mama." Cissy scooted off the tailgate and went back to polishing.

"I need to know if she loved us," he said stubbornly.

Cissy turned, startled to realize he was crying. She put down her rags and went over to him. "We have a mother who loves us." She rubbed a soothing hand up and down his arm. "And a daddy."

"You were just a newborn, but I was a year and a half when you were born. I was old enough to walk around and hug her neck, and *she gave me away*. Why would she do that? I need to ask her why. Maybe she's sitting someplace hoping more than anything that we will find her. Please help me find her, Cissy. Please."

"Buddy, you're not making sense. What if you found her and discovered she's an awful woman? Maybe the police took us away from her because she wasn't a fit mother. Did you ever think of that? No, I will not help you. It would be going against Mama."

"I WISH they weren't making such a fuss," Buddy said as his mother smoothed down his hair and straightened his collar.

"The whole town is proud of you, son," Martha Claire said.

From their backstage vantage point Buddy could see the lectern onstage, a row of chairs behind it. The audience was filled to overflowing. The band was playing "King of the Road."

When the coach told him there would be a public announcement, he had no idea it would be like this. His father had even come home midweek to attend. Dad hadn't come home in the middle of the week since Grandma Stewart broke her hip. Buddy glanced over at his grandmother in her wheelchair. She lived with them now, in the downstairs room that had been Grandma Polly's after she got too weak to go up and down stairs. His mother looked slim and pretty in a flowery yellow dress. She was talking to his dad and straightening his tie, even smiling at him.

The principal was lining them up to march onto the stage. Cissy was to wheel Grandma Stewart out last and sit with her on the end of the row. Cissy looked pretty, too, with her dark, curly hair worn down for a change and not in its usual ponytail. She was smiling at him, offering a thumbs-up from her position behind the wheelchair. Buddy returned the gesture and felt a lump in his throat. This should be Cissy's day, too. He never would have passed anything except P.E. and shop if she hadn't coached him all the way.

The band played the school song as they marched to their places. Buddy felt his neck turning red. He couldn't believe it. Half the town must be there. He bowed his head while Reverend Huxley offered a prayer that made it sound as though Buddy had gotten a football scholarship to Texas A.&M. because he was a God-fearing boy. He squirmed a bit at that. Buddy only went to church because his mother made him. He stared down at his large hands. His birth father was probably some dumb farm boy with hands just like these, not someone who was expected to go to college.

Buddy kept staring at his hands while his high school coach had his turn at the lectern, offering a lengthy chronology of Buddy's high school football career, ending with his triumphant senior season, when he was recruited by every college in Texas.

Then it was Mr. Lemkey's turn. Lemkey was the A.&M. assistant coach who had recruited Buddy. His words were less glowing. He called Buddy a solid player who had a lot of potential if he worked hard and made his grades. Then he called Buddy to the lectern. "And now, it gives me great pleasure to announce on behalf of the Texas A.&M. athletic department that Buddy Stewart of Columbus High School has accepted our offer of an athletic scholarship and will be playing for the finest football program in the entire nation." The band struck up the Aggie War Hymn, and the audience rose to its feet, clapping and singing.

When everyone once again was seated, Buddy was left alone at the lectern. In a quivering voice he thanked Mr. Lemkey and said the words he had rehearsed with Cissy the night before. He had chosen A.&M. because of its great traditions and because it was his father's alma mater. He promised to work hard and do his best. He thanked his coach, the school, his team, the town. Then he surprised himself by adding words that had not been rehearsed.

"My mother always said Columbus, Texas, is the best place in the world for kids to grow up, and I think she's right. I guess all of you know that my sister and I are adopted. We grew up in Columbus because two good people took us in and raised us. Cissy and I are the luckiest kids in the world to have ended up in this town with Grayson and Martha Claire Stewart as our parents. We owe them everything, and I love them very much." Then he hugged his parents, who both had tears in their eyes. Buddy was crying, too. And Cissy. His words about his parents had been heartfelt. He did love them and was grateful to them for the life they had given him. Maybe they weren't perfect, but then neither was he.

After the assembly Cissy said, "You were wonderful," as he held her close.

"Cissy, what if I'm not good enough for this?" And suddenly he wished he had turned down A.&M.'s offer and signed on at one of the small state schools where they didn't expect football players to do much more than show up for class. But everyone told him he'd have a better chance of a professional career if he went to a Division I school. And Mr. Lemkey had promised he would have tutors to help him study and advisers who would make sure he enrolled in classes taught by professors who understood the importance of football to the school. Mr. Lemkey didn't know, however, that Buddy never would have gotten through high school without his sister's help. If only Cissy could come with him to College Station, but she wouldn't graduate from high school for another year, and she was hoping for an academic scholarship to the women's college in Denton, where she could study nursing.

"What if I can't hack it at college?" he whispered to his sister. "Everyone will hate me if I screw up."

Cissy put a finger to his lips. "Just do the best you can. No one can hate you for that."

DURING *Buddy's three semesters at Texas A.&M., I came to realize that I had not done my brother any favor during those nightly study sessions at the dining-room table. As soon as I was old enough to take over the evening homework sessions from my mother, I became the most diligent of tutors. I'm not sure he ever would have graduated from high school without my help, but maybe that would have been for the best. A big strong boy like him could have gotten a job on the docks in Baytown or Texas City. He could have joined the army or the merchant marine.*

After he left for college, I did what I could over the telephone, but Buddy simply was no good at memorizing things—historical dates, the Gettysburg Address, multiplication tables. He went to college counting on his fingers and moving his lips when he read. He did modestly well on the freshman football team, but he was beginning to worry that he didn't have a prayer of completing four years of college, no matter how many tutors the athletic department provided. I think he wanted to quit school then, but the whole town was expecting him to become a football legend.

His sophomore year he played in most of the games and was cited in newspaper articles as a "promising" defensive player. I was a college student living in Denton by then, with studies of my own. I told myself that as long as Buddy went to class, he'd be all right. And maybe he would have been, but he frequently cut classes. I suspected his cutting had to do with all the beer he drank. His roommate bragged to me that Buddy had the team record for consuming the most six-packs at one sitting.

I spent my childhood watching over my brother. The time had come for me to find other purposes in life, but it was difficult. It felt as though I was succeeding at my brother's expense.

TEXAS A.&M. won the Southwest Conference in 1967, earning the right to face Alabama in the Cotton Bowl on New Year's Day. Buddy found himself constantly looking down at his right hand, imagining the Southwest Conference championship ring that would soon reside there. He went home for Christmas, but the team was required to return to College Station the day after to prepare for the bowl game. *The Cotton Bowl.* His family and all his friends would be there. Millions of people would be watching on television.

In the locker room before the game he received a telegram from Justine and Iris. They wished him luck, said they loved him and would be watching and cheering for him and the Aggies. Buddy got tears in his eyes. They loved him. In his mind he dedicated the game to Justine and Iris. And to Cissy. Always to Cissy.

The game was a close one, and Buddy didn't get to play as much as he thought he would. By the fourth quarter, however, there were injuries. Buddy knew he would play the rest of the game.

With the Aggies ahead 20 to 14 in the waning minutes of the game, all the defense had to do was hold the Crimson Tide for one last possession. But on fourth down the Alabama quarterback broke loose. Buddy realized that he was the only Aggie with a chance of catching him. He ran like he had never run before, closing on the Alabama player as he crossed the thirty, then the forty.

Buddy's lungs were bursting, but it didn't matter. This was going to be his moment. He was aware of crossing the midfield stripe. *Now,* he told himself, before the guy reached field goal territory. Buddy reached deep within himself for a final burst and flew at the guy, knocking his feet out from under him.

Almost instantly Buddy was engulfed by his fellow players. Hugs that lifted him off his feet. Backslapping. Cheers. All around him yelling and cheering. The cheering from the stands was deafening. All for him. All for Buddy Stewart of Columbus, Texas. He thought of his parents and Cissy watching in the stands, of Justine and Iris watching in New York. He hadn't let them down.

After the game, in the shower, with hot water washing over his bruised body, he cried with the emotion of it all. It was a day he would never forget. A beginning. From now on he was *someone.*

The next day his picture was on the front page of the Colorado County *Citizen.* When he walked downtown, people stopped him on the sidewalk to shake his hand. His mother had a picture of him in his Texas A.&M. football uniform framed and put in the store window. His dad and sister were proud, too, but they reminded him that finals were coming up, that he needed to spend the rest of the Christmas break studying. Cissy had exams of her own to prepare for, but she made out a study schedule for him and outlined the main points that would be covered on his finals. Buddy never ceased to marvel at his sister. How could she know what would be covered on the final exam in a class she had never taken? But she would look over the course syllabus, run her finger down the textbook's table of contents, and start writing. He should learn the major muscle groups and the basic food groups. He needed to review the rules for field hockey, badminton, and rugby. She wrote out a number of math problems for him to solve.

Buddy promised himself he would spend at least three hours a day studying, but whenever he opened a book, he would find himself replaying the Cotton Bowl game. He would stare down at the Southwest Conference championship ring on his finger and thank God he hadn't gone to a smaller school. Playing football for Texas A.&M. was a dream come true. After a time he would give up on studying. Surely none of his professors would flunk a player who had made the game-saving tackle in the Cotton Bowl.

He was wrong. The first week of second semester the coach called Buddy into his office. "Stewart, we told you that you had to at least show up for your classes," he said in disgust, shaking the grade report for the first semester in Buddy's face.

"But I only missed Monday morning classes," Buddy insisted.

"You only had classes on Monday, Wednesday, and Friday mornings. That's *one third* of your classes you didn't show up for."

"I thought all my professors supported football."

"Yeah, they're supporters. They could have flunked you, but they didn't. Each one of your professors gave you a D. You made straight D's! That means you are now academically ineligible." The coach took a breath. "I'm sorry, Stewart, but you're finished here. If you still want to play football, you'll have to raise your GPA and apply at a Division II school. I wish you well."

Buddy shook the coach's extended hand and walked back to the athletic dorm in a daze. What was he going to do now? How would he ever be able to face his parents?

He threw himself onto his bed, where he stayed for three days, getting up only to go to the bathroom and stumble down the hall to get a candy bar and soda pop from the vending machine.

Finally his roommate, Clive Fredericson, a linebacker from Lubbock, pulled a chair over to Buddy's bed. "The coach asked me to talk to you," he said softly. "You've got to leave, Buddy, before they send the campus police to kick you out of here."

Clive helped him pack and drove him to the bus station. "You got enough money to get home?" he asked. Buddy nodded.

He didn't go home, though. He traveled to Denton. To Cissy.

DENTON was a long way from College Station, almost to the Oklahoma border. He looked out the window at the passing landscape and thought about Cissy. Staring at the ceiling the past three nights, a major truth had evolved. He and Cissy were not related. When night fell, Buddy studied his own reflection in the bus window and found reinforcement for this theory. Other than the fact that they both had dark hair and brown eyes, he and Cissy weren't alike at all. He was built like a refrigerator, and she was as slim as a reed. He was good-looking, he supposed, in a big, rawboned kind of way, but Cissy had a look of quality about her. She was as delicate as the china figurine that graced his mother's parlor. Cissy was an angel. A princess. She was as dear to him as life itself.

The phone at Cissy's dormitory rang and rang before a sleepy-voiced housemother finally answered. Was this an emergency? She wanted to know. "This is her brother," Buddy said.

The woman let out a "Humph," not believing him. He would have to call back in the morning.

"Please, just tell her that Buddy is at the Denton bus station."

Yes, she would do that—*in the morning.*

Using his duffel bag as a pillow, Buddy stretched out on a bench and fell asleep. When he woke, Cissy was standing over him. He leaped up and hugged her. "Am I glad to see you."

"Buddy, what's going on? What are you doing here?"

He led her to a corner booth in a nearby coffee shop and explained that he was finished at A.&M.

She cried a little and told him she was sorry. "What will you do?"

"Get a job here in Denton to be near you. I thought maybe we could rent an apartment and live together." He reached across the table and grabbed her hands. "I can't go back to Columbus with my tail between my legs."

Cissy frowned and shook her head. "Undergraduates aren't allowed to live off-campus," she said. "I'd be kicked out of school."

"Then come away with me," he blurted out.

"Buddy, what are you talking about?"

"We don't have the same parents, Cissy. I don't know why it took me so long to figure that out. I'm oversized and stupid. You're little and smart. I'll take care of you. I love you more than anyone."

More tears welled in Cissy's eyes. "Oh, Buddy, whether we're related by blood or not, we were raised as brother and sister. I love you like a brother. I'll always love you like a brother."

"Then just let me be with you. I need to be with you."

She covered her mouth with her hands and slowly shook her head back and forth.

Buddy wondered if his life was over, if it would be better to die. Numbly, he allowed her to buy him a ticket to Columbus.

"I'll call Mama and explain everything," she said, hugging him good-bye. "It's just as well. Mama needs you at the store."

As Cissy watched the bus roll out of the station, she wondered if she could have gotten special permission to live off-campus. After all, Buddy was her brother. She had not been totally surprised by his words, however. She had sensed something like this might happen. Sometimes her feelings for her brother were confusing. There had been moments when she was deeply aware of his big, strong body. And yes, she, too, had wondered if they were truly brother and sister. But all that wondering and adolescent attraction was just a phase she had passed through. Now she was genuinely in love. Randy Calhoune was a senior premed student across town at North Texas State. She'd met him at church. Yesterday, after the eleven-o'clock service, he'd asked her out, and she'd been floating ever since.

For the first time in her life she was turning her back on her brother. But Buddy was twenty years old, she reminded herself. He needed to start solving his own problems.

Cissy went to a pay phone. When her mother answered, she said, "Buddy is on his way home, Mama. He's flunked out of school."

Martha Claire drew in her breath. "Oh, Cissy, are you certain?"

"Yes. He was just here. I put him on a bus for Columbus."

"What was he doing in Denton?"

"He was afraid to come home. I told him you and Daddy would be okay about it. Tell him how much you need him, Mama. He needs to feel important. Tell him you want to make him assistant manager of Stewart's Dry Goods." Cissy fished around in her pockets for a tissue. She was crying hard. "Oh, Mama, it just breaks my heart. He's like a lost little boy."

She could hear her mother blow her nose. "It will be all right, dear. Thank you for letting me know."

"His bus is scheduled to arrive at four fifteen."

"I'll be there."

"I love you, Mama."

"I love you, too, Cissy. You are the greatest blessing of my life."

MARTHA Claire hung up the phone and cried for her little boy. Her poor Buddy. She understood well the message of Cissy's call. Buddy needed to be built up, not torn down, which she might very well have done if Cissy hadn't prepared her.

She dried her tears on her apron, then walked across the backyard to the garage and climbed the stairs. Buddy would live here, she decided as she inspected the empty apartment. He needed both the comfort of his home and the dignity of a place of his own. As she ran her finger across the dusty table, she remembered that awful day when she'd carried Justine's possessions down to the backyard incinerator and burned them. Justine and Iris had been gone for almost seven years now, and Martha Claire still didn't want to ever see her sister again, unless maybe it was her dead body in a casket. She hated her that much.

When Iris wanted to come back for a visit that first summer,

Martha Claire had not allowed it. Iris never asked again. Martha Claire knew that Cissy and Iris had middle-of-the-night phone calls. When she realized what was going on, she had wanted to jerk open the closet door and pull Cissy out of there, but she hadn't. The girls had talked once a month for years now. At Denton, Cissy didn't have to crawl into a closet to talk to her cousin. Martha Claire was glad they had each other. She herself had no one to talk to. She had invested all in family. Her best friends had been her husband, her mother, and her sister. Now all she had left was two children who were careful in her presence.

Martha Claire worried that her children thought of her as a mean old woman who made their father's life miserable and had deprived them of their beloved cousin. She longed to tell them what their father had done and see some understanding in their eyes, but she and Grayson and Justine had sworn they'd never tell anyone. No one was ever to know that Grayson was Iris's father.

Grayson's mother had died last spring. Martha Claire hadn't wanted her to come live with them, but what could she say? Her own mother and grandmother had lived with them for years. Maybe if Martha Claire had still loved the woman's son, she might have felt differently, but there she was, taking care of someone she didn't really like. When Grayson told her how much he appreciated what she was doing for his mother, she simply shrugged.

After Lily died, they moved the bed back upstairs and put the television, sofa, and easy chairs back in the morning room. Most nights she sat there by herself, her dinner on a tray. She didn't hate Grayson like she used to, but she didn't love him, either. She missed her children and didn't like being alone at night. As a result, she looked forward to Grayson's being home on weekends and wasn't such a slave driver anymore. Sometimes they would cook hamburgers on the grill and walk downtown for a movie.

She glanced at her watch. It was time to go to the store. Assistant manager, she thought with a smile. Her Cissy was a clever girl, no question about that. Grayson was going to be disappointed about A.&M., but they'd always known the boy was no student. Surely Grayson would see that home was the best place for him.

FRIDAY EVENING, WHEN HE arrived home, Grayson was surprised to see a light on in the garage apartment. He got his suitcase from the truck and started across the yard. The back door opened. "Buddy's home," Martha Claire said through the screen door.

"Is he okay?" Grayson asked.

"He was expelled because of his grades," Martha Claire said, holding the door open for her husband. "He's telling people he has a bad knee and decided not to stay in school if he couldn't play football. He's going to work for me at the store."

Grayson went into the bathroom to wash up, and he stayed for a while to grieve in private for the death of a dream. Grayson knew Buddy was a marginal student at best, but after three semesters he'd convinced himself that the school would look the other way and let him play ball. Maybe he could even earn a degree. With a degree he could have coached high school kids, could have held his head up for the rest of his life. Grayson splashed water on his face, then went to have dinner with his wife.

"You look tired," Martha Claire said.

"I'm just hungry, and if I'm not mistaken, that's pot roast I smell. Isn't Buddy eating with us?" he asked.

"Some of his friends came by. They went to a basketball game."

"Is he okay?" Grayson asked again.

"I think he will be," Martha Claire said as she lifted the Dutch oven from the stove and set it on a trivet.

"I don't think having him work at the store is a good idea," Grayson said, and watched Martha Claire's spine stiffen. He should have sounded more tentative, Grayson realized. Now Martha Claire would dig in whether she had reservations about his working at the store or not. Grayson tried to backtrack. "It's not the store, really. It's the town."

"What's the matter with the town?" Martha Claire demanded.

"There's not much opportunity here. Buddy needs to learn a trade. He can't stay here forever and let his parents support him."

"We won't support him. I'll *pay* him for working in the store."

Grayson shook his head. "He's never shown any interest in that store. We practically had to threaten him to get him to wash the windows or help take inventory. You work hard, but Buddy won't. He'll put a sign on the door and go fishing."

"I didn't realize you had such a low opinion of your son."

"Not low, just realistic. A storekeeper he is not."

"Like father, like son. Is that what you're telling me?"

Suddenly more angry than tired, Grayson glanced toward the door. He didn't want to sit here in this unhappy home with his unhappy wife no matter how fine the food might be. Maybe he should just leave.

She put her hand on his arm. "Please don't go."

He looked at her for a long moment, then put his hand over hers and nodded. He would stay.

"Poor Buddy," Iris said. "School was always such a struggle for him, but football made him proud. Is he just devastated?"

Iris was twenty-three now, in her second year of medical school. She had had lots of boyfriends over the years and even had been engaged once in college, but the young man had second thoughts about her plans for medical school.

"Yes," Cissy was saying. "He wanted to move to Denton and rent an apartment for us to share."

"I can see him wanting that," Iris said. "He wouldn't have to go home and would have you to look after him."

"I told him I'd be kicked out of school if I moved out of the dorm, but maybe I could have gotten special permission to live with my brother," Cissy admitted. She was sitting at the one-armed student desk that sat by the third-floor dorm's only telephone. "Do you think I should have him move up here?"

"No, sweetie, I don't think you should do any such thing. You'd end up cooking his food, washing his clothes, picking up after him. You'd turn into his little mother when you should be having fun and enjoying college life."

"He's decided that we're not really brother and sister," Cissy said softly, checking to be sure no one was within earshot. "He thinks he's in love with me."

Iris said nothing for a long minute. "Buddy adores you, Cissy, because you're a sweet, precious girl who has made life easier for him. But the only kind of love you owe him is that of a sister for her brother. He'll find some other girl to take care of him."

"I'm not so sure. He's not very nice to other girls. He doesn't trust them. He's afraid of ending up browbeaten like Daddy."

Iris sighed. "Buddy has to work out his problems on his own. If you don't let him, he'll end up ruining both of your lives."

After the cousins said good-bye, Cissy wondered why she hadn't told Iris about Randy Calhoune. She hadn't told anyone else, either, in case he turned out to be not as nice as she thought he was. Still, Iris's words gave her courage. She had done the right thing for both herself and Buddy. Randy Calhoune had come along at just the right time. Thinking about him gave her resolve.

Was Randy thinking about her? Had he already begun to imagine a future with her? She wasn't sure she wanted to be a doctor's wife, though. Doctors' wives didn't practice nursing. Yet the idea of marrying Randy and living a comfortable life filled with children and a lovely home was not altogether unattractive.

Randy was tall and slender with wavy brown hair and matching brown eyes. He had a sensitive face and elegant hands—like a piano player's or a surgeon's, Cissy thought.

After her freshman year in Denton she planned to take the remaining three years of her nurse's training at Parkland Hospital in Dallas. Randy would be in Dallas, too. He had grown up in Dallas and planned to go to medical school there.

Dallas. A real city with skyscrapers. The thought of living there both scared and excited Cissy. She wanted to visit museums, libraries, even the fabled Neiman Marcus. Now she wondered if she would do those things with Randy Calhoune at her side.

IT WAS only three in the afternoon when Martha Claire returned earlier than expected from a funeral in Rosenberg for her father's cousin Trudy. Arriving at the store, she found the lights off and the door locked. With a sigh of disappointment she fished around for her key and went inside. The merchandise on the sale table was in a jumble, and the cash register drawer was open.

How much had Buddy taken? Martha Claire wondered. She couldn't get it into his head that she paid him what she could afford and he absolutely could not help himself to more money whenever he felt like it. He didn't pay rent and ate most meals at home, so he should have enough money to make payments on his used Ford pickup and to manage his few other expenses. But she knew he was already behind on the truck payments.

Buddy went out with his friends almost every night and didn't come back until all hours. Sometimes he didn't show up at the store until noon or later. He was a good salesman, however, when he put his mind to it. Male customers would linger after they had made their purchase to talk sports, often thinking of something else they needed to buy while they rehashed Buddy's game-saving tackle in the 1968 Cotton Bowl game.

It was just going to take time, Martha Claire told herself as she folded the sweaters on the sale table. Buddy still wasn't over the disappointment of being dismissed from A.&M. Eventually he would settle down and assume more responsibility for the store.

Grayson didn't agree with her. He kept insisting that Buddy was going to have to leave Columbus. Grayson thought Buddy should join the army or learn a trade, like welding or auto mechanics. Only last week he'd told Buddy that he was going to kick him out of the garage apartment if he came home drunk one more time.

"This is my property," Martha Claire reminded her husband.

Buddy had smirked at his father. "Hear that, Dad? Guess we know who wears the pants around here, don't we?"

This weekend Martha Claire didn't want to fight about Buddy. She planned to tell Grayson that. There wasn't anything he could say that would make her send Buddy away, so there was no point in discussing it. She would cook a pork roast for dinner.

Grayson called Friday morning to say he was making a call in nearby Sealy and should be home by six. "Tell Buddy I expect him to have dinner with us. If you go to the trouble to cook a meal, he should be there to eat it. And I thought we could sit down after dinner and look at some of the brochures I've sent for. There are some excellent vocational programs around the state."

Martha Claire started to say she had no intention of sending Buddy away, but she held back. She wanted a nice evening. Besides, Buddy wouldn't show up for dinner. He never did when Grayson was home. He didn't want to hear his father's lectures.

Sure enough, right before closing time, Buddy left the store. Martha Claire knew she wouldn't see him until he dragged himself out of bed Saturday morning.

The first thing Grayson said when he walked in the door was, "Where's Buddy?"

Martha Claire couldn't help herself. She put her hands on her hips and told her husband that Buddy was having a hard time adjusting. Yes, he drank too much, but he just needed time to get himself straightened out. Maybe someday he would learn to drive sixteen-wheelers or become a welder, but it had to be something the boy decided and not something his father dictated. And she didn't want to hear another word about sending him away.

"It probably doesn't matter anyway," Grayson said, tossing a packet of brochures in the trash. "He's probably going to be drafted. He'll end up crawling around a jungle in Southeast Asia."

BUDDY'S draft notice came in the spring. After basic training at Fort Hood, he came home for one last weekend before he left for Vietnam. I drove down from Dallas to tell him good-bye. I cried and told him to take care of himself. I wondered if I would ever see him again. I prayed I would, and that the army would make a man of him. Something sure needed to. If that war didn't destroy him, I feared he would end up doing the job himself.

My father had now moved back into Granny Grace's old bedroom, and I suspected he would never again be welcome in my mother's bed. Their war over Buddy seemed to have eroded whatever goodwill they had reconstructed in the years since Iris left.

My dad had inherited forty acres of bottomland from his mother and sold off most of it to a cotton farmer, saving a river-hugging sliver for himself. He used the money from the sale to bulldoze a narrow lane, buy construction materials, and dig a well and an outdoor toilet. After my brother left for Vietnam, Daddy built a one-room cabin with a porch that overlooked the river. I knew he wanted a retreat, some-place to which he could escape from Mama.

Buddy was assigned to a quartermaster unit in Saigon. He never wrote, but he did call home every couple of weeks. Mama said that he liked it there and actually seemed to be enjoying himself. No one shot at people in the quartermaster corps.

After a year and a half he returned to Columbus and the rent-free garage apartment, seemingly unchanged from his time in a war zone. He was as irresponsible as ever. I suspected my brother had become an alcoholic or worse. I knew I should go home and confront him, make him see a doctor or join A.A., but I didn't. As I finished up my last year of nurse's training and spent as much time with Randy Calhoune as our schedules allowed, Columbus and the problems there seemed very far away.

Randy wanted to give me an engagement ring, but I told him I wasn't ready. I loved him, and for two years now I had lived for his phone calls, his presence. True love was supposed to be forever, but the lesson I had learned from my parents told me that was not always so. I wondered how I might feel about Randy in fifteen or twenty years—and how he'd feel about me.

THE last Sunday in May my parents and Buddy drove up to Denton for the Texas University for Women commencement ceremony. I graduated with highest honors and even won the Florence Nightingale Award for most exemplifying the highest ideals of nursing. I had worked hard to make my parents proud.

Randy sat with them. He had given me a birthstone ring as a graduation present. A friendship ring, he called it, because I still wasn't ready to be engaged.

Eventually my foot-dragging turned into a decision of sorts, and he found someone else. Even as I suffered the pain of rejection, I felt as though a burden had been lifted from my shoulders. My future no longer was laid out in front of me like a road map.

I was a better nurse after that. I became a professional, not just a girl biding her time until the wedding bells rang. I began to think about maybe training to become a nurse-anesthetist. With Randy out

*of my life, I could do it in Houston. With the interstate highway,
Columbus and Houston were now just an hour apart.*

*I actually looked forward to being the dutiful daughter again. My
parents needed me, and I needed them. If Buddy had been a more devoted son, if Iris wasn't lost to them, if Justine still came to visit, if
they had a joyous marriage, I might have felt less connected to them.
As it was, I was needed.*

Six

BOB Anderson regarded Martha Claire from behind his large, very
cluttered desk. "What does Grayson think about this?" he asked.

Martha Claire shifted in her chair. Grayson wanted to sell the
house. He called it an albatross. "He's not crazy about the idea,"
she admitted. "But it is my house."

The portly bank officer picked up Martha Claire's loan application. "This is a lot of money you're asking for."

"That's what it will take to fix up the house," she said. "The
plumbing has to be replaced, the kitchen modernized. I'll want to
finish out the attic and put two bedrooms, a bathroom, and a sitting
room up there. The estimates are attached."

"A lot of money," Bob said. "And what if this bed-and-breakfast
idea catches on? Other folks might rent rooms. The town could end
up with more guest rooms than it can support."

"Mine would be the best," Martha Claire said with a lift of her
chin. "I can make the house pay its way, Bob. I know I can."

"Maybe so, maybe not," he said, leaning back in his chair. "But if
the bank does agree to finance this project, I'll have to have a mortgage on the house, Martha Claire. And I will need Grayson to sign
the note."

"But the property belongs to me," she protested.

"Yes, but it's going to take both of you to make this project work,
and we've got to have a cosigner. If you really want to do this, you'd

better sit down and talk it over with Grayson. It's a big undertaking and a big debt to assume. Unless you both are completely behind it, I think you better forget about this loan."

She felt hot anger rise to her cheeks. She had mentioned it on and off to Grayson for a couple of years, but he always changed the subject. Martha Claire wanted to tell Bob Anderson never mind, that she would take her business elsewhere. But if her hometown bank wouldn't loan her the money, how could she expect anyone else to? She stood. "I'll talk to Grayson," she said.

MARTHA Claire and Grayson still had their Friday evening dinners—just the two of them. Buddy was seldom around. Strange how she looked forward to them. Martha Claire doubted if she and Grayson would ever again sleep in the same bed. But Friday morning she would wash her hair, and Friday evening she would prepare something nice for dinner. Over dinner they would share any conversations they'd had with Cissy. Martha Claire would give Grayson a report on the store. Buddy was mentioned only in passing. If they talked about Buddy or spending money on the house, they argued. And they tried not to argue on Friday evenings.

This Friday night, however, Martha Claire couldn't wait. She passed Grayson the bowl of mashed potatoes and told him all in a rush that she needed for him to co-sign a mortgage so she could turn the house into a bed-and-breakfast establishment.

"Right now we are without debt, Martha Claire," he said, putting down the bowl. "That is one of the few things we have going for us. I know how much you love the house, but we're too old to take on a debt like that. I'd never be able to retire. If we sold the house, we could buy a smaller place and maybe go to Europe. Just think of how tied down you would be with a bed-and-breakfast."

"I want it more than anything," she told him. "And you owe me this, Grayson."

He met her gaze. "So if I sign this note, does my penance end?"

Martha Claire regarded her husband of more than thirty years. All she had ever wanted was to marry this man and have his children. If she had never discovered the truth about Iris's birth, she could have lived the rest of her life in blissful ignorance. Then maybe this dilapidated old house wouldn't be so important to her. As it was, however, all her dreams were invested in it. Her only chance for happiness was to turn her family home into a bed-and-breakfast.

But Grayson wanted to strike a bargain. He would sign the papers at the bank if she would agree to renew their marriage. How remarkable to think that he still cared about her enough to want that. She should be flattered, she supposed. She could tell him yes, that she would wipe the slate clean if he would only sign that note. He could return to her bed and her arms.

But he had made love to her sister, and for ten years she had had to live with that image. The two of them meeting someplace, kissing, undressing one another, exploring each other's bodies. She could see it all. She could see the act that had given her sister a baby when she herself would never have one.

CISSY'S elderly landlady stood in the middle of the tiny apartment and clasped her hands to her meager bosom. "You have made it very pretty," Mrs. Tran said in her very precise English.

Cissy looked around, seeing it through Mrs. Tran's eyes. In the past week she had painted the walls and ceiling, installed a ceiling fan, and sanded and varnished the floors. It did look nice, she decided. A garage apartment, no less, just like back home. It was only a ten-minute drive to Houston's Baylor Medical Center and cheap enough that she didn't have to have a roommate.

She had disappointed her mother terribly when she accepted a position in the intensive care unit at Baylor. It was nursing at its most intense, triumph and loss on a daily basis. Maybe someday she would be satisfied with working in a small-town hospital, but right now she wanted challenges.

The dynamics of her parents' marriage had shifted once again since her father had refused to mortgage the house and let Mama start a bed-and-breakfast. Her father no longer automatically did everything her mother asked and spent more and more time in his fishing cabin. He had visited Cissy in September, and she had taken him through the intensive care unit where she worked. Later they had toured the Houston Museum of Fine Art, where he had lingered in front of the paintings by European masters and told her how, after the war, he had spent many afternoons in the Louvre and traveled to Rome to see the Vatican art treasures.

"You always said you were going to go back to Europe someday," Cissy said, and immediately wished she hadn't. The look of pain on her father's face made her look away.

"Yes. I always wanted to take your mother there, but I don't think she really wants to go. Once maybe, but not anymore."

"I'll go with you," Cissy said. "Maybe Iris could come with us."

"Do you still talk to Iris?"

"Yes, but not like before. She's doing her residency, so she's as busy as I am. We're lucky to catch each other every other month."

"Please tell her that I think about her every single day."

Cissy realized her father had tears in his eyes and reached for his hand. "I will," she promised. Then she added, "I love you, Daddy. Iris does, too. She says you are the finest man she's ever known."

CISSY didn't arrive home for Thanksgiving until almost eleven o'clock Wednesday evening, but her parents came out to greet her as always. Her father carried her bags up to her room, and her mother insisted on putting out milk and cookies. Buddy was out. He had left directions to a roadhouse on the Brenham highway if Cissy wanted to drive over and meet his friends. Saturday night she would go, Cissy promised herself. Tonight she was tired.

Her parents sat with her at the kitchen table, quizzing her about work, the performance of the used Volkswagen bus she had bought. As she watched them, she thought how handsome they were. Life had disappointed them, but as they sat here talking to her, their faces were filled with the pleasure of her company. Cissy felt guilty that she didn't come home more often.

That night Cissy awakened to the sound of the phone ringing. She rolled over and stared at the clock. Three fifty-seven. Then she looked out the window to see if Buddy's truck was parked by the garage. It was not. She rushed into the hall. Her father was already hurrying down the stairs, an anxious expression on his face. Her mother had come out of her room. Cissy stood with her mother at the railing. *Let it be a wrong number,* Cissy prayed. *Please.*

When he hung up the phone, Grayson looked up at them. "There's been an accident. Buddy was coming back from Brenham. They're taking him to the hospital there."

"Was he badly hurt?" Martha Claire asked, her voice trembling. Grayson nodded.

Cissy drove, with her mother in the front seat and her dad in back, heading up Highway 109. Near Kearney they passed a wrecker towing Buddy's hideously twisted pickup. Martha Claire cried out, "Oh, my God!" and began to sob.

Cissy clutched the steering wheel and prayed with all her might that her brother would survive. She should have driven to Brenham tonight to meet him, no matter how late it was. She should have let him move to Denton. Insisted he come live with her in Houston. Buddy wasn't strong like she was. He needed her to take care of him. Yes, she would do that. She would nurse him back to health, help him get himself straightened out.

The nurse looked up as they rushed into the emergency room, and she paged the doctor. Cissy knew at once that Buddy was dead. It was too quiet. There was no activity, no ER staff racing around.

The slim young doctor introduced herself and explained that Buddy had been dead on arrival. He had been thrown from the car, his neck broken. He had not suffered.

"Where is he?" Martha Claire demanded.

The doctor walked over to a door and opened it. "I'm sorry," she said, and stood aside to let Martha Claire and Grayson enter.

Watching from the doorway, Cissy gasped as her mother pulled back the sheet, exposing the face of her dead brother. Martha Claire caressed Buddy's lifeless features, kissed his brow, and called him the dearest little boy in the world. Then suddenly she whirled to face her husband. "Go ahead. Say it's my fault. I should have sent him away before it came to this."

Tears streaming down his face, Grayson shook his head. "No, it's my fault. I saw this coming and didn't stop it." He approached the body of his son with halting steps and kissed his lips. "Oh, God, my poor Buddy. My poor Buddy. We didn't do you any favor when we made you a member of this family. No favor at all."

Then, with sobs that felt as though they were ripping open her chest, Cissy approached her brother's body and lay her own across it. She was so sorry. So very very sorry. And there was no way to make amends.

AFTER they said their farewells to Buddy, Cissy told the nurse at the Brenham hospital the name of the funeral home in Columbus. Then there was nothing else to do but go back home.

Once there, her mother said she wanted to be alone. Cissy helped her into bed. While she covered her with a quilt, she heard her father's footsteps on the stairs. The door to his room closed.

Cissy went downstairs and picked up the phone. It wasn't Sunday. She didn't hide in the closet. She didn't call collect.

Iris answered at once with a crisp "Dr. Dover."

Cissy began to cry. "It's Buddy, Iris. Buddy is dead." She heard her mother's door open, then her father's. She knew they were looking down at her as she told Iris, the banished child, what had happened to their Buddy, heard her pour out her heart, how she could have saved him, taken him in and watched over him.

"Yes, you could have become his little wife," Iris said, "but would that have turned him into a man? You need to remember all the reasons why you love him and bury the rest."

When Cissy hung up, she heard her mother's door close, then her father's. She sat there in the hallway of her childhood home, where three happy children once had lived. She could almost hear their voices, their laughter. Why had it all changed?

THE morning of the funeral arrived bright and fair. Cissy insisted that her parents come downstairs and eat breakfast. When the funeral-home limousine arrived, they were ready.

Cissy wanted her parents to hold hands or walk arm in arm, but there was no touching between them, not as they walked down the front walk, not in the limousine. Not a word passed between them as they rode to their son's funeral.

The sunlight was intense, and once inside the church, it took Cissy's eyes a minute to adjust to the dusky interior, to realize the smart-looking young woman standing in the vestibule was Iris. Stunned, Cissy's hands flew to her mouth. *Iris!* She took a few halting steps; then suddenly they were embracing. It was really Iris, after all those years. Tears flowed once again, her sadness mingling with joy. Iris had come to help them bury Buddy.

Then Cissy felt Iris pull away, and she stood to one side so Iris could approach Martha Claire and Grayson—the aunt and uncle who had raised her. Martha Claire was standing erect. Grayson looked as though he was about to faint. "I had to come," Iris explained. "Buddy was like my little brother. Mother and I cried together. I know how you both must hurt." Martha Claire nodded and allowed Iris to kiss her cheek. Grayson stood like a statue while she embraced him, but tears were running down his cheeks.

They sat together in front of Buddy's open casket. Cissy clung to her cousin's hand on one side, her mother's on the other. Behind them every seat was taken, and men were standing in the back. They had come to bury the boy who helped give them some of the best years of football Columbus High School had ever had.

At the graveside Martha Claire grew faint and almost fell off her chair. Grayson grabbed her and held her close, but she pulled away. Reverend Huxley hurried to the end of his prayer.

The ladies of the church brought lunch to the house, and people came throughout the afternoon to offer their condolences.

"I remembered them all," Iris said later as she sat with Cissy at the kitchen table, drinking first coffee, then bourbon. "Some of them asked about Mother, but only when Martha Claire wasn't listening. They all must wonder what happened."

"Don't we all?" Cissy commented.

They sat into the night, reminiscing about Buddy, about life as it once had been. "I used to think this was the best house in the whole town," Iris said, looking around the kitchen—at the worn linoleum, the cracks in the ceiling. "It makes me sad to see it like this. Maybe they should sell it and move someplace smaller."

"That's what Daddy says, but I don't think Mama will ever sell it.

She was going to leave it to you someday, since you're blood kin, but then you went away."

"And you don't want it?" Iris asked.

"Probably not. I don't really know what I want. Sometimes I think I should move back home."

"Don't sacrifice the rest of your life for them, Cissy."

Cissy sighed. She didn't try to explain her need for atonement. Iris would not understand. She had failed her brother, and now he was dead. She didn't want to fail her parents, too.

They listened while the mantel clock struck twice. Then Iris pushed an envelope across the table. "What's this?" Cissy asked.

"An open-ended plane ticket to New York. You can use it any time. I'm not leaving here until you promise that you will."

Cissy picked up the envelope. "I always wanted to come visit, but I knew how it would upset Mama."

"I realize that, but I'm tired of only phone calls. Martha Claire's not going to disown you, honey. You're all she has."

"Don't I know it," Cissy said. "I *will* come, though. I promise."

BUDDY *had been dead more than two years when Iris called to say it was time for me to see if that plane ticket was still good. If it wasn't, she would send another. She was getting married.*

I was shocked. I knew she kept company with a German physician who had been one of her teachers in medical school, but I had envisioned a kindly old soul who took a fatherly interest in her. "But isn't he the man who was in a concentration camp?" I asked.

"Yes. Hillel lost his wife and baby. His parents, brothers, everyone. He was the only one of his family to survive. He finished his medical education here. He's quite brilliant—a neurologist."

"So he's Jewish?"

"Yes, but our beliefs are more alike than different."

"Are you in love with him?"

"In a romantic way? Not really. But I do have tender feelings for him. He's a good person, and I respect him terribly."

"Why did you decide to get married?" I asked.

"Because we need each other. We'll make a baby or two. He hasn't

had a home and family for a long time. You have to come, Cissy. It will be just a small wedding at Mother's apartment. You will be my only attendant—my maid of honor."

I agreed to go, of course. But I dreaded telling Mama.

We were having coffee at the kitchen table when I explained that Iris was getting married and I was going to be her only attendant. She looked out the window for a long time. "I used to dream about her getting married in the rose garden—as I had done."

I wanted to ask if she had ever thought of me getting married in the rose garden, but I didn't. Instead I asked the larger question. "What happened, Mama? Why did it all end?"

She pushed her chair back and took her cup to the sink. "Go to New York if you must. But don't come back with wedding pictures for me to look at. I don't want you to speak of it at all."

TWO weeks before Iris's wedding Cissy boarded a plane for New York. Justine, Iris, and Hillel greeted her at the airport.

Justine was an older version of herself—long, lean, graying hair going every which way, wrinkled white shirt tucked into expensive brown slacks. She engulfed her niece in a huge hug.

Hillel looked like her idea of a typical professor, with a tidy beard and a baggy brown suit and tie. His hair and beard were sprinkled with gray. He told Cissy he was honored to know her.

They had dinner at Justine's apartment. With its high ceilings and wooden floors, it reminded Cissy of her mother's house. Justine's photographs covered the walls of the long hallway, but the walls of the living room were covered with watercolors, obviously all by the same person. A friend of Justine's, Iris said.

Over coffee Hillel explained to Cissy the high regard he had for her cousin. "I want you to know that I would have been content the rest of my life simply to be her good friend."

"Getting married was my idea," Iris interjected. "I was looking for a nice man to have children with, and one night we were at our favorite Chinese restaurant. I looked across the table at him and thought, Why not Hillel? He came to America with nothing. The neighborhoods where he grew up no longer exist. He needs a family, too. Our kids will be smart. I'm going to insist he speak only German to them. And when they are old enough to understand, we will tell them what happened to this whole other family in Europe they will never know but must never forget."

"And what about the family in Texas they will never know?" Cissy asked. "What will you tell them about Columbus?"

Iris said nothing for a minute, then looked to her mother.

Justine said, "I will tell my grandchildren about two sisters who didn't get along and spent the rest of their lives being sorry. Or at least one of them was sorry."

Then she opened a bottle of brandy, and they sat out on her little balcony, which overlooked Central Park. Cissy listened to the street sounds. She was actually here, actually in New York. With Justine and Iris. It seemed a miracle.

The next week passed in a blur for Cissy as Iris showed her the sights. They went to the Metropolitan Museum of Art, the Empire State Building, the Statue of Liberty. They prowled through Greenwich Village; they toured the U.N. and saw the Mets play the Phillies.

Cissy spent the second week of her visit at a women's clinic Iris had helped establish in Brooklyn, located in a former grocery. Curtains hung from the ceiling to create examination rooms. The first day, Iris and two other female obstetricians saw more than a hundred pre- and postnatal patients and forty-seven sick children. They desperately needed a pediatrician, Iris said.

The wedding was simple. An elderly judge officiated. Iris and Hillel vowed to be honest and treat each other with respect. A friend of Justine's played the cello. The woman who had painted the pictures in Justine's living room made the luncheon. Astrid was her name. She looked like Ingrid Bergman—Scandinavian, large-boned, incredibly beautiful.

The apartment filled as the evening went by—people coming to offer their congratulations. It was the most eclectic group Cissy had ever seen—artists, rabbis, professors, physicians, students, nuns, social workers. As the evening went on, Cissy saw Hillel begin to weary. Iris saw it, too, and began telling people good night. She and Hillel needed to get some sleep before they left for a brief honeymoon in Toronto, and Cissy had an early flight in the morning.

Finally it was time for the cousins to say good-bye. "I'll pay your way through medical school," Iris said as she hugged Cissy.

"Don't be ridiculous," Cissy said, wondering how many years it would be until she saw Iris again.

Seven

"WITH your grades and experience, any medical school would have to accept you," Iris insisted.

"But what would I tell Mama?" Cissy said. She stared down at the four-page application form that Iris had had sent to her.

"Just tell Martha Claire that you won a scholarship," Iris said.

"I never said I wanted to go to medical school," Cissy said. She carried the application form and the phone to her bed and wearily propped herself against the headboard. She had worked a double shift. She often worked double shifts to keep her weekends free for trips home. Tonight she'd barely had the energy to climb the stairs to her apartment, which was in sad need of cleaning. She couldn't remember the last time she'd dusted. Or changed the sheets. She really should have her car serviced before she drove another mile. And she had promised her mother she'd be at the church in Columbus by six for the covered-dish supper honoring Reverend Huxley, who was finally retiring to his books and fishing. He had a standing invitation out at her father's place on the river as long as he didn't bring up the issue of Grayson's immortal soul.

"You always said you wanted to be a doctor when you grew up," Iris reminded her. "When you were in high school, you told me you'd like to be a pediatrician, but it would cost too much. Well, here's your chance. You don't have to move to New York and practice with me, although that invitation will always be there. I just want you to have what I have, Cissy. It's really quite selfish of me. I can't enjoy my life until I get yours straightened out."

"I wasn't aware that my life was crooked," Cissy said dryly. "Look, Iris, I truly appreciate your offer, but I don't have the time or energy for medical school."

"You would if you didn't go home every weekend," Iris pointed out. "Martha Claire and Grayson are never going to be happy, Cissy. You need to look after yourself. That's why I decided on a school in Dallas instead of Houston. Dallas is far enough away that Martha Claire and Grayson can't expect you home all the time."

Cissy stretched out her aching legs. "At least when I'm home, Mama and Daddy sleep under the same roof and sit down at the same table. It's really quite selfish of me. I can't enjoy my life until I get theirs straightened out," she said, parroting Iris's words.

"Well, aren't you cute!" Iris said sarcastically. "Martha Claire and Grayson have forgotten how to be anything but miserable. And you're not doing much better. If you want, specialize in psychiatry and dedicate your life to healing alcoholic young men before they kill themselves behind the wheel of a car. You also can make enough money to fix up Martha Claire's house. So many more things are possible if you have an M.D. after your name."

"Why isn't it good enough that I stay a nurse?" Cissy demanded. After all, most of the time she loved what she did. At times, of course, she got tired of following orders and wondered what it would be like to be the person giving them.

"I've already told you—I want you to have what I have. I feel guilty, too, sweetie. We all are suffocating under piles of guilt. I could have told Mother that I didn't want to leave Columbus. After all, Martha Claire and Grayson raised me and loved me as though I was their own. I don't know why our mothers started hating each other, but maybe if I had stayed, things would have turned out differently. As it was, I left you and Buddy there to deal with all that misery by yourselves."

Cissy closed her eyes and rubbed her forehead. "I'm too tired to talk about this now. I'll call you in a few days, okay?"

"At least tell the folks that you've been thinking about medical school, that you've been offered a scholarship."

"It's not a scholarship."

"Yes, it is. I am awarding a one-time-only scholarship to a practicing nurse who graduated from Columbus High School and Texas Women's University. Fill out the application, Cissy."

TELLING herself that it was more to appease her cousin than because of any pressing desire on her part to enroll in medical school, Cissy filled out the application form. Writing the one-page essay made her realize just how much she wanted to be a doctor. She hadn't had the money or the courage to go down that long and difficult road before, but now she was older, less fearful, and Iris had offered to pay her tuition. As a nurse, she could find part-time employment to help meet her living expenses. She still hadn't told her parents. Maybe it wouldn't be necessary. Maybe her application would be denied.

The letter from the dean's office arrived four weeks later. Cissy tore it open and read that she had been accepted for the fall of 1977. Enclosed was orientation information and her class schedule.

Iris was delivering a baby when Cissy called. She left a message and called her mother. "I thought I'd drive over for dinner," she said. "I've got something I want to tell you."

"Are you engaged?" Martha Claire said hopefully.

"No, Mama, nothing like that. Is Daddy there?"

"No, he's out at that place on the river."

"Would you drive out and ask him to come home for dinner? I'll pick up a pizza. I want to talk to both of you together."

Her parents seemed almost relieved when she told them her news. Apparently they had been worried that she had become too dependent on them since Buddy's death. A young woman needed a social life and friends her own age, they said.

"Our little Cissy is going to be a doctor," Grayson said with pride. For an instant she thought he was going to reach for Mama's hand, but Martha Claire got very busy closing up the pizza box. "How did you find out about this scholarship?" he asked.

"A doctor told me about it. It's for a practicing nurse."

They sat on the porch for a while. Several neighbors called out hellos, and Martha Claire told them the news.

Before she left town, Cissy stopped by her brother's grave. In the moonlight she knelt on the damp grass and touched his tombstone. If she had taken care of Buddy, she probably wouldn't be going to medical school. Nothing made any sense.

As she drove east on the interstate, the euphoria rose in her breast. Her parents were pleased! Everything was going to be all right. She was going to be a physician. *Cecelia Claire Stewart, M.D.*

"WELL, well, well, if it isn't our soon-to-be Dr. Cissy Stewart," Doc Hadley said, holding open the screen door for her.

Cissy was stunned at the sight of him. The man who had looked after the health of their town for half a century was himself wasted and ill. She hadn't seen him in years but had found herself thinking about him more now that medical school was in her future.

He led her past the parlor and down the hall to the kitchen. He now lived with the oldest of his three daughters, Trudy.

"Trudy said you'd called," he said. "She's off at one of her meetings, but she left lemonade and cookies."

"Well, well, well," he said again as he poured the lemonade. "Your folks are certainly busting their buttons over you. You know, over the years, lots of youngsters told me they were going to be a doctor when they grew up, but you're the only one to actually do it. Course, you were always the most inquisitive. Just listening to your own heart wasn't enough. You wanted to listen to mine and your mama's. You had to watch when I lanced your brother's boil and cut out his ingrown toenail."

Cissy smiled. "You remember all that?"

He nodded. "You and your brother weren't just any other patients. I had a hand in your family like no other and always felt a special responsibility toward the Stewarts. I was almost glad when you kids got colds and measles, so I had a chance to hover."

"Did you always want to be a doctor?" Cissy asked.

"No. I had grown up thinking I would be a vet. Then I worked for one and got kicked in the head by a sick mule. I figured it was a sign and decided I'd better find something else to do."

"But why medicine?"

"Same reason as you, I suppose. You want to do something more than just make money."

"What about when people died, though?" she asked. "Didn't that bother you?"

"Depends. Sometimes letting people go ahead and die is the only cure you can offer. Other times you'll wonder if you couldn't have done something differently that would have saved a patient, specially the young ones. After I'd have a mama bleed to death during childbirth, I'd swear I was going to move to a city where there was a real hospital with fancy machines and specialists, but I never did. People in little towns need someone to look after them."

They talked for a while. Then she got him settled in front of the television. She thanked him for everything he'd done for her and her family, and walked down the hall to the front door.

Her life had been set when Doc Hadley bundled her up and found her a home. Now he was at the end of his life. She might never see him again. She retraced her steps. He was waiting for her. "If you're going to ask me about your birth parents, don't," he said.

"I'm not even sure I want to know," Cissy said from the doorway. "Buddy wondered about them more than I did. But sometimes I wonder if my birth mother knows about us or if she even cares."

"Buddy got to where he asked me every time he saw me. The last few years he kept trying to get me to say that you two weren't related by blood. But secrets are the one thing I get to take with me. Physicians usually end up with lots of them, specially docs like me with a small-town practice. Hippocrates even put keeping secrets in his oath for us docs. We all have to promise not to divulge the things we see or hear in the lives of men."

"But have you ever talked to her over the years?" Cissy persisted. "Does she know that Buddy died? Will you tell her that I'm going to medical school?"

He shook his finger at her. "You go on now, Cissy, and make the parents who raised you proud. You'll be a fine physician."

DOC Hadley died the following month. The funeral was held in the high school gymnasium, the bleachers filled to overflowing.

Everyone cried, of course. Cissy had come prepared with pockets full of Kleenex. She cried for the loss of the man himself and for the thread he represented to her beginnings, to her birth mother. That thread was now forever broken.

WITH her parents' help and a rented truck, Cissy moved her possessions to Dallas, back to the city where she had lived during the three clinical years of her nurse's training. She rented a three-room duplex in a shabby neighborhood near the medical center campus. Martha Claire cooked their meals in the tiny kitchen. Grayson installed chain locks on the door.

They stayed for three days, with Martha Claire sleeping with Cissy in the bedroom and Grayson on the sofa. When they finished cleaning and painting, the place looked livable.

The three of them agreed that Cissy would not come home until Thanksgiving. It was a six-hour drive from Dallas to Columbus, and Cissy would need weekends for her studies and nursing.

They all blinked back tears when it came time to say good-bye. Grayson insisted on giving her a wad of bills. "I don't want you skipping meals," he said.

Cissy stood on the curb and watched her parents drive away. How she loved them. If only she could fix whatever was broken between them and make them happy once again.

With her parents gone, her new home seemed deafeningly quiet. Cissy turned on the radio and stared at the clothes her mother had hung in her closet, pondering what to wear to tomorrow's orientation. She decided on a sleeveless black dress and sandals.

Cissy washed her hair, shined her shoes, filed her nails. And felt as if she had gone backward in time, preparing for the first day of school. New books. New teachers. A new beginning.

The first-year class was welcomed by the dean, who told them they could expect to work harder over the next four years than they had ever in their lives. Then he gave a rundown of the class demographics. Of the one hundred twenty class members, one hundred two were men and one hundred ten were residents of the state of Texas. Ninety-eight had come directly from an undergraduate program. The remainder included six military veterans, two accountants, a commercial pilot, five paramedics, four pharmacists, two schoolteachers, a Presbyterian minister, and one nurse.

"Are you the nurse?" one of Cissy's classmates asked during the break. She had noticed him earlier—the good-looking guy wearing a sport coat, jeans, and well-worn cowboy boots.

"Does it show that much?" she asked, reaching up to pat the top of her head. "I could have sworn I left my white cap at home."

"Just a guess. The other females look too young and affluent."

He looked to be about thirty, with white teeth, a square jaw, and close-cropped blond hair. With his lean, tan body and west Texas drawl, she would cast him as a cowboy, but there weren't any cowboys on the dean's list. "Are you a veteran or the pilot?" she asked.

He saluted. "Captain Joe McCormack, at your service."

At lunch they ate in the cafeteria together. He had grown up on a cattle ranch outside Lampasas and gone into the army after college. Cissy gave a perfunctory rundown on herself, including the part about her cousin paying her tuition. "I am definitely not one of the affluent," she said. "I put my name on the special-duty roster at every hospital in the metro. I'll be doing most of my studying at the bedside of the comatose and dying."

That afternoon they were introduced to their cadavers in the gross-anatomy lab. Cissy and her three lab partners were assigned the body of an elderly black woman. Her lab partners were the pilot and two young men freshly graduated from the University of Texas. It was disquieting for Cissy to see the cadaver's emaciated body exposed for all to see. She was as flat-chested as a boy, and the formaldehyde had turned her skin a leathery gray. One of the U.T. grads laughed nervously. "This old gal looks like she's been rode hard and put up wet."

"Shall we name her?" the pilot asked.

"What's a good name for a teacher?" Cissy asked. "We will need to learn a great deal from her."

"What about Grandmother?" the other U.T. student asked.

The others nodded. Grandmother it would be.

At the end of the day Joe McCormack caught up with Cissy and invited her out for a hamburger. They sat on the outdoor deck at a west Dallas restaurant and talked the evening away. His group had named their cadaver Teddy Roosevelt. "The old guy must have weighed three hundred pounds," Joe said.

Over their second beer they talked about aspirations. Joe wanted to be a family doctor back in Lampasas or some other west Texas town. He would run a few cattle, raise a few horses and kids, have family dinners at a big round table in a kitchen with wooden floors. And laugh a lot. "I forgot how to laugh for a while," he said.

"Vietnam?"

He nodded and called for the check. "I'm in the middle of a divorce. She said I changed too much in Nam. She didn't care for the nightmares, I guess."

"I'm sorry. That must have been difficult for you."

"Still is. What about you?"

"Almost engaged once—to a medical student. Sometimes I have regrets. I hope I'm more suited to be a doctor than a doctor's wife."

Joe drove her to her car. "Good night, Cissy Stewart from Columbus. I hope we're both still around four years from now."

"Me, too."

It had been a good day, Cissy thought as she drove home, in part because of Joe McCormack.

Cissy was surprised at the ease with which she made friends with her classmates—especially her three anatomy-lab partners. But then, they saw each other several hours a day as they slowly dissected Grandmother. Cissy gave up trying to scrub away the smell of formaldehyde, which clung to her hands and the inside of her nostrils. Their evening sessions in the lab were often followed by a beer, often with Joe and his roommate, another Vietnam vet.

Cissy often studied with Joe. They quizzed each other constantly. Name the ligaments of the hand. The nerves of the axilla. Cissy hadn't known there was room in her brain for all the things she learned in just that semester. She never listened to the radio or watched television, never read a book that wasn't a textbook. She didn't see *Rocky*. She kept wondering who Laverne and Shirley were. Sports, politics, current events all but ceased to exist for her as she immersed herself in anatomy, physiology, biochemistry, and genetics.

It wasn't until she was on the highway, driving to Columbus for Thanksgiving, that she came up for air. Her mother was preparing a traditional Thanksgiving feast for the first time since they lost Buddy. Tomorrow was the fifth anniversary of his death.

"It's good to be home," she said when she arrived just before eleven. In spite of the hour, the three of them lingered at the kitchen table, drinking milk and nibbling on cookies. Cissy enjoyed telling her parents about Grandmother and Teddy Roosevelt, about her classes and friends. She didn't mention Joe.

The next day her father carved the turkey as always, but there weren't enough people at the table, not enough words and laughter to fill the room. Cissy knew her parents, too, were remembering other Thanksgivings with family all around—good memories that made the present poignant and sad.

SHE started sleeping with Joe after spring break.

They had talked about it off and on all through that first year. They both confessed to being horny. Joe said he had been all but asexual since he and his wife split up. But as consumed as he was by school and studying, he was always having sexual thoughts.

Cissy was tired of her virginal state. Back in college she and Randy Calhoune had petted for hours but never went all the way. Initially she thought she would save herself for marriage, but now she wondered if she would ever be any man's wife. She certainly didn't want to be the sort of wife Joe said he wanted. But she felt herself responding when he touched her arm. She was always pleased when it was his voice on the phone. He was the first guy she had met in medical school, and she had spent more time with him than anyone else. It seemed only right that they go the next step.

She got a prescription for birth control pills. Soon they were having sex at every possible opportunity. They would meet in his van for a quickie between classes. He spent nights at her house, going to his own place only to change clothes.

"We have created a monster," Cissy said finally. "I fell asleep in class again today."

They rationed themselves. They'd have sex on Wednesday and Saturday nights only. Cissy missed his presence in her bed but was relieved. She didn't want to think about him all the time. She was here to make a physician of herself. But when she wasn't with Joe, she still thought about him, and the thoughts began to take a different turn. She imagined herself in a wedding dress.

But when they were studying for their embryology final and Joe asked if she thought they should get married, Cissy didn't know if she should feel hopeful or unbearably sad. She would marry Joe in a flash if she thought it would work, but she feared she was no more the right woman for Joe McCormack than she had been for Randy Calhoune. She liked Joe better, loved him more, resented him just as much—resented the fact that he wanted a traditional wife who would look after him and the kids. If she had to choose between Joe and becoming a physician, she would choose the latter. But what she truly wanted was to practice medicine *and* for Joe to change his expectations for marriage.

The morning of their embryology final she parked her car and was crossing the street to the basic sciences building when she saw Joe being dropped off by a young woman driving a new Mercedes. He pretended that he didn't see Cissy, but she knew he had.

She didn't realize she had stopped in the middle of the street, until a car honked at her. Very carefully she walked to the curb, then to the steps. She lowered herself to the bottom step, put her head between her knees, took several deep breaths, and convinced herself she wasn't going to die, that she was going to get herself up the steps and to the nearest ladies' room.

The cold water felt almost erotic on her hot face. Again and again she splashed her face. Then she looked in the mirror. "Okay, Cissy Stewart, you get your ass down that hall and make a better grade on that test than Joe McCormack." She was the last one in the room before the proctor closed the door.

It was almost midnight when he called. He spoke so softly that at first she thought it was an obscene phone call. He wasn't alone, she realized. *She* was there, asleep or in the bathroom. "Coward," she said. "You could at least come tell me in person."

"My wife wants us to get back together," he whispered. "She's moving up here."

"With some of Daddy's money, I take it. How nice for you—home cooking *and* a Mercedes. You can't beat a deal like that."

"Don't, Cissy. I am really sorry, but I guess I never stopped caring about her. She's a good person. She will devote herself to me and our children. Maybe I'm selfish to want that, but I do."

Cissy hung up and threw her coffee cup against the wall.

Eight

WHEN the first year of medical school ended, Cissy ranked fourth in her class. By the end of the second year she had slipped a few notches but was still in the top ten. Her classmates and professors all knew who she was—Cecelia Stewart, the nurse from Columbus who had made top ten two years running.

With the two years of basic sciences out of the way, the time had come to leave the classroom. For the next two years Cissy would follow attending physicians around, learning from them at the bedsides of actual patients. Her first clinical rotation was surgery. The first day she and another third-year student scrubbed in on the amputation of a fifty-five-year-old diabetic male's left leg, just above the knee. The sound of the saw and the putrid smell that rose from the gangrenous limb were too much for the other medical student. He started weaving back and forth, then grabbed hold of a nurse's arm for support. The assisting surgeon yelled at him to get out of there.

The operation lasted more than two hours. Cissy concentrated on the hot shower she would take as soon as she got home—a very long shower that would wash away the smell of rotting tissue and the tension that pressed like a vise across her shoulders and neck. But she also felt satisfaction. Because of her nurse's training, she knew that she was better prepared than her classmates for the experiences that awaited her over the next two years.

Her second rotation was internal medicine, which was run by the first and only female department chair in the history of the medical school. Daisy Cunningham was barely five feet tall, pushing sixty, and formidable. The first day of the rotation Dr. Cunningham marched her new crop of students from bedside to bedside as she examined patients.

At the conclusion of rounds she encouraged the students to speculate about the patients and describe any significant symptoms they had noticed. When one hapless young man referred to a patient as the fat lady at the end of the hall, she told him in a frosty voice that the woman had a name. "On my service *all* patients have names. They are human beings and will be treated and spoken of with dignity. Now, does anyone remember this patient's name?"

When no one answered, Dr. Cunningham looked in Cissy's direction. "Dr. Stewart?"

"Mary Sinclair," Cissy answered.

"What else can you tell me about Mrs. Sinclair?"

"Her diagnosis is acute pulmonary edema brought on by congestive heart failure."

"No, no, no," Dr. Cunningham said impatiently. "I mean, what else can you tell me about her as a person?"

"She is a retired secretary, married, and has three children."

Dr. Cunningham nodded. "How do you know these things?"

"They were on her chart."

"Did you learn anything else about this patient at her bedside?"

"She has the beginning of a bedsore on her right elbow, and I suspect that she is lonely," Cissy said.

"What makes you think that?" Dr. Cunningham asked.

"She was admitted last Monday, and there are no get-well cards on her dresser, no magazines that people have brought by."

"Thank you, Dr. Stewart," Dr. Cunningham said. "Would you please come see me this afternoon?"

It was after three when Cissy was escorted into Dr. Cunningham's cluttered office. The first thing Cissy noticed was the quilt that hung on the wall. Another was draped over the worn leather sofa. "The wedding ring pattern," Cissy said. "It's beautiful. My mother has one. My great-grandmother made it for her as a wedding present. Who made this one?" she asked, indicating the quilt on the wall.

"I bought it at an estate sale. I have more at home. They comfort me, especially the old ones made from feed sacks and old clothes. When I think of the women who made them to warm their children and beautify their homes even if the home had a dirt floor, I am reminded that people are more than systems and symptoms." She waved Cissy to the sofa, then poured water from an electric kettle into two waiting china cups and bobbed tea bags up and down. Dr. Cunningham placed the cups on a wicker tray next to a plate of sugar cookies. She set the tray on a small table, pulled her chair from behind her desk, and sat across from Cissy. "I've been waiting for you, Cecelia Claire Stewart."

"I'm sorry," Cissy said. "I didn't think you had specified a time for me to come."

Dr. Cunningham shook her head. "I wasn't talking about today. I've been waiting for you for two years."

"I don't understand."

"I was a nurse, too. I went through a three-year hospital program when I got out of high school, and I put myself through medical school, like you're doing."

Cissy nodded. "I earn most of my living expenses. My physician cousin paid for my tuition and books the first two years. Now I've got a scholarship."

"How many hours a week do you nurse?"

"It varies. Usually about twenty, mostly night shifts, obviously."

"Is that why you never joined the Women's Student Medical Association?"

Cissy knew that Daisy Cunningham was the founder and sponsor of the organization's local chapter. Still, she answered honestly, "Not really. I prefer to think of myself simply as a medical student, not a woman medical student."

"There are too few women in medicine," Dr. Cunningham pointed out. "We have to band together. If we don't, we're overlooked. Women aren't elected president of their medical school class. They don't serve as medical school deans. The best residencies go to men. That has to change. If you don't learn anything else from me, I want to teach you to look after other women and not be one of those nasty creatures who claws her way across the drawbridge, then pulls it up behind her."

After that first meeting the two women became friends. Cissy joined the Women's Student Medical Association, and she dined in her mentor's home many times.

Daisy Cunningham lived in a vintage house in a lovely neighborhood. Her home was indeed full of quilts. The walls of the hall were lined with them, and they were folded on benches and draped over the arms of chairs. The rooms of the spacious house were filled with American antiques. The backyard was shared by a swimming pool and a vegetable garden.

"Are you happy living alone?" Cissy asked her one Sunday evening over sherry, wondering why she had never married.

"No, but I wasn't happy living with a man, either. A man wants a woman to fuss over him. I never fussed."

"My mother liked doing that for Daddy and us kids," Cissy said. "I always thought I would grow up and be just like her."

"Why didn't you?"

"I almost did. I came very close to marrying a medical student back in my nursing school days," Cissy said. "I would have put my nursing degree in a drawer and devoted myself to being a good doctor's wife and a good mother to his children. It might have been okay. It might even have been wonderful."

"Do you still think about him?" Daisy asked.

"No. I think about the man who came after him," Cissy answered. Randy Calhoune was history. She would go for days, even weeks, without thinking about him. But she did still think about Joe McCormack.

After dinner that evening Cissy took a short detour on the way home, driving by Joe's house, then circling the block and parking across the street. Light came from a side window and pooled itself on the lawn. A dining-room window, perhaps. They could be having dinner right now. A lovely home-cooked meal for the harried medical-student husband. Cissy wondered what service Joe was on now and at which hospital as she put her head against the steering wheel. What if there was never another Joe in her life?

THE next day she began dialing Joe's phone number. Every time Cissy had a chance, she dialed—to see if *she* answered. Cissy didn't even know the woman's name. She was simply Joe's wife. With her finger hovering above the disconnect button, Cissy would listen as the ringing went on and on.

All day Tuesday, even though she had promised herself that she wouldn't, Cissy once again repeatedly dialed Joe's house. His phone number became a litany, replaying itself endlessly in her brain. She was out of control. She had to get a grip on herself.

After the fourth day of such insanity she bought a bottle of cheap wine on her way home. Sitting on the back step, she drank from the bottle and watched thunderheads form overhead. When the rain began, she carried the bottle inside and watched from the kitchen window as hail beat down on her tiny backyard.

With the noise of the storm, it took her a minute to realize the phone was ringing. It was Joe. He was just around the corner. Could he drop by?

Cissy didn't know what to do first. Comb her hair? Pick up the clutter? She just stood there clutching an empty wine bottle until he came to the door. He was drenched, his hair plastered to his head, a puddle forming around him on the floor.

"How's your wife?" Cissy asked.

"She's pregnant and throwing up every fifteen minutes. She went home so her mother could look after her."

"Then what the hell are you doing here?" she screamed at him.

"I can't stop thinking about you."

"Just leave, will you, before I throw this bottle at you."

"Are you sure that's what you really want? I saw you sitting out in front of the house the other night. I haven't been able to think about anything else since."

Of course she didn't want him to leave. What she wanted was for him to stay forever. "I hate you," she said as he grabbed her and wrapped his wet arms around her. It felt so good to say those words that she said them again and again. She did hate him. But her body didn't know that. Her body felt as though she had just come home after a long and perilous journey.

Afterward he told her she was beautiful.

"No, I'm not. I'm ordinary."

He propped himself up on one elbow and looked down at her. "No, you are not ordinary. You are the most extraordinary woman I have ever known. You are lovely and so brilliant."

"So why did you leave me if I am so extraordinary? Is *she* extraordinary?"

"No, she's not. But I knew if I survived the war, all I wanted was a sweet wife who would look after me and our kids. A pretty house. Financial security. That's not the way it would be with you and me. Lynette needs me, Cissy. You don't need anyone."

Lynette. She had not wanted to know that name. "So you get what you want, and I don't? Do you love her that much?"

"I love her," he said, "but not like I love you."

"I hate you," she said again, trying to push him out of the bed, but he began touching her again, pushing his face against her belly.

Finally they both lay paralyzed, a sheet pulled over their damp bodies. She knew he wouldn't be there when she woke up. "Don't come back," she told him. "Not ever."

In the night she heard him leave and knew she was supposed to feel sad. But the pain of too much wine throbbing behind her eyeballs precluded other feelings. She needed to sleep some more; then she would feel sad or angry or whatever.

Toward morning she awoke again, and it occurred to her to wonder when her last period had been. She had stopped taking birth control pills, but she wasn't mid-cycle. Close, maybe, but days off. Surely she was in the clear. But a shiver of fear shot through her body. She should have at least insisted on a condom.

She stood under the shower for a long time, symbolically and literally washing away Joe. "No baby, please," she whispered.

CISSY waited three weeks before giving up hope. And then, in spite of morning nausea, tacked on another week just in case. She wanted to hate Joe, to blame him, but when he called that fateful night, she had allowed him to come over.

An early abortion was the only way out of this mess. It was legal now, in the wake of *Roe* v. *Wade.* But what if she never married? What if this was the only time her body would ever be pregnant?

Cissy thought about her own origins. She wondered if her birth mother had considered abortion. Maybe this pregnancy was an opportunity for Cissy to come full circle with her own life—a paying back of sorts for her mother's not ending the pregnancy that resulted in her own birth. Cissy could carry the child and give it up for adoption as her birth mother had done before her.

Cissy also thought about Justine and Iris. If Justine had given Iris away, how different her own life would have been. Iris had been the most joyous part of her childhood. Iris was the reason she was in medical school. If Cissy screwed up medical school because she had gotten herself pregnant, she would be letting Iris down.

Iris was pregnant now—and deliriously happy, as pregnant women should be.

Cissy's thoughts led her around and around in an endless confusing circle. There was no easy answer. No answer to be found by reexamining the past. The past was a maze of secrets and unhappiness. So much unhappiness, and she didn't know why. It had killed Buddy. It had made Justine take Iris away. It made her too afraid to make this all-important decision about her own life. Her mother would never explain the past. Martha Claire would insist that nothing had happened, that marriages wear out like cars, that hers and Grayson's was simply an old, tired marriage.

Finally Cissy made the six-hour drive home—not to the house on Milam Street, but to her father's cabin by the river.

WHEN Grayson heard the crunching of car tires on gravel, he thought that Paul Huxley had been able to get away after all. The retired minister came most Sunday afternoons to fish. And to sip a bit of Jack Daniel's—their little secret. Paul always brought a lemon to suck on while he drove home. His wife, Amanda, was a past state president of the Women's Christian Temperance Union. If Amanda thought he'd had so much as a sip of demon whiskey, she would probably kick him out of the house.

Last week, however, Amanda had fallen and broken her hip. She was hospitalized in Houston, and Paul had planned to visit her this afternoon. Grayson hadn't been expecting him.

He put down his book and walked through the cabin to greet his visitor. The cabin was less primitive now, with interior walls, a secondhand refrigerator, and a pump mounted over a metal sink.

Monday, Wednesday, and Friday were now his days to tend the store. Grayson and Martha Claire kept the store open more because it imposed a needed structure on their days and weeks than for the modest income it produced. Grayson was surprised that they had any customers at all. The store wasn't outdated enough to be quaint. Martha Claire insisted on keeping clothing on the racks long after it should have been sold at the sidewalk sale at fifty percent off the last marked-down price. Not even the sports corner attracted much business. Fishing lures and shotgun shells were cheaper at Wal-Mart.

Grayson was surprised to see Cissy's battered Volkswagen bus rolling to a stop behind his own elderly pickup. He smiled and waved, but apprehension prickled its way across his forehead. He hadn't expected to see his daughter until Thanksgiving. "This is an unexpected surprise," he told her, wrapping her slight body in his arms, laying his cheek against her soft hair. How he loved this darling girl—the only child he had left to love.

She touched his hair. "A few more gray ones, I see," she said, teasing. "You look very distinguished."

He looked down at his ragged T-shirt and laughed. "Yes, Grayson Francis Stewart, Esquire, at home on his country estate." He linked arms with her, walking up the gravel path. "If I'd known you were coming," he said, "I would have had fish to fry."

"I can't stay long. I just drove down for a few hours."

He opened two cans of beer to take out on the porch. "You didn't spend the night with your mother?"

She shook her head. "No. I came to see you."

Grayson felt a heaviness settle in his chest. Something was wrong.

"It really is pretty here," Cissy said, staring out at the river.

"Sit down and tell me what's on your mind," he said.

Cissy leaned back in the dilapidated wicker rocker and closed her eyes for a long minute. When she opened them, she said, "I came to ask what happened to our family."

Grayson opened his mouth to speak, then closed it for lack of words. He tried to clear his throat but could not. He just sat there, feeling like a fool. Had he actually thought he might live out his life without his daughter's asking that particular question of him? Maybe he should have left years ago to prevent just such a moment. Or died. To have been spared this. And Buddy's death. "Have you talked to your mother about this?" he managed to ask.

"No, but she wouldn't tell me if I did."

"No, I suppose not."

"I've reached an impasse, Daddy. I need to know what happened before I can get on with things."

Grayson sucked in his breath, then let it out slowly. A heron, with a silvery fish in his mouth, rose gracefully from a stand of cattails. From across the river a crow cawed noisily. A perfect day. In the summer it was too hot for comfort and the mosquitoes were ferocious, but even then he stayed out here to avoid the pain and censure that still resided in his wife's eyes. For so long he had hoped that he would be able to work his way back into Martha Claire's heart, but he had hurt her too deeply for any hope of redemption. Maybe if he'd known that forgiveness would never be forthcoming he would have driven away and never come back. But he never could bring himself to abandon Cissy and Buddy to a mother whose spirit he had shattered.

Slowly he rose from his chair and went inside. Such a cliché, to keep money hidden under a floorboard. His secret cache. He tucked away bills now and then, telling himself he was going to take that trip to Europe someday, with Martha Claire or not. But there would be no trip to Europe, no trip to anyplace.

He didn't know what had happened in Cissy's life to precipitate her question, but the need in her eyes was real. He only hoped when she had her answer she could forgive him. He had lost Iris and Buddy. The prospect of living the rest of his years cut off from Cissy was too sad to contemplate. He handed her a wad of bills. "Go see Justine," he said. "I'll let her know you're coming."

"Is it that difficult for you?" Cissy asked.

He nodded. He had gotten medals for bravery, but he didn't have the courage for this.

AT THE airport Justine almost didn't recognize Cissy. She seemed deflated, older, and so thin. Justine opened her arms and wondered if this would be the last time she would embrace her niece. How would Cissy feel about her when she knew the truth?

"Are you all right, honey?" Justine asked, reaching for Cissy's carry-on.

Cissy smiled. "Sure. Just tired."

As they headed for the car, Justine explained that they were going to spend the weekend at her friend Astrid's house on Shelter Island. "It's not a long drive," she promised, glancing at her niece.

"I'm fine. Really," Cissy insisted.

Justine found herself talking about Iris, of course. She was thrilled about the baby and worried about Iris—four months pregnant and taking a trip to Europe. Hillel had sworn he would never return to Germany, but last year he located an elderly male cousin who had survived the Holocaust. The man was in failing health; if Hillel was ever going to see a member of his family again, he would have to journey back to the place where they all had died. Iris wasn't about to let him face that emotional journey alone.

It began to rain, and Justine became preoccupied with finding the right turnoff. Cissy sat with her hands in her lap, her face blanched an unnatural white in the light from oncoming traffic.

Justine had begged Grayson not to send her up here. Cissy was *his* child. *He* could explain their sordid history himself. Or lie to her. They had taken a vow with Martha Claire that their children were never to know the secret that had destroyed their family.

"I know," Grayson said. "But Buddy is dead, and Iris escaped. Cissy is bearing the burden of the past on her own, and it's gotten to be too much for her."

"What if she never speaks to you again?" Justine was in her darkroom, bathed in the red glow of the safelight. She almost hadn't picked up the phone, but it might have been Iris calling from Europe. Grayson's was the last voice she expected to hear but had recognized it almost at once.

"I can live with that if it helps Cissy get on with her life. Please, Justine, talk to her. I don't have the courage."

"Then let Martha Claire do it."

"Martha Claire's version would be vindictive."

"And my version?" Justine demanded. "How will it be?"

"Kinder, I hope, than Martha Claire's."

Justine sank onto a high stool and stared down at an enlargement of one of her wartime London photographs as it slowly materialized in the developing tray. A Manhattan gallery had scheduled a retrospective exhibition of her work: "Justine Mayfield-Dover—Thirty-Five Years of Photojournalism." For months now she had been spending hours in her darkroom reliving her career.

She didn't want to do this thing Grayson was asking of her, didn't want to relive those confusing two days when she had tarnished her soul and created the daughter who had given her life meaning.

"Will you talk to Cissy if I send her to you?"

Justine sighed deeply. "No promises," she said. "I don't know that I have the courage, either."

On the ferry, Justine babbled on a bit about the island. How property values had soared. Astrid had spent summers here when she was growing up. The house had once been a farmhouse. "We come here a lot. I take pictures and she paints."

After they had carried in the suitcases and groceries, they prepared a simple meal. Justine lit candles and poured wine. "We'll eat first and save the serious stuff for later," she said. She had several glasses of wine to calm her nerves.

Cissy only took tiny sips of wine but ate a bowl of pasta and two slices of the chewy French bread. She looked fragile, Justine decided, with weariness in her eyes. She wondered where her niece found the stamina in that small body to face the rigors of medical school and long hours of special-duty nursing.

"Tell me about my sister," Justine said. "What are her days like now? What gives her joy?"

"Well, she has the church, of course," Cissy began, "but it's less important to her now that Reverend Huxley has retired. And she still loves to garden. She was never able to turn the house into a showplace, but the yard is on the annual Garden Club tour."

"Iris tells me your father spends most of his time by the river."

Cissy nodded. "Yes. He and Mama see each other, though. They trade off days at the store. And he has dinner at home on Friday nights and stays over—in his own room."

"Does she ever go out there—to the river?"

"Not that I know of."

"They got married out by the rose garden," Justine recalled. "When I saw them together, Martha Claire in Grandma Polly's wedding dress, Grayson in his uniform, with such hope in their eyes, I thought my heart was going to burst inside my chest. They were so beautiful and so much in love. I wish they could rekindle some of what they were feeling that day."

"Me, too," Cissy said, "but I don't think they ever will. Mama is not one to forgive."

Justine nodded. Yes, her sister was not the forgiving sort. But Justine wasn't so sure if she herself would have been able to forgive such a crime if their positions were reversed. And now the time had come for her to confess that crime to her sister's child.

THE rain had put a chill in the air, so after they tidied up the kitchen, Justine built a small fire in the stone fireplace. She brought a cup of tea for Cissy and more wine for herself.

They pulled their chairs close and stared at the flames for a time. If she were a praying woman, Justine would ask that Cissy change her mind and let sleeping dogs lie. But Cissy was gathering herself to speak, and Justine waited with a heavy heart.

"Since I was twelve years old," Cissy began, still staring at the fire, "I've been navigating a maze without knowing how I got there. I have tried to heal my parents without knowing why they're the way they are. I have tried to make up for not being Iris and tried to help us all come to terms with Buddy's death, all the while wondering if I had been a real daughter and not an adopted one if things would be better. What happened to us, Justine? I need to know. I'm pregnant, and I have to decide what to do about it."

Then she burst into tears. Justine knelt beside her and held her, smoothed her hair. "Precious little Cissy," she said, her voice soothing. She handed Cissy a napkin and watched while she wiped her eyes. "What about the man who got you this way?" she asked, her knees creaking as she rose and returned to her chair.

"I got myself this way," Cissy said wearily. "It was so dumb. But to answer your question, he's married. He doesn't have a clue about what's going on, and I intend to keep it that way."

Justine sighed. "I had this same conversation with my mother when I came back from the war. Does Martha Claire know?"

"You're the first person I've told," Cissy said. "Before I decide what to do, I want to know what happened to our family. Why has Mama never been able to forgive Daddy for whatever it was that he did? I spent my whole life trying to make my mother love me, but she was more dedicated to *not* loving Daddy and you and Iris than she was to loving Buddy and me. Now, I wonder, if I have this baby, would Mama think it is yet another way that one of us had failed her, that I was a misbegotten child bringing another misbegotten child into the world for her to deal with?"

Justine took a sip of wine. "I don't know where to begin."

Cissy began for her. "I grew up believing that you were a widow, that a British soldier named Philip Benston Dover was Iris's father. But since there was never one shred of information about this man, I decided that you had to get married and didn't really love him. Now I wonder if he ever existed at all."

"He didn't," Justine said softly. "Your grandma Polly made him up, and Martha Claire put his obituary in the newspaper."

"Does Iris know?"

Justine shook her head. "No."

"I also thought for many years that Daddy was my birth father," Cissy continued.

"What made you think that?" Justine asked.

Cissy shrugged. "I was casting about for a damning secret. That one seemed to fit the bill. I decided that Doc Hadley knew all about it. Maybe Daddy even asked him to give me to them so he could raise me. Probably it was Doc Hadley's idea to tack Buddy onto the deal. Then in those last weeks of Grandma Polly's life, Mama somehow found out. When you came home for the funeral, you stuck up for Daddy and told Mama she should forgive him. The older I got, however, the more difficult it became to believe that story. I couldn't imagine Daddy sneaking off behind Mama's back. Still, I thought of every lady in town who might possibly have given me birth. Eventually I gave up. No one could hide a pregnancy all the way to term in Columbus."

"So now what do you think?" Justine asked, her fingers curling around the arm of the chair, waiting for the axe to fall.

Cissy hesitated. "It wasn't until Daddy told me to come see you that the pieces began to fall into place. Now I think my daddy fathered a child, but it wasn't me. I think he is Iris's father."

"Why do you think that?" Justine asked.

"Mama has never forgiven him," Cissy explained. "If he'd had an affair with anyone else, she would have given him a hard time but eventually gotten over it." There were other things, too, she went on. "Iris and Daddy both got hiccups when they laughed too hard, both chewed on their thumbnails when they were puzzled. Did you ever hear them sing 'La Vie en Rose'? Their voices blended so perfectly, like syrup and melted butter."

Cissy paused, waiting for Justine to confirm or deny. Justine sat motionless, saying nothing.

Finally Cissy broke the silence. "How did Mama find out?"

Justine took a deep breath. "I think the same way you did. She realized how alike they were. Then she looked for proof."

Cissy lifted her chin. "Were you in love with my father?"

Justine wondered, if she had been in love with Grayson, would that mitigate her sin or worsen it? The night they sought shelter from the bombs, in the cellar under her favorite pub, as she clung to him for what she thought was the last bit of human comfort she would ever feel, maybe then she understood that Grayson Stewart was a man she could have loved if he wasn't married to her sister. But did such feelings have any relevance now?

Then Justine began to speak in a great outpouring of words. She told Cissy about that awful night, waiting in the pub for Billy to come through the door as he always did, with his hat at a jaunty angle and a grin on his darling face. Instead two mates from his wing came to give her the news. Her Billy Boy was dead.

"I never made love with him," Justine said. "In the middle of a world war, with planes being shot out of the sky on a daily basis, I had clung to my virtue like it was the most important thing in the world. My sister had been a virgin on her wedding night, and I would be, too, by golly. But when Billy died, I slept with every man who came along. For months I did that. Then I picked up my camera and took pictures instead."

She had her camera with her the evening she saw Grayson in London, she explained. He was in England for medical treatment. He had a bandaged eye when they met for a drink. Then the bombs started falling and they were trapped for hours, clinging to each other as the fire from burning buildings crept closer. She told Grayson about the boy she had loved. He told her he didn't want to go back to Columbus, that he wanted a different sort of life but knew Martha Claire would never agree to it.

When they finally were rescued, they spent the rest of the night and the next day walking through the ruins. She took pictures until she ran out of film. Then they found a pub where they could talk until it was time for him to leave.

"It was an extraordinary twenty-four hours," Justine said. "We had faced death together and shared our innermost secrets. After the armistice Grayson came back. I took a train to Dover and met him there. The war was over, but we were still scared. I was scared that after all my bravado about wanting to live a different kind of life, I didn't have the guts. And Grayson was afraid of going home to spend the rest of his life tending the family store. He wanted to stay in the army, and he wanted me to tell him that he had a right to do that even if it meant not going home to his wife."

Justine turned her face toward the fire. "I told Grayson he would never find anyone who loved him as much as my sister, but he had to make her understand how he felt. Then I went home and realized how determined she was to stay in Columbus."

"Did you go to Dover knowing that you would make love with him?" Cissy asked.

"I'm sure I didn't. We planned to go just for the day but missed the last train back. The innkeeper assumed we were married. We downed one too many pints. But excuses don't count. It was the worst thing I could have done—my own sister's husband."

"When you discovered you were pregnant, did you think about not having the baby?"

Ah, so now they had arrived at the heart of things, Justine thought. "Of course I thought about it," she said. "That was my plan. I wasn't about to have my brother-in-law's child. As soon as I got home, I would go to Freedmantown for a kitchen-table abortion, but my mother decided otherwise. And I must admit it was a relief to have her take charge. When I was in high school, a neighbor girl died after having an abortion. I didn't want a baby, but I didn't want to die, either. Eventually I resigned myself to having it, but I never intended to love it. Strange how things turn out. Being Iris's mother has been the best part of my life." Justine leaned forward. "Before you decide on an abortion, you need to ask yourself why. Would you be doing it because it's what you want or because you are afraid to tell your mother?"

"Both, I guess. I don't want a baby unless I have a husband and my mother can hold her head up. I'm all that Mama and Daddy have left. How can I disappoint them like that?" Cissy stood abruptly, putting an end to the discussion. Justine rose to her feet, and the two women stood facing each other. "Thank you for talking to me," Cissy said, her tone formal. "I know this has not been easy for you."

"Your parents and I swore that you children would never know who Iris's father was," Justine said. "I still don't want Iris to know. And please, don't tell your mother that you know. She hates me enough the way it is." She paused. "Do you hate me, too?"

"A little," Cissy admitted. "Just like I hate myself. But I have loved you for my entire life. And Daddy. I can't go back and change that. My mother did that, and look what happened to her."

At the door to the guest room, Justine wasn't sure if a hug was in order, so she kept her distance. "Let me know what you decide. Either way I'll pay your expenses." Cissy started to protest, but Justine wouldn't let her. Whether she had the baby or not, she would need money. "Should I tell Iris?" Justine asked.

"No. She would want a say. I need to decide this on my own."

"I love you, Cissy," Justine said. "I haven't told you that in years, but I do, and I've always felt guilty about taking Iris away from you. I know how you suffered for what your father and I did."

"Yes, but what you and Daddy did gave me Iris in the first place. I don't so much forgive you as accept that it happened. Okay?"

"May I hug you?"

Cissy slid into Justine's arms. Such a little slip of a girl, Justine thought once again.

I WENT to New York thinking I was entitled to have the sins of the past revealed to me so that I could find some justification for the mess I had made of my own life. I learned that my father and my aunt made love while my mother was anxiously waiting for their return. I ached for my poor mother but wished she had been valiant enough to rise above what had been done to her, to either send my father packing or help him earn her forgiveness. My father had stayed on in their loveless marriage out of remorse, and because of his love for me and my brother. Together our parents condemned us to bear silent witness to their rotting marriage.

I tried to imagine how it might have been for Justine and my father in Dover. Had they simply allowed liquor to push Martha Claire out of their minds? Or had they acted out of anger at my mother's unwillingness to go forth with them into the larger world?

I had not asked those questions of Justine. But then, I'm sure she could not have answered them. She would not have been able to recall her exact feelings, her exact motivations. Just as I had no earthly notion of why I had thought I would die if I did not have sex with a man whom I knew loved his wife and was committed to living the rest of his life with her. But at some level, though, my father and aunt had knowingly committed a vengeful act against my mother, just as Joe and I had figuratively screwed his wife. We had been raging against the person who represented limits for what had been seemingly limitless lives.

Nine

CISSY took the middle road. She would have the baby and give it up for adoption. Her parents must never know. Nor should Joe. Or Iris. Anyone who might try to change her mind.

The thought that Joe would find out filled her with dread. What if he saw her pregnant and realized how she had gotten that way? She imagined him demanding that she have an abortion, thrusting money into her hands. Or offering to perform the procedure himself. Their shared secret. A secret that would bind them for life.

One evening she heard two residents talking about the baby of a third-year medical student one of them had delivered and realized they were talking about Joe's baby. A live birth, but at only twenty-three weeks. The infant wasn't expected to live.

Suddenly a new fear struck arrowlike through Cissy's heart. With the death of this infant, Joe might hire a lawyer and lay claim to the one she carried. If Cissy wasn't going to raise it, he and his saintly wife would. Cissy placed her hands on her abdomen. No, they could not have her child. She did not want this baby raised by a mother who would always have a reason not to love it.

DAILY, Cissy inspected her body from all angles, trying to decide if anyone might guess. She could make it to the end of the semester, she decided, then go someplace else before she began to show. Other than Justine, the only other person she would tell was Daisy Cunningham, and only because Cissy needed her help in salvaging the second half of the academic year.

Over dinner one evening with Daisy, she confessed.

"I wondered when you were going to tell me," Daisy said.

"How did you know?"

"All of a sudden you stopped wanting a glass of wine with dinner. So what happens now?" Daisy asked.

"I don't want anyone to know, including my parents. Can I transfer to an out-of-state school for just one semester?"

"It would be unusual, but I'll see what I can work out."

"You must be terribly disappointed in me," Cissy said.

"Not so disappointed as shocked," Daisy said. "You're not some dumb little high school girl, Cissy. You know better than to have unprotected sex. What were you thinking?"

"I wasn't," Cissy said.

"And the baby?" Daisy asked.

"I'll give it up for adoption."

"You're sure?"

"Yes, quite sure."

Daisy nodded her agreement. "You won't have time for motherhood—not for years," she said.

"No time or money," Cissy added. "I have to work at a paying job to pay my rent and eat. Already there are twenty-four-hour stretches when the only time I'm at home is to shower and change clothes. I've gone too far to just give up on medical school."

"I would think that went without saying," Daisy said.

Daisy poured herself a glass of wine and Cissy a glass of iced tea. From her perch on a barstool Cissy sipped the tea and watched Daisy bustle around her wonderful kitchen. Cissy loved the room. Maybe someday she would have a lovely home herself. She hoped that she would be able to fill it with people on occasion as Daisy did. Not a bad life. A worthy profession. A lovely home. A safe existence. No great joy, but no agonizing pain, either. Maybe she would enjoy this good, safe life more knowing that out there someplace there was a child to whom she had given birth.

THE following Thursday afternoon Cissy received a summons from Daisy. When she arrived at her office, Daisy closed the door.

"You will spend a semester of clinical training in Tulsa. The University of Oklahoma medical school has opened a branch campus there. You're being offered a special one-semester fellowship in family medicine. You will have to pay out-of-state tuition, though."

"My aunt has offered to help me financially."

"Well, let me know if you need any additional help," Daisy said. "I hope I can do something wonderful for you someday."

Daisy waved her away. "Go home and get some sleep. You look like a scarecrow with two black eyes."

CISSY had worried needlessly about what she would wear when she went home for Christmas. Other than snug waistbands, her clothes still fit fine. She warned her mother that she'd had a bout with an intestinal virus and didn't have much of an appetite. Actually, though, with the nausea of early pregnancy fading, Cissy arrived home feeling reasonably well. Her mother's pork roast and mashed potatoes had never tasted better.

Christmas morning her parents emerged from their separate rooms. Grayson fixed waffles and sausage, which they ate in the dining room so they could see the lighted tree in the parlor. After breakfast they gathered around the tree. Just the three of them. Cissy remembered when their family had filled the room. Her mother sighed and said, "What this house needs is children."

The next morning, before leaving for Dallas, Cissy explained about Tulsa. It was a wonderful opportunity—a fellowship. Her expenses would be paid. She planned to sublet her duplex.

"Tulsa is so far away," Martha Claire protested. "We'll never get to see you."

"It's just for a few months," Cissy told them.

CISSY enjoyed her solitary journey to Tulsa. With each mile that rolled by, she felt calmer. Tulsa was six hours from Dallas and twelve hours from Columbus. Her secret would be safe there.

She arrived before dark and had no trouble finding the rooming house where Daisy had arranged for her to live. Her room was spartan, with a tiny bathroom and a window that overlooked a church parking lot. She spent the evening putting away her things. Pictures of her parents and Buddy occupied the top of the bureau. Her quilt was spread on the bed.

By the end of the first week she had settled into a routine, spending her days at a family clinic on Utica Avenue and at sprawling St. Francis Hospital. She was able to conceal her pregnancy much longer than she would have thought possible. The mandatory white jackets that all medical students wore helped.

It wasn't until her seventh month that women started asking when the baby was due, whether she wanted a boy or a girl, if she had selected names. Men seldom commented.

Justine had insisted that Cissy not do any special-duty nursing in Tulsa, and sent more money than Cissy really needed. Cissy was grateful. She felt well enough but was always so very tired.

Justine called often. Did she like her doctor? Had she talked to Martha Claire this week? Did she need more money?

"You don't have to feel responsible for me," Cissy told her.

"Yes, I do. I abandoned you once. I'm not doing it again."

Justine called from the hospital after Iris had her baby—a beautiful little girl with big eyes. Cissy talked to Iris, who sounded exhausted but happy. "You'll have a baby one of these days," she told Cissy. "Our children will grow up together."

For the first time Cissy felt the sting of regret. But she dismissed it. The infant she was carrying would have another family.

Now that she was in her last trimester, she went to the women's clinic every two weeks. At seven and a half months the physician who examined her also delivered a lecture. She needed to take better care of herself. She was anemic. Her blood pressure was elevated. She hadn't gained enough weight. Getting enough rest? Drinking milk and eating plenty of fruit and vegetables? Just popping a prenatal vitamin every day was not enough.

Cissy used the leftover money from Justine's checks to buy a tiny refrigerator and stopped by the grocery for juice, milk, carrots, apples. When she got home, she fell across her bed, exhausted. She knew she had a responsibility to the life she carried. She had failed to keep her brother alive. She would not fail this child, too.

THE FOLLOWING FRIDAY afternoon Cissy began experiencing intermittent contractions. The ob-gyn resident who examined her said she was threatening to go into premature labor. He gave her a shot of terbutaline and prescribed bed rest with bathroom privileges for the rest of the pregnancy.

Cissy protested. She couldn't just go to bed. She needed to finish the semester.

"Try bed rest for a week, and we'll see how you're doing," the physician said, compromising.

How much time could she miss without losing credit for the semester? Cissy wondered as she headed for her car. On the way home she stopped at the convenience store for a quart of milk and a ham sandwich. Later she would go to the grocery.

She dozed through the evening news, then ate part of the sandwich with a glass of milk. She drifted back to sleep, then woke a couple of hours later and nibbled on the rest of the sandwich. She tried to study a bit.

The next time she woke, she felt a bit queasy and chewed on a couple of antacid tablets. She tried to go back to sleep but lay there feeling her stomach grow progressively more rebellious. She was relieved when she finally threw up.

When next she woke, she threw up again. It was the sandwich, she realized—either the mayonnaise or the ham had gone bad. Maybe both. By tomorrow she would be fine. Salmonella, probably. It shouldn't hurt the baby at all. She just needed to stay hydrated. She drank half a glass of water and went back to bed.

The water stayed down less than five minutes. She rinsed out her mouth, then carried the glass to her bedside table.

She awoke the next morning to her neighbor tapping on her door. She had a phone call.

"What took you so long?" Justine's voice asked.

"I was in bed," Cissy said.

"Why? Are you sick? You don't sound like yourself."

"I ate a sandwich that made me sick. The worst is over."

"You sure?"

"Yeah. I just need to drink water and sleep."

Cissy listened while Justine spoke rapturously about Iris's baby. She had mailed Cissy the latest pictures. Then she stopped mid-sentence. "Would you rather I didn't talk about the baby?"

"Of course not, but right now I need to get to the bathroom."

"Call me tomorrow," Justine demanded.

Cissy barely made it to the toilet.

Before she went back to bed, she dutifully took several tiny sips of water. She hoped some of it would stay down. If it didn't, she would have to go to the emergency room for IV fluids. She woke several times during the day, going to the bathroom, sipping water, throwing it up in the metal wastebasket beside her bed, but not all of it. She was sure of that.

When she woke to darkness, she turned on the lamp and looked at the alarm clock, but she couldn't focus her eyes. Reaching for the glass of water, she knocked it over. Her head hurt like hell. Her stomach, too—high on the right, under her ribs. Really bad pain.

She half crawled from her bed to the desk chair and used it to pull herself to her feet. She took three shaky steps to the door but collapsed against it. She knew exactly what the trouble was. After all, she was a third-year medical student. She was suffering from serious dehydration. Food poisoning. But her main problem was the toxemia of pregnancy. She had all the symptoms. Lights were even flashing in front of her eyes, and her legs were beginning to twitch—just like the textbook said. She put her hands on her belly. "I think we're in trouble," she said.

"Help! Will someone please help me?" she called out. She could barely hear her own voice, though. How was anyone else supposed to hear her?

SOMETHING was hurting her left arm. Cissy reached down to pull it out. But whatever it was, it was covered by a piece of tape.

She opened her eyes and stared up at a bag of IV fluids. She was in a hospital. A patient. She'd never been a patient in a hospital before. It was good she was here, she thought as her eyes closed again. But what about the baby? She reached down and touched her stomach. It was soft. Like a pillow without its stuffing.

"It's a boy," a voice said. Her father's voice.

Cissy opened her eyes. "Daddy?"

"I'm here, sweetheart. You gave us quite a scare."

"How long have you been here?"

"Since yesterday."

"How did you know? What happened? When—"

"Justine tried to call you. She made the landlady unlock your door and check on you."

Cissy touched her stomach again.

"Yes, you had the baby. He's a tiny little thing but moving about. They have him in an incubator, but he's breathing on his own."

"Does Mama know?"

"Yes, Cissy, your mother knows."

THE ring of the phone in the middle of the night had cut through Martha Claire's chest like a dagger. She rushed downstairs, thinking of the last time the phone had rung in the night—the night that Buddy died. Her hello was breathless. Then she listened while a woman explained she was Cissy's landlady in Tulsa and Cissy had been taken to the hospital in an ambulance.

"Why?" Martha Claire demanded. "What happened to her?"

"I'm not sure," the woman said. "She was unconscious. Her aunt insisted that I look in on her when she didn't answer my knock."

"Her *aunt?*"

"Yes. She had called several times, but Miss Stewart never seemed to be in her room. Finally the aunt asked to speak to me and said she was worried about her niece and asked me to check on her. Miss Stewart was unconscious, lying on the floor right next to the door. I thought she was dead. Scared me half to death. We called the police. When I called the aunt back, she asked me to call you and gave me your number. They took your daughter to St. Francis Hospital. I hope she's all right." The woman paused. "And the baby, too."

"The *baby?*"

"Yes. Her aunt said you didn't know. Your daughter was pregnant, Mrs. Stewart. She came to Tulsa to have the baby and was planning to put it up for adoption. She's a lovely young woman, your daughter. So polite. Not the type at all you'd think would get herself in a situation like that."

Martha Claire hung up and immediately called New York information for the number of Justine Mayfield-Dover. With a trembling hand she punched in the numbers. Justine answered immediately. "What is going on with my daughter?" Martha Claire demanded without identifying herself.

For two heartbeats there was no sound. Then Justine said, "I talked to her the day before yesterday and thought she sounded shaky. Then I kept calling back to check on her. Finally I convinced the landlady to unlock the door and see if she was in there."

"How come you know about my daughter's situation and I don't?"

Justine sighed. "She came here last November, wanting to know the family secrets. She told me she was pregnant."

"The family secrets?" Martha Claire's throat was dry. It was suddenly hard to speak. "What did you tell her?"

"She had pretty much figured things out on her own. All I did was confirm them. She seemed to think that understanding what had happened between you and Grayson would help her decide if she wanted an abortion or not. The only thing she knew for sure was that she didn't want you to know. She couldn't bear the thought of disappointing you."

"You had no right to tell her," Martha Claire said. "We swore those children would never know."

"Cissy asked me. I wish I had told her years ago. She has suffered because of what happened. She has a right to know why her mother hates her father, why her brother turned into a drunken bum who ultimately managed to kill himself, why I ripped Iris out of her life. She has a right to know why no matter how hard she tries she will never be able to make you happy. How could I not tell her?"

"If the past was so important to her, she should have asked me."

"She knew you wouldn't tell her. She went to her father, but poor Grayson didn't have the nerve. He won medals for facing the Nazis, but he didn't have the guts to go against you and tell Cissy what she wanted to know, so he asked me to do it."

"You have talked to Grayson?"

Once again Justine sighed. "Yes, I talked to him. It was the first real conversation I'd had with him since England. He was all torn apart inside back then, and he still is. You've really done a number on that man. I'd think you'd be tired of it after all this time."

"Don't you go heaping blame at my doorstep. You were the one who took the axe and chopped this family in half."

Martha Claire heard Justine draw in her breath. "Yes, you have every right to hate me. But you should forgive Grayson."

"Why?" Martha Claire demanded, spitting out the word.

"Because, God help him, the man still loves you. Are you going to Tulsa and see about Cissy? Because if you're not, I will."

"You leave my family alone!" Martha Claire said, spitting out the words. "I will look after my daughter."

"Good-bye, Martha Claire," Justine said, and the phone went dead.

Martha Claire slammed down the receiver. "I hate you!" she screamed, her voice echoing in her big empty house. "I hate you!"

GRAYSON awoke to the beam of headlights shining through his curtainless window. He pulled on his pants and grabbed his shotgun. A couple of weeks ago he'd had to scare off some teenage boys intent on pushing over his outhouse.

Martha Claire was standing in the beam of her headlights. "Cissy's in the hospital," she called. "We have to go to Tulsa."

"What happened?" he asked, stepping down from the porch.

"I'll explain on the way. Pack some things and let's go. Hurry."

Grayson stumbled up the steps, then stood in the middle of the room trying to think of what he should do first. But his only thoughts were of Cissy. *Please don't let anything happen to her,* he silently implored to a god he had not addressed in years.

He didn't have a suitcase out here, so he emptied a box of magazines and threw in some underwear, a few shirts, a pair of khaki pants, his shaving things and toothbrush. Then he put on shoes and a shirt, picked up the box, and went back outside.

Martha Claire had moved to the car's passenger side. Grayson put his box in the trunk and got in. "Tell me," he said as he backed down the rutted lane.

"Did you know she was pregnant?"

Grayson shook his head. "No, I didn't."

"She went to Tulsa to have the baby and put it up for adoption. I called the hospital. She was unconscious when they brought her in. She had an emergency C-section and is in intensive care. The doctor I talked to said her kidneys had shut down."

"Will she be all right?"

"He wouldn't say."

"And the baby?"

"Alive."

"A boy or girl?"

"I didn't ask."

He heard the rest of the story in bits and pieces. About Justine getting worried. The landlady checking Cissy's room. Martha Claire had called Justine—not a good conversation apparently. His wife was angry at him for sending Cissy to Justine, angry at Cissy, angry at Justine. But her anger was tinged with weariness. And fear.

Whenever they stopped, Martha Claire would call the hospital. "No change," she would tell him.

Grayson wanted desperately to talk about the baby, but he didn't dare. Why had Cissy kept it a secret? Had some boy hurt her? Grayson's hands tightened on the steering wheel at the thought. He would want to kill anyone who hurt Cissy. Finally he had to ask. "How do you feel about the baby?"

"Angry that she got herself that way. Angry that she didn't tell me. Angry that she told Justine instead."

"But the baby itself. How do you feel about it?"

"I don't know."

It was late afternoon when they reached the hospital in Tulsa. Cissy was still unconscious. They stood by her bedside, weeping, begging her to live on. "We need you so," Martha Claire said, clinging to her daughter's limp hand.

Then they went to the nursery. Martha Claire tapped on the door next to the viewing window. Five bassinets were lined up in front of the window. Grayson stared at a baby in an isolette that was pushed into a corner, separated from the other babies. The word "confidential" was written across the name card. When the nurse opened the door, Martha Claire explained that they were Cissy Stewart's parents, that they wanted to see their daughter's baby.

"It was a confidential delivery," the nurse said, glancing at the lone infant in the corner. "I can't let you see the baby."

"Our daughter is in a coma. We need to see this baby," Martha Claire said. Then she added a soft, imploring "Please."

"Stand in front of the window," the nurse said. "I may need to move the babies around. His isolette might pass by the window."

"Then it's a boy?" Grayson asked.

"Yes. A boy. A scrawny little thing, but holding his own."

She closed the door, and they watched while she rearranged her charges. Then she looked around furtively and pushed the isolette to center stage. Grayson watched his wife. He knew that any future he might have with this infant depended on what happened in the next few seconds. He watched his wife standing in front of the window, watched as tears began streaming down her cheeks, as her face took on a look of such rapture he had to look away. Only then did he focus his attention on his grandson, who was stretching, clutching tiny little fists over his head. Martha Claire was weeping now, holding on to Grayson's arm for support.

THEY waited through the evening. About ten o'clock Martha Claire went downstairs to find them some coffee. When she got back, Grayson was standing by the bed. Cissy's eyes were open.

"Mama, I'm sorry. I didn't want you to know," Cissy said.

"Shhhh," Martha Claire said. "We saw him. He's a beautiful baby."

"Oh, God," Cissy whispered.

"You go back to sleep, honey," Martha Claire said. "We'll talk about it in the morning."

One of the nurses directed them to a nearby motel.

"Do you want me to get two rooms?" Grayson asked as he pulled up in front of the office.

"Two beds will be fine," Martha Claire said.

She waited until she was sure Grayson was asleep, then went to sit by the window. She parted the drapes and stared across the highway at the hospital, where Cissy was. And the baby. Martha Claire hadn't wanted to leave her daughter's side, but Grayson looked as though he could sleep standing up. She needed to get some sleep, too. She had to be clearheaded when they talked to Cissy in the morning. And Grayson—she would need to talk to him first. He had to be a part of this.

Her hands were resting on her belly. Even after all this time she could feel her barrenness as surely as she felt hunger or thirst. "Please," she prayed into the dank darkness of the cheap motel room. "I'll forgive Grayson if You'll let us have that baby."

A baby could heal them, could make them happy again.

GRAYSON watched while Martha Claire explained. She was standing at Cissy's bedside, holding her hand. "Your father and I have it all worked out," she said. "We will take care of the baby while you finish school and serve your residency."

Cissy was frowning. "But what would you tell people?"

"That you had a baby," Martha Claire said with a shrug.

"When Justine had Iris, you made up a story," Cissy challenged.

"Times were different then," Martha Claire said. "If a girl had a baby out of wedlock, her family could never hold their heads up again. Bea and Jim Hawkins's daughter isn't married, and they're all there at church on Sunday morning, proud as peacocks, with their granddaughter all dressed in ruffles and bows."

Cissy sighed. "I don't know, Mama. That baby connects me to a man I'd just as soon forget. I'd worry that he'd find out and that someday the baby would demand to know who his father was."

"Neither the child nor the man will find out unless you tell them," Martha Claire said. "Don't forget, the baby would be living in Columbus, at least until you've finished your medical training. It's not like you'll be wearing him around Dallas in one of those baby slings."

Cissy stared out the window. "Do I have to decide right now?"

"No, of course not," Martha Claire said too brightly. "You take your time, honey. This is a very important decision."

Grayson stood. "We should leave. Cissy needs her rest."

A peeved look descended onto Martha Claire's face. She didn't want to leave until Cissy promised not to give away that baby.

"Are you sure you and Daddy want to take on a baby?" Cissy asked. "You're not as young as you used to be. What about night feedings and all that?"

"We have had a great deal of experience," Martha Claire said softly, hopefully.

"And the expense. We're poor as church mice."

"I'll sell the house if I need to," Martha Claire announced.

Cissy let out a little gasp. "You'd do that?"

Martha Claire pulled back her shoulders. "In a flash."

Silence settled over the room. Then Cissy looked at her father. "What about you, Daddy? You haven't said a word."

Grayson took his daughter's hand. "I think you should listen to your heart. It might help for you to see the baby, but that's up to you." Then he half pulled Martha Claire from the room.

"We can't just leave her," Martha Claire sputtered as he guided her toward the elevator. "What if someone from the adoption agency comes? If Cissy gives that baby away, I'll hire a lawyer, Grayson. I'll fight her with every breath in my body."

"I know you will, Martha Claire. And that might even be the right thing to do. But let's see how things play out first."

They went to Cissy's rooming house. Martha Claire had called the landlady and arranged for them to stay there while Cissy was in the hospital. A fold-up cot was already waiting in the corner.

Martha Claire was a caged lion for the rest of the afternoon. Keeping the door ajar so she could hear the phone, she paced about the small room. Grayson had made a deal with her that they could return to the hospital after dinner if they hadn't heard from Cissy. Martha Claire waited until five thirty and prepared some sandwiches. Silently she ate hers and pretended to watch the evening news, then went into the bathroom to groom herself for what lay ahead.

Cissy was out of bed, sitting in a chair, the IV still in her arm. "Is it all right for you to be out of bed?" Martha Claire asked.

Cissy smiled. "I'm fine, Mama. Did you have a nice afternoon?"

Martha Claire glanced at Grayson. "We rested."

"Good," Cissy said. "Me, too. And I saw the baby."

Grayson held his breath. Martha Claire's hand flew to her breast.

"He's a skinny little thing, isn't he?" Cissy paused, as though she expected them to say something.

Grayson was afraid to speak. Martha Claire, too, apparently.

Cissy's expression softened. "You poor darlings. You really want this baby, don't you?"

Like two puppets, they both nodded.

"I guess it will be okay, then."

"Thank God," Martha Claire said, sinking onto the bed.

Grayson knelt in front of his daughter and put his hands on her shoulders. "I hope you're not doing this just for us."

"I'm not, Daddy. I promise that I'm not."

"Well," Martha Claire said, "we need to think of a name."

Cissy actually laughed. "Mama, something tells me you have a name already picked out."

"He's such a little angel," Martha Claire said. "I was thinking about Gabriel. We could call him Gabe."

GRAYSON drove back to Columbus to tend the store and prepare for the arrival of his grandson, with Martha Claire staying behind to look after Cissy and the baby. It was with much pleasure that he refinished the crib, Polly's rocking chair, and a chest of drawers. He chose Buddy's room for a nursery.

Clearing it out had been heart wrenching. This had been Buddy's room throughout his childhood, and his possessions remained pretty much as he had left them. As he boxed up trophies, athletic paraphernalia, yearbooks, photographs, model planes, baseball hats, Grayson talked out loud to his dead son, telling him how much he had loved him, apologizing for not being a stronger father, for not keeping him alive.

Once the room was empty, he painted the walls a soft white. He put the crib by the window so Gabe could see the trees and the sky. In the store's back room he found the picture of Buddy in his Texas A.&M. uniform, which Martha Claire once had displayed in the store window. Grayson carried it home and hung it over the chest of drawers. He didn't think Martha Claire would mind.

Grayson called Martha Claire and Cissy every night, first at the hospital, then at the rooming house after Cissy and the baby were discharged. The phone calls were a foolish luxury, but after spending most of his evenings alone for the past eighteen years, Grayson found he needed a daily connection with his wife and daughter and through them the baby. Martha Claire did not chastise him.

He drove to Tulsa when Gabe was four weeks old, to bring him and Martha Claire home. Cissy had already returned to her duties. On the drive back, they had just crossed the Red River when Martha Claire asked him to move back into the house. "The boy will be needing his grandfather," she pointed out.

"Yes. I'd like that," he said.

They drove straight through, pulling into the driveway in the middle of the night. While Martha Claire fed Gabe, he was all eyes, looking around. Such an alert little guy. After he had been fed and changed, Grayson carried him upstairs and rocked him to sleep in his great-grandmother Polly's rocking chair.

Martha Claire seemed pleased with the baby's room. She watched while Grayson carefully lowered Gabe into the crib and covered him with a baby blanket. "It was hard going through all of Buddy's things," he admitted. "Is the picture all right?"

"It's perfect."

They stayed there for a time, side by side, staring worshipfully down at the tiny boy who already filled their hearts.

Later Grayson stood under the shower for a long time, trying to bring some ease to his aching muscles. In his room, he gingerly stretched out on the bed. Home, he thought. He was home to stay. He closed his eyes, wondering how long the baby would sleep and was surprised when the bedroom door opened. Martha Claire stood in the doorway, the light from the hall backlighting her body in her nightgown. "You don't need to sleep in here," she said.

MARTHA CLAIRE'S DECISION TO invite Grayson back home had been carefully thought out. She needed his help with Gabe, and a fatherless boy needed a close relationship with his grandfather.

She had not planned, however, to invite Grayson back into her bed. The sweet moments they had shared putting the baby to bed had softened her, she supposed. She had watched while Grayson stroked Gabe's tiny back until he fell asleep. Grayson had always had all the patience in the world with children. She wanted to touch Grayson's arm and tell him she was remembering their first night with Cissy. She didn't, though. She had stopped touching her husband during the years they warred over Buddy's future, had not reminisced with him since they lost Iris.

From her room she heard Grayson come out of the bathroom, heard the sound of the door to his room closing behind him. Martha Claire had left her own door ajar, to hear the baby. She had bragged to Cissy about their experience tending babies, but she was out of practice. When her children were small, she heard every whimper in the night. But that was a long time ago. Iris was almost thirty-four. Cissy would soon be thirty. What if she had lost her knack? What if she didn't wake up when Gabe cried? But if both she and Grayson left their doors open, one of them would surely hear the baby when he woke for his feeding. She got out of bed, padded across the hall, tapped on the door. "Grayson," she said, turning the knob.

The light from the hall fell across his bed. He had propped himself up on an elbow and was waiting to see what she wanted. She meant to tell him to leave his door open, but those other words had come out. *You don't need to sleep in here.* Words that indicated she wanted him to sleep in her bed. Did she? Martha Claire no longer thought about sex, no longer needed or wanted it. How could a grandchild change that? It was crazy. Grayson was still Iris's father. That would never change. Still, she felt giddy. Feverish, even.

She went back to her bed with her heart pounding. *What had she done?* She heard him coming across the hall, felt his weight on the side of the bed—the wrong side, she realized. In the past, when they shared this bed, their positions had been reversed.

"Good night," she said.

"Good night," he responded.

She wished she had her robe on. She was naked under the thin fabric of her nightgown. She lay motionless, hardly daring to breathe. Then she heard the sound of muffled sobs. Grayson was crying into his pillow. She sat up and touched his arm.

"I'm sorry," he said into the pillow. "Oh, God, Martha Claire, I've missed you so. How I've missed you." He grabbed her hand and kissed her palm. "I wish I had died in the war," he whispered. "Then I wouldn't have hurt you like that." He said her name again. Softly. As though it were the most beautiful two words in the world. Then he asked if he could hold her in his arms.

She said yes. There were no more words after that. They kissed for an incredibly long time, as they had back in their courting days. She felt beautiful, like that girl back then, like she had been on their honeymoon on Galveston Island before her husband went to war, before he went to England to be with Justine. Yes, she was on Galveston Island, with the sound of the waves, the night breeze coming through the open window and cooling her warm young flesh as she made love with the only man she had ever loved.

Ten

MARTHA Claire bent over to pull an offending shoot of nut grass from the lawn, then climbed the front steps, put her pruning shears and straw hat on the table, and seated herself in her favorite wicker rocker. She tried to decide if she should start breakfast or just wait out here for Gabe and Grayson.

Martha Claire rocked back and forth. She loved this porch. When Gabe was a baby, Grayson would sit out here rocking him, often singing the old songs they once had sung around the piano: "Jacob's Ladder," "On Top of Old Smoky." It was only in the past year that the boy had finally learned to fall asleep on his own, without his grandfather rocking and singing or stretched out with him on his bed, and then only because Martha Claire reneged on a previous ruling and let Puppy Dog sleep with him.

Puppy Dog had been a tiny little thing when they found him near Grayson's shack. The poor animal had been half dead, with every rib showing, but he made a beeline for Gabe and started licking his face. Puppy Dog was now a big, ungainly creature who left a trail of slobber everywhere he went, but Martha Claire often found herself wishing she'd let Buddy have a dog.

She paused a minute in her rocking, studying an overgrown branch on a holly bush. But she resisted the urge to take up her shears and snip it off. The offending branch would still be there tomorrow. Cissy liked to say that she and her mother both made rounds in the morning. Cissy marched up and down hospital halls with a stethoscope, and her mother marched around the yard with her pruning shears. It was true, Martha Claire thought. That was how she started every day, grooming her yard.

And such a wonderful yard it was. The crepe myrtle were in full bloom now, and the rose of Sharon. The beds of coleus, caladium, and impatiens were in full foliage under the trees. Cissy said that one of these days, when she had finished her residency and she was finally in practice and making all that money everyone said she was going to make, the first thing she was going to do was replace the handsome iron fence that had marched its way around the yard in all those old photographs. Cissy wanted to do all the things to the house they never had been able to afford, and sometimes Martha Claire let herself revive the old dream of restoring the house to its former glory, but mostly she lived from day to day, enjoying what blessings came her way. When the time came, she probably would tell Cissy to put on a new roof and forget about the fence.

Martha Claire lifted her apron and wiped the sweat from her brow. Already, at eight in the morning, it was muggy and still. But what else could one expect in south Texas in July?

Soon she saw them coming up the street—grandfather and grandson. Grayson had their fishing poles over his shoulder. Gabe saw her sitting there and began to run, holding up the morning catch. "I caught two, Grandma! I caught two!"

At four Gabe was an undersized little boy. He had started life small and would always be small, like his mother. Small but mighty, his grandfather liked to say. Mighty curious, for one thing. Gabe was a boy with a million questions. He kept his grandfather constantly going to the encyclopedias to find out what was the largest bug in the world, why Texas was named Texas. Gabe wanted to know if fish kissed, why worms didn't have legs, what held up the moon and sun. He was the exact opposite of Buddy, who had been a big athletic boy with few questions.

Gabe came running up the steps holding his catch in the air. "Can we take the fishes to Houston and show them to Mommy?"

"They would smell up the car, honey, but we could take her some vegetables, though. Why don't you and I go around back and pick some things for her. I bet she'd like some okra."

"My mommy likes okra a lot," he said.

Martha Claire had to take his dirty little face between her hands and kiss it. Such a dear boy. Her love for this child filled her up and made her a better person. If only she could have allowed herself to love her children this way. "Yes, your mommy likes okra," she agreed. "But do you know what she likes even better?"

His face broke into a big silly grin. "She likes me better than anything," he said proudly.

"Oh, indeed she does. That mommy of yours is looking at the clock right this very minute and thinking that in only three more hours her Gabe will be there to spend two days with her."

"And after two days she's going to put me in the car and drive us back to Columbus, and she'll stay here for five whole days. We'll pick blackberries, visit Reverend Huxley at the nursing home, and put on a show for you and Granddaddy in the attic."

"You got it!" Martha Claire said. "Now give those fish to Granddaddy, and let's go pick those vegetables."

"And some strawberries, too. Strawberries aren't vegetables. They're a fruit."

"My, what a smart boy you are!" Martha Claire said, remembering another summer day when she had waited on the porch for Grayson and Iris to return from an early morning fishing excursion. She looked at her husband, thinking to share her memories with him, but he was just standing there, staring down at the fish, a puzzled look on his face. "Grayson, are you all right?"

He shook his head, as though to clear it, and looked at her with questioning eyes.

"Are you going to clean the fish?" she asked.

"The fish? Yes, I'll clean the fish," he said gratefully, and followed her and Gabe around back.

THE party was Cissy's idea. She insisted that Stewart's Dry Goods could not close its doors after more than eighty years without a bit of fanfare. She decorated the walls with old snapshots she'd had blown up to poster size—of Grayson's grandparents standing behind their cash register, of his parents behind the same cash register, of Martha Claire and Grayson in his army uniform standing in front of the store. She'd also had posters made from some of the old newspaper ads—shoes for two dollars and fifty cents, men's socks for a quarter. And she'd borrowed the picture of Buddy in his A.&M. football uniform from Gabe's bedroom.

A steady stream of people came all day. The punch and cookies ran out in the first hour. Cissy rushed off to get more. Then she went to the nursing home to fetch Reverend Huxley, and ended up making several trips back and forth when other residents wanted to come. The store was a part of their memories.

When the last of their guests had finally taken their leave, the family took down the posters and folded the tablecloth. Martha Claire cried as she locked the door. Wal-Mart finally had put them out of business. She hated Wal-Mart and had vowed she would never set foot in the ugly, sprawling store that was ruining downtowns all over America, but she also felt a sense of relief. She didn't want to spend her days down here anymore, and Grayson no longer could manage the store on his own. He would forget how to make change and sometimes got lost on the way home. The store had represented such a major part of her life. It became who she was—

Martha Claire Stewart from the dry-goods store. Even so, they probably should have closed it when Grayson's father died. She should have let Grayson have a go at another sort of life. She told him that as they walked home.

Grayson didn't answer for the longest time. They walked half a block before he said, "I never was a good storekeeper, but maybe I wouldn't have been a good army officer, either. What I should have been was a teacher."

"You could have had a fine military career," Martha Claire said, taking his arm, "but you would have been a good teacher, too. You could have taken students to all those places you never got to go."

"Cissy wants to take me to Europe," he said.

"She what?" Martha Claire said.

"She found a tour for veterans and their families."

They walked along in silence, past the house where he had grown up, past the little house where they had lived as newlyweds. So, here they were, Martha Claire thought, two old people walking down the street toward what was left of their lives. So much time wasted, so many regrets. And such a sense of missing. She missed her parents and Granny Grace, but most of her missing was for Buddy and Iris, who both should still be a part of her life, along with Iris's daughter and any children Buddy might have had.

"You should go," she told him as they turned into the white gate of their own home.

"To Europe?"

"Yes, you should go. Tell Cissy about the war. Tell her all the things you felt and learned. Someday she will tell her son."

"I love Gabe," he said.

"I know you do," she said as they climbed the steps.

FOR years I had thought of taking my father to Europe. Then, when Gabe came along, I thought maybe I'd wait until he was old enough to go with us. I began to realize, however, that Daddy couldn't wait that long. He often forgot what he was about to do, stopping in his steps, a puzzled frown creasing his forehead.

So we made the trip, joining our fellow travelers in Rome—old men, some with old wives, others with sons and daughters. There was a pair of aging brothers who had traveled together from Wisconsin. A middle-aged woman from Oklahoma had come alone, fulfilling a lifelong promise to herself that she visit the place where her father had died. In all, there were forty-five veterans, two dozen wives, twenty-one children, and two grandchildren. The men moved with shuffling steps and apprehension in their eyes. They had come seeking to ease the grief they had carried all these years for fallen comrades and the guilt of having lived into old age when others had died so young. A sometimes suffocating blanket of poignancy hung over our bus journey through Italy, Germany, Luxembourg, and France.

Daddy couldn't remember yesterday's news, yet he recalled vividly his war years and recognized many of the places he had been: "That little stream was red with blood when we waded across." "Over the crest of the next hill is the town where my sergeant got hit."

It was the cemeteries, of course, that tore us all apart. Cemetery after cemetery. Seas of white markers, each one representing a young man who didn't get to go home to the rest of his life.

When we were planning the trip, I had asked Daddy if there was anyone buried over there whose grave he wanted to visit, and he told me about Fenton Crutchfield, the young driver who had died in his arms. It was the first time I'd ever heard him speak the name of any of the men he had known and fought with over there. Fenton had grown up in an orphanage in Iowa and planned to marry a girl named Sally when he got back home.

I had done my homework and knew that Fenton Crutchfield was among the ten thousand servicemen buried in the American cemetery outside Lorraine. You can't imagine what it was like climbing down from that bus and looking out over ten thousand white headstones. My poor father was overwhelmed to the point of speechlessness. With a map sent to me by the American Battle Monuments Commission, I led him up and down the rows until we found Fenton's grave, where he would pay homage to the driver who had died in his arms and to all the men he had known who died. For all those years he had carried that unbearable burden, of living while most of the men in his command had died. "I would have died to save any one of them," he told me. "I always wondered, If I had made better decisions would fewer of them have had to die?"

He knelt in the grass and embraced the cross that marked young Fenton's grave and wept. I wept, too, of course. How could one not? I wept for the burden my father and all these men had carried with them into old age. I felt privileged to share my father's sorrow, but my mother should have been the one to make this journey with him. Maybe then she might understand how hideously difficult the war years had been for him, how he might have sought refuge in a woman's soft arms, even if that woman was his wife's own sister. I myself fully forgave him; I would have forgiven any of the men on our bus just about anything. They had suffered for me and my son.

In Paris, with hugs and tears, we bade our traveling companions farewell and stayed on for four more days of sightseeing. Our last night we went to the top of the Eiffel Tower and looked down on what must be the most beautiful city in the world.

While I had forgiven my father, the sinner, I found it difficult to forgive my mother. I blamed her more for what had happened to our family than I blamed him—or Justine. Which wasn't fair. Technically Mama had done nothing wrong.

I remembered asking Mama about inviting Iris to my graduation from medical school. Mama said she wouldn't come if Iris did. "What did Iris ever do to you?" I had demanded.

"She left."

"But Justine was her mother. What did you expect Iris to do?"

"She should have told Justine that she belonged here in Columbus with you and me and Buddy," Mama had replied, real anger in her voice. "I was the one who raised her while her so-called mother went trekking all over the world. Iris was sixteen years old. She could have told Justine that she wouldn't leave us."

I never told Mama that my medical education had been Iris's idea and that she had helped me financially. And I never told her that Justine had provided the money for me to live in Tulsa until Gabe was born. I suppose I was afraid she might withdraw her love from me the way it had been withdrawn from them. Maybe being adopted had altered me more than I realized, but I needed for Mama to love me, no *matter how conditionally. I had lived my entire life seeking her approval.*

I did a general internship at Texas Medical Center in Houston, then a three-year pediatric residency, also in Houston. My salary was pitifully small, but I sent my parents whatever I could. I had become my aunt Justine, sending checks every month and sweeping in and out of my child's life. I missed Gabe terribly and called him several times a week, but I had made my choices. Someday I would make it up to him. When it came time to decide if I would continue my postgraduate training or enter private practice, I decided to go home to Columbus. I wanted to be with my son and didn't have the heart to take him away from my parents.

Martha Claire Stewart might not have given me birth, but as surely as if she had, perhaps even more so, I was and always would be my mother's daughter.

GABE was five when I bought the building where Doc Hadley had practiced for almost fifty years and hung out my shingle—CECELIA C. STEWART, M.D., FAMILY MEDICINE AND PEDIATRICS. I hoped eventually to limit my practice to pediatrics, but I needed all the patients I could get. At that point I probably would have treated puppies and kittens. My parents had sold the building where the store had been. My father had a small pension from the shoe company and another from the National Guard. They got by. Getting by had become a way of life for us.

But that would change. I would never be rich, but I would earn a good living. The bank didn't hesitate to loan the money to buy a clinic to someone with an M.D. after her name.

The decision to practice in Columbus had not been an easy one. I was offered a fellowship in pediatric urology, which probably would have led to a faculty appointment and the opportunity to practice and teach at a university medical center. For months, every time I drove home, I practiced explaining this to my parents—that I wanted to buy a house in Houston for Gabe and me, that I loved the challenge of the medical center, loved saving the lives of children who would have died if they hadn't received the level of medical care provided there. In

Columbus I would be the front line of medical defense, not the last resort, the generalist, not the specialist with residents following me from bedside to bedside, hanging on my every word. But how could I turn my back on my parents and their dream of having me practice in Columbus, of having me and Gabe with them for the rest of their lives?

Iris said I was a fool. After I told her I'd bought Doc Hadley's clinic, we didn't talk for several months. Then finally she called to apologize. "But it is such a waste," she amended.

It was and wasn't. Duplicating Doc Hadley's life would not be a waste, and being a good daughter was its own reward. Being a good daughter had been my destiny all along. I would live a full, rich life in the town where I had been raised, the town where I would practice medicine and raise my child.

Eleven

MARTHA Claire pulled an afghan over her legs and studied her needlepoint—a wall hanging of Texas bluebonnets—then glanced over at Grayson dozing on the sofa, Puppy Dog curled at his feet. The two of them spent a lot of time on the sofa these days, an old man and an old dog dozing away what was left of their lives.

Martha Claire picked up the remote control and changed the channel from the football game Grayson had been watching to an old black-and-white movie. Movies had changed so, she thought. The old ones seemed overly melodramatic, but the stars had such style. Years ago she had thought about being an actress herself. That notion had ended the day Grayson marched up on a stage and sang "When the Moon Comes Over the Mountain."

The memory made Martha Claire think of Gabe. She wasn't sure she approved of all the time he was spending with the Caldwell girl. But she and Grayson hadn't been much older than Gabe when they had pledged undying love to each other.

Martha Claire put down her needlework and went to the kitchen, where she put some apple cider in the teakettle to warm. Cissy and Gabe would be home soon from the high school band concert. Gabe had given up football in favor of the band, which was a wise move. He played the clarinet much better than he could catch a football.

Martha Claire put a blanket around Grayson's legs, then returned to her chair and tucked the afghan around her own legs. A freeze was expected tonight, the first of the winter.

On nights like this she wished for a fireplace so that she could pull her chair close and toast her toes. If she had allowed Grayson his military career, probably some of the houses they lived in would have had a fireplace. As life turned out, though, except for the few years she and Grayson lived in the rented house next door to his parents, Martha Claire had spent her entire life in the house her mother had inherited from her own parents. There was a bronze plaque out front now, mounted next to the front door, stating that the house was a historic landmark. By next year Cissy planned to have the house completely restored and listed on the city's annual Magnolia Homes Tour.

If Grayson had stayed in the army, Martha Claire wondered if she would have kept the house for them to return to when he retired. That was hard to say. But one thing she did know—if they had not been living in Columbus, she never would have had the opportunity to raise three children. She wouldn't have had those years with Iris and wouldn't have been here for Doc Hadley to drop off two little waifs in need of a family. If she and Grayson had come back to this house to live out their years after retiring from a military career, they would be living here alone. So it didn't do one bit of good to wonder how things might have been. This had been her life, and there was no going back.

Only last week she and Grayson had been watching a documentary about England on PBS, when suddenly there was a shot of the white cliffs of Dover. Martha Claire studied Grayson's face, but he showed no reaction. "That was where you went with Justine after the war," she told him.

"With Justine?" he asked with genuine puzzlement.

"You don't remember going there with her?"

He shook his head. "I remember France. I remember the war."

Martha Claire didn't know if she should laugh or weep. *He didn't remember Dover.*

Now, as she picked up her needlepoint, she wondered if he had also forgotten the aftermath. Should she ask him? Before she could decide, the front door burst open and Cissy and Gabe came rushing in, along with a blast of cold air. Grayson blinked himself awake.

"I've got some apple cider warming on the stove and some freshly baked oatmeal cookies," Martha Claire said, ready to herd them toward the kitchen. "I want to hear all about the evening."

Gabe put his arms around his grandmother and rubbed her cheek with his cold nose. He was taller now than she was. He was not handsome, but pleasant-looking, the sort of person you knew by the look of him was kind and good. Not that he was perfect. Gabe had a real lazy streak. He put off mowing the grass until Martha Claire shamed him by getting out the mower and threatening to do it herself. But he was silly and happy and made her heart swell so that at times she thought it would pop right out of her chest. If only she could have loved Buddy the way she loved Gabe, maybe things could have turned out differently for him.

IT GOT even colder in the night, but Grayson kept kicking off the covers. Martha Claire would pull the covers back up and rub his shoulders to soothe him. "Where am I?" he asked at one point.

"Here with me," she told him.

"Will you stay with me?"

"Always," she promised.

"Thank you," he said before drifting back into a fitful sleep.

Finally he stopped thrashing about, and Martha Claire felt herself settling into a few hours of real sleep.

Toward morning, when she woke and reached for her husband's warmth, she knew the instant she touched his flesh that he was dead. In the same instant the smell of his bowels filled her nostrils.

Quietly, so as not to wake Cissy and Gabe, she went downstairs for rags, a basin, and garbage bags. She cleaned her husband's body, changed the bedding, dressed him in clean nightclothes, and carried the soiled linens out to the garbage cans.

Then she washed herself and got back into bed with him, to hold him in her arms and weep and say all those words she never told him in life. She was so sorry for all those wasted years, so sorry for the years she had banished him from his family, so sorry she hadn't let him manage Buddy. She stroked his hair and kissed his face. "You were the handsomest boy in all of Texas," she told him. "And you were the best father those children could have had. I never told you that, and I should have."

Finally Martha Claire heard Cissy stirring and knew it was time for her to relinquish her husband's body and tell Cissy that her father was dead. Carefully, as though she might wake him, she kissed his lips, told him she loved him, and went to Cissy's room.

The door was open. Cissy was sitting on the side of the bed, dialing the phone—the hospital, probably, to check on a patient. She looked at her mother's face and returned the receiver to its cradle. "Your father is dead," Martha Claire said, her voice catching.

Cissy looked at her with disbelief, then went rushing out of the room. Martha Claire followed and watched while Cissy knelt beside the bed, buried her face against her father's chest, and cried out loud. Her cries brought Gabe, who knelt with his mother and tried to comfort her, but he was crying too hard himself.

Grayson had been loved, Martha Claire thought proudly. Her husband had been a good man and he had been loved.

A PERSON'S punishment for living so long was all these funerals, Martha Claire thought as they walked toward the church. Grandparents, parents, in-laws, friends. And Buddy. Buddy's funeral had been the saddest of all. Grayson wouldn't mind her thinking that. Grayson was seventy-four, and his time had come.

But oh, how she would miss him. Never again would she be able to reach for his hand or kiss his lips. Every day she would think of something she wanted or needed to tell him, and all she would have was a gravestone in the cemetery. And memories. She had lots of those. Trouble was, so many of them were upsetting.

It was a cool, crisp day. She had insisted on walking the three blocks to church, as she always did. She was arm in arm with Cissy and Gabe and counted herself fortunate indeed to have them with her. Someday they would be doing this sad task for her. But not for a long time yet, she hoped. She wanted to live on, to see how Gabe turned out and know her great-grandchildren. And she still hoped that someday Cissy would fall in love and they could have a wedding in the rose garden. She would even invite Iris if Cissy wanted her to. *Iris.* Martha Claire wondered if she would come to the funeral. She was sure Cissy had called her. Martha Claire wanted Iris to be there. When she had appeared at Buddy's funeral, Martha Claire had been distant, then regretted it afterward. If Iris came today, Martha Claire promised herself that she would not be distant. She would take her arm and march up the aisle with her. She paused for a minute to take a deep breath.

"Are you all right, Mama?" Cissy asked.

"I have to know. Did Iris come?"

"I don't know," Cissy said. "She didn't say one way or the other, but her husband isn't well."

It was hard to believe Cissy was forty-four. Her dark hair shone in the sunshine. There were a few gray hairs, but not many, and a few lines around her eyes, but not many of those, either. It was a dear face, always so full of concern for others. Martha Claire said, "Do you know what your father's last words were? He said, 'Thank you.' And I want to pass that thank-you on to you and your son. Because of you and Gabe the last part of your father's life was full of love. I thank you for that. For the rest of my life I will thank you for that." Then, with her Cissy on one arm and her Gabe on the other, Martha Claire marched up the steps of the church to her husband's funeral with a prayer. Please, let Iris be there.

She was.

Just as she had been when Buddy died, Iris was waiting in the vestibule. It took Martha Claire a couple of heartbeats more to realize that the older woman with her was Justine.

Before she could absorb this stunning event, Iris stepped forward, and Martha Claire opened her arms.

"I loved him so," Iris said. "He was like a father to me. I wish I could have seen him one last time."

But because he *was* her father, Iris had not been allowed to see him one last time, Martha Claire thought.

"Oh, Martha Claire, I've missed you so," Iris was saying through her tears, relief on her lovely face that she was not being rebuffed.

"And I have missed you," Martha Claire managed to say, even though she was only a few feet away from her sister, Justine, who had betrayed her as no sister ever should. How dare she come here for Grayson's funeral! The old hate rose in Martha Claire's throat. She felt Cissy tense beside her. And Iris.

Justine stepped forward. "I had to come. I needed to come back. Not because of Grayson, but because of you."

Martha Claire had to be civilized. She could not make a scene at her husband's funeral. She nodded at Justine, then walked up the aisle to the front row, reserved for Grayson's family. His casket was there. She had debated about whether to have it open. She was glad now she had said no. Justine would not be able to look on his face and remember the time when they had made love.

Paul Huxley, leaning on his son's arm, offered a eulogy for his old fishing buddy. "Grayson Stewart was not a religious man, but he was a spiritual one," the old minister said. "He knew the name of every bird, knew the habits of God's small creatures. He told me once that he had no expectation for a hereafter. He had killed men in the war and didn't feel like he had sent them on their way to some great reward. 'They were pretty damned dead,' he said. But those of us who do believe in a hereafter would like to see Grayson there. I myself can't imagine a paradise that didn't have a fishing hole and two spare fishing poles for me and my dear, dear friend Grayson Stewart, who was, in spite of himself, a godly man."

That was nice, Martha Claire thought. Such an unlikely friendship: a minister and an agnostic. But it had been a good one.

At the cemetery, as she watched Grayson's casket being lowered into the ground, she wanted to cry out, to tell them to stop, that she had to touch him one more time and tell him that she did love him, that she forgave him completely. But it was too late.

THE afternoon passed in a blur, with Justine and Iris the center of attention. The kitchen and dining room were full of food.

Finally, when the last of the mourners had told Martha Claire one final time what a good man Grayson had been, they were alone. Just the five of them. Two old sisters and two younger women who had been raised as sisters. And young Gabe, for whom his grandfather's funeral had been his first.

"Go," she told her grandson. "Go find your friends. Celebrate life." He had looked to his mother, who nodded and smiled, and he rushed up the stairs to change his clothes.

Martha Claire had meant to go back to the cemetery alone, but at dusk all four women were in the car, with Cissy driving.

The evening was crisp and still. The four women lined up in front of the fresh gravesite. Martha Claire began to sob first. Suddenly, with a feeling of panic, she realized that Iris and Cissy were walking away, arm in arm, leaving their mothers alone.

"I don't want to be here with you," Martha Claire told Justine.

"I know. I'm sorry I came, sorry I have upset you so. When Iris told me about Grayson, all I could think of was coming back here to you. I'd like to start over, Martha Claire, if you will let me."

Shivering a bit, Martha Claire began walking, and Justine followed her. They walked among the tombstones that presided over the graves of their parents and grandparents, of friends and acquaintances. And Buddy.

"It still hurts so much," Martha Claire said, with a hand on Buddy's tombstone. "Grayson wanted to make Buddy leave, to make him grow up, and I wanted him to stay. Grayson blamed himself because he didn't stand up to me. I blamed myself because I didn't have the courage to do what was best for my son. And Cissy thought if she had done a better job of looking after her brother, he wouldn't have been driving drunk along that country road. Until Buddy died, I thought that finding out about you and Grayson was the worst thing that could happen to me. It wasn't."

"Can you ever forgive me?" Justine asked.

"Not forgive so much as give up," Martha Claire said. "I am weary with hating you."

"I'm not well," Justine said. "When the time comes, I'd like to come back here to die—and be buried here with Mama and Papa. And darling Buddy."

"And Grayson," Martha Claire reminded her.

"Yes, and Grayson."

Martha Claire led the way back to Grayson's grave. Where did she go from here? Justine's and Grayson's betrayal had given her Iris. Because of Iris, she and Grayson had the need and the courage to adopt Cissy and Buddy. And in spite of the heartache children bring, they had defined her life. How does one unravel it all and come to terms? "I could've forgiven Grayson and saved my family, but it became who I was—a woman betrayed. I became a very ugly person." She paused, then asked, "Are you really dying?"

"Yes, so it seems."

Martha Claire sighed. "Feels like all I do is bury people."

"Then it's all right for me to come home?"

"You couldn't wait to leave Columbus. And now you want to come back. It doesn't make sense."

"A part of me never really left. I thought of you always, Martha Claire. You are my roots. My sister. If there was only some way—"

"Hush up, will you," Martha Claire barked. "I have my sins, too. Every time you went off to some faraway place, I thought how nice it would be if the plane went down. Then I could have Iris all to myself. I couldn't stand it when you took her away. I prayed that you would die so that she would come back to us."

As it turned out, my aunt Justine lived on for almost two years. Iris insisted it was because Mama refused to let her die. She had come home to Columbus at Christmastime, the month after Daddy died, and she never left. Iris and her daughter came to stay with us the last month or so. Strange how life can be, with sadness and happiness drawn in with the same breath.

My mama's house is still there. My son and his family live in it. I returned to Houston—not to a brilliant career as a university-based specialist, but I am with a medical group that looks after very sick kids. Mama lives with me. I have a beautiful garden because of her.

We drive to Columbus every Sunday, and she inspects the garden there. Gabe earned a degree in landscape architecture at Texas A.&M. and designs gardens all over the state. But the one in Columbus he keeps as it was. He doesn't dare change it.

I ran into Joe McCormack a few years ago at a medical conference. He practices in Lampasas, a widower now. We see each other once or twice a month and go on trips together. Joe doesn't know that Gabe is his son, and I don't plan to tell him.

To this day Iris doesn't know who her father is, and I will honor the promise I made to her mother. With the advent of the Internet and all the possibility for tracking down birth mothers, Gabe wanted to launch a search for mine. I told him no, he absolutely wasn't to do that.

Martha Claire Mayfield Stewart raised me, and I am her dutiful daughter. Every year on my birthday she tells me that the woman who gave me birth is thinking of me that day, and I know if that woman is still alive, those words are probably true. On that day I think of her and thank her for giving me life.

But the other three hundred and sixty-four days of the year my allegiance is to the woman who had the courage to take me from the arms of a wise old country doctor who wasn't afraid to play God.

JUDITH HENRY WALL

"I wanted to write a book about forgiveness and what happens when it is not forthcoming," says Judith Wall from her home in Oklahoma. The result was *My Mother's Daughter,* her nineteenth novel. Wall began her career as an author in the early 1970s, writing children's books while raising her own three kids. Later she tried her hand at romance novels and mysteries. Finally, she turned to the kind of books that she herself loves to read—women's fiction.

For Wall, the joyous part of writing novels is creating flesh-and-blood characters. "Good characters stay with you always," she says. "They never go away; you may forget elements of a plot, but you never forget a good character."

To learn more about Judith Henry Wall and
My Mother's Daughter, visit the Select Editions website:

📖 ReadersOnly.com
Password: *happy*

Even Steven

John Gilstrap

Susan Martin thinks the little boy is the answer
to her prayers. Her husband, Bobby, isn't so sure.
    They don't know it yet, but the time to pray is
just beginning. . . .

One

BUNDLED tightly against the cold, the young couple lay on an out-cropping over the Catoctin River, looking up at the cloudless sky and wondering which of the countless millions of stars was truly the one that delivered wishes.

Bobby pulled his bride of five years even closer and kissed the top of her head. "Happy anniversary."

Susan snuggled in, burying her face in his jacket.

The calendar had lied. After such a brutal winter April should have brought warmer temperatures. Out here in the West Virginia mountains, though, the air still smelled of February.

This wasn't at all how he'd planned it. The spot was perfect, yes, and the night beautiful, but he'd hoped the sadness would have dulled by now. There had to be a way to make the pain go away. There *had* to be. If he were a better husband, he'd know what it was. Susan's thick brown hair—invisible in the darkness—felt warm and soft against his hand as he gently massaged lazy circles on her scalp. She liked it when he did that.

"We'll just try again," he whispered, hoping she didn't hear the tremor in his voice. "And again and again, if we have to."

Susan just burrowed her head deeper. Her anguish felt like razor blades in Bobby's gut. This was to be their weekend of healing. The tears were a part of it, he supposed, as was the pain, but he worried about the anger. Sometimes when he was alone, he raged about the injustice of it all, cursing God and Susan and himself for denying them the one blessing that would make their marriage whole. Sometimes on nights like these, as his best friend succumbed to wave after wave of grief, he wanted to hurt something just to exorcise the rage.

Time was the answer. He knew this, but it was the one element in the world that he could not manufacture.

"Time heals all wounds." What a crock.

The river ran fast and loud just below them, swollen by melting snows. The thunderous noise filled the void of the night, bringing to Bobby a momentary glimpse of the peace he'd hoped they'd find out here. What is it about water, he wondered, that settles the soul?

On a different night he might never have heard the rustling in the bushes that bordered their secluded outcropping. It was a tentative sound, bigger than a coon or a possum.

"Oh, my God, it's a bear," Susan breathed, speaking their common fear. And it stood between them and their campsite.

Bobby was way ahead of her. Rolling quietly to his side and then onto his feet, he rose slowly. "I'm gonna scare him off," he said.

"You're gonna *piss* him off. Just be still."

Bobby had never actually encountered a bear in the woods, but the common wisdom agreed that they'd much rather run away from a noisy human than face him down.

"Go on!" Bobby shouted at the top of his voice. "I see you there in the bushes. Get out! Run away!"

Susan pulled at his pant leg. "Bobby!"

As the rustling stopped, Bobby turned and grinned. "See?"

Then it charged. Squealing like a frightened pig, the beast bolted out of the trees, coming straight toward Bobby at first, then breaking off to the right, toward the river. Only it wasn't a bear.

"Oh, my God," Susan yelled, "it's a little boy!"

And he was scared to death. Screaming, he ran in a blind panic toward the edge of the rocks, and the roiling waters below.

"No!" Bobby shouted, and took off after him. "No! Don't!"

But the kid darted with amazing speed, turning at the last instant away from the water, back toward the woods, screaming all the way.

"I didn't mean it," Bobby called. "Stop! I didn't mean it." His words only seemed to make the boy move faster.

Finally an old-growth oak tree ended the footrace. The boy looked over his shoulder long enough to see if Bobby was closing in on him, and slammed into the tree. A glancing blow on his shoulder sent him ricocheting into a sapling, then onto the ground. He just sat there, stunned, then started to cry—a wailing that went beyond pain, combining fear and anger and frustration.

Bobby stooped down and hesitantly reached out a comforting hand. "Hey, kid. I didn't mean any harm."

"Here, let me in." Susan shouldered Bobby out of the way and scooped the boy into her arms. He fought at first, but then he looked into Susan's face, and he liked whatever he saw. He seemed to meld with her; his face burrowed into her shoulder.

Susan shot a look to Bobby, but he didn't know what to say. The boy was tiny—maybe three years old—and filthy. Dirt caked his hair and his ears; his skin was crusty with it. He wore only a pair of footy pajamas, with little red choo-choo trains stenciled on the flannel.

"What do you think?" Bobby whispered.

"I don't know. He's so small. And he's freezing."

Bobby looked around, hoping to see a terrified parent somewhere, but all he saw were woods and sky and water. He stripped off his down jacket and wrapped it around the boy's shoulders. "Here you go, tiger. Let's get you warm." To Susan, Bobby added, "Let's get back to camp."

During the walk back, Susan tried to talk to the boy, asking him his name and how old he was, but all he'd do was cry and hang on.

"This is bad, Bobby," she said. "What's he doing out here without clothes in this kind of cold? And how did he get so dirty? Look at him. This isn't just a little dirt. This is weeks of dirt. Months, maybe."

She had a point. This kid looked as if he'd been rolled in mud.

In two minutes they were back at their campsite. Primitive was the name of the game here. Their Explorer was parked a good mile away, at the bottom of the trail. What little they had in the way of creature comforts they'd packed in on their backs. The campfire had burned down to a pile of shimmering red embers.

"I'll build this back up," Bobby said. "Why don't you sit with him for a while inside the tent, Sue?" he suggested. "Wrap him up in a sleeping bag and just hold him. He must be scared to death."

"Then what?"

"I don't know. I guess we hike out with him in the morning and take him to the ranger station." Bobby stayed in the doorway for a moment, watching the two of them settle into a sleeping bag. "Tell you what," he said, "I'll make some hot chocolate."

The camp stove was a single-burner job, fueled with white gas, and it took Bobby about three minutes to put it together, the blue flame telling him that he'd done it correctly. He poured water from his canteen into a pot, put it on the burner, and set about the business of resuscitating the campfire. Within minutes it burned freely, the flames reaching a good foot above the pile of sticks.

This whole thing had him spooked. Why in the world would a toddler be wandering around the woods in his pajamas? If he'd indeed been separated from his parents, where were the teams of rangers and police that should be out here looking for him? A sense of foreboding prickled his skin, and he found himself obsessed with the notion that someone was watching him.

A loud snap drew his attention to the right, toward the darkness that lay beyond the illuminated circle cast by the campfire. He heard it again. Whatever it was—*who*ever it was—was approaching cautiously. Bobby closed his hand around a club-size piece of firewood and stood casually, keeping it hidden behind his leg as he moved to the edge of the light circle.

"Bobby?" Susan asked from the tent. "Is something wrong?"

"Shh. I don't know. Be quiet for a second."

There it was again, only this time a rustle of leaves preceded the snap—and again the movement stopped.

"Hello?" Bobby yelled. His words seemed five times louder in the silence of the night. "Who's out there?"

SAMUEL cringed at the sound of the breaking stick and froze without waiting for Jacob's hand signal. He knew he'd screwed up again, and he knew that Jacob would have one of *those looks* on his face. He hated those looks. Samuel Stanns wasn't nearly the idiot that his brother thought he was.

Okay, so he'd let the boy get away. That was a big mistake, and Jacob was pissed, and when that happened, the whole world had better start paying attention. Ever since they were kids, Jacob'd had a temper, and everybody who knew him knew to stay away from it.

"Are you listening to me or what?"

Jacob's harsh whisper brought Samuel back to the present. He nodded yes—that he was listening.

"You just stay here," Jacob commanded. "Don't go anywhere and don't say anything. I'll take care of this."

SUSAN poked her head through the tent flap. "What's going on?"

Bobby waved her back inside. To the woods he said, "Howdy. You scared me. What can I do for you?"

"Well, I'm hoping you can help me find my son."

At the sound of the loud, gravelly voice, the boy bolted upright in his sleeping bag and made a keening sound. Susan tried to quiet him, but it was useless. The boy was utterly terrified.

Outside, Bobby recognized the boy's cries for what they were, and he caught the flash of contempt in their newest visitor's eyes.

"I'm Tom Stipton," Jacob said, extending his hand. "I see you found him. Quite a handful, isn't he?"

"I'll thank you to keep your distance," Bobby said, tightening his grip on the club. The stranger was six two if he was an inch. He looked like someone who'd been in his share of fights, and he moved with the confidence of one who usually prevailed. Bobby's mind raced with possible bluffs, but with the kid making so much noise, he wasn't sure what he could do. "How did you lose him?"

The visitor seemed amused, as if he knew that his lies were transparent but decided to humor Bobby anyway. "Oh, the wife and me was drivin' down the road when we broke down. I fiddled with the engine for a while. When I looked up, dear little Samuel was gone."

The words sat wrong with Bobby. "Dear little Samuel" had a troubling ring of sarcasm. This guy should have been ecstatic to be reunited with his son. Instead, he seemed angry.

Bobby needed to do something. None of this added up and—

The gun came from nowhere, materializing in the visitor's hand as it swung up to point at Bobby's chest.

Bobby reacted without thinking, ducking to his left even as he swung his club. He connected with the man's hand just as the weapon fired, the explosion deafening him momentarily as he rolled to his side and struggled to find his feet. He waited for the agonizing impact of a bullet, but instead saw the stranger on his hands and knees, brushing through the leaves on the ground.

The gun! I must have knocked it out of his hands.

Bobby charged, with his club raised high over his head, but the stranger saw him coming and drove a fist deep into his belly, knocking the air out of his lungs. Gasping for a breath, Bobby never even saw the vicious backhand that buckled his knees.

His consciousness wavered. The whole world spun at a weird, tilted angle. As he attempted to find the ground and grab on to it, he knew with absolute clarity that if he passed out now, he'd die.

He tried standing once, fell back again, his hand landing in the fire, triggering a yelp of pain. The singed fingers helped him to focus, though, and as his vision cleared, he saw the stranger back in the leaves, trying to find his pistol.

The fuzziness in Bobby's head evaporated. This man was going to kill him. Him and Susan. And the boy. He had to stop him.

With a rush of clarity he remembered the pot of water simmering on the small stove. Scrambling to his feet, he staggered toward the dim blue flame and snatched the boiling pot from the burner.

At that instant the stranger made an odd growling sound as he triumphantly snatched his gun from the leaves.

Bobby never even slowed down. Charging full tilt, he slung the scalding water, catching the intruder squarely in the face. Jacob howled. Bobby kept coming, catching him full in the throat with his shoulder and sending him sprawling into the dirt.

"Samuel!" Jacob yelled. "Dammit, Samuel, help me!"

Bobby scrambled back to his feet. He needed the gun, but it was still clutched in the stranger's hand.

"Samuel!"

Bobby went for the weapon. He grabbed it by its barrel and pulled. It fired. Bobby yelled and fell to the ground, certain that he'd been hit, but surprised by how little it hurt. His right forearm felt as if it had been set on fire by the muzzle flash, but as he glanced at the damage, he was shocked to see that he'd come away with the gun.

Still blinded from his burns, Jacob turned onto his belly and thrust his hand out to close with crushing force around Bobby's ankle. "I'll kill you. I swear, I'll kill you. Samuel!"

Terrified, Bobby tried to kick himself free from the man's grasp, but there was no getting away. He sighted down the barrel of the big pistol at the top of Jacob's head.

He'll kill me. He'll kill Susan . . .

But his finger wouldn't work on the trigger.

Then the scalded eyes found him. The man looked straight at him. Even through the blisters, the coldness of his eyes chilled the night air. "I'll kill you!" he yelled, and lunged forward.

The pistol bucked in Bobby's hand, blinding him with a brilliant white flash, and then it bucked again. He couldn't even see what he was doing anymore, but he had to kill this monster.

SUSAN shrieked at the sound of the gunshots, and so did the boy. They desperately hung on to each other inside the tent as she tried to make sense of it all, to figure out what she should do.

If Bobby was dead, then so was she. And the boy, most likely.

All she heard now was quiet. After so much noise the quiet was most terrifying of all.

SAMUEL felt the tears coming, and he fought to stop them. Only pussies cried. He'd heard Jacob say that a thousand times.

He'd said not to move, dammit! And he'd said not to say a word, so when he started calling for help, that was really really confusing.

But from where Samuel stood, it sure looked as if Jacob needed help—the way he just lay there, not moving. He couldn't be dead, could he? Jacob was too tough. He'd never die. He'd always be there for Samuel, no matter what. He promised.

But he sure wasn't moving.

Samuel started to cry in spite of himself, but quietly enough so no one would hear. He was more frightened than he'd ever been.

"Come on, Jacob," he whined in as near a whisper as he knew how. "Come on and get up. Please get up, Jacob."

BOBBY couldn't take his eyes off the man on the ground. He just watched, numb, as the blood leaked out of him, forming little rivulets in the mulchy forest floor. The trembling started from Bobby's shoulders and raced down his body, uncontrollable spasms that made him sit down heavily.

"Bobby, are you all right?"

He looked up to see Susan staring at him, horrified.

"I think I killed him," he said.

Susan put the boy down and sat next to her husband, gathering him into her arms.

It was more than Bobby could comprehend. What had happened? Not a half hour ago he was comforting his wife in the moonlight.

Susan jumped to her feet, as if shot with electricity. "No, don't!" she yelled. "Don't do that!" She darted over to the body, where the filthy little boy straddled the man's back, pounding him as hard as he could with his fists. "Stop it!"

As she wrenched him away, the boy continued to flail and scream. Susan just held on to him, and in time he settled down some, his panic dissolving to sobs and then a muffled whimper before he finally fell asleep in her arms.

She held the boy tightly in the crook of her shoulder, patting his back. To keep him turned away from the body, though, she had to face it, and what she saw made her stomach churn. The man lay so still. She saw blood leaking through his thinning hair, blood staining his denim jacket. She shuddered.

"Who's Samuel?" Bobby asked out of nowhere. "He kept calling for help from Samuel."

"Isn't that what he called the baby?" Susan asked. "He said they turned around, and Samuel had run away."

Bobby nodded pensively. That's right. So was he trying to get this tiny little boy to come to his aid? Not likely.

"We need to get out of here," Bobby said. "I think he's got friends, and I don't want to meet them."

"It's dark! The trail's too dangerous at night."

"Well, it's safer than staying here." Bobby nodded toward the body on the ground. "Besides, the sooner we report this, the better off we're all going to be."

"But what about the baby? He can't walk all that distance."

"We'll carry him, then. But we've got to get out of here." Bobby looked at the pistol he still clutched in his hand, then stuffed it into the waistband of his jeans. "It's just not safe."

Susan scanned the woods for more gunmen. A giant fist squeezed her stomach. "Okay. We'll come back later for our stuff, right?"

Bobby nodded. "Right. Just leave everything."

As Susan wrapped the boy up in a jacket and a sleeping bag, Bobby couldn't take his eyes off the corpse. He'd killed a man, damn near been killed *by* him. Why? What the hell was going on?

He realized now that he needed to know who this guy was. He needed a wallet or a driver's license from his attacker—some name to give to the police. The corpse's wallet bulged plainly from his back pocket. Bobby gathered the courage he needed to take the next step. Straddling the body, he used only his thumb and forefinger to reach in and grab a corner of well-used leather.

"What are you doing!"

The suddenness of Susan's words made him jump a foot. "Are you robbing him?" Susan said as she stood there at the opening of their igloolike tent, the bundled boy in her arms.

"No, I'm not robbing him!" He was aghast that she would even ask such a question. "I want to get his ID."

"Oh, honey, I don't know. . . ."

"It'll only take a second." He pulled the wallet clear of the pocket and opened it. He couldn't see much in the darkness, but the bill-fold had an odd shape and weighed more than he thought it should. When he turned it over in his hands, he saw why, and for just a fraction of a second his heart stopped beating.

A gleaming silver badge stared up at him. He reeled and sat heavily on the leaf-strewn forest floor.

"What?" Susan said, moving toward him. "What is it?"

"He's a cop. Oh, my God, Sue, I killed a cop."

Terror bloomed in Bobby's chest. Cop killers went to jail, pure and simple. Provided they lived long enough.

"But so what if he was a cop? Self-defense is self-defense."

But was it *really* self-defense? The cop came to their campsite looking for a child to whom the Martins had zero rights, and when Bobby resisted, the cop drew his gun. Whose self was being defended?

No, don't think that way. He was going to shoot.

But he didn't *shoot, did he?* At least not until Bobby lunged at his gun and started to fight with him.

"Bobby? Bobby, what's wrong? It *was* self-defense, wasn't it?"

All at once it crystallized for him. They had to get out of there. They had to disappear, make it look as if they'd never even been there. Stuffing the wallet back into the man's pocket, Bobby stood and whirled to face his wife. "We've got to go. Take everything. And I mean *everything.* I don't want to leave so much as a trace."

"You're scaring me," Susan whined. "Tell me what's happening."

"Think about it, Sue. I killed a *cop.*"

"In self-defense." She said the words as if she were speaking to a dense child. "He didn't identify himself as a cop. I was here. I heard that. You had every right—"

"What about the other cops, Sue? The ones who investigate all of this? They're going to see a dead cop, and they're going to hear about a child we don't know from Adam, and a story about an attack that's making less and less sense, even to me."

"So what do we do, then?"

"We get the hell out of here." Bobby stepped over the body and started policing the area. "For all I know, this is the worst thing we could do, but it's the only thing that sounds right. Now put the kid down someplace and let him sleep. I need help here."

He moved at a frantic pace, darting around the campsite, playing his L.L. Bean miner's light over the ground, hoping to find any trace of themselves that they might have left behind.

While the little boy slept at the base of a tree, Susan shoved their belongings into their backpacks. Bobby's sense of urgency had infected her. She wanted to be off this mountain and on to someplace safe and friendly where she could talk some sense into his head. They had nothing to hide, dammit. To run was to admit otherwise. She knew that Bobby would know this once he started thinking straight again. For now all that mattered was getting back to the car.

SAMUEL hadn't moved in a half hour, and neither had Jacob. It really was true, wasn't it? Jacob was really dead, and these people had killed him. If it hadn't been for those two nosy Nellies, everything would be just fine.

But why are they nosy Nellies? He whirled at the sound of Jacob's voice, only to find himself staring deeper into the woods.

"Jacob?" He looked nervously toward the campsite again, and at the body, which still hadn't moved. "Where are you?"

No answer. Jacob was like that sometimes, asking questions just to get Samuel thinking straight. He stewed the question over in his mind. Why were they nosy Nellies?

Because of the kid. That damned kid, who refused to do anything he was told to do. That kid who would scream and whine but never say a word to anybody. For the life of him, Samuel couldn't figure out why Jacob had wanted the kid in the first place.

You let him get away. You fell asleep.

That time, he knew the voice came from inside his head. The picture that Jacob wanted him to see started to focus in his mind. If the kid hadn't gotten away, if Samuel hadn't fallen asleep when he should have been watching, then Jacob wouldn't have been shot.

Samuel gasped, clapping a hand over his mouth to keep anyone from hearing him.

Oh, God, oh, God, oh, God, it can't be. I killed my own brother.

FINALLY they were ready. The backpacks were full, and the woods where their campsite had been looked pristine.

Susan wanted to carry the boy, but with her full pack she couldn't manage the weight, so Bobby took over. Cradling the boy in his arms, he led the way, illuminating the path with his headlamp.

The boy couldn't weigh much more than thirty pounds, but dead to the world as he was, he felt much heavier. That, combined with the fact that Bobby could no longer see where he placed his feet on the narrow, steep, rocky trail, made the thirty-minute walk to the Explorer seem an hour and a half.

"I see the car," Susan said from behind.

Bobby shifted his head, and sure enough, he caught a flash of white through the trees. "Thank God." The little boy now felt as if he weighed three hundred pounds.

"Okay, little guy," Bobby said as he walked around to the side of the truck. "I've got to put you down for a second." The boy woke up and stood as Bobby lowered him to the ground. With two presses of the little button on Bobby's key fob, the locks popped up. He pulled open the door and hoisted the boy onto the back seat, where he instantly curled onto his side and stuffed a thumb into his mouth.

"I'll ride in the back with him," Susan announced.

Thirty seconds later they were heading down the treacherous, unpaved switchbacks that would lead to the road home. Bobby found himself riding the brakes even after shifting the transmission into low. If anyone had asked Bobby yesterday, he would not have been able to imagine a circumstance in which he would make this drive after dark. Not unless someone was gravely ill.

Or dead, with a bullet in his brain.

Finally they made it to the bottom, and Bobby let out an audible sigh. They were back on solid pavement, and they had put plenty of distance between themselves and whomever the cop might have been traveling with. For the time being, the worst was over.

SAMUEL had taken a trip. That's what he called those times when he left the real world and traveled off to think thoughts that no one else could understand. And when he got back, the campfire and the flashlights were gone, and the darkness pressed in all around him.

Samuel didn't like the dark. But at least in the dark it was okay for him to cry. No one could see, so no one would call him a pussy now. Certainly not Jacob. Samuel sagged to his knees and sobbed there in the darkness. Jacob was never coming back. He was dead. And there was nothing Samuel could do about it.

It took another half hour for him to summon the courage to move out of his spot and do what he had to do next. The moon didn't provide a whole lot of light, but it was enough for Samuel to pick his way through the trees. He moved a step at a time.

Through the bushes an iridescent white rectangle drew his attention. He bent down for a closer look and found a piece of paper with writing on it. Samuel liked paper, and he liked writing, so he stuffed it into the pocket of his jeans.

You're not out here to pick up trash.

He knew that, and it angered him that he could so easily be distracted. Returning to his original course, he took only six more steps, and then he was there. His brother still hadn't moved; he was just a black stain against the night.

Samuel knelt as close as he could and rested his hand on Jacob's shirt. "I'm really really sorry, Jacob," he said. And then, choking back a sob, he leaned down and kissed his big brother good night.

ONCE the adrenaline high subsided, leaving only the monotony of a long drive in a quiet car, reality began to sink its hooks.

My God, he'd killed a man. You can't murder another human being and just walk away. Besides, he was a cop.

"But I didn't know that, Judge," Bobby imagined saying in a future courtroom. "It was self-defense. He scared me so badly that I rushed him, and then, when he pulled his gun, what choice did I have?"

His stomach tumbled at the very thought of it. They'd never believe him, not in a million years. But they didn't see the man's eyes. They didn't hear the boy's reaction to the sound of his voice. Things that seemed perfectly logical were going to sound ludicrous. Surely they would all understand that. They'd *have* to understand it, because it was the truth.

"Innocent people don't run, Mr. Martin."

And that's the truth, too. Ask anyone. The truth is a powerful weapon, they say. It will set you free.

So long as the evidence bears out your story.

And so as long as your victim is not a cop.

God Almighty, what was he going to do?

The gas gauge had dipped below the one-quarter mark, and a lighted AMOCO sign caught his attention. He slowed the Explorer smoothly, slapped the turn signal, and slid behind the row of pumps closest to the road.

Sensing the change, Susan mumbled something, then set her head back down on the headrest. An instant later she was asleep.

"Must be nice," he grumbled as he carefully and quietly opened his door. The way he felt now, he doubted that he'd ever get a restful night of sleep again. He walked between the truck and the pump, reaching for his wallet as he went. He had his credit card in his hand, ready to insert it into the gas pump when the sensibly paranoid lobe of his brain reached out and gave him a good slap.

If ever there was a bad time to use a credit card—with all of its traceability—this was it. It'd have to be cash. He checked his reserves, found two twenties, and went ahead and set the pump. He lifted the nozzle, flipped the lever, and nothing happened.

The speaker popped in the roof of the pump island, startling him. "You've got to pay first," said a groggy adolescent voice.

Bobby made his way toward the squat glass building that advertised itself as a minimart. As he opened the door, a zit-faced kid behind the counter wrestled himself to his feet.

"How much do you want? Whoa, are you okay? What happened to your face?"

Clearly the visual effects of his fight were worse than the physical ones. "Just born ugly, I guess." No way was he going to explain anything to this kid. "Let's shoot for twenty bucks' worth."

A picture of a smiling baby on a box drew Bobby's attention. They sold Pampers here, too. Well, he could sure use some of them. And some of those wipe things, too.

He brought his booty to the checkout counter and nearly fell over when the kid said, "With gas, that'll be forty-four dollars and thirty-seven cents."

"Holy cow," Bobby gasped.

The kid smiled. "We ain't the cheapest, but we're the only place open for thirty miles."

"Tell you what, then," Bobby said. "Put me down for fifteen dollars in gas, and then the rest here."

Susan still had not moved by the time he wandered back to the truck, though she stirred as he opened the back door.

"What's going on?" she asked.

"I just stopped to get some gas and essentials."

Susan saw the diapers and smiled. "That was sweet." She drew one leg under her and closed her eyes again.

The Explorer drank every bit of the fifteen dollars' worth, with thirst to spare. Bobby returned the nozzle to its slot in the pump and was on his way back to the driver's seat when he saw the pay phone at the far edge of the parking lot. This was his chance, he told himself, his chance to do the right thing.

But what would he say? "Hi, there, my name's Robert Martin, and I just killed a police officer."

No, that wouldn't do at all, would it? Truth be told, he didn't have to say anything to anybody. He could just go on his merry way, and maybe nothing would ever come of any of this.

He found himself approaching the phone booth even before he knew what he was doing. Just let it go, his brain screamed. Just drive on and take your chances.

But a man was dead, dammit. And none of this even touched on the issue of the boy. What were they going to do with him?

He placed his hand on the phone. "Okay, Bobby. You can do this," he said aloud. He made his phone call.

April Simpson offered up a little prayer of thanks that she'd been able to drive all the way home without falling asleep. She feared sometimes that this pace might kill her. Eight hours at McDonald's followed by another four cleaning offices downtown were only half of the available hours in a day, but as the baby in her belly continued to bloom, she needed more sleep than she could find.

Some nights she lay awake in her bed crying, wondering how she was ever going to get by with two children to care for. She remembered those endless nights when infant Justin refused to sleep, crying and crying. Now her son was nearly three, but still terribly two, and she was going to have to find a way to deal with another infant. She wasn't sure she could do it.

Not that she had a lot of choice anymore. She'd decided to keep the belly squirmer, and that's all there was to it. To hell with what William thought. William was a pig. He'd been a pig for as long as she'd known him, and if it hadn't been for the night of drunken passion that had created Justin, she'd never in a million years have married him. William wasn't the father, but he was a man, and at the time that's what she thought she needed most.

April pulled into her space at The Pines and scanned every compass point for signs of trouble before turning off the ignition and climbing out of her tiny Geo. Her little car served as her symbol of freedom—her statement to the world that she wasn't completely useless. It also was the only asset that she owned outright and in her own name. One day it might just be her ticket out of here.

As she crossed the dark playground on her way to her building, she kept her hand in her coat pocket, wrapped around the tiny .25 that she'd bought six years ago but never fired. William liked to say that she could empty a whole clip into someone and only piss him off, but if that bought the time she needed to avoid a rapist or a weapon bigger than hers, then that was just fine. Killing wasn't her bag. Surviving was.

She kept her eye on the cluster of kids over by the sliding board, watching without turning her head, as they did the same to her. What were they doing outside at four in the morning? Where were their parents? And why would they want to be outside on such a cold night? Here in Pittsburgh, spring felt too much like winter.

Twenty, thirty yards away, the kids posed no immediate danger, but as one of them took a step closer, her hand tightened on the pistol's grip. When it turned out that he was merely moving around to sit on the end of the sliding board, she relaxed.

She'd once counted the steps from her parking space to her front door, and the number 182 remained burned into her brain forever. One hundred eighty-two steps, exposed to the whims of whoever might decide to take advantage of her. Yet, no one ever had. She wondered sometimes why that was. Maybe it was because she stayed clean and sober and never hassled those who could not make the same claim.

Finally she arrived at her apartment door, relieved to find it locked. That meant that William was reasonably sober.

April turned the dead bolts, and as the door swung open, she nearly screamed. William was waiting for her on the other side, sitting in the La-Z-Boy opposite the door. In the blue light of the television he looked like somebody's ghost.

"You scared me to death!" she exclaimed.

William didn't seem startled at all. "Sorry," he grunted. "I've been waiting up for you."

"What's wrong?" Call it woman's intuition or a premonition or whatever, but she knew that something terrible had happened.

He didn't say anything. He just pivoted his head, and then she saw the bruises on the left side of his face, swelling his eye shut.

"William, what—" She took a half step closer, then froze. "Justin," she breathed.

Dropping her purse to the floor, scattering keys and change everywhere, she bolted down the short hallway toward the baby's room. Justin slept on a mattress on the floor, and that mattress looked for all the world to be empty. "Justin? Justin! Where are you!"

He was gone.

"William!" she screamed. "William, where's Justin?" She bolted back into the living room, panic boiling hot in her belly. "Is he dead? Please tell me he's not dead."

William shook his head, a barely perceptible movement. "He's not dead. At least, I don't think he is."

"Tell me! Tell me what happened."

William winced and took a deep breath. "They took him."

The words hit like razors. "*Who* took him?"

"Two men," he said. "I think they were working for Logan."

Suddenly the room seemed short of oxygen. April had to breathe hard to keep from passing out. "Why of all the children in the world would Patrick Logan want my little boy?"

"I—I d-don't know."

"Don't lie to me!" Suddenly the .25 appeared in her hand.

"Whoa, April! Okay, okay. I'll tell you. I owe him some money."

"You owe Patrick Logan money? You borrowed money from that drug-peddling son of a bitch?"

"I didn't borrow money from nobody. I rolled a guy last week who turned out to be one of Logan's mules. He wants the money back, and he took Justin as insurance."

"How much?"

"About a thousand dollars."

"A thousand dollars! A thousand dollars? You had to know it was Logan's money. Or Ortega's or somebody who runs drugs."

William shrugged again. "I guess I wasn't thinking."

"You weren't thinking. That's what you have to say?" A thousand dollars was more money than April had ever seen in one place in her entire life. "Give it back, and we'll get Justin back."

"It's not that simple. I don't have it anymore."

"You spent a thousand dollars in a *week?*"

Another shrug. "Well, there's interest, too."

This was too much. April couldn't believe what she was hearing. "How can you spend that much money in a single week?"

"It just went. I don't know. I bought a couple of rounds at Wilson's, and I guess my luck wasn't so good at cards there one night."

"You lost my son over booze and cards? Are you *crazy?*"

William became angry. "Hey, it's not like I offered him up for sale. They *took* him, April. And they kicked the hell out of me in the process."

Without a word April turned on her heel and headed for the kitchen. "I'm calling the police."

William hurried after her. "No. You can't."

"The hell I can't. I don't give a damn if you go to jail."

William grabbed her roughly by the arm. "That's not it. They told me that if I called the cops, they'd kill Justin."

April's knees sagged, and she leaned against the wall for support. Until that instant the reality of it all had not hit her. Her son—her beautiful little boy—had been *kidnapped*. By people who wouldn't hesitate to kill him. "So what are we supposed to do?"

"He gave me a week to come up with the money. His men promised they'd keep him alive that long. But not a day longer."

The wave of hopelessness started in a place deep down inside April's body, and it spread with amazing speed, until her hands quaked uselessly and the gun clattered to the parquet floor tiles. Images of her adorable little boy bound and gagged flooded her mind. "Then what are we going to do?"

"We'll have to get the money back. I have a week."

"We *don't* have a week! I will not allow my little boy to be handled by that man and his people for a single second longer than it has to be."

William scoffed, "Well, we're gonna have to be a *little* patient, anyway. It's not like I can come up with that kind of money overnight."

The smugness of his tone made something snap inside April, and she smacked him across his face. "How dare you—"

Then, just as quickly, he fired back, a stunning blow to her cheek. Stars flashed behind her eyes, and she fell to the floor.

"Don't you ever lay a hand on me, bitch," he snarled. "I'll get the money, all right? And I'll get your damn kid back, but don't you ever *ever* hit me again." He disappeared into the bedroom.

April couldn't bear it anymore. Lying there on the floor, she buried her face in the crook of her elbow, and as a door slam shook the apartment, she started to cry.

SUSAN'S nap didn't last long after the Explorer started moving again. Her mind reeled with all the countless things that needed to be done. The diapers were a good first step. She had cleaned the boy's bottom and replaced the tattered pajamas with a clean T-shirt from Bobby's backpack. He was still caked with dirt, but she felt as if she could at least hold him now without cringing against the stench.

Through all her fumbling in changing him, he never really woke up, though he never seemed fully at rest either—no doubt pursued in his dreams by the same people who'd done this to him.

Well, he was safe now. Susan would make sure that nothing bad could happen to him anymore. He lay with his head in her lap as they traveled in silence down the highway toward home. Toward their house, really. It wasn't a home yet, would never be until they added the sound of a child's laugh. As it was now, the Martins' rambling brick colonial—their dream home, set in the woods of Clinton, Virginia—stood merely as a shrine to what might have been, to what nearly was.

Susan had known grief in her time—from the death of her mother just a few years ago to every one of the three miscarriages that had plagued the early years of their marriage. She thought she could be strong, that she could handle grief as it came her way. To lose Steven, though—to lose him the way they had—was a sharp, enduring, Technicolor kind of pain that just never dimmed.

Because of Susan's history, that pregnancy was monitored more closely than a moon shot. She visited her ob-gyn weekly for a while there, and she endured every test known to God or babies. Over the months, they'd assembled an entire album of sonogram photos— none of which were legible to her, but that didn't really matter. They were *finally* going to be parents. All systems go. Everything A-OK.

They learned the baby's sex—it was a boy. Bobby's dream come true. Nothing else mattered back then. The entire world revolved around the hyperactive baby as he boogied without pause, ultimately finding a rib with his foot and thrumming it in rhythm to a tune only he could hear. Bobby made it a point to be in the bathroom for Susan's nightly baths, just to watch Steven wriggle in response to the hot water.

They were the happiest and healthiest days of Susan's life.

Then, two weeks before he was due to be born, Steven had died inside her womb. Her son—the son she knew so well, despite never having seen him—had somehow tied a knot in his umbilical cord.

"I just wanted you to know that you did nothing wrong," her ob-gyn had told her. "Perhaps it will help to remember that he died playing."

Died playing. Susan loved that phrase, and she loved the image that it conjured. But then the sadness came with the force of a collapsing wall, crushing her soul.

Every morning, afternoon, and evening the pain lived on, its edges just as sharp as they'd been six weeks ago. Susan knew from her shrink that six weeks was nothing on the grief timetable, but she didn't know how much more of it she could take. Sometimes it seemed that the very next minute would edge her into lunacy.

Those were the times when Bobby miraculously appeared for her, his strength restored, his optimism unblemished. God, how she loved him.

She found herself watching the back of Bobby's head as he piloted the truck through the night, studying the strong set of his chin, his unshakable concentration on the road. Watching him brought a glimmer of warmth. All of this really would pass, she told herself, and if she emerged whole on the other side, it would be because Bobby had never let go of her hand. She used these thoughts to edge the other horrors out of her mind as she leaned back against the headrest and closed her eyes.

An hour later, as the Explorer swung the turn into the long, wooded driveway, Susan was sound asleep, the fingers of her right hand tangled in the boy's filthy mop of hair. In her dream Steven was with her again, his head on her lap and listening intently as they read together from *Winnie-the-Pooh*.

RUSSELL Coates cinched the seat belt even tighter and willed himself not to look out the window.

"Are you okay, Agent Coates?" the chopper pilot asked.

He did his best to smile. "Peachy."

"I've been doing this for years, sir. Since Vietnam, in fact, so you can relax. There's the crime scene down there." The pilot pointed through the windows. "Now, we can lower you on a winch, or—"

"You're out of your mind."

"The alternative is a long walk, sir."

"Always my preference over a long fall. Just land this thing and let me out, okay?"

Russell's headset crackled. "State police chopper, this is the FBI ground unit below you. Is Agent Coates on board with you?"

Russell recognized the voice of Tim Burrows, his A.S.A.C., and he beat the pilot to the mike button. "I'm here, Tim. We're just looking for a place to park."

As police agencies go, the Charleston, West Virginia, field office of the FBI was not exactly Murder Central. They did their share, of course, but most murder investigations fell within the jurisdiction of local police forces. Because this particular killing had occurred in Catoctin National Forest, however—on federal property—it was a federal issue. Moreover, because it had occurred on Russell Coates's first day back from a Bahamian cruise, it had become the Bureau's version of a welcome-home fruit basket.

A hiker had discovered the body and made an anonymous phone call to the nearest ranger station. A ranger, in turn, had called the local police, who notified the FBI. Someone thought to rouse Russell out of bed on his last day of vacation to catch a state police chopper out to the middle of nowhere.

That Tim Burrows, the wonder boy, had been standing in for him all week didn't help matters. At thirtysomething Burrows sported that kind of raw ambition that made Russell nervous. Never a group known for low self-esteem, the young agents of Burrows's era had had their egos pumped with helium, and they floated somewhere between annoying and insufferable.

Of course, it could just be that Russell was getting old, but he refused to believe that. Outside of the National Football League, forty-three didn't meet anyone's definition of over-the-hill.

On the ground below them Russell saw four smoke trails rising from where someone had used road flares to mark out a makeshift landing zone. He held his breath as the chopper approached from upwind and then flared gracefully before touching down without so much as a bump.

"On the ground safe and sound, sir," said the pilot.

Russell reached across the center console and shook his hand. "Nice job. Glad it's not mine." He ducked low under the rotor disk as he jogged away from the big machine.

Russell headed for a group of rangers gathered around a Park Service vehicle, and as he did, one of the cluster—a mid-thirties blonde with that hearty woman-of-the-earth look that seemed so common among park rangers—broke off from the pack and walked out to meet him.

"Sarah Rodgers," she said, offering a hand. "I'm shift supervisor."

Russell grasped her hand, noting her grip. "Russell Coates, FBI. Special agent in charge."

"You're the S.A.C. I've been hearing so much about. I guess I was expecting something in burlap."

Sack. Burlap. Funny. First time he'd ever heard that one. He smiled. "Actually, it's the Secret Service that pronounces the word. We only spell it. It's S period, A period, C period. What kind of resources we got working up here now?"

"Well, there's a few of your people up at the scene with the body, and a few local and state police thrown in for good measure."

Too many people. "Is the area closed off to hikers?"

The question amused her. "This is a national park, Agent Coates. If you're asking if we've shut the gates, the answer is no."

Why did he have the feeling that they'd gotten off on the wrong foot? He smiled as best he could. "Look, Ms. Rodgers, I don't mean to offend, okay? I'm just a little disappointed that the whole world might have traipsed through this crime scene before I've had a chance to see it."

"Ditto about the offense," Sarah countered. "Please understand that my people are trained in all aspects of running a national park, but homicide investigations are a bit out of our league."

Fair enough, Russell thought. "So where am I?"

Sarah retrieved a weather-beaten, plastic-laminated map from the back pocket of her green trousers. "Here's the spot where we found the body." She pointed to a place on the map next to a meandering river. "That's about a mile up that trail"—she pointed to his left— "which is right here on the map. We call it Powhite Trail. Currently you're standing right here, on fire road 7. Technically, people aren't supposed to drive up here, but many do."

"You don't ticket them?"

Sarah shrugged. "Not so long as they stay off to the side and don't block fire equipment access. Frankly, we don't get but five or six parties a month that come up this way. It's not an easy hike."

"Okay, Ms. Rodgers—"

"Call me Sarah, please."

"Okay, Sarah. I need to head up there and see what's happening, but while I'm gone, I'd like you to make sure that none of the vehicles I see here are moved. And I want you to make sure that no other vehicles are permitted to come within a hundred yards of here."

"What am I supposed to tell the police and the media when they come flooding in here?"

"Tell the media whatever you'd like and send them away. If the cops are halfway professional, they'll understand."

Sarah looked at him as if he were crazy.

"Look, if our bad guy parked along the side of the road, his tires likely left an impression. That means we have to make castings of every tire print around here, and I need you to keep your vehicles in place so I can rule out their prints from all the others."

"How long is that likely to take?"

He shrugged. "I don't know. Probably the better part of the day. Welcome to police work, Ms. Rodgers. Now, can you spare someone to escort me up to the crime scene?"

ONE glance at the scene told Russell that Tim Burrows had a good handle on things. Judging by the hundreds of feet of barricade tape that had been stretched among the trees, he saw that the crime scene was a big one, roughly defined as the entire mountain.

Tim looked more like a jungle grunt than an FBI agent, dressed as he was in camouflaged BDUs with his H&K 9-mm strapped low on his thigh in a Velcro-and-nylon holster.

"Hey, Tim," Russell opened as he approached his A.S.A.C. "Bring me up to speed."

Burrows smiled and led with his hand. "Hey, Russell. How's the golf game?"

"Didn't even bring the clubs. Decided to rip the lips off fish instead." Russell would take a smooth lake over golf any time.

Tim handed Russell two heavy rubber bands for his shoes—all investigators wore them to differentiate their footprints from the others—and led the way toward a blue paper sheet that had been anchored against the breeze with a half-dozen stout rocks. As they approached, a potbellied deputy kicked the rocks off one long side of the sheet and let the wind flop it over to reveal the corpse.

"I figure time of death at twelve to eighteen hours," Tim said. "He's rigored up tight, and you can see the lividity for yourself."

Indeed, Russell could. The dead man lay on his stomach, and all the low spots of his body had turned purplish black from the stagnant blood pooled in his tissues.

"The guy's a cop. Thomas Stipton from Pittsburgh, Pennsylvania. We found his badge and ID in his back pocket."

Russell's right eyebrow scaled his forehead. He nodded toward the empty holster on the corpse's hip. "Where's his weapon?"

Tim shook his head. "Haven't found it yet."

"Shot with his own gun, you think?"

"Hard to say till ballistics gets done with the bullets. Here, take a look at the entry wounds." As Tim spoke, he pointed out the different holes with the point of his pen. "We've got one here in the shoulder, between his shoulder blade and his collarbone, one here at the suprasternal notch, and another here on top of his head."

Tim dug using phrases like suprasternal notch. Russell would probably have called it the base of the throat.

"High, downward angles," Russell observed. "You figure the killer was hiding in a tree?"

Tim shook his head. "I thought that at first, yes. But look down there in the woods. You see that orange evidence marker? That's a stray bullet lodged in a tree trunk."

Russell could see the scar itself, gouged in the base of a tree about twenty feet away. "So what are you telling me? The guy was crawling?"

"Well, that's the million-dollar question, isn't it? I figure maybe it was a foiled rape attempt. Judging from the powder burns, this guy was shot, like, point-blank."

"But his pants are up," Coates noted.

"Maybe he was still trying to subdue her when he got shot."

Russell's head bobbed as he considered that. "Okay. So why didn't she call the police when she got down off the mountain?"

"Scared, maybe?"

"Maybe." Russell strolled in a small circle around the body, trying to imagine a scene as it might have unfolded.

"There's something else—"

Russell silenced Tim with a raised finger. He saw something. Not sure what it was, exactly, but it was *something*. Call it insight, call it intuition—whatever it was, he'd learned to trust it. Something about the arrangement of the leaves right over there—a cleared spot among the mess of rocks and leaves. If he used his imagination a little, he could almost see a faint circular imprint in the ground.

He walked over to the spot and knelt, feeling along the ground for a telltale sign of—

"Here it is," he announced. "The stake hole from their tent." Removing his pen from his pocket, he gently probed the hole. From the angle he could guess where the other stakes had been. "There was a campsite built here last night. I want plaster casts made of these stake holes, Tim. And I want casts made of every footprint and of every tire track down there on the fire road. You were going to show me something else?"

"Oh, yeah. Damnedest thing. Parker over there found these." Tim led his boss farther into the woods. "Look."

Russell followed Tim's arm down to two more footprints. "These prints are deeper than the others, and they're unusually close together. Parker thinks the depth can only mean one of two things. Either the guy is really heavy or he stood here for a very long time."

"Or both."

"Right. Don't you think that's odd? Somebody standing out here watching somebody else get killed?"

Russell shrugged. "I don't know. If I had stumbled by a murder in progress, I might be inclined to stand real still and be quiet. Better than being drawn into the fight."

"So that puts at least three people on the scene of this thing now.

And of those three, one of them is dead, another did the killing, and a third stood by and watched."

"How do you know he didn't stand here before or after?"

"I don't know that for sure, but what would be the point? I mean, who's going to stand out here in the middle of the woods long enough to make an imprint this deep? And as far as hanging around after the murder, that doesn't make sense either. This guy has a dead body on his hands. He's going to get the hell out, isn't he?"

Russell nodded and walked back toward the campsite. "It's also interesting that they took plenty of time to clean up before they left. I mean, they even scattered the ashes from their campfire. Seems kind of odd to me that someone who's just been attacked would have the presence of mind to cover their tracks so well."

Tim thought it over. "Okay. So why not conceal the body?"

Good question. "How would you do that? I mean, as a practical matter, you could bury him, but that would mean a damn big hole. I figure they saw the futility of it and decided to use the time to concentrate on doing away with all vestiges of themselves."

And how naïve a decision it was, he didn't say. Even the smartest criminals leave something behind. Beyond the footprints and tire tracks, there might be cigarette butts, toothpicks, hair or blood samples. All he had to do was piece those things together, use a little imagination and logic, and with a little luck, he'd have himself a murderer in no time.

Three

Bobby Martin shot upright in bed, instantly awake and instantly aware of all the horrors the new day brought.

Had he really killed a cop and called in and reported it? So much of what was happening jumbled in his head like somebody else's terrible dream. But none of it was fantasy, was it? Every detail, every mistake, every second was bona fide, certified, USDA-choice reality.

Whipping off the covers, he swung his feet to the floor, surprised to see that he was still wearing his pants and socks from yesterday. He'd been so exhausted when he lay down he hadn't undressed.

He didn't bother to call out to see where Susan was. He knew. She'd be right where she was the last time he saw her: in the baby's room, watching the little boy sleep. The hallway still smelled of fresh paint and new carpet, and as he crossed the bridge that separated the grand foyer from the expansive great room, he walked gently, hoping not to wake anyone.

He still didn't quite understand how he'd allowed himself to be talked into buying this barn of a place. What good were five bedrooms when you had furniture for only two? But it was the house that Susan wanted, purchased in the frenzy of dreams about Steven.

What wonderful times they were. Finally, after so long, they were going to be a family. A *real* family, with kids and messy diapers and toys underfoot. Everyone they knew offered good wishes. They were inundated with baby showers, providing them with enough clothing and paraphernalia to keep the kid going for the first three years.

Since the baby had died, however, they'd heard precious little from anyone outside the family. People didn't know what to say, and truth be told, Bobby didn't know how to reach out to anyone. If one more person tried to comfort him with the adage that miscarriages happen all the time, he was going to throttle them. At full term it's not a miscarriage, it's a dead son. Why couldn't people recognize that?

He found Susan in the nursery, where she hadn't moved since last night. She still sat in the rocker, stroking the sleeping boy through the crib rail. She looked up and smiled. "He's beautiful, isn't he?"

He was, indeed. Even through the dirt that caked his face, the boy would have been the darling of Madison Avenue. His dark brown hair and olive complexion gave him a Latino look, but with the long, slender features of a Scandinavian. He looked like the very picture of contentment.

Bobby smiled back. "Has he awakened at all?"

"Hasn't moved. He was exhausted."

Seeing Susan this peaceful made Bobby feel warm in a place that had been cold for too long. But he also felt fear.

"Honey, we have to talk."

"Later." She didn't bother to look at him this time.

Bobby moved around and knelt next to his wife. "What are we going to do with him, Suz?"

She looked at him as if he'd lost his mind. "What do you mean?"

Bobby's jaw dropped. "What do I *mean?* We have to turn him over to the authorities. Someone must be looking for him."

"Whoever did this doesn't deserve to have him back."

The finality in her voice shot a chill the length of Bobby's spine. "Honey, he's not a stray puppy. You can't just keep somebody else's child. We don't even know his name."

"Then we'll name him."

Bobby closed his eyes tightly and shook his head, as if to rattle a loose chip in his circuitry. "Do you hear what you're saying?"

Her jaw was set. "Don't ask me to explain it, because I can't. But I prayed to God for a child, and even as I was praying, there he was, standing there, wanting only me. God sent him to me. I don't know why, or how, but this baby belongs to me now, and there's nothing you can do or say that will change my mind."

"How about if I say kidnapping, Suz?"

"You say kidnapping, I say murder," she shot back. "You can't prove one without admitting to the other."

The words hit like a fist. "Susan, are you threatening me?"

For a long moment she just glared, as if weighing her words, and then her eyes cleared. She shook her head. "I'm sorry. Of course I'm not threatening you. Think of the box we're in, though. We need to think everything through before we do anything."

"That's what I wanted to talk to you about."

"I know. And I guess I just don't want to deal with it right now. Let me sit here for a while longer, okay? Let me just be here when he wakes up. After that we can talk."

Bobby didn't know what to say. Surely she didn't believe that they could just keep this child and pretend that he was their own. Even if she talked herself into it, how could they possibly explain such a thing to friends and relatives?

Seeing the dream painted on her face, though, he couldn't bring himself to shatter it. Not now, not with her looking the way she did.

"Okay," he said finally. "We'll wait. But just for a while."

She smiled and turned back to the boy. As Bobby exited the nursery, he heard her start to sing a lullaby.

He thought about showering, but decided to unpack the Explorer first. As he passed through the kitchen, he was shocked to see that it was only seven fifteen. He'd slept for only three hours.

He put on a pot of coffee, then headed out to the garage, thumping the button for the overhead door as he descended the short flight of steps. Thank God for three-car garages. He and Susan were both pack rats, and he had to step carefully through a minefield of junk that was scattered all over the floor of the center bay to get to the Explorer.

The morning chill still had a bite to it, and he found himself wishing that he'd put on a jacket. No matter, he had one in his backpack. After lifting the tailgate, he reached inside and pulled his navy-blue pack closer to him so he could dig into the main pocket.

As he eased back the flap, his palm landed on something sharp, and it recoiled from the delicate silver wire that stood up from the angle of the tubular aluminum frame. There were two strands there, braided together with a half-dozen twists.

He felt something tumble deep inside his chest as he realized that the paper camping permit that the wire had once fixed in place was no longer there.

By TEN o'clock Russell Coates was about ready to move on. The crime-scene technicians had arrived in a swarm around six, and he'd learned a long time ago that the smart man stays out of their way. By the time they finished, half the mountain would be bagged, tagged, and catalogued.

In the meantime, Ranger Sarah Rodgers had already approached him twice about speeding things along and releasing her vehicles and personnel. The first time she did her best to conceal her annoyance, but apparently didn't feel so compelled during round two. Russell thought it was kind of cute how her ears turned crimson when she shouted. Now here she was again, striding up the hill toward the yellow corral of barricade tape, carrying a sheaf of papers in one hand and a portable radio in the other.

"I think she digs you," Tim said softly from behind.

Russell groaned. "I'm a magnet for chicks who can bench-press me." He walked carefully through the maze of evidence techs to meet her at the tape. "Sarah, we're working as fast as we can."

She looked confused. "What? Oh, that. They finished with my folks a good hour ago. They've all gone back to work. Thanks."

So much for round three. "What can I do for you, then?"

She handed him an enormous stack of manila-colored cards. "These are the park registrations for the past week."

Russell took them and smiled. "Thank you."

Then Sarah took them back and spun them around so that they could both see. "You asked for them all, so that's what I brought. Five, six hundred registrations." She shuffled through the cards until she found a smaller stack. "But look here. We've only had about three dozen parties in here to camp over that time, and of those, it looks like only fifteen or twenty of them entered at a spot that would likely bring them this way."

Russell looked closely at the registration cards. "Why, thank you, Sarah. That was very . . . helpful."

She laughed, and for the first time he saw that under all that Ranger Rick crap was a beautiful smile. Russell was a sucker for beautiful smiles. "You don't have to seem so surprised."

He laughed uncomfortably and shrugged.

"Now I must warn you that not everyone registers," Sarah advised. "There's a five-dollar fee that goes along with it, so it's not unheard of to find the occasional hiker who tries to dodge the system."

Russell nodded. "Especially the ones who are here to commit murder. Gives us a place to start, though."

"Agent Coates?" Another ranger approached, with two backpackers in tow: a man and a woman, both in their twenties, who looked disgustingly healthy and about three days overdue for a bath. "These people have some information that might be useful."

Russell slid under the barricade tape and approached the young couple. "I'm the agent in charge of the murder investigation."

"Gary Combs," the man said, offering his hand. "This is my wife, Mandy."

Russell shook her hand as well. "Pleased to meet you. What have you got?"

The couple exchanged nervous looks.

"You start, Gary," Russell prompted.

"Okay. Well, I don't know if this really means anything, but last night around midnight we heard some yelling out here, as if somebody was trying to hurt someone."

"We can't say for sure anyone was being hurt," Mandy corrected.

"No, no, well, of course not, but now that I think back on it—"

"You heard yelling," Russell interrupted. "We'll just keep it at that—yelling, but you can't say for sure what it meant."

"Yes, exactly," Gary said. "It sounded like a little kid."

Tim came under the tape now and stood shoulder to shoulder with his boss. "Now, that's interesting," Russell said. "Could you make out what they were saying?"

"No, not really. In fact, I'm not sure they were really saying anything. That's one of the reasons I think that a kid was involved. You know how they just sort of yell, but don't really say anything?"

"How close were you to these screaming people?"

"Oh, I don't know," Mandy said. "I'd guess they were probably a hundred, maybe a hundred fifty yards from our campsite."

"And how far was your campsite from here?" Tim asked.

Gary turned to the ranger. "Well, we were more or less where you first saw us, so how far is that?"

"Half a mile, maybe? Straight up this path."

Russell paused, giving his brain a chance to make something of this information. How could an argument with a child cause a shooting all the way down here?

"When did you hike in?" Sarah asked.

"Last night," Mandy said.

"From the top of the mountain or down below?"

"Down below."

"So did you pass the people who were camped here?"

Gary said, "I remember seeing a camp here, but I don't remember seeing the people. I'm willing to bet, though, that at least one of them was a woman."

"They had a cute little flower wreath hanging on the front of their tent," Mandy volunteered. "We saw it when we passed."

Russell looked down at the cards in his hand. "Ranger Rodgers, I don't suppose you remember how many of the campers on our short list checked in as a couple, do you?"

She answered without hesitation, "Six."

"Really?" Russell couldn't keep the surprise out of his voice. "You know this?"

Sarah smiled. "Photographic memory. Four point oh business grad from Harvard."

Why did this surprise him so much? He stuffed the cards into his jacket pocket. "Six. Well, that really will narrow down our initial search, won't it?" Then to the young couple: "Let's hike back up to where you were when you heard this yelling."

APRIL Simpson checked her watch, then walked to the tall windows to see if the used-car manager was anywhere in sight. It had been fifteen minutes since he'd taken her Geo on a test drive, and he should have been able to make a decision. April prided herself on the condition of that car, and she expected a top-dollar offer.

Scanning the horizon, past the sea of parked cars, she saw no sign of the fat manager in the ill-fitting suit. Across the lot a pair of old folks drooled over a champagne-colored Caprice while a hot-shot sales guy drooled over them. What did you have to make to afford a boat of a car like that? A hundred grand a year? And April was trying to scrape together enough pennies to buy back her son.

The shame of it all gripped her insides with an iron claw. How could everything have gone so wrong in her life? What had happened to the days when she and her dad used to dream about her acting career? God knows she had the looks for it, and she'd been the star of every show her high school produced.

The plan had always been clear: Her father would continue to work double shifts for as long as it took for her to graduate from the North Carolina School for the Arts, and then, when she finally made it on Broadway, she'd build a special wing for him in her home in the Hamptons. Her dad needed to escape the mills, and after all the sacrifices he'd endured since her mother died to make their life together decent and respectable, she owed him something better. She could see the desperate hope in his eyes whenever they dreamed aloud.

Never in all its thousands of iterations, however, did the dream include a tumor. She'd just completed her second week of college when she got the call to fly home. Her father had collapsed in the front yard, and the prognosis was as bleak as it could get. Cancer had been entwining his brain stem for years, the doctors told her. They gave him two months to live. He took only three days.

Just like that, she was an orphan at the age of eighteen. With one deft swing of his scythe, Father Time had left her an adult, and with adulthood came all the realities: Her father was broke. Worse than broke, actually, with debts far exceeding his ability ever to dig himself out. He had already missed three payments on the mortgage and was technically in default when he died.

In sixty days she was out on the street. Thus began the thrill ride down the toilet, spiraling ever faster toward the ultimate darkness that was her future. She marveled that the memories were still so clear after nine years; how the pain they brought hadn't dulled a bit. She missed her father unspeakably, and she missed the comforts of her life growing up, but more than anything, she missed the hope that had once dominated her childhood and kept driving her toward her dreams.

The sudden appearance of her Geo just outside the glass snapped April back to the present. She watched as the used-car manager pried his girth from behind her steering wheel.

The door opened, and Mr. Simenson waddled back inside the sales office. "I don't suppose you have maintenance records, do you, ma'am?" he asked, wedging himself into his chair.

April shook her head.

Mr. Simenson's fat fingers worked his calculator, and he jotted some numbers on a pad. She tried to read them, but he shifted just enough to block her view. When he reached for his blue book, April leaned forward in her chair.

"I took a look in the library before I came here. The blue-book value on the car is about fifty-three hundred."

Simenson laughed. "Well, I'm not gonna offer that kind of money. I've got to turn a profit, you know."

April's eyes narrowed. "How much then?"

He smiled from the nose down. "I can give you seventeen fifty."

April's jaw dropped. "Seventeen fifty! But I've taken terrific care of that car! It's in great shape."

Simenson shrugged. "The mileage is a little high, and the paint is beginning to fade. You can't get top dollar with it in that condition."

"But seventeen fifty? You've got to do better than that."

Simenson raised his hands as if surrendering. "I'm certainly not the only game in town. If I were you, I'd try selling it myself. That way you can get retail price. It's your call."

Something in Simenson's face put April on edge, as if he knew something that she didn't. Then she got it. He sensed her desperation, and in his business, desperation meant weakness.

"Unless you're in a hurry for the money," he added, and for the first time the grin became genuine.

SUSAN awoke with a start, frozen with fear and not sure why. A scream rose like a siren from the darkness of the room. The boy!

Instantly she launched herself out of her chair, eyes wide open, scanning the room for whoever or whatever was harming the boy.

God only knew how long he'd been like that, shrieking his head off, the bars of the crib clenched tightly in his hands as he rocked his body violently back and forth.

Susan was on him in seconds, scooping him up and hugging him tightly to her.

The boy was beyond hysteria, beyond anger, in a place where she'd never seen anyone, let alone a child so young. At first he struggled to free himself from her grasp, but then he seemed to recognize her, and he finally hugged her back. While the fear seemed to have drained from him, he still fought for control of his breathing, each inhalation coming in halting, choking sobs.

"Shh, shh, shh," she cooed. "You're fine. Everything's fine."

But nothing was fine. Things were as bad and as terrifying as they'd ever been. Whatever unspeakable traumas this boy had endured, they both knew that they wouldn't go away merely with a hug and a place to stay. Susan made a silent pledge right then and there never to lie to this helpless child again.

"I don't know what happened to you, sweetie, but I promise you that no one will ever hurt you again so long as I am here. You'll be safe." As she rocked him and whispered in his ear, his breathing returned to normal and she could feel his little muscles relaxing.

Within five minutes he let go completely and was looking curiously around the room. But God, did he stink!

"What do you say we clean you up?" she asked lightly.

"No!" he yelled, and he arched his back, sliding out of her grasp and landing on his feet.

The reaction startled her, even as she was pleased to hear a voice out of the little guy. "But you stink, little buddy. We need to give you a bath."

He stomped his foot once and shook his head. "No!"

"I won't hurt you."

"No, no, no, no." And he took off for the door.

"Wait!" she shouted. What had she said to frighten him so? By the time she got to the door, he was already halfway down the stairs. "I'm sorry!" Susan yelled. "Come on back."

Then she caught the look on his face. That wasn't fear she saw; it was a smile. He was playing the chase-me game.

"Come back here, you stinker!" She laughed and hurried down the steps, hoping to catch up. No way. He was already across the foyer and into the library.

"Where, oh, where, might that little boy be?" she asked. "I guess I'll just have to have those cookies all by myself."

When she heard a giggle, she spun around and clasped her face with both hands. The boy was peering around the corner. "There you are!" she exclaimed.

Turning toward Susan, he giggled and brought both fists to his mouth—a gesture of pure glee.

"Would you like a cookie?"

The hands stayed in front of his mouth as he nodded.

"Are you going to let me give you a bath?"

Another nod.

"Okay, then. Come with me."

Susan held out her hand. The little stranger showed no hesitation at all as he hopped over to her and grabbed on to a finger. As they touched, Susan felt a rush of warmth and her eyes filled with tears. This little boy, who was so frightened and alone just a few hours ago, was trusting her now.

She did a funny little Charlie Chaplin walk as she led him into the kitchen. The three vanilla wafers she offered to the boy disappeared in seconds, prompting her to offer three more before declaring, "That's it for now. Nobody needs more than six cookies." She heard these words and smiled at how motherly she sounded.

As she placed the box on the cooking island, she noticed for the first time a note, written in Bobby's nearly illegible hand:

Dear Suz,

I couldn't sleep and I couldn't sit still, so I decided to go out and grab a few supplies. Be back around noon. Luv ya,

B

So that was where he'd gone.

"Okay, Mr. Stinky Pants," Susan announced to the boy. "It's time for you to get cleaned up."

She halfway expected another romp through the house but was pleased to see that the little guy understood when a deal was a deal. He led the way back up the stairs, using both hands to steady himself as he scampered up to the second floor.

By the time she caught up, he was already back in the nursery, staring eye to eye at a stuffed tiger someone from Bobby's office had bought for Steven as a shower gift, and the little boy with the filthy body and stinky diaper had obviously fallen in love.

"Do you like that tiger?" The boy's head whipped around to display a huge smile, and he nodded. "Would you like to keep him?"

The nod became even more enthusiastic.

"Okay, then. Tiger is officially yours."

The purity of the joy brought tears to her eyes all over again.

"Okay. Now it's time to get you clean."

This time Susan led the parade as they marched toward the bathroom. In a wild, disjointed thought, she wondered if bathing a child without a parent's permission constituted a crime during these times of hypersensitivity to children's issues. In an instant her pulse rate doubled. The list of laws they'd broken in the past few hours spun wildly through her head, making her dizzy.

Oh, my God, she thought, I'm going to jail. She felt a kind of paralysis looming over her brain. But what had they done wrong? All they had done was rescue a child.

And kill a man.

Well, what else were they supposed to do? She couldn't just leave this baby out there all by himself. And she certainly couldn't let that terrible man have him.

"You want to tell me your name, sweetie?" she asked as she ran the bathwater.

It was as if he couldn't even hear her.

"Well, silly, you've got to have a name. Everybody has a name." She tickled him, and he giggled, but he still refused to say a word.

"Okay. Then I'll just give you a name, how's that? A special name. We'll call you Steven. And you can call me Mommy."

APRIL'S purse felt hot against her shoulder, as if everyone on the bus could see the wad of cash inside. In her mind the money glowed, a great neon beacon to everyone in this miserable neighborhood who wouldn't hesitate an instant to kill her for seventeen dollars, let alone seventeen hundred.

She should have haggled more. She should have left the dealership in a fit of moral outrage, and tomorrow, after she had her son back and everything was safe again, she would undoubtedly kick herself for being such a wimp. But for the time being, it was worth a thousand dollars a minute just to keep Justin from enduring any more fear or pain or misery than he had to.

The bus driver looked oddly at April as she made her way to the door, as if to ask if she knew what neighborhood she was stepping into. It was a kind gesture, and she acknowledged it with a little nod before climbing down the steps. How was it, she wondered, that everyone in the world knew where Patrick Logan lived and what he did for a living, but the police could never figure it out?

The neighborhood looked even worse than when she'd last left it, nearly four years ago. Just being here brought a flood of memories that April thought had been permanently exorcised from her brain. Thanks to the drugs that ran her life in those days, the memories were more visceral than visual. She'd made a living then, such as it was, dancing in the sleazy strip joints that lined the block, but she'd never once succumbed to Patrick Logan's daily entreaties to join his band of whores. It was her one source of pride from those awful times.

A half block ahead, on the opposite side of the street, three punks in bulky winter coats talked at the base of the steps leading to a brownstone that was conspicuously devoid of graffiti. This was Patrick Logan's house, and those coats on his bodyguards concealed more firepower than a SEAL team. As April approached, the three of them closed ranks.

"I need to speak to Logan," April said.

The two thugs on the outside turned to the taller thug in the middle. "Yeah?" said the middle one. "Well, I don't think Mr. Logan is taking visitors this morning."

"What's your name?" April asked him.

He answered, "Ricky."

"Look, Ricky, I don't want to make a big deal out of this, okay? Just do me the favor of telling your boss that April Simpson is here to give him the money he wants, and that I want to discuss the return of something to me." A frigid icicle of guilt stabbed her insides as she heard herself refer to Justin as an inanimate object.

Ricky considered this for a long moment, then finally nodded and made his way to the top of the concrete steps, where he disappeared behind the massive door. Two minutes later the door reopened, and Ricky beckoned for her to join him.

As she got to the top, he blocked her path, lowering his voice as he said, "Move funny and I'll kill you. Do you understand?"

She nodded, and Ricky let her pass, stepping in behind her.

Logan stood waiting for them in the foyer, wearing slippers and a bathrobe. Nearly as wide as he was tall, Logan combined all the worst elements of his Irish bloodline. His red hair might have looked violet in a different light, and his big round face joined his shoulders directly, seemingly without the intervention of a neck. A bulbous red nose showed his affection for whiskey.

Logan's eyes narrowed as April stepped into the foyer, then widened again as he placed her face. "April!" he exclaimed. "Well, well, I never thought I'd see you again."

April found herself embarrassed by the recognition and said nothing. She reached into her pocket and withdrew the manila envelope stuffed with cash. She counted out ten hundreds and thrust them toward her host. "Here's your money."

Logan looked confused. "You're here to buy something?"

"I'm here to pay my husband's debt."

"Who is your husband?"

April's blood pressure shot up. *My God, he doesn't even know.* "He's the man your goons stole my son from."

"I'm not sure I know what you're talking about," Logan said.

"Kidnap that many toddlers, do you, that you can't keep them all straight?"

Logan's eyes hardened. "Be very careful, April. Perhaps you've forgotten who you're speaking to."

"I haven't forgotten anything, you pig. I want my son back."

Logan chuckled. "Is your husband so afraid of me that he sends the missus to do his work?"

"I want him back," April said, not about to get sidetracked.

Logan held her eyes for a long moment, then gestured for the money. He counted the bills, then frowned. "There's only a thousand dollars here."

"That's what he owed you."

Logan laughed. "The amount he stole from me was more like eighteen hundred. With reasonable interest, that comes to more like twenty-two hundred. Plus another thousand for expenses."

April felt the blood drain from her head. "Expenses. What kind of expense is there to take a little boy from his mother?"

"Surely you don't think I would take care of such a messy business myself," Logan scoffed.

Suddenly all the fight evaporated. "Please," she begged. "I only want my little boy. My little Justin."

Logan handed the bills to Ricky, who stuffed them into his jacket. Then the big Irishman moved closer to April and put his hand on her shoulder. "You can have him as soon as you come up with the extra twenty-two hundred. Twenty-seven by this time tomorrow."

The feel of his paw made April shudder. "How can you do this?"

"How can I do *what?* Your husband robs me of my money, and you ask *me* how I can do this? All I want is my money, sweetheart." To his buddy, Logan added, "Ricky, grab her purse."

April didn't bother to fight as the giant thug stripped the bag from her shoulder.

Logan accepted it from Ricky and opened it. "What do we got here?" Logan counted the bills. "Another seven hundred and fifty bucks. See, April? Only two grand more and you're home free."

April couldn't take it anymore. Her fear and her grief poured forth in a choking sob. "But I can't get that money," she gasped. "I already sold my car to get what you have. I have nothing left."

At a signal from Logan, Ricky took April by her arm.

"Look at me, April," Logan said quietly. Her eyes came up to meet his. Where anger had burned just moments ago, her face showed only sadness. "You've got to find it." He stroked the underside of her chin with his forefinger. "Rob a bank if you have to, I don't care. But you've got to find the money, because I'll only keep him alive for a week. And did your worthless husband mention what happens if you go to the police, April?"

April nodded.

"You'll never even see the body, April. You'll never, ever know for sure. And that will kill you, too."

RUSSELL Coates had released the Combs couple as soon as they'd pointed out their campsite from the night before. If he found himself with questions later, he had their address and phone number.

Starting from that spot, he and Sarah had looked for something that might possibly explain the sounds the couple had reported. Sarah's presence at the crime scene bent the investigation protocols a bit, but truth be told, he enjoyed her company.

About thirty minutes into their search, they struck the mother lode. Russell walked to the edge of a roughly rectangular pit— maybe four feet by eight feet, and six or seven feet deep. Dirt had been stacked up high on both ends of the hole, and inside it looked as if someone had done a makeshift job shoring it up with two-by-six lumber.

Sarah joined him. "Is it a grave?"

"Maybe," Russell replied, but he didn't think so.

Sarah leaned forward and looked into the pit. "Is that baby food?"

Russell nodded. "That's what it looks like to me."

"They were burying baby food jars? What are they, squirrels?"

Russell smiled. "No. I'm afraid our victim was being buried alive."

Sarah gasped. "Who would do such a thing? And why?"

"Those are the big questions. When we answer those, we'll have ourselves a killer." He went on, "The baby food is a new twist. Good idea, actually. It's portable, nutritious, and requires no can opener."

Russell strolled around the perimeter of the pit. Over by the edge opposite where he stood, he thought he recognized boot-tread imprints similar to the ones near the body. The forensics people would make that final determination, of course, but he already knew, just as he knew that the key to this case lay with whatever link tied the two crime scenes together. Crime scenes, like accident scenes, were really inanimate witnesses, and once you learned to listen to what they were telling you, the most complicated investigations became obvious.

He liked his notion that someone was being prepared for a live interment. Early in his career, live burials were rare, but in recent years that seemed to be the outcome of virtually every kidnapping. Russell blamed the trend on a couple of high-profile films.

Fact was, if Russell were himself a kidnapper, he'd bury them, too. In the old days, when kidnappers stashed their victims in a basement somewhere, finding the kidnapper almost always meant finding the victim as well. An off-site burial, on the other hand, raised the stakes for everyone. If the kidnapper got an inkling that the good guys were getting too close, all he had to do was keep his mouth shut, and even if he got caught, without a victim to point to, he stood a good chance of staying free.

Russell pulled on his lower lip as he sifted it all through his mind. He'd have to check back at the office, but as far as he knew, there were no outstanding abduction cases out here. What was the deal with that? he wondered. *Somebody* should have noticed that a cop was missing.

Russell turned the third corner around the grave and paused. A big grin bloomed on his face. "Look over there." He pointed toward a small stand of bushes. Something lay in the branches, but from where he stood, he couldn't quite tell what it was. Sarah followed as he moved closer. It looked like a discarded solid-core door, and someone had cut a round hole through the middle of it.

"What is it?" Sarah asked.

Russell didn't answer. Instead, he craned his neck to see past the door into the woods. "Aha," he said triumphantly, and he waded through the undergrowth over to a five-foot coil of what could have been dryer vent hose. He didn't touch, but he knew right away what he'd found. "This is their ventilation system. Once you get your victim down into the hole, you cover it with that door to keep the dirt from crushing the guy, and this tube runs from the hole in the door up to the surface here so your captive can breathe."

"How horrifying," Sarah gasped.

"It beats the hell out of a noseful of dirt." He said that in a cavalier way, but the very thought of it made his stomach hurt.

"So are you thinking that the kidnappers captured the police officer and tried to bury him? And that he got away?"

Russell pulled his lip some more. Is that what he thought? The evidence supported that theory, but something bothered him. Why hadn't word of a missing cop reached his desk? Granted, he'd been away for a while, but surely Tim would have made that connection right away. Any crime that specifically targeted a cop as its victim swept through the law-enforcement rumor mill with breathtaking speed. Yet this one had gone unreported.

Russell wandered back to the excavation. The footprints clearly showed that the victim had walked around up here. Why didn't they just shoot him when he started to run?

"You look really confused," Sarah observed.

He nodded. "I'm just trying to figure out the series of events. Say you're being kidnapped."

"Let's not."

"Just for the sake of argument. You're brought up here, and maybe you see what they're going to do to you, so you panic. You don't say, 'Oh, okay. Let me just climb into my own grave,' right? You're going to fight like hell."

"Right."

"So where are the signs of the fight? There aren't any," Russell answered his own question. "So, instead of fighting, maybe you just run off. Why don't the bad guys shoot you down?"

"Maybe they missed."

"Maybe. We'll certainly look for any signs that a gun was fired, but that would have been the first thing our two hikers would have mentioned. Anyway, shot at or not shot at, you go plunging through the woods with kidnappers right on your tail. How do you end up getting killed a half mile downhill?"

"Suppose the people who pitched the tent were waiting for him?"

Russell nodded. The pieces were beginning to fit together. "Okay. So you stumble onto these people who are somehow in on the plot, and they pop you." A buzzer rang in his head. "No, wait. Remember the burns on the guy's face? They fought first."

She looked horrified. "Burns?"

"I forgot you didn't see the body. Yeah, he had burns on his face. They looked like scalds, actually. But why? How?"

Sarah didn't seem to have a problem with that at all. "I don't know. You're cooking eggs, maybe, and this guy comes crashing through the woods, and he startles you, and you react with the first thing you can get your hands on."

"Okay. Then they *weren't* part of the plot, right? I mean, who boils water in the middle of a kidnapping?"

"So they weren't involved."

"Until they shot him." Russell rubbed his eye with the heel of his hand, and the answer flashed in his mind. When he looked up again at Sarah, everything suddenly made sense.

"We've been coming at this from the wrong direction," he declared. "We've been assuming that the cop was the good guy, and the killer was bad. Suppose that the grave was meant for our campers?"

Sarah's eyes grew big as she fit it all together for herself.

Russell continued, "So our victim goes through his final preparations for this thing he's going to do, and then he sneaks up on our friends down the hill, only all hell breaks loose. They struggle; they douse him with boiling water. When it's all done, our cop is dead."

"But what about the screaming?"

"Huh? What screaming?" Then he remembered the screaming that had brought them up here. "Damn." Okay. So one major detail still didn't fit, but that didn't necessarily trash the entire theory.

Russell's mind re-created a crime scene down the hill: A young couple was minding their own business when this guy with a gun came out of the night, threatening to kidnap one or both of them. One of the campers was able to distract the good officer long enough to douse him with the water, and from there it's all about the ensuing fight. They're on the ground, rolling in the dirt. The good guy gets his hands on Officer Stipton's gun, and he fires. That explained the angles of the wounds, too, didn't it?

Yessir, this was the answer. The campers killed in self-defense. And then they ran. Why on earth would they do that? Well, when he closed that little loop, he'd have the whole mystery solved.

SAMUEL sat atop the big old tractor in the barn, his hand poised over the ignition switch, staring out through the sagging double door at the house across the hundred yards of turfy, unkempt grass. He had chores to do, and he intended to get to them right away, but nothing felt right without Jacob around to tell him what to do.

Leaving Jacob there in the woods like that was the hardest thing Samuel had ever done. But if there was one thing that Jacob had made clear, it was that you never, *ever* touch a body after it's dead. Not without wearing gloves, and Samuel didn't have any of those with him. His brother had told him a million times: "Whenever you touch the bodies, you leave a little of yourself behind, and that's how you end up in the electric chair."

Samuel didn't understand how the electric chair worked, exactly, but it wasn't important that Samuel understood. Jacob had worried about that stuff a lot—a *whole* lot—and if it was real enough to worry him, then it was real enough to worry Samuel.

So who was going to do the worrying now? More importantly, who was going to tell him when it was time to worry? Samuel just wasn't good at that stuff. Hell, he'd almost forgotten to undo the burglar alarm before he walked in the front door. The alarm, for God's sake! Forgetting the alarm was right near the top of the list of worst things you could possibly do.

Stop worrying, you pussy. Jacob's voice seemed to come out of nowhere, making Samuel jump in his tractor saddle.

"Huh? Jacob? Is that you?"

You drove the truck home safely, didn't you? Anybody smart enough to do that is smart enough to do house stuff.

"I left you out in the woods to be eaten." Even as he spoke, Samuel felt stupid. He knew that Jacob wasn't there—he'd seen the body, so why was he talking to him? Samuel's head hurt.

What choice did you have? I told you not to touch me. I told you not to touch anybody, didn't I?

Samuel felt his lip start to quiver.

Stop that crying. Be a man. You have to be the man, now that I'm gone.

"You're gone because I killed you."

Those nosy Nellies killed me, Samuel. That man at the campfire.

"But I watched."

You did what I told you. You did good.

Samuel had been sitting there in the barn for a long time with his hand just hovering over the ignition switch. Finally he kicked out the clutch, opened the choke, and turned the key. For a few seconds it seemed that maybe the battery hadn't survived the winter, but the starter turned and the engine coughed to life. It was like this every year for the first cutting of the season. Certainly, it had been this way for the twenty-odd years that Samuel had been doing it.

Checking once over his shoulder to make sure the mower deck was attached, Samuel gently eased the throttle forward, engaged the transmission, and lifted his foot off the clutch. The big John Deere moved forward smooth as butter.

As he broke out into the cool sunshine, he brought the machine to a halt again. Where should he start? Way off to his left, up on the top of the hill, the little graveyard beckoned him to come and cut up there first. The tombstones would probably be completely invisible by now. For sure, that was where he should start. Give his mama and daddy a chance to see the world around them again. But he didn't want to. He never much liked going in there. The graveyard could wait.

Samuel decided to concentrate on the big field. There was a time—Samuel could even remember it—when their twenty acres was more like a hundred, and they used to keep animals. Once their folks passed away, though, Jacob said that farming work was for suckers, and he let everything but the fields closest to the house and the barn just go to hell.

It'd be another few weeks before the springtime grass took on that deep green color—almost blue—and Samuel couldn't wait. Next to Christmas and Thanksgiving, the fresh smell of newly cut springtime grass was Samuel's favorite aroma in the world.

So who was going to cook the big holiday meals this year? Samuel felt the panic swell inside his chest, and he took a deep breath, holding it tight, to push the fear back down where it belonged.

Samuel got scared a lot—a whole lot, in fact. That's when he'd go on a trip.

He went on trips when things got too big for him to understand, and with all that was happening out there in the woods—between that little boy struggling in the gunnysack, and then all the screaming, and finally with the kid running away—too many things had happened too quickly for him to keep up. Plus, Jacob was *so* mad. Mad enough that Samuel was a little afraid of him, too.

Why did he have to be afraid like this? Why couldn't he be brave all the time like Jacob is . . . was. Oh, God.

Jacob was dead. Oh, what was he going to do now? Out here in the big field with the aroma of grass filling his nostrils, he tried to find peace, but the pain just wouldn't go away.

About the time that Samuel was tracking the bush hog, oh so carefully, along the fence line out on the far edge of the property, the sadness started to change. He realized that he was getting angry—something he rarely did. His mind focused on all that he had lost and on just how quickly it had all gone away. Funny thing about anger. Once you tap that well deep down inside your gut, and the anger starts to trickle out, there's no controlling it. He focused on what those nosy Nellies had done. Forever and ever Samuel would be stuck out here on the farm by himself. If he could just find out who those nosy Nellies were, then get his hands on them, he'd get even, yes siree.

BOBBY thought of the decor in the offices of Donnelly, Wall, and Bevis as lawyer-light. As he passed through the doorway into the wine-colored reception area, the fist that had been clutching his heart all day clenched tighter still. He was going to talk to a *lawyer,* for God's sake. About shooting a man.

Bobby handed his business card to the receptionist. "I need to see Barbara Dettrick right away."

"Is she expecting you?"

"Just tell her who it is, and tell her it's an emergency."

Twenty minutes later the lobby door opened and Barbara Dettrick stepped out to greet her client. "I'm sorry, Bobby, but I was in the middle of a conference call and couldn't get away." She stepped forward and thrust out her hand. An avid outdoor enthusiast, Barbara looked taller than her five feet ten and never failed to be in good humor. "Nice to see you— My God, what happened?" She reached out to touch his bruise, but he shrank away.

"Can you come with me for a minute?"

She looked confused. "Come with you? Where are you going?"

He hooked her in his right arm and guided her toward the front door. "I'll explain in the car."

Barbara allowed herself to be led out into the parking lot and into the front seat of Bobby's Explorer. "Where are we going?"

Bobby climbed in and started the engine. "We're going shopping."

"Shopping? Bobby, what's happening?"

"I'm not supposed to be meeting with you. So I've got to complete the shopping I used as the ruse to get me out here. Understand?"

"Not a word."

Bobby took a deep breath. "I'm in serious trouble. I broke the law but haven't been caught yet. 'Yet' being the operative word here."

"What are we talking here? DWI?"

He pulled out into traffic and headed for the Kmart Plaza. "Kidnapping, and maybe murder."

"*Excuse* me? You're kidding, right?"

"You want to hear the details?"

"God, Bobby." No, she didn't want to hear the details, but clearly she was about to. She surrendered to the inevitable.

Bobby did his best to leave nothing out. And when he got carried away with the emotion of it all and the facts started to jumble, Barbara slowed him down and asked a few probing questions.

"Now I'm stuck with this little kid in my house, and I don't know what to do with him," Bobby concluded. "If I turn him in to the cops, I'm confessing to the murder. If I keep him— Well, hell, we all know I can't do that. So what do I do?"

Barbara Dettrick had been a hair-twister for as long as Bobby had known her—ever since third grade—and now, as they sat in the Kmart parking lot, she worried the strand in front of her left ear into an unruly spike. They were quiet for a long time as she thought things through. Finally she spoke. "How likely do you think it is that this guy you shot was going to do you harm?"

"Well, looking back on it, I really don't know."

"Don't look back on it, then. Tell me about when it was all happening. How fearful were you of him harming you or Susan?"

"I think I was dead certain at the time."

"So he lunged first?" Barbara prompted.

"Well, you see, that's where—" Her eyes flashed, and Bobby cut the words short. "Yes. Yes, he definitely lunged first."

"So you had no choice but to defend yourself?"

"Right." Bobby was getting the hang of this now.

"And what do you think would have happened if you hadn't wrestled the gun from him and killed him?"

"He would have killed me, and the others, too."

Barbara nodded enthusiastically. "That's good. That's the basis for a solid case of self-defense. And let's just hope Susan saw the same events that you did. What about the gun? Do you still have it?"

"No. I stopped on a bridge on the way home and dumped it into the river. Look, do you think we could carry this on in the store? I'm supposed to be picking up supplies for the baby, and if I'm not back soon, Susan will worry."

Barbara nodded but then scowled. Something wasn't right here. "You said that Susan didn't know you were talking to me. Why?"

Another deep sigh, and suddenly Bobby's emotions were like an open wound, raw and weepy. "She, uh, she thinks that God sent us this baby, to be ours to raise."

"Come again?"

"We've had a few miscarriages over the last couple of years, and you know about Steven. It was looking like we'd never be able to have kids. That's really why we were out there camping. We wanted to get things right in our heads, you know?"

Barbara looked away, clearly overwhelmed by it all. But then she was all lawyer again. "Okay. Let's deal with the murder first." Bobby recoiled at the word. "I'm sorry, but that's what people are going to assume when they find this body. From that point on, they'll do their best to identify the killer." Something in Bobby's expression made her stop. "What?"

"I don't think it's a huge stretch for them to figure out who did it. Our camping permit is missing. I think it's probably up there at the murder scene. Maybe it came off during the fight."

"And it's got your name and address on it?"

"You betcha."

"God, Bobby."

"That's why I'm here. Any second now, somebody's going to show up at my door with handcuffs, and I need to know what to do."

"I don't know what to tell you. It's too early to panic, though. It'll take time for someone to discover the body, and maybe—"

Bobby cleared his voice. "I, uh, I called the police on our way out of the park this morning. They found the body a long time ago. Maybe before we even got home."

The attorney looked as if she'd been slapped. "Are you crazy?"

"Excuse me! I'm happy to say I don't have a whole lot of practice at this stuff, Barb."

Barbara looked disgusted. "Bobby, I just don't know what—" She cut herself off. "Wait a minute. How long ago did you call?"

"I think it was around four a.m."

She checked her watch. "Okay. And it's nearly noon now. How come they haven't already come to get you?"

Bobby shrugged. "I don't know."

A smile finally invaded her otherwise bleak features. "I don't think they've found your permit. Here's hoping it fell off on the trail somewhere."

"But they're still going to come looking, right?"

"Sure they will. They'll be looking at everyone who was there last night. The difference is, without evidence to tie you to the scene, they'll come just to talk, instead of to execute a warrant."

"So when they come to my door and start asking questions, at what point do I call you?"

"The instant that they lead you to believe that you're a suspect."

"What about evidence, Barbara? All the stuff that can connect me to the campsite? You know, the tent, the remains of our food, our clothes, that sort of thing. What do I do with all of that stuff?"

Barbara looked at him as if he were crazy. "Bobby, you've got possession of a human being who doesn't belong to you. I don't think that your tent is on your top-ten list of problems."

AT FIVE feet ten, one hundred and sixty-five pounds, Carlos Ortega could have been a movie star, sporting perfect white teeth and a flawless olive complexion. He wore his thick mane of jet-black hair short and combed straight back, and he favored a business-casual look. He sat perfectly still, smiling, as he watched little Christa settle into her chair. Nothing had moved since the last time they'd played together here in the music room, but his daughter was a twelve-year-old perfectionist. The seventh-grader double-checked the strap on her rock stop, eased the point of her cello's end pin into the cup, settled the scroll just so over her left shoulder, then poised her bow over the strings. She was ready.

"Okay," Carlos said. "I'm going to give you two measures of the bass part, and then you come in."

"I know, Daddy." Christa issued her patented eye roll.

Carlos laughed. At the piano his right hand remained on his lap as the fingers on his left stroked the opening notes of Pachelbel's "Canon." As Christa entered exactly on her cue and music blossomed from her bow, his eyes welled with pride. Tonight at the concert the string ensemble would play the piece as a round, with Christa switching in the third verse to the obbligato, playing the solo that was written for a violin. Here in this final rehearsal Carlos played all the other parts on the piano.

Behind him, over his right shoulder, Carlos sensed movement, and he pivoted his head to see Jesús Peña standing in the doorway, his perpetual scowl only slightly less severe than normal. Once eye contact was made, Peña retreated out of sight. Knowing how much his boss cherished his time alone with Christa, this was as close to an interruption as he would dare.

When the final notes of the canon hung about them in perfect harmony, father and daughter shared a smile.

"That was pretty," Christa said.

"That was *beautiful,*" her father corrected, and he slid out from behind the piano.

"Aren't we going to practice some more?"

"Sweetie, I have work to do."

"But this is *our* time. You said so yourself."

Carlos rumpled her hair. "It is. But sometimes things interfere."

Christa tried to pout but couldn't quite pull it off. Gently placing her cello on its side, she stood, gave her father a hug, and then headed for the door. "You can come in now, Tío Jesús," she called even before she reached the threshold. As she passed through the doorway, she playfully stuck out her tongue at him.

When he appeared, he said, "I'm terribly sorry, Carlos."

Carlos waved him off. "Tell me what's on your mind, Jesús."

"Someone is here to see you. She says she knows you from a long time ago, and she seems very upset. Her name is April Simpson. I told her you were busy, but she was very insistent."

"I don't know an April Simpson."

"She said she used to be April Fitzgerald."

Carlos allowed his jaw to drop a bit. What on earth could possibly bring that bitch out to see him? "What does she want?"

"She wouldn't tell me. She just said it was very important. Life and death, she said. I can send her packing if you'd like."

Carlos thought about that. For her to come here, her life must have taken a terrible turn, and something told him that he might just enjoy hearing the details. "Send her in."

Peña left the music room. Carlos moved to a white leather sofa.

Twenty seconds later, in stepped April Fitzgerald. She looked terrible, her once beautiful blue eyes stained red. She'd cut her hair since high school, transforming that shiny long mane into a kind of auburn helmet.

He said nothing for a long while, allowing the discomfort of the moment to make her squirm.

"It's been a long time, April," he said at last. "Please." He gestured to the lush leather chairs across from him. "Have a seat."

She moved hesitantly and gently sat on the very front edge of the left-hand chair. Carlos noticed that the pink frock under her jacket seemed unusually lightweight for days as chilly as these. Her ample breasts jiggled as she moved, and were it not for the obviously pregnant belly, she might have intrigued him.

"I haven't heard from you," Carlos baited. "No Christmas card, no dinner invitations, no nothing."

April remained silent, casting her gaze down to her hands, where she'd worried a Kleenex to tatters.

"Could it be that you still think I am a—let's see if I can remember how you put it—ah, yes, 'a worthless, stinking spick'?"

"You tried to rape me."

Carlos laughed. "When I make a pass, it's rape?"

Silence. She hadn't come here to argue.

He leaned back and folded his hands across his chest. "It must be difficult to be so much better than everyone else." His eyes scanned her appearance. He didn't need to tell her how far she'd fallen from her lofty dreams.

More silence.

"Look, April, I thought you came here wanting something."

It took a moment for her to say the words. Just hearing the syllables was like reliving the nightmare. "My son has been kidnapped."

It wasn't what he'd been expecting. He said, "Go on."

"My husband, William, took some money from a man who works for Patrick Logan. You know him, I assume?"

"I might have heard the name."

She told the whole story, so far as she knew the details, covering William's bonehead mistakes, the kidnapping itself, and her efforts to repay the debt on her own.

Carlos shook his head when she was finished. "This is a terrible thing, April, but why do you come to me?"

"You're a drug dealer, Carlos." He recoiled. April saw the reaction and leaned forward in her chair. "You're in the business of intimidating people. You can talk the same language as Logan."

Carlos recovered quickly. "Oh, I do speak the same language, April, but I conduct my business in a whole different way. Still, what would you expect a man to do when someone steals from him? Merely shrug and forget about everything?"

April slammed her hands down on the coffee table and shouted. "My son's not yet three years old, Carlos! Logan's not threatening to kill the man who stole from him. He's threatening to kill a little boy!"

The outburst brought Peña to the door, but he retreated from his boss's nod.

Carlos thought a long time before saying anything. His anger built like steam in a kettle as his mind raced through all the crap that Logan had pulled over the years.

There was nothing new or unique about Carlos's business dealings with Logan; it was the same compromise he'd negotiated with every other upstart tough guy who'd tried competing against him. Rather than going to war against them, Carlos wooed them to his side. For a fifty percent stake in everything they brought in, Carlos allowed them to live—live well, in fact, if they were any good at what they did.

And Logan was good, regularly turning fifteen, twenty grand a week in crack, angel dust, and meth. But he was a sick, sadistic s.o.b. who couldn't separate his ego from his business sense.

"Look, April," Carlos began, "your hubby made a bad, bad move here. Logan is an animal. What was he thinking?"

"It's not about William. This is about Justin. I have no idea where William's head was. I don't care. I only want my boy back. I'll give you whatever you want. I'll *do* whatever you want." The words made her choke, and she fought her sobs.

"It's not that easy, April."

When her eyes came up, they were as hard and as cold as onyx. "I want my son. And you can get him for me. You were once a nice boy, Carlos, and now you're a powerful man, and that's why I came to you. If I was wrong, then I'm sorry. And I'm sorry for your daughter when she finds out what her father is."

"Did you just threaten me, April?"

"I made a promise," April said. "I swear to God, if I don't get my son back, everybody in the world will know what kind of business you're in. I'll name names. I'll—"

"You'll die."

April nodded, her eyes now clear and animated. "Perhaps. I expect you'll try. That's why the first paragraph of my letter begins, 'By the time you read this, I'll likely be dead at the hands of Carlos Ortega and Patrick Logan.'"

Carlos leaned closer. "Letter? What letter?"

This time it was April's turn to be smug. "*The* letter, Carlos. The one that will be in tomorrow's mail if I don't get my way."

"You stand to make some powerful enemies, April."

"If I have powerful enemies, it won't be because I made them. It will be because they volunteered."

Carlos searched for the sign that she was frightened. All he saw was determination. "Why not go to the police now, then?"

"Logan says he'll kill Justin if he smells police. For right now, though, nothing's happened that can't be undone. I was hoping that you might be the one to talk sense into him."

Carlos took in a deep breath, then let it out as a sigh. "You've got balls, April, I'll give you that. You understand, don't you, that no matter what happens, I won't be able to protect your husband?"

A deal had been struck. "I wouldn't ask you to," April said.

RUSSELL Coates apologized to no one for establishing his command post up at the murder scene rather than down on the fire road, where it would be much more comfortable for the press. The decision frosted Tim Burrows's ass, he knew. Why else would Tim have dressed in his GI Joe suit if not to preen for the cameras?

Russell chose as his own seat a deadfall—oak, it looked like—while the others either stood or sat Indian-style, reminding him of campers gathered around the campfire for a ghost story. Burrows was there, directly across from his boss, and so was Henry Parker, the chief criminologist on the scene. Lieutenant Homer LaRue was supposed to be there, too, representing the West Virginia State Police, but he was still on his way up from the parking lot. At the very end of the line sat Russell's new pal, Sarah Rodgers, unofficially representing the Park Service, and in general helping him to conclude that maybe midlife wasn't such a bad place to be.

"Okay, Henry. Why don't you start?" Russell said.

A big man, with huge shoulders and a thick waist, Henry Parker looked more like a bouncer than one who made his living plucking the magic needle out of ten-story haystacks. "Well, it'll be a day or so before we have a coroner's report back, but I'm guessing the firearm used here to be a big one—I'm guessing .44 or .45. It appears that both the victim and the shooter were on the ground when the shots were fired. In examining the casts of footprints, I've got at least a dozen possible unsubs here, not counting the victim."

"He's not a cop!" a new voice boomed from behind. They all turned to see Homer LaRue hurrying in from the path. "Our dead guy's not a cop. I checked on this Stipton guy, and the Pittsburgh P.D. reported that *their* Thomas Stipton was on duty this morning. He did, however, report his badge stolen about two months ago."

"This puts an interesting spin on things," Russell said. "Now we have an armed man in the woods masquerading as a police officer. Who else knows what you just told us, Homer?"

"Nobody, I guess. I made that call myself."

"All right, then. If I hear it in the press, I'll know it came from this group, and I assure you that I will not be a happy camper," Russell warned. He looked a little too directly at Agent Burrows, then scanned every face before turning back to Parker. "Sorry, Henry."

Parker cleared his throat. "I was saying we have footprints from about a dozen unsubs. Now remember that unsubs are just that—unknown subjects. Here's what's interesting: Of those footprints, only three sets are found both here and at the grave or pit or whatever we're calling that big hole in the ground up there."

"Grave sounds good to me," Russell said. Parker nodded.

"And of those three, one of them appears to belong to a child, maybe two or three years old. I'm guessing from the imprint that he or she was wearing something on his or her feet, but nothing very substantial. Maybe a pair of moccasins or socks."

For the first time Henry consulted a set of notes. "Okay. Now, the second of the three common sets of prints belongs to our dead guy. The third set belongs to that set in the woods, where somebody apparently stood for a long time. Big guy, too, judging from the depth of the prints. Let's call him unsub one. Two will be our non-cop dead guy, and three will be the kid. Y'all with me?"

Everyone nodded.

"Good. Unsubs four and five are a man and woman, or man and adolescent, I guess. How's big and medium? Anyway, prints from four and five are everywhere here at this scene but nowhere up the hill. Curiously, though, I found prints from four and five *and* the kid down on the fire road, next to some tire tracks that I'm guessing belong to some kind of sport-utility vehicle. That's it, at least until I get lab reports back."

Russell closed down Henry's turn with an abrupt nod. "Okay, Tim. Tell me what we know about possible suspects."

"Well, I'm not sure there's much there that we didn't know hours ago." Tim recapped the claims of the young hikers Gary and Mandy, who thought they saw signs of a man and a woman down here, but never really eyeballed anyone. From there the short list of potentials had been narrowed down to just a half-dozen couples.

"Oh, wait a second," Tim said. "Henry, did you say the vehicle with the cluster of unsub prints was a sport-utility vehicle?"

Henry looked up. "Yes, that's what I said."

"Well, I've run all the names on that list, and only one of them owns an SUV." Tim shuffled through his notes. "That would be a Robert Martin, 7844 Clinton Road, Clinton, Virginia."

Russell's eyebrows danced a little. Sometimes this police work wasn't as difficult as they liked to pretend. "What's his history?"

Tim shook his head. "He doesn't have one. Not so much as a parking ticket. I can call the Richmond or Alexandria field office and have somebody at their doorstep in a couple of minutes."

Russell thought about that, then rejected it. "No. I think I'd like to pay a call on them myself. If I'm gonna be building a case, I'd like to look them in the eye."

Next Russell turned to Sarah. "Ranger Rodgers, I need you to get these names and tag numbers to all of the entrance stations and tell your rangers to keep an eye out for them."

"You think they're coming back?"

"It's a cliché, I know, but it happens enough that we really should keep an eye out for it."

Russell clapped his hands. "That's it, then. Our work here is done. Ranger Rodgers, you can have your park back."

"I appreciate that," she said, noticing he had a nice smile.

"Thank you, ladies and gentlemen, for a good day's work. Henry, the instant you know any helpful details—"

"I'll get them to you, Russell."

Russell turned to Agent Burrows. "Timbo, I want you to make

sure that everything we've done here is documented and assembled. If I find a bad guy, I don't want our case kicked out because of something administrative."

Tim's face darkened. "I thought we were going to talk to that couple on the registration form."

Russell shook his head. "No. *I'm* going to talk to them. You're staying here to make sure the scut work gets done."

Five

APRIL Simpson stepped off the bus without even knowing where she was. Farther out in the suburbs, to be sure, but which one or which direction, she wasn't sure. She'd chosen this stop because of the shopping mall across the street. She needed to be with strangers for a while. She needed to be with people whose concerns today dealt with topics other than death and missing children.

It was nearly three o'clock, and it occurred to her that she'd forgotten to call in to work this morning. She was supposed to be running the lunch shift, too. No doubt there'd be hell to pay for that in the morning.

As she walked across the street and then across the expansive parking lot, she drew her jacket closer and tried to control the shivers. He'll be okay, she told herself. Carlos promised.

Inside the mall, the heat had kicked in, making it ten degrees too warm. April was surprised by the crowd, by the numbers of shoppers with nothing else to do on a Monday afternoon. The pace seemed different, too. These people—these ladies, really, because there wasn't a man in sight—seemed to be out for a carefree stroll, each of them with a little boy or a little girl in tow.

Everyone looked so happy. That was the hardest part. They had their children in backpacks or in strollers or tethered to their sides by a tight handhold. Everyone was so normal. What she would do to change places with any one of them.

Wandering the wide avenues of this indoor palace of a mall, past the Macy's and the Bloomingdale's, April caught sideward glances from a few of the shoppers. She supposed she represented a part of the world that these ladies with their hundred-dollar slacks and thousand-dollar baubles couldn't possibly understand—a world they wanted to know nothing about.

She watched these pretty, rich ladies and their babies and somehow knew that they'd blame all of this on her. They'd all assume that she'd been a bad mother, that she'd somehow brought this misfortune onto herself. They didn't hang out with the likes of Carlos Ortega, and they didn't allow people like William into their lives.

I had no choice! April's mind screamed. But suppose she had known that Justin would be taken from her one day at gunpoint. Would she have been able to find another option then? You bet she would.

Suddenly the mall felt too small. April needed to get home, regroup, and come up with an alternative plan of action. She'd placed the fate of her baby in the hands of killers and drug dealers. My God, was she crazy? She was Justin's mother, not Carlos Ortega. It was *her* responsibility to get him back.

What was it that Logan had told her about the money? Two thousand dollars by tomorrow, and he didn't care how she got it.

Rob a bank if you have to. Those were his very words.

Suddenly the little .25 in her jacket pocket weighed twenty pounds. Could it really be that simple? Could she really just march into a bank and walk out with all the cash she needed? People did it all the time. They got caught, sure, but all she needed was a couple of hours. Just long enough to get the money to Logan and to get Justin back home. After that, they could arrest her or do any other damn thing they pleased. Justin would be safe.

April had wandered into Macy's and found herself staring at a rack of men's dress shirts. Along the back wall, over the display, she saw the words credit department, written in pewter-colored relief over a squared-off archway. The same letters went on to announce customer service, public phones, and rest rooms, but April didn't care about any of those other things. The credit department was where they kept the cash. So far as she knew, robbing a credit department was a local crime, not a federal one. Two thousand dollars would mean nothing to these people. They had dresses here that sold for more than that.

The lights were brighter on the other side of the archway. Only two tellers worked behind the elevated bank of windows, both women. Only one seemed to be receiving customers; the other, younger than the first by at least thirty years, seemed lost in counting money for her drawer. Cash. Thick stacks of it.

The older woman, who looked maybe fifty years old and needed a trip to the hairdresser to take care of a root problem, sat closest to April. She lifted her drugstore-issue reading glasses from their perch on her breasts and planted them on her nose so she could squint at whatever it was that the customer had slid over to her. She started shaking her head even before she started reading.

"No, dear. This is the letter that you sent to us. I need to see what we sent back to you."

The customer, who appeared way too young to have three children clinging to her legs, looked as if she might cry. "But I couldn't find my copy. Don't you people keep copies of your own letters?"

The lady behind the cage laughed. "Oh, sure. I happen to keep copies of every letter the company writes right here in my pocket."

The words and the tone with which they were delivered angered April. This mother was late on her debts, and the store was making her life miserable. They'd make sure that no credit card company would trust her. If she was more than a few weeks late, they'd start calling her home every night.

April tried to look like the very essence of calm as she strolled over to the little writing podium across from the teller cages, where she found a Customer Comment form with enough space at the bottom for her to write what she needed. The block she chose on the form read, "Please tell us any way that we can make your visit to our store more enjoyable." In big block letters, and with an amazingly steady hand, April wrote, "Give me all the money in your cash drawer. Do not panic, and do not set off any alarms. I have a gun."

Once done, she slid into line behind the woman with the squirming kids. It's for Justin, she told herself. Anything's legal when your son is in jeopardy.

"I can help you over here, ma'am."

Startled, April looked up to see the young lady in the other cage flashing a bright, genuine smile at her. She sidestepped out of the line and walked over to the teller whose nameplate identified her as Debby.

"What can I do to help you?" Debby asked.

Oh, God, she was friendly! April didn't want to have to look into the eyes of someone who was friendly. How could she go through with this?

"Are you okay, ma'am?" Debby asked.

April managed to nod. She looked down at the slip of paper in her hand and then back to Debby. Hesitantly her hand slid forward.

As soon as the note left her touch, April knew that she'd made a mistake. "No, wait," she started to say, but Debby had already unfolded the note and read it. Color drained from her face.

"Oh, my God." Debby brought a hand up to her mouth. Her eyes filled with tears. "Oh, my God!"

The old bitch next door heard her. Instantly she recognized the look for what it was and moved quickly to open Debby's cash drawer. "Just give it to her," the older teller said urgently.

But Debby continued to unravel. "Please don't kill me," she begged. "Please, please don't shoot me."

Now the mother with the kids understood, and she pushed the little ones behind her. "Oh," she moaned. "Ohhh . . ."

The older teller pulled handfuls of bills out of the drawer and shoved them onto the counter, not saying a word and studiously avoiding eye contact. "Here. Take what you want. Take it all."

April still hadn't moved, frozen in place by the fear of the others. In her jacket pocket her hand closed more tightly around the little .25, and as it did, she felt a dash of panic herself. The money stacked up on the counter—mostly twenties and smaller bills, it looked like, but she saw a couple of hundreds, too.

"Take it," the woman said again. "Just don't hurt us, okay?"

That's when someone screamed, a piercing scream that made

everyone whirl to face the door. A young mother with a baby stroller had just entered and, at the first sight of what was happening, yelled and dashed back out toward the men's department. When the mother was out of sight, April heard her shout, "Somebody's robbing the store! She's robbing the store!"

April realized she didn't have a chance anymore.

"Take it!" the old teller insisted.

April reached for the money, then hesitated. She needed two thousand dollars. Every penny of it. Eight hundred or twelve hundred wouldn't do it. She'd never be able to grab that much and still get away.

"Take it!"

No. It wasn't enough, and taking too little would ruin her life for nothing. She decided to leave it there.

Saying nothing, she turned for the door.

Back in the men's department again, April moved quickly, winding her way through the maze of racks. Maybe by not running, she'd be able to slip out of the store unnoticed.

"There!" someone yelled. April whipped her head over her left shoulder to see a small army of young men and women approaching. Store security people. She broke into a run.

It had been a long while since April had run full tilt, but in the old days she'd been pretty fast on her feet. Despite the baby in her tummy, the racks of clothes flew by as she zeroed in on the big opening leading to the mall. Behind her she could hear the pace of footsteps pick up as the security people closed in on her.

April focused on a lady at the front entrance who was talking into a shopping bag. The undercover guard stood flat-footed, hoping to block her quarry's path. April never even slowed down. She kept her shoulder low, and the impact barely made her stumble as the guard went airborne.

April darted out into the mall as everyone else slowed down long enough to see that their co-worker was all right. April knew those few seconds could mean a lifetime for her. The store security people were essentially out of the race now, leaving her to beat three uniformed guys from out in the mall. April charged toward them.

The uniforms were all men, so they had her beat on strength, but when she pulled the little .25 from her jacket pocket and held it up, their will dissolved.

"She's got a gun!" one of the guards shouted. All three slid to an abrupt stop.

Off to April's right a lady screamed. Some shoppers dropped to the ground; others took off. The security guards seemed most frightened of all, dropping to the tile and shouting frantically into their radios.

April sprinted through the stupid-looking fake park in the middle of the mall, easily dodging the loosely rooted trees and oversize synthetic rocks. She plowed through the arrangement of pansies and marigolds, past a small cluster of dogwoods, and finally came out on the other side. Now there was nothing between her and the doors leading to the long hallway to the emergency exit. Behind her an army of security guards was in pursuit.

She turned her body sideways at the emergency door to hit the crash bar with her hip. It flew open as if it were made of cardboard. A tiny speaker on the lock bleated an ugly screech of an alarm.

Finally out in the daylight again, April headed for the parking lot, still wishing that she had a plan. Running was an option for only so long. Her legs had grown as heavy as her belly, and her wind was giving out. To surrender meant losing Justin, though, and she wasn't about to do that. Not without a fight.

But what kind of fight would it be? The way she figured it, in fifteen seconds, thirty at the most, they'd be on her. So she fired a shot. Into the ground at her feet. In the vastness of the open parking lot, it sounded tinier than a firecracker. But the pursuing footsteps stopped. This was good. This was her chance.

Her legs had grown rubbery by the time she reached the end of the long row of cars. Directly in front was a road and, beyond that, more parking lot. How on earth—

She never saw the guy coming. From off to her left—could it have been over the top of a parked car?—she saw a flash of blue shirt. She felt a beefy arm around her waist, and the momentum of the tackle drove her sideways into the back panel of a sport-utility vehicle. As her ear rammed into the back window, she heard a crunch and was instantly bathed in a shower of tiny glass beads. She found herself on the ground, covered with glass, and surrounded by people who were all shouting at her to do something. When she tried to stand, the glass beads bit deeper, and she saw blood on her hands.

Finally she was able to raise her head high enough to see a face or two. She recognized the flashes of blue uniform, and curiously, she noted that the boy closest to her—that's what he was, too, a teenager—had pretty eyes that nearly matched the color of his shirt. Handsome, too, with teeth that sparkled when he smiled.

Only, this wasn't a smile, was it? No. This was a sneer, and the boy had a stick in his hand. As April saw the stick coming toward her head, she tried to say something to make him stop, but there really wasn't any time.

BOBBY turned off the radio and closed his eyes. He sat still in the Explorer for a long time before pushing the button to activate the garage door. As the door rumbled upward, he wondered just how long he had. Kidnapping. Murder. Both capital crimes, and he was guilty of both. What was he going to do?

He and Susan could move away, he supposed—just disappear from everyone they knew and then raise the child as if they'd always had him—but what would be the point of that? Bobby's whole desire for children was rooted in his need for family, his need to project and absorb even more love than he already felt for his parents and his wife and his siblings. To have a child merely to disappear made no sense. No sense at all.

But to stay meant facing the music.

Finally Bobby's foot released the brake and he glided into his parking space. As he opened his door, grabbed the bag of purchases he'd made at Kmart, and stepped out into the garage, he realized that he was all alone; Susan's aging Chrysler Concorde wasn't in its slot. The butterflies in his stomach grew three times in size. Where could she have gone? He left the bag on the concrete floor and hurried toward the door. His key found the lock, and he rushed into the kitchen, closing the door behind him. "Susan?"

No answer.

"Susan? Where are you?"

Instantly paranoid, he headed first for the nursery, where once again he found no sign of people. Next he tried the master bedroom. Boxes lay strewn about the bed, some opened, most not, and he recognized little bits of festive wrapping paper from the day of the baby shower his staff had thrown for Steven back in December.

Then he got it. She was digging for baby clothes. But why? Where could they possibly want to go?

Samuel. The name popped uninvited into his mind.

The mysterious Samuel, who refused to help his friend. Maybe he'd finally figured out who they were, and he'd come to get his revenge. Maybe he'd come and taken them.

No, that was ridiculous. "Stop it, Bobby," he told himself. He spoke aloud. "Just stop it. There has to be a logical explanation."

He scoured the bedroom for a note, for some indication where she might have disappeared to. He searched the nursery next and finally the entire downstairs. Not a trace.

In the family room he sat heavily on the blue tapestry sofa and eased his head back onto the cushions. This problem got worse with every passing second. Nothing in nineteen years of schooling or in his captainship of the debate team or in the succeeding years of excellence in the business world as an account manager for a prestigious software firm had prepared him for this.

He tried to figure out his next step. Their first problem was the baby. Specifically, where to deposit him. Bobby liked the idea of dropping him off at a church. With luck a set of parents out there were frantic with worry over the loss of their little boy, and recovering him would make everything all right again. Unless, of course, the kid's father was a cop who just happened to be lying dead in the middle of the West Virginia woods.

The telephone rang, and the sound of it went through Bobby like a shot. He jerked up from the sofa, dashed to the kitchen, and lifted the receiver. "Hello?"

"Hi, Bobby, it's me," Susan said cheerfully. "I just wanted you to know that Steven and I are okay, and that we'll be out for the better part of the afternoon."

A chill raked Bobby's back. "Steven?"

She gave a naughty little giggle. "That's what I decided to call him. I've always liked the name Steven."

Bobby leaned against the edge of the counter and struggled to control his breathing. "I like the name, too. That's why we were going to name the baby that."

"And now I have." Bobby could see her beaming smile as she spoke. "He's so beautiful."

"Look, honey, where are you? We need to talk about some things."

"I'm at the mall."

"The mall! Are you crazy? What if somebody sees you?"

Susan laughed. "I'm at White Flint. I wouldn't go anywhere we might know anyone. Bobby, you should see how Steven interacts with people. He's such a charmer. I just love being with him."

Bobby's heart pounded a timpani beat against his breastbone. This was bad. This was really really bad. "Just stay where you are, okay, Sue? I'll get in the car and come and join you."

"Oh, no, that's okay. We're having a terrific time."

"Honey, I can be there in—what, forty-five minutes? It'll be fun."

"No, Bobby." This time, her tone was unequivocal, harsh. "This is our special outing, okay?"

Okay? Hell, no, it's not okay! He needed her home. He needed the boy home. Now. "Honey, listen—"

"Time to go. Steven's getting antsy in his stroller. I love you, Bobby."

Those words came all in a rush, and before he could take a breath to argue, he heard the line go dead.

"No!" He yelled it loudly enough to echo through the house that he suddenly hated more than he'd ever hated anything in his life—the place that weighted his life like an anchor. He slammed the receiver into its cradle on the wall, then picked it up again and smashed it into the granite countertop, launching a shower of plastic shrapnel across their shiny kitchen floor.

PITTSBURGH DETECTIVE TOM Stipton rubbed his temples. Sooner or later the teasing would stop. He was sure of it. Problem was, with twelve years to go before retirement, it probably wouldn't happen while he was young enough to enjoy the break.

It had been five whole hours now since he'd found out that he'd been shot to death in West Virginia, and all things considered, he felt pretty good about it.

The shift commander had fielded the telephone call. "Hey, Tom, there's a West Virginia state trooper on line three. Steel yourself. I'm afraid it's not good news."

Tom punched the blinking button. "Yeah. Hello?"

The voice on the other end was downright grim. "This is Lieutenant Homer LaRue with the West Virginia State Police. I'm investigating the murder of one of your police officers."

Tom gasped. "One of ours? Who?"

The voice faltered. "A Detective Stipton."

Tom's face apparently displayed the expression people were waiting for, and the squad room erupted in laughter. Then Tom explained to LaRue how his badge had been stolen from his locker at his health club.

As part of the punishment for losing his badge, Stipton had been removed from the homicide division and placed on the petty crimes unit. He liked to think of it as the humiliation that kept on giving. Now he glanced across the squad room and saw his next case arriving. She appeared tall for a woman—five ten—and she looked like death in her bloodstained secondhand clothes. An enormous bandage all but obscured her left eye. The effect of it all was particularly startling given her obviously pregnant belly. The uniformed officers on either side led her to an interrogation room, where they removed her handcuffs and ushered her to a chair.

Tom met the officers as they were on their way out. "Is this our armed robber?"

Sergeant Sammy Feitner was the older of the two officers. "This is her. Hasn't said a word since we picked her up."

"Looks more like a victim than a perp. That bandage on her head your doing?"

Feitner scowled. "Not my style, Tom. One of the security guards got a little carried away."

Tom winced. "Ouch. She been to the hospital?"

The big sergeant shook his head. "Refused treatment."

"How about her sheet? Did you pull it?"

Feitner took a computer printout from his back pocket. "Not much there. A possession arrest a few years ago, but she walked."

Scanning the sheet, Tom noticed her address in The Pines. That in itself was nearly as good as a conviction.

"Here are the statements from the store security folks," the second officer said, handing over another set of papers. "And here's a copy of the video from the security cameras."

Tom signed the chain-of-custody slip. "No request for a lawyer?"

Feitner shook his head.

"Well, thank you, gentlemen, for a job well done," Tom said.

April didn't look up as Tom came in and walked to the table.

"Ms. Simpson, I'm Detective Stipton with the Pittsburgh Police Department. Can I get you anything? A soda? Coffee?"

April didn't move. Her chin was touching her chest.

Tom nodded. He had infinite patience at times like these. Truth be told, given the case against her, keeping silent wasn't a bad strategy. He paused, then leaned his arms heavily on the table.

"Hey, April," he said softly. "Could you look at me, please?"

She hesitated, then rocked her head up to full height. Beneath the bruises, she was a beautiful woman.

"That's a nasty knock you got on your head there. Are you sure you don't want to see a doctor?"

Clearly, movement hurt as she shook her head.

"Was it one of our people who did it?"

"Does that matter?"

"Well, I think it does," Tom answered with a shrug. "I don't like the notion of my officers out there beating on civilians."

She shook her head again, ever so gently. "I don't think so, no. I think it was one of the rent-a-cops at the mall."

Tom pulled a notebook from his inside jacket pocket. "Would you like to consider filing charges?"

April scowled. "Maybe I will. I'll have to think about it."

Tom made a note. "Okay, fair enough. Now, what about a lawyer, do you want to have one here while we talk?"

April inhaled deeply and closed her eyes against what seemed to be a jolt of pain. "I guess not. I don't intend to say anything."

Another note. "Okay, fine. Now, let's watch some television together." A television and VCR sat on a rolling cart in the corner, and Tom pulled it closer to the table. He turned it on and slid the tape of the crime into the player. Then they were watching in color from a high angle as April walked into the credit office and over to the writing carrel, where she took a piece of paper from the stack and wrote something down.

Tom stopped the tape, then fished through a manila envelope for a Ziploc bag in which someone had placed the Customer Comment form. "Just so you know," Tom said, "the person we see there is writing the following note: 'Give me all the money in your cash drawer. Do not panic, and do not set off any alarms. I have a gun.' "

He started the tape again, and they both watched the entire episode in the credit department. Two more edits tracked the woman throughout the store, all the way to where she tackled a lady at the door and then charged out into the mall. Tom pushed the STOP button.

"I noticed that she didn't take any of the money," April said softly.

Tom nodded. "I noticed that, too, just as I noticed that she never produced the gun that she talked about in the note. I might even find that encouraging if it weren't for this." Reaching into the manila envelope again, he withdrew another bag, this one containing the little .25-caliber pistol. He laid it on the table.

"April, I've got to tell you that none of this looks very good for you, okay? We can make a case here for armed robbery and the use of a firearm in the commission of a felony. That's twenty, thirty years right there. If we pushed a little, we could probably get you for attempted murder, too."

April's head snapped around, her eyes showing terror.

"That shot you fired in the parking lot. In a strict interpretation of the law, that meets the definition of attempted murder."

April looked even more miserable.

Tom rose from his chair and walked to the water fountain near the door, where he pulled a Dixie cup from the dispenser and filled it. He set it on the table in front of his prisoner. "Let me put all of my cards on the table here, April. I need you to sign a statement that says you did what we both already know you did."

April brought her gaze around to meet his. "What if—"

Tom held up his hand for silence. "I don't want you saying anything yet, okay? Now, I can't make any promises to you, but if you make this easier on all of us by signing a statement, then I'll do whatever I can to convince the prosecutor to take it easy on you."

April stewed for a long time. Then she said, "Assuming I were to confess to doing this—which I'm not—would it make a difference if I had a really good reason for doing it? Would it matter that in the end I changed my mind and that the only reason I fired that shot—if I fired it at all—would have been to get the people to back off long enough for me to get away? Would any of that matter?"

Tom smiled gently. They were coming close to an agreement. "I suppose it could. But I'm not the guy who makes that call."

April considered it all carefully.

"You know, I figured when I saw you that there was more to this case than it seems. I mean, look at you. You're a good-looking woman—with a baby in the oven, no less—and with the exception of that one drug thing a long time ago, you've lived your life within the law. I asked myself when I first saw you: Why would this woman choose this day to ruin her life?" Tom leaned closer to her and lowered his voice. "What did happen today, April? What was it that drove you to rob that store?"

She was so close. She opened her mouth as if to begin, then shut down again. She looked away. "It's not easy deciding to confess to something you didn't do. I'm going to have to think about it."

Tom sighed. The moment had passed; there'd be no confession today. "Okay, April, suit yourself. Take some time. And while you think, I'll just go ahead and have you booked on the burglary, firearms, and attempted-murder counts."

"But I'll be able to change my mind later, if I decide to, you know, confess to that crime I didn't commit?" The edge of panic had returned to her voice.

Tom didn't answer. This was psychological warfare, after all, and he didn't want to just walk away from his advantage. Instead, he gave a little shrug, as if to say, "We'll see."

As the door closed behind him, he peeked once through the wire-reinforced window. He felt a twinge of guilt when he saw her start to cry.

six

WHO does that greaseball spick think he is, anyway?" raged Patrick Logan, slamming another hole—his fourth—into the drywall. The big man's lip was split, his nose was shattered, and his neck still bore the mark of Peña's garrote. "He comes into *my* house and disrespects me in front of *my* people! Who does he think he is?"

Ricky Timmons had seen his boss on plenty of rants over the years, but this one was off the scale.

An hour ago Carlos Ortega and his thug, Jesús Peña, had stiff-armed their way past Ricky and into Logan's office.

"You're an idiot, Logan," Carlos had said as he loomed over the big man's desk. "A stupid, worthless idiot. Don't you understand why we've been able to achieve such quick success? It's because people fear me and because they know I'm good for the community. Me, I'm the United Nations and the Teamsters all rolled into one. We have rules for how we conduct business, and anyone who doesn't follow the rules gets taken care of. You know this, right? Tell me that you know this."

Logan had gasped for air and nodded spasmodically as Peña tightened the thin nylon cord around his neck. Yes, he understood.

"That's good. It's good you understand. When word gets out that one of the people who works for me is targeting two-year-old children, do you think that the police will continue to look the other way? Do you think that the people in the neighborhoods will continue to be our friends once they realize that you're willing to kill their children over a few dollars?"

This time, the gasp meant no.

"I agree. That's why you're going to contact your buddy who has this child and tell him to bring the baby home. Tonight."

Logan gasped. "I can't. Not tonight. He's too far away. Tomorrow. I can have him home tomorrow."

Carlos's eyes narrowed. "Where is he?"

"Someplace out in the mountains."

"In the *mountains!* What mountains?"

"W-West Virginia. I d-didn't want, you know, for the body to be found." Then, Logan added quickly, "If it came to that."

Carlos slapped him, splitting the Irishman's lip. "You're sick," Carlos growled. He followed the slap with a punch that shattered the big man's nose. "You've got eighteen hours, Logan. Eighteen hours. By ten o'clock tomorrow morning, that baby had better be home with his mama and not a mark on him, or I swear you'll wish that I had killed you here today. Right now, that little boy is all that's keeping you alive."

"Dammit, Ricky, I asked you a question!" Logan hollered now. "Who does he think he is?"

Ricky jumped. "I don't know. I guess he thinks he's Carlos. I guess he thinks he's the boss."

"The boss! He has the balls to think that he's the boss of *me?*"

Ricky said nothing, fearful of where this might go. In Pittsburgh, Carlos Ortega was *everybody's* boss.

Suddenly the raging storm seemed to subside. In its wake Ricky saw a calm that was almost more frightening than the fury.

"I think it's time things changed, don't you, Ricky? I think it's time for someone else to start giving the orders."

Ricky closed his eyes against the inevitable. This was where he'd feared Logan was headed.

"This is our chance, Ricky boy. Our chance to take it all."

"This is our chance to get killed and lose everything."

The smile disappeared. "Are you afraid of Carlos, Ricky?"

Was it possible that Logan didn't get it? Everybody was afraid of Carlos, because Carlos had surrounded himself with an army of loyal people. Hell, even the users on the street would stand up for him. But that's not what Ricky said to Logan.

"I think there's a time and a place for everything. Right now you're pissed off because he and his goon came in here and dissed you. But you've got the whole city to think about. Are you prepared—I mean *really* prepared—to fight for it all, block by block? Do you really want to do that?"

Logan glared at his lieutenant, his eyes hot. "What I want," he said carefully, his voice quivering with rage, "is for that s.o.b. to be dead. I want him to know that you never mess with Patrick Logan and get away with it. I want the world to know that."

"That doesn't answer—"

"The hell with the others, Ricky!" Logan boomed. "If we take out Ortega the others will fall in line. It's time for me to start running my business the way I want to run it."

Ricky's shoulders drooped, as if deflated.

Logan went on, "If we don't act first, Ortega is going to come at us."

"That kid," Ricky said. "You're not giving him back?"

"Hell, yes, I'm giving him back. I'll have the bones in one bag and the guts in the other."

"Cripes, you heard what Ortega said about—"

"Would you shut up about Ortega? He's dead, okay? He doesn't matter anymore."

"But about the Simpson bitch—"

"She's dead, too. And her husband, too. The whole family."

"That's a lot of bodies. The cops are gonna clamp down on us."

"You're afraid of gettin' caught, aren't you?" Logan asked.

Ricky shrugged, suddenly embarrassed. "That's part of it. Plus, I'm not so hot on doing the kid."

"You don't have to do the kid. I got other people to take care of him, okay? That leaves you to take out the Simpsons, and me to do Ortega. We can be done and home by nine o'clock."

Ricky sighed. In Logan's mind, this was all a done deal.

TIM BURROWS WATCHED AS Henry Parker supervised the cataloguing of the evidence they'd collected that day. The evidence bags were logged onto a master sheet, carefully verified, then placed into various bins, for transport either to the Charleston field office or back to headquarters in Washington.

"Hey, Agent Burrows!" someone yelled from behind.

Tim pivoted to see Homer LaRue on his way up the hill, waving a thin file folder in his right hand. Tim strolled down the path to meet the state trooper halfway.

"Take a look at this," LaRue said. "We found out who the stiff is."

Tim opened the folder Homer gave him and read for himself what LaRue told him anyway.

"It took the computer a little while to spit out the identification from the prints we took, because it looks like the guy tried to carve 'em off a few times. His name popped out as Jacob Stanns, from up in Wetzel County, near the Pennsylvania border. He was in and out of trouble a lot as a kid, and on into his twenties. Had a thing for weed and for boosting other people's wheels. He was arrested on a murder charge about fifteen years ago, but the state's attorney let him walk for lack of evidence."

Now Tim's eyes came up to stay. Nothing like the mention of a previous murder to get his attention. "So is he married?"

Homer shook his head. "Don't think so. The file says he lives with his brother, Samuel, out on the family farm. Samuel, apparently, is a few cards short of a full deck. That's one of the reasons they went easy on that murder charge. Seems if Jacob went to jail, there'd be no one to take care of the brother."

"What do we know about the brother, other than the fact that he's a little slow?"

"Nothing, really. He doesn't have a record."

Homer related some more about the results of the autopsy, getting into the details of impact angles and time of death, but Tim found his mind wandering back to the footprints in the woods—that separate set, where someone just stood and watched.

"Agent Burrows, are you even listening to me?"

Tim snapped back to the present and smiled sheepishly. "I'm

sorry, Lieutenant. I was just thinking about the footprints in the woods and wondering if maybe they belonged to this brother."

Homer recoiled from the thought. "What kind of man would just stand there while his brother was getting shot to death?"

"I don't know. Be interesting to find out, wouldn't it?"

Homer returned his gaze to his papers. "Well, we traced the nine-one-one call that led us up here in the beginning. Turns out it was made from a pay phone at a convenience store outside of Winchester, Virginia. The night clerk remembers only one guy who wasn't a regular coming in after midnight. Said he bought gas and diapers."

Tim's head cocked. "Diapers? As in for a baby?"

"As in Pampers. The guy was surprised how much they cost."

"Tell me he paid by credit card."

Homer shook his head. "No such luck. Cash."

"The Pampers bring to mind those little footprints, don't they?"

"I was thinking the same thing," Homer noted.

Tim lifted his fatigue cap to scratch his scalp. "Tell you what, Lieutenant. What do you say you and I take a trip out to Wetzel County to pay a visit to Samuel Stanns? Let's see if he can shed any light on what happened here."

"Why don't I just have a trooper bring him in?"

Tim pretended to consider that for a moment before shaking his head. It wouldn't do to tell this hillbilly that he didn't want to share the credit with a bunch of locals. Instead, he just said, "I'd kind of like to see their place for myself."

NEVER *touch the little phone.*

It was the thought that jolted Samuel out of his nap. With the lawn finally done, and with all the excitement and tragedy of the night before, he finally just couldn't keep his eyes open any longer.

The cell phone chirped again. That was Jacob's phone—the one that the Boss always called on, the one that Samuel was never, *ever* to touch, except to plug it into its charger.

The phone chirped again.

He wasn't supposed to answer, dammit!

The phone chirped.

He had no choice, did he? He had to answer it. Rising from the sofa, Samuel walked slowly over and lifted the phone.

"Hello?"

The voice on the other end was nasty. "Burn the package."

Samuel scowled. "What package? Is this the Boss?"

The voice stopped, as if he were suddenly suspicious of something. "Is this Moonlighter?"

Moonlighter! Samuel had heard Jacob use that name before. "Um, no, th-this is his brother."

"I want to talk to Moonlighter."

Samuel gasped. He was going to have to tell, wasn't he? "Jacob— I mean, Moonlighter—Moonlighter is dead."

Another pause. "Well, what about the package?"

"What package? I don't know what you're talking about."

The man on the phone sighed. "You don't remember picking up something last night? Something about three years old?"

"You mean the little boy?"

"Hey, shut up, you dwid. This isn't a secure line."

Samuel said nothing. He didn't have to talk to anyone who spoke to him that way.

"Well, were you there for the pickup, or weren't you?"

"Yeah, I was there."

"And you know where Moonlighter put him?"

Samuel felt himself blushing as he shifted feet. This was the embarrassing part. "Well, I know where he tried to put him."

"What do you mean, 'tried'?"

Samuel stuffed his hands in his pockets, the phone cradled into his shoulder. "He sort of got away."

"What the hell do you mean, he got away!"

Samuel's mind raced, trying to come up with something he could say that would make the Boss less angry. "I—I mean, we had him, and then . . . well, he got away. He ran through the woods. We tried to catch him, and that's when Jacob—I mean, Moonlighter— got into the fight with those people and then got killed."

"So you don't know where the package is?"

While Samuel was talking, his hand found a piece of paper all crumpled up in his pocket. On that little sheet of paper—the one he remembered picking up—he saw a name and address. The little slip of paper said Bobby and Susan Martin, and Samuel remembered the nosy Nellies calling each other that. And the slip of paper had an address in Clinton, Virginia.

"I know where he is," Samuel said triumphantly. "I can get him."

Silence from the other end while the Boss thought about things. "Tell you what," he said finally. "I want you to get the package and meet me tonight at midnight at the place where you lost him. Do you think you can find that place? You're not too stupid for that?"

"I'm not stupid!" Samuel shouted. "I drove all the way home from there all by myself. I can find it."

"Good." The Boss's voice did sound a little lighter. "Then you meet me there with the package—with the boy—at midnight."

Something in the tone of the voice made Samuel feel funny. "You're not going to hurt him, are you? Because we never wanted to do that. It was all a game. Jacob told me."

The voice laughed. "Jacob told you that, did he? Okay. Well, we're not going to hurt anyone. You just be there at midnight."

"I'll be there," Samuel said, but the line was dead.

He hoped that he could get where he needed to go and be back in the park by midnight, but he wasn't completely sure.

Samuel liked maps. He was good with them, just as he was good with some numbers, such as lock combinations and telephone numbers. He got the atlas off the shelf in the living room and found Virginia. Sure enough, there was Clinton, just outside of Washington, D.C. It looked like maybe a four-hour drive.

He checked his watch. If he moved quickly, he could be there and then back to West Virginia in no time at all. He'd make the midnight deadline easy as pie.

RUSSELL cursed as he slid the heater control on the dash to OFF. Again. Never in his life had he been in a rental car where everything worked properly. Today the gremlins resided in the heater, which cycled between only two settings: sweat and freeze. The good news was, he was almost there.

Clinton, Virginia, was the shopping hub of the surrounding horse country, where people paid big bucks to live in a Disneyfied vision of small-town America. They couldn't quite afford to live among the old-money foxhunters in Leesburg or Middleburg, but this place teemed nonetheless with all the trappings of nouveau wealth.

Russell piloted his rental Chrysler through winding roads where huge homes dominated the rolling landscape, but where nobody seemed to be home. The owners were still toiling away at their downtown jobs, preparing for the daily commute. This far out, Russell figured they spent a solid hour, hour and a half each way. Welcome to the new millennium, he thought. His own tastes ran more toward the two-bedroom condominium, where three thousand dollars furnished the whole thing.

Russell felt in his gut that this Martin couple were the people who could answer all of his questions, in all likelihood on the heels of having their rights read to them. He was still missing motive, but opportunity was there, and he'd just learned via cell phone that the SUV they drove was a late-model Ford Explorer.

He nearly missed the house he was looking for—number 7844— and he hit the brakes hard to keep from blowing past it. From the road, there was no house, just a mailbox next to a long driveway that curved up a steep incline and disappeared behind the trees.

Pausing to verify yet again that he had the right address, Russell started the long climb up the hill to visit the Martins.

BOBBY was a wreck. Where the hell were his keys? He had had them just a couple of minutes ago. Oh, there they were, right in his pocket.

He tried to remember what Barbara Dettrick had told him: that even if they caught up with him, he had a perfectly good explanation for what had happened. And he did report the body, didn't he? That had to be worth something.

With his keys clutched in his fist, he quickly walked through the kitchen, pausing to arm the alarm system before opening the door and walking outside.

He'd almost made it to the door of his Explorer when he saw a

Chrysler climbing up his driveway. The man behind the wheel bore a look on his face that ruled him out as a salesman or a welcoming neighbor. Ten bucks would get you twenty that this guy was a cop.

SOME people are natural criminals. Russell had spent hours with suspects who had committed horrendous crimes, but to talk with them, you'd think that they were deacons of their local church. Russell believed that supreme criminals are supreme liars.

Robert Martin was not one of them. This guy looked like the proverbial kid in the cookie jar. As Russell drove up the sweeping driveway, he caught his prey in the garage, clearly in a hurry to go somewhere. In an Explorer, no less. As he saw Russell's car approaching, the guy nearly jumped out of his skin.

Russell took his sweet time getting out of his car. He noted that the guy didn't come forward to meet him. Nor did he run away. He just stood there, watching. Russell wondered what that meant, just as he wondered what the bruises on the guy's face meant.

Russell finally strolled over to Bobby. "Hi, there. Beautiful house."

Bobby either winced or smiled. Russell couldn't tell. "Thanks."

"Are you Robert Martin?" Russell had closed the distance to an uncomfortable three feet of separation, effectively trapping his suspect against the Explorer's tailgate.

Bobby circled around his visitor and stepped outside onto the driveway. "Yeah, I'm Bobby Martin."

Russell made a point of keeping his back turned for a moment as he scanned the inside of the garage. As he turned, he reached into the pocket of his suit coat and produced a leather wallet with his credentials. "I'm Russell Coates with the FBI."

For the first time in his career someone actually reached for the creds and pulled them closer to get a better view.

"So you are," Bobby said. "Why are you here?"

The initial fear seemed to be gone now, replaced by a wariness that told Russell that his visit did not come as a total surprise. "I'm investigating a murder."

"Oh, that," Bobby said, nodding. "Terrible thing. I guess I've halfway been expecting you to call."

Russell raised an eyebrow. "And why would that be?"

"You're talking about the killing up in the park, right?"

"You know about that?"

"Well, my wife and I were camping up there last night, so when I heard about it on the news, I figured that sooner or later somebody would want to talk to us. I can save you some trouble, though. I don't have anything to offer."

"Why don't you tell me what you do know."

Bobby shrugged. "I know I was there last night, and then I heard that there'd been a killing."

Russell pulled out his notepad. "Who were you there with?"

"My wife."

"No one else?"

"It's just the two of us."

Russell eyed the box of Pampers in the Kmart bag on the floor.

Bobby caught his gaze. "We lost a baby a few weeks ago," he explained, looking down. "We, uh . . ."

He didn't bother to finish the sentence, and Russell decided not to push. This Martin guy was either a hell of an actor or he'd tapped into a genuine source of pain. "What's your wife's name?" Russell asked. A softball, nonintrusive question always helped to bring people back on track.

"Susan."

Russell wrote it down. "So you saw and heard nothing?"

"A lot of dark and a lot of cold," Bobby said with a chuckle.

The suspect's words were just a little too glib. "Did you see or hear anything related to the murders?"

"Like what?"

The guy was good. Russell was supposed to be the one putting his suspect on the spot, not the other way around.

"Tell you what," Russell said, closing his notebook. "It's kind of cold out here. What do you say we go inside and talk? It won't take very long."

The panicked look flashed again behind Bobby's eyes as he shook his head. "I'd rather not."

"Why not?"

"I need a reason for you not to come into my home?" Bobby said it as if he'd never heard of something so appalling.

"Do you always entertain guests out on the driveway?"

"You're not a guest," Bobby said. "You're the FBI, and I can tell that you suspect I had something to do with this mess in the park."

"Your behavior isn't doing much to make me think otherwise."

Bobby shrugged. "All the more reason not to talk to you anymore." He turned to walk back into the house.

Russell almost laughed at the absurdity of the situation. "You know, we don't *have* to do this the easy way. I can take you into custody as a material witness and question you all night long."

Bobby stopped and turned back toward Agent Coates, taking his time as he formulated his response. "I don't think you intend to do that," he said. "Else you would have come here with an army of agents and a lot of big guns. Instead, it's just you on a fishing trip."

Russell allowed himself a smile. "And a suspect who's doing everything he can to make himself look guilty as hell."

Bobby's head bounced noncommittally on his shoulders, as if to acknowledge the point. "I think you need to call the ball here, Agent Coates. Either you've got your probable cause, and you're going to haul me in, or I'm going on inside to watch television."

Russell cocked an eyebrow. "What about your trip? When I was driving up, you were headed to your vehicle. I assumed you were about to take a trip somewhere."

Bobby looked as if he was thinking of a retort, but he ended up letting it go. "Have a nice day, Agent Coates."

Russell watched as Bobby strolled self-consciously back toward the house and pushed the button for the garage door. The overhead door started its downward trek. Russell yelled over the noise. "I see you've got the same tires as the prints we found at Powhite Trail." He enjoyed watching the words land on his target.

"I'll see you in a little while," Russell called, but by then the door was all the way down.

BOBBY made it only as far as the mudroom before he grabbed the wall and slid down onto the floor. To keep from passing out, he sat Indian-style and gulped huge lungfuls of air, keeping his eyes clenched tight until the spots stopped dancing.

It was all over now. It had to be. The tires were the key to it all. Soon there'd be the army of cops with their search warrants. Everything would come crashing down in—what, two hours? There'd be the shame of the mug shots and the television camera crews. There'd be the announcements from all of his neighbors and co-workers about how surprised they were that a guy as nice as Bobby Martin could turn out to be a murderer and a kidnapper.

Why hadn't he just come clean? Why hadn't he just sat Agent Coates down and told the whole story? At least then the truth would have been on the record. Now no matter what he said to anyone, whether under oath or just in passing, it would be judged as just another lie told by a frightened criminal.

Climbing back to his feet, Bobby wandered into the kitchen and helped himself to a tall glass of orange juice. He hadn't realized how dry his mouth had become. The cold juice felt great, even if it sat a little uneasily on his stomach.

"You know what you need to do," he told the room. It was time to make his phone call.

Judging from the sound of the receptionist's voice, Barbara Dettrick had alerted her to be ready for his call. The lawyer picked it up on the first ring. "Bobby?"

"The FBI just left," Bobby said. "I think he knows it's me."

"It doesn't matter what he knows, Bobby," she said sharply. "And it doesn't matter what he thinks. All that matters is what he can prove. Now tell me what he asked and what you told him."

Bobby recounted the conversation as best he could. He told her he admitted to being in the park last night and that he thought he'd done a stunning job of never straying from the truth.

"Don't be so proud of yourself, Bobby," Barbara admonished. "This guy isn't some hayseed deputy. He's the FBI, and he knows when he's being evaded. What about that permit thing you were so worried about? Did he ever mention anything about that?"

"No, he didn't. What do you think that means?"

"Well, I hope it means he never found the damned thing.

Frankly, with that kind of evidence you'd be under arrest now. How about a search warrant? Did your FBI buddy mention anything about coming back with one of those?"

"Not in so many words, no. But he did say that the tires on my Explorer were the same as the ones at the crime scene."

"I thought you parked down the hill from the crime scene."

"I did. About a mile, I guess."

Barbara nearly cheered. "A mile! He's bluffing. A mile might as well be a light-year. Besides, every Explorer on the street is probably using the same tires. I don't think we've got a lot of exposure there."

"So what happens next?"

"That depends. At this point the next move belongs to the other side. We just sit and wait."

Bobby fell silent. There had to be more than that. Just waiting for the other shoe to drop would drive him over the edge. "I want to turn myself in. Explain it all and see where it turns out."

"I think that's a mistake. The feds have a death penalty now, and they're always looking for a place to test it. Until I know more about what they know, then I think we should just hang tight and keep our mouths shut."

Bobby made a growling sound. "How long will this stretch on? I don't know if I can take it."

"You can take it. You have to. Now let's talk about this stray human being you have on your hands."

"I've made no progress there. Susan took him out shopping while I was meeting with you."

"Shopping? Where people might see her? Is she out of her mind?"

Bobby closed his eyes. "Right at this second? Yeah, I think she is. And I'll be damned if I know what to do about it."

RUSSELL Coates was negotiating the narrow road out of the Martins' neighborhood when his cell phone rang. It took him a whole two rings to find the thing in his jacket pocket. He opened his Star-TAC with one hand and brought it up to his ear.

"Coates."

"Hi, Russell. This is Tim," said the familiar voice. "I thought I'd catch you up on a few details. We got a positive ID on the stiff. His name was Jacob Stanns, and he lives out in West Virginia with his brother, Samuel. I'm heading out there to chat him up."

"Okay, good. Anything else?"

"Not much. The nine-one-one call was traced to a convenience store outside of Winchester. Some state troopers talked to the kid who was working last night. They didn't have any pictures to show, but the description the kid gave of the customer came close to the Martin guy's driver's license."

"What did they buy at the store?" Russell asked.

"Other than gas, the clerk said he bought a box of diapers."

seven

LIKE the little lady that she was, Christa Ortega waited patiently in her seat while Tío Jesús walked around to open the car door for her. Carlos could barely contain his pride as he watched her take Peña's hand and then rise like an angel out of her seat. Once Christa was out on the sidewalk, Carlos's wife, Consuela, followed, sliding across the seat and likewise accepting Peña's hand. Carlos himself stepped out last, from the front seat, and walked his ladies down the long sidewalk toward the school. Peña followed closely behind, Christa's cello dangling from his left hand.

He kept his right hand free.

"Carlos, this is so silly," Consuela said, laughing. "You'd think that we were arriving at the Oscars."

"This is better than the Oscars," Carlos said. "This is my daughter's big chance to show everyone how talented she is."

"Dad-dy." Christa blushed. "I don't even have a real solo part."

Carlos and Consuela parted company with their daughter at the music-room door. Christa accepted the cello from Peña and headed on in to tune up and get ready.

The St. Ignatius School orchestra was big. Between the string ensemble and the larger concert orchestra, over a hundred kids would play tonight. Given two parents per kid, more or less, along with faculty and staff, there had to be upward of two hundred people in the auditorium. Despite their early arrival, the Ortegas found that third-row seats were the best they could manage.

"She's nearly as beautiful as her mother," said a voice from behind them.

The Ortegas turned to see Father Eugene, his smile beaming. "Father!" Carlos rejoiced. Father Eugene bore the single-handed responsibility for keeping Carlos near the church. Ever kind and always willing to listen, the aging priest hated everything about what Carlos did for a living but still managed to treat him as one of his flock.

At seven sharp the houselights dimmed and the children filed onto the stage. When all the seats onstage were filled, Carlos's heart rate doubled. "Where's Christa?" he whispered.

Peña saw the look on his boss's face and stood. The set of his eyes and his jaw told everyone that he was prepared to fight.

Consuela pulled on Peña's suit coat. "Sit down!" she hissed. "These are the beginners. Christa won't be out until later."

A man dressed all in black stepped into the rear of the auditorium. Filling the doorway as he did, he drew looks from people in the quick-exit seats, but they thought nothing of this man wearing a clerical collar. The bushy mustache made him seem rather unlikely as a priest, but not so much that anyone would inquire.

The man could see a seat about halfway down in the center section, three seats from the end. When he arrived abreast of the row, he stooped till his mouth was inches away from the occupant in the aisle seat. "Excuse me," he whispered, "but would you mind scooting over so I don't have to climb over you?"

The man did mind, but what could he say to a priest? He nudged his wife, and they each scooted over one seat.

The priest nodded his satisfaction. "Thank you so very much."

No one would ever think to ask the priest why he never took off his gloves.

WILLIAM SIMPSON WAS furious. He wasn't April's secretary, and he was tired of fielding all of her phone calls. How were they supposed to make ends meet if she didn't show up at her jobs?

He needed a drink. Grabbing his keys and jacket off the sagging little table in the hall, William headed out.

This playground was a problem. He had never liked walking through such a wide expanse of open space with no place to duck and run. It wasn't so bad during the day, but once it got dusky like this, he began to feel uneasy.

Out of nowhere an invisible horse kicked him in the gut. The impact knocked him backward a good three feet and landed him in a twisted pile of arms and legs. When he tried to straighten himself out, his legs wouldn't work.

What the hell . . . ?

As he struggled for a handhold on his pant leg, the horse kicked him again, and he shrieked in horror. He'd been shot! That had to be it. It *had* to be.

His breathing wasn't right. He felt an odd pressure in his chest. Not a pain, really, but every bit as oppressive as if someone heavy were sitting on him. That's when he saw the blood.

He tried to scream out for help, but the weight in his chest had filled his throat, rendering his vocal cords as useless as his legs.

As he lay there, staring up at the black sky, he wondered where all the stars had gone.

A block away, in the third floor of a condemned rattrap, Ricky Timmons had watched through his rifle scope as he made one of the easiest hits of his life.

But it bothered Ricky that no one in the neighborhood had seen the woman April. The woman was a loose end, and sooner rather than later it would need to be tied.

BY THE time Bobby saw Susan's headlights sweeping up the driveway, his anger had blossomed to rage. He'd never before endured the kind of fear he'd lived with over the past twenty-four hours. And when he turned to his best friend—his life partner, with whom he was supposed to grow old—she wasn't there. She was off shopping. She was off in some make-believe world where she could claim a lost child as her own, as if he were a lost puppy.

She was calling him Steven. How sick was that?

Now that he saw the headlights, though, the jumbled emotions all drained away, leaving behind only a miserable sense of dread. He stood framed in the living-room window, the space behind him darkened so he couldn't be seen. Ever since Agent Coates had left him, he couldn't shake the feeling that he was being watched. What was the word from the cops show? Oh, yeah. Surveilled.

Susan opened the garage door but got out of the car while still on the driveway and walked around to the back seat on the passenger side. For a second Bobby wondered what she was doing, but then he saw the little boy's head bobbing in the glare of the dome light, and he remembered that Susan probably didn't have enough room on that side of the garage to wrestle him out.

The way she moved and the way she smiled as she lifted him out of the car, you'd think she hadn't a care in the world. Going back to the trunk, Susan took out half a dozen shopping bags before closing the lid again. She handed a bag to the boy, and he hugged it to his chest, beaming. A stuffed tiger dangled from his left fist.

Bobby headed back toward the kitchen to meet them. He and Susan arrived at the door at the same time.

"Oh!" Susan exclaimed. "Bobby, you scared me."

"Sorry," he said, but he didn't mean it.

"Steven and I had such a wonderful time! You wouldn't believe how many mothers are at the mall this time of day. We just shopped and shopped." She gushed on breathlessly, the whole way ushering the boy into the family room, where he zealously tore into a package, which, as it turned out, contained a Pooh bear. He beamed as Susan sat down next to him on the floor to play.

"The FBI came by this afternoon," Bobby said.

"Oh, really?" She didn't even look up. "What did they want?"

Bobby's eyebrows launched up to his hairline. "Excuse me? They wanted to talk about a certain dead body they found up in the woods last night, remarkably close to where our tent was."

Susan had the tiger now, and the stuffed animal tickled the boy's tummy, competing with Pooh for attention. Giggles bubbled up from the toddler.

"Susan, are you listening to me? We need to do something."

She lifted her face. "I am doing something. I'm playing with my son. You ought to come down here and join us."

"Your son? Susan, stop it! Dammit, just stop it."

Susan's voice took on a condescending tone. "What you keep forgetting, Bobby, is that God sent this child. He's not going to let anybody take us away from him. Not the FBI or anyone else."

Bobby's jaw dropped. "I don't believe this."

"Where you have fear, I have faith. It's that simple." She turned away from him again. "And I don't think this is something that we should be discussing in front of Steven."

"He's not Steven!" Bobby roared. "Steven is dead."

The boy started to cry, and Susan gathered him into her arms. "Shut up, Bobby." She rose to her feet. "I'm not going to sit here and listen to this."

"Yes, you are!" Bobby boomed. She tried to push past him, and he grabbed her arm. "These are capital crimes, Susan. You can't just climb into some fantasy world and pretend it will all go away."

Susan yanked hard to get her arm free. "You keep your hands off of me. And you keep your hands off of my son, do you hear? He's mine. He's my Steven. I don't care what you do. Leave. Turn yourself in. But nobody's taking my little boy away from me again."

Bobby let Susan's words just hang there, hoping that she would hear them for herself. "Look," he said softly, "I'm sorry I yelled. I'm sorry I got mad. It's just that things are so wrong now."

"Don't take Steven from me."

Bobby looked at Susan hard, saw the commitment in her eyes.

"Okay," he said at last. "I won't take Steven away."

"Ever."

He hesitated. He loved her too much to lie to her. "I can't say that, Susan. I promised I wouldn't give him away, okay? Not tonight, anyway. That I can swear. Not tonight. But I can't vouch for *ever*. I've already talked with the FBI today, and I'm telling you that they're getting close. Sooner or later they're going to come back. Don't make me swear now to what might happen then, okay? That's just not fair. I can't do that."

Susan's eyes narrowed as she considered his words. After a long moment she finally nodded. "Fair enough," she whispered. "But for tonight we're a family, right?"

Bobby took a deep breath. Certainly, this was no time to argue about what defined a family. This was a time simply to nod and smile. "Okay. Tonight we're a family."

ONE look at the jailer's face told April that something was terribly wrong.

She sat among a dozen other women, who had made it perfectly clear that she was not welcome in their group. She didn't care. All she could think of was Justin. When would Carlos make good on his promise to bring him home?

The other prisoners turned as the jailer approached with her keys.

"April Simpson, front and center," the guard called.

April stood, knowing instinctively that something terrible had happened. "I'm April Simpson. What's wrong?"

"Detective Stipton asked to speak with you again."

April stepped through the door, and the guard shut it behind her. "Is there something wrong?" April asked again.

The guard grasped April's elbow. "The detective will tell you everything you need to know."

This was about Justin. She could feel it. Something terrible had happened to him. What else could it possibly be?

Detective Stipton was waiting for her when she arrived in the interview room, his back turned to the door. When he turned, his face looked grave. He gestured to the seat he'd occupied during their last session together. "Please have a seat."

The politeness rang warning bells throughout April's body. God. Oh, God. She sat. So did Stipton, directly across from her.

"April, I wish there were an easy way to tell you this."

Tears rushed to her eyes. Poor Justin. Oh, please, God, take care of my boy.

"I'm afraid your husband's been shot. He's dead."

April scowled as her brain struggled with the words. Did he say my husband? William?

"He was walking out of your apartment. Someone was waiting for him and shot him three times. He died on the spot. I'm sorry."

On a different day, under different circumstances, this might have been terrible news—and judging from the look on Detective Stipton's face, it *should* have been terrible news—but for the moment all April wanted to do was let out a whoop of joy.

Justin was still okay!

ST. IGNATIUS'S auditorium erupted in applause. As one, the audience rose to their feet, cheering with the kind of enthusiasm that only a group of proud parents can generate.

Logan joined them, of course, if only to blend in. He thought he'd spotted Ortega early on, but he couldn't be sure until the ovation started and everyone stood. Logan didn't recognize the woman who stood between Ortega and his pit bull, Peña. He could only assume that she was Ortega's wife.

Logan followed his target's gaze up to the stage and picked out which child belonged to him. The star of the show, of course. Logan kept applauding with the rest as the conceited little bitch blew her father a kiss.

The houselights came up as the children filed out, and Logan suddenly felt terribly self-conscious of his gloved hands. He shoved them into the pockets of his black overcoat and stepped out into the aisle, fighting against the flow of the exiting crowd to make his way closer to the stage. As Logan edged through the crowd, he saw Ortega disappearing behind the heavy velvet curtain.

The thought flashed through Logan's head that his target might get away, but then he noticed the kids filing out in the same direction, and he put it all together. As the audience bottlenecked at the rear exits, Logan walked purposefully up the four steps to the stage. From there he joined the tail end of the musician parade as it made its way down the long beige-and-white hallway to the music room.

Up ahead he noted the red EXIT sign and nearly laughed out loud. Easy hit and easy escape. What more could he have asked for?

A woman Logan recognized as the director shouted as he entered the music room, where total bedlam reigned. His hand tensed on the weapon in his pocket. But she was yelling at the kids, not at him.

Ortega stood across the room with his wife and his human bull-dog, watching his kid putting her stuff away. As Logan entered the room, Ortega actually turned and looked right at him, but then looked away, back to his little girl. Peña looked, too, but he wasn't so easily distracted. The bulldog's brow knitted as Logan held his gaze just a second too long.

Logan's mind screamed, Now! But by the time he brought the weapon up to fire, Peña was already moving.

"GET down!"

Peña's beefy hand sent his boss stumbling forward. Instinctively Carlos knew this was a hit. He watched in horror as Peña charged, his hand disappearing under his coat and emerging with a gun.

"Tío Jesús!" Christa yelled. "Look out!"

Carlos grabbed his daughter's wrist and pulled her down to the ground with him. "Stay down!"

A gunshot fractured the air, sounding more like a grenade in the acoustically enhanced practice room, and the crowd panicked. Carlos heard screaming. Shrieking. It was the sound of raw terror. A second shot seemed somehow even louder than the first, and out of the corner of his eye Carlos saw Peña's gait wobble. A third shot dropped Peña where he stood.

Carlos gathered his daughter closer to him and rolled on top of her, shielding her body with his own. His instincts, honed by years on the street, told him that he needed to charge the gunman at full speed, but if he got up, he'd leave Christa exposed. He waited.

Logan didn't. He fired.

The bullet hit his target's knee. Carlos felt as if his whole body had been slammed with a hammer.

Consuela darted forward to help Carlos, but froze in place as Logan wrapped his fist in Christa's hair and dragged her to her feet.

"Daddy!"

Logan held the girl in front of him, his left hand gripping her throat. "You know who I am now, don't you, Ortega?" Logan asked. "Say my name, though, and I'll blow her head off. Just nod. You know who I am."

Once he put the priest's size together with his voice, Carlos recognized Patrick Logan. He nodded.

"Good," Logan said. "It's important that you know that."

"Please don't hurt Christa," Carlos moaned.

This time he didn't even hear the gunshot as the bullet slammed into his face.

AFTER two hours with Homer at the wheel, Tim Burrows couldn't wait to put his feet on the ground again. Lieutenant Homer LaRue seemed to believe that every tire rut and pothole was a target to be rammed at not less than thirty-five miles per hour. The more nervous Tim became, the more Homer seemed to enjoy it.

The Stanns place turned out to be about three miles past nowhere, way out in the wilds of West Virginia. But for the mailbox at the end of the driveway, they'd have missed the house entirely. Even at that, they had to extrapolate that ST N S really meant Stanns.

Even in the sparseness of early spring, the woods still owned the driveway. Unpaved and still muddy from rains that had fallen days ago, it bore tire ruts deep enough to prompt even Homer to slow to a crawl. Branches and dangling vines slapped and screeched along the windows on both sides of the vehicle.

"How spooky is this?" Homer mused aloud as tree limbs and bushes loomed white under the assault of his high beams.

It went on like that for a good two hundred yards. At one point they even had to ford a stream.

"How sure are you there's a house at the end of this?" Tim asked.

Homer shrugged. "We keep going as long as the road does. Ain't no turnin' around in here."

Interesting point, Tim thought. A driveway such as this would be a nightmare in a hostage-rescue situation. A terrorist would merely have to wait until all of the law-enforcements assets were committed to the road, then attack with impunity. What exactly did they know about this Samuel Stanns? That he was "slow." What did that mean? This was precisely the kind of knowledge vacuum that could get you in trouble.

"You're looking pretty stressed there, Agent Burrows," Homer said. "You got something you're not telling me?"

Tim said nothing for a long moment. It wouldn't do to admit even an ounce of fear to a yokel like this. "No. I've told you everything I know."

"Kinda makes you wish we had backup, doesn't it?"

Tim snorted. "I'm not sure how the West Virginia State Police handles things, Lieutenant LaRue, but at the FBI we don't bring an army to ask a few questions."

Homer laughed. "I gotta tell you, Special Agent Burrows, I've met a lot of people in my time on this planet. But being a jerk comes easier to you than any five people I've ever met."

Tim glared at LaRue. "Thanks for sharing that, Lieutenant. I'll be sure to pass your sentiments on to your commander."

Homer's smile grew even bigger. "I appreciate that. Just make sure you spell my name right on the report, okay?"

The cruiser climbed another hill, and suddenly the trees disappeared. They found themselves at the edge of a wide-open field. In the light of the crescent moon they saw the dark outline of a one-story farmhouse. Hundreds of feet off to the left of the house—it was hard to judge distances in this light—stood the classic silhouette of a barn.

The place looked empty as they pulled to a stop out front, thirty feet from the porch. No lights burned anywhere. Homer trained his high beams on the front steps so they could see where they walked, and he pulled his long-handled Maglite from its clamp on the edge of the front seat, right next to his 12-gauge shotgun—or riot gun, as they still called it.

"Ready?" Homer asked.

Tim answered by opening his door and stepping out into the cold air. A single breath brought the heavy odor of freshly cut grass, and Tim drew his weapon. Someone was home, all right. They just wanted it to look as if they weren't.

Homer and Tim approached the porch steps shoulder to shoulder, both of them in a half crouch.

"We don't look too paranoid, do we?" Homer whispered.

"There's a difference between paranoia and caution."

Homer sighed. "How about you lighten up?"

Tim Burrows had no desire to lighten the moment. He had no desire to do anything but concentrate.

Homer paused at the base of the steps, so Tim decided to go first. He'd made it to only the second riser when LaRue again interrupted his concentration.

"Yo, Burrows," Homer said. "Take a look at this."

Tim didn't move, but instead grumbled, "What is it?"

"It's what we country boys call evidence," said Homer.

Keeping his eyes focused on the front door, Tim retraced his steps, then looked down just long enough to see what had so captured LaRue's attention. It was a footprint, embedded in the soft, muddy grass at the base of the steps.

"Look familiar?" Homer taunted.

Sure enough, the print looked identical to the one they'd found in the woods, where someone had stood and watched a murder. Just that quickly Tim Burrows knew that Samuel Stanns was either a killer or a material witness. Either way, this was a big moment.

Tim started back up the stairs, his weapon out front.

"What are you doing?" Homer whispered.

"I'm going to make an arrest."

"The hell you are! We need backup."

"No, we don't." Tim's mind conjured images of a dozen potbellied deputies pouring down that driveway and clamoring for credit at a time when the career spotlight was rightfully his. "It's not your call. This is a federal operation."

"What is wrong with you, Burrows? Let me call for assistance."

"No. While we wait, he can dig in and build himself a hell of a defensive position, turn this into another Ruby Ridge. You want that? I'm going in." Tim climbed to the porch.

"Damn know-it-all feds," Homer grumbled as he brought his .44 to arm's length and hurried up the stairs after him.

With Burrows already standing on the knob side of the door, Homer took the hinge side, both of them standing with their backs pressed against the front wall. Tim shot a glance to LaRue, who said, "This is your game, buddy. I'm just here to take notes."

Tim hammered on the wooden door. After about fifteen seconds, when no one answered, he did it again, this time calling out at the top of his voice, "Samuel Stanns, this is the FBI. Open the door."

Another ten seconds passed.

"I'm breaking the door," Tim announced at a whisper.

Homer scowled. "Why don't you try the doorknob?"

Tim looked embarrassed for not having thought of that himself. He put his hand on the knob. Sure enough, it turned. He saw Homer's big grin but refused to acknowledge it.

"Now cover me, will you?"

Homer's .44 was up and ready. "You going in fast or slow?"

"Watch me." Tim settled himself, took a deep breath, then in one smooth motion shoved the door open and swung his weapon down to confront whoever might be lying in wait for him.

From the corner of Homer's eye the muzzle flash looked like a camera strobe in the darkened foyer, and the noise of the blast was deafening. He watched, horrified, as Burrows bent at the waist, then stumbled backward down the porch steps. Homer yelled and launched himself away from the wall. A lifelong hunter, he knew a shotgun when he heard it.

Scrambling for the porch rail, he fired blindly over his shoulder, then sort of rolled himself over the rail, dropping like a sack. Five feet away Tim Burrows lay sprawled on his back at the foot of the stairs, the left side of his camouflaged BDUs soaked black.

The agent's lips worked as if trying to say something. Homer cursed as he slapped the eject rod and dumped spent casings into the dirt. Reloaded now, he threw two more quick shots toward the front door and scrambled to where Burrows lay.

"I got you, Burrows," Homer said. "You've been hit, buddy. You've been hit. And we're out in the open here." Homer grabbed the agent's shirt collar and pulled. Burrows wailed in agony. "I know it hurts," Homer said, "but we've got to get you under cover."

The ground was more gravel than grass, and the sharp stones dug at Homer's hands and knees, drawing blood from both as he dragged Tim around to the back of his cruiser. "Okay, buddy," Homer said hoarsely. "We got you under cover now." He dared a peek over the trunk lid, and when nobody took a shot at him, he ducked down again. "You just wait here. I've got to get some help."

Grabbing Homer's sleeve, Tim grunted, "No."

The look Homer saw in Burrows's face was unlike anything he'd ever seen. He gently pried the agent's fist from his jacket. "I gotta get you a chopper, kid. I need to get you flown out of here."

With that, Homer laid Tim's hand back on his chest and duck-walked down the passenger side of the cruiser, keeping the vehicle between himself and the shooter. Since the initial exchange the gunman hadn't fired a single shot, and Homer didn't know what to make of it. It was possible that the bad guy was moving for a better angle from which to finish what he'd started.

Homer pulled open the car door and was instantly awash in the cast of the dome light. He might as well have been onstage. Three swings of his heavy steel Maglite took care of the problem.

Relieved to be back in the blackness, he found the microphone on the dash and pulled it free. "Four seven seven to control!" he shouted at a whisper. "Signal thirteen. Shots fired. Officer down!"

APRIL wanted to feel sad about William, felt that she *should* feel sad about him. As much as she tried to conjure the image of a warm, loving man—and, yes, there'd been times when he'd been exactly that—all she could see was the useless drunk he'd become. The man who'd let her baby be used as collateral. So now William was dead, just as Carlos had warned.

But what about her? What was April going to do about this armed-robbery charge? Such a stupid thing to do! If she'd just waited, she'd be at home waiting for her son to return, rather than stuck in a police station.

Maybe the judge and the jury would take it easy on her when she explained how she'd been in fear for her child's life and that she'd had no choice—

In a flash of realization a brand-new wave of panic overwhelmed her. She gasped as she realized that she'd *never* be able to tell the real story of what had happened. That would mean implicating Logan and Carlos, and if she did that, they'd kill her for sure.

Detective Stipton had left her alone in the interview room, presumably to allow her to deal with her grief. After a half hour the door opened, and she wasn't surprised to see him standing there, but his expression unnerved her.

"April, I'm sorry, but we're going to have to continue this conversation tomorrow."

"Is everything okay?" Clearly, it was not.

Stipton looked at her for a moment, considered not saying anything, but then said, "There's been a shooting at a student concert at St. Ignatius School. There's at least two dead."

"Oh, my God!" April exclaimed. In a rush she remembered the sound of cello music wafting from Carlos Ortega's library while she waited in the hallway to be announced. She remembered the beautiful little girl who wore a sweatshirt with an elaborate school crest, under which were the embroidered words ST. IGNATIUS SCHOOL.

Panic rushed toward her. April brought her hands to her head, and her eyes grew huge as she understood what had happened. She screamed, "They're going to kill him! They're going to kill my baby!"

Until this moment Stipton hadn't even known she had a baby.

"Who, April? Who's going to kill your baby?"

"Patrick Logan," she said, and then the look of panic deepened. "The shooting at the school. That was Carlos Ortega, wasn't it?"

Tom took his old seat, crossed his legs, and laced his fingers around his knee. "How did you know that?" he asked. If April was ready to tell a story, he was ready to listen.

HOMER grabbed his portable radio from its charger and returned to his wounded partner. Burrows was slipping away, and Homer could do nothing to stop it. The hole in Tim's gut was huge, about the size of a fist.

"C'mon." Homer searched the night sky for an approaching chopper. "C'mon, guys, or there won't be nothin' to save."

Beyond the hammering of his own heart, though, combined with Burrows's raspy breath, the night brought nothing but the sound of uninterrupted silence. Even the shooter remained still. Why? Why would he shoot a man and then not even attempt to finish the job?

What was that? He listened carefully and thought that maybe it was the beat of helicopter rotors, but the sound disappeared.

No, there it was again! That was definitely a helicopter. But was it *the* helicopter? Was it Life Flight?

Homer scanned the sky, but when he saw only blackness, he picked up his portable radio. If the medevac helicopter was approaching, it should be trying to raise him on the radio.

Homer twisted the knob on the top of the radio and was instantly greeted by the sound of an electronic voice. "Four seven seven, this is Life Flight One. Do you copy?"

Homer brought the radio to his lips. "West Virginia State Police unit four seven seven to Life Flight One. I copy."

"How is your patient, four seven seven?"

"I've got a pulse, but he's been hit pretty bad. Lost a lot of blood."

"I copy that, four seven seven. Do you have a visual on us yet?"

"That's a negative, Life Flight One. No visual."

"Okay, four seven seven. By the way, is your scene secure?"

Homer hesitated. "Uh, negative, Life Flight."

"Be advised, our procedures require a secured scene before landing."

Homer's heart sank. He'd been afraid of that. They were medics, not soldiers or cops. They were defenseless.

Homer hated the thoughts that were knocking on the door of his brain. Why shouldn't he just do what they should have done from the very beginning—wait for backup to arrive. But a federal officer lay beside him dying.

God, how he wished there was a better way.

He checked to make sure he had all six chambers loaded. Next, he checked the magazine on the shotgun. Full to capacity. Suddenly he was out of time killers.

He keyed the mike on his portable. "State police four seven seven to Life Flight One. I'll be securing the scene. Stay close."

There were two ways to make an assault such as this one: You could go in fast and noisy or you could go in slow and stealthy. Frankly, Homer didn't think his nerves could handle stealthy.

He rose to his haunches, steadied himself, checked to make sure that he could handle the Maglite and the forward grip of the shotgun in the same hand, then leaped forward. A loud, guttural, animal yell rose from his throat as he dashed straight up the stairs, across the porch, and on into the foyer, the shotgun ready at his shoulder.

He saw the gun before he saw the gunman and fired. The riot gun bucked hard. He fired again.

Gun smoke choked the air. He'd expected return fire and got none. He felt both elated and frightened. Where was this guy?

Homer allowed himself the luxury of lowering the riot gun to his hip as he searched through the wreckage. He saw no body on the floor, no signs of blood. The shotgun that had wounded Burrows was still there, or, rather, bits and pieces of it were—mostly just the barrel. The shredded weapon appeared to be floating in the air, a gun with no one to fire it.

He took a step closer, and as he did, he got his first glimpse of the heavy fishing line on the floor and then of an elaborate arrangement of pulleys mounted near the door—and another near the stairs, where someone had lashed a shotgun to the post.

"Well, I'll be damned!" he said. It had been a trap. A booby trap, and Special Agent Burrows of the FBI had charged right into it.

SAMUEL waited in the truck for a long time before walking into the little restaurant for directions. He hated asking for directions. Not just because he scared people sometimes, but because when they started to tell him, the words oftentimes came too fast.

A thin lady stood at a podium. "Can I help you, sir?"

"Yes, ma'am," Samuel said, scraping the filthy John Deere cap off his dirty hair. "I was wondering if you could point me toward an address." He pulled the rumpled camping permit out of his pocket and read the street number to her.

The lady knew exactly where that place was. "You drive straight across the railroad tracks there and around the curve and at your very first opportunity, hang a left. That will put you on Clinton Road. Then you just go straight for a mile, maybe a mile and a half."

Samuel closed his eyes as he listened, trying to visualize what she was saying, and when he opened them again, he thought he had it.

"Thank you very much." He walked back out to the parking lot.

He drove slowly, following the lady's directions and examining the house numbers that were posted on trees or posts or rocks. Lots and lots of driveways, but no houses that he could see.

There! That was the number right there! He saw it on a post next to the mailbox.

Drive in slow now, Jacob told him.

He wasn't sure why Jacob had decided to come driving with him, but when he'd first heard the voice, he nearly drove the truck into a tree. He couldn't see him, but he could sure hear his voice.

Turn your lights off. Surprise means everything, Samuel.

"You just hush up. I know what I'm doing."

Bright carriage lights on either side of the front door made the night seem like day up near the house, so Samuel decided to park in the shadow of the trees, where no one would see him.

Samuel pulled open the truck's door, swung his legs around, and lowered himself to the ground oh, so softly.

Don't forget the gun, Jacob told him.

"I'm not forgetting anything," Samuel whispered sharply. He stuffed the Ruger automatic into the waistband of his jeans.

Jacob had taken him on a lot of the jobs he used to do and shared in detail every little thing. Only before—well, you know, *before*— Samuel's job was mainly just to keep an eye out. One of Jacob's most important rules was to always enter from the rear of a house. Samuel made an effort to stay in the shadows as he worked his way around the left side of the enormous brick home.

"I need to find the phone line first," he whispered as he clicked on his flashlight, looking along the foundation for the telltale wire to the gray box. He giggled with glee when he found it within seconds. Sure enough, there was the raised picture of a telephone with a bell in the middle of it. He used a Swiss Army knife to turn the screw that kept the little plastic cover closed. Inside there were the phone connections: two wires with little plastic clips on the end. Noiselessly he slipped the blade under the wires and cut them cleanly away from the plugs.

Now it was time to find a way inside.

RUSSELL Coates had finally gotten around to checking in with the Fairfield County police, a courtesy that should have been his first order of business. As it turned out, he needn't have been concerned. The duty shift commander, a Captain Himler, made him feel right at home, granting him a desk and a phone, free access to all the files he needed, and all the coffee he could drink.

"Why don't you just reach out and touch this guy if you're so sure he did it?" Himler asked after being filled in on what Russell had found so far. "I mean, you've got the tires, and you can put him at the park and at the convenience store where the shooting was called in. What more do you need?"

Russell thought for a moment before answering. "I guess I'm just not comfortable with it yet. It's like I've got all the pieces, but none of the glue to hold them all together."

Himler shrugged. "If it were my case, the guy would've been in interrogation for two hours now."

Russell shook his head. "Not this guy. He's smart and he's rich. He'd lawyer up before you even thought of the first question."

Russell's cell phone chirped. He snapped it open. "Coates."

"This is Chuck Wheatley." Russell recognized the voice from his field office. "We just got word that Tim Burrows has been shot."

Russell gasped reflexively. "Oh, no! Is he all right?"

"We don't know yet. He was checking out a lead on your murder case, and he opened a door that was rigged with a shotgun. He's still alive, but he's lost a lot of blood. He's in surgery now."

Russell checked his watch. "Damn, I'll never get a flight at this hour. I'll catch the first one out in the morning. When he gets out of surgery, give me a call."

"You got it. And there's one other thing. You said you were looking for any reports of kidnappings. We just received an all-points from Pittsburgh about a little boy—a two-year-old named Justin

Fitzgerald—who was yanked from his stepfather last night and is apparently being held as leverage in some drug operation. Since then the stepfather's been whacked by a sniper, the mother's been arrested robbing a department store, and the whole deal is somehow tied in with the murder of a drug lord. Think it has anything to do with your park killing?"

Russell shrugged. "I don't know. The kidnapping I was looking for was an adult. I don't know how a little kid could fit—"

The footprints. The Pampers.

A door in his mind opened and shut again, teasing him with the solution. "Thanks, Chuck. Remember to call me about Tim."

Russell slapped the phone closed and leaned forward with his elbows on the desk. The answer was so close.

What did he know? He knew that a child was kidnapped from Pittsburgh. He knew that Jacob Stanns was shot dead while either being buried alive or burying someone else alive. But the murder was so far away from the burial site.

Could this Justin Fitzgerald be the key? Could this be the boy for whom Robert Martin shelled out more money than he expected for a box of diapers, at the same convenience store where someone happened to report a murder?

Russell still didn't have his arms completely around it, but he sure knew enough to bring this Martin guy in for questioning. Rising from his desk, he headed toward the shift commander's office.

It was time to see about some reinforcements.

Eight

EXHAUSTION crushed Bobby's body. Mentally and physically, there was nothing left. And now, as they lay together in the bed, the three of them—Bobby, Susan, and . . . Steven—his body demanded that he sleep, but his mind wouldn't let it happen.

This was their truce. They would spend the night as a family together. But there it would end. Bobby simply couldn't take it anymore. In the morning he would telephone Agent Coates.

What was that?

Something startled him, jolting his heart. He realized now that he'd dozed off, if only because he was so conscious of being wide-awake. He must have heard a noise.

He sat there for a long time, listening to the night. But he heard only the syncopated rhythms of Susan and Steven breathing.

The longer he listened, the safer the night seemed. He strained to see the security alarm's annunciator panel on the wall. His heart skipped again as he saw a green light glowing where there should have been red. He'd forgotten to set the damn thing.

He swung his feet around to correct his omission. He froze in place, though, even before his feet touched the floor. This time, there was no mistaking the sound he heard.

Somewhere downstairs a door opened and then closed.

CLIMBING in through the basement window had been Jacob's idea. *Houses this big always have alarms,* he'd told Samuel, *but a lot of times, they don't hook up to the basement.*

Letting the flashlight beam lead the way, Samuel quietly crossed the basement to the wooden stairs. He tried not to let himself be distracted. He had a job to do. The Boss said so, and you don't mess with the Boss.

The staircase creaked under his weight. If this place had an alarm, it would probably be hooked to the door at the top of the stairs. He opened the door quickly and laughed a little when everything remained quiet.

He lost concentration, though, as he stepped out into the huge kitchen, and he let the door close too quickly behind him. It didn't slam exactly, but it made a lot more noise than he wanted.

His mouth gaped as he took in the hugeness of this place. How was he going to find Justin in a place this big?

People sleep upstairs.

He followed his light beam around to the right and on into the short hallway that led to the foyer, and there he found it. In the mottled artificial light a curved stairway seemed to be floating in the air.

He started up the treads, keeping the aim of his automatic focused at the top, where anyone who wanted to stop him would have to appear.

Get the boy. Just get the boy. Don't worry about anybody else. Do whatever you have to do.

"I will, okay? Just let me think. Just let me think. . . ."

CAPTAIN Himler was nodding his head even before Russell had finished with his explanation. He made a quick phone call, then hung up. "I can get you six patrol officers if you can wait a couple of minutes."

Russell checked his watch. "Sure. A couple of minutes can't hurt, and I'd like to have the manpower, just in case."

THE footsteps were in the foyer now.

Bobby couldn't believe it. He jostled his wife sharply. "Susan! Wake up! I think there's somebody in the house."

"What!"

"Shh." Bobby snatched the telephone off the nightstand to call the police, but it was like listening to an earmuff. "It's dead!"

"We've got to get out of the house," he said. Bobby's mind raced. If they tried to go out the front windows, they'd fall two stories; out the back, it'd be three.

The back porch! That was it! They needed to cross the bridge over the foyer, and if they made it to the nursery, they could climb out onto the porch roof. From there it was only ten feet to the ground. They could survive that. But they had to get there first.

"Come on," he said, leading the way to the bedroom door. "Quickly. It's our only chance."

Susan didn't want to go, but she didn't argue either.

When she had gathered Steven into her arms, Bobby pulled the door open and stepped out into the hall.

SAMUEL had just been wondering which room to start in, when he heard people talking and moving around quickly.

He quickened his pace, the gun outstretched. Just as he reached for the handle, the door flew open. There in front of him, not five feet away, was the man he remembered from the woods. The man yelled as he saw Samuel, and Samuel yelled back.

Shoot them! Jacob told him.

Without thinking about it, he brought the weapon up and pulled the trigger.

BOBBY saw the stranger's arm move and somehow knew what was going to happen next. Intuitively he launched himself at the burglar, hitting him square in the chest. For just an instant he wondered if the explosion that rocked his body was the sound of his bones shattering.

The intruder seemed as surprised as Bobby, and off-balance, too. The impact drove him back toward the railing and the marble foyer below. The wood of the railing cracked on impact, but it held.

Gathering the fabric of the man's jacket into his fists, Bobby hauled him away from the railing and then tried to heave him back toward the same spot on the rail. But the surprise had evaporated by now, and the intruder was having none of it.

"Susan, run!" Bobby yelled, just before a punch to the side of his head left him feeling rattled. He refused to let go. "Go, Susan!"

The intruder roared, "I'm not a pussy, dammit!" And then he hit Bobby with everything he had.

SAMUEL felt the guy's grip loosen on the first punch, and on the second he went reeling across the hallway. Regaining his balance, Samuel brought the pistol up. But then he saw the woman and the little boy darting down the hallway.

Shoot!

"I can't! I'll hit Justin!"

Instead, he charged after them. He didn't know where they were running to or why they'd try to get to another room on the same floor, but then again, he didn't much care. They never had a chance.

He took the woman off her feet simply by snagging her hair in his fist.

SUSAN FELT HERSELF GOING down and hugged Steven in close. They hit hard, and the boy leaped to his feet, screaming. He turned and started toward the stairs.

"I got you!" the intruder yelled. He got Steven around the middle, but the boy squirmed so severely that Samuel couldn't hang on. The boy fell, rolled to his feet, and scrambled for the steps.

He'd nearly made it when Samuel went for an ankle.

"Leave him alone!" Susan shrieked, and she launched herself at the gunman, digging her nails deeply into the flesh of his face.

SAMUEL yelled as the nails slashed his cheeks. He hadn't expected this kind of fight. Jacob was right again. He should have just shot them when he first saw them. Now this bitch was on his back, where he couldn't get a shot, and little Justin was getting away.

Get the kid, dammit!

"I'm trying." But the woman wouldn't let go. In fact, it seemed that the more he struggled, the tighter her hold became.

Through a haze of tears Samuel saw the boy nearly at the stairs and lashed out with his foot.

HE WAS kicking the boy down the steps! Bobby couldn't get his vision to clear completely, but he sure saw Steven teetering at the top step. His wife was screaming. The boy was hysterical.

A fall from here would kill him; that's all there was to it.

Bobby scrambled drunkenly across the carpet and snagged the little one's nightie-night the very instant he began to topple. The material held, and he was able to pull him in to safety.

"Oh, my God! Bobby!" Susan's shrieks reached a new level.

Bobby whirled to see the stranger standing upright again, his forearm tucked tightly under Susan's chin, his pistol at her head.

"I only want Justin," he said. "I don't want you, and I don't want her. I have to take Justin back."

An icy hand gripped Bobby's insides as he realized that he could no longer win this. "Please put the gun down."

"Give Justin back to me, and I will."

Bobby wondered if the man was drunk. His words seemed thick.

Not slurred really, just labored. Drugs maybe? "Who's Justin?" Bobby asked, a play for more time. Time to think.

"You know who he is. Give him to me, and I won't hurt her." The man pressed the muzzle in harder to emphasize his point.

"Let him kill me," Susan sobbed. "I can't lose my baby again."

Bobby's breaths came in quick, short gulps. He looked from his wife to her captor, wondering what to do.

"I'll do it," Samuel said. "I'll count to four, and then I'll kill her and I'll kill you, and I'll still get Justin. Let him go."

"No, Bobby! Please."

"One . . ."

"I'll do it!" Bobby shouted the words and hurried forward with the boy. "Here, take him. Let her go."

"Bobby, no!"

Steven went nuts, squirming and kicking.

"Bobby!" Susan shrieked. "You can't give up our baby!"

"Take him!" Bobby yelled. "Do it now and get out of here."

In one quick motion the man let go of Susan and scooped Steven out of Bobby's arms.

Susan charged at the intruder, screaming, eyes filled with murder.

Samuel started around with the pistol, but Bobby tackled his wife, wrestling her to the ground.

"Go!" Bobby shouted. "I've got her! Just go!"

Samuel tried to hold his aim, but the squirming boy was giving him fits. "I heard you!" he shouted angrily, and at first Bobby thought he was talking to him. Then he realized that this man who'd broken into his house was embroiled in a shouting match with someone who wasn't even there.

"The boy's the most important!" the intruder ranted on. "You said so yourself. I've got him, and I'm gonna take him back."

He shouted on like that the whole way down the stairs and on out the front door, his voice ultimately drowned out by Steven's— or Justin's—high-pitched squeals.

Bobby would never have guessed that his wife could be so strong. Hanging on to her was like riding a bucking bronc in a rodeo. She squirmed and twisted. She tried to bite him.

"Susan, stop! Dammit, stop!"

"My baby! You let my baby go! You gave him away!"

"He's not our baby, Susan! That man was going to kill you and then take him anyway!"

"Let me go!" She got a wrist free and pummeled him, pounding his face and his ears, the blows landing with stunning force. Bobby felt the fight drain out of him in a wave of agony. He let go and rolled himself into a protective ball.

Susan didn't hesitate an instant. She jumped to her feet and tore down the stairs, taking them two, three, four at a time.

She dashed through the foyer and the opened front door, shrieking to the night. "Bring him back, you bastard! Bring back my baby!"

RUSSELL Coates opted to ride in the lead cruiser. Captain Himler was at the wheel, leading a procession of four vehicles through the downtown center of Clinton. Out here reception on his cellular phone was fragile, and he had to keep a finger pushed into his other ear to hear the latest on Tim Burrows's condition.

Himler waited until Russell hung up to ask, "How's he doing?"

"They don't know yet. It's a pretty bad belly wound, and he's still in surgery."

Himler shook his head. "Damned shame. And you think these folks we're after had something to do with it?"

"That's what my instincts tell me, yes. I think the Martins are up to their eyeballs in something they shouldn't be involved with."

A few minutes later the police vehicles were scattered around the Martin property, their light bars shimmering.

"It's your scene, Agent Coates," Himler said as they approached the front door. "You may do the honors."

Russell nodded, then stepped up and rang the bell. Ten seconds passed, and he switched to the knocker. "Robert Martin!" he yelled. "This is the FBI. I have a warrant to take you into custody."

This time he didn't even wait for a reply. If the suspects hadn't answered by now, to hell with them.

Two patrol officers stepped forward with a battering ram, and after one practice swing, they sent the decorative cherry-stained door exploding open in a hailstorm of wood fragments and broken glass.

Two minutes later the primary search was completed and the house was declared empty.

So I spooked them, Russell thought. Where would I run if I were them?

A patrol officer yelled from above, "Captain Himler, I think you might want to take a look at this."

Every eye turned to the cop on the bridge over the foyer.

"We got a bullet hole and signs of a fight up here."

SAMUEL hit the sack with his flashlight, and it stopped squirming. "Quit making me do that!" he scolded. "Just be quiet and enjoy the ride. This is a game, okay? I don't want to hurt you. I don't want to hurt anybody—so just settle down."

Why did they call the boy Steven? he wondered. If his real name was Justin, why would they call him Steven? It didn't make sense.

Just like a lot of things didn't make any sense. Like, why did Jacob have to die? Why couldn't he have won the fight and gone on to do all of this stuff with the Boss? Samuel hated this stuff. Every time he thought about the Boss, his heart would hammer in his chest.

On the days when Samuel allowed himself to be brutally honest about everything, he knew very well what Jacob's business with the Boss was all about. He knew that these nighttime outings were sometimes about killing bad people. He wondered, though, about this stuff with Justin. Jacob said it was a game. But Samuel didn't much like this notion of stuffing a little boy in a sack and putting him in that room underground. He didn't like that at all. Part of him wondered just how asleep he really was when the boy got away the first time.

Now that he thought back on it, he could almost remember watching the boy struggle out of the hole and take off into the woods. He remembered thinking how nice it would be if the boy got away.

Of course, that was before Jacob had come up and seen that he was missing. That was before he got so mad and told Samuel to stand still in the woods while he got himself shot.

Those were all really bad memories, and that same part of him that remembered them also wondered why he was going back out to the same woods all over again.

BY ALL indications, it had been a hell of a fight. The railing over the foyer was barely holding together anymore, and the bullet hole in the doorframe spoke volumes to Russell. The bags of new children's clothes and toys intrigued him as well.

"I'm entertaining any theories you might have," Himler said. "Do you think the Martins were the shooters or the shootees?"

Interesting question. Russell still couldn't make the link between a foiled kidnapping and all of the bloodshed that had followed. He supposed that the Martins might have surprised an intruder and fired off a shot, but it seemed equally likely that the intruder surprised them with the intent to murder. Of course, the second case begged the question: Why and how did he flub it so miserably?

"I don't know what to tell you." Russell pinched the bridge of his nose, hoping to ward off a headache. "What I need is a way to snap my fingers and be in Pittsburgh. Whatever's going down here, that seems to be the common denominator."

"What'll it take, four, five hours to drive?"

"Something like that. But I'm dead on my feet. I need to crash someplace for a couple of hours before I head out."

"I can get you a ride," Himler offered.

Russell waved the offer away. "I can't put one of your officers through a drive like that just so I can sleep in the car."

"I wasn't talking about a car. I was talking about a helicopter."

"WE'LL get him back, Susan. I swear it."

She refused to speak to him. Instead, she stared out the car window at the passing darkness.

"Dammit, Susan, don't do this. He was going to kill you!"

"And now he's going to kill Steven," she shot back. "God—"

"Yes, God sent him to us. I hear you. That doesn't mitigate the fact that you can't just take possession of another human being."

"Well, you *killed* a human being. There's your big problem. It's not Steven, and it's not me. It's how are you going to get away with killing a police officer?"

"He wasn't a police officer," Bobby said.

"How do you know?"

"Well, I guess I don't *know*. But there's been no mention of it. Not in the news, not when the FBI guy came to the door this afternoon. If he were really a cop, we'd have heard something by now."

"Then who was he?"

Bobby shrugged. "I don't know that either. But remember when he and I were struggling out there in the woods? Remember he kept calling out for Samuel? I think that Samuel just came and took Steven away."

Susan's scowl began to show fear. "But why?"

"I suppose to finish off whatever it was that his buddy had started. Whatever we interrupted."

"But the dead guy had a badge."

"So what? Anybody can have a badge. Go down to the army surplus store, and you can have one, too. If I'm right, the guy I killed was a kidnapper. He wasn't shooting to protect the boy; he was shooting to get him back."

"So is that why you think they're heading back to the woods?" Susan asked. "To finish off whatever they were going to do?"

Bobby nodded. "Yes. Did you hear what Samuel said to Steven in the hallway? He said they were going back. To me, that means back to where all of this started. Whatever he's got planned, it has to take place back there. I'm just hoping that it turns out to be the woods."

They drove in silence for a long time before Susan said, "Do you think we should call the police now?"

Bobby had to laugh. Where was that question ten hours ago? "No, not anymore. If we call it in, they're going to want us to sit down and talk through it all. We don't have the time."

As they drove on through the narrowing roads and deepening woods, Susan found herself watching Bobby drive, watching that hard expression that she'd never seen before they lost Steven the first time and now seemed never to leave. That expression said it all. He'd worked so hard to be the rock that suddenly Susan wasn't sure that she'd ever given him the room to grieve on his own. Suddenly she saw things with a remarkable clarity. What once seemed fuzzy and confusing now seemed perfectly sharp. She realized for the first time what he must have gone through these past hours, these past weeks. She understood that she was alive now because he'd been selfless enough to throw himself in front of a madman's gun. That scene back on the bridge in the house wasn't about giving up Steven. It was about saving her.

And now here he was, every bit as terrified as she, driving through the night to rescue a little boy he'd never even come to know.

"You know," she said. "I really do love you."

"I love you, too." He tossed a forced smile her way.

"It occurs to me that I've been something of a jerk today."

"Have you?" he asked, a genuine smile finally cracking through that look of stress and gloom. "I hadn't noticed."

As IT turned out, discovering the body in the woods and all the attendant nonsense surrounding it was the best part of Ranger Sarah Rodgers's day. Ten minutes after Agent Coates drove out of Catoctin National Forest, she'd received a report of a brush fire on the far southern end of the seventy-three-thousand-acre facility. A cold front had brought rain, but by the time they were able to contain the blaze, it had charred over twenty acres of old-growth hardwood.

But even that wasn't the low point of the day. According to the Weather Service, they could now expect the temperature to drop through the night to an unseasonable twenty-five degrees, with snow that would accumulate up to six inches by morning.

All of this would mean stranded campers, short staffs, and a sixty-five-hour workday for Sarah. Even now, as she piloted her green Chevy pickup into one of the parking slots in front of the ranger station, she noted the big heavy flakes that tumbled through the beams of her headlights.

Ranger Gardner Blackwell looked up from the papers on his desk as Sarah walked through the door. "Coffee's on the burner," he said, offering a big buck-toothed smile. "Just made a fresh pot."

"You're a lifesaver, Gard." Sarah poured coffee into a heavy white mug, then helped herself to a chair in front of Gardner's desk and watched him sift through park passes. "Got any murderers in there tonight?"

"Only three that I know of," he replied without dropping a beat. "But I sent them all down to area one. Thought the Tourist Center could use a little excitement."

"Kinda weird, though, isn't it?" Sarah mused. "Chances are we've handled paperwork that was filled out by a killer."

Gardner cocked his head as he regarded her. "How weirdly morbid. I think it's time for you to take a nap."

"That time passed unnoticed about twelve hours ago."

They shared a laugh before Gardner changed the subject. "Oh, before I forget, we've got to get some new chain strung at the entrance road at the top of Challenger Trail. It's busted again. I just noticed it on my last rounds."

Sarah tried to remember precisely where Challenger was.

"Connects to Powhite," he said. "Leads to Route 630."

Of course. She never ceased to be amazed by the extent some people would go to save a few bucks on a permit. "Put it in tomorrow's briefing for everybody to be hard-asses on permits for the next few days. No excuses. Any signs of who might have broken the chain?"

"I just assumed it was kids. You think it had something to do with the murder?"

"I think I should include it in my next chat with my FBI contacts. What have you heard from the patrols about the condition of the roads?"

Gardner rose from his chair and carried her empty cup back to the coffeepot. "None of them have mentioned anything, so I guess things are still in good shape. I'll ask them when they check in."

He didn't bother asking her if she wanted a refill. She'd already fallen asleep.

IT HADN'T occurred to Samuel until he cleared the pass at the top of the mountain that he'd forgotten to put the bolt cutters back into the truck. If someone had replaced the chain across that road, he'd have to think of something pretty quickly. As he pulled off

Route 630, he nearly cheered when he spotted the barricade right where they'd left it, lying in the dirt.

He tried turning off the headlights the way his brother had done the night before, but he turned them back on after barely missing a tree. Fifty yards later he realized that even the headlights weren't enough to see properly, so he parked the truck and turned it off.

Walking around to the passenger side, Samuel opened the door and lifted the sack from the floor down onto the wet ground.

The boy didn't move while he untied the cord that knotted the mouth of the bag, and for a brief moment Samuel worried that maybe Justin was hurt. As the fabric fell away, though, he saw that the little boy was just fine. He lay on his side, with his eyes open, his thumb stuck into his mouth.

Samuel squatted down. "Hey, little boy," he said cheerily. "We're almost there, okay? You gonna be a good boy this time?"

Justin said nothing. He didn't even make eye contact.

"I need you to stand up now, okay, Justin?"

But the boy did not move. Maybe he was just too tired. "Want me to carry you instead?"

Again the boy didn't respond, but Samuel got him up anyway. His little butt rested on Samuel's forearm, and the mussed mop of hair rested on his shoulders.

Justin smelled like babies always do, kind of sweaty, but tonight, there was a new smell. Baby powder. That was it. And it smelled delightful, filling Samuel's head with the kinds of memories that never seemed to come anymore. Each night when he closed his eyes, all he saw recently were the jobs he'd done with Jacob. Those people were all bad, he thought, and the Boss said they had to be taken care of.

But what kind of game makes you bury a little boy? That was a new voice in Samuel's brain. That was his *own* voice.

Samuel found himself hugging Justin closer to his chest as he worked his way through the thick woods. The boy's little body trembled in his arms. "Are you cold?"

That was a stupid question, wasn't it? Of course the boy was cold. It was snowing out! Samuel unzipped his coat and wrapped one of the flaps around Justin's pajama-clad body.

"Just a little bit further. Just a little bit further, and we'll be with the Boss. Then everything will be just fine."

The Boss is going to hurt him. There was Samuel's own voice again.

"No, he won't," Samuel insisted aloud. "He's not going to hurt anybody. He told me so. Isn't that right, Jacob?"

He waited for an answer, but none came.

THE shriek of the telephone nearly launched Sarah out of her chair. Gardner brought the handset up to his ear. "Area five. . . . Oh, yeah, she's here, but it may take me a minute to get her fingernails out of the ceiling."

Sarah stuck her tongue out at him and reached for the phone. "This is Sarah Rodgers. Who's this?"

"Jerry Bartlett down at entrance four. Thought you'd like to know that your favorite Explorer is back in the park."

Sarah was instantly awake. "You mean the one from last night?"

"Yeah. I just finished collecting the entry permits, and I happened to notice the license number matched the one we were told to look out for. Once through the gate, I don't know where they headed, but I thought you'd want to know right away."

She couldn't believe it. Criminals really do return to the scene of the crime! "Okay. Listen to me, Jerry. I need you to make a phone call for me." She read a number to him off a business card from her pocket. "Call that number, tell whoever answers exactly what you told me, and then meet me at the bottom of Powhite Trail."

Dropping the phone into its cradle, she turned to Gardner. "Grab a shotgun. I think this evening is about to get really exciting."

THE Bell Jet Ranger was all over the sky. Near the Blue Ridge the fine, chilly weather of northern Virginia had quickly turned. What had once been clear, starry skies now looked like thick gray ink as the heavy clouds reflected the chopper's blinking strobes.

Russell sat in the back of the chopper this time, watching over the shoulders of the two pilots for signs of panic. "You're sure it's safe to be up here, right?" he asked over the intercom.

The uniformed cop on the right—the command pilot—half turned as he keyed his intercom. "Agent Coates, you need to relax. It's a little rougher than usual, but you're perfectly safe."

Russell loved the way pilots practiced the art of understatement. And the edge of annoyance was not lost on him. They were flying through this crap as a favor to him.

According to Russell's latest information, Tim Burrows was out of surgery, and the doctors had sent out word that there was every reason to be optimistic. Russell said a little prayer of thanks.

"Agent Coates." The pilot's voice cracked in his earphones. "I've got a call for you here. I'm gonna patch it through to your headset."

Russell heard a brief burst of static.

"Agent Coates? This is air-traffic control in Charleston, sir, with an urgent message from your office. Ranger Sarah Rodgers reports that the Martins' Explorer has been spotted in Catoctin National Forest."

Russell's eyebrows nearly left his forehead.

"Do you copy, sir?"

"Affirmative, I copy. Thank you very much."

In another hiss of static Russell's headset was disconnected from the main radio. Now this was damned interesting. Why would an attack in their home bring them back to the woods?

"Okay, guys," he said into his intercom. "We need to change the plans a bit. . . ."

THE accumulating snow masked many of the landmarks that Bobby remembered from last night. It was colder, too, and while his jacket kept his body warm, he wished he'd brought a hat.

"Suppose this isn't where they went?" Susan asked as they walked up the Powhite Trail, her hands tucked into her armpits for warmth.

"This is it," Bobby replied, hoping that saying it firmly enough would make it true.

Bobby's logic for being here was simple: Last night, Steven had come running to them from upstream, which meant that wherever his ordeal had started was centered somewhere uphill from where they'd camped. His plan was to go there and wait. It was that simple. Now that he was here, though, it seemed *too* simple, too driven by coincidence. These woods were big even on a clear day. On a snowy night they felt even bigger. The more he thought about it, the more stupid and hopeless it all seemed.

Suppose they're not even here? Suppose they went to an airport?

These thoughts tortured him as they continued up the steep incline. If he was wrong, then he supposed it would be time to make that phone call to the FBI.

As for Steven, it would be time to pray. Hard.

It NEVER occurred to Samuel to wonder about the other car. He saw it sitting there among the trees, and he assumed it belonged to the Boss, but he kept on walking toward the special place in the woods where they would play their game. The snow fell and fell, the big flakes accumulating on the outside of Samuel's jacket. Little Justin curled tighter and burrowed deeper. He still hadn't said a thing.

Samuel's doubts grew steadily. Maybe he didn't want to continue working Jacob's job. Maybe this would be the last time that Samuel ever dealt with the Boss. So why keep going at all, then? Why not turn around and take Justin home?

Because the Boss knows where you live, you dummy.

"Don't call me that! Just keep your mouth shut."

At the sound of Samuel's shouting, Justin started to cry. Instantly Samuel felt terrible. "Oh, it's not you. I was just talking to Jacob."

It was Samuel's turn to jump when a voice boomed from the shadows, "Who the hell are you talking to?"

He whirled around, leading with his flashlight. "Who is that?" he yelled. He shifted the boy and the flashlight to his left hand while he dug the Ruger out of his pocket with his right.

"Whoa, there, Sammy," said a new voice, this one coming from farther over to his left. "You just be careful with that gun."

Samuel shifted the beam accordingly and caught a glimpse of a young man standing in a clump of trees, holding his own pistol. He thought he recognized the voice. "You're the Boss."

"No, *I'm* the boss," said the first voice. A big man with red hair stepped forward. "And you have a package for me."

Give him the boy, Jacob told Samuel.

Samuel shook his head. He didn't like the looks of this. Didn't like the looks these men had in their eyes. He stepped back.

"Not thinking of leaving us, are you, Sammy?" asked the man with the gun.

Actually, that's exactly what he was thinking.

IN FIFTEEN years as a park ranger Sarah had never once pointed her firearm at another human being. In fact, she had always seen her obligatory pistol as more of an ornament than a weapon—no more threatening than her Smokey the Bear hat or her badge.

Gardner seemed impressed that she'd known exactly where to find the Explorer parked. "I figured there was only one place for them to be," she explained.

As they climbed the Powhite, following the steadily filling footprints on the trail, she found herself wishing that she hadn't been quite so aggressive. These people were murderers, after all, and she felt unprepared for a midnight shootout. Gardner's 12-gauge helped, but even a hail of buckshot wouldn't do much to stop a well-aimed bullet from piercing her unarmored body.

"Well, I'm scared," Gardner said as lightly as he could. He made no bones about his distaste for the law-enforcement aspects of his job. "You sure we can't just wait for the sheriff's deputies to take care of this?"

As much as she wanted to say yes, she found herself shaking her head no. "In good weather it takes them twenty minutes to get up here. Tonight it'll be twice that. Look, Gard, if it helps, I'm not feeling particularly suicidal or heroic this evening."

"Makes me feel all aglow and comfy."

TORN STUBS OF CRIME-SCENE tape still clung to the trees all around them. Without those clues Bobby wasn't sure that he could even have found the old campsite. It seemed so different. In the distance they could still hear the rush of the river, but with the snow muffling everything, even that sounded different.

As they walked into the tiny clearing, Bobby hesitantly illuminated the area at the base of the tree where the body had lain. He felt a sense of genuine relief when he saw that it was gone.

"Steven!"

Susan's cry made him jump a foot. "Where? Where is he?"

"I know you're out there, honey. Come to your mommy!"

He understood now that she didn't actually see anything. She was hoping. And drawing a lot of attention to herself if their attacker was out there. Still, if everybody stayed quiet, no one would find anything.

"GIVE us the boy," said Ricky Timmons, his voice menacing.

Samuel took a step backward. These men wanted to hurt the boy. "You—you stay away," he stammered.

"Oh, for God's sake," grumbled the tall, redheaded man. "Just end this crap."

Samuel saw Ricky's gun hand arc up, and he raised his own. Ricky fired first, an enormous muzzle flash that seemed to rock the whole forest. The Ruger split the night as well, kicking hard against the heel of his hand as Samuel pulled again and again. In the strobes of the muzzle flashes Samuel thought he saw the other man fall.

He thought it, but couldn't be positive, because now he was running, plunging through the woods downhill. From behind he heard still more gunshots, but he never even glanced around to see. There was no time for that. He had to get little Justin back to safety.

The flashlight splashed through the woods, casting weird shadows as he ducked and dived past branches and over rocks.

And the boy was cooperating now. He stayed perfectly still, allowing himself to be hugged tightly to Samuel's chest.

The very same chest that glistened black and wet in the night.

SUSAN SCREAMED AT THE cacophony of gunshots. They sounded so close, but as they echoed and deflected through the forest, they could have been coming from anywhere.

"I think it was from up there." Bobby pointed up the trail.

Susan pointed more to the left. "No. From there."

They split the difference and left the trail, heading toward the river. Susan wanted to run, but Bobby held her back. "If we make too much noise, we'll never hear anything."

"But Steven!" she breathed. "I know he's hurt. I *feel* it."

"I hope not," Bobby whispered. "But if he is, we'll never be able to help if we can't find him."

DOWN the trail Sarah and Gardner recognized the sounds for what they were and quickened their pace, breaking into the closest thing to a run that the steep slope would allow.

"Sounds close," she gasped. "Keep your eyes wide-open."

"I'll keep them open for the deputies is what I'll keep them open for."

"OH, GOD, little boy, are you hurt?"

Even as Samuel stumbled through the forest, he brought the boy out from under his jacket and held him out to get a better look. The lower half of his nightie-nights was soaked in blood.

"Oh, no. Oh, no. You're hurt, aren't you?"

But Justin didn't seem to be. Now that he was exposed to the snow and the cold, he started wriggling all over again.

It's not him, you idiot. It's you.

Samuel gasped, and as he did, a terrible pain stabbed him deep in his guts. He yelled out, an animal-like howl.

"You lied to me, Jacob. You lied to me!" Samuel choked the words out of his throat as he continued his downhill stumble. "You promised me it was a game. You promised!"

Suddenly Samuel's legs weighed a hundred pounds each. Sheer force of will kept them moving down the hill, and it took all the concentration he could muster to keep from falling face first.

If he fell, he'd hurt the boy. Can't do that.

His stomach hurt bad. There was blood in his throat, making him cough. And still he plunged through the woods. Tears streamed down his face as he realized just how stupid he'd really been.

"THAT sounds like a person," Susan said hurriedly as the two of them jolted to a halt.

Bobby agreed. That's exactly what it sounded like. And they both knew exactly the direction from which it came.

Finally it was time to run.

RUSSELL handed the pilot the sheet of paper on which he'd jotted down the radio frequencies from that morning. "Dial these into your radio," he said over his intercom.

For the first time the pilots seemed unnerved by the weather. They didn't say anything, but Russell could see it in their faces.

When the frequency was set, Russell heard the familiar pop in his headset. He opened with, "Fairfield County Helicopter Eagle One to Catoctin National Forest ranger units, how do you copy?"

A tinny, breathless voice came back. "Go ahead, Eagle One."

Russell smiled. "Ranger Rodgers, I presume."

"They're here!" she shouted. "They're here at the murder scene from this morning, and shots have been fired."

This got everyone's attention. The copilot started digging for the map that would show the layout of Catoctin National Forest.

"Is anyone hit?" Russell asked.

"I don't know. The shots were not directed at us, but they were close by."

"Do you have backup on the way?"

"That's affirmative, but they're still a long ways out."

"Okay, Sarah. Stand by." This time he keyed the intercom button. "Hold that map up so I can see it."

The copilot shifted the map and the gooseneck light while Russell leaned in closer. It took him a good thirty seconds to get himself oriented, and then he pointed to the spot where he'd spent the morning investigating. "That's where she is. Now, where are we?"

The copilot pointed to a spot east and south of Sarah's location.

"That's about seven minutes from here, but I'm not sure about flight conditions—"

Russell keyed the radio mike before the copilot could finish. "Sarah, this is Coates. We'll be there in six minutes."

EACH step felt as if somebody were running a hot knife through Samuel's guts. His head had begun to feel funny, and while he knew that only pussies cried, he couldn't help himself.

And somebody was following him.

He couldn't bear to turn around and look.

His steps had slowed to a virtual stagger, though in his mind he was still running as fast as he could. He heard people.

Were they coming up behind him? Were they coming to hurt little Justin? He couldn't let that happen.

He'd die first.

BOBBY heard the big man approaching at the exact same instant he saw him. Recognition came instantly. This was the man from the hallway, the man who'd threatened to kill him and his family.

"Steven!" Before Bobby could stop her, Susan bolted forward to retrieve the boy, who wrenched himself free of his captor's hands and dropped to his hands and knees in the mulch.

The big man struggled to get a hand on the boy, but he never had a chance. He stood there for a long moment, listing off to the side and trying to gather the strength to lift the pistol that just barely dangled from his right hand.

"No!" Bobby shouted, and lunged at him, just as he'd lunged the night before, only this time his opponent fell easily.

The man howled in agony as he fell. "Help him," he gasped. "Help the little boy."

Bobby wrenched the pistol from the big man's hand. He threw the weapon into the woods. Curiously, Bobby noticed that the man was crying the way a child cries when he's ashamed. He tried to cover his face, but it was as if his hands were just too heavy to move.

"I'm so sorry," he sobbed.

Bobby leaned in closer. "You're hurt. Is your name Samuel?"

Samuel's lip trembled as he nodded.

Bobby knelt up straight and looked back over his shoulder to see Susan locked in an embrace with Steven. Well, whatever came of all this, at least they were finally safe.

Three inches from his head a two-inch gash exploded from the side of a tree at the very instant that the woods shook from another gunshot. Susan screamed and tried to shelter the baby while Bobby scrambled toward them. Two more shots passed within inches.

"Who is that?" Susan screamed.

Bobby ran full tilt, grabbing a fistful of his wife's coat and dragging her away. "Run!" he hissed. "Run! Run! Run!"

Susan had difficulty finding her balance as Bobby pushed her through the woods. "Let me carry him," he said, reaching out to grab Steven, but Susan turned away.

"I've got him."

"Fine. Then move!"

The worst part was not knowing where the shooter was. In the darkness they could be running in circles and never know it.

The river beckoned Bobby. The sound stood out above all others, and as long as he knew where that river was, then he'd at least know north from south. As they plunged through the woods, he found himself drawn toward the water at an oblique angle.

If this were a different time of year, the rushing waters might provide them with a means of escape, but here, in the frigid cold and the snow, the river was a death sentence in itself.

Please, God, just get us out of this alive. I'll take whatever's coming to me, but just let us escape from this alive.

Another gunshot split the night. Bobby didn't know where this bullet went, but he knew that they weren't running fast enough.

SARAH instinctively ducked at the sound of the last shot. It was that close. "There!" She pointed ahead and to her left. "It's coming from over there."

Startled that she'd heard no answer, she turned to face Gardner, but he was no longer next to her. Terrified that he'd been hit, she whipped around, the beam of her flashlight illuminating hundreds of falling snowflakes, which cast confusing shadows on the forest.

Then she saw him. He stood over in the trees, trying his best to stay out of sight. He wasn't hit; he was just scared. "Gard!" she called. "Gardner, come on!"

He shrank farther away.

"Try not to wet yourself!" she shouted, and she took off again in the direction of the running shoot-out.

Footing was becoming treacherous now, and as she ran through the punishing branches, she found herself reaching out more and more to keep from falling.

She heard another shot and this time saw the muzzle flash that came with it. She killed her flashlight and drew her .38, cursing Gardner for being such a wuss. With luck maybe he'd at least be able to screw up enough courage to point the way for the sheriff's deputies when they arrived.

THE woods ended abruptly at the rocks, and from there the Martins had no place to go. Susan took one step out onto them, and her feet went right out from under her. Airborne acrobatics kept her from landing on Steven.

"My God, Bobby, we're trapped." Susan had to nearly shout to be heard over the roar of the water.

He hadn't counted on the ice. Where the raging torrents splashed up, the rockfaces froze solid and invisible, impossibly treacherous. They couldn't stay here. To stay was to die.

This time he didn't ask for the boy; he just took him from her. "We've got to move on," Bobby shouted.

"Where?"

"This way!" He eased himself onto his butt and scooted across the slick surface. Ahead and below he could just make out a complex tangle of rock outcroppings. If they could make it that far, he thought they'd be safe for a while.

Clutching Steven to his chest with his left arm, he tried to control the speed of his slide with his right, but to little avail. Once he got on the far side of this first rock, he dropped feetfirst a good yard, straight down, landing up to his shins in a puddle of standing ice water. The chill took his breath away. He had to steady himself against the rocks to keep from falling over into the river itself.

Susan inched down the rock as he had, on her backside. She had two hands with which to control her descent, so things went a little better for her.

He'd just grabbed hold of her hand when the gunman fired again. The report was nearly as loud as Susan's yelp of pain.

SARAH had just gotten into position to see what the gunman was aiming at when she heard the shot and saw the woman on the rocks drop out of sight.

"Freeze!" Sarah yelled, bringing up her pistol.

But her target didn't freeze. He spun quickly around to face her and fired off two quick shots.

Sarah retaliated with three shots of her own, but they were wild. Diving for cover, she cursed herself for not staying behind to hide in the trees with Gardner and decided it was time for a full commitment. Rising to a squatting position, she fired off her last two rounds in the shooter's general vicinity. As she'd hoped, he dropped to the ground.

Yes! She had the break she needed. She took off like a sprinter, heading back in the direction of protective ground cover.

She ran for maybe thirty yards, until she found herself comfortably ensconced in a thicket of evergreens. Somewhere she heard movement. She froze as the sound of cracking sticks came ever closer, their sounds still masked by the roar of the river and the quiet hiss of the snow falling through the trees.

Moving as slowly as she knew how, Sarah thumbed the release on her .38 and flopped the cylinder off to the side. She cringed as she pushed the eject rod, praying that the noise would be slight. She caught the spent casings in the palm of her hand. How she wished she'd listened to the warnings of her instructors! How many times had they warned that more bullets were better than fewer? That automatics were better than revolvers? Other revolver-toting rangers at least equipped themselves with speed-loaders. Instead, she found herself slipping spare bullets one at a time out of the loops on her belt. They were located behind her hip—cowboy style—and she had to work by feel, pushing each bullet up with her forefinger and catching it in her palm.

She'd slipped out the last of them when she heard the sound of rotor blades. Thank God, she thought. Help was finally—

"Sarah, this is Eagle One," crackled her radio. "We need help zeroing in on your position."

She'd never heard anything so loud in her entire life.

SUSAN clutched her face as she toppled toward Bobby. She fell like a tree. He tried to catch her, but with his left arm filled with a panicked Steven, he could work only with his right, and that just wasn't enough. He spun, too, under the force of the impact, and as he tried to recover his balance, his feet tangled.

He yelled as he fell backward, grasping at the air for a handhold, then clutching the boy tightly to his chest.

The frigid water registered as fire against his skin, agonizing needles of cold gouging his flesh as the torrent engulfed him and swept him downstream. With Steven clutched tightly in both arms, he struggled to roll onto his back, even as the little boy fought desperately to break free. But Bobby refused to let go.

This is it, he thought. This is the end.

He sensed more than saw that the current had ripped him away from the riverbank and into the main channel. Rocks pummeled mercilessly as he shot blindly through narrow chutes and over four- and five-foot waterfalls. He wasn't sure how he managed it, but somehow he'd gotten himself oriented feetfirst and on his back, clutching Steven on his chest the way an otter cradles his food.

He felt as if he were moving sixty miles an hour through the water, and as his butt and back scooted along the bottom, he thought for sure that the heavy impacts had to be breaking bones.

This couldn't go on. The frigid water siphoned away his energy. He could already feel his feet getting more clumsy as he used them to push away from approaching rocks. If he didn't find a way to shore soon, then he wouldn't find it at all. He and Steven would either drown or die of exposure.

Up ahead—it was nearly impossible to judge distances in the dark—he could just barely make out the silhouette of a deadfall across the water. It stuck out about halfway, extending from the right-hand bank. If the big old tree—it looked like a pine from here—had fallen recently, the branches that extended down toward the water would still be pliable enough to cushion their impact and slow them down enough for Bobby to grab hold of something. If it was old, however, those same branches would be so many spears, waiting to run them through.

Bobby kicked and paddled, spitting out mouthfuls of water that now tasted like blood, but the current wouldn't relent. It had them in its grasp, and it had no intention of letting go.

He didn't see the last waterfall until he was right on top of it. Two boulders guarded its entrance, skulking just under the surface. At the spot where the two rocks were joined, Bobby's ankle jammed to a stop and the rest of his body kept going. The bones connecting his knee to his ankle twisted against each other and snapped.

Bobby howled in agony as his driving momentum carried him completely over the rocks, which finally released their grasp.

Not until he splashed back down into the water and his brain was swimming in agony did he realize that Steven was no longer in his arms.

THE spare bullets scattered as Sarah moved quickly to slap her hand over the radio speaker. The gunman reacted with frightening speed, firing off a panicked shot. She could tell that he still didn't know where she was exactly, and he couldn't know that right now she was essentially unarmed.

She quickly twisted the dial of her radio to the OFF position. Her heart hammered as she patted the dark ground, searching for the bullets she'd lost. The movement outside her little thicket started up again, suddenly sounding much closer than before.

He'd circled around! He knew where she was hiding!

Please, God, just one bullet. Just let me find one bullet.

Overhead the sounds of the approaching chopper drew closer. He knows, Sarah thought. Somehow Russell knows where we are.

A stick cracked immediately behind her hiding place, and Sarah froze. He was right there. He was right outside her hopelessly thin wall of vegetation!

In all the distraction of the helicopter and the gunman who was close enough for her to feel his breath, her fingers almost passed right over the stubby little cylinder. A bullet! She'd pay a million dollars for four more, but one would give her the chance she needed.

She felt the beat of the rotor blades in her chest now as Eagle One closed in on her. Suddenly she was bathed in the blinding white light of the million-candlepower searchlight. Shadows circled and danced around her as the beam cut the night. She looked down, and as she did, she saw a pair of shoes, and they stood not a yard away from her.

A gasp escaped her throat, and the feet moved, taking five quick steps backward.

Sarah jumped to her feet and brought her weapon up. At this range she couldn't miss.

"Sarah, no! It's me!"

Realization came instantly. "Gardner!"

"I heard—" His eyes changed as he focused on something behind her. He brought his shotgun to his shoulder. "Look out!"

Sarah dived to the right as the night erupted in gunfire. Both men fired and both men fell, the 12-gauge spinning off into another stand of trees. Just from the way he dropped, Sarah knew that Gardner had been hit.

"Gard! Oh, no, Gard!"

Still on her hands and knees, she scrambled over to where her friend lay, a crimson stain spreading quickly across his chest. He was alive, but his expression seemed empty, confused.

A racking cough seemed to bring him back to alertness. "Oh, God, that hurts," he moaned. Then a look of horror appeared as he focused past her again. His mouth tried to form words, but Sarah didn't need them. She spun on one knee, her weapon extended to the full reach of her arm.

Ahead of her, in the whirling shadows of the searchlight, a huge man with flaming red hair struggled to his feet. The whole left side of his down coat looked as if it had been through a shredder, and as he raised himself to his full height, he sagged to the side of his wounds. A pistol dangled from the fingers of his good hand.

"Drop your weapon!" Sarah yelled.

But the man appeared not to hear. He took a step closer.

"Freeze! And drop that weapon. Now!"

The man raised his weapon. It looked as if it took an enormous effort for him to lift his pistol.

Sarah pulled the trigger. And nothing happened. The snub-nosed just clicked. When she'd loaded her one bullet, she'd obviously not put it in position. She was going to die. Right here in the woods she loved so much.

The big man smiled, revealing a mouthful of red teeth.

Sarah pulled again. This time when the hammer fell, it launched a bullet right through the bridge of her attacker's nose.

Seconds later she was on the radio. She had a life to save.

PAIN knotted every muscle in Bobby's body as he jolted against even more rocks.

"Steven!" he cried into the night, and from somewhere he heard a choking cry. "Steven!"

The water here was much shallower than it had been in the channel. The boy had a chance, he thought. "Steven!"

There! Not five feet away, he caught a flash of baby blue as it shot past him, heading back out toward the center of the channel. It was him! That blue was the new pair of nightie-nights.

Bobby lunged, his hands missing the boy by inches. He tumbled sideways in the water. With the deadfall zooming in closer by the second, this was his last shot at saving the boy. And himself.

Bobby launched himself one final time at the boy, who was now bobbing on the surface of the water. Bobby came all the way out of the water, looking like a frantic basketball player struggling to score a slam dunk on his belly.

There was nothing to protect Bobby's face as he crashed back into the water, where more rocks awaited him under the surface.

But he had the boy. He pulled Steven close and hugged him tightly.

There was the deadfall—only yards away now! Bobby spun onto his side, protecting Steven from a direct impact with the fallen tree. He hit hard, the branches snagging him in a hundred places.

Oh, God, his leg! He shrieked as the bone ends scraped against each other, and his mouth filled with water. Now that they were no longer moving, the current was like a battering ram, pinning them both against the tree.

Hanging on with one hand to the thickest part of the trunk he could find, Bobby hoisted Steven into the air with his other hand, the tiny, limp body making no move to fight him. By heaving himself up a little, he could get the boy high enough to wedge him into a kind of cradle that nature had formed in the twisted boughs of the old pine tree.

"Up you go, sport," he grunted as the boy rolled out of his grasp. "And don't you dare die on me." In his heart, though, he knew that it was already too late, whether from the cold or from a lungful of water. He harbored no hope that the boy would see another day. Any more than he harbored hope that he would see another one himself.

The best Bobby could do—and it took an amazing effort—was to lift his right arm maybe three inches out of the raging water, just far enough to wedge a medium-sized branch into his armpit. He hoped that it would be enough to keep his head out of the water when the oncoming unconsciousness finally overtook him.

As the darkness engulfed him, his thoughts turned to Susan. She was out there somewhere, too. He hoped that her next husband would be able to provide a better life for her than he had.

THE light of heaven was blinding. Bobby tried to look away, it was so bright, but it got still brighter. And it was cold. Oh, so impossibly cold and windy. And noisy. Heaven roared with an unspeakably loud growl, a thrumming noise that sounded every bit like a . . .

Helicopter!

". . . hear me? Mr. Martin, can you hear me?"

Of course I can hear you, Bobby thought, but his mouth wouldn't work. As he forced his eyes open, Bobby thought for sure that he could see the face of that FBI agent—what was his name? Oh, yes, Coates!—staring straight at him.

"I'm gonna need your help, Mr. Martin!" Coates shouted. "I need you to slip this collar over your head so we can both get out of this water."

Water. The river! This wasn't heaven. He was still in the freezing Catoctin River. He was still in hell.

"B-boy," Bobby managed to say. "B-boy."

"We got him! He's already in the chopper. And if you don't coop- erate, sir, I'm getting back in there myself. You understand? In a couple of minutes, we're all dead!"

Bobby nodded. He managed to let go of the deadfall long enough for Russell to slip the collar over his head, from which point the agent had to manipulate Bobby's arms to bring them the rest of the way through. From there Bobby just lay back silently while he was manipulated some more: a strap here and there.

And then the darkness returned.

SAMUEL wouldn't let himself cry.

Now that the helicopters and the lights were gone, he was left there all alone in the dark, among the trees. His belly didn't hurt him so badly anymore. That was good. But he was *so* cold.

He wished that Jacob was with him now. He'd know what to do.

"I'm so sorry, Jacob," he tried to say. "Please help me."

And then, there he was, staring right down on him, shining a light in his eyes. Jacob was alive again, wearing a heavy green jacket with a fur collar around his neck. It looked warm. But the hat looked stupid—like something Smokey the Bear would wear.

Jacob was shouting something at him, and then he talked into a radio, but Samuel couldn't make out any of the words. He tried to lean in closer to listen, but it felt as if somebody were pulling him further and further away.

"You'll be okay, buddy."

That time he heard it, but the sound came without pictures. He slipped further away, smiling even wider. Jacob said he'd be okay. And he'd called him his buddy.

BOBBY Martin awoke slowly, his steady movement toward consciousness driven by the terrible ache in his leg. He inadvertently flexed a toe, and a bolt of pain launched like a missile all the way up into his groin and beyond. The crystal-like clarity of the pain vaulted him over the wall of wakefulness and landed him squarely in the middle of reality.

He knew instantly where he was and why he was there, and a knot of panic seized his insides. He raised himself up to his elbows from the medevac cot and took a swipe at the man whose back was turned to him, hoping to get his attention.

The man whirled around, startled, revealing the now familiar face of Special Agent Russell Coates.

"My wife!" Bobby yelled over the thunderous vibration of the rotors. "We have to go back for Susan!"

Russell smiled and moved out of Bobby's way so he could see the patient on the other side of the narrow aisle. Susan lay under a huge pile of blankets, her eyes closed.

"Is she okay?" Bobby shouted.

"She'll be fine."

"But she was shot!"

"Medic says it looks like a ricochet." Russell pointed to a spot over his ear. "All three of you are hypothermic as hell, and your leg's going to need mending, but you'll all be fine."

"What about the boy?"

Russell nodded toward Susan. "He's breathing fine and sleeping away on the other side of your wife. Everybody will be just fine."

Bobby saw another supine form on a cot that was actually *under* Susan's. "Who's that?"

Russell's features dimmed. "That there is Ranger Blackwell with the Park Service. He was shot."

Shot trying to save me. "Is he going to be okay?"

He didn't know how to interpret the look he received in return, but he knew better than to pursue it. Instead, he laid his head back

down and tried to relax, wondering whether his nightmare had finally ended or if it was just beginning.

APRIL knew the instant that she heard the heavy door open at the
end of the short cellblock that the approaching footsteps were coming for her. Her bare feet landed soundlessly on the concrete floor,
and she was waiting at the barred wall when Detective Tom Stipton stepped into view.

"You know something," she said anxiously.

He looked so grim. "Before I go into the details, April, I want
you to know that Justin's going to be just fine."

"You found him?" she gasped.

Stipton nodded. "Yes, but—"

"And he's alive?"

"Well, yes, but he's had a tough go of it. Apparently, the plot to
kidnap him was interrupted by—"

"Wait," April said, holding up her hand. She smiled, and her vision
blurred with tears. "Just tell me that first part again."

The grimness left Stipton's eyes, and dimples formed in the corners of his smile. "He's going to be just fine, April."

TOM Stipton pulled his unmarked vehicle up to the curb and threw
the transmission into park. Neither he nor April said anything for a
long time as they took in the war zone that was The Pines. "You
could do better than this," Tom said.

April offered a half shrug. "Hey, it's better than the digs I almost
had, right? At least here I can come and go as I please."

Tom forced a chuckle. "Well, I think I'd avoid that mall for a
while. They're still not real happy about the D.A. looking the other
way on this."

"That reminds me. I need to write him a thank-you note."

Tom cringed. "Um, I'm not sure that's the best idea. He is, after all, an elected official, and this decision is going to be controversial enough without a record of your thanks."

"Can I thank you, then?"

Tom smiled. "Sure you can. It's not necessary, though."

April leaned across the seat and gave him an affectionate peck on the cheek. "Thank you, Detective Stipton. And that comes from Justin, too." They both looked to the back, where the boy was sound asleep in a car seat.

"Can I tell you a secret?" Tom asked with a conspiratorial twinkle. "He's the one I really did it for. He's been through too much to lose his mom just because she was a little crazy one day."

April held Tom's gaze long enough for it to become uncomfortable for both of them, and then they both broke away. "Why does a cop car have a kiddie seat anyway?" she asked as she climbed out of the car.

"We keep them in the trunk all the time," he answered, climbing out himself. "You know, just in case."

April laughed at the absurdity of it. "You mean you keep it back there with the bulletproof vests and the tear gas?"

Tom laughed along with her. "Don't forget the road flares and shotgun." He waited while she lifted out the sleeping boy and rested him on her shoulder. "Want me to walk you to the door?"

"You know, I really don't need a bodyguard."

"But you're not armed anymore."

"Well, don't tell everybody, okay?" She laughed. They stood there together for a moment. "Tell you what. You want to escort me, then you call me for a date and escort me to a nice dinner."

Tom's smile became bigger. "I might just do that."

She bounced her eyebrows playfully and walked away.

Turning the lock on her door, April stepped into her dingy little apartment and instantly knew that something had to change. Tom was right: She didn't belong here. These two bedrooms and roach-infested kitchen were a shrine to William and all the misery he'd brought into their lives. She had dreams and she had talent, dammit, and where the talent fell short, she had drive. It was about time for her to start believing in herself as much and as deeply as her father had believed in her.

It was time for a *huge* change.

The first step was to exorcise the remnants of her worthless husband from this place. Laying Justin gently on his mattress, she watched him sleep for a moment before heading into her bedroom. She wanted to feel sad as she gathered up William's clothes from where they lay on the floor and draped over the footboard of the bed. She'd have settled for something other than hatred.

She finished on her knees, straining to reach all the way to the back wall of the closet for a stray white athletic sock, which, for some reason, appeared to be stuck to the wall. More accurately, she supposed, it appeared to be stuck *into* the wall.

"What is this?" she asked the room. She reached in even farther and had to tug hard to pull it clear. But it wasn't just one sock, it was four of them. As the socks tumbled free, a twenty-dollar bill tumbled out, too. April frowned.

As she moved in close enough to see into the hole, more money came into view. Wincing at the thought of what her fingers might find, she reached in and touched stacks of bills. She pulled out first one, and then two more: twenties, tens, fifties, and hundreds. There had to be hundreds of dollars here. Thousands, maybe!

Gathering up the money, she hurried out to the living room and piled the bills onto the coffee table. Even as she separated the stacks by denomination, she knew that she was looking at more money than she'd ever seen. William must have—

The realization of what had happened nearly made her scream, and she fell back on the threadbare sofa. He'd had it all along! The bastard had had the money from the very first minute! None of this had had to happen to Justin.

They were going to bury her baby alive! April's entire body went cold, and grief descended like a great black cloud.

"Oh, God!" she whispered.

When Justin walked into the room, she felt racked with shame.

"Mommy?" Justin said hesitantly. "Don't cry, Mommy."

April held out her arms, and the little boy ran to her. She gathered him in and kissed his hair and his face. "Oh, baby, I love you *so* much. I'm so sorry." The tears burst from her in a rush.

"Be okay," Justin croaked. "Be okay."

"You bet we will."

April wondered if she'd ever be able to let go of her little boy again. Holding him close felt like perfection. She held him there on the couch until she lost track of time.

When someone knocked on the door, she nearly didn't answer it. But the visitor was persistent, and when she finally caved in to ask who it was, Tom Stipton's voice greeted her.

"Just a minute!" she called. Moving quickly, she scraped the cash onto the floor and from there shoved it all under the sofa. That was drug money, she knew, and she didn't yet know what she was going to do with it. Until then, she didn't need anyone asking questions.

When she opened the door, Tom greeted her with a huge smile. "I'm back." he said. He held a shoe box in his hand.

"So you are," April said nervously. "Would you like to come in?"

Tom shook his head. "Um, well, not now. I'm on duty. This came for you in the mail today, addressed care of the police department. Thought you might like to have it."

Curious, she took the box and opened it to reveal an orange stuffed tiger. From behind, Justin recognized it instantly and squealed with glee. He rushed up and grabbed the toy, giving it a big hug. As he pulled it free of the box, a note fluttered to the floor.

"Have you read this?" April asked as she bent to pick it up.

"Well, under the circumstances, we didn't want it to be a bomb or anything."

It was written in blue ink on expensive stationery:

To whom it may concern,

Our lawyer tells us that you wish to remain anonymous, and we therefore are sending this in care of the police department. Meet Tiger. He once belonged to a very special boy who never got a chance to play with him. Now he belongs to your little boy, whose name we're told is Justin.

We hope one day that you'll feel comfortable enough to drop

us a line, just to tell us how he is doing. You probably already
know this, but you have a terrific little boy. It was an honor to
call him ours, if only for such a short time.

> Very sincerely yours,
> Susan and Bobby Martin

I THINK this is the one," Bobby said.

Susan shook her head. "Nope. If it were, I'd know it. A woman
can feel these things."

"I can feel things, too, you know."

They sat on the hardwood floor, just outside the bathroom off the
foyer, waiting for the timer to ring.

Susan teased, "Not every shot hits the target, you know."

"But this one did. I'm telling you, this one did."

Susan cocked her head and frowned. "But suppose it didn't?
We've been disappointed before, and I don't want—"

Bobby took his wife's hand gently into his own. "If it didn't, then
we'll try again. But this one did."

She smiled and shook her head. He was hopeless.

When the timer dinged, they both jumped a little.

"Think we should give it another couple of minutes?" Bobby
asked quickly.

She gave him her scolding look. "I already put an extra thirty seconds on the timer."

They stood, and Susan opened the door. Bobby put his hand on
hers and pulled it closed again. "Hey," he said softly. "I love you.
No matter what, I love you."

Susan kissed him lightly and hugged him. "I love you, too."

And then they stepped inside together.

JOHN GILSTRAP

ROBERT CUMMINGS

Former firefighter, EMT, explosives-safety and hazardous-waste expert, John Gilstrap sounds more like the hero of a thriller than the author of one. During an unhappy stint as managing editor of a construction trade journal he joined a volunteer fire service to have something more interesting to do. He later earned a graduate degree in safety engineering.

Through it all, Gilstrap wrote fiction. His first published novel, *Nathan's Run* (1996), became a commercial success, and today he writes full-time. Currently he is creating a screenplay of Norman MacLean's book *Young Men and Fire,* a true account of a Montana forest fire that killed twelve young firefighters in 1949.

To read an exclusive interview with
John Gilstrap, visit the Select Editions website:

ReadersOnly.com
Password: *happy*

The volumes in this series are issued
every two to three months. A typical volume
contains four outstanding books in condensed
form. None of the selections in any volume has
appeared in *Reader's Digest* magazine. Any reader
may receive this service by writing to
The Reader's Digest Association (Canada) Ltd.,
1125 Stanley Street, Montreal, Quebec H3B 5H5.

Some of the titles in this volume are also
available in a large-print format. For information about
Select Editions Large Type, call 1-800-877-5293.

ACKNOWLEDGMENTS

Pages 6–7, 8: illustrations by William Low
Pages 142–143, 144: illustrations by John Hersey
Pages 284–285, 286: illustrations by PhotoDisc
Pages 434–435, 436: illustrations by Cheryl Cooper

The original editions of the books in this volume are published and copyrighted as follows:
The Rescue, published by Warner Books, Inc.,
distributed by H.B. Fenn and Company Ltd. at $29.95
© 2000 by Nicholas Sparks Enterprises, Inc.
Code to Zero, published by Dutton, a member of Penguin Putnam Inc.,
distributed by Canbook Distribution Services at $37.99
© 2000 by Ken Follett
My Mother's Daughter, published by Simon & Schuster, Inc.,
distributed by Distican Inc. at $37.00
© 2000 by Judith Henry Wall, Inc.
Even Steven, published by Pocket Books, a division of Simon & Schuster, Inc.,
distributed by Distican Inc. at $36.95
© 2000 by John Gilstrap